OCT   2012

❧ THE ZENITH ❧

Translated by
Stephen B. Young and Hoa Pham Young
with the editorial assistance of Nguyen Ngoc Bich

THE ZENITH

DUONG THU HUONG

VIKING

VIKING
Published by the Penguin Group
Penguin Group (USA) Inc., 375 Hudson Street, New York, New York 10014, U.S.A. • Penguin Group
(Canada), 90 Eglinton Avenue East, Suite 700, Toronto, Ontario, Canada M4P 2Y3 (a division of Pear-
son Penguin Canada Inc.) • Penguin Books Ltd, 80 Strand, London WC2R 0RL, England • Penguin
Ireland, 25 St. Stephen's Green, Dublin 2, Ireland (a division of Penguin Books Ltd) • Penguin Books
Australia Ltd, 250 Camberwell Road, Camberwell, Victoria 3124, Australia (a division of Pearson Aus-
tralia Group Pty Ltd) • Penguin Books India Pvt Ltd, 11 Community Centre, Panchsheel Park, New
Delhi – 110 017, India • Penguin Group (NZ), 67 Apollo Drive, Rosedale, Auckland 0632, New Zealand
(a division of Pearson New Zealand Ltd) • Penguin Books (South Africa) (Pty) Ltd, 24 Sturdee Avenue,
Rosebank, Johannesburg 2196, South Africa

Penguin Books Ltd, Registered Offices: 80 Strand, London WC2R 0RL, England

First published in 2012 by Viking Penguin, a member of Penguin Group (USA) Inc.

10   9   8   7   6   5   4   3   2   1

Copyright © Duong Thu Huong, 2009
Translation copyright © Penguin Group (USA) Inc., 2012
All rights reserved

This is a work of fiction based on real events.

LIBRARY OF CONGRESS CATALOGING-IN-PUBLICATION DATA
Duong, Thu Huong.
   [Đinh cao chói loi. English]
   The zenith / Duong Thu Huong ; translated by Stephen B. Young and Hoa Pham Young.
   p.   cm.
   In English; translated from Vietnamese.
   ISBN 978-0-670-02375-2
   I. Young, Stephen B. (Stephen Bonsal)   II. Young, Hoa Pham.   III. Title.
   PL4378.9.D759D5613 2012
   895.9'22334—dc23 2011046011

Printed in the United States of America
Designed by Carla Bolte • Set in Monotype Perpetua with Linotype Aperto display

FOR LUU QUANG VU

AND ALL THE INNOCENTS WHO HAVE DIED IN THE BLACK SILENCE

AUTHOR'S NOTE

It is beyond me to write only from my imagination. Everything I have ever written has built upon true events. Even so, one needs to remember the hard fact that fiction is still fiction. A novel is neither the divulgence of self-referential musings nor the stringing together of episodes from an author's life.

Like all my published books, *The Zenith* is truthful to this rule. But, to avoid all unfortunate misunderstandings that might occur, I must emphasize this once again with respect to the character Tran Vu and those related to him. The inspiration leading to the construction of Tran Vu's character came from the real story of Mr. Vu Ki, the former curator of the Ho Chi Minh Museum. On the other hand, the character of To Van is not at all related to Mr. Vu Ki's actual wife or her family. The fictional juxtaposition of such a man and such a woman is not far from the realities of high-ranking Vietnamese during those years. Such juxtaposition is only a timeworn novelist's invention. There should be no special inferences arising in this case.

In reality, I did not have the honor of knowing Mr. Vu Ki for I had no intention of ever inserting myself in to the ranks of the Communist dynasty. Though I had a serious prejudice against all the frivolous maneuverings and red tape of that environment, curiosity mixed with admiration in my unsettled mind and made it hard for me to control the urge to meet him. Only when I heard that he had become frail did I mingle with a group of underlings to have a look at him from afar. That was the first and also the last time. The following year he passed.

For me, Vu Ki was one of a tiny group of people who could preserve some sense of chivalry and loyalty among teachers and friends—those extremely beautiful Vietnamese virtues which the Communist regime successfully destroyed during fifty years of rule.

Vu Ki's wife and her family have every right to feel proud to have had such a husband, a father, and a man.

THE ZENITH

DUO

1

"Oh, Father, Father, Father . . ."

The scream of a child wakes him up, and instantly it seems as if a blow from the back of the head knocks him emotionally off kilter.

"Oh, Father, Father . . ."

The scream rises up from the valley, the sound reverberating between the rocks, shaking the top of the trees, creating an invisible wave that agitates a large, still space.

After composing himself, he understands the screams belong to a different child.

"It's not him, it's not the little one . . ." he tells himself.

The painful feeling at the back of his head subsides and so does his anguish. The president stands up, steps out, and asks the security guard, "What happened?"

"Sir . . . it could be an accident in the valley. Someone has fallen from a tree or a rock, or the cliff."

Just then, the strident sound of a siren rises from the security unit camp below. In the calm wind he can clearly hear the bustle of a soldiers' posse gathering for the rescue . . .

"Oh, Father, Father, Father . . ."

"Oh, Father . . . will anybody save my father? . . . Hey, folks . . . Anyone, please save my father . . ."

This time he hears the desperate call of the child. The call of a boy entering his teenage years. That cry oscillates between the innocent feeling of youth and a turning to the ways of adulthood. In the cry, he can hear many different heartstrings vibrating all at once—moving with the accumulated love of months and years, reciprocating love and so many other invisible obligations, the pain of the unplanned separation, the terror of an uncertain future . . . All these feelings converging at once, like many different rays of light meeting at one spot. That rendezvous, he understands clearly, provides our fundamental link in the chain of our life, a hook that can tie us to the highest sublimation as well as to the last stage of depravity, a relationship that can spill much ink in the history of mankind. Such is the binding quality of the love between father and son, the oldest melody in the symphony performed by all living creatures. A kind of antique music that the tides of time have tried in vain to destroy.

"He must now be about the same age as this boy—same age but less fortunate."

He wonders, and visualizes the face of the kid now. The son that he tries to forget but can't put out of his mind. The son to whom, for a decade, he has refrained from coming close and yet who returns to rule over his heart, the most secure place for a child but not secure for himself. There, the image of the child is embroidered by his imagination as well as by his melancholy yearning. In this same place, his presence ignites a hellish fire that burns him daily.

"Who does he look like, I wonder? She or me? Does he look intelligent?" he has asked himself so many times. Many times, the silence alone answered.

He remembers clearly that from birth to six months the boy resembled the president's eldest sister, from the bridge of the nose to the lips, especially in the thick hair falling and covering the temples and forehead. But then from the seventh month to one year, strangely, all the features changed and the child came to resemble its mother. This change surprised everybody, himself first, then the mother; and after that the mother's older sister.

"Wow . . . He's already at puberty . . . the years fly by like arrows . . ."

Instinctively, he sighs, not noticing the bodyguard behind him.

"Mr. President, do you have any instructions?"

"Instructions?"

As he replies, he realizes how distracted he is.

"You see the men down there already gathering to go help? . . . Just you and I are standing here . . . We are the useless ones."

"Sir, Mr. President . . ."

The soldier is uneasy, his neck turns red. Then his face and both hands slowly become red, too. He backs up, looking at the president with wandering and puzzled eyes. The president suddenly realizes his careless oversight.

"Oh . . . I mean to say at this moment, you and I are not useful because we can't run down to the valley to help the victim. But otherwise, we are all useful people, with each carrying his own duty . . ."

"Yes, sir."

The soldier sighs in relief. The fat face shines sweaty and red.

The president pats his shoulder. "I am just joking, don't take it seriously."

Then he smiles and points to the temple, which, since early morning, has been emitting incessant sounds of praying and a mallet knocking on a wooden gong.

"There is nothing to do right now. Why don't you go to the temple and relax?"

Then he returns to the inner room and throws himself on the pillows. In the outer room, the plump soldier quietly closes the door and leaves. Feet heard stamping on the steps and temple yard fade into the knocking on the wooden gong. The rhythmic knocking resonating in the air makes him remember the sound of dripping water in a cave filled with stalactites. That is the sound of time passing, an eternal tune. This morning when it was still dark and he was lying in bed, he heard the nuns and the two bodyguards whispering by the door:

"Today, the temple must begin the prayers early because of an important occasion. Just wondering if it will annoy the president or not?"

"Oh, no! You cannot pray so early. We must let him sleep peacefully," said the bodyguard.

"Please bear with us. In a year of 365 days, the temple dares disturb the president with unusual praying this morning only. . . ."

Hearing this, the president roused himself and put on his quilted jacket to intervene:

"Just let the temple pray. I've been up a long time."

"Hail to Buddha! We appreciate your kindness."

The nun clasped her hands together and bowed her head deeply in thanks. Then she backed away. She took the kerosene lamp she had placed at the foot of the wall and returned to the temple. It was still dark outside and the enveloping fog was like smoke; the panels of her brown robe flapped in the fog, creating a strange distraction. And the lamp swinging in the night reminded him of an image long buried in the past.

No longer wanting to sleep, he lit his lamp to read a book. But no words registered as he kept hearing the prayers and sounds of the wooden gong. Sitting this way for a long time, in a state of complete emptiness, he mechanically turned the pages of the book, listening to the melancholic, monotonous music from the temple, which sounded like a calm river or a gently flowing stream that gurgles between grassy banks. At last, he understood that the image from his past for which he was painfully searching was that of his mother. One frigid and foggy winter night, his mother had also carried an oil lamp across a courtyard, the panels of her dress similarly flapping in a foggy night. She was going down to the water buffalo shed to add more rice husks to the pile of kindling. During such extremely cold nights, if you didn't keep the fire alive, the buffalo could easily die or get frostbite on their feet to the point where they couldn't plow. He was then four or five, snuggling in his mother's arms until she got up; then he would sit and cuddle the blanket, following his mother with his eyes . . . the dainty profile of a country woman, the panels of a brown dress flowing softly . . . The warm arms and sweet smell of mother's milk . . . The perfume of a far distant past returned. An inexpressible emotion surfaced within him. And with it, an unexplainable sadness. . .

"No! It's absurd!" he cried out. Then, closing the book, he reached for the stack of newspapers. But the news was the same every day, as he had long known. What was the point of eating the same dish, from the same cook, day after day? Disappointment overtook him from his head down to his toes. The image of the woman in the brown dress returned, reminding him again of his distant youth. A five-year-old child in bed looking at his mother brought up an unrequited longing for another child; and in that way he paced back and forth in the hell of his heart.

By nine o'clock, he feels out of breath. Waiting for the chubby bodyguard to take away his morning tea, he says:

"I wish to go to the forest for a stroll. Get ready and in a few minutes we'll go."

"Sir, that's impossible!" the panicked bodyguard blurts out, and seeing the unhappy face of the president, explains in a low voice:

"With respect, Mr. President, today we cannot go to the woods. Please understand . . ."

"It may be cold but it's dry," the president replies, controlling his anger. "It's enough if I wear my quilted jacket . . ."

"Mr. President, today is an inauspicious day. Yesterday, the nun told me this. This is the worst day of the year; that's why the temple prays so early today"

"Is that so! But you're a young lad, you believe in this kind of thing?

"Yes, sir . . ."

The bodyguard hems and haws as if something were stuck in his throat, but an instant later he suddenly adds: "I believe . . . I'm not afraid for myself but I have the duty to protect you. We just can't go into the woods."

This is the first time he sees the sweet youth display such unusual decisiveness. He smiles quietly. A silence out of respect. Whether he likes it or not, he has to admit that this young man is a gift from heaven. However, he can't believe that such fear could ever become real. From the day he arrived at the Lan Vu temple, eighteen months ago, no accident had ever occurred until today, the accident of some father. And the cries of that unknown child bring him back to his own hell: the absence of his son jabs at him like the excruciating pain of a cancer, torturing him without mercy. His heart is like a reddish, unfeathered young bird falling into a thornbush.

Lying in bed, he covers his eyes with his hands and thinks quietly to himself:

"I wonder if the child will cry of pain when I die? Will he cry inconsolably like that boy in the valley?"

A contemptuous voice rises from the depths of his soul like a brutal slap right to his face.

"Forget it! Nobody has ever told him who his father is. How can he possibly find out who he is when his very own father erases every trace that would make it possible to locate him?"

He addresses himself to an imagined, and thus unimpeachable, judge, suddenly feeling like a cowardly weakling before such authority.

"But at the same time . . . I hope . . . that with time . . ."

Turning his back, the judge throws at him a contemptuous silence. In spite of himself, the president moans and feels the color of his face changed by shame. He quickly hides his face in the pillows, fearing that someone might unexpectedly walk in. A fit of repeated contractions squeezes his chest excruciatingly, as if it were being kneaded by iron hands. Then, suddenly, he wants to cry. A kind of longing he has not experienced since his youth comes over him at this moment. A strange kind of desire, urgent, intoxicating, and painful. He wishes he could cry out loud, in broad daylight. He wishes he could cry to his heart's content, cry inconsolably, cry copiously between the high heavens and the deep earth. Wishes he could cry incessantly like a woman or a child. Wishes he could scream in the midst of the jungle and the mountains like that unfortunate son of the man who had just fallen into the ravine. But instead of calling out "Father!" he would cry "My son!"

"Son, my very own son."

"Son, my very own blood, the one who will carry on my line, my very own flesh. The fruit of an untimely love between me and her."

But he can't cry, because there is a knock at the door and immediately Le, the commander of the bodyguards, enters.

"Mr. President, are you feeling unwell?"

"I have a splitting headache," he replies without moving from the bed. Le's even-toned voice drips as if from a faucet and resonates in the room. He feels each word as a stab to his nape.

"Mr. President, the tea is ready. Please drink it while it's hot."

"Please just leave it there for me."

"Mr. President, please allow me to call the doctor."

"Not necessary. Everyone has headaches from time to time. I can assure you that it's not my blood pressure."

"Mr. President, you are still under treatment."

"I have stopped for two weeks already."

"Mr. President . . ."

He is forced to turn over and sit up. Le shows no special emotion. He stands firmly in the middle of the room with the tea tray in his hands. Once a day, either in the morning or in the afternoon, the commander personally attends the president to check on his health or to inspect the guards. An unusual diligence. An icy concentration. His ordinary features, his many large freckles, give a dark brown hue to his complexion so that people might assume he had Indian or Arab ancestry.

"Mr. President, the tea contains Lingzhi fungus jelly and medicine for your heart. The doctor has urged you to drink it while still hot. That's why we cover the tea with a special cozy."

"OK. Leave it on the table for me," he replies, thinking, "Poor me; not a moment without being watched."

The commander puts the tray on the table and repeats, "Please drink it while it is still hot."

"Thank you. I just heard the scream of a small child down in the valley. Do such accidents happen often?"

"Not often; but every year, according to the local people. Mr. President, you need not overly concern yourself about it. It's not good for your health. I already sent my deputy to take some guards down the mountain to help."

"Can't the government do something to prevent such accidents?"

"Yes, of course. But . . ." the commander replies with some surprise, his eyes shining with a devilish light and irreverence.

Once again the president realizes he has blurted out an unwise question.

"I know that acts of God or destiny are beyond human intervention. Nevertheless, the government should do as much as it can—"

"Yes, it does!" Le interrupts him. "The government will certainly take the victim to a clinic. From here to the district town is very far. The family alone can't do it. And the government will help with the funeral if the victim is too poor. First the Youth Brigade, then the village Party secretary, after that others as well."

"I would like to visit the victim's family," the president says, surprising himself with this sudden thought. Le stands still for quite a while. Then, attempting a smile, he politely says, "Mr. President, you are still under treatment and still in a situation where you must pay strict attention to the pace of your recovery. Attending the funeral at this moment would be very unhelpful. In addition, from the top of the mountain down to the valley is more than three thousand feet. A young soldier would feel tired, so for you . . ."

"You brought me up the mountain and now you are reluctant to take me down?" the president says coldly.

The commander, again shocked by the unusual reaction, says, with a stupid look and his voice rising,

"Mr. President, when we bring people up the mountain, we must mobilize military aircraft. At this moment, every aircraft has been sent to the front to carry the wounded."

"What?" He raises his voice in retort, not hiding his anger. "Every week I receive a report from Central Party Headquarters. Each report is full of news of successes. What are you trying to tell me?"

"Sir." Le bows. It is hard to read what is behind the narrow but square forehead that thrusts up like a cliff, a notable forehead resembling Stalin's. Le often bragged and threatened his comrades: "Don't cross me! Don't you see this forehead—one exactly like the Great Stalin's!"

At this moment, the commander lowers his head in thought. After a moment, his back stooped low, he says, "Mr. President, if you have decided, I will report back to Hanoi."

The president stands up and walks to the garden, realizing that the brown-faced fellow is slowly stepping back and away. Now anger squeezes his heart; a wave of suffocation surges up his throat. At the same time, his lungs fill with a hot steam, like that rising out of a steamship's boiler. Both the steamship that had taken him from the country and the one that had brought him back had had the same fire now burning his breast.

A plum branch stabs at his temple. He quickly closes his eyes. At this instant, the cry of the boy in the valley rises again. This time the boy stops screaming. His cry is now only a moaning floating in the wind. He thinks, "I guess perhaps help has arrived."

Out of the garden he heads toward the gate with the three arches. The wind blows from all directions. After halting a moment, it thrusts through the clefts in the mountain, chasing the clouds over to one corner of the sky to unveil a space of sweet blue. Thanks to the clear sky, the president now sees the clumps of woods below. In the space among the pines, the bodyguards' quarters look like matchboxes lined up in a row. Next to that is the weather station, built from stones quarried during French times. There is a winding road that leads down deep into the valley where a medical team can now be seen taking the injured one on a stretcher back to the village. The group walks one by one like a file of ants.

Looking from up high, the president thinks he is watching ants holding on to each other while climbing a reed stalk.

"Father, oh, Father."

The wind changes direction, blowing from the valley up the mountain-side. The cry of the boy swirls up and unfolds. He cries without stopping. Perhaps the father did not survive. Pity the one with the unfortunate destiny and pity the child who is about to endure life as an orphan.

He thinks and instinctively closes his eyes. The sound of the wind in the pinewoods throws itself into a vast space.

The president feels the wind touch his face, feels the damp cool of spring, of old forests, and of all the wildflowers on the mountain's flank.

"Father, oh, Father."

Suddenly, he opens wide his eyes because of a pressing question: If I die, will the child cry? Will he love me like that son of a woodsman, crying for his father?

This thought stops him in his tracks, his feet planted before the three-arched gate, as if he had just banged his head on a stone wall or been hit by an ill wind.

Obeying orders, the young bodyguard had been sitting in front of the temple but never ceased to watch the president. Seeing his pale face, the guard rushes up:

"Mr. President, please return to your room. You might catch cold or slip and fall. Since morning, the ground has yet to dry."

Then he grabs the president's shoulders tightly and guides him toward the house. The president wants to brush off the guard's grip but his own arm is warm. His entire body is also warm, and, when pressed against him, that warmth gives vitality and gladdens the soul. All you need is to stand beside such a person and you will get this feeling. A good and healthy youth. He thinks and agrees to follow him into the room. There the tea has been cooling. He sits and drinks his tea with bitter thoughts.

"He will never cry for me, because he doesn't know whose child he is. Forever, he will never know who is his birth father."

Then he mocks himself for being wrong when he thought that the woods-man was the unfortunate one. Who is the more unfortunate?

Now he understands why he had the sudden desire to go down to visit the victim.

A bitter longing mixed with a searching curiosity flowers in his heart; he wants to attend the funeral of the woodsman because he wants to experience the funeral of a real father.

Even the Lingzhi tea cannot suppress the suffocating heat in his chest. He has a hard time breathing even though his room is large and he has opened the windows to let in the cool air of the mountains and forests. An electric heater had been placed at the foot of his bed; it gives warmth and has no smoke from charcoal. Compared with the old days, such comforts make people feel good.

"Not to say it isn't a touch of luxury." So he thinks to himself as he remembers the bamboo and the dried branches that the two temple women use for heating.

The frame of his electric heater holds a picture of Snow White and the Seven Dwarfs dancing near a fire. The blinking flames illuminate the dwarfs holding hands, endlessly circling around the beautiful young girl with blond hair. With dull eyes the president, gazing a bit long at these fairy-tale characters, suddenly stands up and goes to the window. The wind now blows along the ribs of the mountain, singing through the forests he has visited. The sloping forests threaded throughout with pine trees sweep down from the high mountain peak to the foot of the Lan Vu pagoda and rise again to the foot of the sky to the north. Lower still on the second ridge is the forest of bamboo, all kinds of bamboo—yellow ones, lime-green ones, interwoven with thorny ones, making for an unending royal symphony in the summer nights. Bamboo covers the mountain slopes as far as the woodcutters' village, flowing down to the foot of the mountain, there connecting with fields of tea and cassava. Then follow the terraced fields, themselves followed by fields over which the white herons can fly straight like those in the delta, fields that are cut up like patches of a fresh green dress; dotted by little hamlets and extending to the southern horizon. Before, at the New Year, people from all around would climb three mountain terraces to attend services at Lan Vu pagoda when the plum-tree orchards around it were in full bloom, a blanket of white flowers that looked like a cloud, and the wild plums also blossomed along the well-worn trails. Those who worked from dawn to dusk with mud on their feet and hands waited for this pilgrimage at a miraculous moment of their year, the moment that triggers all the secret longing, the moment that calms all the pain and loss of life that has passed to nurture the breath of hope in those who seek to ascend the trail. Is it possible that the pure white of the plum blossoms, the delicate whiteness of the apricot blossoms, the spring fog, the white clouds on the mountaintop, and the flickering white steam in the crevices could create a magical sight—an intoxicating symphony of unsullied whiteness making one feel the power of purity and eternal rejuvenation?

Or could it be that the sounds of the temple bells and the chanting of Buddhist prayers are a balm to soothe the never-ending dark and difficult incarnations of humanity?

For whatever reason, he thinks of himself as guilty because since his arrival, the government, to ensure his safety, had forbidden the local people to come up to Lan Vu. They had thus confiscated a little joyfulness from those people, robbed them of something unique: romantic and sacred moments in the isolated lives unfolding in this place.

Lan Vu used to have twelve monks and nuns. The government ordered all of them to move down to two minor temples in the bamboo forest. He had to protest vehemently before the resident head nun and an assistant were allowed to stay. These two women, one young, one old, tended the garden all day, cleaned the temple, and prayed. It seemed as if they never took a break, except for sleep and two quick meals a day. A reluctance kept him from ever crossing over the paved courtyard, which became the boundary between his world and that of those who had taken vows of faith. From time to time, from his isolated world, he would discreetly glance over to see the two nuns sitting face-to-face on two old bamboo benches. Between them was a tray of food aligned exactly on a table, also made of bamboo. Even from afar he could guess how meager were those meals.

An unwieldly curiosity obsesses him: Is it possible that they don't feel pain and fear? Is it possible that they are completely detached from the feelings and needs of a normal person? That they hold no desire or anger; feel neither affection nor hatred, elation nor discouragement? No wishful anxiety; neither happy nor hopeless. Their lives flow like water in a canal—no falls or storms. If their lives really are that bland, he thinks, it would be an unimaginably heavy burden.

Every time he looked at the faces, as calm as still water, of the two women in the temple, this question returns like a refrain—a math problem without a solution.

"Mr. President, you should not stand in the wind too long," says the chubby soldier who has just finished cleaning the two rooms and now stands behind him.

"Don't worry. I want to get some fresh air."

Then he looks at the bucket full of dead ephemera in his hands, and says: "Oh, there are so many night butterflies . . ."

"Yes. Because it's warm."

Suddenly the wind stops, then, as if by some coincidence, the sounds of the wooden bells and the praying stop as well. The branches of the plum trees are no longer moved by the wind, staying still as if fixed by a curse. After a split second, the old nun walks out of the temple, followed by her assistant.

The president asks: "Your Reverence, today you pray past noon?"

Each time he sees the abbess, he speaks first to greet her. When he was a young child, his mother had taught him to respect those older than he. The nun is possibly in her eighties, so she must be at least seven years older. Though she is small and slight, she is still quite strong and thoroughly alert.

The nun turns to the president and replies, "Sir, this morning we cast the I Ching and learned that a misfortune would befall the people in the area, so we had to pray sufficiently for their protection."

"Then, Your Reverence, those with unlucky fortunes will be saved?"

"Sir, we cannot answer that. Whether those marked for danger will live or not depends totally on their inherited karma and their preordained destiny. We pray to ask that the Buddhas alleviate their bad fortune somewhat. If their destiny is still weighted down with this world, then we ask for them a quick recovery so they may return to their families and share this life with their wives and children. If their current destiny has reached its end, we ask for them a quick liberation, so that they can leave this worldly existence without too much pain and suffering, allowing their families and loved ones to feel some relief, and they themselves to benefit from the good karma that will bring them to a quick reincarnation into their next lives."

The president remains quiet, but thinks, "If it is so, then the praying does not really help humanity that much."

As if she guesses his secret thought, the old nun continues: "Mr. President, you are a country-saving hero, the great father of the land, the one whom we Vietnamese completely respect and to whom we are grateful. From another perspective, we are cloistered: we live in a world in which leaders like you don't live; we believe in things you neither know nor trust. That's why, with your permission, I would like not to reply to questions that we cannot answer."

"Your Reverence, please don't take offense. My concerns don't merit any attention, I only wish to fully understand the Buddhist scriptures."

"You will if you are so destined."

"But if I am not . . ." He lets out a question he cannot stop: "If I don't have such a destiny?"

The old nun smiles, not offended by the question, which is a bit provocative: "Sir, if you are not destined, you will never understand, even if you read a thousand sutras in ten thousand volumes, or if you sit a thousand times to hear erudite sermons."

After speaking, the nun points her hand toward the western part of the valley, where a mountain ridge runs straight in front of their view. "Do look at that mountain in front of us: the people here call it Sword Mountain, because of its shape. Now, please focus on the beaten paths running along the sides of the mountain—those paths that run parallel to each other and can never meet. This image is similar to the paths taken by those who are in the world. Without a different destiny, we will forever walk on only one side of the mountain."

With no more to say on the point, the nun steps back, bows, and apologizes: "Merciful Buddha, we humble ones should not so disturb you."

The attendant who stands behind, who always stands behind, also bows. Then the two turn back to the temple on the other side of the yard.

The president looks after them in a casual manner: two women wearing brown cloth; neither particularly pretty nor charming. To be fair, during their youth they might have been girls who deserved stares, but one could not say that they were beauties. If a majority of people believe that beauty gives strength, then in their cases, they probably could not have had much confidence in having any impact. Intelligence gives another kind of power, but also one with which they would not have bested very many others. But there was a kind of strength firmly lodged in them that made them unflinching in the face of great authority.

He knows keenly that there are very many people of great learning, those carefully trained abroad, who have real ability and are considered the brains of scientific studies, yet they are ever ready to do all that is bad and they never feel shame. Worldly power crushes their conscience as well as their self-respect. Under orders from the Party, these PhDs can easily demonstrate that it's better for pigs to eat water buffalo manure than bran, that water spinach is more nutritious than beef, or that children should not eat more than 200 grams of meat in a month to avoid risks of getting ill. Their writings made his face turn red but he could not dissuade them. Once the wheel starts to turn . . . Doesn't this wheel carry his very own imprint?

He sighs deeply, a habit he had acquired in the last few years. Many times he had tried to get rid of it but without success.

The young soldier comes right up before him and clicks his heels in greeting. "Mr. President, I report to ask your permission to go down the mountain."

He asks, "It's already time to change the guard?"

"Yes, sir, in three minutes and ten seconds, but the other team is already up here," the soldier replies, lifting his wristwatch to check the time in an attentive and proud manner. For sure, this is his most valuable possession, an article the government provided for his professional use.

"Indeed, it is five o'clock." The president speaks as if talking to himself while glancing out and around. The two night-duty guards have come up to replace the chubby soldier, their footsteps clunking on the gravel. Because the wind is calm, the noise is amplified in the mountain isolation. The two soldiers approach together and solemnly bow to the president. He makes a familiar and gentle gesture, responding to their formality, to allow them to perform their duty as assigned. Meanwhile, the chubby soldier leaves the temple yard, turning down the beaten path. Because of his weight, the sound of his retreating steps is louder than was that of his two ascending colleagues. He hears small stones being kicked loose from the sides of the path, rolling down and hitting the mountainside.

The president returns to his lodging just as the food-service team presents his evening meal. As it is not convenient to prepare his meals in the sparse temple kitchen, they are prepared in the guards' kitchen, and someone brings them up to him. A doctor regularly eats with him, to check the quantity and quality of his meals, and sleeps in one of the three rooms on the right side of the temple.

When the president walks into the room, the head cook steps up: "Mr. President, please eat your meal while it's hot."

He looks at the dishes set on the table and says, "You work hard all day, and you still climb up here. Why bother? It's OK to let others bring the meal up to me."

"Mr. President, I want to personally inspect whether the food is good or not. . . . If there is disappointment, I must change the menu to your satisfaction."

"You know that I am not picky about my food."

"I am fully aware that you never want to trouble anyone. But your health is a national treasure. We are honored to serve and to protect you."

The president silently sits at the table and says nothing more. The assistant cook sets the electric rice warmer on the table and, along with the cook, steps out. Naturally, he knows that they are watching him discreetly from behind the door. Because they really respect him and truly worry about his health, he feels forced to pretend that he enjoys the food, while in reality, he can't taste any flavor in what he is chewing and swallowing. Then he waits for them to clear the table, blurts out some compliments while sipping the white longan pudding, and listens to their respectful farewell before they return to their base. Sitting alone, he listens to the footsteps of a group of people mixed with their laughter. Turning off one light, he looks out into an empty space framed by the window. In the dark, the tree branches take on peculiar shapes. The light shining on the leaves makes a thousand bright eyes, and every time the wind shakes, these eyes blink with a look, sometimes playful, sometimes dangerous.

At this time, his heart no longer has that unsettling feeling. The heat in his lungs dissipates, leaving him with an incredible emptiness. His heart is like an abandoned house, where the wind freely and playfully blows, chasing the residing ghosts. His heart is like an uninhabited island after the birds have gone, leaving behind a heap of feathers on the grass.

He sits disengaged for a long while, not knowing what he is thinking. But suddenly a frigid shiver runs through his flesh, bringing up goose bumps all over his body. Some muttering cry behind him. He turns around. The incoherence won't stop. When he turns right, the cry comes from the left wall, and when he turns left, the cry changes its place; like a child's game of hide-and-seek. He stands up and looks at all four directions, seeing nothing but the set of four lacquer vases: Spring, Summer, Autumn, Winter. Then the cry comes directly from the top of his head, hanging there, disconnected, fleeting . . .

"Is it my own cry? My own quiet scream coming from beyond the horizon, or her final cry, my beloved?"

He wonders.

But he does not want an answer.

A truly painful cry from the girl or a silent scream from himself, it doesn't make any difference. For a while, for a very long while, he has had the habit of suppressing his thoughts in silence. Those thoughts are like sunken boats, piled up at the bottom of the ocean, buried in slimey mud, where aquatic plants thrive. For a long time, his words have been murdered like unfortunate sailors beheaded by pirates, their bodies thrown over and left on the sea bottom; and the unceasing waves become moving graves, screaming and whispering nonstop to let the ghosts settle in the womb of the dark sea.

The dead calm sea.

For a long while, too, he has had a habit of looking at his own thoughts as if they were someone standing out in the hallway and peeking back in through the keyhole, curious and ashamed of the indiscretion.

In coldness and hatred, his thoughts run away like a shivering little snipe in the field, beset by the sounds of people in pursuit, fearfully hiding in furrows and thornbushes. Under pressure and feeling oppressed, his thoughts sink as if in a muddy field or marsh. As the months and years pass, these thoughts fade like a newborn in an incubator with little oxygen, dying slowly.

But now, some upset is breaking out. Some sort of disturbance like an earthquake or the warning signs that a tsunami is coming or an insane volcanic eruption is on its way. He realizes the thoughts are distant, having faded away, but now like a thousand tattered pieces of an old shirt are suddenly coming together, trying to reassemble their former shape. Those dying newborns suddenly open their eyes and cry in the incubator. Those months and years suddenly, hurriedly return. Is this a miracle of the gods or a sorcerer's curse?

He does not know. He cannot know. But the calm sea erupts. He understands that the person from the past has returned . . .

Someone knocks at the door. At first gently, then with more urgency. He suddenly realizes that it's time for the doctor's visit. He will take the president's pulse before he retires to his room across the temple patio.

"Today, I would like to go to bed early," he says before the doctor appears in the door frame. "Why don't you get a good night's sleep? I will call if I need something. Is the telephone in your room working?"

"Yes, Mr. President, the technician fixed it. It rings loudly . . . In any case, please allow me to check you."

"There is no need, you checked me carefully last night. Twenty-four hours can't knock out a life. Go to sleep. And I'm telling you ahead of time that I will smoke one or two cigarettes."

"Mr. President . . ."

"I haven't touched the cigarette box for three consecutive weeks. But tonight, I will smoke. Once in a while, we should indulge a habit."

"But, Mr. President . . ."

The doctor hesitates. He wants to say something but stops. Maybe he wants to say that cigarettes are the president's enemy . . . that the president must stop, the sooner the better, that his own duty is to put an end to the craving whenever it develops. But it's like water off a duck's back for both he who speaks and he who listens. The doctor realizes that his speaking would be useless. After a few minutes of hesitation, the doctor bows slightly and says:

"Mr. President, I wish you a good night."

"I wish you a good night, too."

The doctor disappears in the darkness.

A few minutes later, a light comes on in a room across the temple yard. A baritone voice is heard singing: *"My love! How long before we see each other?"*

The president tilts his head, listening. For quite a long time, the man has not sung this love song. The doctor likes to sing but perhaps because he lives so close to the president, he shyly sings only marches or folk songs. Perhaps tonight, since he gave the president permission to smoke, he now gives himself permission to sing a love song.

"My love . . . Where are you now?"

Word follows word; the light sounds fly like a twirling kite in the summer skies. That faraway summer . . . That summer, the wind from Laos blew through the western mountains, wildly hissing on the dry and cracked plains, where large cracks turned into huge ones, zigzagging like the veins of unfortunate mountain gods. Thirsty birds had stopped singing, but, in exchange, kites flew up in flocks. Wheat-colored ones, green ones, and yellow ones; the colors of the spring butterflies . . . Those kites danced close to one another in the skies, like intersecting dreams, like fires of moral purpose burning in the very last seconds for a warrior falling into the abyss.

"My love . . ."

The smooth voice takes him to another summer, with the cool shade of trees and the sounds of flowing streams. To sunsets in the fields shining into the house . . .

"Where are you now?

"Our love is from a distance, but our hearts miss each other . . ."

The night is now calm because the wind has stopped blowing. There is no moon. Not even stars. Only a mysterious black color. The mountains, the waterfalls, the forest, the gardens, the woodcutters' village down below, and the faraway fields are all submerged in the silence of the thick night. A vast, suffocating, black space. In this still time, each word of the song spreads like the dissemination of ringing bells.

The president lights a cigarette so he can hear the song more clearly:

"My love . . . When are we going to see each other? . . ."

Now he hears sobbing from right behind his neck. This well-known sobbing makes him sit dead still. He dares not turn around. Three times he deeply inhales the cigarette smoke, believing the smoke will clear his mind, chasing away all fancies and confusing visions. He is wrong. The sobbing does not disappear but resonates clearly by his ears to the point where he can hear panting as well. A face all wet with tears leans against his cheeks. A flood of tears; freezing tears. He lights his second cigarette, then a third, letting out the smoke continuously, but he still feels the cold tears.

"Oh, my love . . ."

The singing voice still rises. But no, it is not the singing, but his own calling out. However, he dares not say the words out loud, so all they are is a singing in silence.

"Please, little one, forgive me . . . please, little one . . ."

His eyes are burning. In a dreamy moment, a faint warmth crosses his eyelashes. The cigarette smoke is dispersing with a flicker; it rolls out like clouds in a stormy wind at dusk; the fading smoke spreads like fog over pond water in the spring. Is his life nothing but ethereal mist, the movement of clouds and whirling wind? Is his authority no more than the fleeting enchantment thrown by opera-house lanterns?

"Please, little one, forgive me . . ." He speaks with bowed head, not knowing that the doctor is at the door.

"Mr. President . . ."

He looks up and it takes him a second to recover.

"Why aren't you singing? I really like your singing. You have a fantastic voice. You could be a professional singer."

"Mr. President, you are too kind."

"I am not being diplomatic with you."

"Thank you, Mr. President."

"Why did you return?"

"I was told that you didn't smoke just one or two cigarettes, but many . . . It's extremely dangerous to your health."

He looks down at the pack of cigarettes and realizes he has smoked half of it. Thick smoke still fills the room. The doctor stares at his face. Maybe he sees the stains of the tears. The president takes a handkerchief, wipes his face, then clears his voice: "I indeed smoked too much. The smoke burns my eyes."

"Mr. President."

"It does not matter. I will stop right now." He squishes out the cigarette in the tray right in front of the doctor. Then he stands up, stretches, covers his mouth with his hands as if he is yawning:

"Now I have to do tai chi if I want to fall asleep."

2

Vu returns home precisely at noon.

He just wants to dunk his head in a bucket of water to cool off and then go to sleep. The weather is cold but his rage is boiling; his face feels so hot it might have been fried in oil. Even though he has drunk two pots of tea, on top of one morning cup of coffee, he does not feel hungry at all. He keeps thinking of the bed in the corner of the room, behind the curtain with a pale blue flower design. In just a few minutes, he will roll onto it, in the silence closing his eyes so that he doesn't have to see anyone, and give those extremely tense threads in the mind an opportunity to unwind. At this instant he realizes how much he is attached to his room with its old-fashioned bed and its old flowered curtain. Many times his wife had wanted to replace the faded cloth curtain with a fancy lace one, but he had firmly objected. Perhaps because we are human, we all have our personal preferences, sometimes strange, weird, or utterly illogical. In his spacious house everything had been changed. From the color of the walls to the furniture, to clothing and food, to pots for plants, paintings, the clothes rack, the box of medals . . . Only the old curtain remained, surviving as if lost in its new surroundings. It is made of plain cloth, the inexpensive kind, of which the long days and months have whittled down its threads to their core and have faded its color to the point that the tiny wild grass flowers now float like blue dots crowding in upon one another. But Vu likes this curtain. Its presence offers him some consolation. Its blue color brings him a feeling of peace. He cannot explain this to his wife, except to sum it up as follows:

"This curtain is really unattractive, but it was hung on the occasion of our third wedding anniversary. Don't you remember that the liaison courier who brought this curtain up to the maquis later died that winter on his way back to Hanoi to get more news?"

"Yes, I remember. But all things only last for a time. There is a saying: 'One life of ours is much longer than the lives of a million things.'"

"If anything brings ease to those who use it, then it should endure. We aren't forced to follow the crowd. Don't put too much emphasis on stuff. You are educated; you're not like that low-class Tu."

"You dare compare me with that broad Tu, the fishmonger?" his wife cried out in anger.

He waited until he could have the last word: "I don't compare you with those kinds of people. But don't forget that only those people care a lot about things. They don't know what to do other than boast about their wealth."

His wife went quiet, her face turning red. From that day on, she let him be. Perhaps more out of pride than from a real understanding of the meaning of things. Whatever the reason, he won that round and the curtain remained. For him it was more than a simple souvenir; it was a life-saving talisman. It brought him calm during times of danger. It brought him necessary clarity in times of confusion. It soothed his soul. Whenever he was sad, in pain, he locked the door to his room, lay on the bed, and pulled the curtain all the way over to the far wall to hide everything, leaving in view only the blue that calms. It was a faded color, but it was the color of his youth. It echoed the years and months of the past, but those sounds carried a vitality that could revive his tired soul. That was the vestige of a season that had closed. A trace only, but one strong enough to re-create thousands of worn footpaths in the old forest. As that, it allowed him to find again the vision of himself, regaining the strength he used to have, the courage and the victories he used to be so proud of, the happiness mingled with danger he had enjoyed.

Many years ago, Vu found a tight bond between the blue curtain and his favorite song from his high school days, "Come Back to Sorrento."

This Italian song was first imported by the French schools, then it spread to the local schools until it intoxicated all the boys and all the girls in their flowing white school uniforms. The song inspired a vague conviction that everybody should put down anchor at some shore, someplace where they could heal their wounds, where new skin could grow over an open gash, and you could wait for the scar tissue to harden. A place where they could find again a source of life. A place where they could be reborn. A place called the old home . . .

For him such an old home was now just a few yards of faded cloth. He had nothing else besides that.

He thinks: "In a few minutes, I will crawl onto the bed, into the familiar corner. The blue curtain will protect me and I will find an escape . . ."

The sudden braking sound of the Volga startles him:

"Chief, we're home."

"Thank you."

"Tomorrow, what time is convenient for me to pick you up, Chief?"

"I must leave earlier than usual. Perhaps six fifteen would be ideal."

"Chief, will you eat breakfast at home?"

"Correct; I'll eat at home to make it simple."

He gets out of the car; walks as if running into the house; hurriedly climbs the stairs; hurriedly strips off his outer clothing to change into pajamas; falls crumpled onto the bed with a sick person's collapse such as one who has been overcome by a seizure and would just drop anywhere on the sidewalk or in the bushes. Familiar feelings and the soft blue color help him regain regular breathing. He closes his eyes, waiting for calm composure to return to his soul just like a farmer listening to the raindrops during the dry season. Downstairs, there are the sounds of china being broken, of chairs being pushed, then the screaming of Van, his wife:

"What's going on?"

. . .

"I ask: Who broke my plate of boiled meat?"

"Trung did."

"Throwing away food? Then in three days you will eat nothing but salt. . . . Who allows you to create havoc in this house?"

. . .

"I ask: Who gives you the right to pillage under my roof?"

Van's voice shries like a knife scraping slate. He has never heard his own woman's voice so terrifying as just now: "Why is her voice suddenly changed so oddly?"

"Trung, answer my question!"

He hears the loud sobbing of the child. And this sobbing is suppressed into the sound of sniffling. Leaning on his arm, he gets up. Downstairs, his wife continues to scream:

"Did you hear what I said? Answer me, Trung!"

At this, the child bursts into tears. It is no longer a sniffling sound but the low crying of a teenage boy whose voice is changing. Vu opens the door and goes downstairs. In the dining room, his wife has her hands on her hips, a position that he despises most in a woman; a position that he considers most unattractive, from the point of view of both beauty and morality. In that position, even a beauty queen could not inspire positive reactions from a man, especially from those who have been well educated. For a long time, his wife had not dared to so stand, a stance he often condescendingly called "the manners of that fishmonger, Tu." For a long time, too, his wife had understood that his disposition was quiet and humble, but that once he became angered or enraged, it would be a tragedy for the family, as a breakup would become unavoidable. For a long time, she had also known by heart those areas into which she should not trespass, which he had formally established, knowing it would be like a deadly minefield if she ever stepped into them . . .

Thus, today, what insane spirit had crossed their threshold or what defect of memory had prematurely arrived to make her forget so completely?

He stands right next to his wife and asks, "What is going on?"

Van is startled and turns. She points to the corner:

"Look over there, Trung is fed up with meat and he threw the whole plate on the floor. And Vinh did not have any . . . From today until next week, I will let them eat rice with salt."

"That's OK," he says softly, then slows each word, as with students who are just starting to learn spelling. "In the next three years, I will not touch any meat with chopsticks. That way nobody will be missing anything . . . Are you satisfied now?"

"Ah . . ." His wife drops her arms, looks at the smile on his lips. Her red face turns purple then white.

Having lived with him over thirty years, she knows very well that insipid smile is reserved for his enemies. She backs off, opens her mouth to say something but can't. Suddenly, she turns away in an unusual provoking and rude manner. Leaving the dining room, she goes straight out to the courtyard, where the jade plant is waiting to be groomed.

Vu stops and asks Vinh : "What happened between the two of you?"

"Nothing . . . nothing happened," Vinh replies awkwardly. Then he dashes out of the dining room into the courtyard

Without even glancing up, he knows that Vinh is looking for his mother. That is his only refuge in this house, the place where he can hide from all his sins. Waiting until Vinh disappears, he bends over and asks Trung:

"What did he do to you?"

The adopted son bursts out sobbing. He obviously had repressed his cries, but now the water overflows the dike, and he cries profusely and uncontrollably like a three-year-old, but with the low tone of a teenager. Vu waits for his cries to end, and pulls him to his bosom:

"You and Vinh are the same age but you are ten months older. There is an old saying: 'Older by one day only, you are still the older brother.' You ought to behave like one, right?"

"Yes. I remember your words. But today Vinh insulted me."

"How did he insult you?"

"He told me that I am a bastard, and a moocher."

"Suddenly he said that?"

"We sat down to eat dinner because Mother said you wouldn't be home for quite a while. At first, nothing happened. But when I was about to pick up some meat, he blocked my chopsticks and screamed: 'You're a moocher, a bastard. Your kind only deserves to eat vegetables and peanuts; you have no permission to eat meat or fish. Letting you sit and eat with us is honor enough.'"

Vu is mute. His face is sweating and his heart grows cold. He feels as if it stops beating for a few seconds. A thought runs across his mind, burning it as if someone is guiding a hot iron across his flesh: "Vinh couldn't have thought of those things all by himself. He is a rude boy but not too smart. Those cruel words must have come from his mother. From my wife? How could she be so low class?"

After a while, he calms down and says:

"You should not bother with Vinh. He is greedy and he lies. You are actually my own son. Your mother's name is not Van, but the blood that runs in your veins is mine. The skin covering your body is surely my own as well. If Mother Van and younger brother Vinh do not accept you, we will leave them and live separately. Just you and me. Do you understand?"

"A . . ."

The boy opens his mouth; his eyes open wide. In the boy's state of utmost astonishment, Vu detects suspicion and fear mingled in opposition to a sense of great good fortune. He knows that what he has said has surpassed all the boy's expectations, and is his dream of all dreams.

"You are my own child. Do you understand this?" Vu says again.

Trung still stands dumbfounded, his face pale and his lips turning white. Vu sees clearly all the waves of emotion that surface in Trung's beautiful eyes.

A bitterness fills Vu's heart: "My gosh! . . . How he longs for a father! Having a father is really an ordinary fact for millions of other children, but for him it is the ultimate dream, or maybe just an illusion. Pity this poor orphan prince."

He looks deep into Trung's clear brown eyes, a doe's eyes. Gloriously beautiful, yes, but a bit effeminate. Is it merely because of this stunning beauty that he must endure a hard fate? This fleeting thought arises as a light wind. Vu holds tight the hands of the adopted son and repeats each word: "You are my child. For a long time I didn't want to disclose this for fear of many issues. But now, Son, I have to tell you the truth. Because you have reached an age of mature understanding."

"Father!"

The boy rushes into his arms, the sudden happiness making him burst into sobs. He leans his head against Vu's chest, tears pouring down his face, soaking wet like a stream. Vu quietly squeezes the child. Together, both tenderness and bitterness invade him and his throat chokes.

3

The clock on the wall leisurely rings twelve times. Vu continues reading, as if nothing has happened. His wife comes up behind him and tries to close the book.

"You should go to bed, it's getting late."

Vu turns back to the page and says, "You go to bed first. . . . I need to read."

"I apologize . . ."

"You didn't do anything wrong. . . . To be truthful, the mistake is the forced union between us . . . I regret . . ."

"What do you mean . . ." Van says, raising her face, which is warming at his calm but painful words. She wants to debate, to persuade, to show her goodwill. But Vu turns around, raises his hand, and points at the four surrounding walls. Van knows that they cannot talk in here, where recording bugs are placed everywhere, from inside the house to the big trees in the yard. She finds a piece of white paper and writes:

"We will talk about this tomorrow."

He writes his reply right underneath: "Tomorrow, I have to leave at 6 a.m."

"Then when can I talk to you?"

"When I return."

"Sleep well."

"You, too."

Van crumples the paper and burns it, a longstanding habit of theirs. Then she goes to bed. Remaining in front of the table, he turns the pages but not a single word registers. On his chest, the tears of the adopted son are still warm; in his ears, still the sounds of a sobbing boy. He can guess what kind of storm had roiled the child's soul that afternoon:

"Poor little one . . . For so many years, he silently sought traces of a father. No matter how much I loved him, no matter how hard I fulfilled a father's role genuinely, with dedication and with passion, that lack would leave a huge hole which could never be filled. Blood ties are the invisible strings that unite the generations.

"You are my own son. The blood that runs in your veins is my own blood. The skin that covers your body is mine as well!—Why did I speak so? Was it the inspiration of spirits or the temptation of the devil?".

Whatever it was, the words had been said. Words once spoken, four horses chasing them cannot catch up with them. From today on, the fate of the boy is bound to his by this secret relationship. The mystery of this fate arises to hide another mystery.

Really, he doesn't know if he behaved rightly or wrongly when he told Trung that he was his son—a child born out of wedlock, to be exact. But that afternoon, he hadn't had the opportunity to think, nor the time to ponder. He had acted in the manner of a poet caught up in compulsive inspiration, even though he is not a poet, and is not even familiar with acting on such compulsion. But he knew what to do when his own wife and their own son had pushed the adopted child into bitter despair.

"Am I responsible for letting this shabby and bad situation develop?" he wonders.

And his soul fills with darkness.

He cannot measure the complexity of life. He feels too powerless to steer the family vessel. Perhaps he has insufficient insight and lacks the courage to possibly understand the natural inclinations of the woman and his own son?

"Perhaps I lack both, both clarity and courage. I lack both of the most necessary qualities in a man, in a father and in a husband. It seems someone once told me that."

Perhaps . . .

Sounds from the past always follow the word "perhaps," and with those sounds one turns pages yellowed with the stains of time. Vu knows that inside him is a man from the past, one who is concerned with family traditions and the values that cluster around them. For this reason, a son, someone to sustain the lineage, was his most secret and most earnest longing after he had married. After seventeen years of failure, the day Vinh was born was for him a celebration, "shedding tears of happiness," as they said thousands of years ago. Vu remembers staying up with Van for three consecutive nights as she went through her labor pains. He sat up so that she could lean on him when she did not want to lie down; he gave her his arm so that she could pinch and scratch when the pains tortured her. After the birth was over, both his arms were covered with scars that took a month to heal. The other women in the room had looked at Van with obvious jealousy. They had looked at him with unhidden envy. His wife certainly had not forgotten that. She couldn't have forgotten that it was he who readily took on the responsibility to launder and cook, to serve her, even though the families on both sides, as well as his office, had plenty of people to help out. Everything he had done flowed from a clear realization that his wife must feel the utmost happiness when she became a mother, when bloodlines mix to create a new human being, the one with the mandate to maintain and prolong the names, the corporal images, and the reputations of the two family lines.

When Vinh was still young, from one to six years old, his features were dainty, his face was beautiful like a "lady from Hong Kong," and he looked more like his mother than his father. The two then thought he would grow up to become a movie star, if not as famous as one from Hollywood, at least like an Yves Montand or an Alain Delon. But from the age of ten, his features totally changed. Vinh lost his movie star look, and took on the features of a tough guy. Then, when Vinh came in second in an elementary school athletic contest, he and his wife changed their dream of an artist to one about a sports champion. Besides changing in appearance, the boy also revealed a character that few parents would wish for. First, he became an awful glutton. His son became sickeningly avid when sitting down to eat, at which time he would not see anybody or pay attention to anything, except bending down to get his food. On special occasions, his wife would invite chefs over to cook unusual dishes. On such occasions Vinh would skip school to stay home, dashing to the kitchen to help himself to the food even before his parents and the guests. Many times, Van tried to persuade Vu that a child who eats well is something to rejoice at, because he will grow big and strong. But when he looked at his son hunched over the table and eating while hardly swallowing or breathing, Vu felt his face heat up. When Vinh was twelve, the hair around his mouth grew bushy and his voice broke low; his mother asked Vinh to eat separately with Trung in the kitchen so that Vu would not feel ashamed.

It was probable that when she had to face reality on her own, his wife also suffered. But in front of him, she never backed down. At all costs, she had to protect her son, the only masterpiece of her life as a mother. Often, too, he wanted to go along with her, to believe that their son would become "someone very famous in the future."

He often told himself that a person's abilities could mature late, bloom late in the season, kick in as needed like slow-burning coal, imitate the Chinese mandarin Lu Wang, who sat fishing on a rock for more than eight years before he lifted a finger to help rule his country. In such fashion, his son might someday become a famous scientist, a designer of airplanes, of boats, a creator of special new chemical formulas, or a doctor who could cure nasty diseases. It was completely possible for the boy to become someone helpful to the people, bringing honor to his ancestors. With the condition that he would have to change his personality and become someone who loved to study.

"With the condition . . ."

Oh, what a supreme and impossible dream for a father and a mother!

Though in pain as if each segment of his intestines had been cut, Vu realized that his hope was every day moving farther away. Moving away toward infinity. In this bitterness, each day his son more and more resembled Tung, Van's spoiled younger brother. From appearances, this resemblance drew surprised comments from both families. First, the nose spread too large on the face, with both nostrils large and thick, and with a tip shaped like a garlic clove, always shiny. Then two tiny eyes under extremely bushy brows, the kind people call "caterpillar brows." Due to his appetite he very quickly grew fat. The fatter he got, the more prominent became his cheeks, erasing all remnants of his once attractive youthful features. Vu did not much believe in the art of physiognomy, but his son's appearance gave him despair because, from experience, he knew that physical changes to one's features are often followed by changes in one's spiritual life and one's morale. Not much later, his suspicions were proved right. During grade school, Vinh had always been ranked as an outstanding student. Crossing over to the first year of high school, he dropped to the rank of only an average student. The very next year, he fell into the category of "special needs students," and it was all downhill from then on. Vinh was often written up, and his wife had to visit the teachers almost daily. Vu noticed that his wife always brought gifts along, some that he had bought when abroad on official business; some from the countryside, where special local delicacies were available such as garden-raised chickens, fresh ocean crabs and shrimp wrapped in banana flowers, fresh fruit, and homemade candied fruit.

Once, he couldn't help telling his wife: "You're going to spoil our son one hundred times over if you keep doing this. Vinh doesn't have any inner drive. I've seen it many times: he pokes his head into the packages you bring to the teachers, like a circusgoer, careless, as if it's all a joke. He seems to think that he can spend his energies having a good time and being stupid while his parents do everything to give him a life. Please stop it; if you don't, your son will become a totally useless person like his uncle. That ugly resemblance is already on display."

Blushing red from her face down to her legs and arms, his wife turned around and lamented: "I know that my family is inferior to yours. My brother was a dumb student. Why didn't you pick a wife who was well educated, with writing covering her from head to toe?"

"Don't be petty and proud. You should think seriously about our son's future. To do that we need to look straight at the truth. The truth is that the more Vinh grows up, the more he likes to play around. His uncle Tung comes by to take him out at any time. And you keep protecting both of them. To study like this, sooner or later he will be a social misfit."

"Nobody in this family is a social misfit. Don't be too strict with your son. He is a stubborn child, so we have to pick a certain way to bend him. Look around. How many successful people passed through this kind of naughty childhood? There are illiterates who became successful. It is said, 'A good horse often has flaws . . .' "

Vu was forced into silence. Fed up but silent. What else could he say? He felt powerless. What could he do to turn the situation around?

The child was their joint product, but her contribution was the larger. All during the pregnancy, she vomited and always felt sick. Her pregnancy was a thousand times more difficult than that of others. She was not born for getting pregnant and giving birth. This boy child was her life's lucky lottery. There would not be a second chance. For seventeen years she had often been pregnant but then miscarried. She would miscarry one month and become pregnant again a few months later. This unhappy sequence kept on repeating, to the point where her family and even her colleagues thought of her going to the maternity clinic like a common chore. No pregnancy survived its fourth month. With the magical assistance of heaven and earth, when she was forty-one, at the age that ends all women's hope of becoming a mother, she succeeded in having Vinh. That was why, for her, this child was like a king without a throne. The peculiar thing was that this circumstance could turn around entirely a mother's point of view. During the early years of their courtship, Van often showed open contempt for her brother by referring to him as "Tung the pig." Now that their own son so resembled "Tung the pig," her feelings for her brother grew more affectionate and tender. But for Vu, each time he watched uncle and nephew chat, or play around, or flirt, or eat, he could not but feel terrified. A man past his forties with no beard and a teenager with thick bushy hair around the lips. Both had fleshy, bloated faces. Both had such bushy eyebrows that their eyes were left as slits hiding in shadowy darkness. Both had a voluptuary's gaze when their eyes gauged a young girl or a woman. A horselike, hissing laugh was identical in both and so unbearable that he had to leave. At twelve his son already had a fat belly, just like his uncle in his youth on the day when Vu had set foot on the threshold of Mrs. Tuyet Bong, the village seller of fish sauce.

"How can we tell to which port life's boat will sail? How could I have guessed my only son would inherit all the disgusting traits of his maternal family? I loved Van, believing that her essence flowed from her father, Mr. Vuong, the teacher, not knowing that along with the delicate and dainty traits of her father, she nevertheless was filled with the seeds of her mother's character, that seller of fish sauce famous for her bad temper and unattractive presence. Is this marriage the greatest failure of my life? A failure without redemption?"

The Phu Luu district was known for its prosperity. When they reached their full-moon years, they were known as a handsome young man and a pretty gal. Then they were sent to Hanoi for middle school, dandy and sophisticated students with ironed clothing, well supplied by their families so that they might keep up with their peers. Romance happened easily when they all were in the same boat; she read a novel while he turned a newspaper's pages. Romance also blossomed easily when they were together in summer camp as "boy scouts" and "girl scouts," when they sang foreign songs such as "Serenade," "Come Back to Sorrento," or "Santa Lucia." Furthermore, Van was pretty. She was known as the beauty queen of Phu Luu. And to top it off, both of them were at an age to dream of love. Moreover, they had no worries about making a living and the stormy wind of revolution had yet to touch them. Besides . . .

Oh! How many more such "besides" for him in resuming an analysis of a marriage some three decades old? But he remembers the first time he took her home to surprise his parents, in the style of young men in those days. His parents stood dumbfounded for a while before they were able to return the greeting of the beautiful guest who was such a good match for their son.

That night, his father called for him and gently told him: "Times have changed. Now nobody would dare marry off a son or daughter without their consent. I find this practice in harmony with what is right. But for one person to live with another is the most difficult thing in this world. Don't forget that. Once you promise to live with a woman, you have promised to carry half of the responsibility for that person's entire life. That is why you have to be careful."

"Father, are you referring to Van's family circumstances?" he somewhat passionately queried directly. "But the two of us have the same values. Even Van herself recognizes that her mother lacks proper virtue. Once Van admits this, she must know how to behave correctly."

After hesitating for a moment his father replied: "It's your decision." Then he suddenly emphasized: "In the old days, people said that when you choose a wife, you look at her family; when you choose a husband, you look at his genes. Son, should you not consider whether or not they had it right?"

"Yes, I will mull it over," he replied at once.

He did think about it. But a young man's thinking can't last more than twenty-four hours. The thinking of a young man in love is even shorter. A word from a beautiful person can overcome all barriers of prejudice and suspicion.

The very next afternoon, Vu hurriedly looked for Van and asked her casually: "Do you think your father and mother's marriage is a satisfactory one?"

"No, a thousand times no," Van replied without hesitation. The reply was direct and straightforward. The whimsical marriage between the teacher Vuong and the fish sauce wholesale dealer Tuyet Bong had been a subject of constant comment for several decades in the community, so, unwillingly, Van had heard every derisive word since she was about five. Looked at from every angle, from physical appearance to character, Van's parents presented a rare caricature. A very proper teacher with a sparkling and noble countenance, never speaking but politely, with pleasantly open gestures, living with a heavyset woman, avaricious and caustically argumentative. Behind her back people called her "the fat bitch with the filthy mouth." And they ranked her principally according to the way she used her loud mouth with its thin, haughty lips: "Pay the price" or "No credit: settle in cash"; quarreling with or swearing indiscriminately at the neighbors' children and grandchildren. She also constantly stuffed her mouth with junk food—a never-ending indulgence. Without taking into account her maliciousness or her way of putting on airs with money and wealth, just considering her mother's appetite, many times the daughter blushed in front of her friends.

As if to have her boyfriend know full well her resolution, Van explained: "When my dad's father was very sick, he called my grandmother and father into his room to ask that he marry my mother, Bong. A week later, before he died, he spoke of this again. So, after the mourning period, grandmother arranged the marriage for them."

"Why did your grandfather force your dad that way?"

"I don't know. Because my grandmother didn't know and my dad didn't know."

"Even though your father didn't love your mother?"

"Everyone—in the family and in the neighborhood—knew that."

"In the family, grandfather was God. One word from him was an order."

"Now would your father demand that you marry someone you don't love, like your grandfather once did?"

"Never!" Van replied right away, automatically. "I would never accept that."

"Why?"

"Because the times have changed. Now modern women wear shorts in public. I'm not that modern but I don't live in feudal times either."

They laughed chokingly, seeing how lucky they were to live in a new age, with freedom to love and to marry each other according to their own desires. He returned home, repeating to his parents their funny exchange, assured that every suspicion had been resolved. Nevertheless, his parents sought every excuse to thwart this marriage. The prospect of an alliance with the teacher Vuong and his wife the wholesale fish sauce dealer brought numerous anxieties to their hearts. His father looked for causes because, according to custom, there had to be some hidden and awful connection if one were to force a child to repay a fearful debt. No one misunderstood this truth: that Mr. Vuong had to live with Tuyet Bong was the same as accepting the harsh conditions of hell or purgatory for the rest of your life, an entire life bartered away in an exchange. And the last point was the important one: every such marriage—strange and unfortunate—often left behind destructive tendencies for future generations.

Popular speculation had provided many theories to explain all this. Some held that Old Mr. Secretary, father of the teacher Vuong, had once gone with Mr. Licentiate, father of Tuyet Bong, to Laos to dig for gold. Once, when the pit had collapsed, the latter had saved his friend from death. Then, out of gratitude for saving his life, Old Mr. Secretary had promised to marry the only daughter of his savior to his only son.

But many others instead insisted that the story of panning for gold was too far-fetched: both men grew their fingernails long and couldn't even hold a knife securely—how could they have found the strength to follow a group of miners to pan for gold?

Gold always flows in the same veins as blood. In this line of work, if you are not the chief honcho of a pit, having bags filled with cash and a brain filled with devilish schemes, then most likely you take up working in the pit as an ordinary ruffian or rascal, unafraid of quarrels with guns and knives, or you might be at a dead end, without another livelihood, ready to throw your life away as so much straw or grass . . . In actuality, both "old men" were born gamblers. Year-round they gambled, winning a lot but also not infrequently losing. During one unlucky year, Old Mr. Secretary lost continuously throughout the winter. But the more his pockets emptied, the more he craved filling them again, with a bitter passion, so he pledged his house with its lands and gardens, in town as well as in the countryside. All his wealth, both hidden and visible assets, was placed on the gaming table in the mad hope of getting back the money lost. But destiny abandoned him, leaving only bad luck, the two stuck together like shape and shadow. At last all the wealth was consumed in the fires of gambling. At New Year's Old Mr. Secretary envisioned the scene of his wife and children being thrown out of their home, to seek refuge in street corners or marketplace nooks. Afraid and tormented over his wrongdoing, Old Mr. Secretary tried to kill himself. At that precise moment, Old Mr. Licentiate settled his friend's debts large and small, with only the wish that later, after their children had grown up, they would become in-laws.

All intriguing rumors are always just that, intriguing rumors. Such theories are only theories because those who had lived with the two are no longer alive to certify the truth with any finality. Besides, all history is only a book reporting theories when behind each and every theory is a multitude of mysteries. The history of each family is no different. Secrets always exist to embellish and to cover our lives in mystery. Vu's parents did not much like such mysteries, but after a year's hard work of investigation they could not find any truth. Thus they had reluctantly agreed to the proposed marriage. And so the wedding had gone off smoothly, though there had been some awkward moments. Indeed, Vu's parents were classy people, expertly knowing how to hide the awkward aspects to the utmost extent possible.

During its beginning years, the young couple's married life unfolded as one might wish. They lived by themselves, partly because of their work and partly because his parents lived with his oldest brother's family. A separate house for them was provided before the wedding. However, during their years of passion, his family was always a warm cradle never out of his mind. His old home was a place to which he often returned. His wife had to accept this. In her heart of hearts, she wanted to monopolize his time as well as his love but knew that this was impossible. Routinely, at the end of every week, they went back to Vu's family home. Everybody came together around meals of familiar home-cooked dishes that could satisfy more than those in fancy restaurants. Vu's mother, despite her age, was still an extraordinary cook. She made snail stew with banana stems, frog stir-fried with pepper and bamboo shoots, catfish soup with vegetables, shrimp braised in rice wine, or eel braised in turmeric. Additionally, not only was the food good, the family atmosphere was warm, reflecting genuine affection among people coming from the same root. Only once each year did they visit Van's home, for Tet, the New Year. That could not be avoided; it was a hallowed tradition. Vu was obliged to go along for a few meals. He could endure that duty, even though he had to see his mother-in-law. He felt as if he were being tormented by sharp thorns every time he witnessed her abrasive manner: when she shouted demands at the servants, her obnoxious way of handling money, or the unattractive, unrefined way by which she expressed her contentment—while still chewing, she tilted her face and laughed, showing all the food mixed up in her big open mouth in a gross display.

The fish sauce distributor was fully aware of all this. One time, she blurted openly: "I know I don't appreciate the two of you. But the two of you don't appreciate me either. It's best that everyone eats as they like and each sleeps in his own bed. It's enough that, once a year, you just bring gifts for the altar."

"What are you saying? It's so petty . . ." The teacher rolled his eyes in anger.

Mrs. Tuyet Bong closed her eyes and kept her mouth shut. Even though she could be quite vulgar, could pull up her skirt and start a fight with anyone over a penny or let loose a string of toxic curses with any neighbor who dared touch her or her son, she still feared her husband a lot. To him she was like a loyal dog. Her extremely thick lips always shut when he raised his voice. Her tigress eyes flipped into those of a meek rabbit whenever he glared at her. When he gave an order, immediately she had to jump off her high horse, even though just a minute before she had been prancing around on it as if off to do battle. Neighbors said that she was born under the sign of the rat and he under that of the snake, thinking that, while a rat can taunt a cat, in front of a snake it will become completely paralyzed and just wait for death. Others of meaner spirit would say that the zodiac made no difference; a person like her, thanks to a mysteriously predetermined fate, could only sit and daydream . . . of a guy with torn pants and shirt, barefooted, with infected eyes, whose job was to chase after hogs down country roads.

And so, for many years they lived by this principle: a daughter-in-law belongs to you; a son-in-law is a guest. Van had never showed annoyance when her husband criticized the bad habits of her beloved younger brother, Tung. But recently, everything had changed. Ever since their own son had grown up to become a second beloved Tung, there was a risk that he would become worse than the original one. The rottenness that grows on the tree of power is a thousand times worse than any mold that sprouts from plain dirt or just pops up or in the middle of the hay.

"Alas! Children are golden chains, fetters . . ."

A plaintive thought suddenly popped up in his mind. Simultaneously, his heart was pierced by two arrows. Two faces appeared all at once: that of his own son and that of another man's son.

"I will die . . . I will die because of this tug of war . . . for this pain is something I cannot share with anyone . . . in this dark tunnel there is no escape . . ."

He moaned. He suddenly remembered that his wife was in bed and for sure was still awake. He hurriedly gnashed his teeth to put a stop to his moan. Then another face appeared, along with a thought as sharp as a sword's blade:

"But no, I have no right to die; at least not now. With my death, those scoundrels will have a free hand. With my death, too many people will be affected. I wouldn't know what misfortunes will occur. No, I have to live. I don't have the right to give up . . ."

Holding his head in his hands, he groped as if he were injured and found his way to bed.

4

The airplane cannot take off due to thick fog.

The fog hangs like white silk swatches twisting over the airport and the green grass turns dark as it drunkenly absorbs moisture from the low-hanging fog. A young woman brings a tray of tea and politely places it in front of Vu:

"Sir, please drink some tea. It will be a long while before the plane can take off."

"Thank you, miss. How many times this month has the plane been delayed?"

"Three times already. Today is the fourth."

"Usually how long is the wait?"

"It depends on each day's weather, but on average until past noon."

"You know that proverb, too?"

"Yes, the elders said: 'Rain does not last past noon; wind not past three p.m.' . . . My maternal grandmother taught me that." Saying this, the girl turns the teacup faceup on the saucer, and pours tea. The fragrance of the jasmine tea rises and makes the room less desolate and empty, as guest houses and railway stations often feel.

"In one hour the cafeteria will sell beef soup and sesame balls. But if you need them now, I will fetch some for you."

"Thank you. I have already had breakfast at home," he replies, but then changes his mind.

"If it is not too much trouble, could you bring me some sesame balls? What kind do they sell at the canteen?"

"We have three kinds: one with savory filling, one with mung bean and cane sugar filling, and one with honey."

"Please bring me those with mung bean and cane sugar."

"Yes, I will bring them up right away," the young woman replies and briskly leaves the room.

His eyes follow her while he ponders: "She must be well connected to get work as an airport employee."

All girls from the countryside with muddy feet and hands who are selected to work for the government or in the big city have this enthusiasm and dedication. Their bodies are full of life, their faces are tanned by the sun; their enthusiasm is that of those who have twirled in a tense tempo under the utmost hard work to then fall into a life with a slow pace and many amenities.

"But in only a short while, they will change. From their appearance to their character . . . With the years, everything will change slowly . . ." he melancholically thinks while sipping his tea.

The young woman returns with a plate full of sesame balls. There are so many, he would need to be thirty-five years younger to be able to consume them all. The airport canteen's regular patrons are young pilots and mechanics with active stomachs or new soldiers who pour in from the countryside.

Placing his plate properly on the table, the young woman bows her head once more and leaves.

"Thank you, miss."

Vu smiles and starts to nibble on the sesame balls. With the cup of tea, his appetite unexpectedly returns and he eats two. To his surprise Vu drinks several more cups of tea. That very morning, his wife had served him a bowl of noodles as usual. That bowl of noodles had had the same ingredients and flavors as always, but he couldn't take more than two spoonfuls. Perhaps because the two of them had had a sleepless night; an empty and cold night that hardens your heart and soul. When a man and a woman share a bed but won't or can't make love, or they do not want or have anything meaningful to share, then their hearts turn in different directions and their brains are filled with different thoughts. To be bound together in such torment is frightening.

That morning, when the alarm clock rang, he got up and immediately went out to the garden, knowing full well that he could catch a cold. Walking aimlessly among the trees for a while, he then had gone in to get dressed. Then he sat down at the dining table in front of the bowl of noodles that his wife had prepared. He suddenly looked at Van's face, swollen with lack of sleep. It appeared exactly like that of Mrs. Tuyet Bong.

He thought, "I am getting old; I can't see clearly. Nobody ever said that Van looked like her mother. People always commented that she was a carbon copy of Teacher Vuong, just like Tung was a copy of the fish sauce wholesaler."

Then he had looked and looked at his woman—the person who had shared his life for more than thirty years, the one he was so familiar with, from the way she brushed her teeth and combed her hair, to the style and color of her favorite clothes, the way she picked up her food or put on her charms. He had then looked at her with some doubt, in the state of someone who cannot rely on his own senses. Because from a certain angle, he did see that his wife did have some of Mrs. Tuyet Bong's features. It was not the shape of the face, nor the bridge of her nose, nor her walk or smile, but an invisible resemblance that eluded any verbal description.

"It's not my imagination, but the weakness of my mind in analyzing . . . or a simple habit of forgetting. I have seen Van standing with her hands on her waist, arguing with a cadre managing supplies, in a strident and vulgar way just like her mother. That was long ago. Sixteen or seventeen years ago. That time she was extremely ashamed of herself. Now, it happens again and she is no longer ashamed. With the months and years, everything rots away . . ."

"Sir, let me pour more water in the teapot."

The young woman has come back with a thermos of hot water in her hands. She is about to pour water into the teapot, but she hesitates and asks:

"Sir, do you need new tea?"

Vu looks up and answers: "Thank you. The tea is still strong, you can just add more water for me."

He fills his cup with the new very hot tea. He brings it up to the level of his chin, where the steam spreads across his face and a whisper repeats itself again and again:

"With the years, everything slowly rots away . . . With the years . . ."

He does not know what causes this thought to take over his brain, something like those hungry leeches that stick tightly to the thighs of miserable water buffaloes. Vu's family owned no rice fields, but rural life had been familiar to him since youth thanks to summer vacations. Later, when he committed himself to the revolution, he was forced to become familiar with paddy fields. During that entire period, the image that terrified him most, a fear he could not acknowledge, was the sight of leeches in low-lying fields. Every time he saw a pack of leeches darkening the water's face and chasing after bait, whether the bait was him or someone else, Vu's skin grew goose bumps. He despised leeches not because they sucked people's blood, because mosquitoes as well as other insects did likewise, but because, most frightening to him, their slimy bodies evoked uncertainty, a kind of elastic and free-floating danger, a threat about which one could not predict either its origins or its end.

There is a kind of pain that tugs like the leeches do, that grabs the heart tightly at its deepest recess and never lets go. Real leeches are not that dangerous; you can let them suck the blood of water buffaloes until they grow as fat as your big toe. Once satiated, they just fall off. You can drop those blood-filled leeches into a pit of active lime, and in that way most effectively massacre these parasites. But when facing a lingering pain, people become paralyzed, unable to pull the parasite out from a bleeding heart.

Vu does not remember in which book he read about this. But suddenly the thought returns, like smoke from smoldering hay hanging over the field of memory.

Suddenly, cheerful laughter catches his attention: popping out of the door frame between the canteen and the kitchen is a group of four young girls, each one round, with red cheeks, twinkling eyes, and a face full of happiness. The two in the front carry a big basket with a heap of sesame balls. The two behind, even more hefty, carry the largest size of army pot, probably with broth for the beef noodle soup. Behind the four girls comes a fellow with skin dark as a burned house pillar and shoulders square as a Tet rice cake, carrying a basket of sliced noodles. It's time for the canteen to serve the morning meal to the soldiers at the airport. Vu looks down at his watch; at that moment a gong is struck briskly.

After three slow and three fast rings, the airport soldiers happily enter, every single one of them with his hair well groomed, his uniform well pressed, his complexion smooth and pinkish, clearly the most important, pampered group of soldiers in the corps. They walk while joking around, exchanging stories and conniving looks.

Out of curiosity Vu follows them with his eyes, thinking: "In this group of good friends, who, I wonder, will take a knife and stab whom? Who will pour poison into whose glass of water? And who will lure whom into a spot that has been mined?"

The young soldiers see him. They stop chattering, raise their hands in salute, and follow one another to sit at a row of tables on the right side of the room, an area reserved for middle-grade meals.

The canteen is only one room, serving only one kind of sesame ball and one kind of beef noodle soup, but it is divided into two sections. The area where he sits is reserved for higher-class meals, the floor having been raised some six inches by a platform that has had a veneer carefully applied, one that shines like a mirror. Also, the chairs and tables here are made of good wood and the tables are covered with white tablecloths. The cups, plates, and bowls are nice, thin Chinese porcelain. The area on the right, at a lower level and reserved for middle-grade meals, has a brick floor. Here the furniture is of plain wood, there are no table coverings, the cups are aluminum and the bowls and plates of Hai Duong porcelain, the kind that is thick like tiles but chips easily. Dividing the two areas, as if to clearly mark the separation, is a row of carved wooden posts hung with strings of paper flowers in various colors. In a disdainful, aloof manner Vu looks at the strings of shiny flowers and smiles cynically as he thinks to himself:

"What is the difference between a bowl of upper-grade noodle soup and middle-grade soup? Maybe the first bowl holds twelve pieces of beef and the other only six or eight pieces. Is it that the first bowl gets more sliced onions than the second, or that its broth might have more fat or more pepper? Oh, this practice is so far from the ideals of all those who joined the revolution. After many bones have been broken and much blood spilled, all so that life falls back to counting the pieces of meat put in a bowl of pho or on a plate of food . . ."

He quickly gulps a mouthful of hot tea, suddenly recognizing the familiar path that leads to purgatory. But the shiny paper flowers grab his attention. The thought of caste division, of the dominion of power, of precarious and unchanging conditions of man's existence . . . all of these permanent tensions rip and tear his heart like a pack of leeches.

Yesterday morning, as soon as he had arrived at the office and before he could even put his briefcase on the desk, the young secretary had hurriedly run in to report that the administrative office of Central Party Headquarters was summoning him unexpectedly. This secretary, skinny with a pale, greenish face and an anxious disposition, looked really pathetic:

"Chief, please leave immediately, Leader Sau is waiting."

Vu laid the briefcase on the desk and said slowly: "Who gives that order?"

The secretary looked up with big, round eyes and lowered his voice as if he had to whisper: "Leader Sau himself called by phone not ten minutes ago. He called not just once but twice."

"He called twice because he likes to exercise his voice," Vu replied.

But when he saw the shocked face of the secretary, confused and terrified, he quickly added: "Prepare my documents."

"Yes, Chief. Leader Sau said that it's a special meeting, so you don't need to bring any documents as usual."

"That's fine."

Vu put the leather briefcase in the cabinet, and folded some newspapers to bring along. He had planned on such reading to pass the time while driving. But once in the car, he felt anxious so he threw the stack of papers in a corner.

"What special development could have happened today?" Vu thought to himself. "For a long time he hasn't called me urgently like this, not since the day when the pack of cards was flipped open."

On getting out of the car, he passed the guards—bones and flesh standing as still as wooden statues, faces held up at a right angle, chests extended as ordered, rifles pointing straight up toward the sky. Their profession was to be just like that: a display of earthly force, a means of threatening and menacing outsiders. Such display was familiar to him, so why had he suddenly felt different, surprised and unfriendly? For a long time now, he had seen in this daily exhibit only a boring presentation. But today, he realized that it had been set up solely for him, designed to warn him alone. The emotionless faces of those wooden statues hid a danger that he couldn't yet detect. As if there were some kind of unseen plot filling up space; as if there were some kind of suffocating gas in the air, or a snake's venom, or a poison . . . an invisible killer slipping into his lungs. He abruptly turned around to look at the soldiers even after he had already stepped inside the garden. Then he tried to analyze his strange sensations but was unable to come up with any satisfactory explanation. In such a state, he walked through the garden full of vibrantly colorful spring flowers, while his mind searched in the midst of a dark tunnel of bewilderment and suspicion. Before climbing to the third floor, he glanced up and saw Sau already standing there, looking down on the garden. He waved at Vu. Vu's face flushed as he thought that Sau might have witnessed him turning around and looking at the soldiers; and very likely had guessed at the secret thoughts being born in his brain. The soldiers were Sau's, chosen by him, paid by him personally, and he personally designed their privileges and applied disciplinary fines. Those soldiers without question would follow his personal orders. That was a reality known to all.

Sau waited for him in the hall so that they could together walk into the reception room, which was very spacious, more like a place to play pool or ping pong. Next to some couches set beside one another, there was a table along the left wall, also ridiculously large, on which there were many assorted glasses and cups from different countries lined up in a long file for tea and filtered coffee. A young lad was busy there preparing drinks.

Stepping into the room, Sau ordered: "Stop, leave it all there."

The servant disappeared at once like a ghost. Then Sau's hand pointed him to a low armchair: "Sit down. Today I have business to take up with the Department of Foreign Affairs. I can't receive you as long as usual. We shall work together quickly."

Having already sat down, Vu stood up at once, saying: "If you are busy, I will leave. We can meet another time."

"The matter is urgent; that's why I summoned you so hurriedly."

"Even if urgent, I will still work according to procedures. I don't want to bother others. I don't accept working in a patchwork manner."

Sau stopped and looked at him attentively, as if stunned. Apparently nobody had dared talk with him that way for a long time. Apparently, too, it was very hard for him to swallow. And, apparently, he was not prepared to react to such a situation. An awkward moment passed.

He suddenly smiled: "Why, now, do you get angry so easily? In the past people said you were cool like Jell-O . . ."

"However you are born, you die the same way. That's how it was put."

Playfully, Sau shook his head: "That's not true. Your character changes with time. I have changed, not to become angry like you, but more playful. There's this interesting point . . ."

He started laughing loudly, a very delighted laughter: "What I am going to say is not easily understood by those like you who have Confucian blood running thick in you; in fact, it even seems absurd . . . Listen here . . ."

Sau approached close to his armchair, bent over, and laced each sentence with a delightful and unhidden malice: "In my old age, I suddenly like to look at pretty girls. It's like cigarettes or pipes—you stop for decades then suddenly you crave them . . . If not for my work, each morning I would go to West Lake. There, at sunrise, groups of girls come to exercise and row boats, all of them about sixteen or seventeen, all pretty as if in a dream."

As he finished talking, he turned and went to the table against the wall, to pour coffee into two black cups. Vu quietly looked at the crow's-feet around his eyes, realizing he had aged even though he still had that big and tall body with a light skin, the gift of a princely body bestowed by heaven, that he usually assesses half seriously and half in jest during casual discussions: "My body has enough strength to hold twelve different lifetimes, with enough agility to serve thirty-six women with dedication, from nubile ones to middle-aged beauties."

Behind every one of his jokes there is always someone buried in some deep forest corner, on some isolated trail, or in some dark prison cell. Vu looks at his pink, fat nape reaching up from the collar of his black shirt and wonders: "This morning, who is implicated in all these flirty jokes?"

Sau had come back with two cups of coffee in his hands. The aroma diffused throughout the room. He squinted and asked: "Don't you find this coffee exquisite?"

Vu replied: "I've only smelled it, not yet tasted it."

"Silly, you only need to smell coffee to know its quality. You are not yet a connoisseur."

"I have never held myself out to be a connoisseur of anything. But, based on my experience, there are many foods that you only smell and don't eat. Like fried fish marinated in poison, for example. When I was still living in the small town at home, I saw my neighbor bait a dog that way."

"Ha , ha . . ." Sau burst into laughter, laughter that resonated throughout the room and then out into the hall. A girl poked her head in, then disappeared at once. Sau put a cup of coffee in front of him and said, "Drink . . . You do have a gift for argument . . . Really, I should have assigned you to run the Ministry of Foreign Affairs."

"Really?" Now Vu also laughed. "Then correct the mistake; it's still not too late . . ."

He started to sip his coffee.

On the other side of the table, Sau also began to drink quietly. A huge gold ring on his fourth finger, about the size of a railroad screw head, reflected on the black glaze of the imported cup.

Vu ponders as he looks at the twinkling reflection on the porcelain glaze. Black coffee in a black cup. How exquisite! You really should be an interior decorator for private homes or a painter for the stage. That way fewer people would die unjustly. Meanwhile, Sau had put his cup on the table and stretched out against the low armchair. The collar of his black shirt contrasted with his fair and pink complexion, still full of sensuality even though blotted with age spots. He likes the color black. He has dozens of black shirts. In receiving foreign guests or when appearing before the people, he has to wear white shirts and suits, but on other occasions he always wears black shirts. This is a preference worth noting. It could be his careful way of grooming, caring for his smooth skin. It also could be to create an image of a gangster in black dress or of historical martial artists dressed in black. No one dares to discuss this openly, except Vu. One time, he opened the topic, going on the attack:

"You are really very seductive in a black shirt . . . contemporary and youthful, too . . . in a black shirt, you look ten years younger . . . that way you cheat life out of ten extra years," Vu had told him once during a lunch break at a conference when all the delegates had sat down at their tables. Sau had appeared shocked, he couldn't believe all that his ears had just heard. But Vu had carefully added: "I think that it's the way you use colors to shine over the others. It's an old game, been around since the beginning of the century, actually, nothing new to it at all. Furthermore, what you do is already enough to create an impression. The mechanisms of power are in your hands—with the power of life and the power of death. Why do you still need to wear black shirts?"

"You, you . . ." Sau had stuttered, his face pale with anger. The people around them were also pale from fear. But Vu had calmly looked at him. A split second passed; Sau smiled. Responding to this smile, Vu had smiled, too, the smile of someone about to step up to the gallows. In that moment of dead silence and cold animosity, Sau had said with warmth and friendliness: "Have you been stung by a bee? How does the wearing of a black or white shirt have any influence on the people's welfare?"

Vu had smiled cynically: "It does! Wearing black shirts saves on soap. That way, you are a good role model for young people. The only thing is, ten kilograms of soap cost less than a bottle of French perfume, which I see you bring home from every trip abroad. You carry a suitcase full for your primary and secondary ladies inside and outside your home."

"I give up," Sau had politely replied but then added: "You need to be more understanding of others. Not everyone can live like a monk as you do. Men are like roosters; they must know how to show off their combs and wiggle their tail feathers." At this, he smiled faintly and left. The other delegates had sat dead still while shuffling their chopsticks and passing bowls around . . .

Three weeks after this, Vu's oldest brother came up from the countryside. He didn't rest after the drive and together they went to the flower garden by West Lake, where the rock jetties are covered with duckweed roots and dead ephemera. Right away, without any hesitation, his brother said:

"Someone told me everything. Do you plan to die?"

"I am still alive because I don't fear him. Otherwise, my grave by now would have been covered with green grass."

"He is an unusually dangerous type. His kind only comes along once in a while. Have you already forgotten the lesson of Le Dinh?"

"I have not. But I am not in the same situation."

"I am very worried for you . . . If something should happen to you . . ."

Vu squeezed his brother's hand and looked at his face with great warmth and trust:

"Dear brother, in such a situation, we can only rely on family loyalty. We will do all that we can. Success or failure is up to heaven."

The elder brother choked with emotion: "I only worry about you; as for me, I will pass. In our family, you are the only one with hair, I am bald. They won't pay any attention to me."

"I am no different from you. We have no line of retreat."

They held hands and said nothing more, because at that moment, from the Quan Thanh temple, a couple emerged. They crossed Co Ngu Street and walked toward the brothers.

Sau's voice suddenly rose and startled him: "Why, by now you must be able to assess things accurately, yes?" Immediately Vu put down his cup of coffee.

"Good! Indeed, it's very good."

Sau leaned completely back against the chair, in a posture of commanding nonchalance, his arms positioned symmetrically on the arms of the chair.

"Are you hooked on coffee or on tea?"

"I like both, but I'm not hooked on anything. Now, tell me what you have to say."

"Obviously something's up."

He stopped as if waiting for Vu to continue asking.

Fully familiar with Sau's tactics, Vu distractedly looked out the windows, as if he had forgotten the matter, or the subject was nothing to be concerned about.

Finally, Sau drank the last of his coffee and said:

"The office just informed me that the Old Man has requested to go down the mountains and visit with some citizen."

"What citizen?"

"A woodsman who fell into a ravine and then died on a stretcher on the way back to the village. I've asked you to come so that you can go and advise the Old Man to give up this idea. Right now we are in the middle of a hundred, a thousand things to do. The Old Man shouldn't complicate matters."

"The Old Man is president of the country. He established the Party . . . How can I mentor him? Who came up with this weird idea?"

"This is not a weird idea but an intelligent recommendation. Brother Ba has decided on this. It is also Ba who had the idea, right now, that you are the only one who can explain things to the Old Man."

"Explain things to the Old Man!"

Vu dropped the cup of coffee and sprang up. An anger burned away inside his body, spread to his veins, pulled at all his muscles, and tightly squeezed his heart. He suddenly found himself shaking, his voice also shaking accordingly.

"What are you saying? For me to tell the Old Man what to do?"

"No . . . No . . . I apologize."

Sau also jumped up and he suddenly stuttered, out of some confusion:

"I spoke badly . . . I forgot the right words . . . I sincerely apologize to you. But Brother Ba said, at this time, you are the one closest to the Old Man, the one who can sway him."

"I am not the only one, the whole people are close to him. That's the honest truth. If all of you have forgotten that, then I want to remind you."

"I know! I know!" Sau replied, and all of a sudden his lips turned white, the drops of coffee forming clear brown spots on them as he drank.

"I am sorry I used the wrong words. This happens to lots of other people as well, because we are just Party cadres, not thinkers or writers."

"What do thinkers and writers have to do with this? They're just clowns who dance around in roles written out for them," Vu shouted inwardly, wanting to spit this out into Sau's face, but an intuition about the need to be moderate stopped him. Pretending not to pay any attention to what Sau had said, Vu lifted his coffee cup and sipped to the last drop. Then, as if he had regained his equilibrium, Sau cleared his voice and said:

"The truth is, I am thoughtless sometimes because I am too busy. I keep thinking that the Old Man is convalescing, so it's best to let him rest. Besides, at the moment all helicopter units are activated for combat duty. The Old Man needs to be understanding toward us. The country is at war."

Vu looked straight into his face: "You really think that I can tell the Old Man what you told me earlier? Do you think that's possible?"

"Oh, no! I don't want to say that you must report back to him those naked concerns just like that, but in a different way and with different words."

"With more honeyed words, more polished words? Is that what you mean? I am like the rest of you, not a writer."

"Talking with you is damn hard. You intentionally don't want to understand. It is clear that the Old Man is fond of you and trusts you more than the rest of us. Once people like and trust each other, they become more sympathetic. The war is getting tense; we have to draft all soldiers and enlist the entire people. The Old Man needs to rest, to take care of his health, so that he can receive delegations of heroic soldiers returning from battles. No one can do this except the Old Man."

"I'm not clear if I really have the honor of being loved and trusted by the Old Man as you said, but the truth is, besides him, nobody can do it. That's the plain truth; even the blind can see it. If this were not the plain truth, your grave would be green with grass. And not only yours."

Vu laughed silently in his stomach: "You really are an honest fellow sometimes, Vu. Either that or you are a second class actor."

Lifting his empty coffee cup, Vu tilted his head and slowly said:

"You run the Party's organizational machine; you know the personal history of each person like the back of your hand; you should know very well that before I joined the revolution, I had been well educated. My ancestors taught me that whenever someone truly cares for you, you must respond with fundamental trust and with loyalty. If the Old Man likes me, I cannot reciprocate like a thief or a traitor."

Sau laughed, even though only faintly: "Oh, for sure you are a stickler for words."

That said, he abruptly got up as if a scorpion had bit his butt and started pacing with big steps in the room. Like a mirror the glassy tiles reflected his tall and hefty image. His shoes were polished to a shine. Vu had the impression that Sau listened carefully to the knocking sound of his heels on the floor, as if he were counting each footstep . . . One of Vu's colleagues with the same rank had once told him that in a meeting with Sau, he had let Vu's colleague sit tight in a chair for an entire half hour, while he circled around and around without seeming tired, like a salesman showing off a new style of shoes.

Vu thought: "You don't have the smarts to understand that all tricks grow tiresome if overperformed. All contrived threats from literature and the arts need to change."

Looking him over from head to feet, Vu said:

"You appear still quite limber. You can still serve the ladies for a long while . . ."

Looking at Vu's playful eyes, Sau realized that he had made a wrong move. His face hardened, but he smiled and sat down in front of Vu, stretching his arms behind the armchair, as if his recent display was only part of his early morning exercise, a habit to invigorate the start of day for those who must rub the seat of their pants on office chairs.

"I thank you; thanks to heaven my machinery still works well. That's without using herbal medicine."

Then, as if to avoid a blow from Vu, he suddenly cried out as if he had just remembered something important:

"Damn, I've been so busy lately, I forgot to call the Old Man. And you?"

"The Old Man has not called me for a long time as well," Vu replied coldly.

Sau rushed to say:

"If so, I will arrange for you to visit him. Every now and then, it's good to go back and visit the mountains."

"It's up to you," Vu answered summarily and stood up.

At the same instant Sau, too, jumped up, quickly like a cat, to grab Vu's arms tightly:

"Let me phone to have them make arrangements. You can leave tomorrow."

That's why Vu is here, at the domestic airport reserved for the air force, right at seven o'clock in the morning. Now, seated, he drinks his tea and stares at the bloated fog on the other side of Dinh Cong Lake. Waiting.

5

Since waking up, the president has stared into the east, waiting for the sun to rise. But white clouds cover all four directions.

The clouds submerge the mountaintops in a vast white ocean. From the crevasses to the deep ravines, the watery mist curls upward like smoke, a kind of wet, cold smoke infused with the smell of forest tree and the fragrance of wildflowers. Those gigantic moving mists look like blind dragons feeling their way toward an unknown destination. Those dragons at times crawl across the rows of mountains by stretching out their strange bodies, at times crunch together and pile up in the valleys, forming images of fighting monsters. The sky has no horizon; unseen are the swaths of forests, high or low, over three ridges of mountains. Even the temple garden is immersed in fog. The white mist hovers just outside the window of his room.

Seated and looking at the sea of fog, the president puts a finger on his pulse and counts . . . ninety-five, ninety-six, ninety-seven . . . the numbers jump without stopping. At this age, it's hard to master one's body. The president knows he is waiting for one person, and the apprehension keeps coming on even if he does not want it to:

"Why, for no reason, am I in this awkward situation? A few years ago, everything was different . . ."

He wonders but knows he has no answer.

About five or six years earlier, he had thought that all things were settled. The chess game was over. The old gown wasn't even in the trunk but had been burned up. All the pictures, too, had turned into ashes to be mixed with dust. Even with all that, still his heart is beating hard. .

He thinks to himself: "Whatever; from every perspective there is no way to salvation. Once the path has become entangled with thorny vines and the well has been filled in, no longer is there any reflection off the water in which to look for a vision of the one who was . . ." But all of a sudden, an opposing voice speaks out in his soul:

"It was a wrong move. It was the most humiliating move that could happen in the life of a person, especially for a man."

The president sighs. "I had no other choice."

The opposing voice says: "It was not that you didn't have an alternative way. The problem was that you didn't have the courage to choose another path."

He replies: "But now, one door has closed. What has passed is over and done with."

His mysterious opponent bursts into despising laughter: "Everything is not finished as you imagine. Every failure always brings along consequences that the loser cannot fully measure. This is a warning from me to you!"

The clouds have not dissipated.

"Why so much fog this morning?"

Unable to stay seated, feeling half paralyzed and half anxious as if he were perched on charcoal, the president stands up. As soon as he puts his feet down on the steps, the chubby soldier rushes in from the temple patio and stops him:

"The fog is very bad for you; please stay inside."

"I've sat here since this morning."

"Please wait a few moments, when the fog clears you can go out to the patio."

"Did you see the abbess and her attendant? . . . One is seven years older than I am and the other is a weak woman. Both have been out on the patio since early morning; they didn't wait for the sun to be over the mountains."

"Yes, but . . ."

"Let me go out for a while for some fresh air. Staying in the room too long, I will suffocate from sadness and my limbs will be paralyzed."

"Sir . . ."

But he has forcefully brushed the soldier aside and decisively stepped down onto the patio. There by the cherry garden he stands fixed like a stone. The fog comes over his face cold and wet, with a faint and fresh smell of the mountains. In the main temple, the candles flicker, the sound of the wooden gong mixes with the normal chanting of prayers, a kind of music that has become familiar to him. Every so often when the prayer chanting stops, the dripping sound of dew on the tile roof is clearly heard, a mossy roof that has turned blackish. With time, the wooden door frame has also taken on a darker shade. In this desolate and enchanting setting, the light from the candles grows more iridescent and vibrant.

"Oh! The light of a fire . . . Why is it like firelight?"

His heart breaks with a savage cry. The candle flames in the pagoda remind him of another flame, years back in the deep forests of the north . . . the distant flame of the maquis . . . flames that danced, that popped and exploded like so many eggplant and mustard flowers. A huge house, with strings of multicolored paper flowers cut by the clumsy hands of kids who hung them on the pillars. Spaced among the flowers were sheets of glistening gold paper. He knew well that in order to have those glistening sheets, for an entire year the young man in charge of the youths had had to collect and save the wrapping paper from his cigarette packs, the sole luxury he allowed himself.

He remembers as if all the youthful faces illuminated that night by the flames were shining bright with happiness.

But, what year was it really? It couldn't be the year Binh Tuat (1946), because that year the resistance movement had taken shape, material requirements were mostly in place, even the printing plant for making Blue Buffalo notes was up and running. It must have been Dinh Hoi (1947). Yes indeed, the year Dinh Hoi.

One afternoon, at approximately three thirty or close to four, judging by the slant of the sun's rays through the leaves, he had had his head bent down in reading a document when he suddenly heard continuous chattering. When he looked up, he saw the chief office administrator smiling broadly:

"Mr. President, in a little while please join our celebration."

"What's the occasion?"

"Don't you remember that we are still celebrating the Children's Festival?"

He was briefly surprised and said: "I thought I had done this and had distributed candies to the children."

"Mr. President, you did celebrate and distribute gifts to children from two to ten years old. But today it's the turn of older children, those over ten, especially the young cadets from fifteen to seventeen who study together to prepare for travel to friendly countries."

"Ah, is that so?" he replied, then thought of the two thick piles of documents waiting for him on the shelves.

"I still have so much work."

"May I report that those youth are eagerly waiting for you. They have practiced their songs and dances for a month to welcome this day of celebration. Should you not come, I am afraid . . ."

"Why didn't you organize it all in one day?"

"If we did, it would be too crowded, the auditorium would not hold everyone. The other problem was that the other day the organizers did not have enough candies. We had therefore to split into two sessions."

After he finished talking, he smiled broadly, showing off his teeth, uneven and tainted the color of dirt from smoking pipes. Looking at him, the president laughed:

"Fine. I will work a little more. When it's time you come and get me."

Then he bent over and continued reading documents, completely calm. He had had no idea that fate was waiting for him underneath the pillars of his plank house.

"*Love, when will we see each other again . . .*"

The familiar song from the doctor again comes into his mind, like the electric prod that jabs at his heart. Pain spreads all over his body. He feels as if not only his heart is being crushed but that every cell in his body is being crushed as well. He suddenly thinks of that picture of Cupid, the blindfolded child with wings. The image brings on goose bumps and shivers: "Who knows who in this world will be your love? Who knows when fate's hammer will break open your heart?"

On that night long ago when his chief of staff had come to pick him up, he had still tried to finish the report. Neatly putting away the pile of documents, he had walked to the door. But when he put his foot on the stairs, he had turned around to cover the typewriter with a piece of cloth, fearing dust or some insect dropping from the roof might ruin his work machine. There was no rush in his movements, no stirring emotions in his heart. He had executed each movement with the self-awareness and calm necessary to his status——the leader of a country at war.

The chief of staff had waited for him at the foot of the stairs to take him to where all the sections camped in common. The women's section, the youth section, the National Salvation children, the Democratic Party, the Socialist Party, the Agricultural Society . . . All were arranged into one assembly. The zone for families was also nearby, the area of spouses and children of high-ranking cadres who participated in the resistance while tending to domestic duties. The camp was away from his house across a valley with a stream. By the time the president and his guide reached the valley, it was pitch dark. The chief of staff had swung back and forth a flashlight wrapped in thick cloth, exposing a pinhead of light only the size of a firefly. The valley lacked cover from tall trees. The trees bordering the trail were conifers or narrow-leaved, not providing enough protection against curious eyes in spy planes above. To compensate, there were many wild fireflies, and patches of phosphorus from decaying wood shone like a guiding light for the mountain god or ceremonial lanterns for forest spirits.

They had to rely on such natural lights to walk. In about thirty minutes, they came to the stream. After crossing it, only a short descent remained until they arrived at the encampment. He asked the chief of staff:

"Last time I told you what you need to do when you cross a stream. Do you still remember?"

"Mr. President, you said . . . that . . . that . . ." He chewed on his words between his teeth. It made the president laugh.

"I reminded you to pee on both feet before you cross. That's the old way to prevent arthritis which I once learned. Your generation is still young and doesn't know the laws of heaven. You all take your health for granted. But health is the big asset which we all need to preserve."

"Mr. President, because my brain is thick, I learn now but forget later."

"It's not a question of education: it's not a lack of intelligence but of taking precautions."

The chief of staff smiled, then stepped rearward behind him, and put into practice what he had just learned. Hearing a loud sound of splashing urine, the president had a quick thought:

"For sure, he is healthy. Youth really is a time of paradise."

It took them a while to feel their way across the stream, because the bottom was quite slippery, though the water was not that deep. The rocks were not sharp but the big ones here and there were quite mossy; one needed only a small false step to fall down. Having to go to the clinic was a real bother, especially in the deep mountains and forests, where not all equipment and medicines were available. This very real worry prompted him to always remind himself and others:

"This war is in a very difficult phase. We all must take care of our health. In other words, we have no right to get sick. Clinics and medicines should be reserved for wounded soldiers. Caring for your health to the utmost is discipline; it is the spirit of responsibility to the nation as well as to our own selves."

In the middle of the stream, the chief of staff suddenly grabbed him:

"This spot is very slippery, let me hold your hand and lead the way."

"Thank you, but I have passed the most dangerous spots."

"Do you find the water too cold?"

"Cold or not, we are close to the bank."

The president smiled and said: "Next time, if you mean well, you should ask to carry me before I put my feet in the water."

"Oh, oh, oh . . ."

The young assistant had no way to answer so he cried out like a lamb.

In the darkness, a large group of people straggled forward into view.

"The president . . . the president has arrived . . ."

"The president has arrived."

He raised his voice: "I am here!"

The group cried out and ran down to the stream, where the water was only about a foot deep. Water splashed all over the president's clothes. Lantern light glistened back and forth on the water, and arms grabbed his shoulders, his back. One touched his shirt, another his shoulder. The president recognized these people by the smell of their sweat and breath.

"Are you tired, Mr. President?"

"Sure, I'm tired. But not so much that I have to ask you to carry me to camp," he replied and briskly went up the slope. From here on, the forest was dense. Everybody uncovered their flashlights. Between the two sides of the path, rays of light intermingled in front of him. He felt enthusiastic. He thought of the joy waiting for him. Meeting young people was relaxation to him, like recess for elementary students.

Ahead, lodgings were bright with burning lights. The door frames were burnt orange, a vibrant color in the night. The sound came of children singing to the beat of clapping hands. When he stepped forward, they all stood up and sang loudly to the clapping instead of using words of welcome:

"Our mountains and rivers will be grateful to you generation after generation,
We hear your voice resound among the rivers and mountains,
Let's all go together, advancing down the road to liberation,
Let's all go together, listening to the sacred soul of the southern land calling
  out to us . . ."

All those fresh and youthful faces, those bright eyes, and the bright fires of that night . . . he remembers them clearly to this day. Was it because they had registered at the same time with one face, a couple of eyes, a smile as red as if it carried lipstick, a flock of shiny black hair? Was it because all this had registered at the same time with the image of her?

Oh, no, no!

Maybe time had dyed everything the color of a magical cloud. The truth is, that after that night, he hadn't longed for anything else. The exact truth is, that when his sleep came on, he would recall that glorious night with a light and floating joyfulness: people singing, fires, the *xoe* dance of the mountain folk, and skirts fashioned from scintillating cellophane paper. A boy of about twelve had sung "Song of the Mountain Girl" in a marvelous tenor voice. And finally, a pair of clear brown eyes had looked straight at him across the fire.

Oh, those doe eyes, doe eyes!

His heart sang a high note of admiration:

"How could there be such beautiful eyes? I never saw any other such eyes. A rare gift from the Creator! Are not heaven and earth extraordinary?"

It is so true.

Exactly so true.

After that, he could not remember anything, as work had pressed down on his shoulders. A campaign; then another campaign. A battle front collapsed on the east but expanded to the west. A vitally essential operation was put in motion. An opposing operation brought problems. A network of enemy agents was discovered with half of its members caught and held in jail and the other half reduced to inactivity, widely dispersed or hiding in the shade. The internal situation gave rise to problems that needed redress. The country had a dire lack of culturally able cadres who could handle proselytizing missions and foreign affairs.

He really did not remember anything else.

The months and years passed.

And so passed the vicissitudes of a life. Each life is like an uncharted river, with no one able to foresee its twists and turns, its corroded passages or filled embankments, where its waters will run calm and where they will become rough. Are we not each trapped in fate's long, wide net? Are not the twirlings and turnings inside each of us nothing more than a clown's performance?

If only he could have guessed his fate, he would have turned in another direction . . . If only he could have foreseen his future, he would have avoided heaven's net.

But every "if only" is just a long sigh coming at the end. Every "if only" is like the sound of falling rocks. One hears the loud noise and the breaking only when the rocks are about to hit bottom. Who can raise hand or foot to stop rocks when they fall from mountaintops into deep ravines? Who?

This question might be a bit lame, and he does not want to believe he has a soft heart. The brave resolve of a revolutionary coupled with pride in dialectical materialism stops him from believing in fate. However, his continually nagging mind still awaits an answer. And the answer is buried in the fog along the horizon before him. Thus, whether he likes it or not, he still has to remember one occurrence, one point in time, when, suddenly, his aging heart was pierced.

That had been a fateful summer day.

That noon, General Long had invited him to review plans for an upcoming military campaign: the 1951 fall-winter offensive against French bases. He had been satisfied, from the beginning of the resistance up until that very moment, and felt he could now breathe lightly with relief as he thought to himself:

"The wheels start to turn. We have passed through the wobbling phase of the war, a phase with a thousand difficulties. This summer opens up a new phase."

That summer was in the year of Tan Mao.

He had been born in a Tan Mao year. Summer had come late but was not too muggy. He had planned to wear a set of maroon civvies, but after a few minutes of pondering, he changed into a military uniform. He knew that in uniform he looked younger and more handsome. His slight carriage fit well with either civilian or military clothes. In uniform, though, he could easily assert his charm and power of attraction. In uniform, his features seemed fresher and softer, and in his mind all the songs of his youth rushed back. Those verses lingered on, hidden away within him and bringing him an elation that only he knew. After changing into uniform, he had told his bodyguard that he would go to General Long's cave all by himself, a very short and familiar walk. He had wanted to reclaim for an instant the freedom that had been confiscated. A forest road, the sounds of birds, monkeys, leaves . . . but most of all, to walk alone, to think by himself, to admire the scenery by himself . . . such was truly happiness when one's life was so tightly tied up with a group.

Completely happy, he walked briskly without paying any attention to his surroundings. About halfway along, suddenly someone cried out in panic:

"Stop! Please, Mr. President, stop!"

"Don't take another step. Please, Mr. President, don't!"

Looking up, he saw two girls dangling from a large branch of a fallen tree. They were frantically looking for a way down, their faces very red, their mouths spattered with fig grains. He knew they had been up there sharing the figs, so busy with eating them that they did not see the pedestrian inadvertently invading their world and breaking up their rare opportunity to snack well. When they had suddenly recognized him, they had no time to get down, therefore they had frantically called out to stop him. Then the pair desperately sought a way to escape.

"Be careful! Be careful or you will fall."

It was his turn to cry out in fear when he saw the two of them hugging the tree, sliding down at one scoop like little monkeys.

"Careful!" He cried out and could not help smiling.

"Why don't you come down slowly? Sliding like that, you might fall easily and tear your clothes."

Now on the ground the two girls looked down at their roughed-up clothes.

"Mr. President!"

One girl spoke out and looked up at him.

The president was stunned: it was that pair of eyes! Those doe eyes; the final fixation on that night of celebration four years ago. He recognized the young girl from years past who had stared at him across the fire. In an instant, the images, the colors, the sounds, the memories of that evening's walk with the chief of staff were reborn. Completely. Revivified. After four years, suddenly the ashes of forgotten memories were cleaned away by a gust of wind.

"The late children's festival. That night of celebration moved to the fourth day of the sixth month." The thought moved like lightning. At the same time, a succession of thunderclaps exploded, pressing his head to burst open: "Then she was fifteen! Now she is nineteen!"

Yes, it was her!

It seemed that he had stood there silent for a long time, embarrassing the girls. They looked at each other, then at the tree, then down at the ground.

"We're sorry, Mr. President!"

"We didn't see you, sir."

"We . . ."

He didn't understand her babbling words. He only saw her delicate doe eyes, which looked like deep lakes or dewdrops dangling on a leaf, her curved lashes blinking incessantly like the fluttering of a sparrow's wings. He saw clearly only her full red lips tainted with pieces of fig innards that highlighted her two rows of teeth as bright as pearls. He found her face filled with innocence but having as well that special seductive magnetism given by heaven to a woman who would be known as capable of "rocking the nation and upsetting a city."

He cannot remember what he did to calm the girls down. He also cannot now remember how the girls bade him farewell and how they took their leave. He cannot remember now what he had said to her at the parting moment. His spirits had been topsy-turvy. His heart had beaten as hard as if he had been in his twenties. In that stormy state, sounds coming from all four sides had sounded like a huge choir singing around him—the singing of an invisible, imaginary crowd. Could it have been a forest ghost or a mountain god? The happy cries of a forest lord or dangerous screams from a gaggle of old sorcerers? A fleeting fear had made him stand still. He had stood like that for a while after the girls were long gone. He had listened carefully to the singing of the mysterious choir, had felt the air trembling and twirling, had seen gigantic and shapeless waves curve around and soar. Miraculous space was an ocean and he was a boat that had been thrown to the waves without his consent, without his calculation, without his hesitating . . .

A . . . a . . . a . . .

A . . . a . . . a . . .

He had listened to the sounds ringing from the four points of the forest, following him as a wake follows a ship that has been jolted and pushed into misadventure, some cruel melodrama authored by destiny.

That night he had written in his pocket diary: "Tan Mao Year."

In the Mao month.

Noon. I had . . .

But even the most intelligently curious mind could not have completed the unfinished sentence.

"Mr. President, please come in for your meal."

For a while now the chubby guard has been standing behind him.

"You all have already eaten a while ago?"

"Sir, the company cook is preparing lunch."

"Oh, is that so?" he mutters. For a time he had been eating irregularly, not even three meals a day. Often he even forgot to eat, and eat well, so that the people could trust in his good health. Forgetfulness is the faithful friend of old age, a friend we can't shake off no matter how much we try. He turns and enters the room to sit down before the tray with his breakfast. A bell-shaped bowl has a lid covering it. He turns over the hot lid, moist from steam:

"Ah, so today the cook gives us rice gruel."

The fragrant smell of onions and herbs arises; that fragrant smell so familiar to cooks of long ago. Rice gruel with onions and herbs is light on the stomach as well as a remedy for flu. He has known this fragrance since early childhood.

"Sir, please take your food before it cools," the chubby guard reminds him, his eyes not leaving the president's hands.

He bends his head down to see the finely sliced scallions and the herbs as nicely cut as Chinese bean thread noodles, sharply reminding him of the time when he was sick and the girl showed off by cooking rice gruel for him. The gruel unskillfully cooked by the girl had whole rice grains in it and the scallions were still on their stems.

"Little one, you're a girl from the mountains . . . ! Mountain Girl: you are our nightmare, little one, our private nightmare . . ."

"Oh, please, Mr. President . . ." the soldier blurts out, tilting his head to hear some low noise. After a minute:

"An airplane is coming up, Mr. President, do you hear it?"

"I don't hear anything. The ears of someone over seventy can't compete with those of an eighteen-year-old," he answers with a smile.

He looks to the east. The sun had already been up for some undetermined time. It is a completely ordinary day; the sun wants to hang just like a ripe orange suspended in the air, as a gentle sun, not one of sheer brilliance. A sun still undecided in the middle of a dream; a drowsy sun that could signal something ordinary like a burning areca nut or something like a carriage furiously bringing fire to burn all the land on a cursed planet. The white clouds still swirl like the sea around the mountaintops, but around the sun is a light blue halo. A blue completely surrounded by a strange darkness.

That blue was the color of endless summers. Why has it appeared today?

While he stands looking at the sky to the east, the phone in the corner of his room rings stridently. The chubby guard runs in to answer and comes back to report:

"Mr. President, sir, the helicopter has arrived. The office invites you to go down to the landing strip."

"Has Chief Vu come up?"

"Yes, Chief Vu will accompany you with a bodyguard to take part in someone's funeral in Tieu Phu hamlet. After that, Chief Vu will follow you back to the pagoda. The program has been set."

"I will change clothes."

"Sir, you need to finish all your rice gruel, as the day is very cold. The first squad of guards will come up here to accompany you down to the landing strip.

"Clothes must be chosen.

"Mr. President, sir, all is ready."

6

The mountain roads curve back and forth like a chicken's entrails. Hearing the sound of music, one might think it was close at hand, but the curved road makes its source rather far off. On both sides of the way, bushy bamboo blocks a traveler's progress. But the special singing to send off a soul is continuously melodramatic. First notes from a one-string zither, then those of a flute and a two-string fiddle. As the first refrain ends, up comes the voice of a male singer, low in tone:

"*. . . Soul, oh soul, don't you turn your head back*
Soul, oh soul, don't regret your earthly life"

Like blossoming buds in spring, like colorful and fresh leaves in the summer, turning yellow in the fall or in frigid winter, life on earth is in the Master Craftsman's hands. Who can escape this great game?

From nothingness, our parents give us human incarnations; we cry as we greet life; we laugh the laugh of a child; we set off on our way, under the burdens of carefree youth, and put them down when our breath weakens and our health evaporates.

"Water runs down and hair changes color.
The Master Fisherman spread his net over the four seas.
Life—a vagabond—is like the flashing wings of the butterfly . . ."

He listens to the singing, quietly surprised because this is the first time he has heard such verses, even though he has lived in his own country for so many years now:

"Why only now do I know of these folk songs? Did they just pass by like a wind and I didn't pay attention all those years? Had the government forbidden the people to sing such sentimental lyrics? But life is both birth and death, melancholy is the living twin of happiness."

"Mr. President, please let me carry your overcoat."

A guard steps up to take the overcoat he has just taken off. He gives him the overcoat; then suddenly a throbbing pain runs through his spine. Sweat wets his forehead; he dabs at it with a handkerchief but it won't subside. As the hour of Sending Off the Soul approached, he had intended to visit the unfortunate family, but he had no right to make them wait. Besides, so many people had to accompany him. To his front, the first squad is walking with the village chief, a tall, lanky woman who looks partly French, having shoulders broad like a cross and so bulging with muscles that any man looking at her would feel intimidated. She wears traditional clothes, a long hanging blouse made of thin blue cloth, trousers of shiny black satin; but then she had put on canvas shoes with white laces, the kind athletes wear. Her face is large with slanted eyebrows and jaws spread wide on both sides, and a neck thick like a column but red. Her strength and her firmness would overwhelm the powers of ten men combined. At his back walks the second squad with the deputy village chief and the village policeman, the two men equally small and short and similar in age and dress, wearing cadre shirts and green khaki pants. But the police chief has a large leather belt to hold his pistol. The two squads form a small detachment of four rows. The path is narrow, but on his left is Vu and the medical doctor and on his right the commander of the guard company, Le. Thirty yards behind them is an armed platoon to fend off kidnapping by aerial assault.

"Mr. President, please take your medicine before attending the funeral."

It's the doctor's turn to make the request. The president stops and swallows a handful of medicine with a cup of ginger water Then they continue walking. This portion of the road is more rugged. On both sides, the bamboo does not bend over but intertwines into a wall. The leaves weave themselves into a bright green roof. It's high noon, thanks to the roosters crowing from the hamlet to the east to the hamlet on the west, from the higher villages down to the lower ones. The crowing of the roosters, like the melancholy sounds of the singing, doesn't stop, as if they cannot break the unseen silence that rules over the scene, reinforcing it instead. This silence is uncompromised like clear crystal and more unyielding than steel. A vast silence. It seems as if it hides some forest over the sky's horizon.

"Soul, oh soul, please look ahead
Let the dust of life settle behind your back."

The sound of singing now sounds very close, but they still have to cross a turning, curving stretch before they can arrive. A crowd has gathered right at the compound's entrance, waiting for him. Teenagers in proper uniform line up in two rows of honor, holding flowers and flags, with camouflage umbrellas on their shoulders. Behind them are all the residents of Tieu Phu hamlet, men and women from middle age and older. There are no young men left in the village, for they have been drafted to fight or have enlisted in units of the Fighting Youth in support of the front lines.

"A true wartime scene. When the men are gone, when only women washing clothes on riverbanks and plowing the fields are left. As the 'Chinh Phu Ngam' poem described—in isolation, the village is lonely . . ."

His thought abruptly ends as the crowd recognizes him.

"Long live the president, long live, long live!"

"The president will live forever with the mountains and rivers!"

"Long live the Democratic Republic of Vietnam!"

"Long live the president!"

He realizes that the singing to send off the soul has stopped, because all the musicians with their flutes and zithers have stood up to get a better look at him. Those wearing headbands of mourning with their eyes still swollen also come out to welcome the honored guest:

"They have left the corpse alone in the house. My visit, it turns out, has brought disruption to this family."

At first the cheering is awkward and reserved but then turns more heartfelt as if everyone forgets that they should be in mourning. This thought makes him feel that his presence is inappropriate. Waiting for the crowd to be less enthusiastic, he gestures with his hand to signal for silence. In an instant, everyone is dead silent. His heart palpitates as he recognizes his ability to persuade and the power of his personal presence. That strength has not been lost with the years.

"Dear kith and kin."

As he speaks, he observes the eyes of the people. In those eyes there is a foolish adoration, an unconditional submission that he has known all too well. Now, that longstanding perception no longer excites him.

"Why can't they love me differently? Why can't they both love and respect everyone equally?" he thinks to himself as he continues to address them:

"Dear kith and kin, please let me thank you sincerely for the heartfelt words of welcome with which you greet me. Don't forget that we are here to attend a funeral, not a meeting or a conference. I am just an ordinary visitor like everyone here. I suggest that we all be quiet, everyone returning to their places so that the funeral can proceed smoothly."

Always his words command; commands full of supernatural might or saintly power, even he doesn't know for sure. The people quietly disperse, so quietly that he can hear his own breath. The family returns and stands around the coffin. The musicians resume the melodramatic singing to lead the departure into eternity:

". . . *From dust we return to dust*
The turning around comes as it must . . ."

The guards stand outside. The village chief and Le accompany him to call on the host representing the bereaved family. They have to cross a huge patio, one covered not with tiles but with slabs of green stone each about two feet on a side, placed in perfect alignment and giving the area in front of the house where the funeral is to take place the look more of a temple patio than a country villager's front yard. The residence compound is built in the form of a "gate": the main building in the middle, with five very large rooms and antique tiles on the roof, and two houses, one on either side, no less grand, each one also with five rooms facing the large patio. As he quickly looks around, he thinks:

"The doors are high and the rooms are large but when you leave for the last time, you have only your empty hands." Then, in spite of himself, he sighs deeply.

From behind, Le steps up and gives him an envelope: "Mr. President, this is the money to donate in consolation."

Mechanically he takes the envelope, not knowing how much money it holds or how much is enough. The memory of generous country customs, the fleeting images of funerals, weddings during his youth, all now faded, have not left a single mark. In his daily life now he never touches money or any other kind of expensive object. In reality he has never had money in his hands though his picture is on every piece of paper currency used throughout the entire nation. But he sees that the eyes of the villagers are discreetly looking at the envelope in his hand, and, for the first time in his life, he is confused about the real value of those flimsy pieces of paper that one can spend.

A suspicion makes him frightened: "How much did they put in it? Will they disappoint these people?"

It is true that life asks us only for hard, practical value. But only far too late do we ever understand just what such value is and where it lies.

"Always after the fact," he thinks in French.

Another silent sigh resonates within his heart.

"Please, Mr. President, approach the altar."

The female village chief guides him, going up first with him following; this tall woman with the broad shoulders of a very practiced martial arts adept could be a professional bodyguard.

"Why hasn't the Ministry of the Interior recruited her for a bodyguard? That is a waste of talent," he thinks as he steps up before the altar. It is a large standing chest, the upper part for an altar and the lower part for storage, made from four special kinds of wood, elaborately carved with dragons, unicorns, tortoises, and phoenixes with mother-of-pearl inlays, more a work of art than something for household use. The cabinet is placed against the middle of the wall opposite the main door. A large bronze incense burner is smoking. Two vases are filled with amaranths and peonies and varieties of wildflowers. He places the envelope on a large porcelain plate with a deep-jade-colored glaze, filled with other envelopes handmade from all kinds of paper scraps.

"I, your humble servant, am very grateful, Mr. President."

"I, your humble servant, thank you."

A woman and a young boy come up before him, formally bowing down on their knees to him. He feels disturbed because people kneel down like that only before sainted spirits or the altar for their ancestors.

"Don't; no need. Please have the family stand."

He lifts the child up, realizing that what he had suspected yesterday was correct: the child is about twelve or thirteen. The loosely fitting mourning shift hiding his body makes him look smaller. The mourning headband has slipped down to his nose, but when the boy looks up, he sees a lovely face with long, finely drawn eyebrows and the eyes of a man.

"The child is good-looking; he will be very handsome when he grows up."

Yesterday, on hearing the child cry out for his father, he could not imagine the boy's face. To him the boy had been only some child without a name calling out to him but one nevertheless associated with some other child. Now, the boy's fine face forces his heart to race. That face recalls another face from long ago. A face that has disappeared. His throat suddenly becomes dry. He turns from the child, planning to say something, but he can't find the right words. Maybe he cries a bit then; Vu comes up and gives him a handkerchief.

"All of us, your humble servants, are grateful to you, sir."

The voice of a young woman in his ear startles him and he looks up.

The widow had come up right in front of him to thank him. He sees her face drowned in tears under a mourning headband made from plain cloth. She looks young with an attractive face. She appears to be about thirty and no more. Her sudden loss has not diminished the beauty or the vitality of a woman in her springtime. Her complexion is blush white, without a freckle or a brown spot as most country people have, those who spend all day in the rain and the sun on the mountainsides or in the fields. The widow's peaches-and-cream complexion seems to belong to someone with overflowing good fortune. A face that is extremely difficult to find in a war-torn country. Her eyes are black and full of spunk, graced by long eyebrows that touch her temples—for sure an asset that she had passed down to her son. Those eyes, too, are not frequently found in countrywomen, because they do not reflect any hint of the endurance that marks the character often found in the women of Vietnam. Those eyes look directly at him, without any hesitation or fear.

"With such eyes, she can do anything she wishes," he thinks and scrambles to find some appropriate words in response:

"We offer our condolences to your family, hoping you and your son will quickly pass through this difficult time. Make sure your boy completes all his studies."

"Yes, we will carry out your instruction," the widow replies right away, as if her answer had been prepared in advance.

Then the village chief asks him to retrace his steps and visit the deceased. He follows mechanically, not knowing the customs and proceedings of an ordinary funeral. This is the first time in his life he has been to the funeral of a common person. After an instant and very suddenly, wailing breaks out behind him:

"Father, oh, Father, why are you leaving us?"

At that moment he notices some twenty more people also in mourning dress; some are in their thirties and forties but there are also younger ones. They push their way forward, cuddled close to one another to form a gang that could overwhelm the widow and her son. They form up as a choir, voicing their laments as a song accompanied by instruments. This group stands to the left of the coffin, the young mother and child to the right.

"Two forces, two children; this point seems uncontested," he reasons, and his eyes wander, looking for a picture of the deceased. He immediately sees a chair with an intricately carved back close to the coffin; on it is a large framed picture bordered by a black cloth.

"Ah, here he is! It's not a father still in his thirties or close to forty like I guessed yesterday . . ."

The commander of the two watchful companies to the right and the left of the coffin is in his fifties, or older. Only his face does not reflect the weariness, or the equanimity, poise, patience of the faces of other men his age. His face is square, with trace lines of adventures, and reflects both pride and vitality. His eyes stare straight out with a confrontational and provocative look mixed with a touch of malice. The bridge of his nose is large and straight like a bamboo stick. A beautiful mouth, with regular lips, is seated in a long and bushy beard, curly like that of a Caucasian, and jet black.

"This face testifies to what has happened to this unfortunate one, even right in this house."

He is shocked: all his guessing, his thoughts, his emotions, are put in play like boats bouncing on the water. An old understanding about oppression also immediately pours out like waterfalls wildly rushing down to sink those boats. A burning liquid enters into his nostrils. Smoke floats in front of him, with gray colors of storm clouds and the hazy purple of poppies.

"Eldest brother, we should leave!" Vu says behind him.

Feeling a hand gently touching his, he suddenly understands that he must awake. Turning to the group in plain white gowns and with white head-bands to the left of the coffin, he says:

"I offer my condolences to the family. I hope we will all overcome this very painful and sad circumstance and quickly regain normal lives."

It's the turn of this family to acknowledge his consoling words with all the adamant and resentful feelings they have stored in their hearts. Patiently, he waits for the wailing to subside before he takes his leave. But it seems that his comforting comments only give an excuse for those strong, repressed feelings to reveal themselves after the loss. The cries, the whining, of some twenty people only become more intense.

"Oh, Father, Father, how could you leave us in the middle of a terrible situation? Father, you left, but all the problems were not explained, all the resentments were not revealed."

"Father, oh, Father, please come back and listen carefully . . . your children, your grandchildren, all your own flesh and blood are here . . ."

At this moment it is the village chief who swiftly helps him escape this complicated situation: "Stop. Every pain must have its limits. Besides, the president needs to preserve his health to serve national priorities. I propose that the family disperse so that we can take the president back to rest."

After speaking, she pushes out her muscular arms to back the mourners away on both sides, with all the strength and precision of the edge of a bull-dozer's blade. Before he realizes what is happening, he finds himself cross-ing the stone-tiled patio to the compound gate. A few bodyguards gather close around him. The four musicians stand and play the national anthem to bid him on his way.

The familiar tune arises. The president is now forced to stop in the middle of the patio with his guards, seeing at a glance that the village chief is glaring at the musicians, not knowing whether to compliment or threaten them. In any case, everyone has to wait for the song to stop.

The national anthem! The national anthem!

He is as dumbfounded as if he were hearing it for the first time; for years the verses with their deep meanings had been imprinted in his mind. Is this the impact of the funeral or have his own mental abilities changed over the years? Or do the folk instruments bring on a peculiar expression to a quite familiar piece of music? It's impossible for him to explain this clearly, but a terror invades his soul as he hears the national anthem played on a one-string zither, a flute, and a two-string fiddle. Why is the melody so very sad? A patriotic song for a nation but one so sentimental and so full of melancholy? As if this upbeat and energetic melody hid within its notes evening temple bells and the howling of night owls. As if this provocative singing brings out parallel images that befit its ambience: dark, foggy horizons, deserted and cold streams, banks full of rubbish, a cemetery that spreads itself out infinitely under the sheltering wings of flying crows.

"Is it old age that makes me easily melancholic, or do these folk instruments bring to the national anthem a sadness that it does not usually promote? Because music for Sending Off the Soul is only appropriate for traditional songs like 'Lan Tham, Sa Lech Chenh, Sam Soan'?"

He can't find an answer. A pain twists in his heart. He looks up to the blue sky beyond the tops of the bamboo, trying hard to chase away such distressing thoughts, but to no avail.

"Let me know who your friend is; then I will tell you who you are. As such, I can say that: let me hear a people's songs and I will tell you that people's fate! Could it be true that a people's fate is determined by its songs, by its oldest forms of dances, by songs that accompany a people like a companion for eternity, like your shadow, like the entwined male and female sides of some asexual fish? Can human beings change their fate or not, and in life can their efforts bring on no more than a small percentage of all that will accumulate in a lifetime?"

"Mr. President, please step along," the chubby guard, who stands close behind him, whispers.

The president turns around and waves his hands to bid farewell to the musicians, then heads toward the gate. There the two platoons of guards are ready. They resume their previous formation to head back to where the helicopter is waiting.

7

"Venerable Abbess, we bother you too much."

"Mr. President, we are honored to serve you."

"Venerable Abbess, it might just be that our discussion will go on all afternoon. If so, your afternoon chanting will be interrupted."

"Mr. President, as ordained people we pray throughout our lives. When we need to stop, we stop. Buddha's spirit is within us even in our silence."

"Venerable Abbess, aren't you afraid that the sacred one will scold you?" he asks, half joking, half serious, with a smile that hides multiple meanings.

"Honorable Sir, if a Buddha did that, then he'd no longer be a Buddha," the abbess replies with a smile, a gentle smile, then walks out of the room.

He and Vu step aside as the nun passes by. The smell of soapberry spreads in the air, because the nun's clothes are washed in soapberry. There are three old soapberry trees in the corner of the temple, healthy and bushy, with lots of pods all year long. He often saw the nuns go to the garden and bring back full baskets, then line up the berries to dry them on a steel grate resembling a huge fish grill. On afternoons with pouring rain when vapors from crevices rose up to mix with the white cloud, the two women would sit silently while the berries were drying, their silence stretching on until the evening meal, when a nun would light altar candles and tweak the oil lamp on the old bamboo table.

"What are they thinking in that lingering silence? Maybe they don't think about anything at all; many people can't imagine that they are really so simple and intellectually empty that they don't have much at all to think about. Because those who don't think, cannot act with so much courage . . ."

Many times he has asked himself that question. He has never found a satisfying answer. He remembers that the first time he was at the temple he had seen all the doors locked like in a warehouse. He had summoned Le and the administrative officers for a discussion. When he had learned the truth, he had hurriedly ordered that the guards let the abbess and at least two novices return. This had been his primary condition in agreeing to stay at this place for rest and recuperation. Two days later, the guards had brought a group up the mountain. He knew that they were implementing his instructions, but he did not know why such a large group was needed.

"It can't be that they have agreed to let twelve venerables and nuns return to the temple," he had thought.

But he had rejected that hypothesis right away because it was improbable. He had backed into his room to observe. It was true that twelve venerables had appeared in the temple patio, but they did not have permission to return. They had come only to accompany their superior back to the old place. According to tradition, that was a way by which students could show their respect to a teacher. He saw ten tall and healthy monks, full of life; because only those with enough physical and mental health would be able to meditate in such isolated mountains. Those ten hefty men surrounded a tiny old woman, not taller than five feet, with a calm face and the very ordinary features of an average Vietnamese woman. She held a bamboo pole in her hand.

"With this very pole, the old lady went down the mountain after the officials forced her to leave the temple, and now, with this same pole she climbed up a mountain over three thousand feet high, needing no one to carry her on their back. And this tiny old lady is over eighty years old!"

Perhaps because the abbess was seven years his elder, he felt embarrassed and sad simultaneously. Perhaps because the legal might that had forced her into exile was his very own political system, of which he was the official spokesperson. He couldn't find a precise explanation.

In the yard, the abbess had climbed up to the third terrace and given her disciples instructions:

"Hail to Buddha, we again stand on the ground of our house. All of you please open all the doors, clean all the shelves, and light incense and candles. And you, nun, your duty is to arrange the flower vases. We will chant prayers to welcome our honored ones back to the old abode."

"Hail to Buddha, we will comply as you direct."

He had noticed the respectful manner of all ten monks in front of an old and tiny nun, and a thought had invaded his mind:

"Later on, of all these respectful disciples, which one will push the old lady down the ravine to replace her as the boss of this temple? Which one will put arsenic in the bean-braised tofu or in the cabbage soup?"

But on the far side of the patio, temple bells were ringing. The sounds of a beaten wooden gong and the chanting of the twelve disciples followed. The air filled with the fragrant smoke of incense. He had listened to the regular and continuous chanting, knowing that there was another force residing within our lives, an invisible force, of a kind that was not to be measured by integers as one can calculate the strength of human muscle power.

These memories suddenly coming to mind make him contemplative for a moment. But he also realizes that Vu is waiting for him. He says: "The abbess gave us permission, we can enter the temple."

"Big Brother, you've never been inside?"

"Never. I don't dare intrude into the land of the ordained. The fact that we've pushed ten monks down to the lower reaches of the mountain bothers me. Why don't they choose another location?"

"I don't know for sure who chose this spot. But surely this is the best one for Sau and the others to prevent everyone from coming to see you."

"They are brilliant with respect to those things."

He smiled while imagining that anyone who wanted to ascend all the way up Lan Vu mountain must appear in the lens of the guard company not for just a few seconds or minutes, but for more like half a day even if they were athletic or professional climbers. Under these conditions, only a wild hare or squirrel could hope to escape surveillance. His enemies in the Party had thought carefully when they had chosen the peak of Lan Vu instead of a dark tunnel as in an old European "oubliette" where people were sent to be forgotten. Here even on top of a magnificent mountain, he had no way to gossip with trusted associates either in his own room or in his doctor's quarters. All the walls contained listening devices. Each time Le led a technician to change a "bug" he knew it, because each time they carried a canister of mosquito spray on their back. Le would invite him to "take a walk in the woods to stretch his flaccid legs" while Le would "spray for mosquitoes." He always had to wait for a few hours before the smell of the spray would dissipate, then he could return to his room. Since he never crossed the brick patio to enter the temple proper, the Buddha statues were lucky not having to taste the insect spray. Today, they could use Buddha's domain to chat with each other for a while.

"Are you are sure that we can talk safely here?" Vu asks for the last time to bolster his confidence.

"Trust me; I'm old but not yet senile," he replies, looking straight in the eyes of his loyal follower, the only one left who had survived life with him.

"I apologize . . . but . . ."

"I understand."

They are silent for a moment, as memories have returned with each word, each thought. Then trembling, Vu asks:

"Big Brother, do you cough a lot?"

"Don't worry, I am much better. The remaining problem is my heart. But it's rare to reach seventy, I have lived long enough."

"You must take good care of yourself."

"You, too. But, on second thought, neither of us have any way of prudently taking care of ourselves. Life's just a gamble."

"Yes, just a roll of the dice."

"Whether we like it or not, we have to accept that life has its limits; so, too, does our health. I cannot do anything more at this time, but I still want to know what is going on in our nation."

"But . . ."

"Just let me know. We have endured the most dangerous times. I hope you haven't forgotten that?"

"But you are now very weak, Elder Brother. We who must die cannot hold off the destruction that time brings on."

"But I am not yet blind, or deaf, and my brain is not yet paralyzed. I still want to know what's going on outside of here, outside these walls of white clouds, outside this enchanting prison."

"I don't have enough courage, please forgive me."

"I am the one who must apologize to you. I am the one who owes you a debt. I put too much hardship on your shoulders."

"Brother, please don't say that. This entire nation is indebted to you. Even if I took on more, it would still not be enough."

From each shelf of the altar, red wooden statues touched with gold leaf look out at them intensely. The president thinks that his secret conversation with Vu does not go beyond the wooden eyes and ears. The smell of incense slowly rises up, and, for the first time, he understands that he is stepping up to another, a new, realm, entering a new space. He suddenly utters a sigh.

"What is the matter, Elder Brother?"

"Nothing. Tell me so that I clearly understand what's happening in our country."

"But . . ."

"Don't worry. I can take it."

"The situation is very bad. Our strength was not enough but they decided on a general offensive. General Han met me and told me that, in the battle at Nam Phai, the entire command staff was wiped out, except for General Han, who escaped because he was in Ha Tinh. The bodies of soldiers clogged the ravines; the streams could not flow through."

"I had guessed that when they keep urging me to write poetry to inspire the people."

"The terrible thing was not only that. Han returned to the front for only two days before his family received word of his death."

"He must have been killed while on the road, for sure in Thanh Hoa province."

"I suspected that, too."

"For a long time Thanh Hoa has turned into a bandit haven."

"Yes, many know this."

"Pity his whole family."

"Yes, his young child is not yet ten while his wife has suffered a serious joint ailment for three or four years now."

"Is there any other reason? Or was it just because he kept in touch with us?"

"For sure. The paper and the radio talk only about victories. Deserting soldiers were stopped at the crossroads on the forest road from Quang Tri to Ha Tinh and were brought to the reeducation camps for deserters. Nobody in the north knows the truth about the battles. But I believe Han was assassinated for another reason."

"I understand," he replies, and suddenly feels a frigid wind blowing up

and down his spine: "Too many people have been hurt because of their connection with me."

"You cannot say that."

"But it's true. Even me. I have been hurt for being me. It's the truth."

"Elder Brother, don't torture yourself."

"As you see, I am not blind or deaf, nor losing my mind. I must bear some
responsibility before the people."

Vu looks at him angrily: "There is nothing more you can do for 'this'
people—the people to which you belong must bear responsibility for themselves."

"Aren't they your people, too?"

Vu sighed: "They are also mine, true. But oftentimes I feel so dispirited.
Because we can't change our race like we can change our clothes."

"But it's our nation. Even if we want to reject it, we can't."

"Because we cannot reject it, we suffer."

"On this planet, surely there are other peoples that deserve to be as miserable as we are. But many cannot recognize that they must be miserable
due to some cause or some condition. As long as they don't yet realize that
something true and real is justly causing their misery, then that sense of
misery doesn't last."

The President drops this very vague comment, prompting Vu to look
inquisitively at him. He seems to be pursuing something in his mind, his
eyes aimlessly looking at the temple patio. Vu waits a few seconds then says:

"You said . . ."

"What I want to say is that every nation has its strengths and its shortcomings. But to accept and to look straight at the core of our shortcomings
is an extremely difficult thing to do."

The two of them remain silent. Vu anxiously looks at him:

"You are too old and have had too much suffering to think about such
things. Life runs within set banks; better to let the stream run its course."

As for the president, he pensively recalls a spring day in the war zone of Viet
Bac along the Chinese border. Then, exactly at the lunar New Year, everyone at headquarters competed in cooking traditional dishes. Among all
these, the foremost was congealed duck's blood with pig intestines. Not
only the cooks but all the headquarters staff it seemed had jumped in to
prepare those important dishes. At noon, his staff brought him the duck's
blood with pig insides on a tray. During wartime, a mere mouthful of meat
was considered a banquet, because there were long periods when everyone

at headquarters had only cassava instead of rice. The previous year, a soldier in the intelligence company went crazy from eating only cassava for six months in a row. He was from a well-to-do family, and so had no experience in enduring scarcity. Six whole months without a grain of rice or a piece of meat or fish for your stomach, just cassava every day, first eaten boiled, then for a while eaten broiled, and then afterward boiled again but now in a soup of salt and wild leaves; this man from town took sick, his complexion turned green, his stomach extended as if he were pregnant. One morning, when seeing his adopted brother bring up a basket of boiled cassava, he suddenly jumped up crazed in the yard, screamed as if a devilish spirit had entered him, stripped off his clothes, took hold of his head, and ran into the woods.

This incident had obsessed him. Therefore, his mind opened to all those happenings that carry life forward. And so he couldn't eat those nutritious traditional dishes anymore. He looked at the bowl of duck's blood on the tray with disinterest—a tureen full of dark red blood, coagulated like Jell-O, with chopped peanuts and herbs spread evenly on its surface. In addition there was a very small bowl of fresh chili peppers. The guard had carried in his tray of food to respectfully place it in front of him and then had waited to see whether he would enjoy the special dish, because for everyone this was so obviously the most elegant meal in the entire year.

"Just leave it for me. Go down and eat with your friends," he hurriedly said to the soldier so that he could retire at ease.

Left with him was the bowl of blood. He thought of ways to discreetly get rid of it. Since his youth, he had dreaded the smell of blood, even if it was camouflaged under all the various flavors of herbs such as basil, mint, and cilantro, green onion, shallots, roasted peanuts, and minced fresh pepper. Each time his family had drawn pig's blood, he would slip away into the fields. Nobody could force him to eat that horrible dish, a dish that many had coveted the most whenever a pig was slaughtered, a dish that both male and female elders esteemed as good for having both "yin" and "yang" auspicious properties. They used to make fun of him:

"Smart in his studies but stupid in his eating."

He never really knew why he was so put off by this traditional dish. Once, when he was a young man living in Paris, he had gone to a movie about the customs of Africa. Watching the local people draw blood from the cow, whose head bobbed in the vat of blood, then drink the still fresh and hot blood, his skin suddenly burst out in goose bumps, sweat dripping wet on his back. His face took turns being hot then icy cold. He imagined that the people around him were looking at him, noting his strange mental state and guessing all the thoughts hidden in his mind. He had sat paralyzed in the theater until the end of the afternoon, waiting for everyone else to leave before he got up. Outside it was freezing cold. The sweat on the back of his shirt was wet and cold, making his body shake uncontrollably. He had turned around and found the restroom, where he picked up a newspaper and used it to pad his chest and back before going home.

At night his dreams were splattered with red. Animals were slaughtered; blood squirted up; they screamed, jerked, and shook in crazy and desperate ways. All the people had their mouths splattered with fresh blood; all their smiles were also bloody. These images all appeared at the same time, on top of one another, tumbling, twirling in his mind. This had been the first time since childhood that he had experienced such fear. It was like the first time he had held a flashlight to clear a tunnel in which eternal darkness threatened one's life. Thanks to that movie on African customs, he had found a comparison, a point of reflection. He saw that realizing the shortcomings of a nation was like having a fever: you must endure before you can cure.

That night he could not close his eyes, so he had read until the streetlights became pale white in the dawn light.

Then the storm of revolution had sucked him into turbulence. For years, he had thought he no longer needed to concern himself with what he considered his people's "shortcomings." He had had too much work on his hands. The struggle of his people against foreign aggressors was always unbalanced, with the scale permanently tipped in favor of the foreigners. In such circumstances, he could not possibly pay attention to all the details. He had to mobilize the citizens, because their unity provided the highest-quality strength, the kind of power most likely to bring victory in this unequal contest. For this unity, he had to accept things that he found to be "shortcomings." For this unity, he had many times pretended to be blind in the face of coarse behavior and petty reprisals, which he was quite certain were habits of rebellion against culture itself. For this unity, he had to ally with those who belittled him as "someone with Bordeaux wine in his blood."

On that New Year's Day in the war zone, he had poured the bowl of duck's blood into the bamboo tube he used for water, waiting until the afternoon when everyone left to play volleyball in the field before he dumped it out in the privy.

"Are you all right?" Vu suddenly asks.

The president understands that he has just put his hand to his chest to feel a pain in his heart: "Sometimes the tightness recurs," he answers, smiling.

"With old age, everything is fixed in place, even death. Therefore, it's smartest of all to learn to coexist with disease. And with disappointments . . ."

"First come the disappointments."

They are silent. A floating moment spreads through the springtime, a moment when dampness mixes with sunlight to make a band of shining sea bubbles. They both hear a pair of larks singing somewhere. Then the chubby guard appears before the temple's front door.

"Mr. President, the office just called to ask Chief Vu to go down to the landing field."

"What time does the plane leave?" Vu asked.

"The office did not say when."

"Please call them back to ask the exact time of departure."

The soldier left immediately.

On the patio, the sunlight spreads like honey, calm and still yellow from the mountain peak. In that yellow, there is not the muggy environment often found in the low plains of the north, but a delicate, pleasant freshness, like the kind of fall weather found in Europe. He closes his eyes to find himself strolling along the river Seine when the leaves are changing color, where on both banks rows of reddish yellows and light reds burst into the sky like vibrant but fragile flames. The white bridges that appear out of the fog were not made for pedestrians but for painters and poets. He remembers the green slopes of Montparnasse; the lights along the streets, the arrows pointing to sidewalk cafés. Europe: part of his life happened there. He recognizes it by all the emotions that had been engraved deeply and permanently in his being, by the taste of cheap red wine on his tongue and the noise of the streets in his ears, by the remembrance of the colors of sunlight and sky. The warm memories of youth are tainted by the sadness of having been away from his country. When living there, he had recalled his homeland, missing it as a void, as a madness. Why now do his thoughts go back to that faraway land? Why now has it become something missing within him? Day by day that feeling is becoming more and more passionate, more and more filling his heart with emotion. So sad, so very sad! Nostalgic, so very painfully nostalgic! Europe! Europe! Is it that Europe is only a subterfuge to remind him of his now finished youth? Maybe he recalls Europe because he recalls all the dreams unfulfilled, all the journeys not completed. Was not Europe a land with both foe and friend and thus a companion both silent and nagging, until the moment of burial? He felt very tightly and permanently attached to a land that did not belong to him. Is this his own private drama or is it some eternal pain for every person?

"Chief, the office says that the plane will take off at four p.m. sharp," the soldier announces, reappearing.

Vu replies in a very curt manner: "Tell the office I will be down there at four; a five p.m. takeoff is not too late."

"Yes, sir."

The president waits until the soldier leaves and says to Vu: "Why are you tense with them? Functionaries are functionaries."

"Sometimes we have to slap their face so that they remember who we are. Not everybody becomes their servant."

"That is not the fault of the little people."

"You forget that every golden lord was toppled by his closest guards; they may be little people but they have big dreams. You forget Quoc Tuy? He started out as a professional pickpocket in the Sat market. He was whipped close to death because he did not give up his share to the boss. One night he sneaked in and stabbed his boss, who was in bed at a brothel. He then left his hometown and wandered south to become a plantation worker. There, he got class consciousness and chose to follow the revolution. He became Sau's follower when the two shared a bunk in the Son La prison."

"I thought he was much younger than Sau."

"Exactly so. They are at least a dozen years apart. In prison, Sau turned himself into Quoc Tuy's protective mentor. That's how they treated each other. Quoc Tuy cleaned his pot, washed his clothes, and even scratched Sau's back. That's why Sau later appointed him minister of the interior. That was the most important ministry, with the most power; everybody knows that. At that time, many comrades saw the danger and protested, but Sau repressed them without mercy. His power was in knowing just how to use those whom you call little people. Then the time comes for the little people to use the littler people. The credentials most in demand are: uneducated, with a criminal record. Secondary credentials are being truly poor and stupid, of which the husband and children of that broad Tu of the fish market make perfect examples. Those two kinds of people become Sau's main pillars of firm support. They will do anything he wishes. Have you forgotten Brother Le Liem's report?"

"Everything is too late."

"Yes, too late!"

He hears his younger friend swallow, as if he is swallowing the rage in his throat. He wants to say something to Vu to comfort him but can't find the words for it. What could he do for Vu and what could Vu do for him now, under the circumstances? No alternative is satisfactory. At least while they sit next to each other they gain some unspoken comfort to soothe the heartaches. On the patio, the wind blows and the trees look naked. The singing of wild birds on the far side of the ravine mixes with the high-pitched chirping of nightingales on the patio, creating a soft, natural mountain harmony. Why are the mountains and rivers so beautiful but the people's hearts so sad? When had he turned criminal toward himself and toward those others bound up with him? Oh, this question has not ceased to torture his aging heart, and it will torture him until he dies.

Another gust blows by from the sky. The yellow leaves that it catches are spinning around the patio. It seems the air has turned colder; or is it the misty clouds surrounding the temple that make him shiver? The sunlight has muted into a weak yellow. It is very possible that a spring rain will pour down in a few minutes.

"You'd better get down the mountain, I am afraid it will rain."

"Yes, I must go, as a lot of work awaits. Besides, the plane is only booked for today."

He then looks straight at the president. "Elder Brother, please take it easy and rest. Everything is as usual. Although he lives in a distant place, the little one is an excellent student. He just won the Marie Curie math award in the all-city high school competition."

"Thank you, brother."

"There is another thing I need to tell you truthfully."

"I am listening."

"Trung is reaching the age of thinking for himself. To spare him pain, I told him that he is my own son, out of wedlock."

"What you did was correct. A child out of wedlock is a thousand times happier than a child without a mother and a father."

They both stand. One looks down at the old tiles of the temple floor, and the other looks out at the layers of clouds forming a white wall.

8

That night the president goes to bed really early.

When the doctor arrives to take his pulse, he finds the door closed and the lights off. The two guards who are on watch all night stand in front of the veranda. The watch lights illuminate half the temple patio and the trees at the garden's edge. Not daring to sing and disturb his sleep, the doctor returns to his office, gets some cards, and asks the guards to play.

"Remember not to laugh loudly or shout. If you get too happy, keep your lips tight and cover your mouth if you want to laugh. The loser will have a mustache drawn on his face with soot, but must absolutely remain silent, OK?"

"Absolutely, Doc, whatever you say; we are under your command."

In the room, the president hears the whispering, the shuffling of furniture, and the doctor's footsteps crossing the patio to the kitchen area of the temple. Most likely he is fetching a pot to use its soot for drawing the mustache on the loser. When all has been arranged, the group sits down, pleased with their harmless game of luck, and the cards are dealt. From that point on, he hears no sound other than the screaming of his own soul:

"My child; oh, my own child! My own son!"

Tears on both of his temples are wet and cold. He presses the pillow down on his face to suppress the sobbing:

"Why am I crying like an ordinary woman from a most ordinary family? When did this ridiculous thing start to happen? It must be old age, which brings changes to a person, making one act in this silly way."

He scolds himself, but a few seconds later, his heart starts crying out again:

"Oh, my child, my own son!"

Simultaneously a burning longing to see the little boy's face tortures his abdomen:

"Is he taller than the son of the woodcutter, or the same size? And what does his face look like now? I only remember him when he was three months old. Nobody thought that would be the last encounter."

He remembers the loft in an old street. One had to walk a long corridor to reach the entrance, where there were always three guards dressed as civilians. The corridor was narrow and very dark alongside a thick wall, and served as a divider with another house, that of a shopkeeper. The shopkeeper had a storefront on the street level, and lived upstairs with an older sister. A huge spiral staircase with a wooden balustrade rose from the dark corridor to the upper floor, to a high and aerated room painted in light blue. For a short time that room was to have been his warm love nest; a nest, however, that had had no time to warm up before it was destroyed by a windy vortex . . . Like the transit of a shooting star, happiness had passed him by. He hadn't even had a good look, and it was gone. Happiness: only sand grains in the palm of his hand. Before he could grab them, they had slipped through his fingers. . . .

Even with all that, it had been happiness. . . .

He thought he had forgotten, but it returned. The vision of an ancient spring day. For an instant, the brightness brought forth the scene of a past paradise—the old room; the old bed. The little one kicking wildly in the white diapers. The baby had smiled at him. Its red lips curled up, trying to say something. And her! She sat at the end of the bed, her fingers rolling up red yarn. All around were small skeins in many colors. What did she do with all that yarn?

Now he remembers: she had rolled up the yarn to make new dolls to hang around the bassinet for the baby boy to play with. The old doll had been damaged by his older sister a couple of weeks before. She had told him so, because every two or three weeks he could visit the mother and her child.

While listening to her chat, he asked where his daughter was. She said she went to sleep with Auntie Dong. He didn't ask of her further, and she pouted that he loved the boy Trung more than the girl Nghia, that he respected men and disparaged women, still living by feudal values. He smiled because she had repeated to him the exact propaganda lesson taught her by the cadres. And he himself had taught them:

"The revolution will establish a new society, in which everyone will be equal before the law, with no distinction based on ethnicity, religion, or gender."

He didn't listen to what she said, for he was attentively looking at her young pouting lips, recalling the pair of doe's eyes staring at him through the fire in the forest night. He smiled while she was lecturing him, while the little one wildly kicked in the white diapers. Intensely he looked at the baby, realizing that the boy had inherited the best traits of both him and her:

"He will be really handsome. He will become an elegant and stylish young man."

She was certain of his bias and one more time reminded him:

"Mr. President, you must love them both equally."

"Oh, of course. Each one is our child . . ." he replied to please her.

In reality, he cared for Nghia very much, as the girl resembled the older sister he liked best of all in his family. They were as two sickles made from the same mold. Because Nghia carried his very own image, she had to bear misfortune. In the little boy he saw her resemblance, his beloved.

Now she was no more. No one left to pout about his impartiality, a bias that he recognized in himself.

"I have two children, a girl and a boy; one is only a year older. Why do I remember only the boy? I, who always taught people about equality between men and women?

"But danger hovers over the boy more than the girl. Thus, probably, my sin through him is proportionately larger. Thus, this constant obsession about him," he reasons to himself.

Even if his rationalization is extremely weak, he does not go deeper to question what is in his heart. It would be useless. All the paths in his rationalizing always return him to the old resting point. He misses the boy like crazy. After ten years he thought he could forget, but suddenly memories return and become a permanent pain, a gaping tear in his heart. The dream of being oblivious had dissipated like a cloud before the sun, leaving now only a burning longing:

"How is my son doing now? Does he worry about where he comes from? Or does he live safely under the protection of his 'uncle' Vu, believing that he is the son of some unknown person, an out-of-wedlock child living with an adoptive father? He will believe that. Believing so will provide an anchor for him. An out-of-wedlock child? Fate must have predestined it, because his affair with her had been outside the law. That kind of illegal affair would naturally produce children out of wedlock. Pity all of us, all victims of an unjust game. Now what is happening to my out-of-wedlock child? Does he look like me or her; does he keep intact all those features he had at three months? Is his complexion fair like that of his mother? Is there a Mongolian birth mark on his back like the one on mine, because older sister Thanh said that the mark appeared only when I was ten years old . . ."

All these concerns could only be shared with her. He knows that people would dissect every word that came from him. Even if he ventured to tell Vu, Vu could not bring up any photo of Trung, as Vu, too, is being watched closely. If he showed the slightest sign that his heart was still passionate, the child would be used more effectively as a weapon in the hands of his enemies.

Knowing all this, he still cannot suppress his anxiety:

"An old father and a young child: that is the reality. Is the unfortunate woodcutter as tormented as I am at this instant? No! No! . . . because he died right on the hammock, on the way home. That way, even if he were worried and in pain, he only had to put up with it for a couple of hours, not to mention that during so short a time, the pain had paralyzed his brain."

Love between father and child runs deep; for the first time he thoroughly understands the meaning of this.

When he was young, still a child, his spirit had not yet sought the far distant horizon, his ears heard only the wind blowing over the homeland, and his eyes looked only at the roof of the ancestral cottage. The work of the father, the responsible love of the mother: he knew these only as an average person would. Later those bonding kinship emotions grew fainter and fainter, easily forgotten when his heart had turned to a larger and more theoretical love: the country, the people, the nation . . .

These terms describe something grand, something wonderful. All great things are abstractions. The revolution was something even more gigantic, even more wonderful . . . and more shapeless . . . and more inhuman . . .

He recalled the year when the revolution succeeded, how his sister had come up from Nghe An to visit him. He did not set aside even a moment to chat with the woman he considered to have been his second mother when he was young. That woman was a virgin all her life; a virgin until she crawled into the coffin. Her life had been one of complete sacrifice for all her relatives. Not being received by the younger brother, she quietly returned home without a word of complaint. That day, for once, his heart was torn apart. Then he was forced to forget and he had forgotten. All his life he had adapted to accepting and practicing forgetting. A forgetting that had been ordered; a forgetting that was carefully formalized; a forgetting that was deliberate.

But this time, he does not succeed in forgetting. The boats that had been sunk pop up to the surface of the sea. A ghostly corpse from underneath the ocean's mud, which has ceased decomposing, appears on the surface, rising and bobbing on the peaks of the waves. This is his hell.

Suddenly he wants to be a father! Suddenly he can no longer accept forgetting. Suddenly he remembers the son and hourly visualizes his features. Suddenly he craves seeing him, even from afar, even hidden behind a tree or some wall; nameless, shapeless, and ashamed like a fellow that squanders then repents in his old age, trying now to find a way to his own lost drop of blood.

All this nagging, this wishing, this longing confines him within the cage of an inexorable fate. A prison of his own making. His own legal system, wherein he is both criminal and judge. Why does heaven so torment him? From where does this rushing madness come that brings chaos to his mind, pain to his body, and agony to his heart?

The necessary psychology of a father toward a son!

Only now does he understand this reality. Of old, it was said: "Tears run downward." So true.

"Filial love for parents can't equal the ties of anxious love in a father's soul for a child. Because when we love our parents we look up but when we love our children we look down. And, according to the laws of heaven and earth, tears always flow downward. Especially whenever we recognize that as fathers we have done wrong. Hell itself will then open a door straight into the heart."

Such angst is as old as the earth. He had thought that he could avoid the ordinary waves of feeling that come with being human, but now those same ordinary waves are drowning him. For a long time he had assumed that he could just forget his own small affliction, believing that he could concentrate all his energies to better serve his country. There had been times when he had fairly succeeded in such forgetfulness. But forgetfulness was an opponent with a long memory and ferocious tenacity. Now he receives its reciprocating blows. Because life is always a stream flowing between the banks of forgetfulness and longing—a frail human vessel needs only a change of wind or some rough water to bounce it around and beach it on one side or the other.

"I thought life had calmed down. . . . I thought I had solved the problem and there were no more worries. But just now, everything has changed."

Now the ship that is his life has been pulled by the wind from forgetfulness to longing. He can no longer pretend to live like a saint. He must now face up to every ordinary pain, the pains that run in all the channels of an ordinary life, a life that for so long he had refused to live.

Might it be that because ordinary people see beforehand the kind of hell that now confronts him, they easily avoid it? For him, could the pain now be appearing when his strength has diminished, making its taste more bitter?

Damn those old, penetrating and sad songs. He now really hears them only when his sun has almost set:

"Father, oh, Father, why do you leave the little ones?
Summer's sun has not gone, but fall is here.

Then the winter brings the north wind back.
Father has left, the house has lost its roof.
Who will spread their arms to protect the little ones?"

Before him he visualizes almost thirty heads, each circled with the white cloth band of mourning; pairs of red eyes, swollen with crying; wailings rising in concert, in the harmony of a farewell song; the whole company standing on both sides of the coffin; beyond are dripping candles and bowls of rice each with a boiled egg on top and flowers amid the incense smoke.

"When I come to die, will any of my children cry for me like all those children of the woodcutter?

"Oh, no; my two children will stand among a noisy crowd and whisper: 'The president is dead.' Or a little more elegantly if they have been well educated: 'The president has passed away.' If they would shed a tear or two, it would only be infectious drops picked up from the common sadness; only a chain reaction, as when people sneeze because the one next to them has sneezed, or one laughs loudly, losing one's breath, following the spirit of the surrounding crowd.

"My children will never know that this president was the one who created them, that the blood flowing in their veins is his, that their skin and flesh are no different from his, that their hearts, brains, livers, lungs, all their genetic diseases or their idiosyncrasies are from that same person. They will never know all this.

"My fate is much worse than that of the woodcutter in the Tieu Phu hamlet, because at the very least, he had blessings. A real father, with real power. Did he not know well what he wanted, what he could do, and what needed to be accomplished?"

The portrait of the deceased reappears before his eyes. He remembers clearly the handsomely curved eyebrows above eyes both welcoming and taunting. A defiant look: a seasoned life and a firm disposition marked the corners of his mouth with chiseled insets and the straight bridge of his nose with bamboolike resilience. Special is the bushy beard, jet black and curly like that of a European; it frames his square jaw, like that of the folk hero Tu Hai, which was dubbed a "swallow's jaw."

"This peasant dared confront his fate. Even lying in the coffin, he still had this resolved look of someone who defies all obstacles that block his way. And those sad songs sending off his soul, could they break the heart of the one who has just closed his eyes? Oh no, absolutely not. The woodcutter was a blessed father, because he brought good fortune on his son. These chants should be for me, just for me!"

He thinks this bitterly, and this bitterness makes his tears continue to flow. The tears flow in zigzags on both temples, through his hair:

"This woodcutter was a worthy father. At least, he had raised his youngest son until the boy was thirteen. Those thirteen years, in stormy times, in sunny times, in the winter rain, he had provided protective arms. That son had tasted the sweetness of a father's love; he had been secure, enjoying a warm childhood. That woodcutter deserved to be a father. That genuine father is a model putting me to shame as long as I shall live. Why did I put on earth those lost drops of blood, those children without father or mother? Giving birth to children that you cannot protect is not even worthy of animals. From that point of view, I am an irresponsible and incapable father. Moreover, I allowed those unscrupulous people to pursue them like wild animals after prey. Death runs behind them like a shadow. Therefore, not only am I an incompetent father, I have no conscience either."

The pain comes in waves, as if someone is punching him from down below all the way up to his heart. And those punches are at times jabbing, at others nonstop. The president recalls a first-class African-American boxer, one who was famous everywhere when he was young. In his training room, this boxer had the habit of puckering his mouth each time he threw a punch. Each time the sandbag got hit, his face was all frown, and his lips shook, an action resulting from either an uncontrollable smile or the pressure of some state of mind; and his face had the look of his going through extraordinary pain.

"My heart is like such a sandbag being punched by an invisible person. And this invisible person smiles after each punch. A real smile, instead of some contortion brought on by a twisted mind."

Should he get up, turn on the light, and call his doctor?

But, if he does so, the doctor will discover his tears. Not only that he had cried, but that he had cried for a long time, and that he had cried a lot. The hair on both of his temples is still wet; the pillow on which he rests his face is also wet; the lids of his eyes are swollen. Those things cannot be erased quickly.

"I am too old; why should I live any longer under these circumstances?"

Suddenly, a thought comes upon him, like a sigh arising from an incredible depth. He is not surprised. Nothing should take you by surprise. This is totally contrary to his own feelings when he had first heard the panicked cries of the son of that unfortunate woodcutter. That cry now blends into another, silent cry. The muffled cry of his own son. The son whose face he does remember; the son he purposely abandoned and intentionally forgot.

9

"Ha, ha, ha, ha."

The laughing of some ghost exploded by his ears. More accurately, it was a fit of laughter like pouring rain on a stormy day battering a corrugated roof; a very strange kind of laughter, accompanied by a hoarse reverberation in the throat like the shrieking of a bunch of wildcats. The laugh seemed to come from deep down out of an immense grave or from an abandoned castle buried in the core of the earth:

"Who's that? Who has such a terrifying laugh?"

He digs in his memory. Who had had that strange laugh and where? That laugh contained the growling of wild animals as well as the hissing of a twisted wind inside a deep dark hole. Both strange and familiar at the same time, it seems . . .

"Ah, ha, ha, ha, ha."

The pain disappears as he concentrates his memory to find this ghostly laughter . . . But he can't find anyone. At this moment, the laughing one says:

"Really, you don't remember me?"

He lifts the pillow from his face so that he can intensely peer into the room's darkness. The electric light outside still clearly shines its rays through the cracks around the door. The giggling of the card-playing group can still be heard softly in his room. Nothing much different:

"Sorry, I don't recognize you," he replies.

"Won't you try one more time?" the laughing one responds, his voice soft and high-pitched like that of some homosexual.

"Sorry, I can't," he repeats gently.

The laughter bursts into long waves, and this time, he recognizes the big fat face, round like the dumplings eaten by truck drivers in the north. Chairman Man, the most powerful man under the eastern sky. He has not seen him for a long time, therefore he is a bit confused. Actually, Chairman Man, born in the year of the Snake, two years after him, a man full of demonic plots leading China's Cultural Revolution, is still alive. More precisely, he is conducting the most terrifying campaign of elimination ever seen in the history of humanity. This extraordinary emperor has displayed all kinds of acts to awe the people with his championship mettle, the most well-known being swimming across the Yangtze River. Why is he now appearing as a ghost? Why is he borrowing the features of some resident of the underworld? Curious, he strains his eyes to look at the face opposite him and slowly starts to make out the features of the king of the north. Chairman Man's face floats in space, his eyes squinting with joy, his lips turned up to provide the melody of a provoking smile.

"Greetings, Comrade," says his visitor from the north.

He interrupts: "Where did you come from, Great Older Brother?"

"I am great indeed, but I am no brother of yours. And don't call me Comrade either because my once brilliant patina is faded. That other one is dead and he turned into a decomposed corpse a long time ago."

"Sorry."

"Sorry?" Chairman Man asks most condescendingly. "Thank you. If that would please you. Oh, all the diplomatic forms you know by heart! Oh, the Western cheese gives out a smelly scent to the nose!"

Chairman Man starts to laugh louder, and this time he shows two rows of small and yellow teeth like those of some rural woman who lacks hygiene and is lazy with her grooming. His eyes squint small in a look that both teases and despises:

"You are very polite . . . the useless and fake politeness of the white men. Me? I challenge all protocol, step on all opinions and customs. I impose my own rules on everything."

He starts laughing even louder, and now a foul smell comes out of his wide opened mouth. Normally, Chairman Man never opens wide his mouth. When he speaks or laughs, he opens it just to the degree he has calculated. Everybody knows that Chairman Man never brushes his teeth, believing that the tiger has its strength because it never brushes its teeth. Maybe he thinks such mimicry will bring him saintly power, make him a champion like some strong wild animal. The only difference is that, usually, a tiger opens its mouth really wide when it yawns as well as when it roars, while Chairman Man acts in reverse. Is that some mysterious artifice that only he understands?

Ending his provocative laugh, the great helmsman from the north continues:

"The word 'comrade' is dead and dead with it are all those past formalities. Between you and I, what remains forever is the emperor of China and the vassal of Vietnam. A rock cannot turn into a blade, even if people call it so. Only idiots believe the magic trick that turns white paper into a dove. I thought you were smarter than that."

" 'At seventy,' our ancestors taught us, 'if one is not yet blind or crippled, one does not boast of being good.' Everyone can still make a mistake before standing in front of the grave."

"Humility—whether it is sincere or fake—is only a game of those without talent or who have short necks and small throats. Throughout history did you ever see any powerful emperor who was reserved in front of his people? Maybe you would remind us of the Sage Kings Yao and Shun? Those two imaginary ghostly corpses were invented to comfort dirt-poor scholars. Yao and Shun—they are no different from communism. Just votive paper clothing that people burn to please the ghosts. Those alive can't wear it. Just things to play with or to fool the people. As toys, they are not without purpose. Just as farmers use rakes in the paddies and sickles to cut the rice when ripe, we use these special tools to lure the people to where we want them to be and to force them to do what we want them to do. Communism is much better than Cao Cao's plum orchard."

"This I know well, because you called the soldiers 'Red Army comrades' when you needed them for the Long March. Then you called the farmers your 'peasant comrades,' 'pillars of the revolution,' 'the future launchpad of the nation' when you needed them out in the fields to shout, to chase away the birds like half madmen or wooden puppets . . . When you forced them to pull up the rice stalks and feed the pigs water buffalo manure, or abandon the rice fields to the wild and dig pits to make iron, they were sung as 'the class of saintly peasants,' as 'humanity's progressive force.' With such a clever way and with such beautiful words, you carried out the most crazy and cruel games, games that no former lord or king had ever dared attempt. Those lessons I remember very clearly. Because we once followed you and we had to pay a price, though that price was less than the one your people had to pay."

"The people? Just wooden pawns on history's chessboard. Whatever they do must contribute to the game. When they are no longer useful, just throw them in the fire as kindling."

"Yes, this I know. Millions of Red Army soldiers eventually became firewood when they no longer had a place in the game. Also, this same lesson I learned at the beginning of the Cultural Revolution up north, in your country. Many times has China's history applied this slogan: 'In military matters, it's OK to sacrifice soldiers'; but with the scale of the Cultural Revolution, you will become the greatest gangster in that history book."

"No brutality, no heroic greatness! Don't you forget this."

"I won't forget. Maybe I lack the capacity. From my position, I would be terribly shocked to see our people eat corpses or fight each other over food . . . Sometimes I have doubts, I don't have enough courage to believe what is happening right before my eyes. Don't you know that the peasants in many Chinese cities are dying of starvation; that in those places, people eat grass like buffaloes and wild pigs; that families exchange the corpses of their loved ones so that they won't eat those dear to them?"

"The race of humans is a race that eats its kind. This has occurred regularly in the history of mankind and of China. Have you forgotten the story of Wu Song, who inadvertently ate a dumpling filled with human meat?"

"No, I have not, but that story, I thought, happened thousands of years ago. And with people having struggled to make progress, they have left such savagery behind them. The border between man's barbarism and civilization stands at the abolition of cannibalism and incest."

"Really, you are a good student of some blue-eyed and high-nosed teacher. All kinds of reasoning can lead students by their noses. Me, I don't believe in any kind of reasoning, other than what I create."

"You exaggerate. It was thanks to Stalin's support that you got your throne."

"Did I get Stalin's support or did I use him to build a throne for myself as, in the old days, Egyptian pharaohs used the slaves to build their pyramids? Either way, it's true. It's called the art of using one's tongue here."

"Chinese history has no lack of devious people. But you must be its most extraordinary example."

"I don't look backward; neither do I look forward. I am the only such animal on this planet. There is no second."

"I agree. As far as cruelty and the degree of fooling around with the victims, you are tops. When you forced peasants to the fields to scream at the birds or to become amateur steelworkers, or when you indifferently look at them eating grass or each other, you unite those two traits into one."

"I choose the jest of cruelty just as you choose the dramatized pain of a coward."

"I am a coward and a drama queen, is that what you are saying?"

"Exactly! I will show you right now: any emperor from the East at all worthy of being an emperor would never cry up and down over leaving behind a little drop of blood. You know that I have scattered my seeds all over the land like peasants scatter rice husks at harvest time. I don't remember and I don't want to remember how many children were dropped along the roadsides. I have no duty to remember them. Others must take care of them. One thing is for sure, among those children, anyone who wants to betray me will get cut down quickly and firmly, just like when I cut down those with no blood ties who reach for power. Power cannot be harmonized with ordinary feelings of conscience."

He sees the large face as if it inflates and darkens in seconds. Then it turns phosphorescent. The chairman's small eyes squirt out dark green sparks:

"For sure our game will end. Then each can open his eyes wide to see . . ."

He doesn't have time to open his mouth. Chairman Man has already gone.

He stares straight into space for a while, but the big man doesn't return.

"The word 'comrade' is dead! And with it all the games of that past. There: Chairman Man said it openly. Whether one wanted it to end or not, the curtain had dropped. It was not unintentional that Balzac had named his novelistic productions *'La Comédie humaine,'* the Human Comedy. But Chairman Man might be right when he said that power cannot be harmonized with conscience. Because a king has only the responsibility of protecting himself, his own governing power. Anything else is just grass to trample on.

"How can I treat like grass those on whose behalf I sacrificed my life? And her, too, her and her children; how can I treat those three lives like earthen graves along a road, or as rabbits dumped in a stew after I have looked them in the eyes? Can I ever imitate the great powerful one in the north?

"If I can't do exactly as he does, I will be stuck between two cutting boards, power on one hand and feelings on the other. I will be crushed because of my entanglements.

"But it's too late to change. Whether I like it or not, it has all happened. The wheel of time doesn't roll in reverse.

"But the issue at hand is as in the beginning. But if . . .

"There must be no 'if.' With an 'if,' one can put Paris in a bottle.

"Man knows that there is no 'if,' but they still have to invent the word in searching for the truth, just as heaven gives us the opportunity to make choices."

At this moment, he hears clearly a sad scream down in the depths of his heart: "If heaven gives me the power to start over again, I think I will never act like the powerful one up north."

He understands that Chairman Man is Chairman Man while he is only who he is. None can change their character or their fate. All words of advice in life are worthless!

10

The sun up just enough to reveal faces, Vu and his wife, Van, take each other out along the streets, like a pair of lovers most intensely involved. She sits quietly behind as he quietly pedals, each absorbed in their own thoughts. The streets are still deserted, one sees only groups of newly recruited soldiers walking along inexorably, perhaps on their way to an assembly point. Half an hour later, the Red River dike rises up and blocks their view.

"Let's get off here," he says, and she nods in agreement.

They get off the bike and climb the Yen Phu slope, looking for a sidewalk teahouse where they can leave their bike, then quietly cross the dike to the cornfield. At that moment the sun shows its top on the other side of the Long Bien bridge, spreading its light in the shape of a fan. The cornfields are still wet with dew. Strings of dewdrops run down the sides of leaves, twinkling like strands of glass beads, as the leaves shimmy in the wind. This year the spring wind is blowing late, as if there were a campaign to change the color of the sky and the season of the wind. Bursts of wind run along the sides of the river, then all of a sudden whisper along the cornfields as if hesitating out of fear. Far off, a pack of sailboats reflects on the pink water, turning it silvery white. The sandy shore is so quiet that one can hear clearly from the boats the sounds of children fighting and of a fisherman coughing. A bent corn plant rubs his arm with all its dampness amid its roughness. He shivers lightly and turns to her:

"Careful, don't get your clothes wet. It's still a bit cold."

"Yes, I know . . ."

Her response contains some unhappiness but he doesn't pay any attention because he is busy watching the children on the other side of the river. There are more than a hundred of them, of elementary school age, every single one of them wearing a hat made of hay, with a backpack or a handbag. They cling to one another on a barge. Perhaps students of some school evacuated out here:

"If the planes come, where can they take shelter?"

He is fully aware that the shelters, whether personal or communal, have no real value other than that of a sedative drug. A pad of reinforced cement not bigger than a large bamboo tray covers the opening of a trench not deeper than eighty centimeters. It might shield you from grenade shrapnel, but how could it protect you from heavy bombs dropped from airplanes? But nevertheless people need the shelters to provide some sense of security. War is like a game. A terrible game in which the first victims are ordinary people like those children across the river. Squinting his eyes to see better, he gazes at all the straw hats dotting the morning sunlight, the tiny backpacks and the handbags inside which he knew mothers had packed their own monthly food ration. They had to scrape together the last grains of sugar, save the last of the dry food to give their children a chance to survive at the far-distant destination; a high sacrifice for people living with privation. The endless suffering of a history bespattered with war. Is this the fate of his people? It's like they are people who are skinned and then made to face tearing winds or searing flames.

He hears her warning and remembers that she is sitting next to him. They are out here so that they can talk more easily:

"Perhaps Elder Brother is right; this country is ours. Even if we want to deny it, we can't. We belong to a people who have been skinned open, therefore we have to endure all the pain that comes to those who have been skinned; to each his or her own measure. Now we have to go back to our torment!"

Smiling, he says: "I let you go first."

"No. You are the man."

"In our time, man and woman are equal."

"I don't believe that."

"You did. Everything that happens in our household shows not only that you believe women are equal to men, but also that women can influence men with their feminine ways."

"I only act exactly as other women do."

"But I married you and I didn't marry the others. And this we agreed with each other before we got married . . . have you forgotten?"

She is quiet because she has not forgotten. With all the months and years of living together, and especially after they had a son together, why is he absolutely not conceding?

"I have not forgotten. But I don't understand."

"What don't you understand?"

"Why is a father so indifferent to his own child, then so affectionate with one of another?"

"One of another?"

He turns around and looks straight into her eyes for an answer. Unable to avoid his gaze, she replies slowly:

"Suppose he is the Old Man's son. It's still not like having your own natural son, one who carries your family name, one who will carry a stick and roll on the ground during your funeral and mine, one who will light incense at our altar as well as those of the other ancestors, on both paternal and maternal sides. Is that what you want? Your adopted child doesn't have the Tran family name; the blood that runs in his veins is not Tran family blood."

Now he understands: pride is the most powerful feeling in life. Any child is a very important product in which one can place all hopes and surround them with so many deep emotions. Any child, no matter how he turns out, is a sacred idol for a father and a mother. Because he no longer accepts this blinding conviction, he has hurt her sense of pride. This is what makes her angry. She can't forgive him or the unfortunate child either.

He recalls an old verse that his high school teacher had read during a discussion at the end of one week: *A person's self-centered heart is a wild animal, a cruel and blind animal. No proper consideration can stand steady before such a beast. No breath of conscience can make a dent because such a beast has no heart.* That skinny teacher with eyeglasses thick like the bottoms of glass cups had imparted so many useful things. The older he grew, the more he missed his old teacher as the fisherman misses the lighthouse.

Seeing him silent, she continues: "Do you think I'm missing the truth?"

She looks at him intensely, not hiding her sense of victory.

Then he turns around:

"Do you believe that our son will live up to all his responsibilities as you hope? Just take his uncle as a mirror and you'll see a true reflection. Please try to look straight at the truth, at least this once. Though you hope that Vinh will be better than his uncle Tung, can he not become a duplicate of your younger brother, and so another reflection of your mother?"

Immediately her face reddens brightly, the red spreading to the roots of her hair by her ears and on her temples. He knows that he has hit the target, that she cannot deny that their son is the exact duplicate of his uncle, a kind of unintelligent urban playboy, selfish and without scruples. Many times he has had to embarrass himself to intervene so that her incompetent and lazy brother could have a place to live. For sure, in a not too distant future, their son, too, will have to hide in his father's shadow to find a place to stay. This eventuality even the neighbors already know. But she cannot accept defeat. A mother's pride is stronger than wild animals. Standing up, she shouts in his face:

"Even then, he would still be your son, your very own son. He is the eldest son, who will carry on the Tran lineage!"

"This is your last card, right?" he asks in a calm manner, a bit exasperated.

That calm is what she dreads the most. His eyes look to the river's far side, where the sunlight spreads brilliantly all along the sandy shore and on the rows of leaning houses that stand beside the ferry.

"First you should sit down because I do not want to see you behave like that vulgar seller of fish sauce, Tu."

She sits down, in tired fashion. Her face turns a darker shade. And while he does not have any anger in his voice, his soul has changed its tenor. What's left there is an indescribable pain. Without looking at her, he says:

"I am like other fathers, I long for a son to carry the family name. I have tossed and turned and have been torn for many years watching our son grow. I also dreamed up so many hopes. The more I despaired, the more I dug in to build up more new hopes. Maybe men are different from women; their love always has limitations when it comes up against the truth. A man's love cannot, all of a sudden, become unconditional. At some point it must break down when it hits a wall of reality. Then people speak of 'broken dreams,' or 'illusions.' In general, one must have broken dreams to grow wise. When a dream breaks, one can't just close one's eyes and walk into the muddy pond. They have to open their eyes to see the path clearly and avoid falling into the slimy mud to die there a stupid death. I have no more hope for our son. From the day he first screamed at Trung in the middle of a meal and in front of everybody, that he had a right to hold a bowl only when he had handed over his ticket, I understood that my son and your son does not carry any Tran blood, but only that of the Phams. I have no hope that he can bear my family's name.

"So you carry hopes that later Trung will carry a stick and roll on the ground for you?" she asks with obvious bitterness.

"No. I don't hope for that," he replies slowly. "Perhaps I no longer have such a need."

She bursts into tears. First, she tries to suppress them. Then, afterward, she lets her rage go. It has been a long while since she has cried, cried without holding back, cried like a peasant, with all that sobbing and wailing, with the intensity and manner of one who is jealous, who has been disappointed, enraged, and oppressed for so many years that now it all needs to come out in a cleansing. He quietly listens to her crying and blowing her nose noisily and forcing herself to cough and cough.

The time just passes.

The sun reaches the horizon. The reflection of the Long Bien bridge on the water now turns to the faded pink of the crab apple flower. The cornfield around them is dry of dew, the leaves shaking crisply. A child's laughter coming from the fishermen reminds him of happy days in his own childhood, leaving him thinking:

"I had a good family where discord over selfish interests did not undermine affections. But that was just luck. To talk of luck is just to say that people don't have enough power to make it happen. Luck is a gift from heaven or a blessing from some holy spirit. Who can know if we will pick up or not pick up some ripe fruit that has fallen in our path? When I married Van, I hoped that our child would take after the teacher Vuong in the event he was not fortunate enough to inherit the good qualities on his paternal side. Who could suspect that he would end up with the character and traits of the notorious woman who sold fish sauce? He is the heir of Mrs. Pham Thi Tuyet Bong.

"That's what they used to say: 'It hurts like hell.' Only one lost hope can bring you down. A child is a most fragile bridge connecting everyone to the future. Children are a lottery, such that all who buy a chance to win can't guess what kind of prize will come on the morrow."

Taking out a pack of cigarettes, he lights one and slowly exhales. Cigarettes are a diversion appropriate to the situation, while waiting for her to cry her heart out and looking for a new approach to their marriage.

A stuttering child sings among the fishermen. He stands up and walks toward the sandy beach. There he finishes his cigarette and returns:

"Are you done crying?"

"Yes, I am," she replies, but in reality she has only just exhausted her feelings.

Now she learns that everything has its proper limits, even a fit of crying to release frustration and rage.

"Now we should speak openly like two friends."

"Like two comrades."

"Oh no. That status was appropriate in the old days, in the northern war zone . . . nowadays it's used before people kill each other."

He went on in a humorous manner before her curious eyes: "I don't want to kill you, we've shared the same blanket, the same pillow, for many, many years."

"I am listening."

"I know you have put up with a lot of grief after the arrival of Trung in this family. I have to be grateful to you for taking care of those two children at the same time, all these years, even with the help of your sister Nga. Honestly speaking, those were very hard years, but we were happy because together we suffered and did as best we could. Things got worse when Vinh grew up; a poor student, the more spoiled he was, the more unstructured and boorish he became. And more and more he resembled his uncle Tung, both in character and appearance, so much so that I had to turn my face away when they stood or sat next to each other. You must understand me on this point, right?"

Quiet, she looks elsewhere. He continues, melancholic:

"Bringing this up does not make me very happy because I, too, like you, am made of flesh and bones. However, after many years of hesitation, I know that the truth can't be avoided. And, in truth, you can't accept that your child is inferior to the child of another, no matter who that other is."

"I didn't mean to say that. I was too angry."

"You didn't mean to say that, but you thought it for a while, a long while. We live under the same roof; we should not let frustration wound our feelings. We are no longer young. You can live separately with our son. I can raise Trung because that is what I promised before my conscience. I will save him at any cost, even that of my own life. I told you that at the very beginning, nothing hidden. Now the decision is up to you. You have complete power to decide."

"You're filing for divorce?"

"I am not doing anything. But people can live separately even if the law still keeps them tied. Because the laws have no control over the heart."

"Do you love someone else? Is there another woman in your heart?" she blurts out suddenly, and instantly blood rushes to her face, turning it bright red like the face of someone carrying a heavy load up a slope in the middle of June.

He looks at her: "Are you serious or are you joking?"

"I didn't mean that you love some girl in your office or in this town."

"Because you know as well as the palm of your hand the backgrounds and personalities of all the women in my agency, young or old, married or single. And you have a network of spies to follow them and thwart them. Isn't that right?"

"I am not talking about those who work with you."

"Do you mean to say it's some woman in an embassy that I met during one of my official trips? You often open up the lists to check. I can provide you those lists directly. If not, you can find them at the foreign ministry, or even in Sau's office. As I know, he receives you quite warmly every time you make a call on him. Everyone knows the scheme: the wife of your enemy is your best ally."

"You suspect me?" she bursts out, and it makes him laugh.

Immediately she knows she has overstepped, and his laugh makes her furious. He is one who is never jealous. If he were, even once, the situation might be different. But he is a straightforward man, with self-respect, and he does not allow himself to have feelings he finds demeaning, according to the moral criteria he has learned.

"Are you asking seriously or not?"

"I am sorry, I didn't mean that."

"So, what do you mean?"

"I am not talking about anyone alive."

"So, you are talking about . . ."

He stops because he cannot continue to talk, because of all the shock, the confusion, and the fear that she incites in him. But when he sees her eyes looking down, he understands most of it: not only is his wife jealous of the adopted son because he is more intelligent, better-looking, and has more character than her own, she is jealous of Trung's mother. His mother was younger than her, prettier than her, not once but a thousand times more, even though she herself had been known as the beauty queen of the war zone during the resistance.

"She is jealous of the dead," he realizes to himself. "How can jealousy create something so irrational and loathsome? She has nurtured these unwholesome, illogical thoughts for how long and I wasn't aware? But I couldn't have known, as this is totally outside my way of thinking. No one of ordinary mind would give in to such a sick and shocking emotion. It can only be a new thought. But my wife is strong; in her family no one has yet to . . ."

He looks at his wife intently, his jaw locked, his mind unsettled. He feels like one struck dumb or paralyzed by an ill wind, a dangerous and hidden sickness that could not be foretold, neither by a doctor nor the patient.

"A wicked wind."

This is a sickness that can threaten a person from the neck down. Now he himself has been hit, engulfed in a state half awake and half paralyzed, seeing everything turning dark purple, half the color of the *chan chim* flower, half the color of eggplant. The face of his wife also turns faint purple, each elastic feature agitated as if she were looking at herself in the face of a pond being hit by stones.

With glassy eyes he looks at the familiar face as it changes, all its features growing thin, breaking, quivering, and wonders if it is real or a dream. What is happening before his eyes?

"What is it, what is it that has happened to our lives?" he wants to ask, but his lips won't open. His hands and feet can't move either, though in a second he would have raised his hand to violently hit his wife. He freezes comatose in his emotions. Like a living corpse. Completely like that. Because he has a clear intention about his own survival.

At that moment, she recovers just in time. After pouring out all that had accumulated like a volcano, she has deflated like a beach ball, like a tire losing its air. She looks at him staring down, grasping that her words had come out of unconscious jealousy. Now it is her time to fear. She stands up and heads toward the dike.

He stands there for a while, absentminded, unaware that the sun is becoming very bright. On the river, the barge suddenly blows its whistle. The strident sound brings him back to the present. The numbness slowly dissipates and he can feel his legs and arms and warmth on his face. The wind from the river brings the smell of grass and the water, mixed with the warm and organic smell of trash decomposing in the waves that push against the banks.

A tickling feeling makes his throat itch. As his hand touches it, he gets hold of a praying mantis. The little creature waves its swords like mad. Even after he catches it in his hand, it does not stop moving its thorny legs in the air:

"You are pretty wild—a young horse fond of kicking, a young praying mantis fond of fencing, a young dog fond of barking, a young cat fond of scratching . . . What are you fond of doing?"

Next to his ears, he suddenly hears a children's song that he used to sing when he was six, on those summer days in the countryside when he followed the village kids to ride water buffalo and fly kites. It has been sixty years. One's life is like a dream. Instinctively he bends down and looks at his shadow on the corn rows:

"How many more springs will I see this shadow?"

The question just popped up in his mind, the reply already bouncing back with a sad laugh:

"Oh, of what importance is that? The longer you live, the more shame you endure, it was said of old."

Lifting the mantis, he observes it for a last time before throwing it in the cornfield. The tiny insect disappears among the rows of green leaves that wave without tiring. His nape again erupts with an itch. This time it's not because of a mantis or a grasshopper on him but the heat. The roots of his hair also start to sweat. Vu takes the soft hat, puts it on his head, and then returns to the Yen Phu dike.

The road is deserted, so he can see right through the entire little town. People shouldering goods in baskets quickly walk by. Smoke from electric generators blows out black dust that turns part of the town dark. To the other side is West Lake, a huge expanse of water behind rows of purple flowers along the Co Ngu road. A little farther on, he can see the Tran Quoc pagoda with little buildings unevenly arranged close to the water. A boat bobbles in the distance, most likely belonging to a fisherman, because every now and then a net is thrown in the sunlight.

"Where am I going now, home?" he asks himself, but he knows he can't return at this time, even though he briefly thought of that blue curtain as his last refuge where he could recover his balance. She holds the key to the motorcycle; for sure she had driven home first. And right now she has changed clothes and is getting ready for lunch, unconcerned as if nothing had happened. He knows this clearly. He knows well that women recover rather quickly after every tormenting crisis, that their ability to fend for themselves in these emotional outbursts outdoes that of men. Maybe their hormonal disposition provides them with sufficient capacity to overcome such stormy episodes, such extreme emotional pain, and this ability creates for them a gendered reflex to emotional and spiritual chaos. Another cause might be that their skill in thoughtful consideration has limits, therefore they are less prone to the feelings that nag away at men. In each woman survives a part of primal humanity, quite powerful in the ability to sidestep the conscience. Their broodings as well as their regrets normally pass like a summer rain. Therefore they can stand more pain than men:

"Women are the strong ones, not men. This is the Creator's biggest mistake." He visualizes the calm face of his wife, at times stubborn, whenever she is scheming something. Tears always accompany some small objective, such as when to defend her younger brother's mistakes, to run around trying to correct his misdeeds, or to justify her son's academic incompetence, and when to paint new hopes for the one who will carry on the family name. He is familiar with all her tactics and campaigns even if he appears not to be paying any attention. In reality, all such maneuvers by women seek only to protect those who are close and to protect their own interests: "Mine, where is mine?"

There is the number one focus of all women.

Not only women, but all of humanity. Selfishness, a basic instinct, sits deep within all living things.

When he is tired of his wife's petty tricks, he usually thinks:

"Rats, life is like that! She is just a woman, an ordinary woman among thousands of women, born that way among thousands of beings."

Besides, he knows that living in any family demands negotiation. Without compromise, no community is possible. But he knows for sure that he cannot live with a woman who lacks morality. An ordinary woman with all the ordinary shortcomings would be acceptable. But an immoral or cruel woman, that would be another story. Like this side of the river or that side.

Today's conversation has pushed him over to the other side. The danger is obvious. Already he can see the roof of his home torn off and its walls cracked open.

"No one can measure the depths of a woman's heart. No one knows for sure what thoughts are buried in their minds, what feelings hide in the deep, secret recesses of their hearts. And I have lived with her for more than thirty years."

Decades; so many ups and downs; so many warm memories; so much shared sadness. How can he count all the times at his wife's bedside during her many miscarriages? How many paths had they walked; how many forests and streams had they crossed? Under how many temporary roofs during nine years of unsettled living in the resistance, with the sky as a tent and the dirt as a mat? How many times had he boiled water with herbs for her to wash herself and her hair? How much rice soup had he cooked for her when she was ill? How many days and how many nights?

He finds it so vast—all those eventful years, that stretch of a life now gone forever. He feels a lump in his throat as he thinks of the path ahead: a lonely life, like a desert spread far to the horizon, with no shelter, no shade trees. An invisible and shapeless desert that leads straight to the grave.

"From where and since when did this venal jealousy arise? It can't have been an ugly feeling that developed from disappointment in the son, an obvious failure of a mother. It can't be that simple. So if this cause makes no sense, then this jealousy has been nurtured for a while, since those days before the resistance was victorious, and all that had to have happened in the Viet Bac resistance zone."

—————

All these wandering thoughts bring him to the intersection where the road forks: to the left is the road that leads to Quang Ba; to the right is the curve of the Yen Phu dike leading all the way to the northern part of the city. In the middle of the fork, a group of concrete pillars has been erected to support gigantic panels that display the government's strategic slogans. Striking red letters shine on a white canvas that is stretched on a steel frame a little higher than ten meters. One has to bend over backward to be able to read them. He knows by heart all those sorcerer's sentences. In truth, he had imprinted them in his heart and mind with a frightening determination:

"All the cadres, all the soldiers, all the people resolve to defeat the invading American bandits."

"If the mountains remain, if the rivers remain, the people will remain. Once the American bandits are defeated, we shall restore the mountains and rivers tenfold more beautiful than they were."

A gigantic panel holds a portrait of the president in military uniform, his finger pointing to the zigzagging road along the Truong Son Mountains heading into the south. Above the picture is written:

CROSSING THE TRUONG SON RANGE TO SAVE THE NATION!

Under the picture is written the echoing reply:

UNCLE, NEPHEWS, AND NIECES ALL TOGETHER INTO BATTLE!

The huge, blown-up portrait of the president on that highest panel was his, actually his. The National Museum had asked to put it in an exhibition called Vietnam Is on the Road to Victory!

He had taken that picture unexpectedly while accompanying Elder Brother to the battlefield, with a very old Conrad that a Russian reporter had given him before going to China on his return home. At that time Elder Brother had just recovered from a bout of dysentery. There were no vegetables; meat and fish were only for display; for many long months there had only been salted fish and boiled bamboo shoots, bringing more than half the people on staff down with dysentery. At the end even Elder Brother, a little better treated, but older than most, had to endure the same disaster. A disease shared fairly. Then, Elder Brother had joked:

"Everybody is equal before dysentery!"

On the way to the front, the Old Man always joked like that. His jovial way of speaking, full of images and hidden meanings mixed with gestures, made him especially magnetic. The Old Man knew that he had magnetism; Vu had witnessed more than a few people intensely listen to him with their mouths wide open. He recalled that Ms. Xuan had loved the Old Man during that time. The fateful romance had begun in the 1953 campaign. 1953; definitely that year. It was said that was the year of the Snake: Quy Ti, the green snake. The resistance had one more year before it was over.

He remembered the stream over which he took Xuan for the first time on the way to the Old Man's house. He was the first and the only person this mountain woman had confided in. That stream had been as transparent as glass; one could see clearly the fish that swam around the mossy plants, the crabs that suddenly crawled out of cracks between the rocks.

"Oh, oh, oh!" The girl had exclaimed with joy and immediately bent down to catch some crabs and put them in the Cham cloth bag on her arm:

"Let the cook make sour soup for the president . . . we have enough for a pot."

He didn't know what to say but was obliged to wait and watch her check all the cracks to catch any unfortunate crab that came within her sight. It must have been at least fifteen minutes later before they resumed their walk. Xuan shook the bag in her arms and smiled happily:

"Tonight the president will have a good bowl of soup."

"Right. Crab soup with wild watercress. What a perfect dish!" he replied as he took in her beaming happy face.

There was a spontaneous naturalness, a simple angelic presence in this woman like wild grass, a freshness like a wildflower. She stirred the young souls of men. She brought together spring and youth—a priceless gift, something heavenly that neither power nor money could obtain. Not to mention an exquisite beauty that made birds fly and fish dive before her.

He understood why Elder Brother loved Xuan, even though he never spoke of it in words.

Nothing is more difficult to hide than love. One can hide big spending, wealth, dreams and wishes, hatred or pride. But nobody can hide love. Love is like poverty, if you consider it from that point of view. That's what he had learned from Elder Brother's convoluted love; even though he was a leader, even if he had passed through many past romances in his wandering life. But this girl was his greatest love, his last love in an unhappy life.

———

Gusts of wind blow on his face, dreamingly.

And the sounds of birds singing rise from the guava trees along Quang Ba road, sounding both real and unreal. He pensively looks at the huge picture, the image of a person to whom he is bound more than to his own blood and flesh. The sunlight gliding on the oil brushstrokes makes the portrait become lively, as if someone had poured on it a layer of silver sparkles. This kind of technique is more appropriate to theater art and this makes him uncomfortable. But it presents the old features fully: that gaunt face in profile, with cheekbones and nose bridge, those bright shining eyes with which he can read every glance:

"His arms are bone skinny in the loose sleeves of the shirt. Exactly from when we were starving, when bowls of cooked cassava were flavored with bright red pepper and salt."

He remembers the black piece of soap that looked like dog feces, made by the local shop, using ingredients that, if disclosed, all the soap producers on earth would be ashamed of. Eventually, that miserable time passed. Every time one stepped into a stream to wash clothes, the soap foam floated dark gray like bubbles of sour earth from the fields; it was horrible. But making up for that were the sounds of young military cadets singing loudly and of wild birds chirping. And hopes rested on a victorious tomorrow. Our people had never lived in a present reality. We lived only with and by hope. That never-ending resistance survived thanks to hope.

But then what about this war? Perhaps the companies of soldiers who today advance down along the Truong Son mountains separating North Vietnam from Laos are just as we were in the old days: hoping and thinking of a bright tomorrow. The saintly Old Man who still leads their way shows the same face and bearing of that saint of the old war in the Viet Bac. With just one difference: he is no longer a true saint but only an embalmed corpse on a short leash—a zombie!

"It was I who gave them that picture; now they exploit it like a weapon of amazing power. Who could have predicted that?"

That particular angst has been stewing for a long while.

"Who could have predicted that?"

No longer is that picture in his family album. The negative was lost with the Conrad camera on the day of victory in the fall of the year Giap Ngo.

When the troops had marched in from the five gates, all the units and organizations had excitedly set off for Hanoi . . . Hanoi, Hanoi with its beloved thirty-six old quarters, the cherished city that had been taken from us for ten years. Nobody had wanted to be late even by a day.

"On to the capital! On to the capital!"

That had been the cry in everybody's heart in the chaos of good fortune. When happiness fills up your soul, a few items will be forgotten, or a few things will be misplaced or lost. That is normal.

But if that photo had been used in an exhibit of portraits or for any other artistic purpose, maybe he would not have felt such remorse. But it was being used in the war against the Americans, a pot of war that boils flesh, a war that Elder Brother had predicted and had tried to avoid from the beginning. Therefore, a bitterness never ceased to gnaw away at his heart. Yet he recognizes at the same time both the shameless games that people play and his own failure. That state of mind is more terrifying than death itself.

A convoy of trucks approaches from the Quang Ba road, each one completely covered over. Crossing the empty space to enter the city, the trucks throw up thick dust. He knows for certain that the convoy carries supplies to the front. All day, every day, convoys carry ammunition and food toward the south. Every day ships carry cadets south to Thanh Hoa and Nghe An. From those two provinces, the units will disperse in different directions according to their orders.

And this fact is certain: every day blood will spill.

But spilling blood has been the norm of life over the long history of the Vietnamese people, a people for whom each era has been delineated by war. Furthermore, for this particular war, those in command offered a compelling logic to for their orders:

"Our people are heroic; such a people will defeat every enemy; such a people cannot lose very much in a war."

With that kind of logic, blood spills in silence, bones will fall in silence, the names of the fallen will be enveloped in darkness and fog.

Is this just fate?

Is this just fate or is it a choice?

Fate: because the Americans had chosen the south as a dike to contain the Communist wave.

Fate: because the north had fallen into the hands of one inflicted with insanity. He wanted this war at any cost: a war that would build for him a colossal monument, the most colossal one in the history of all wars.

"The war against the Americans must be ten times bigger than the war against the French, so the monument will be a thousand times more imposing!"

This end had been fixed right from the start.

The memorial had been built in the imagination and in daydreams since the beginning of the war.

How damned! History's game pitting red against black; the most facetious black comedy of all is the spiritual punishment of a whole nation planned secretly inside a madman's skull. And how many millions had voluntarily given their lives believing that their sacrifice was necessary for the future of their motherland, for the honor of their race, when in reality they are only a pack of sheep led into a gigantic incinerator to justify the theory of a ghostly corpse that has decomposed under the black dirt?

"Does he truly believe in Marxism or does he only borrow Marxism to achieve his dream of conquest?

"Marxism is nothing more than a large cloak in which to hide this dream of imperial glory. He is nothing but a traitor who usurps a throne using the oldest tricks in the book."

These thoughts drill through his heart as usual. These thoughts had left a well-trodden bare path in his brain. In recent years they obsessed him more intensely. Many illogical points can be understood only as time and space retreat. Now he has no doubt. The one who had harmed Elder Brother was the one the Old Man had most loved and trusted. But this one cares not for the people, and is not moved by the sincere guidance of the leader. He needs only power and glory.

He needs glory at all costs.

He is the one who at any cost must throttle his teacher.

He is the one who must find any means to kill his father. He can accomplish all this because the people admire him unconditionally. That is the price that has to be paid for being ignorant and cowardly. This reality is not fate but belongs to the phenomenon we call "victimization through collusion!"

For a long while, plagued by doubt, he questioned himself many times. But never did a true answer arrive; not until the Ninth Party Conference. At that landmark conference, all the cards were turned faceup. The majority of the delegates sided with Ba Danh and Sau. They wanted a victory more worthy than that won in the resistance war against the French. They wanted this new war. It was an addiction; an addiction beyond their control. A fateful romanticism that seduced an entire people in a mad rush. The passion to be a hero is fiercer than any sexual fixation. In the burning fires of sexual desire, no logic survives. When Sau decided to move the resolution for the war, Elder Brother walked out into the corridor to smoke alone. He returned to the room, looking out through the window, smoking nonstop. His heart pounded hard in his chest. An invisible fear weighed on his mind. An unnamable concern churned his stomach. A dreamy sadness like gray clouds filled the four corners of the sky. Vu had wanted to go stand behind Elder Brother but didn't dare. Even Elder Brother himself could not explain his cowardly action, although those around him all looked at him as if he were the last hero of the epoch.

"Is it human nature to cling to a group and otherwise to lose one's balance and feel insecure when standing all alone? Is that why I stayed in the meeting room with all the rest?

"No! I stayed there because I could not and did not want to do any little thing that would console Elder Brother in front of them all. That display of formality or that naked complicity was the most debased act in both our lives."

Exactly so!

Perhaps, so.

No, exactly so!

He had confirmed it but for years he had tortured himself:

"I should have stood behind the Old Man. I should not have let Elder Brother stand all alone in the hallway at the moment when he saw so clearly his betrayal by those cretins. A betrayal in broad daylight."

He recalls that he had glued his eyes on the window frame, where part of the president's back could be seen inside circles of cigarette smoke, while his own brain and soul were paralyzed. He understands that, from then on, history's path had turned sharply; that the image of the other was an irreversible stigma of loneliness, of a hero fallen from his horse, that from that day forward the fates of everyone, including his own, would change with this lonely man's falling off a horse.

Another convoy of trucks comes.

This time it's an artillery unit.

But the barrels are lowered, covered with parachute fabric and braided leaves. Red road dust coats the tires as well as the soldiers' faces. He waits for the artillery unit to go then turns into the Quang Ba road. He has not walked on this street for ages, partly because he has been busy but also

"Yes, sir."

"Too many insects, right?"

"Yes, I can't sweep them all."

"Spring insects for you. Clean them up then bring me some tea."

"Yes, sir."

He looks at the young man carefully picking up the broken glass, reflexively bringing his hand up to rub the back of his head. How many times had he felt that he had been hit from behind right in the middle of his skull just above the neck, where one blow can kill a man or a woman. This time again at that same point and only at that point:

"Only one blow; never use a second one to take someone's life. Even if the victim stands one meter and sixty tall and is equal in weight."

That had been the modus operandi of One Stroke Tam, the special aide of Quoc Tuy, minister of internal affairs. Nobody had ever told him that it was Tam who assassinated her, not even Vu. But he learned the truth in his dreams. Through his dreams, he knows for sure that she was strangled. Through his dreams, he knows they assassinated her the same way they eliminated members of the rival People's Nationalist Party in the old days. Ever since then, One Stroke Tam had been notorious. He had never met this thug face-to-face, but more than once during the resistance years, when the Party had fought with rival nationalist leaderships, Sau had bluntly described this hooligan, recounting and not concealing his pride. Later on, after the resistance had won, Sau rarely mentioned this person's name, but he knew that One Stroke Tam had been made head of a senior police unit and that mysterious deaths of Party enemies and those who contradicted Sau happened as regularly as lunch. All in silence. Nobody dared bring up the topic, except Vu. Was it because of this openness that Sau had pushed Vu aside? So many people had talked about this in whispers. Sau's relationship with Vu still remains a secret. Everybody knows Sau's personality. The recent death of his youngest brother, Le Dinh, is still hot news in palace circles.

Sau is the oldest son of a wealthy family. After him came two younger brothers. Both were tall and stocky like Sau, keen for food, women, and power. But of the two, the older one was more accommodating, even though before joining the resistance, he had killed someone in a gambling match. He had therefore fled the village to follow his older brother into the resistance to avoid arrest. Under the protective arms of his older brother, he first escaped imprisonment while the resistance was still covert, and then, when the day of victory arrived, he enjoyed every privileged advantage suitable for his cheating mind. Therefore, he idolized his older brother. The youngest brother, rather unconventionally straightforward and having no criminal past, was not bound to take orders from his elder. The tradition of the eldest brother's power replacing a father's authority did not enter his head. Many times, he publicly announced:

"You eat your own rice; you do your own work; you are responsible for what you do."

At one anniversary of their father's death, the three brothers gathered. They discussed many topics, including national affairs, because all three were highly placed palace retainers. The least senior, Le Dinh, was minister of industry. At the anniversary, there would be good wine, fatty pork, and all the delicacies of the ocean, even though the country was at war and the people had to tighten their belts. When wine goes in, words come out. So, at some point, inner thoughts come to light. The youngest brother pointed at his brother's face and shouted:

"Brother, don't be too cruel. If not, later on people will dig up Father's grave. And Father belongs to all of us. He did not sire you alone, he sired me, too."

"Shut up," Sau growled in a hushed voice. He did not want those around them to hear their argument, even though the three brothers were eating separately in a private room, but there was still a risk that their conversation could be heard outside it. Besides, servants went in and out to pour more wine, refill water glasses, or bring in new dishes.

"I order you to shut up."

"I won't shut up."

The youngest brother shouted even louder:

"I don't want my father to have his grave desecrated and his body exposed because of your wrongdoings. You enjoy great power and senior rank; you enjoy seafood delicacies; our old man lying in the ground never had a taste."

At this point the middle brother intervened. Two sisters came from another room to plead with Le Dinh to lower his voice. Sau did not utter another word. More than a month later, Le Dinh took two followers hunting in Thanh Hoa. It was a pastime of which he never tired. Many times he had left cabinet meetings if hunting was still possible. He was a first-class hunter. Perhaps heaven had created him in the first place to be the boss of the wild animals. In his trophy collection were five tigers, more than twenty bears, not to mention wild boars, deer, and various other creatures.

During that particular hunting trip, Le Dinh had died right in the car, on the stretch of road between the cities of Ninh Binh and Thanh Hoa. It was officially reported afterward that his hand had itched to take out a gun to clean it, when, unfortunately, it had gone off.

The bodyguard crosses the temple patio carrying a tea tray. His round face is hot and red; sweat drips from his forehead. After climbing several steps, he kicks the door wide open and respectfully places the tea tray in front of him:

"Mr. President, please drink your tea. It took me longer because the electric kettle is broken. I had to boil the water in the temple kitchen."

"That is all right. Leave it there for me."

"Sir, these are fresh bean cakes. The Hai Duong provincial commissar just sent them over as a gift."

"Thank you."

The guard steps away, the back of his shirt soaked with sweat. He must be very miserable to have to use the temple's tiny kitchen. Because of his size, anytime this guard is close to fire, he drips sweat. He remembers last summer when the guard had to accompany him on a walk around the mountain surrounding the temple while waiting on Le and the "mosquito spraying" specialist, sweat not only soaked his back, but also the back of his pants over his round and curvy buttocks, which resembled those of a woman. Sweat dripped continuously on his forehead and face. He had a large towel on his shoulder to wipe it off. Then, he had said:

"Lucky for you that I am the president of Vietnam. If I had been born in Africa certainly you would not survive the heat."

"Of course I would. To protect you, Mr. President, I would go any- where!" he replied instantly.

After that, they did not talk until they had returned to the temple.

But he brings up this little memory. His life does not lack such appealing recollections, just as he never is without those who admire his resolute faith. But he doesn't understand why he always recalls such trivial memories of this particular plump soldier. Is it because among isolated mountains, one needs a familiar presence? Or is it because he is too old, and, with old age, it is easy to slip again into emotional immaturity? Or is it because after so many vicissitudes, so much uncertainty, he needs to cling to a certainty of human goodness to make his final years less excruciatingly painful? He has no idea. He no longer needs to analyze everything clearly. By instinct, he knows that this person has good karma, and so is worthy of his trust. By instinct, he feels personal warmth having this awkward and large lad by his side. It seems as if the space around him is heated by an invisible light; the light of innate goodness, innate loyalty, and innate affection.

"Did you taste the bean cake yet?"

"This is for you, Mr. President. We will get our share at the last meal of the week."

"Waiting until the end of the week is too long. Go and taste half of the bean cakes today. Our elders always said: 'Don't put off today's work until tomorrow.' Eating is the same."

"Not so, sir. I don't dare . . ."

"This is my command. You must take half of the responsibility. If I eat all the cakes on this plate, I will skip my evening meal or have to take a laxative."

He gives half of the cakes to the guard and watches him go to the other side of the patio. The night watch requires two people but during the day one is enough. He chose him for the day watch, because once in a while he needs to leave the room, to escape, by walking aimlessly on the trodden paths surrounding the temple that lead into the woods behind it or to the mountains on the other side.

"I am like a prisoner. I don't eat stale rice, but my compulsory labor is many times more arduous than the work given to other unfortunate inmates."

During those aimless walks with the chubby guard at his side, he feels his sadness somewhat alleviated. All that he is reluctant to share with others, he is able to share with the guard easily and without calculation. Yesterday just that very guard had gone down to the village of woodcutters to visit the family of the deceased and then returned to tell him everything. Right at the start, he had recommended to Le exactly how much money should be put in the envelope when the president would go to pay his respects. That fellow's awkwardness told him what he predicted was on target. The envelope was large but the amount of money was quite meager. He asked Le to arrange for an additional amount and gave it to the heavyset guard to take down to the village.

The guard having left, he realizes his own misstep: people could question his special concern for the unfortunate family of that woodcutter, when every day thousands of people die in the war, of bad luck, of diseases. He, the president of a country, should have as his primary concern the interests of the entire people and the fate of the country; for what reason should he be so concerned about one individual? This is wrong and a failing in the quality of his responsibility, or a weakness in his ability to think and to decide. An excessive curiosity comes only from an idle, lazy life or from a brain in malfunction. An excessive curiosity is a flaw that should be over-come by all ordinary men, and even more so with him, the supreme leader of a nation.

All of a sudden anger oppresses him, visible on the pale face of a traveler. An elderly man, both stranger and friend, looks at him with frowning brows and says:

"What meaning to all this? All this subtle questioning and necessary cau-tion fit for an old king in a dark cave? What meaning to concealing a wounded heart and an imprisoned mind?"

And he suddenly realizes that this stranger in front of him is none other than himself smiling a sad and teasing smile. Without looking at him, he replies:

"You are right! I indulge this curiosity because I want to, because the position of national president no longer preoccupies my soul, because the sufferings of a father force me to look straight at my sins, because all the regrets of a husband compel me to consider that woodcutter as a mirror reflecting my own conscience. I have the right to regret; I have a right of redemption; a right to love whom I want to love; and therefore, the call of my conscience is justified."

His eyes follow the soldier, who appears smaller and smaller on the road down the mountains until he totally disappears behind rugged stones and mountain tea bushes. And the streaks of white clouds, gossamer like but-terfly wings, gently weave around the mountaintops, haphazardly conceal-ing the spring sun.

"My beloved! I know that everything fell apart; that the boat was shat-tered beyond repair with its planks bobbing on the waves; that the felled trees can never grow anew; that those in the ground can never find their way back. But I still want to probe my own mistakes to their depths, facing your ghost and never forgetting the lives of the two children. I will not and need not stand before any earthly tribunal, but I have to face you before a tribunal in the next world. I know that you will be waiting for me there."

The other man turns around, stands directly before him, and looks at him with condescending eyes. His pride bruised, the president's temples burn hot. He looks straight back at the one who taunts him. This time he realizes he looks just like him, like twins; worse, like two drops of water—from the body frame, the skin tone and hair color, the gestures, the clothes, to the eyes. The only thing is that the other's face is indifferent, the "I don't care" kind of indifference of a samurai who is ready to toss away his sword under the moon to satisfy some dream and then perish.

"Why do you still demur in belated regret, in hopeless repentance?"

"Because I am a person like millions of others. I cannot escape from the need of a father, of a husband, to love and to be loved. It's a legitimate entitlement."

"But you did choose to deny those ordinary feelings. It's you who accepted emasculating a normal man's life to please your comrades, those who gave you the great role of Father of the Nation but who assassinated your wife and destroyed your children's chances in life, and also with that acceptance you gained access to all the conveniences that came with your grand role as the nation's great, respected elder."

"No, no, I never accepted that. Everything happened behind my back, in the dark. I was betrayed."

"If that was true, then you must have fallen into one of these two types: one who is overly trusting or one who lacks good judgment. Both types share a common denominator: lack of intelligence; bluntly speaking, simple ignorance."

"Maybe . . . maybe I was stupid; very stupid. One thing about this humiliation is that my mistake was recognized too late."

He munches on the cakes to alleviate the bitterness of this last thought.

The morsel of the traditional bean cake is so sweet that he has to wash it down with piping hot tea. Then the thought of using sweetness to dilute the bitterness in his soul brings up a sour smile. Now he is reminded of fallen dynasties, gold spilling out, jade broken; so many garments and crowns, so many splendid costumes that will eventually just rot away, like corpses that are food to maggots. Those who lived in the red towers and polished chambers of the past, who had many times polished pearls or drunk nectar out of deer horns to nourish their beautiful bodies or to decrease the astringent taste of their souls. The dramas that come with power are as old as the earth. The only difference between kings of old and him today is the way they are named: the kings are those who inherited power from their forebears as people inherit wealth from their ancestors as gifts. But he, he has no inheritance—neither material nor spiritual. He is one who gained a throne with only his empty hands, who made a lake with drops of water. His only asset was the admiration and love of the people. That is his legacy! It is also his prison!

THE STORY OF
WOODCUTTERS' HAMLET

The road leading to Woodcutters' Hamlet curves like a chicken's intestines.

"Woodcutters' Hamlet"—people still call it that without knowing whether its name is outdated, or, to be more accurate, whether its name is consistent with the facts. In reality Woodcutters' Hamlet is not a small hamlet but a village proper with ample lands and many residents. One time, its leaders thought about changing its name from Woodcutters' Hamlet to "Victory Village," but that proposal didn't get anywhere because the locals were too familiar with the old name, as were people in the surrounding areas.

Woodcutters' Hamlet was founded, how many generations ago it was not clear, by three families headed by three brothers who had left their birthplace in old Bac Ninh province to come up to seek a living by cutting wood. The history of this migration is somewhat a mystery, and it has become more mysterious over the generations from when the hamlet had a mere twenty residents. Woodcutters' Hamlet became a large village with three neighborhoods and more than two thousand inhabitants, who make a living not only by cutting wood and selling charcoal, but also by planting dry rice and wet rice, and by producing other farm products like honey and noodles, and by growing tea plants. Its history is passed down on moonlit nights with the sound of mortars pounding flour to make cakes, on house patios with women sitting around fires kneading bread while the men sit smoking pipes and drinking tea while chatting.

That history is tied mysteriously to the name of the old land: Bac Ninh, which was the capital in ancient days. The special quality of residents in a capital city is that they consume more than people living elsewhere. The traditional Bac Ninh banquet was usually described with the word "tang," stories, as in a house with two, three, or five stories. Bac Ninh banquets come in numerous categories: two-story banquets, three-story banquets, five-story banquets (four-story banquets are rare). Each story is one full brass tray of food. A two-story banquet presents all the food on two brass trays. Just extend that definition to visualize a three-story banquet or a five-story one. Surely no one stomach can hold all the food of a three-story or a five-story banquet, but serving such banquet trays can be looked at from two points of view: respect for guests or ostentatious display of wealth (actually, it is the same thing whether done graciously or crassly).

The second characteristic of residents in a capital community is that they talk. They like to talk, to carry on about life's vicissitudes, and their ability to so talk exceeds that of those who live elsewhere. Sometimes that ability develops to extremes, leading to the habit of embellishing everything. Anyone could become an amateur writer or an almost poet. Such need to create can only propel itself through a unique window frame: building on precedents. Thus, one can find many different versions of the history of the three families who started Woodcutters' Hamlet, transforming a desolate mountainside into a busy community with the sounds of people walking, the crowing of cocks, and happy singing. The people of Woodcutters' Hamlet built the Lan Vu temple and two others lower down the mountain, the northern region being well known for its numerous pagodas and shrines. The need to contemplate a temple landscape is one way to embrace nostalgia for traditional environments.

Woodcutters' Hamlet consists of three parts: the upper, middle, and lower sections. The upper part sits right at the foot of the mountain range, where the first three families settled and built their commune. Many generations passed, young people got married, gathering husbands and wives from many walks of life, set up farms, and erected houses on the surrounding slopes, configuring them into the middle and lower sections of the village. Up in the hills, inhabitants of these two sections plant both dry and wet rice along with tea bushes while growing cassava, cauliflower, and kohlrabi on the lower slopes. Families who live in the upper commune are considered pillars of the village and are naturally respected according to a set of old customs about which nobody knows for certain when they were established or by whom. Thus, Mr. Quang, the unlucky woodcutter, was one of those personages who always sat on the foremost mat, who were always listed in the first rank of those who had the most power in Woodcutters' Hamlet, one of those who the village chairmen as well as party secretaries had to ask for their opinion, had to get their approval, when something needed to be done. Fifteen years ago, around 1954 when the following story occurred, his eldest son had been village chairman. Mr. Quang was then both a village elder and had sired a person of power.

In the autumn of that year, his wife had fallen ill. She was then close to sixty and had given birth to eight children, so her strength, though not completely gone, was like a lamp without much oil. At the Mid-Autumn Festival, her personality had suddenly changed. She became extraordinarily ravenous. In the past, she had always disdained food and drink, eating only two bowls for show at each meal. At banquets, she raised her chopsticks only to please her husband and children. Suddenly, that mid-August night when the kids started in at the banquet, everybody saw her dash to the tray of rice cakes, fill her plate, then go sit in a corner to eat them in a flash without drinking a single cup of tea.

Everybody knew that rice cakes made for the kids at the Mid-Autumn Festival are usually very sweet. Even those who have a sweet tooth can finish only two of them and they have to drink at least a potful of tea to wash them down. But she finished eating a full plate, which meant at least six large cakes, of which in the past she could eat only one corner before shaking her head in disdain. This sudden development rippled throughout the village like an earthquake. But it was strange that she did not care to pay any attention to those nosy eyes around her; she acted like one distracted. She had only one real concern: for the foods she suddenly craved madly. Her obsession with food slowly became a mysterious terror for everybody, beginning with her children. She doted on honey from young bees. Each morning she poured a cupful of honey, sat and consumed it glumly with a stack of sesame rice sheets or with half a basket of boiled cassava. She devoured pork, beef, then chicken and duck, then shrimp and fish. At lunch she would eat an entire pig's leg or a whole steamed rooster. At dinner, she would wolf down eight or nine bowls of rice accompanied by salty braised fish or brined small shrimp with roasted peanuts and a basketful of watercress or stir-fried cabbage. One day when the family's flock of one hundred chickens was almost gone, with only a few very young chicks and two old hens left for breeding, she went into the coop and took out more than two dozen eggs to make pork omelets to have with two plates of sticky rice, which she ate voraciously like a wild animal. The capacity to eat like that was three times that of a farmer from the south whose job is to dig the ground, five times that of her husband, and twenty times that of herself only a few months before. Because the family was well off, Mr. Quang spoiled his wife. The whole family found ways to satisfy all her peculiar requests. But her kids were frightened and the village people whispered *hush hush* behind their backs:

"It is not really her; it's a hungry ghost that has invaded her. Look closely, her eyes are glazed like one who has lost her soul, and when she eats, she does not look at anyone at all. Our elders taught: 'when eating, watch the pot of rice; when seated, look around you.' A wise one would glance here and there before raising their chopsticks. Only those who are taken over by a ghost would bend their head and eat like a duck being filled with snails, like a pig being forced to eat mush, without caring to see if the one next to you can get a bite or not!"

"My God, next to her are her husband and children; at times she doesn't even care to pay them any attention."

"What about the night of the Mid-Autumn Festival when, despite her husband and children being there, she took for herself the whole plate of cakes and went to eat in the corner? Only weird people would do that."

"Yeah, that was really strange. But I don't believe a ghost did it; neither a ghostly apparition nor a hungry one."

"If it was not a ghost, it could have been a demon's spirit! Only if invaded by a hungry demon could someone eat like that. If ordinary people ate like that, they would die from burst stomachs."

"True indeed. If one could digest all that, it would still be a strange thing. The other day the kids boiled some eggs then left for a youth organization meeting. I didn't want to waste the food so I forced myself to eat three. My stomach was heavy until midnight; I had to drink some wine with candied ginger."

"That woman didn't eat to live but ate to die. There are always people like that."

"I'll bet she'll live for a long time. But eating like that will consume even a mountain of wealth. I can't guess just how Mr. Quang will manage."

"The mouth eats; the mountain collapses! If ordinary people who just eat and don't work can collapse a mountain, just think of someone taken over by a hungry ghost!"

"Don't be silly, there's no ghost, only a disease that until now the doctors are unable to cure."

Mr. Quang remained silent. He quietly went into the mountains to look for honey whenever the honey jar in the house was empty, but what the bees made wasn't enough to collect. He also took money from his savings to buy pork and beef for his wife, after the hundred chickens were all gone. Even a hundred young geese could not keep up by laying new clutches of eggs. All over the region, when anyone slaughtered a wounded buffalo or an injured calf, or old and sickly cattle, they would all call on him, because he was the most reliable customer. Nobody spent like him.

He told his children:

"I don't care what people in the village say, your mother narrowed her mouth all her life, to raise you all; now it's time for her to nourish herself."

"Everything is up to you, Father," replied the oldest one, who was village chairman.

Almost forty, married with three children, he lived in a separate house, but visited his parents every day. Two younger brothers had enlisted, leaving only the youngest son officially living with the parents. The couple gave birth to eight children, but now had only these four sons. Each was named with the letter Q like his father. The village chairman was Quy; then followed the twins, who together enlisted on the same day, Quyet and Quyen; and the youngest one was Quynh, the best-looking of the brothers and, it seems, the biggest flirt. Barely fourteen, he was already chasing girls with more than a little passion. Several times his mother had to run from the upper section down to the middle and lower sections, even to villages half a day away from Woodcutters' Hamlet, looking for him. Of the four brothers, the mother spoiled the youngest the most; from food to clothing and books. Quynh was completely cared for to the point of creating jealousy among his friends. He looked most like his mother. His voice was soft like a girl's. Maybe that was why the mother spoiled him so much. The village people said that she didn't have hands that could raise a daughter; all those who came to her bosom perished after some months, none surviving as long as a year.

That year the winter was painfully cold; every kitchen kept its fire bright day and night. Old people dared not leave their kitchens. At night they slept around the fire like Montagnards. Fog from the mountain spread a white net around the garden, forming a floating mass over roofs and trees. Many days the fog hovered until close to noon, with no time to dissipate before the afternoon brought down new fog. Then, following those foggy interludes, came days of continuous rain with northern winds. The trees in the yards bent their bare trunks under the whipping of the winter wind. The hissing wind leaped from the crevasses, first quietly, then roaring down upon the hamlets, bringing with it ageless laments. It was so cold that if you got a cut and didn't have time to treat it with medicine, blood would coagulate right away, then the open skin would not heal because the skin would shrink. During that time, the people of Woodcutters' Hamlet gathered around the kitchens of the big families, the wealthiest ones that had stored enough logs to last several winters, who had enough sticky rice and honey to offer guests without causing frowns or complaints about wasting resources.

In previous winters, Mr. Quang's kitchen had always been full of guests; they said that both his doors and his heart were open wide. Wide doors, a tall house, both plain and sticky rice, jars of sugar, jars of cane sugar, jars of honey—all piled up in the five large rooms of the outbuilding on the right of the compound. Peanuts, mung beans, white and black sesame seeds were stored in baskets. Mr. Quang was generous and gracious to guests. During the days of continuous rain and wind, of gray clouds hovering, what happened outside the house made a sad contrast to the festivities taking place on the inside. Neighbors, unable to go up to their terraced fields or down to their rice paddies, or to climb the mountain to make charcoal or cut firewood, all gathered in the kitchen and the three main rooms of his personal residence. There the fire was popping, the charcoal was red. The men prepared pipes, cigarettes, and tea, and conversation exploded like firecrackers. In the kitchen, women pounded flour to make cakes, or boiled sticky rice or sweet porridge, depending on their mood. When the lower door opened, several women would be carrying baskets of rice or containers of honey and lard. Rice cakes, sesame seed cakes with meat fillings and sweet bean fillings covered in honey, sticky rice with peanuts, sticky rice with mung beans, sticky rice with steamed chicken or grilled chicken—every kind of sticky rice. One could say that not even royal and princely delicacies could bring such joy and happiness during those cold winter days when people from the hamlet gathered in his kitchen. From the bedrooms to the kitchen, laughter burst out as if canned for a television comedy. Guests would laugh once, the host twice. Mr. Quang had a hearty laugh that everyone secretly admired. Those who prognosticated fortune from facial appearances said he was wealthy because of his laugh.

Even though he was from the countryside, he knew many trades and many ways to make money off others. As soon as he came from the woods having cut wood for charcoal, you could see him with ruler in one hand and knife in the other going with a group of carpenters and workers down to the city to work on a public project. As soon as his hands were dry from farming, you could see him with a horse cart hauling tea or dry cassava to market. From there, his cart would carry all kinds of goods to sell to the cooperatives of the Zao, San Ziu, and San Chi peoples in the south and in nearby districts. From the mountains to the plains, from the plains to the seashores, he bought dry fish, dry squid, and all kinds of fish paste, traversing hamlets in the highlands where there were only mountains and hills and vegetation. Like a sea horse, he never stayed long in any one location. That was why, even though he came only from woodcutters, even during his young adulthood he had eaten in all the four directions.

His adventuresome looks created a strong presence that made others envious and fearful. Additionally, the way he treated people made the villagers admire him. Such worldly qualities were surely rare occurrences where people are bound tightly to mountainsides. Good hearts are also hard to find there; but if found, they can't do much good where standards of living are so marginal. In the most brutal winters, so many widowed mothers and orphaned children could rely only on his help, because the public social welfare budget, at the most, could provide no more than twenty kilos of unhusked rice. Mr. Quang never gave unhusked rice. He didn't want to annoy anyone. Where the cooperative gave unhusked rice, he donated kindling, polished rice, fish sauce, sugar, lard, and money. As such, it was advantageous for both the giver and the receiver. Too many people were indebted to him. But he placed no demands on them, as if he couldn't help but assist them. That practice seems a bit strange, but it gave lighter hearts both to him and to those in his debt. And his imposing house took on the role of a small village shrine, a place providing everyone with the warmth of a living community and moments of relaxed happiness; the cheerful ambience of a summer festival that brightens hard and sad lives in the mountain fastness.

That winter, with those bone-chilling rains and interminable northern winds, out of habit people looked toward his house, but there no more did a fire burn brightly. Though nobody passed the word, no one dared come to his home. They knew that he had left with his knife and his ruler more than a month before, after relinquishing the house and its money to his youngest son. He had to go down to the town to work because the family's wealth was gone. Nobody dared empathize with his sadness or console him. Nobody dared bring up the subject of his wife's strange condition. For those who are humble and unsophisticated and who are used to living frugally, such a disease is a curse. It is similar to typhoid fever, tuberculosis, or dysentery in the old days. Bereft of a familiar refuge, the villagers had to turn to a family in the middle section that had newly become wealthy, that of Miss Vui, the Party Committee secretary.

Miss Vui was thirty-two years old, never married, destined maybe to never fall in love with anyone. Or, to be more accurate, it seems most unlikely that anyone would ever fall in love with her, not because she is bad in character or in looks, but because she is several inches taller than even the tallest men in the village. With such stature, she also has massively square shoulders, as if she were made for carrying baskets on a pole, with overly developed and rock-hard muscles. Her shoulders would fit well on a first-class martial artist. One of her hands could easily knock over a guy her age. She is in the mold of her father, Mr. Vang, formerly a famous martial artist in the three provinces on the western side of the Red River, who earned quite a bit of money prize-fighting all over the north. The village residents all agree she so resembles her father that if she shaved her head and stripped to a loincloth, she could enter the ring and make opponents shake with fear, as her father did when he was famous. Mr. Vang had a mole larger than a black bean in the middle of his neck. On this mole, hair always grew, each strand longer than three inches. Miss Vui also has a similar mole, but under her chin; each day she has to look in the mirror to cut the little tuft. If she gets lost in her work and forgets this task, the hairs grow long, oddly twisting. Perhaps all these peculiarities leave her unable to have a husband like other women. She turns every male fainthearted. Her looks as well as her strength are hot topics for the village men to discuss when they work on the cassava grass under the hot June sun or sit and smoke water pipes on rainy days. There are a thousand ways to bring up a funny story about her, usually with just a question, some fact common to both men and women in the upper hamlet:

"Yesterday I saw Vui carry beehives up the hills. Her legs moved differently."

"Different how?"

"Her legs shifted out on both sides, as if something were tucked inside."

"Something stuck between her legs, unless she tied there a coolee or a fox?"

"You crazy old man, just like a saint who lies . . . I think someone has crossed into paradise."

"Fairy heaven or paradise: you black peasant who tries to be literary! Just say bluntly that someone jumped on her belly. Who would so dare risk his life? Maybe you? I see your face looking kind of guilty!"

"Me? It would be such an honor! Many times I wanted to try, but when I saw her my penis just shrank down like one on a three-year-old. Hey, I'll step aside for you."

"I'm very grateful to you; but not enough guts. I am afraid I might just turn off in the middle. And my kids are still chicken and duck eggs with nobody to raise them. I'll step aside for anyone with stronger willpower."

"Let's bet: whoever dares touch Vui's cavern will be feted for one whole month. The losers will take turns paying for good wine and juicy chickens."

"Never; what value would your wine and chickens have?"

"OK, how about a young calf?"

"No young calf is worth the loss of half of one's life."

"How about three of them?"

"Three cows or ten cows, add in three bars of Kim Thanh gold, I will still decline."

"Don't joke around: three gold bars would build five brick houses."

"So, then, why don't you try?"

"I don't bet on bluffs. If you all put in enough money to buy the gold, I will put my life on the line immediately."

"You'd sacrifice yourself in public? Nobody believes that. Your wife is barely five feet and only ninety pounds yet she pouts and tells everybody that you are hopeless, that you pump three times and fall out of bed; before you get to the market, all your coins have already dropped out. Like that and still you boast."

"Don't believe a woman's mouth. Are you in the bed with me to know anything?"

"OK, someday let's have a contest. We'll call out the administrative committee to judge; we'll borrow Mr. Quang's watch to check the time. You and your wife on the left, me and my wife on the right. Whoever loses must give up a cow. I won't eat that cow alone but will grill it for everyone in the hamlet. So, are we on?"

"You are a little smart-ass. My hair is in two colors, I won't be stupid enough to lose a cow to an oversexed guy like you. OK, I concede. If you believe you have an iron rod, why don't you try it on Vui just once? Her family must have hundreds of gold bars, not just three. Everybody says that after Vang passed away, she pulled in the money. The old man must love his daughter to watch over her day and night. If you can get into bed with her, right away your life will really improve. Not like a mouse that falls into a basket of rice, but like one who lands in a jar of gold."

"No way, not for money, gold, or jade, I won't do it. I dare only to get on my wife's belly or on some equally silly woman. But with Vui, we speak in the presence of Martial Artist Vang's spirit: if I were to test her strength, for sure I would perish in the middle of the struggle. Perhaps I can only duck my head into the cavern and pop out again or put my foot into it for a little kick."

Such chatty sessions could go on and on before becoming boring. No doubt the tedious, hard work in the countryside drives people to seek such distractions, even when they suddenly realize that the joking around can hurt another's reputation or can even be cruel. On Miss Vui's part, she doesn't care what people say behind her back. She lives just like a man, doing all that only men can shoulder. She shows no sadness or loneliness like other women dreaming of happiness. Because they are married and have children, happy fortune rarely comes to them while hardships quickly arrive to wear them down. Sometimes when out briskly walking, with a face full of confidence, she makes even the most successful men envious, leaving them with an inexplicable hurt as if an invisible force has crushed them flat like a runaway fox killed by a horse cart. Especially after Mr. Vang passed on, anything she touched turned into money. When alive, he had built houses for his daughter, guessing that she couldn't live an ordinary life. He taught her carpentry, bee farming, tea growing, and noodle manufacturing . . . anything that could turn into pieces of paper good for spending or that could entice somebody's desires. Vui is smart, and has an unusual aptitude: she can learn any trade thoroughly. Her mother died in childbirth; she was raised by her paternal grandmother; and when that grandmother died, Mr. Vang gave up his travels and returned to Woodcutters' Hamlet to be with his only daughter. People did not understand why he never remarried to provide a caretaker for his household, to have someone bear him a son. His only reply to the concerns of his neighbors was this brief comment:

"Is there ever a time when stepmother and stepdaughter will get along?"

When his curious relatives would question his personal situation, he would say casually:

"Having sex is easy; I can have it anytime I wish. Women secretly seek me out before I seek them. But that's just a momentary satisfaction for the body. To remarry is totally another matter. I won't bring trouble on Vui. Because of her birth, my wife died; I have no heart to betray her up in heaven."

A husband so loyal is indeed hard to find; a father with that kind of love for a child is a rare thing in life. When Mr. Vang died, Miss Vui honored him with a three-day funeral commemoration, even though she was a Party Committee secretary and her Party superiors had forbidden people to spend money wastefully on festive celebrations or funerals. But always life bestows on some people privileges that put the law to shame, because beyond the laws set by those in power, there is a kind of law that people just naturally intuit which doesn't need to be written down in black and white. Thus for three consecutive days, the sounds of drums and horns were heard throughout the entire village, and songs to send off the spirit poured down like a waterfall. Each day, cows, chickens, and pigs were slaughtered on the tiled patio. Village people, from old to young, with social prominence and with humbling poverty, leisurely enjoyed this banquet. So the passing of Martial Artist Vang resembled a celebration even though people would be reluctant to call it that. Right after her father's funeral, Miss Vui suddenly gained powers outside the realm of formal regulation. Before, being only a secretary of the village Party Committee, she was the boss of teenagers and kids. After witnessing evidence of her dedicated filial piety, as well as of her uncanny generosity never before seen in a woman, the villagers totally changed their perception of her. Thus, from a girl that had missed her opportunity, who had been a never-ending subject of salacious jokes from the men, she became a village elder who should automatically participate in all important village projects, a role normally held by senior males and never by women. They don't involve her when spouses quarrel, because that is the work of female cadres in the mediation section, but they will engage her when drenching rains flood the roads, when dispute over the land erupts with the next hamlet, when a school or a maternity clinic for the village needs to be built, when the district needs to be petitioned over the distribution of equipment and provisions; in short, for all those necessary and important issues that affect the future of the residents. That winter, for the first time, the kitchen in Miss Vui's house replaced the now cold kitchen of Mr. Quang and his wife.

Village people, especially the women, very quickly became familiar with her storage sheds. She did not have ten spacious sheds as Mr. Quang had. Having long been wealthy, his compound was arranged in the old-fashioned style: three buildings formed a U around a square tiled patio; each building had five spacious rooms, with thick tiles, high ceilings, and wooden doors that shone like mirrors. The five rooms in the left building were reserved for the youngest son, Quynh, who would marry and raise children. The five other rooms in the building on the right were for storing provisions, staples, and every kind of tool. When anyone would ask him where were the rooms for Quyet and Quyen, he would say:

"Those two are destined to live with their in-laws. I consulted fortune-tellers seven times on this and they all said the same thing."

Martial Artist Vang's house, with five rooms, is much too large for Miss Vui, unmarried and childless. That is why she decided to convert three rooms into storage as city people do. In her storage units, everything is organized neatly, lined up like soldiers; from tools for gardening, carpentry, drying tea, making noodles and raising bees to boxes of provisions. Each numbered, neatly and cleanly, in a most professional way. Because of her single woman's habit of extreme orderliness, Miss Vui designates for her guests those dishes that she thinks will not demand too much effort. Therefore, villagers are treated by her only to basic entrees like sticky rice with beans, five-spice cakes, or savory sesame balls. Not to be imagined are steamed or roasted chickens with sticky rice or other more painstaking creations.

Very quickly did the villagers accept the spinster's household rules. Even if they missed the festive atmosphere of Mr. Quang's kitchen as a paradise lost, their practical eyes forced them to value Miss Vui's kitchen as a pleasant inn for tired pedestrians. The smell of *lam ngu* porridge was not as tantalizing as that of sticky rice with chicken, but porridge was still enough to warm one's stomach on cold days. And that year it was brutally cold. No one had ever experienced such a terrifyingly cold winter. People did not exaggerate when they said it was so cold it shrank your ears, froze your brains; so cold it congealed your breath in your nostrils. From October to December, the cold hung on without a break. It seemed as if there was not a single sunny day. Looking up to the top of Lan Vu, not even a green dot of a tree or rock could be seen. It was not snow, but fields of clouds piled up layer upon layer to create a vast, frigid and white sky so that when the wind blew, those fields of white clouds shoved one another, moving and floating to project silvery cold effluent. It was rare for the sun to rise; if it did, it was pale and wrinkly like an orange eaten by a worm, and then it disappeared without a trace.

That year, to be more accurate, there was not one winter but two, continuous without a break. The Lunar New Year passed in a hurry; nobody seemed to remember it because of the cold rains. Nobody cared to celebrate; there were no drums of any kind. There were no games at all; no pigs or buffalo were butchered. No one let the kids run around outside. The only pastime was gathering around the kitchen fire making rice cakes and all kinds of sweet porridges. One day at the end of February, when trees should have started to launch their buds but, because of the lingering cold, were still totally naked, people gathered in Miss Vui's kitchen. The hostess realized that she had two containers of chicken fat of the best quality, used only to make the sweet kinds of sticky rice, with shredded coconut and sesame seeds, and decided to make that special treat, a decision that everyone welcomed.

Immediately in the kitchen, the women briskly started to soak the beans and the rice and to clean the steamer pot, while in the upper part of the house, the men sat and smoked around the fire, munching on five-spice cakes. Out on the patio, the rain continued, a rain with heavy drops accompanied by a north wind; the type of rain that hurts the bones, that holds those who want to leave more tightly than the clinging arms of lovers. Just when the pots started releasing the fragrant steam of red sticky rice, Mrs. Quang suddenly appeared with her raincoat in the middle of the patio. At first nobody recognized the new guest. To get from the upper section down to the middle one has to cross several hills; it was raining relentlessly; the cold cut through skin and flesh. Nobody thought that an old lady of sixty would walk such a road to come here. When Mrs. Quang took off her hat and her raincoat made of light blue nylon, people understood that she sought out this warm kitchen because her own had become cold and empty. A sixteen-year-old boy could not cook and take care of someone afflicted with hunger cravings like her, especially when he was used to being served himself.

The hostess was the first to recognize the uninvited guest. Miss Vui was talking to a group of men in the parlor. She hurriedly took a hat belonging to some guest to protect her head, then rushed out onto the patio to greet Mrs. Quang. She warmly and cheerfully welcomed her to the house. The cheerfulness was special because she realized that just a winter ago, Mrs. Quang had owned the grandest kitchen in the village, to which guests had flocked from three villages, and that, for more than three decades, the name of Mr. and Mrs. Quang were famous throughout the entire district because of their wealth and their hospitality.

Mrs. Quang acknowledged everybody very slowly with a vague general salutation to all at once, as she didn't greet anyone by name. Then she sat down on the corner of the settee that Miss Vui had arranged for her, and turned her face to look out at the patio, where the rain was falling sideways without stopping.

After pouring tea for the new guest, Miss Vui ran to the kitchen to give warning. The storage cupboard had to be opened immediately, enough sweet rice quickly scooped out to cook another pot to eat with roasted pork. The villagers quipped that Mrs. Quang was eating with more salt than before. Her every meal must have meat or fish. She would not be satisfied with varieties of sweet rice like all the others. The hostess, as well as all the women of the hamlet's middle section, prepared everything with evident excitement. This was a rare opportunity for them to observe the mysterious illness that the whole region was discussing. Since the Mid-Autumn Festival, Mrs. Quang had not set foot outside. Along with her hunger affliction, she had lost the habit of working as well as the ability to socialize normally with her neighbors. She would not move her limbs or touch anything, nor take care of the garden, tend to the chickens and pigs, or sweep the courtyard. She only made special dishes for herself. She forgot all ordinary concerns for husband and child. With loss of memory she could not even remember the names of her neighbors. For a while now Mrs. Quang had lived as if cut off from everyone. The two huge wooden doors were always latched tight. People saw her cross the yard only on the rare occasions when her youngest son, Quynh, returned to cook for her or move the beehives. Villagers looked at her with eyes of veiled curiosity, as they would look at one with special mental problems. It was no surprise that as soon as she settled her bottom on Miss Vui's large settee a crowd gathered around her to chat; men as well as women could not conceal their itching curiosity. But as if Mrs. Quang were unaware of where she was, to anyone who asked, she just nodded, then she turned her head to look out at the tiled courtyard while smiling faintly. Silent until she was brought a tray full of sticky rice with braised pork, red rice, and sesame rice with honey, she quietly held a pair of chopsticks and said:

"Please do eat, ladies and gentlemen."

Saying this and not waiting for any reply, Mrs. Quang started eating with intent. People dispersed to other tables, but, while eating, still watched her. The hostess ran back and forth, from the parlor to the kitchen, keeping in charge but never taking her eyes off the patient. Every conversation, every discussion evolved as a commentary behind the back of one person: Mrs. Quang. She herself was unaware of everything. She ate two platefuls of sticky rice with roasted pork; no one else dared to touch them. Then she pulled the plate of sesame rice closer to her. The men lowered their heads, pretending to pay no attention, but anxious glances passed among them. After eating up the sesame rice she looked over at the remaining half plate of red sticky rice at the other corner of the table.

Standing behind her, Miss Vui shouted out alarmingly: "Ladies in the kitchen, please bring up a new plate of red rice."

"Right away, miss."

The women scattered to the kitchen, then one quickly ran in carrying in both hands two plates of bright red sticky rice:

"Madame, here are two plates, not just one."

No one had anything to say, but all understood that once her chopsticks touched a plate, that plate would be contaminated with a germ more dangerous than those causing fever and dysentery. No one would dare touch such a plate with their own chopsticks. Those who had to be at her table ate cautiously while shaking. A nameless fear stabbed them. Even so, there was fair compensation to offset their fear: their curiosity was satisfied. As the four men at Mrs. Quang's table were sharing the last bites on their plates of rice, Mrs. Quang had already cleaned up both her new plates of red sticky rice. To sum up, by herself she took care of five plates of sticky rice along with a large bowl of roasted pork.

The four male guests quickly withdrew from this battlefield of appetites to find a place to smoke. Their fear showed. They were terrified of catching her horrifying condition. Even the hostess did not escape that fear, whispering to her two nieces:

"Take the tray to the back of the garden and bury it, the deeper the better."

At that moment, Mrs. Quang stood up and said aimlessly in the middle of the house:

"Thank you, Hostess. Good-bye everyone; I am leaving."

Without waiting for her hostess, she put on her raincoat and hat and walked out to the patio. When Miss Vui ran out of the kitchen to bid Mrs. Quang farewell, she had already left, so Miss Vui saw only a swath of the light blue raincoat flapping behind the kitchen.

Twenty-four hours later, everyone in Woodcutters' Hamlet heard that Mrs. Quang had died.

It happened on her way home, in the bamboo forest between the middle and upper sections of the hamlet. She had sat down on the side of the road, leaning on a rock, her hat over her face. Sadly, her youngest son had gone to visit a friend in the next village and, having fun chatting away, decided to sleep there overnight. It was a brutally cold day and no one was out on the road. That was why it was not until early the next afternoon that people came along the road to see an old lady sitting and sleeping in the cold rain. Suspicious, they approached and moved the hat. She was stiff like a rock. Because she was the mother of the village chairman, there was no shortage of people who would run fast to the office of the upper section to give word. Quy immediately sent people to the city to inform Mr. Quang while he and other hamlet elders made funeral arrangements.

Always and everywhere, for being the mother of someone with power and position, one automatically enjoys a more ostentatious ceremonial than do average women. Of course, her son was the village chairman. No one person had to prepare tea and betel nut, buy cigarettes, arrange for a band with drums and horns to immediately arrive at the house; sounds of music and singing just rose up all over the hamlet. If you were not the mother of the village chairman, your family would have to take care of the banquet, the betel and tea and the money in the envelopes, before the drum and horn ensemble from the funeral home could be summoned. From the one who played the horn or the two-string zither, to the drummers that sang the soul-sending songs, all the musicians were professionals who started their career in early youth and have patiently preserved their professionalism through many repressive campaigns of the revolutionary government. There had been long periods when they had to hide their instruments, pretending to retire. Everyone duly played the role as ordered with one heart, a common resolution, to obey the order of the district chairman or the village chairman:

"The Party and all the people with one heart carry out the mission of building a new people, a people of socialism."

Following that criterion, a wedding could only have green tea to drink and cakes and candies to eat. To economize, clapping hands replaced firecrackers. As for funerals, it was absolutely forbidden to play drums and horns and there could be no banquet, no funeral cortege, no flags or banners. Most of all no monks could be invited to pray for the dead. All those traditional customs were counterrevolutionary, corrupting people's minds and causing damage to socialist morality.

Time passes; life goes on. Bit by bit, sad affection for those departed encourages people to no longer fear the government so much. Everyone asks:

"No socialist government in the other world? If no one worships our ancestors, they will become roving hungry ghosts. If those buried below become hungry ghosts, how can living people prosper?"

"No drums, no horns, no songs to send off dead souls: How can the dead find the way to heaven? If they cannot get to heaven, their only option is to go to hell and become food for the devils. Thus children and grandchildren turn against fathers and grandfathers, shoving such close kin into the tiger's den and snake's mouth."

"Alas, the revolution is only a few decades old, but our ancestors have lived maybe thousands of years. Who knows the right path, the wrong one? To be safe and sure, we should do as our elders did for years."

Such clandestine discussions began within the confines of each home, hidden behind walls and closed doors. But slowly they began to spread to gatherings around a pot of tea, a tray of wine. Then finally they followed the peasants to the fields, into the gardens, and stoked a hot fire in the heart of the hamlet.

As ever, what is to happen, will happen. Villagers exploded in violent protest when the secret police came to seize the first family who dared call the musicians back to their old ways. The host had paid a special insurance fee far beyond the musicians' wildest dreams, which gave them the courage to risk their comforts. Besides, he hadn't dared challenge the government all by himself. Even when his old father was still struggling on his deathbed, he had gone to each house and appealed to everyone to rise up together. Because every house had an old father or a weak mother, and because funerals held up the sky over each family, everyone wholeheartedly joined him. The protest occurred quietly in the dark. The local officials were totally unaware, thus they grabbed the family of the deceased in a rude and cocky manner, not knowing that the people had prepared to resist. As soon as they saw the chairman and the policeman cross the door into the funeral home, sounds of drums exploded loudly. Hearing the alarm, elders came over and surrounded the courtyard—close to four hundred salt-and-pepper and white-haired heads. In addition, women and children stood in an outer circle like an army of shields. The unusual situation unsteadied the officials' legs. They more humbly asked:

"If you want to return to the old ways, you must answer to the law. We are here just to remind everyone."

"We do not consider funeral rites to be old ways. We consider them as filial piety. You said they are 'old ways,' meaning that for thousands of years now, our ancestors were all a bunch of idiots who did stupid things."

"We didn't mean that."

"Old customs? So, what do you mean? Please explain clearly in front of all the people. Here, sooner or later, whether we like it or not, each family has to arrange this filial responsibility, this reassurance. No one can avoid what is necessary to be human."

"Orders from higher authority state clearly: horn and drum music is an old custom of the past. Our duty is to enforce, not to explain."

"If tomorrow the district commissar orders you to dig up all the ancestors' graves, you will close your eyes and do it, without thinking whether it's right or wrong?"

"You go too far; the Party would never order such an irrational or inhuman thing."

"They sure do! . . . You forget but we don't: the year of the rooster, your superiors ordered the Lan Vu temple to be destroyed and used two temples farther down the mountain for people's education classes. The village elders had to remonstrate with the province commissar, to beg Mr. Loi Den, before the temples were spared. Fortunately, during the dark years Mr. Loi Den needed our donated shelter and food, eating cold rice and salty cabbage brine from our homes."

At that, the head of the village police lowered his voice:

"OK; if you ladies and gentlemen want to follow the old customs, please do it quietly. We will stay out of it."

After saying that, he signaled the village chairman to leave. As soon as the two stepped beyond the door, the drums and horns burst out loudly, partially as an order, partially as a taunting.

The village police chief whispered in the ear of the village chairman:

"Don't play around. There was an old saying: 'When they speak with one voice, even the monk will die.'"

The village chairman was at a loss, not knowing what to say, seeing this guy reputed to be so tough and mean suddenly submitting so easily to a crowd. Three months later, the village chairman's father died and the drum and horn musicians were immediately summoned. He personally brought the musicians offers of betel nut, cigarettes, and envelopes with cash.

From that day until now, there had been many new village chairmen and heads of the village police. But none of them ever brought up funerals and weddings in Woodcutters' Hamlet. All followed ancestral customs as if they were the natural order of things. Higher officials pretended not to hear or see.

Thanks to this political evolution, Mrs. Quang's death brought on every formality: drums and horns, hearse, banners and flags, flowers and incense, and not meagerly either. The compound was squeaky clean after two seasons of the hunger illness eating its way through provisions, but Mr. Quang borrowed three cows and three hundredweight of pork for his wife's funeral. Local opinion worried:

"That debt: when will he ever pay it all back?"

One with a fouler mouth said, "Really, she is a hungry devil: dead already but still demanding stacked trays full of food. Perhaps the husband has to comply in full, fearing her coming back to haunt him."

In any case, everyone on the mountain could not help but bow their heads in respect before such a husband.

For seven full weeks Mr. Quang stayed at home. He asked monks to come and pray for her on the day her soul returned, otherwise commonly known as the forty-ninth day after death. Then, instead of music, chanting and the ringing of wooden gongs were heard throughout the night. He presented thirty trays of food to serve relatives and neighbors. Then, early the next morning when the sky was still black as ink, he took the horse cart down to the town. The neighbors heard the clip-clopping of horseshoes on the patio and saw the storm lantern dangling on the carriage frame, spilling light through the fog:

"He is a foreman on a construction site, why is he taking a horse cart? He must be building houses and selling goods, too, no?"

"Only heaven knows. Someone with as many friends as he has can do anything. Now he is indebted up to his neck. He's got to find ways of making money."

"True, talent comes with bad luck. Heaven gives a way to make money, then it sabotages you with a wife transformed into a hungry devil."

"That's nonsense, as if when a hungry devil afflicts a family, the only way out is to bury it alive."

"What you say, sir, is frightening to the ears. But pity us, it is really terrifying. Since my birth until today, I have never seen such a thing. Just thinking about it is enough to give me goose bumps."

The neighbors gossiped, and every time they did, they felt pleasure about their own situation, whatever small happiness they had was in their own hands according to whatever their fates had allotted them. The cold spring of that year hit like a nightmare. It was followed by an unexpectedly muggy and hot summer filled with thunderstorms. Pouring rains in June and July made the streams overflow, breaking up many sections of road. The cleanup from the storms and the road repairs cost much money and labor. Cicadas popped out in swarms in the late summer. Their singing all day and all night prevented the elderly from sleeping. Children went through epidemics of first flu and then white fever. Their crying sounded like ripping cloth and made the air more oppressive and suffocating. Just as the weather can suddenly change, so, too, can life. Old worries return to the anxious and puzzled minds of the people, relentlessly vibrating like the sound of cicadas. Ignoring the meetings and warnings from the government, the villagers resolved to bring, during the summer festival, the monks from Lan Vu temple down to the two temples at the foot of the mountain to chant prayers and dissipate the bad weather. Usually the summer festival is given only one day, but that year, because of all the many unusual occurrences in heaven and earth as in their daily lives, the villagers celebrated for three consecutive days with flags and banners hung all over the temple courtyard. From old to young, villagers sat cross-legged and respectfully chanted prayers, hoping that the anger of the spirits and deities would disappear.

Mr. Quang returned to the village on the last day of the summer festivities. His horse cart was the only one in Woodcutters' Hamlet to have a top, therefore villagers could recognize it right away. He seemed thinner than before. Wrinkles now framed his eyes but his jovial laugh had not changed. In half a spring and one full summer, he had paid his debts, both capital and interest, and had given each creditor ten meters of cloth as a gift. Neighbors looked at him as if he were a lost soul fallen from the moon. They whispered and speculated among themselves about all the ways he could have made so much money. But the speculations were just that: unanswered questions. No one guided or found the path of this particular person. He lived beyond the imaginations of rural people. Not only did he direct people from Wood-cutters' Hamlet but he also recruited people from neighboring districts to work in wood and cement in district public projects. After arranging tasks for a work crew, he would turn responsibilities over to his trusted partners and disappear in his horse carriage. A few weeks later, he would return to check the quality of the work, to discuss and reach agreement with superiors as well as with the lower-level staff assigned to the project, and then after a dinner with wine for the workers, he would raise and empty his cup along with everyone, laugh loudly at all the funny jokes, and disappear like a magician. No one could ever follow him, but he had a special way of checking up on everyone, even when away. One couldn't expect to fool him. Of course he had never cheated or lied to anyone, and the group of villagers that followed him down to work in the city knew the rules of the game, so no one ventured to cross this successful personage.

After paying all his debts and sharing a meal with his children and grand-children, his horse carriage again clip-clopped down the road one early morning. This time music from the Suong Mao radio he carried by his side could be heard. This machine that looked like a black brick but could pro-duce all kinds of songs, even high-pitched singing, was nonetheless a myste-rious object in the eyes of the villagers. Even the district officials were unable to possess such a strange thing. The neighbors opened the doors, looked at the horse carriage, and listened to the music, which was fading away.

"He is very with it!"

People would comment:

"If you are not with it, you are not the man Quang. Who else could dare to order a banquet of thirty full trays for the forty-ninth-day memorial of a wife? Even after a hungry devil had consumed his wealth."

"If she were a normal, sweet person up until the very minute she jumped into her coffin, he would have ordered three hundred full trays for the banquet!"

"You would have to say so!"

"How old is he to look as firm as a female crab?"

"She was sixty, he is sixty-one. They married according to the rule: a girl is older by two, a boy by one."

"Ah! Already sixty; then he doesn't need to think about remarriage. From now on, his only remaining task is to collect money to put into his pockets!"

That was the point of view among the people of Woodcutters' Hamlet. They wanted a loyal and dedicated husband like Mr. Quang to stay a widower until the end of his life so as to live up to their ideal of a completely moral person. Just so do people need to lean toward a moral ideal, as long as that ideal doesn't apply to them. Then, at the end of that winter—to be more accurate, on the twenty-fifth day of December—Mr. Quang abruptly brought back a young bride. A young woman with good skin and good form, her eyes shining sharply like a knife, her eyebrows long across her temples to the roots of the hair. That first day, she sat on the bar of the cart as it passed along the village road, chatting with him while shaking her legs and laughing out loud. Many mistook her for Quy's daughter:

"What? The girl Mo suddenly fills out so quickly?"

"Your eyes must have a cyst, how could Mo be that big? She weighs no more than a handbag at the most."

"Could it be Man, who is only fifteen? Her laugh is very different and is hard as nails. I am sure it's not her."

They did not have to wait long. Right that evening, his patio courtyard bustled with neighbors. The storm lamp was hung in the middle of the patio and shone out to the front and back gardens. People drank tea, ate all sorts of cakes and candies, and listened to him make a brief introduction:

"This is my new wife. Her name is Ngan."

Nobody had time to say a word before the girl stepped up and smiled broadly:

"I greet all of you as my elders. Thank you for coming to congratulate us. In a day or two we will become neighbors."

The villagers stood mute. The dream of the ideal husband collapsed, dissolving like the lime-plastered walls of a house buried under a fallen mountain. Besides, the bride was too young and too beautiful, to the point that everyone lost their breath. She wore a green silk, short-sleeve blouse; her breasts were full and alive, as appetizing as two bowls of sticky rice firmly pressed. Her buttocks were curved, a nice sight under her shiny, black sateen pants. Just like her legs, bulging every time she walked, and creating excitement among the men each time the wind would blow against them. Her eyes were also black like sateen, shooting out rays of fire that made hearts beat wildly.

Clearly, Mr. Quang understood thoroughly the hidden thought of the men as he said half joking, half serious, "The district town is full of women as beautiful as my wife and more so. For whoever wants it, I can make an immediate introduction."

As if someone pulled on their tongues, the men said:

"Of course we want one, but with no money in our pockets, what girl would take us?"

"A patched heart is no different than a healthy one; I'd take a beauty. If you can find one who is half as beautiful as your wife, I will be your assistant, looking after your fields and gardens without pay until your death."

"Don't believe that guy, he's well known for fraud. Those who lent him money have yet to get a penny back. If you want to help, help me here."

"Ladies and gentlemen, did you hear that? We are old friends, but when it comes to women, friendship is for nothing."

The chattering continued while Miss Ngan withdrew to the kitchen to boil water for tea and bring more cakes and candies to offer the guests. People sat around past midnight. It had been two years that his spacious house had been dark. Now it regained the once familiar warm atmosphere. Even though conversations were bursting like firecrackers, the neighbors' eyes searched around for his sons. Quy was not there, neither was the youngest, Quynh. If it had been someone else, there would be some snide questions put, such as:

"Where did the oldest and the youngest masters go? Not back yet?"

"The family adds a new mouth, so where did everyone go?"

"Today is the day to welcome the stepmother; it's proper for the sons to make tea, open cigarettes, and invite the neighbors over."

Villagers do not lack oblique and twisted ways. But because Mr. Quang had high status and because poor people in the community were indebted to him in more than a hundred ways, not just twenty or thirty, all kept in their throats any word pickled in vinegar and hot peppers.

That night, on their way home, people blurted out:

"The older son doesn't bother to attend; the youngest fled. This family will soon be a mess."

"A mess around Mr. Quang—impossible. One look at his face tells you all you need to know. One like that wouldn't even blink if his house were on fire."

"Baloney! Even with a steel heart one can't eat when children revolt!"

"Let's see who's right! You won't have to wait long. Either today or to-morrow, what is good will emerge. Who'll take my bet?"

There was no need to bet, for on the next day, everyone saw Chairman Quy come to visit his father. He loudly knocked on the door. Annoyed, Mr. Quang asked:

"Who makes such a ruckus?"

"Your son."

"Go away, I'm still sleeping."

"Dad, open the door. I have something important to say."

"Nothing needs to be said this early. I'm just back from far away, I want to lie down and rest my back."

"Dad, wake up. I have—"

"This is my house, I can sleep as long as I wish."

"But I have to go to work in the village office."

"Going to work is your business, sleep is mine."

Chairman Quy stood for a while in front of the closed wooden door, his face intensely red. Then he had to give up and leave.

The neighbors held their breath as they overheard the dialogue between father and son, missing no sentence or word. Older men and women with salt-and-pepper hair fixated on such a rare village melodrama, knowing that the play would have many acts to come.

The next day, the neighbors puttered around, working gardens, picking beans or peanuts, sorting corn—finding any tiny job that allowed them to follow every sound that came from Mr. Quang's house. They saw his doors open out really late: was it nine thirty, ten, or even noon? Probably around then.

"Old Quang is now a city person. Country people don't dare sleep that late."

"Country or city, one has only one head, two arms, two legs, and a third one dangling among the long hairs. In your sixties, even if you are as strong as a bear, you can pound a young wife with hips like that only once and then you will need ten hours to get your breath back."

"Hey, Mrs. Tam, listen to your vulgar husband talk dirty!"

"Not just my old man, every one of you drools looking at Miss Ngan. One thing though: none of you can compare with Mr. Quang. You all are moldy chopsticks. Moldy chopsticks can't be used with a red lacquer tray."

"Silly woman! Admit it: you're a moldy, plain wood tray."

"Of course I'll admit it! If I were not such a moldy tray I would never put up with those old moldy chopsticks all my life."

"You clever broad! Tonight you'll hear from me!"

This conversation took place during the noon meal, when the neighbors were eating while glancing at the garden on the other side to see if Chairman Quy had come again. But he had not. One could only hear a rooster crowing, then afterward Miss Ngan laughing: a rather strange laugh, both worldly and childish at the same time, with something utterly fresh like spring flowers, the laughter of a woman who has just turned eighteen. Then Mr. Quang's voice in the kitchen. Most likely both were cooking; only the two of them because the youngest son, Quynh, had gone to his maternal grandmother's house down in the lower section of the village. Half an hour later, Miss Ngan came first carrying a tray, and Mr. Quang followed with a bottle of medicinal wine, clearly the scene of a honeymoon. They ate their meal in the main sitting room and not in the kitchen as everyone else does. Wealth creates such habits.

The neighbors had to wait patiently until close to the evening meal before seeing Quy return. Mr. Quang and Miss Ngan were cleaning up the five storerooms in the compound used to keep household goods and provisions. Energetically, they were carrying out to the patio a heap of jute bags to sort out those which could still be used for holding grain for the horse or hay. Quy crossed the yard, his face grimacing:

"I want to talk to you, Dad."

Mr. Quang looked at his son and hardened his voice:

"When you want to talk, you go inside a house. When you want to enter a house, you must salute the owner before crossing the threshold. You are a chairman, the head of a village, but you don't even know the most basic courtesies and polite manners. Who can you lead?"

"I did greet you, Father."

"In this house, besides me there is my wife. Before, your mother was my wife. Now she is dead and I have married Miss Ngan. She is mistress of this house."

"I do not have a mother of such a young kind."

"Ah, you do not want a mother who is young, but I do. I married a wife for myself, not for you."

· "You can marry anyone you want, but you should look all around you first. Your head now has hair of two colors."

"I do not need you to teach me. I do what I want."

"But, as the oldest son, I carry on the family's honor and importance."

"The oldest or youngest son in this family makes no difference. My hands brought in everything. I have never relied on any child. Since my marriage, I provided you with a house; when your mother was ill, she ate up all the wealth, but you—the heir to the family's pride—did you ever help me with even the leg of a cow or one hundredweight of pork?"

Quy could say nothing.

"Not a cup of rice, not a penny, not a piece of cloth . . . not even a piece of candy. Do I tell the truth or do I make things up for you? Everything came from my own hands. This family survives thanks to my own sweat and tears. You were not filial enough to give your mother even one meal; you did not give your shoulder to help me with even one kilo of rice; so don't boast that you are the future guardian of this family. Open your eyes to what's going on: What kind of eldest son and family leader only digs for food as you do?"

Again, Quy could say nothing.

"You turn mute, with a stiff throat; you dare not talk back. Because for all this time, it was us who subsidized, who took care of you and your wife; never was the reverse true. You are the kind who always opens his mouth but never gets his hands dirty. Just know your place and stay there. Don't talk about your being the oldest to scare me. Best for you to walk out of my sight!"

The discussion happened right in the middle of the patio. Mr. Quang didn't even bother to lower his voice, but raised it to release his anger. Some said he intentionally spoke loudly so that the neighbors could not help but hear him, so that from then on whoever would wag a tongue would hold it in and close it with a top, not itching to interfere with his affairs. Some thought he pounded his son into submission to shame him deep in his soul so that, in this house, no one would have permission to cross him; and also that this son would forgo any dream of an inheritance. For a long time, his oldest son, Quy—as principal heir to the lineage—had dreamed of this spacious house both night and day. After his wife gave birth to two girls, Quy determined to have a son even if he had to suffer Party discipline for two years and wait two years to be assigned the position of village chairman. Mr. Quang had long known that the length and breadth of the compound, the field and the garden, the beehives, all the obvious and hidden assets that people inside and outside the family always tried to ferret out, were objects of Quy's greed. Some also suspected that, for a while, he had considered every aspect and one day would put all his cards on the table, revealing the calculations that had long since been added, subtracted, multiplied, and divided in his head. This remarriage provided the occasion to express all these considerations.

Therefore, the neighbors held their breath and listened to the confrontation.

That night, everybody poured down from the upper hamlet to the middle one to gather at Miss Vui's house. Leaving no detail out, they recounted the argument between father and son. After the exchange, Quy had stood on the patio with planted feet for a long while. Mr. Quang and Miss Ngan continued to shake the jute bags, making a thick dust. No one spoke. In that silence, the village chairman quietly retreated.

Someone opined: "Lose this round, win the next. Quy won't put up with losing!"

Another disagreed: "There will be no next time. I don't take Mr. Quang's side just because I drink and eat at his house, but I know he was right ten times out of ten. Since he and his late wife arranged Quy's marriage, was a sausage or a roll ever brought over for them to eat?"

"Because Quy assumed his father had money. If you can't rely on a father, who can you rely on?"

"No one should ever rely on others; not even parents or children. If you rely on others, you make a beggar of yourself, so don't try to lecture others and don't demand things beyond your fair share."

"It's easy to talk, but his daughter is nineteen and Mr. Quang brings home a bride of eighteen: How can Quy stand that?"

"The girl Mo is already nineteen? I am shocked!"

"Have you been sleeping? Master Quy is forty-one this year, not less. Mr. and Mrs. Quang married when she was eighteen; that next year they had a son right away."

"Now that you mention it, it's quite awkward. Quy's wife could have given birth to Miss Ngan."

"Each eats from his own bowl; each sleeps in his own bed. Life is so different now."

"No matter how different, when those involved are of the same blood, still sit at the same table, sleep under the same roof, anything unsettling will lead to conflict."

"What do you mean by unsettling?"

"Unsettling means something out of tune with what we normally see or hear in life. You all just imagine Quy's wife standing next to Miss Ngan. On one side is a fat sow, with bony neck and breasts sagging down to the belly button. On the other is a tray full of food, a smooth nape like that of a dove, an arm plump like an ear of corn, skin white like a boiled egg peeled. And you would make the old sow call Miss Ngan 'mother' . . . it's beyond laughter!"

"I think your eyes are searching, digging, more than they should. They call someone like you a dirty old man!"

"Being a dirty old man is not too bad; I do not refuse your compliment. But let's get back to Mr. Quang's situation; I think Quy is jealous of his father. Whoever wants to see a father bite into a succulent piece of meat, while the son has to munch on a bone? This is the very thing that roasts the soul of the chairman."

"That's bullshit! The fire that burns the soul of the oldest son is the estate that he was sure of inheriting. Did you not see, ladies and gentlemen, that after the birth of the boy, Phu, the chairman was elated every minute, every second? Risking Party discipline turned out to be a big win. The father is the firstborn son; his firstborn son is in line to lead the lineage whatever happens when Mr. Quang passes on, and the wealth will flow into his pockets. Even though nowadays the law on paper holds that all children are equal, having equal rights, by common custom people still follow the old law. Now, with an eighteen-year-old stepmother, the dream has dissipated into smoke. For sure, there will be new children born. Miss Ngan could give birth to twelve children, big like stone pillars. Even though he is sixty, with his strength, Mr. Quang could bake five or six kids before he dies. This turns to naught all the efforts of Mr. Chairman to father a son."

"You are such a jerk! Even if Miss Ngan has ten sons, Master Quy is still the firstborn of the lineage. His son carries on the principal family line."

"Ah, you all are dead wrong. In very ancient times, the laws turned upside down. There were laws and then there was that which opposed the laws. In royal families, even crown princes were pushed aside; here we talk about just common people. All laws are born in the minds of the people. The mind is connected to the heart. Wherever veers the heart, so, too, goes the mind."

"Yeah, yeah . . . you are right!"

"I don't believe it! Anything can be said; to act, everyone must look to the village, to the nation. The king's law bows before village rules. So our ancestors have taught for a thousand years."

"In every period, people looked to the village and to the nation; but they also turned around and looked to the people. Ordinarily they acted accordingly to normal understanding, but when necessary they could step on all criticism. Don't you think Mr. Quang is that kind of person?"

"Yeah, yeah . . . you are so right!"

"Now, any doubters left? If so, please raise your hand so that I can count."

"This is no meeting to elect a co-op chairman or an accountant needing us to raise our hands and vote."

"I ask again: Does anyone doubt the points I just raised?"

No one had any doubt, but people were still torn by some concern that was hard to express, an impression that was really hard to put into words. Many thoughts, feelings, so convoluted one with another, that they could not be understood thoroughly and eluded the capacity for explanation. The only recourse was to wait. Clarity would come with time!

Next morning, a youngster from the lower section came up to see Mr. Quang, saying that Master Quynh had asked him to fetch his clothes and books; that from now on Quynh would live in the lower section with his maternal grandmother and two uncles. The neighbors heard Miss Ngan ask her husband to receive the guest. Mr. Quang's reply was pretty rude:

"I don't know which family you belong to. Lately I made my living in the city and so have not had the opportunity to visit other hamlets. Given this, I can't turn his belongings over to a stranger. Why don't you go back and tell Quynh that his clothes, books, and personal stuff were bought with the money from my pocket. If he wants these things, he must bring himself up here to meet me, not ask another."

Of course, the youngster had to retreat, without any sound or noise, according to the neighbor's telling. That afternoon, the late Mrs. Quang's two younger brothers knocked at their brother-in-law's door. Perhaps feeling scared, they decided to come together, hoping the following song holds true:

"Two against one: if you don't lose an eye, you'll break a leg!"

It was time for the evening meal. The neighbors used the excuse of asking for some salt, some lard, to listen in on his affair. The host not only greeted the brothers warmly, he made a new pot of tea and invited them in:

"On the occasion of my wife's brothers' visit, please stay for dinner to make us merry. We should prepare many trays and invite the whole world, but following custom, we have to wait until after the first anniversary of the death of my son Quy's mother. It will be only a month more."

"Oh no, we dare not bother you that much."

"No, you do not; in fact it is I who want an opportunity to raise and empty glasses with you all. We are neighbors with adjoining gardens and share the alley; I am away most of the year. Only in winter is there time to get together with people in the hamlet."

"Fine, since you insist."

The host called down to the kitchen: "Down there, please pluck two more chickens."

"Yes, dear; I hear you!" Miss Ngan replied immediately. Ms. Tu was beside her in the kitchen, making rolls and dumplings while stir-frying dishes. She was Mr. Quang's niece, fifty-nine years old but still a virgin. Her mother died of typhoid fever when she was ten. For two years her father raised her, then he died in a flood. At twelve she was determined to live by herself, not fearing loneliness, ghosts, or spinsterhood. The villagers dreaded the young girl who incorrigibly kept an altar to respectfully remember and honor her father and mother. They said she was a nun who lived at home. There were women in her family on her father's side who lived single like that; some were temple keepers, some organized occult trance dances, and some were hospital volunteers until their deaths. No one ever heard a word about any romances during her youth. In reality, she had neither winsome charm nor beauty. Her body was small, firm, with an ordinary face but without much of a chin and her mouth was missing some teeth. Her own mother endearingly called her the "mumbler," which became her nickname. Ms. Tu was neither ugly nor pretty. Her lips were nicely red; her eyes clear like moving water. Many in the village, far less attractive than she, married as expected. She had to accept a life of loneliness. Was this because in some previous life she had been wayward, with multiple husbands or wives, therefore in this life was now having to pay for that excess? Or had the spirits of her ancestors forced her to become a spinster, caring for the family altar and worshipping the ancestral spirits? No one uncovered the ultimate reason, but in their hearts, they respected her. As for Mr. Quang, he truly cared for her in a special way. Even though it was not made public, everything Tu possessed—from furnishings, to the garden, to horse and cow, to clothing, to gold bracelets—had been provided by Mr. Quang. The two were uncle and niece, as well as childhood friends; then they became friends in the same field. It was reported that the first time Mr. Quang went to do business in the city, he bought for his wife only a one-ounce gold ring while he bought for his niece earrings made from two ounces of gold. Mrs. Quang dared not feel jealous. Mr. Quang knew full well in his heart that his niece without beauty was the one who most deserved his trust and confidence, because they were bound by an unusual kinship, both of blood and equally of friendship.

The very first night Mr. Quang had brought Miss Ngan to the village, when the relatives and the whole village were still tongue-tied not knowing how to address her properly, Ms. Tu cheerfully made invitations:

"All are invited to drink tea and eat sweets. Today is a banquet so that my auntie can be introduced to her new neighbors!"

Then she called out to Miss Ngan loudly: "Auntie Ngan: show yourself and greet the neighbors. Just leave everything else to me; I'll get it done."

Clearly, her stance was authoritative: an official naming and confirmation that no one had the right to question. They then had to acknowledge to one another:

"Young she is, but according to social ranks within the family, she gets to sit on the inner mat."

"That Tu really is so loyal to her uncle!"

In the end there was no alternative other than to accept the female stranger, barely eighteen years old, as a maternal aunt, as a paternal aunt, as a young grandmother—all according to the prescribed generational ranking of relatives—while nevertheless feeling hidden resentment at her status.

Thanks perhaps to a stroke from heaven or to a gift from the earth, Ms. Tu came to assist Miss Ngan cook the meal that evening. In the parlor, tea was not even over before she brought up a tray full of delicacies.

"Please, dear guests, please sit yourselves on the mats. My aunt is still cooking the mung bean dessert, so she'll just eat in the kitchen with no fuss."

"No, please. If she does that, how can we swallow? These days it's democratic, with equal rights, equal powers; men and women must sit and eat together in good fellowship."

"Thank you, sirs; we are not being difficult. The two of us have everything in the kitchen, wine, meat, and all the stir-fried and braised dishes that you have here; nothing is missing."

After she was done talking, she ran to the kitchen to permit the guests to be at their ease.

Then the meal began. All six of them—Mr. Quang, his brothers-in-law, and three neighbors—were quiet because the wine was good and the food was even better. In truth, unpleasant topics don't go with a good meal. They have to wait until the eating is over. When pork, chicken, and fish bones cover the tray, when good wine has reached the veins, then tongues get untied and words slide out from the brain's nooks and crannies. It seems that Mr. Quang's two brothers-in-law waited for the wine to settle in before starting to press their case, something they took as their highest responsibility toward the soul of their sister who had died not yet a year ago.

"Thank you, Big Uncle, for giving us food that's filling and wine that's 'relaxing.'"

The older brother-in-law began: "Now that we have finished eating, we have something to say."

The younger one cleared his throat to continue.

The host smiled: "Please, be natural; it is said that when wine goes in, words go out! The elders said this, so it must be true to some extent."

"Nephew Quynh is at the maternal grandmother's home, in pain, sad and confused. We don't have to tell you why he left . . ."

"You are mistaken, I have no idea why. But when that little twerp left home and dropped out of school, he could have had a hundred reasons. I don't have time to guess what games they keep in their pockets."

"You, Big Uncle, have wined and dined out in the world for decades. We are just hicks who stick near our gardens and mountain. We dare not, but if we dared, we do not have sufficient skill to argue with you. But in reality, Quynh's current situation is driving the whole clan crazy."

"The whole clan crazy? Are you serious or are you joking? But your clan or mine? That fact must be clear."

"The maternal clan, your wife's clan. First is grandmother. Then, the two of us here. People say: if the father dies, there is the uncle; if the mother dies, the aunt will nurse."

"I understand that!" Mr Quang interjects, then laughs loudly.

His laugh resonates through all five rooms, even in the kitchen. Ms. Tu and Miss Ngan strain their necks to listen.

"So, when the mother dies, the aunt nurses; but the mother of Quy and Quynh did not have a younger sister, so the two of you must play that role. Excellent! I have never seen such a deep love being expressed. Now that you show such compassion, please do take care of Quynh. Thus you both can help me, taking some weight off my shoulders. Your nephew has good fortune, having both his paternal and maternal families for support. Having both sides, the left and the right, gives one a lucky fate as red as red sticky rice, and a fortune as firm as a fort. If you two can help him fully, the maternal family's reputation will be so much better. I have raised him all these years; I think I have nothing to regret. Now, if, at sixteen, he wants to enjoy favors coming from the maternal side, it's quite commonplace. Everyone in this life must have both father and mother, not to respect one and despise the other."

He turned to his three guests, his neighbors, and said: "Taking advantage of their presence, my neighbors can be witnesses: I hereby relinquish to both of you my parental rights. From now on, for Quynh, his schooling, food, and clothing, and then, in the future, his marriage, are all the responsibility of his grandmother and you two. Quynh will agree to this. And his mother in heaven will be very satisfied."

The two brothers-in-law did not even have an opportunity to reply when Mr. Quang called out to the kitchen:

"We're finished eating; if you have sweet porridge, bring it up."

"Right away, Big Uncle," Ms. Tu replied. In less than a minute, a tray of sweet porridge was brought out; the six men continued with their dessert. Expecting a riposte from the brothers-in-law, the three neighbors ate with curiosity mixed with despair. But those two only bowed their heads, eating without looking up. The dessert was no longer sweet but bitter to their throats. Before the dessert was finished, Mr. Quang called for his wife to wrap cakes and candies as gifts for his former wife's mother with such a smiling and natural manner that the brothers-in-law could only accept the package then run out into the street without being able to utter a good-bye.

Left were the three neighbors and the host, drinking water while picking their teeth and chatting. Night in the deep woods is always more quiet than down in the lowlands. Mr. Quang turned on the Victrola to let the neighbors hear some music. In half an hour, some women and girls gleefully entered the patio, some waving flashlights, others carrying torches.

"Mr. Quang, please turn it up louder; let us listen, too."

"Say, any candies from the city left? We came to get some sweets to go with our nightly chitchat."

"Where is the new mistress of the house? Please light the lamp so that we can all have some cheer."

The storm lamp, hung in the middle of the patio, lit up the whole house to the kitchen. Ms. Tu carried the pot of sweet porridge, big as a pot of rice soup during the Mid-Autumn Festival, to serve the guests in the communal way of eating: a basket of bowls and clean spoons was put on the table for all to serve themselves. When the pot was empty, Miss Ngan opened new boxes of cookies and candies. In the countryside, eating and drinking are a fixed custom, even when people are condescendingly reminded, "A bite bigger than your mouth can bring you down."

The following days took turns passing by like acts in a disingenuous drama where the actors and spectators disdain the parts they have to play. For certain, the actors were those whose feelings had been bruised. Chairman Quy was not accepting, as everyone had predicted. He had his hands on power. Like it or not, power is a force that can be witnessed but not touched. With his title of chairman, he could easily mobilize his direct subordinates like the head of police, the chair of the women's unit, the secretary of the youth brigade, et cetera. Additionally, there was a nameless, shapeless, invisible power that everyone could feel and even smell: the force telling everyone how to live. Quy believed unequivocally in that force just as strongly as he trusted in the seal of the village government, two talismans that he held firmly in his fists.

First, Quy had to ally with his youngest brother, because every struggle turns on force. The stronger the force, the quicker the victory. In this struggle, the most trusted allies have to be your close relatives. "Brothers are like arms and legs; husband and wife are like shirts you take on and off." In the past, Quy and Quynh had not been close, partly because there was a big gap in their ages, partly because Quy had felt that his parents had favored their youngest son over him. And Quy ran the risk of not inheriting a large portion of the family assets if his naive and flirtatious brother was preferred. According to the common rule, a youngest child has a right to inherit if both parents agree and the oldest son has flawed abilities and attitudes, or has a congenital mental deficiency. The chairman does not feel threatened as to lack of ability, but that very clever mind of his might prove to be a double-edged sword when one's capacities turn around to "kill their owner." But now, the appearance of "a cheap broad from nowhere wearing a green blouse" provided an opportunity to test his youngest brother's heart, to win him over and turn him into an effective right hand, something he had done with almost all of his opponents in Woodcutters' Hamlet since he had become village chairman.

As for Quynh, everything was the opposite. The youngest brother was spoiled, still at a romantic age and more concerned with having a good time than worrying about life. Sometimes, if he were asked, "Who will get the big house?" Quynh would smile and reply: "Yesterday, today, and tomorrow all belong to my father."

They would probe a little more: "Do you mean to say that Mr. and Mrs. Quang do not plan to write a will?"

He would turn red and retort: "My parents can still wrestle water buffalo; they don't need to worry about a will."

After that, nobody could get a word out of his mouth. To be fair, Quynh was a good one, liking only to play and not work. From his birth until his mother's death, Quynh had not thought about anything. Everything had been provided for him by others. Even when his mother had died on the roadside while he had been away, sleeping over at the neighboring hamlet, he was not like others who would have felt torn apart, with remorse so haunting that you can't eat or sleep. But Quynh had not felt a bit shocked. When the family had scolded him, he felt sad for a few hours until mealtime, when with a full stomach his concerns would disappear. At night, he slept like a toddler; just like a three-year-old child. The relatives grew tired of talking, of complaining, to Mr. Quang, who only smiled and said:

"Parents give birth to children, but heaven gives them character! What can I do? In my family, only the twins are concerned about work and think about what comes first and what comes later. But they both enlisted on the same day."

Then Mr. Quang would sigh, sadness filling his eyes; only families with enlisted children would understand him.

"During wartime, tears drop as a waterfall. Weeds grow in the gardens; no ferries cross the deserted river."

These couplets echo his thoughts:

"My family situation is similar; the smart ones leave for war, the stupid and the awkward stay behind."

"It's not just us! Everywhere it's like that. The nation is the same for all. The war comes; the wind blows open every door."

People considered Mr. Quang to be a forgiving and easygoing father. They also concluded that Master Quynh was big but not wise; maybe not that frivolous, but surely not mature enough to know how to be frugal, how to meet family expectations and be polite in general. Especially in his schooling he had made his mother unhappy more than once.

Thus, one could not understand why this awkward, heartless, and silly boy left his home the first day his young stepmother appeared. Perhaps this was the biggest question for the neighbors, and most of all for the chairman. He trundled down to the lower section to find out why. It didn't take long to discover the reason. Just two days later, the village people knew that

Master Quynh was in love with his stepmother. At the very moment Miss Ngan set foot in his home, the young man had been stricken by the blinding beauty of the young woman in the green blouse. In his mind he had thought she was the wife that heaven had sent him, because together he and Miss Ngan fit the golden formula for marriage, "a girl older by two; a boy by one," a formula that had been tested for thousands of years. This dream had come in a wink and then had crumbled away the very next instant. The whole drama played out in the young man's heart in less than half a day; from the morning when Mr. Quang's horse carriage brought the new bride to the village to the disappearing of the sun, when Quynh had quietly left home for the lower hamlet.

In the past, cases of sons falling in love with their fathers' new brides were not rare. In such instances, usually the woman had been condemned for being "loose" or a whore—"those immoral ones who seduce both father and son." Insulting the woman is so very easy; it satisfies the public mind, even when a majority are themselves women. And yet, in Quynh's case, the villagers dared not fault "an immoral city whore who wants to sleep with both father and son." First, because, even if Miss Ngan were "loose," she had been in the community for only half a day with no time to practice her trade of seduction. Second, and this consideration was more important, Mr. Quang stood militantly by her side. Whether the thought was ever spoken or unspoken, everybody knew that this canny old man never feared anyone.

That is why when the chairman put it about all over the village that his youngest brother, Quynh, was in love with Miss Ngan, the story took effect only with a handful of people who needed the hamlet seal on their official résumés or certificates of birth, marriage, and death. And even with these people, they dared to suck up only in order to get their way; afterward they avoided Quy.

"Don't poke your nose in other people's business! Messing around will get your head broken."

The people in Woodcutters' Hamlet told one another to sew up their lips with thread. But in life, everything that they "tell each other" or "keep to themselves" doesn't really avoid or remove the reality. Like children who are afraid of ghosts but love to hear ghost stories or people who appear indifferent but actually burn inside with curiosity and resentment. Their self-restraint lasts no more than twenty-four hours. Then they would blurt out to each other precisely how many times the chairman had come to look for his youngest brother. They told one another everything, how in the end the oldest brother branded his youngest brother as "stupid, a lowlife, someone who would not eat rice, but only shit . . ."

People said the youngest son was rather of a sweet and playful disposition, fearful of his father and ashamed at falling for his stepmother. Therefore when his oldest brother urged him on to do this or that, he only shook his head:

"I will not do it. Heaven will kill me if I do that!"

Therefore Quy's stratagem to make an alliance completely failed. From then on, this existential struggle had only himself on the front lines.

At that time, the old year drew to its last days; every household was preparing to celebrate a new year. This year, the Tet festivities would probably be lavish because the previous year had been so cold and devoid of any joyful feeling of celebration. Everybody was waiting for heaven's reparations so that they could have an occasion to gather and be merry. The open ground at the tip of the upper section was cleaned up, holes were dug for poles in preparation for the flag contest. Next to the holes, people prepared for games of cock fighting and releasing doves. This year, the hamlet had a registration for buffalo fighting. Many people from the mountains would come down to attend. Even though Chairman Quy was burning from anger, he still had to go and get the opera group to perform on New Year's Eve, because providing such spiritual refreshment was one of the important criteria that people used to evaluate the ability of hamlet officials. Two days before the New Year, early in the morning, the chairman asked Miss Vui to go to the district town with him to help organize the evening celebration. When there, he assigned the secretary to "investigate the background of that slut Ngan; everything else I'll handle myself."

Thus, according to the formula that one stone can kill two birds, this expedition down the mountain was to take care of official business, as well as to settle a personal vendetta; it was indeed a well-perfected scheme.

From the secretary's viewpoint, she was complying with an order from her superiors, the hamlet chairman and the assistant chairman, as well as satisfying her curiosity as a spinster, which she had to conceal very tightly, in the elaborate manner that people use to put a top on a brine jar that has started to ferment. In such an excited mind-set, she did not hesitate to display all her skills, which she constantly used in the role of host. If one says "strong and daring due to wealth," then she was indeed a more daring authority than many other women. Therefore, after bidding farewell to the chairman, she ran straight to the district public works compound, where

Mr. Quang was one of the three most reputable supervisors of the cement workers and carpenters and where he had met Miss Ngan. Miss Vui believed that there all relevant connections could be uncovered.

She was not wrong; in just half a day she had collected the whole romantic saga of the couple so far apart in age. At noon, she slipped some money into the pocket of a public works driver:

"Comrade, may I get a ride to Ha Tay? I need to resolve an urgent family matter."

The driver reluctantly replied: "In principle, we are not allowed to let others ride in official vehicles."

After stating the official position, he slowly put his hand inside his pocket, his mouth puckered up to whistle. He carefully felt the envelope Miss Vui had slipped into the oversized pocket of his laborer's shirt, to make sure. When the music stopped, he signaled to the assistant:

"Get in the back, little twerp."

Immediately the little twerp ran toward the truck's cargo platform. There he sat between stacks of cement bags and curing forms. It was not jinxing him to note that if there were a swerve or an accident, he would definitely be squashed like a roach under those gigantic wooden forms.

When the assistant driver relaxed, he tied down a cloth cover, turned the truck around, and said to Miss Vui:

"OK; if you have a family emergency, Comrade . . . get in."

Miss Vui climbed up into the front seat and sat comfortably next to the driver, a deeply dark-skinned fellow as skinny as a frog. With that kind of true bravado, she went all the way to Khoai Hamlet, in Hung My village, Ha Tay province, to discover once and for all the nest of dragonflies.

That night Chairman Quy returned to the village, while Miss Vui spent the night as a faraway guest in order to complete the mission that the chairman had assigned to her. She returned home in the early evening of the twenty-ninth day of the last month of the year that was about to end, her face beaming like a flower, on her shoulder a sack full of New Year's toys and treats. Chairman Quy stood to welcome her at the entrance to the middle section:

"So?"

"In good time. Take it easy."

"Aren't you cocky today."

"Not cocky, but the money for transportation and the inn is worth a ton of rice, dear friend."

"I'll take care of it."

"Never in my life have I taken any reimbursement," she replied with the tight tone of someone who always has a full purse. Quy wanted to help her carry the sack of New Year's goodies into the house, but suddenly realized that it would be silly; if someone saw him, they would laugh in his face. Therefore he quietly followed the woman. Clearly detecting the excitement on Quy's face, Vui cried out:

"Go home. We can keep the story for a couple of days without spoiling it. It's almost New Year's Eve. I have to clean and straighten up my house; get the altar ready for the offering. Besides, I have to boil some water to bathe, too. Two days on the road, living in inns; I am dirty and itch like crazy, with black dust in my nostrils. My hair feels full of sawdust."

"OK. I am leaving, then. Are you going to the opera performance tomorrow?"

"Of course. It happens only once a year. Who would be dumb enough to miss it?"

Quy hurriedly left recalling that this spinster worshipped even her bathing. People often said that if Vui needed to take a bath and anyone tried to interrupt her, she would go crazy and chase after them. Her bathwater was infused with pomelo leaves and peelings, lemon grass, jasmine flowers, and other herbs. They were mixed according to a fixed formula and boiled in a copper pot. When the water started to boil, the fragrance wafted around the neighborhood. Additionally, each time she bathed and shampooed her hair, she lit sandalwood incense so that the mysterious fragrance would penetrate her hair and skin; her bathing brought back to life the habits of royal women in olden times. Yet those palace women took such care of their bodies and their beauty in order to entice love from the king; what suitor was there for Miss Vui that she might pine for in secret? Either time or the demons would tell, not before.

The chairman walked away but could not suppress his discontent: "This old maid respects no one."

He walked and fumed quietly, his face hot despite the cold air. He wanted to forget it, but couldn't; he kept thinking about the curt way he had been dismissed, cowardly chased out of an "Old Maid's" house like any neighbor who came to her door asking for some favor. The veins on Quy's temples pulsated wildly.

"She eats a mullet from the head, and thinks of shit as food. She is really irreverent. She forgets that it was I who first suggested to the subcommittee that she be made its chair. She's the kind who forgets a favor. You can't blame heaven for not finding her a husband!"

He walked once all around the middle hamlet, greeting others by mechanically nodding his head without really knowing who it was he was greeting. His restlessness was burning inside him. At this hour, all his official responsibilities were done and all the rest of the New Year's chores and family offerings were tasks for his wife. Quy's mind was transfixed on only one image, one name, one green blouse, one shy smile, and they all belonged to a whore named Ngan!

"A whore named Ngan, a whore named Ngan, a whore named Ngan!"

He quietly cursed.

Then, while so cursing to himself, he realized that he was cursing someone without having any proof. So, now the main thing for him remained how to prove that the whore named Ngan was "indeed a whore, one hundred percent a whore."

But, sad to say, to prove this point, he needed Vui's help—that old maid who was unpredictable and irreverent. She was the one who could provide the proof. Just as a hungry cat must find a way to scratch the throat of a well-fed cat, so too with women. Forcing this old maid to scramble for clues about this well-bosomed whore would be the best plan. But even the best plans have flaws: Vui deserved her reputation for being capable but she was more conceited and disagreeable than anyone else. These thoughts took Quy to the familiar path returning to the upper section. Suddenly he realized that he was getting close to home. The cold wind during his walk had cooled his rage. At the end, he consoled himself:

"Even if I am enraged to the point of bursting inside, I can't do anything. Vui knows all the ins and outs of the story, not me. And this old maid will not listen. Well, if earth won't give in to heaven, then heaven will have to give in to earth. I have to be flexible with her."

He crossed the entrance just as his two daughters carried the kumquat plant from the garden to the inside patio. Back in the kitchen, a pot of rice cakes boiled briskly, the appetizing smell spreading through the air. Here and there, the sounds of small firecrackers were heard around the hamlet. The feeling of the New Year approaching was starting to spread. Quy went inside the house, threw his leather jacket on the table, and lay down on the settee, stretching his legs. He closed his eyes and visualized what would happen tomorrow night: New Year's Eve, the last night of this unfortunate year. The district opera troupe will arrive here to perform *Thi Mau Will Go to the Temple*. For sure, Mr. Quang and the whore Ngan would stay home and not attend. Their absence would be the best excuse for the villagers to gossip, and, at that moment, Vui would do her thing. Her trip must bring success to him. Tomorrow night would be the night of victory. He stroked his belly, inhaled deeply, and screamed:

"Someone boil me a pot of cilantro water. I have not bathed for the whole week!"

The district Public Works Committee always had three work teams on duty, under the supervision of three general contractors, usually known by the cute name of Managing Cadre Outside the District Organization. Mr. Quang was in charge of the masons and carpenters for the city. The second gentleman had a contingent from Ha Tay province. The third was in charge of the team from Phu Tho. Except for Mr. Quang's team, the two others included many women and girls. These were adventuresome proletarians who had to seek food for themselves far away from their parents.

If you are born in a city, you already know the difference between living in a city and living in the countryside. Such a difference can never be eliminated:

"Being wealthy in the village does not equal being a squatter in the city."

Getting a bowl of rice in a village is extremely difficult; besides rice stalks, what is there that can turn into income? In half mountain and half paddy villages like Woodcutters' Hamlet, cows, water buffalo, bees, and poultry can be raised. But in the lowlands, houses are small, the population is dense. Grass patches are narrow like a panel of a shirt, not large enough to feed buffalo to work the fields, let alone raise cattle. Life depends on the rice stalks, and such skinny stalks will not support many expenses, such as for salt and fish sauce, oil for lamps, gifts for New Year's, funerals and weddings, taxes, clothing and jewelry, education and medicines for the children. Because of these realities, Mr. Quang's work team had not a single woman, while the other two teams had many. These women were given a spiteful name: "Coolie Girls."

More concretely: "Nai Shop Guys and Coolie Girls."

Nai shops were found at the intersection where drivers coming and going from all over the Red River basin stopped to eat, bathe, or seek other needs in the dark. When there is demand, there must be supply, though the government intervenes in all manner of useless ways, even tearing them down sometimes. In the end the government had to permit the residents of the Nai street to erect a row of eateries, noodle shops, cheap boardinghouses, tea shops, fruit and cake stands, and other miscellaneous establishments. Nai Shop Guys were skilled in buying and selling. For a long while used to having money, they enjoyed taking pleasure with women and gambling.

Anywhere a game of chance is found, there too are cheating, trickery, deals, and paybacks. In the eyes of ordinary people who lived lives of lawful order, those escapades of Nai Shop Guys that flounted heaven and pissed on earth, along with their bloody killings and stabbings, appeared as an epidemic, a terrifying pox pandemic that must be avoided at all costs.

Second to the Nai Shop Guys were Coolie Girls from construction sites, peasants who had flown their cages, nicknamed "aspiring peasants" by sharp tongues in the city, or "crazies" by rural villagers who gave them suspicious stares. From those two unfriendly vantage points, those who yesterday had dirty legs and muddy hands from rice paddies or dry fields, but today bent their necks and shoulders to carry timber and bricks in construction sites, were grotesque and unrestrained.

In the minds of villagers who are tied down to one home and one paddy field and who, for generations, have hidden behind one temple roof and a bamboo hedge a thousand years old, the lifestyle of men and women living together, the hustle and bustle of construction work, as well as constant moving from one place to another, deservedly places suspicion on their moral character:

"Taking food from others, temporary quarters . . . vagabonds like traveling opera actors."

An unusual lifestyle, without repose, makes others half envious and half terrified. As things go, whatever differs from us, we first spit on. If you can't remove it, you just throw stones to keep it away.

Given these emotional responses, once they decide to leave, women from the countryside—with one shoulder burdened by heavy family debts and the other with shame thrown at them by villagers—do grow adventurous. They intentionally taunt society, take on a careless air, respond in your face, believing that such reactions give them energy to stay strong.

And so, Mr. Quang's young wife had been one of those women—laying bricks, whitewashing, building—women who undertake the heavy labors that, usually, only men have the strength to accomplish.

One morning Mr. Quang had been crossing a bare patch of land where a temporary fence made of wooden poles had been erected to create a barrier between two work teams—his and that from Ha Tay province. Suddenly he heard the striking laughter of girls. Surprised, he turned around. Seeing no one familiar, he continued walking straight ahead. At that instant, three or four girls called out repeatedly in the Ha Tay accent, which cannot be mistaken for any other:

"Hey, mister . . . hey, you there!"

"Hey, you—Mr. Good-looking Old Man—turn around, someone is calling you."

"Hey, good-looking old guy . . . turn around, a lady wants to talk to you. You, old man!"

Inside, Mr. Quang was a bit annoyed, but he thought if he turned his back, they might think he was a coward, and the next time they would tease him in a worse way. He turned around and walked toward a group of silly girls, altogether more than ten of them sitting close to one another on top of some cement forms.

"Here I am," he said, looking at all the faces covered by scarves, only tiny eyes showing. "Here I am. Whoever wants to talk, please stand up. I am not used to squatting."

The group of women all turned to the girl with a green blouse, with a scarf over her face that was also green. Her eyes were no longer smiling but blinking with embarrassment:

"Here I am. The very one that called you to turn around."

"Miss Ngan, please speak louder!"

"She called you 'the good-looking old man.' "

Now she was totally spent, like boiled meat . . .

At this point, Mr. Quang laughed. Looking at the girl with the green scarf, he discovered her breathtakingly beautiful eyes, a pair of eyes like he had never seen before. To put it in poetic form, they were "the eyes of a songstress."

No one said a word more. He felt the group of women was growing embarrassed, so he turned away.

Two months later, after drinking with his workers, Mr. Quang returned to the boardinghouse in town. It was about midnight. Almost all the lights at the site were extinguished, except for some at the supply warehouse or at other vulnerable spots where burglars could enter. Mr. Quang shone his flashlight on the path through the site beaten down by the workers' feet. Suddenly he heard the screaming of a woman behind a row of houses with finished brick walls that had not yet been plastered. The scream was from a woman from Ha Tay province:

"Let me go! Oh my god!"

"Oh my god! Save me!"

He ran toward the cry for help. The flashlight shone on two fiercely fighting shadows. A woman's hair was disheveled, her pants and blouse ripped open. A man, big and short like a bear, was wearing dark clothes. Throwing the flashlight to the side, Quang jumped forward and struck the man twice like a hammer right into his face:

"Here's for taking advantage of a woman! Here's for raping this woman!"

Another punch struck the man's chin. Then Quang grabbed the man, and using all his bodily strength, slammed the attacker's head against the wall, believing that this would be the finishing stroke.

Indeed, it ended the fight as he had intended. The man slumped down, letting out a cry like a hurt wild animal. To make sure it was over, Quang added two more kicks. Seeing that the attacker had no hope of getting to his feet, Mr. Quang picked up his flashlight to shine it on the face of the one who would rape a woman. A panic immediately rushed through him like a lightning flash: it was the deputy chairman of the district public works office. He did not directly assign any work or set wages for the construction workers, but he was the trusted right hand of the person who had that authority. Because of this, he had been made deputy after only two years as a middle-level foreman so that the big boss could easily take advantage of him.

In this dangerous situation, maybe because heaven guided and earth advised, or maybe at the prompting of a guardian angel, he acted wisely. Pulling out his loudspeaker still dangling on his neck like a talisman, Quang blew noisily and brought a sudden frenzy down on the quiet construction area like villagers running from the enemy in war. The sound of the loudspeaker spread from the workers' camp to the area of the cadres supervising construction. After hearing the loud thumping of running steps coming closer and closer, he then turned to the woman who had been attacked:

"Miss, stay put; do not run away, understand? Keep your torn clothing intact, keep the scene of the man struggling with you untouched. That is what happens, don't be ashamed. You'll get me in trouble if you leave now. Do you understand? If people ask what happened, just tell the truth."

"Yes, I understand," the woman replied, and suddenly he recognized her vaguely familiar voice. But it wasn't until all the lights at the site were turned on brightly that he realized that she was the girl in the green blouse, the one who had nicknamed him "the good-looking old man." Yes, it was her. Thus, just like that, it seemed that fate united them.

What happened next was nothing complicated. Once the bright lights came on, the sight of a bruised woman with torn clothes and a beaten man down on the ground with a freshly bloody face and the fly in his trousers open let the onlookers understand right away everything that had transpired.

No need for too many opinions. After many years of struggling to make a living, Mr. Quang had learned the lesson well:

"To protect the moral authority of the Party and the nation!"

He knew that the situation could flip upside down like the turning of a hand, and he himself would become the sacrificed pawn in that new game. That was why he insisted that the supervising committee for the work site invite the police to come and make an investigative report. And immediately, he mobilized the workers to demand that the local authorities, the construction site supervisors, and the provincial labor union act as official witnesses. Even though it was night, representatives of these three organizations had to come and sign statements. Skilled in speaking, Mr. Quang simultaneously used the situation to announce in front of the crowd:

"We take in wandering wives and daughters who have left their homes to seek a living on the land of others; we cannot allow them to be raped. If we don't do our duty fully, people will spit in our faces. Today it's a woman of Ha Tay, tomorrow it might be one from Phu Tho or from our own community. On everyone's behalf, we insist that the government protect the innocent and punish the thugs. If those thugs infiltrate into the ranks of Party cadres, the government must punish them more severely."

"We are one with Mr. Quang!"

The other two contract bosses agreed instantly, seeing their interests being protected under the circumstances. If the event had happened to them—since they were not like Mr. Quang, "one who went without food and spoke like wind, had a heart hard like cast iron, and tendons harder than steel"—they would ultimately have blamed the woman as "a whore who seduced a cadre" and they would have found a way to kick her out of the work site, the sooner the better. Therefore, hiding behind his back, they bravely repeated the same refrain:

"We are totally of one mind with Mr. Quang. Public Works has the duty to protect its workers."

"To preserve the impeccable moral authority of the Party and the nation, we demand that the culprit be punished."

Like a tsunami, rage swept over those peasants who wore the garb of workers; their rancor thundering all over their tiny world. The disaster Miss Ngan had suffered might well be waiting for them one day. The humiliation that she had tasted could very well be the bitter gift their fates had reserved for them at some dark instant in their future. In the lives of those people with muddy feet and dirty hands, self-pity was like a stove that was always on, with its pilot light of hatred and incipient protest continuously burning. In such situations, feelings of solidarity arose simultaneously as their sense of humiliation was provoked. The men as well as the women saw in the tattered woman a reflection of their own pride, a mirror giving back their own destiny, reflecting back generations of meager lives struggling for existence. No wonder that, after the hard, sharp words from Mr. Quang, their anger exploded, like water rushing through when a dike is broken. A crowd surrounded the deputy head of the construction office, who now raised his head to look at everyone with dull eyes. They screamed; they cursed. They spat at him, they kicked his back. The administrative cadres as well as the head of the construction security unit all signed the report in the face of such worker anger. After that, there was no alternative but for the head of the office to discipline the offender by transferring him to supervise the rock-pile site at Yen Bai. Things transpired the way dominoes fall—one upon another. The head of Public Works seemed perplexed for several days, as if he did not want to understand what had happened. But then with his lazy habit of not thinking, he quickly recovered his ordinary rhythm. Besides, he didn't need to worry himself too much, for there was no lack of willing brownnosers. One subordinate may fail but ten others will line up to take his place. Within two weeks he found another assistant administrator. The new flunky was smaller, handsomer, and worked harder.

After this incident, Mr. Quang became famous, not only within Public Works but also all over the town, as a hero, a Prince Valiant come to life. Thus everybody was happy.

When everything had returned to normal, the romance commenced. Ngan found a way to meet him at the inn, with a gift in one hand and two bottles of medicinal wine in the other.

"Please, let me thank you, sir. If it hadn't been for you, I would not have escaped that guy."

"It was nothing. I am a man; if I meet with injustice, I can't ignore it. Others coming across such an immoral thing as that would certainly do as I did."

"Life is not like that. You just speak humbly," she said with determination, leaving him without a comeback. Then he saw the two bottles of wine that she put on the table.

"You brought wine for me?"

"Yes, exactly right. Why are you surprised?"

He smiled: "Who fermented this wine?"

"I did."

"So, you're an alcoholic?"

"No! Not an alcoholic, but I know how to drink."

"Really?"

"First, nobody thinks women should drink. But we are a bunch of paint-ers. We stretch our arms all day long. At night when we go to bed, we feel pain from our shoulders down to our hips. My aunt steeps a mixture of herbs in wine made from good sticky rice. Drinking one cup at night before bed takes away the pain. I follow her instructions, and indeed there is no pain and I sleep very soundly."

His thoughts quietly wandered. For the first time in all his life someone had given him wine, and it was a girl! In more than forty long years living with his wife and children, she'd never thought of buying him a gift, nor had his children. In this family, it seemed as if he had had to take care of everybody, worrying about everyone else's life, with never a reciprocating concern. Always it had been: "Tell your father, he will decide." "Whatever you want, tell your father. He'll make it work."

To Mr. Quang this had seemed only natural, because he had been the father, the husband, the pillar of the family. All the inconveniences of life had piled so many heavy burdens on his shoulders. In carrying them all, he had had no time to think of himself. Now, at sixty-one, he suddenly felt his heart shifting; within him there was another man who needed attention and love.

While his mind drifted in thought, she looked around and picked up a cup from the inn's tea set and poured it full:

"Please try a sip and see."

He lifted the cup and sipped, finding the wine very good even though the herbs had taken away the taste of the sweet rice.

She looked at him attentively, asking, "How is it?"

"I find the wine really good. Maybe it would be better without the herbs."

"How can you be so simple? My aunt sells her medicinal wine for ten times more than a liter of ordinary young wine."

"Yes, I am still such a simpleton!" he replied, and as he looked at the girl the thought emerged quickly that she had been part of his life for a long while, since before the time he and she had each appeared on this earth. Perhaps, he imagined with some awkwardness, in their past lives lived long ago, lives he could not visualize just as we cannot see the dark side of the moon but know that hidden half nonetheless exists. Even so, those far-off incarnations hidden away among many layers of cloudy memories could be efficacious, even though a person could not apprehend them.

"Real or unreal; unreal or real? Why suddenly do I find life really strange?" he asked himself as he continued to look at the woman who stood not more than two yards away. That day she had also worn a green blouse, the same pineapple leaf green she had worn when he had seen her that first time. Her eyes were strikingly beautiful; now he could clearly see each of her lashes. Her brows, long like two strokes of black ink, extending from the middle of her forehead to her temples, almost touching the roots of her hair.

"This young woman is really beautiful! A person out of a painting!" he thought to himself. Suddenly he felt very pained, knowing that she would leave very soon and he would never see her again. Then she would live out her life, and that life would have no connection to his. And him, surely he would pass his old age in this boardinghouse, or in his old home in Wood-cutters' Hamlet, or in a horse carriage on his trips to and from those two locations, with so many messy and tiring family matters. With all his calculated plans, his worries, all the arrangements he constantly had to juggle among a handful of supposed loves ones—those thought to be so close to him but in reality so far distant, those so used to putting burdens on his shoulders without thinking of all that he must taste, all that he must endure, all the bitter bile and burning peppers that he had to swallow—he could now no longer live tranquilly. After this encounter, life ahead of him would be so lonely. And what of him?

This train of thought left him feeling lonely and lost. He experienced a strange weakness, of a kind he had never before encountered that filled up his soul and burned his nostrils. Fearing that he might cry in front of her, he quickly grabbed a cigarette, inhaled forcefully, and twice lifted his face to exhale. Large tears filled up his eyes and rolled down both temples. He forced a cough and annoyingly cursed:

"The tobacco in this inn is the crappy kind from Tien Lang."

And the young woman, she just stood there, puzzled, looking at the wine cup in his hand, still wondering why he didn't like this medicinal wine but preferred the kind that was ten times cheaper—he . . . the hero who had saved her from a desperate situation.

At that instant, the innkeeper stepped in to remind him that his meal was ready and to ask whether he needed additional food for his guest. He suddenly realized the awkwardness of the situation: she had come all the way from the work site, which had taken her two and a half hours, and now it was high noon. He hurriedly said:

"Please take care of food for my guest."

Then, turning to her, he asked: "Would you care to share the food with me?"

"Why 'care to'?" she asked quite sincerely.

And he smiled: "Because you think of me as a simpleton."

"Oh, I was just blabbering."

"So, really now: What do you think of me?"

"I find you . . . find you . . . a very good-looking older man."

After so replying, she burst into laughter. Maybe because she found her own answer ridiculous. Her laughter took a heavy weight off his chest. In that laughter, in her smiling eyes, he detected a promise. He no longer saw life's desert spreading out before him. He no longer felt threatened by her departure. In his innermost mind, he secretly enjoyed this auspicious gift of destiny. Walking out of his room, he loudly called out to the innkeeper:

"Make me an elaborate meal, OK? I have a special guest today!"

Just as Quy had predicted, on New Year's Eve everyone in Woodcutters' Hamlet, except Mr. Quang and his young wife, came out to watch the opera *Thi Mau Goes to the Temple*. They did not attend for several reasons. First, they were in love—in the steamy, hot phase of love. Miss Ngan had the energies of youth, of course. But for two years Mr. Quang had been deprived of a woman's touch—since the day when his wife had come down with the hungry demon ailment. For both, their marriage was like a downpour during a hot drought. Second, all year they both worked down in the city, where there were constant opportunities to attend theater performances, new music, movies, and singing contests; they were not as deprived of entertainment as were the residents of Woodcutters' Hamlet.

Those were the obvious reasons. In reality, their reasons should have been of no concern to anybody. But in life, differences create envy, whether you like it or not, whether you speak openly about it or conceal it. Even before the curtain rose, village eyes eagerly scanned around, looking for this odd couple, as if their presence would cause the opera to succeed or fail.

"We don't see either him or her! Perhaps they stayed home!"

"For sure they did. They don't care to see a play in the countryside. There's plenty in the city. Down there the theater is many times larger than our hamlet temple, and all the curtains are made of red velvet, very classy."

"Why didn't Master Quy invite a first-class opera troupe for the villagers to enjoy? It might be expensive, but it's only once a year. People would pinch their budgets to afford a ticket."

"Even if we had invited them, they wouldn't have come. The road is too long and bumpy, and all the props and velvet and brocade curtains need to be transported in special cars. You would have to pay a lot for just one trip."

"OK, if you've only got wooden chopsticks, use 'em; don't go crazy asking for velvet and brocade curtains, for what?"

"You talk with your dick. Everyone has skin and flesh; everyone likes to eat their rice with fish. Only the crazy refuse new and tasty dishes."

"No, you're the one who talks with his dick. You want some, but have no money. Empty pockets longing for good food! Under the circumstances, shut up; talking just puts you to shame."

"Enough, gentlemen; I ask you all, it's New Year's Eve, no arguments. The festivities are about to start, what's the point of fighting anymore?"

They all backed off. Women pinched and squeezed their husbands to calm their hot tempers. Then the sound of drums gave a cheerful welcome. The two panels of the red stage curtains, dotted with holes made by roaches, slowly drew open and female singers in loose costumes floated onto the stage like the five tinted winds:

"I come up to the temple and see thirteen little novices, fourteen monks, and fifteen nuns."

The band behind the stage struck up a tune. A flute hit a high note over the two-string zither; the sound of the flute and the drum carried the beat. Life's now smiling face lets people temporarily forget oppressions and emotions.

Two hours later, the opera drew to a close.

Villagers stood around for a long time in front of the stage longing for more. The entertainment had ended much too quickly. And after the fun, sadness is always on duty. It was only eight p.m.; there were still four more hours before the old year ended, four more hours until they could light firecrackers and start their banquets. Four more hours to endure the everlasting quietness of the isolated mountain terrain, after being soaked in an atmosphere filled with the lights, colors, images, and sounds of the opera. It was quite oppressive and extremely difficult to endure. People stood around and watched as performers dismantled the stage and packed away their costumes and props. Suddenly, longing filled their souls; a vague realization of something missing brought heartache. There was only life worn out like a piece of cloth down to its bare threads.

While the crowd was still lingering about, Quy had taken care of compensation for the professional troupe. He said to Miss Vui:

"Now I have to take the troupe to get chicken congee before they return to the district town. The villagers still linger and are not ready to leave. If it's OK with you, could you please invite them to your house before the end of the old year? It's only once a year; we need to provide them with an evening of hospitality."

"Right away; no problem for me. Will you come later?"

"I will come if every task is finished."

"That's all right, take care of your duties," Miss Vui answered. Then she approached the crowd and said:

"If you are not ready to leave, I invite you to come to my house to have tea and eat New Year's candies. Wait for the New Year then return home and bring certain good fortune to your house."

"Fantastic! You're really the best."

"Did you make the candies or buy them?"

"I bought them in town. The watermelon and pumpkin seeds are top of the line; I guarantee their quality. The tea is the fragrant Hong Dao brand— for real!"

"Who'll come with me to Miss Vui's?"

"You don't have to advertise! Whoever has legs knows how to use them!"

Nobody voiced it out loud, but everybody knew that the gathering at Miss Vui's house was to be a second performance for the New Year's Eve celebration: following the traditional opera would be a romance about a mismatched couple. Because they were the wealthiest in the hamlet, because they lived differently from the rest, Mr. Quang and Miss Ngan were a target for all the gossips. Gossip has always been a spiritual food unique to villages, as well as a poison that permeates humanity's bones and marrow.

That night, the subcommittee secretary's house was bright with a storm light. She had bought this light after convincing herself that she had become someone of importance, having risen up as if she were a hamlet VIP. But compared with Mr. Quang, she was still a lightweight going up against a heavyweight. Nonetheless, it was a source of pride that not many women had the right to savor. Besides, she thought that the way to her success had been paved by her father and so she wanted him to be proud in the spirit realm. Thus, in Woodcutters' Hamlet, she had been the second person after Mr. Quang to have a four-horsepower generator, a storm lamp, and all the objects that are indicative of prosperity. For people in the region, after a nice house with a large patio comes a horse carriage, both assets and means to make money; then after a horse carriage, the biggest dream is for a household generator to water the yard and the fields, and to light up the storm lamp during the New Year holiday. That New Year, Miss Vui also had bought three porcelain tea services from Hai Duong, the kind that have a large teapot with brass handles. She used them to serve tea to her guests. One teapot could contain two liters of water and each brewing used half a bag of Hong Dao tea. The villagers were overwhelmed, for in the countryside people tend to be frugal. The average family could make one bag of Hong Dao tea last for at least ten days.

In the bright light of the storm lamp, the shiny new porcelain teacups, small and large plates of candied lotus seeds, watermelon seeds and pumpkin seeds, and all sorts of candies and cookies were displayed upon two large tables placed next to each other under a flowery tablecloth as at a wedding. A warm and festive atmosphere spread through the two sections of the house where the villagers sat close by one another according to their neighborhood or their kinships. Such atmosphere made people easily excited and openly expressive. They spoke loudly like horns and drums, from the story of Mrs. Coi's daughter-in-law in the upper section who had triplets to that of Mr. Tu, the drunkard in the lower section who had intentionally hit his buffalo calf to cripple it and thus have a reason to butcher it; from the story of the actress who played Thi Mau with breasts so small that each time she moved, the rubber lining in her bra went up and down in such a hilarious manner, to the story of Mr. Huan's daughter in the next hamlet who conceived a child out of her uterus and was brought down to the district clinic, costing them lots of money but to no good end: the baby was stillborn . . .

Then some guy spoke up loudly: "Hostess: I have a bad habit of being hungry all the time. Is there any chance I can find a piece of cake or a minced pork roll?"

Miss Vui stood up and said, "Yes, right away."

But the man's wife protested: "You really are ungracious; can't you hold out until midnight?"

The husband replied, "Why should I wait? I am hungry during the death anniversary dinner for my father but I should be full at New Year. We are neighbors and she has the kindness to invite us."

The wife further explained: "The food is no big deal, but they will have to use a knife and cutting board; they will have to clean and wash their hands. It's so cold!"

At this point, all the neighbors jumped in: "Leave him alone. If he is hungry, he cannot just sit there drinking tea and eating candies and cookies like all of you ladies."

"That's right. I agree. Hey, Miss Vui, may I have some wine? We men need to have some wine to feel in business. Our elders taught us: no drinking; no ceremony. I dare put it differently: no drinking; no New Year's Eve. Who's with me?"

"Me!"

"Me too."

"Me also!"

"And me too, aunts and uncles."

"That's fine, nothing difficult. But among you ladies, who is willing to give me a hand?"

"Yes, me here. I shouldn't have married a blockhead, so it's payback time for me."

This voice came from the wife of the greedy guy who had first asked for meat. Three other women, wives of those gentlemen who adhered to the belief that without wine you are not a man also agreed to help. The tea party was thus transformed into a sit-down dinner with minced pork rolls, wine, rice cakes, bamboo soup with spare ribs, braised pork belly, and pickled cabbage. Even though it was a spontaneous meal prepared within fifteen minutes, there were enough dishes so that the men could lift their chopsticks happily.

Two trays of food and two large bottles of wine were put on two large platform beds placed across from each other. The men excitedly dug in. Each table had six people for a total of twelve. Miss Vui placed a chair between the two beds so that she could pour wine on both sides.

"Ladies, feel free to drink tea and savor the candied fruits. I have to entertain the men," Vui declared.

"Just take care of them; don't worry about us."

They said that, but the women brought over their tea and goodies to tag along behind their men and eavesdrop on the conversation. People never forget that this is the best part of the evening, after the opera, of course.

Khoai Hamlet was the poorest hamlet in Hung My village. But for generations Khoai Hamlet had had beautiful women. Its residents had only this as a point of pride and only this to compensate for the hardships they endured from generation to generation. In particular, the girls in this village had very light complexions. Even when they worked long hours in the fields, only their hands were a little darker from the sun, compared with women from other villages. People said it was because of Khoai Hamlet's proximity to rivers and mountains, the clean and breezy air making the complexions of the girls and women fresh all year round. Second, their eyes resembled those of Cham women, large and deep with long and curvy eyelashes. It was said that years earlier, a group of prisoners from Champa had been exiled to Khoai Hamlet to cultivate virgin land for a victorious general given the prisoners by the court as a reward for his services. The defeated Cham soldiers then lived and mingled with local people, and, because they were good carpenters and masons, generating wealth for the general, they gained permission to marry local sons and daughters. The children of such couples therefore had large eyes, so clear but so sad, like autumn's ending.

Miss Ngan was born in this poor hamlet that took great pride in the attractiveness of its women. Her mother was the most beautiful woman in the entire district, but before any provincial official or district worthy could take notice, she fell for Ngan's father, a village teacher. He had grown up in a miserably poor family in a poor village, but because he was the only child, his mother and father had tightened their belts so that he could learn enough words to become a first-grade teacher. He was extremely indebted to his wife for marrying him and not joining the regional organization or waiting for some other wealthier, more upscale suitor. From her childhood on, Miss Ngan had heard her father recollect:

"Your mother had been selected for the regional cultural organization. She was inferior to no one. Only good fortune made it possible for me to marry her."

When fully grown, Ngan's beauty was greater than that of her mother. Her father both taught and worked in the fields and he wove baskets in the evening to earn enough money for her to study up to the junior high level. He nourished an unhidden dream:

"You are more beautiful than your mother was. And you have been educated. Certainly later on you will be happier than Miss Nga from Moi Hamlet; one day you will take a plane or boat to pass beyond the seashore."

So her future was planned in advance, like a painting that had first been carefully sketched before an artist came to apply the paint. She would be selected for the central cultural organization or the central political headquarters. She would go to places like Russia, China, and other countries as naturally as eating her daily meals—what an honor for the entire extended family!

Her parents were preoccupied about their two sons and in their minds assumed that Ngan would apply herself exactly to their plan. By sixteen, her striking beauty was seducing many in her circle, not to mention a few young teachers in the district's junior high school. Like a light that attracts insects at night in the middle of the fields, inviting the moths to come and dance, intoxicating them, then burning them, Ngan's fresh and smiling disposition led to punishment for many classmates, because the school forbade students to follow their affections before they had reached adulthood, which was by law eighteen years of age. After witnessing many young men fall off their horses for her, it was her turn to be thrown down—not by those naive boys her own age, but by a literature teacher, an exemplar, married, with three children: Teacher Tuong.

Nobody really knew how their affair began. Teacher Tuong lived with his wife and children in the family compound for teachers in the district school, a row of houses with tile roofs and narrow patios, divided into small lots, all similar in construction and materials, built cheaply and sloppily. In front of this housing compound there was some open land used by teachers and students for volleyball and basketball. Behind the compound was a vegetable garden that enabled the teachers to make ends meet. People often saw Teacher Tuong with a can watering the kohlrabi and cabbage in the afternoon; and his wife could be seen at dusk with her pant cuffs rolled up, briskly chasing chicken around the pen, or out around midnight with her flashlight, picking up eggs. She was a small woman, very skinny, always with an air of sadness showing on her face, which was somewhat pointed, like a bird's head. They had lived in the commune since their marriage, Mr. Tuong having been appointed to the district school after graduating from the mid-level provincial teacher training college. His wife sold medicines in a pharmacy. They had three sons, the oldest thirteen, the middle one eleven, and the youngest, most likely unplanned, only three. Who could ever imagine a romantic, passionate love affair occurring between a young woman of sixteen, strikingly beautiful like a full moon, and a teacher close to his forties, who, when he forgot to shave, had a face dark like a closed jar, his clothes old and tattered, his teeth and fingers stained yellow by tobacco smoke? When the story broke—that is, when Ngan became pregnant—everyone was beside themselves with astonishment. They all wanted to know the reason for what was to them a totally unjustifiable romance. The story of the teacher and the student falling in love made noise everywhere, pushing forward like fire spreading or water boiling over:

"A devil's work; definitely an evil spirit!"

"There is no evil spirit, that's just old superstition. I think the guy's a smooth talker. People say men fall from their eyes, women from their ears."

"Eyes and ears, yes; still, there must be a reason. Why on earth would a young girl fall in love with an old man the same age as her father? She must be mad! If not, then this guy gave her Love Potion Number Nine. Once my cousin, a laborer in Tay Bac, had a Thai girl put a love charm on him. Each time he tried to find his way back down to the plains he turned mad, rolled his eyes, and mumbled all in Thai. The family had to let him go up and live with that woman."

"Until now?"

"Exactly! His wife had to wait five years to ask the village to give her a divorce so that she could remarry. Their two children were sent to my aunt and uncle to be raised."

"I don't believe in love charms or potions."

"I do!"

"I think this teacher has a way of enticing women and girls that we don't know."

"What way?"

"Maybe hypnotizing. This guy may look skinny, but when he looks at anyone, they feel as if they've been nailed down, no longer able to move. I think that girl's soul was sucked out by those eyes."

"Perhaps. But why didn't he ever seduce others? Doesn't every class have more than a few pretty ones?"

"True. Before this he had no affairs? If it's a question of seduction, of promiscuity, something would have happened long before. Fifteen years have passed; there was no lack of pretty girls; why wait for Ngan?"

"Because destiny planned it. When the month and day arrive, the child comes out of the mother's womb. Just so, when the month and day arrive, disaster also shows its face."

"You think of it as a disaster? I believe it's good fortune. Nothing else: sleeping with a virgin girl as beautiful as a fairy. No different than finding paradise."

"But after paradise comes hell. I just heard that Ngan's father aggressively sued the school, and took a knife demanding to kill Teacher Tuong, who had to flee to the city. I heard he accepted his punishment to relocate elsewhere."

"Relocate where?"

"I don't remember exactly, but for sure somewhere up along the frontier. Up there, he was assigned to a nowhere place, teaching new recruits in a noncommissioned officers' training school. Schools that train high-level officers are usually near big cities, but training schools for NCOs are always tucked away in areas where dogs eat stones and chickens eat gravel. There, even watercress is hard to find. All year long the only food is dried fish and shrimp paste."

"Serves the dirty old man right! What goes around quite rightly comes around. He had enjoyed the gift of virginity, had tasted the body of a girl whose skin is like peeled cooked egg, then for the rest of his life he has to suck on dried fish, that's fair."

"If I were young Ngan's father, I too would take a knife and give him a slash. That was the end of a girl's life! A sad fate for a beauty!"

"You'd give him a slash, then you'd have to sit in jail and peel the calendar day by day. It takes two to tango; it took the two of them . . . why slash him?"

"You are really stupid. By law, eighteen years make you an adult. Ngan is only sixteen. To sleep with her, only the guy breaks the law. That crime is called seduction of a minor. Actually, he should have been indicted and sent to jail for at least four years. But his father's older brother is a judge in the provincial court. For that reason he got no prison time."

"Really, I didn't know that."

"You don't read the law?"

"Where's the time for reading law? I work two shifts, sometimes three nonstop. Six days a week. Sometimes on Sunday I must also make some sacrifices for socialism. When I get home, the only thing I want to do is sleep. I'm too tired to climb on top of my wife, so much for reading law!"

"How old is your daughter?"

"Twelve."

"You should read the law now. If you sleep, just close one eye, the other should be left open to look around. If you don't, there might be some guy your age that would like to call you father-in-law."

"You bastard! Why do you have such a toxic mouth? You wish me misfortune like the teacher in Khoai Hamlet, don't you?"

"I don't wish you any such misery as that. But if you worry about what might come from afar, you can avoid misfortunes closer at hand."

When Miss Ngan's fetus was just into its fourth month, though it was already rather late, her school gave her a letter of introduction to the district clinic, asking that the fetus be removed due to an "accident of morality." Ngan's mother took her to the clinic at night; each covered her face with a cloth, showing only her eyes with a hat pulled down to the eyebrows. Ngan's father announced publicly that she had been disowned and banished from the family, telling his wife, "It would have been better if she had put a knife to my heart rather than put me in this situation. From this day on, under this roof, if she is here, then I am not, and vice versa. It's up to you to choose."

His wife dared not choose, because both the husband and child were immediate family. After taking Ngan to the clinic to have the fetus scraped out, she turned her daughter over to her own mother. There, Ngan lived with her uncle and aunt and her maternal grandmother. A year later, Ngan's uncle, a skilled mason, found her a job as a painter for Public Works.

When Mr. Quang and Miss Ngan decided to unite their lives, they planned to legalize their life as a couple. In her family situation, Miss Ngan did not want a lavish wedding as others do. First, she did not want to stir up waters that were settling. The wound to her father was surely not yet healed. Hamlet people still talked about the goings on when he had left his class and rice fields for a month, how he had smashed all his tools with which to harvest and fish in the river. Night after night, he walked like a madman along hamlet paths, sometimes tilting his neck and howling like a wolf calling for his pack. His uncle, the village chairman, had to pay money to bring a doctor down from the provincial capital to give him a shot. Everyone believed that, sooner or later, he would pack up a sack and enter an asylum. Thanks to the good karma coming down from his ancestors and the skill of the provincial doctor, he seemed to recover his senses, but still, once in a while, he used incomprehensible gestures or words. The daughter had indeed been the glorious dream of the father. That dream had shattered like a mirror smashed into small pieces. The hamlet teacher did not want to accept that painful reality. He found ways to erase all traces of time past, when the dream had been alive. Anything connected with Ngan, he removed to burn or throw into the river: all the beautiful photos that once hung everywhere in the house, her trunks of clothes, her sewing kit from when she had taken home economics, the cloth dolls she had made herself, all her school notebooks.

Mr. Quang had been a father. He understood how wounded pride could drive a person to one kind of hell or another. All these years of struggling here and there in so many places, pushing along so many strange roads, had taught him how to be emphatic and patient. His fortunate happiness must in the end run up against a challenge. He would be the one to carry the burden and not Miss Ngan. After much reflection, he decided to ask Ngan's uncle to invite her mother to the construction site for a visit. On the first night, the girl's mother heard how she had come to fall in love with a man forty-three years her elder but appearing as an ancient hero reborn to protect and save her. On the second day, Miss Ngan took her mom to town to buy for the family all those things that make people's eyes brighten like streetlights. On the third day was the official meal between the girl's mother and the future son-in-law, who was twenty-four years older than she. Then was discovered a coincidence that increased the awkwardness on both sides: Ngan's father had been born in the same month and year as Mr. Quang's oldest son, Quy; only the day of birth was different.

Ngan's mother was a practical person. She understood that her daughter had missed her main chance and could never recover that lost opportunity. It must be her destiny that she could only find happiness with older men. No one can defy heaven's rules and regulations. From Teacher Tuong to Mr. Quang, her life's plan could be found drawn in the lines on the palms of her hands. Ngan's mother sighed deeply but accepted everything she couldn't change. Besides, for residents of Khoai Hamlet, material goods were held in very high regard. Ngan's future husband would well provide her with the material side of life. And that was the compensation provided her by destiny.

On the fourth day, her mother returned to her hamlet with two heavy trunks. She did not say anything to her husband about her visit to their daughter; she quietly put things away and said:

"In a few days the uncle of that Ngan will bring workers here to build a house. Down there, he has saved quite a bit of money."

"I told you: don't ever remind me of her name to my face."

"Oh, I forgot. From now on I only talk about her uncle. Next month he will help us fix the house."

"Do whatever you want. This house is always under your authority," the teacher replied slowly, and with his hand behind his back, went out.

Two weeks later, her brother brought a group of eight workers to Khoai Hamlet. With them came three truckloads of timber, bricks, cement, and other supplies. The villagers gathered to observe, just like children who run out to look at the turning shadow lamps during the Mid-Autumn Festival.

Khoai Hamlet had never had a tiled roof. Throughout the hamlet there was only one style of roof: thatched with straw or leaves. Walls were made of the sides of vats, broken little ones bought from the next hamlet. The Khoai people were used to the odd looks of houses built with rejected materials. But if a wandering adventuresome guest ever stopped there, he would be startled with fright at the sight of walls that were twisted, with bumps, sometimes extended like a big belly, sometimes deflated like the inner cavity of a ball. Such houses evoke in one a fearful hesitation. With their odd forms, they look like caves for bears, horses, or tigers, but not houses intended for humans. For that reason, houses that were straight, pretty, with red roofs, was the ultimate aspiration of people there. Therefore, it is easily understood why people crowded around to see the trucks bringing all the materials and the city workers down to the hamlet, just like visitors to a museum.

The construction work went forward in haste. The uncle stayed to supervise it personally. The two-story house emerged as if from a fairy tale. It was beyond what people could imagine. After her house was finished, the teacher's wife had the courtesy to give to the husband's uncle, also the current village chairman, half of a truckload of leftover bricks and cement.

The day the new house was inaugurated, the teacher's wife prepared a twenty-tray banquet for all the relatives. Even though they had been invited, people in Khoai Hamlet were mad because a fairy tale had become real. Why should it come true for an absentminded instructor and not for them? Therefore, they tried really hard to find the truth.

The investigation was not all that difficult because the eight guys who worked on the house had enough time to glance at the hamlet girls and so become smitten with their beauty. Among the workers, two were still single. These two recognized right away the beauty of the girls in a poor village, far away, at the end of a river and at the foot of a mountain. Both decided to conquer, to follow "the old man's footsteps, the good-looking old man named Quang." A few meals with wine in a house with some pretty ones was enough for the two guys to spill all the secrets about the love affair between "Miss Ngan and Mr. Quang." In the end, people were reassured in finding the fairy wand, the wand that transforms all the frogs into pairs of exquisite shoes.

A couple of weeks after the finishing and inauguration of the new house, it was rumored that Mr. Quang and Miss Ngan would come back to the village to register their marriage. If that were to happen, for sure the village chairman would have to perform the procedure personally. As for witnesses, it could not have been anyone but the bride's mother and her younger brother. Everything went quietly and extremely quickly, so no one outside the event knew anything. Moreover, the village chairman never opened his mouth to say even half a word about it. People could only speculate as they saw the new couple walk to a car waiting for them on the other side of the river to return to the city. Seeing them off were her mother and uncle. Smiling, the village chairman waved his hands together in front of his chest. Miss Ngan cried before getting into the car. She looked a couple of times at the old hamlet, the river, the fields . . . her birthplace, a place of penetrating pain, a place to which she will never return.

The New Year's Eve drinking party at Miss Vui's went past midnight. Firecrackers exploded in all directions but the group of people who were drunk with talking still lifted their cups up and down:

"Is it midnight already? We enjoy talking so much we forget our way home."

"Not only is nothing amiss, we are able to taste the best rice wine. We have to admit that Miss Vui's skill deserves respect. She learned secrets from the parents of Mr. Do. The same yeast, the same glutinous rice, but the rice wine made by this family is smoother than mine."

"Not only do we have good wine, we also have good tea and great stories, too! Hey, Miss Vui, I thought that you were only good at doing things; I had no idea you are good at talking, too. You should be in teaching."

"I dare not, you are too kind! I just told you exactly what I heard about Mr. Quang and Miss Ngan, nothing added or subtracted."

"Telling it as it is also requires the tongue to move into the words. There is no lack of people who understand everything quite well but who cannot make any sense when they talk."

"Well, you guys are just complimenting a prince to his face. She is the secretary of the subcommittee; naturally she must know how to talk."

"The subcommittee secretary only knows how to publicize formal decisions, play up accomplishments, or announce rules, how could she know how to describe the highs and lows of serious feelings and situations?"

"That is true. It's very clear that Miss Vui has a talent for storytelling. But one has to admit that this couple's romance is quite interesting."

"You are right. Mr. Quang's love story is quite something. This year is really fun! Because each year we have only one opera. This year we have two. Miss hostess, more wine, please . . ."

"That's right. Vui, the story you told was splendid. It was worth a thousand times more than your two banquet trays."

The hostess brings out two more bottles of rice wine. Whether or not the compliments of the guests are true, her cheeks are bright red, her eyes are shining, and clearly she looks a hundred times prettier than usual. The men continue to pour wine, but the women suddenly stand up:

"That's enough, it's the New Year and you eat like monsters, worse than those who went hungry in 1945."

"What? Let the men be themselves. If on the New Year you have many guests come to eat at your house, in January your business will prosper."

"Each river has its banks, any garden small or large has its fences. Every banquet will eventually end. Let's go and let the hostess rest."

"Let's go. I am very anxious."

The men may have had firm dispositions, but, in the end, they had to understand that when the women speak up it means the hour has come. One fellow poured a final cup of wine down his throat and then said, "OK, gentlemen, let's empty our cups and get going. There is an old saying: 'A man's order does not equal a woman's heft.' People nowadays add: 'Wife comes first, then heaven.' OK, we must look around at the people and follow them."

"You are really henpecked!"

"I am indeed henpecked, I yield to you to hold your head high. Who else is henpecked like me?"

"Me."

"Me too."

"Me also . . ."

The women clapped their hands in praise, while laughing wildly when they saw their husbands unsteadily stand up. At the end only two unhenpecked husbands were left. They looked left and right and realized that all those around them had stood up, so they were compelled to put their cups down:

"OK, let's go! Darn those annoying women. It was getting to be such fun."

The wife of the unhenpecked guy stood behind the other women, silent until now: "The heart of one is like the heart of another, ladies. Unfortunately, our elders taught us that heaven will give you whatever you despise. After enduring awhile, you get used to it . . ."

"Oh my, today this old broad is pretty gutsy."

The very-sure-of-himself guy looks at his wife with fierce rolling eyes, half surprised, half threatening.

Encouraged by the views of those around her, his wife becomes angry: "We all have skin and flesh. Other women dare; I have to stand up as well."

At this moment, the hostess starts to intervene as she senses the atmosphere growing tense. Taking two steps, she inserts herself between husband and wife, smiling more happily than ever before:

"The lady is right; all humanity should sing strongly, sing out loud!"

Then she looked around, smiling. When she saw everyone taken aback by her too literary metaphor she said, "Among all of you men present here,

I recognize eight Party members in all. You couldn't have forgotten the song swearing loyalty to the Party under the Party's flag, now could you?"

The Party members looked at one another, each trying to trigger the others' memory, but all ended up with the words stuck in their throats. Then Miss Vui clearly spoke each word and each sentence:

"Rise up all you slaves of the world,
"Rise up all that are hurt and poor,
"We must destroy the old regime quickly . . ."

"Well, do you remember now?"

"Forgotten, really."

"We defer to you. The day we joined up, we learned some lines to get by. When we were in, that was that. It didn't brings us rice, clothes, or money, why bother to remember?"

"But I bet you all will remember all the minute details of Mr. Quang's story. Is that true or not?"

"You don't have to say so. Neither will we deny it. We do not have to wring our brains to remember what happens in the village and hamlets; it's like remembering our pillows at the head of our beds. And those songs from somewhere and nowhere, brought back from China or the West, why bother?"

"Exactly!"

At the moment, one of the unhenpecked guys speaks up: "I'll bet all of you: Is the story over?"

The loudmouthed woman answers first: "What else if it hasn't ended. The end: he marries her, she sneaks into his bed . . . What else do you want?"

"That's such woman thinking. Your brain is no bigger than a grapefruit, your eyes can't see farther than two arm lengths."

"Yes, we are indeed stupid, let you guys be smart . . . Clearly you are the haughty ones with your pride big like a large basket."

"Listen carefully here: the drama is just beginning. Don't you all see that?"

"I don't see anything at all. They love each other, they cross the mountains and rivers, they legalize their marriage, who dares to interfere?"

"Miss Vui, have they gone through the process?"

"I'm not sure. I heard people speculate this and that."

"If they have not done the formalities, then the man is a widower and the woman has no husband, what can be done to them? Thousands of years ago our ancestors married, had children and grandchildren; who then needed a marriage paper with the government's red seal?"

"The marriage paper is not a big deal but the garlic bulb is. That's the problem."

"What about this garlic bulb? You mean the pair of testicles that dangle in the crotch of our pants, right?"

"How can you be so dense? Testicles are testicles and a garlic bulb is a garlic bulb; each its own kind. At night do you mistakenly touch your wife's clam and think it's the teapot on that table or not?"

"Your comparison is so damn complicated."

"Complication is a fact of life. Now, who dares bet with me that the story of this family is over? For me, the curtain has just closed on Act One. And Act Two will be full of scenes. Well, who dares play?"

"You guys are timid like the field crabs. Nobody dares speak up?"

"No way, I'm not stupid."

"Why bet with you? If it gets out in people's ears, we'll get nothing, just their cursing. In the past, his family has not harmed anyone."

"Enough! Don't make a molehill into a mountain! Whatever is to happen will happen. On behalf of us all we want to thank the hostess. New Year's Eve this time was fun, really fun!"

The group scrambled to light torches, turn on lights, and put on their coats to leave. When the lights started twinkling along the paths of the middle section, a rooster had crowed to welcome the first hour of the new year. A dog's barking followed people's steps. The sky was black like squid ink and the air was still. Miss Vui turned off the storm light, started to clean up the house under the light of a row of homemade beeswax candles.

In her mind, she anxiously thought: "Whatever is to come, will come!"

She knew that everybody else was also waiting like her. With their cautious attitudes, rural people never dare participate in a messy situation but they secretly follow all the developments and also secretly want them to fall out according to their own analysis. Always holding on to the illusions that make for an analyst, one who has power over people living hard and lonely lives, Miss Vui felt a secret dream stirring in her soul, similar to a fetus kicking in its mother's womb. She felt that "something will happen, if not sooner then later." She remembered the angry pair of eyes of Chairman Quy when she had described to him the two-story house with seven rooms newly built for the old couple in Khoai Hamlet. Because Mr. Quang's house was in an old-fashioned style, one-story high but very spacious and all the framing timbers made of real wood, and Quy's house was much inferior. And now the father of the whore Ngan had a two-story house—how could he bear that image? Intuition told Miss Vui that this love story would eventually bring on a great storm. But what kind of storm, the wind blowing from the top of the high mountains or from the distant ocean, no one could predict.

All of a sudden, the old cat in the kitchen jumped out and curled around Vui's legs.

"Go away, crazy one . . ."

She shouted while kicking with her legs, "Meow, meow, ow."

The animal jumped to one side, crying out miserably, its eyes turning toward her, round with fear and surprise. She clicked her tongue: "I forget. It's not fed yet. All night I was busy with guests and forgot about the cat."

Leaving the pile of dishes she was cleaning, she went to the storage cabinet and took out a large salted fish and put it on the cracked dish reserved for the cat.

"Now it is your turn . . ."

The animal approached the dish, continuing to cry, its eyes always following its mistress as if it could not understand or forget Miss Vui's rudeness. She suddenly laughed:

"Stop meowing and eat . . ."

Then she sat opposite the animal to make it realize that her anger had passed. When the cat lowered its head to the fish on the plate, she suddenly had a strange thought that she was like a cat: a cat waiting for its prey in the dark. But not an old cat—rather a female cat that is very young and full of vitality. That thought made her smile to herself for a while.

After the cat had finished eating, licking its lips with satisfaction then running to the other room to curl up in a bed made out of leftover materials, Miss Vui continued to clean the house and wash dishes. Gigantic candles burned brightly from the house to the kitchen, their light plentiful and wild.

She did not have to live frugally like most women with five or seven kids in tow. This New Year's Eve banquet had satisfied her. While washing the dishes, she hummed the song "Rise Up, All You Slaves of the World." She was proud of her extraordinary memory and because her literary aptitude was suddenly on the rise. When she was done washing the dishes and cleaning the house shiny like a mirror, it was sunrise. It was cold, but damp sweat ran down her spine. She said:

"A bath first! Thus, this year, before and after New Year's Eve, I bathe twice."

That was unusual, because people usually avoided bathing after New Year's Eve. But single people like to worship the patron genie of cleanliness. This genie brings them a pride that those with children, grandchildren, husbands, and wives have no right to enjoy.

When Miss Vui finished her bath, the clock struck fifteen minutes before seven in the morning. Fog still covered the young mountains but the rows of trees started to appear faintly with soaking wet leaves. The mistress looked at the patio for a while, dreamily. Then she locked the door and went to bed:

"What will come tomorrow?" she asked herself while leisurely stretching her large body under the quilt.

What must happen, will happen!

But people don't need to be armed against life with literature and words, and don't need to waste time waiting. That afternoon of the first day of the new year, what-must-happen came to life.

It happened when Vui's house was still shut. Snoring like thunder rose up high and fell down low, like the singing of people dragging timber logs, spreading through all five rooms of her house. What comes to life, life raises up. Act Two of Mr. Quang's family drama that she secretly awaited had begun. Unfortunately she did not witness the curtain rising, even though she was the only person who had climbed ravines and crossed streams to get all the way to the distant Khoai Hamlet.

It is customary on the morning of the first day of the three-day Tet celebration for everyone to dress nicely, to replace incense on family altars, and to make remembrance offerings to the ancestors. In the early afternoon, after the offering, families may bring the offering food down from the altar to partake of a joyful meal that will ensure plentiful rice wine and tea all during the coming year. After the banquet comes the time for welcoming guests to the family home. Then, each family host welcomes his sons and their wives, his daughters and their husbands, and scores of grandchildren. There must be trays of five kinds of fruit for the children to eat to their heart's content. There will be red lucky envelopes with cash inside to distribute fairly among the grandkids, no distinction being made between boy or girl or between the children of sons and the children of daughters. There must be candies and cakes and many kinds of different candied fruit for people to munch with tea.

This year, Mr. Quang's house had only the newlyweds. Master Quynh still lived in the lower section with his maternal grandmother. After the failed negotiations by the two uncles, it was Quynh himself who had come up and asked his father for his clothes and other things, plus a sum of money large enough to pay for his tuition and activity fees. After living with his maternal family for a week, the young man had realized that nice words cannot mint money. The grandmother and the two uncles only provided him with empty advice or ineffective actions. They could do no more. Therefore, Quynh accepted living there as if in a boardinghouse, making monthly contributions for his food. The young man did not want to return to his family home, partly because of pride and partly because of his step-mother's beauty, which inflamed his emotions. Obviously the father understood his son's heart and did not force the matter.

"OK, whatever you want is fine. What about the five rooms reserved for you, what do you want to do with them?"

"Dad, just keep them for Stepmother and the younger siblings. I do not have any intention of returning."

"Please think carefully."

"I only ask you for the money to finish college. After graduation, I'll take care of myself."

"If so, I am happy for you. I'm only afraid you won't qualify for secondary school."

"I know. From now on I will attend public school."

"OK, I'll make sure you have enough money."

"It's what I ask for, Father."

The conversation ended and the youngest son picked up the shiny varnished trunk and left. It was a good separation because, subsequently, Quynh suddenly became more mature and began to do well in his studies. His new grades surprised his whole school.

This New Year, it was Mr. Quang who presented gifts to Miss Ngan. The gift for her was not a red envelope containing a few bills but a pink velvet box. When she opened the box, her eyes flashed like electricity and she jumped up to put her arms around his neck:

"Good-looking old man! This is truly marvelous!"

"Is this gift fit for a girl from Khoai Hamlet? Or are you the literary star from the right branch of the celestial horoscope?"

"Literary star of the left or the right branch does not equal becoming mistress of the house of Mr. Quang in the upper section."

"Are you sure of that, honey?"

"As sure as teak wood is hard."

"If Teacher Tuong returns and entices you to leave me, I will hang myself on the jackfruit tree at the end of the yard."

"Smack that lying mouth. You do want to hang?"

"I'll hang your neck first, then mine; in the same hour, no more, no less. It'll make it easy for the kids to do the funerals."

"That is horrible."

"Why such a faint heart? Just a little joking around."

"Don't be so foolish. We've had our share of bitterness. We will live with each other until we step into the grave."

She held on to him tightly, her tears welling up as if separation were stalking outside just beyond the door sill. He held her tightly, too, to confirm his unconditional protection. At that moment, he had a feeling, extremely definite, extremely strong, like his feeling when he first met her, when she, embarrassed, had put the two bottles of rice wine on the table in the boardinghouse in town: she was part of his bones and flesh, part of his own life, the part that he had forgotten, which he had ditched many incarnations before in someplace so far away, on the far side of the horizon. They stood like that for a long while in the calming New Year's air, both knowing and surprised as to why they were so passionately in love with each other. Then the sound of a barking dog and the footsteps of young men going out for a New Year's stroll on the hamlet road startled them out of their love enchantment. Miss Ngan hurriedly put the two red ruby solitaires in her ears.

"My gosh, it's time to cook food for the ancestors."

"Why hurry? The ancestors witness our faithful hearts. It'll be fine to bring them food at noon," he replied.

There were only the two of them, but the offering meal had to be complete. Besides being smart, Miss Ngan possessed all the necessary skills to cook well in a kitchen. She did not need her husband's help to prepare a ten-course banquet in less than two hours: steamed chicken with lime leaves, fried honey chicken, stir-fried beef with bamboo shoots, stir-fried fish with celery, stir-fried pork with cauliflower, chicken pie, pork pie with fungus, jellied pork hock, shrimp soup with fish bladder, and braised ribs with bamboo shoots. Not counting different pork rolls and rice cakes. Right at noon, a tray was brought up and enticing dishes were put on display all over the altar. There were eighteen plates and bowls for the main and the minor dishes. Mr. Quang stood there, stroking his beard and complimenting his wife. Incense and sandalwood smoke spread pleasing aromas throughout the rooms. The warmth of an invisible fire filled the air. The genies of happiness—which always come to a house where people love each other—smiled invisible smiles.

———

At the very moment when Mr. Quang, dressed in formal robes, stood directly in front of the ancestors' altar getting ready to offer prayers, Quy with his wife and two daughters stepped in. He carried two pink grapefruit from his own garden with a stack of black cakes, the kind that Mrs. Quang had liked to eat the most when she was alive. After putting these offerings on the altar, Quy said:

"May I pray to my mother first? Afterward, I must go and bring good New Year's wishes to the units and the villagers."

"Back away from there! On this altar I have ancestors from seven generations back. After that we have great-great-grandparents, grandparents from both maternal and paternal sides; then come the parents, my uncles and aunts. After that is my older brother who died young. Your mother, that is, my wife, has to wait her turn after him. The order of precedence is settled. There is no authority for a variance."

"But I . . ."

"Back off," Mr. Quang screamed. He did not say it but he knew that nobody in Quy's family had acknowledged Miss Ngan. She had withdrawn to the kitchen on seeing the animosity on their faces.

"This is my house, not the office of the village committee. Wield your authority elsewhere; not under the roof of this house."

His father's determination caused Quy to step back. His wife, always hiding in some corner, reached out to pull her husband's shirt. Quy then had no choice but to wait for Mr. Quang to bow and pray.

His prayer was a long one because he had to invite, according to proper generational sequence from high to low, the spirits of all the ancestors, from five to seven generations back down to his wife who had just died the previous spring. That length of time was hard to endure for a son who is belligerent and has real power in his hands. Chairman Quy stamped one foot then the other, as if there were a nest of red ants biting his feet so that he could not stand still. When his father had finished, he rushed forward to the altar, bowed twice, bending his back as they do in the theater, then raised his voice to cry out loud:

"Mother, Mother in heaven: if you are divine please return and open your eyes to see all the turmoil under this roof. Oh, Mother, it brings shame to us children. Why were you in a hurry to leave and let frogs jump on the table, chickens bring trash into the house, and crows build nests on the top of the grapefruit and orange trees?"

"Oh, Mother, dear Mother . . ."

"Dear Grandmother, where did you go? Like this you left us, Grandmother?"

No doubt having rehearsed beforehand, Quy's wife and children raised their crying voices like the choir at a play singing along with the orchestra. Their cries resonated in the calm atmosphere of the neighborhood. At this hour, neighbors were getting their clothes ready and preparing to go out. All the words back and forth and the crying of the chairman's family had slipped right into the ears of the neighbors on all sides who were always ready to listen in.

Mr. Quang was mortified. He was not prepared to receive this blow. To be accurate, nobody had sufficient imagination to anticipate such a thing. They worked hard all year, waiting for the new year with all its new hopes. The first day of Tet is the first day of a new block of time, of a span of life yet to come, a day that has the special, sacred meaning of an unsullied beginning. For that reason, no one would quarrel with any other on such a day; neighbors, even if they hated each other a lot, would suck down their bitterness to make sweet their greetings and wishes, because if words are not good and the meaning is not kind, then misfortune will come to both sides. Even enemies do not fight during Tet; so how could loved ones and blood relatives? That is why he was in shock when he saw his firstborn son with his family crying in front of the ancestors' altar, turning the sacred New Year's Day into a funeral. After a second of stunned bewilderment, he knew he had to act. Pulling out a pole leaning in a corner, something that had been at his side for twenty years while in the woods, he turned toward Quy's face and shouted:

"Go away! Go away right now! This is the altar for my ancestors, not the personal altar for your mother. If you are filial, I allow you to take her picture back to your house to worship. Your wife and your kids, too, get out of this house. I need children and grandchildren, but not a pack of scoundrels that disturb. I will not allow such ingrates to turn this house into a market."

"Oh heaven, you chase your child and grandchildren out of the house; oh, Grandfather . . ."

Quy's wife continued to scream, while her husband stared at his father with red eyes. His breath smelled full of alcohol; for sure the son had been drinking to draw on the encouragement of alcohol before leaving to pick a fight with his old father:

"My mother lived here; you do not have the right to drive ME MYSELF out of this house."

Mr. Quang stood stiff for a minute as if he did not believe what he had just heard. In his family children of whatever age had no right to use such a self-promoting, personal pronoun with their father under any circumstances. His children as well as the children of his brother and sister all knew this rule and looked upon it as something that distinguished them from other families who were looser in their protocol and discipline. Such a humiliation had never happened in his family. Quy knew that full well. Now he became the first to spit on the ways of the ancestors.

Mr. Quang stood shocked for a long while. A piercing pain ran through his heart again and again as if someone were continuously stabbing a dagger through it. For the first time in his life, he realized that a father's heart is extremely delicate and easily injured, that bitter pain can make the eyes blur and send tremors through one's whole body like the shakings that come with malaria. He knew that the change in his son's use of a personal pronoun to address him marked the last boundary line; that, from now on, they would never be father and son as before. Never as before. The pain kept coming nonstop. At the same time his body suddenly hardened like rock, a feeling similar to that moment when he was seventeen and had first put a house pillar on his shoulders in front of the taunting eyes of some young men from the upper section.

The father considered the face of his son, distorted by hatred and alcohol. Another second passed in silence. Then suddenly the father started laughing:

"Mr. Chairman is drunk."

He continued to laugh but suddenly his voice turned strange, causing the son and his family to look at one another in surprise: they had never heard him talk with all of them in such a soft and formal manner.

"Mrs. Chairman, take him home now or else I will file charges. The chairman is drunk and disturbs the home of a citizen."

"What did you say?" Chairman Quy asked, looking straight at his father. Perhaps he *was* drunk, or more likely he lacked the smarts to understand that his father had changed his tone, a way to mark the crossing of that final boundary line. Enunciating his words slowly, Mr. Quang replied:

"Mr. Chairman is drunk and disturbs the home of a citizen, thus doing harm to the honor of the Party and the government."

"What are you saying?"

"Now you, mister, are no longer my child. You are the village chairman, the government's representative. You are drunk and you take your pals around to disturb citizens."

"I MYSELF, I am not drunk. I MYSELF am humiliated because you brought a whore back to be your wife."

"In the old days, our elders told us: 'You can take a whore to be a wife, but never a wife to be a whore.' If Miss Ngan is a whore, I MYSELF haven't gone against our ancestors' teachings. But if my wife is not a prostitute, Mr. Chairman will be punished for defamation and insulting a citizen. Do you understand that?"

"If your wife is not a prostitute then she is a whore who was pregnant out of wedlock. You think nobody knows the story of the teacher sleeping with a student; Ngan pregnant by the teacher Tuong? You think that you can just pick up a whore at the end of an alley or off a mountain or by a river to bring back here and be able to hide everything?"

"I have always acted in full daylight; I have nothing to hide from the eyes of the world. Mr. Chairman crawls away from this house and has already forgotten—such a short memory. Correct: Miss Ngan was pregnant out of wedlock. She was pregnant by someone she loved—Teacher Tuong. It's like thousands of other women who get pregnant with the men they choose. She was pregnant because she's as fertile as a bantam hen. Many other women not pregnant out of wedlock are lucky because they belong to the class with duck's blood, not dove's blood. Like your mother, for example; she was not pregnant out of wedlock because she belonged to the infertile group—not because she was holding tight to her virginity. Before I married your mother, for a whole year I would take her up to Golden Bamboo Mountain. Do you want me to show you the places where I took her down?"

Right then, it was the son whose mouth was open wide with surprise—like someone being struck by lightning on the ears. And when he realized clearly what his father had said, he squealed like a pig being slaughtered:

"That's not true; you lie about my mother! I don't believe you!"

"Your mother and I were in the prime of life. We cut lumber in the woods together all year 'round. Who could stop us? We didn't have to deprive ourselves of our desire. Why did we have to wait for the right day and month? We were engaged; the two families had an agreement. Sooner or later we would be in bed together."

Quy had no reply.

"You are tongue-tied and cannot answer because you are used to lying. You and your wife, too, my man, yourself with your wife, didn't you mix oil and vinegar with each other for a whole year before I managed to make enough money to pay for the wedding? What about the time you furtively took her for a curettage down in the district? You thought I was blind? The money your mother sneakily gave you was taken out of my pocket, why wouldn't I know? It's lucky your wife could still have kids. In many cases, a curettage of the first pregnancy leads to permanent infertility."

Quy's wife was looking at her father-in-law with her mouth wide open until she burst out crying from shame. The two daughters, both of an age to be married, and the son lowered their heads. All were acting their roles under the baton of the father. At this instant, the cards were turned faceup, the father and the mother were exposed, and the children dared not look up. Mr. Quang lowered his voice:

"Enough: we fought so it was a fight. You were born, but only when you were thirteen did I know what kind of person you were. I tried every which way to turn things around but could not. No one can stand against heaven's plans. From now on, don't ever set foot in my house. We are no longer father and son."

"That is your will."

"You are wrong; people don't choose what they want or don't want. But once we have pushed each other this far, everything must change." Again Quy could say nothing.

"You don't dare open your mouth because you still think of wealth. Being a person is quite difficult, Master Quy. Opening your mouth is easy; opening your hand is much more difficult. Filial piety on the lips—everyone has it. If you don't want to, I MYSELF will continue to perform your mother's death anniversaries as usual. She was my wife and now she is still my deceased wife. She made no mistake with me. But you are different. From this day on, I MYSELF will not have you."

The group stood there stupidly. Perhaps what had happened went too quickly and they had no time to understand how it all had ended. Perhaps they believed that whatever they might do, Mr. Quang would never dare push them out the doors of this house, a house they believed their only son would someday own. But Mr. Quang threw the pole back to the corner of the house, looked at them, and said, lowering his voice:

"Go, go! Go away from here!"

He said this softly, almost murmuring, but within this quiet voice, everything was finished; the water had run its course, the boat had slipped its moorings.

Nothing could return to what it had been.

Quy, his wife, and their children took themselves home, the eyes of neighbors watching them from behind windows and doors, trees and stands of bamboo.

People live rather calm lives in the mountains—like the surface of the lake down the valley imprisoned on all four sides by mountain slopes. But if you throw in a stone, circles will spread without stopping. In the same way, some events, big or small—if they upset whatever is most hidden in the human soul—can start a war, a conflict between old-fashioned understandings and modern innovations. Woodcutters' Hamlet that spring resembled a volcano squirting out lava nonstop because of what was happening in Mr. Quang's family. Or, speaking more precisely, Woodcutters' Hamlet that spring was like a roaring, burning stove with the person throwing charcoal briquettes onto the fire being a beautiful girl coming from a strange place, with sensual eyes, and wearing a green silk blouse.

One o'clock came on the first day of Tet; villagers flowed into the streets to go and present their wishes to their loved ones. According to the old custom, the first day of New Year is reserved for visits to close relatives. Visits on the second day are made to more distant relatives, neighbors, and friends. The third day is for hamlet officials to pay calls on one another: the chairman goes to the secretary's house; the secretary visits the hamlet police commander, then the police commander presents his New Year's wishes to the secretary of the Youth Committee or the secretary of the Woman's Federation—the formal structure holding the community together. That year everything seemed to be wrong side up. Right on the evening of the first day, people rushed pell-mell to knock at Miss Vui's door:

"Happy New Year. We wish you five, ten times more prosperity this year than last."

"Happy New Year. We wish that you get many new things, from your head down to your toes."

"Happy New Year. We wish Miss Vui happiness all year long, always to smile with happiness; every day to be as the first day of Tet, every month to be as the first month of the year, and each season to be as the spring."

From the day she had come into life with a cry, never had Miss Vui enjoyed as many New Year's good wishes worded so beautifully, like flowers and brocade; never had she enjoyed such respect from the villagers. That year maybe heaven had turned its eyes on her, or maybe her devoted father in heaven had come to her aid. Her fortune seemed to change. While opening wide her doors, Miss Vui invited the guests in, smiling:

"Happy New Year, I wish each of you everything you are waiting for."

People poured into the house, not waiting for a second invitation. All intuitively felt that Act Two of the Ngan-Quang soap opera would be performed here.

As for Miss Vui, after sleeping straight through for more than nine hours, she was full of strength; her spirits were soaring. She lit incense at her father's altar, changed the water in the vase of peach blossoms, then sat down and ate two pork rolls and one large sticky rice cake. When the villagers came to her house, she was in a wonderful frame of mind, one of satisfaction and happiness—the most important conditions for generous hospitality. The hostess boiled water to make tea; she put out all kinds of cakes and candies that she had bought down in the town. Meanwhile, more and more guests came in; not only elders but also groups of young men and women from the village committee along with teenagers who liked playing games with tiny firecrackers and fighting cocks, or chess. Thus two rooms of the house were filled to the walls with people as happens only when there are meetings over allocation of work points and distribution of rice. Miss Vui had readily at hand a contingent of soldiers to help serve tea, cakes, and candies to everyone. She sat imposingly at the head table, next to the village mucky-mucks and the heads of the wealthiest families.

"I heard somewhere that it has happened. Thus the husbands who don't play second fiddle to their wives have won the bet. I ask to open a bottle of Lua Moi whiskey to congratulate them."

So spoke Miss Vui to open that evening's gathering. Then she took a bottle of Lua Moi from the altar, along with a packet of fragrant roasted peanuts, half sweet, half savory, which she had bought in town.

"Anyone who wants rice cake or pork roll to snack on while drinking, let me know."

"No."

The most patriarchal of all the husbands replied, "Today is the first day of the New Year, so nobody has enough space left in the stomach to hold your rice cake and pork rolls, mistress. But to have fragrant roasted peanuts with Lua Moi whiskey is exquisite. Who can complain?"

"Townsfolk are real specialists. Just ordinary peanuts, but after they roast them, they taste so sweet to the tongue. No matter how much wine you drink, they still taste good. After eating a handful of peanuts roasted in our homes, our throats choke up."

"They have a secret recipe. Many times I have bought some *hung liu* spice in the hamlet market. I mix it with sugar and salt to marinate the peanuts for six hours, then dry them first before I roast them. So I use all the right methods but at the end they are awful, with that smoky, burned flavor."

"My goodness, if listening alone could make us skillful, then who could make a living as a cook or running a restaurant? They have to keep their secrets. It is said that in Hanoi, some become wealthy just by roasting peanuts, or selling steamed and grilled sugarcane soaked in grapefruit flowers, or cooking green mung bean soup with tangerine peels, calling it in Chinese *luc tao xa*. Each pot of *luc tao xa* can feed seven or eight mouths and build a three-story house."

"With little land and too many people, they must struggle fiercely to make a living, so they are smarter than us rural folk."

"As you said, from the point of view of Mr. Quang and his wife, wasn't it smart of him to tell off Quy and his family this noon? Like it or not, he is the most 'citified' person in this village."

"I knew it right away."

The very patriarchal husband laughed out loud: "Your seat is hardly warm and yet you bring up Mr. Quang's family saga. You're too hot-blooded. Can't you wait for us to finish the first round of drinking?"

His voice was full of provocation and arrogance. The very bitchy lady could not stand it and said, "Everyone has given in to you but that's still not enough? Your ego is not just as big as a basket, it is more like a mountain."

"Stop, stop! You two are just opposites, like water and fire. Good thing you never married!"

"Stop, stop. Turn down your fire, little lady."

"OK, I'll shut my mouth right now."

The bitchy one seemed to be pouting; her husband, who was sitting at the same table as the bossy, unhenpecked man, calmly said, "My wife is still kind of childish. She is a fine person."

Both rooms suddenly became quiet for a second; then, after people had heard what had been said, together they all laughed out loud, the young men shouting and clapping hands loudly:

"Hats off to you; such a wonderful husband!"

"Hail to you, we vote you to be role model for all husbands, getting our votes for 'most well behaved husband' in the hamlet. Hey, you girls, open your eyes wide and look, OK. Just take him as your ideal when looking for a husband."

The laughter, the teasing exploded in all four corners. Previously, few had dared openly to compliment their wives, especially in front of a crowd.

Really, it had indeed been quite rare. But despite the hubbub of both praise and teasing, the model husband continued sitting quietly, sipping his whiskey. Having accepted his henpecked status, all the teasing for him was like water on a duck's back. Maybe, though, he had a distracting thought? The others thought so, and when the bursts of laughter died down, they all turned toward the man who normally was considered the least talkative in the hamlet, who never participated in any public discussions.

"Today the toad opens his mouth; for sure now we will have a big storm! You, dear brother, do you have anything to teach the village at the start of spring? Please speak up."

The man put his cup on the table, but his gaze never moved from the tiny waves reflecting off the strong liquor.

"Put it aside; Mr. Quang's family affair is not an issue about citified folks or country folks. It's between father and son. It could happen to any family, either in remote mountains or down in a city. It should make us think about our own fates."

Everyone turned quiet. They were mute for a long while because no one had thought of this. Now that someone had recognized the fact and had given it a name, they backed off, because a truth had been right in front of their eyes and nobody had seen it, like the traveler who lost his way and had just plunged on to slam against a rock or step right into a ravine. There had been such blindness because people looked at whatever happened in Mr. Quang's family only as an operetta or a play—only as something that they would occasionally watch with much curious excitement and think about as someone else's story, a story involving only actors using lipstick and blush powder, and wearing costumes encrusted with gold, dragonfly-ear hats, and high boots, who spend the year singing and dancing onstage.

Just now someone had pointed out to each of them that such melodramas could just as well play out inside their own homes. This warning was like a crack of thunder hitting them right by their ears. The crowd was silent as if struck dumb. They had to wait for the shock to pass. After a while, when they had regained their calm, their heads started to clear. They then considered whether that story held any danger in their own circumstances.

"You could be right. But you are not Mr. Quang. Neither am I."

"You are not Mr. Quang because your wife's hair is not yet gray. Neither am I, because I am determined to go before my wife."

"Who gives you permission to go before me?" the wife responded immediately in a raised voice, adding, "You have to wait to do my funeral, then you can go."

"Yeah, you are spoiled by the love of your husband, and are used to leading him by the nose. No one can set a time: birth has its fixed time but death has none."

"That's so right!"

"Maybe in our families there will be no scene where a son falls for his stepmother, and no scene in which another son takes his wife and children home to create turmoil in front of the ancestors' altar on the first day of the New Year. But who can guarantee that their children will be filial and treat their parents well? I don't have to say it, ladies and gentlemen; you all have known this for a long time."

"Exactly! There is no shortage of stories. In the past, people concealed and covered up such tragedies; putting up with them while swallowing tears in a kitchen corner. In the old days, our elders said, 'Every family has a jar of smelly fermented fish. You must know how to cover it tightly to keep the neighbors from smelling the foul stink.'"

"But the business of 'covering it tightly' . . . that stuff might be more stinky than stirring up shit in the privy just to smell it. Do you all remember the story of Old Lady Cuu, who starved to death?"

"I do! How can you forget that story?"

"Then any of you ladies here want to starve to death like Old Lady Cuu?"

"No, a hundred times no. We are women with brains like grapefruit who can't see farther than two handspans, but we are not that stupid."

"Old Lady Cuu was not stupid. Her husband died when she was twenty-nine, leaving a thatch house and broken wall. All by herself she went up and down to the fields, made charcoal, gathered wood, and raised bees to gain a living. Someone so enterprising cannot be stupid. Her problem was she loved her child too much, trusted her child too much, when, in return, the child did not love his mother. He listened only to his wife, was completely dominated by her, and let his mother die of starvation."

"Why didn't she let it get out so that everyone could know the facts right from the start?"

"That was the problem! Because she loved her child too much . . . because she already had told everybody that her son was the best in the world, intelligent, filial; then when the situation got nasty, debased, and shameful, she dared not open her mouth but clenched her teeth, bit her tongue, and died. You must have realized that the old lady had done right by the saying 'To cover the jar of smelly fermented fish,' haven't you?"

"Yeah, yeah . . . I only think of it now."

"I am not going to be that stupid."

The wife of the henpecked guy spoke up: "Whether or not we think about it, we must learn that tears always fall down, not up. When a mother gives money to her child, the child is as happy as a lark. Whenever children give money to their mother, their faces look sad and their brows frown; their hearts hurt as if cut. That is why I keep telling my husband that in life we must worry for the children, but, above all, we must take care of ourselves. I dare not open my mouth to wait for the fruit, or hold out both my hands waiting for a filial heart. I keep my money securely in my purse. When we get sick, we slowly open our purse to pull some money out."

"Man, are you fortunate to have a wife who knows how to plan ahead."

"A child who cares for you is not equal to the wife who cares for you. Once husband and wife, when you go down to the ocean to catch crabs, or climb a mountain to pick leaves, you must have glue in your commitment."

"That is right! No one wants to be suspicious, but with a son you get the daughter-in-law; with a daughter you get the son-in-law. Those outsiders invade your home. Good ones are rare and bad ones are a dime a dozen."

"Now I want to go back to Mr. Quang's family situation: Do you find that the way Mr. Quang tells all the family secrets so openly is stupid or smart?"

"I think it was one hundred percent stupid. What is not asked about should not be told. Besides, his wife is dead. One should not spill secrets of the departed."

"Neither smart nor stupid! Something that had to be done. Because the son first started the fight."

"Right, when pushed into a corner, things happen against your will. He's not at all happy to have to tell all those things."

"I am not close to that family, but I am in-laws with Mr. Quang's youngest brother. He tells me that even when Quy was still young, Mr. Quang told the brothers that later in life he did not expect ever to rely on his first-born son. But he would fulfill all the responsibilities of a father to ensure a good future for his child. Everyone saw that Mr. Quang had done exactly as he had said. It was Quy who quit forestry high school to return to the village and work in the fields while his father looked for every way to help him study more."

"Not only forestry high school; before that he managed to get the boy in the school of metal weaponry, but that kid could not study. That brain is impenetrable; even if you took a metal rod to smash words into his head, nothing would enter."

"Besides, he is pretty snotty and full of sneaky maneuvers."

"Sneaky maneuvers are one thing, being intelligent is another. Like thorny eggplant and cabbage—how can you mix them together?"

"Yeah, the father shines brightly; so why is the son so bad-looking? He resembles the mother but is not as fresh and pretty as she was. It's really odd; the same features as Master Quynh, who is so good-looking while the brother really is unattractive—shrimpy body and deep-set eyes. Looking into his eyes is like looking down a dark ravine—you don't know where to step."

"People say that with eyes like that your heart is really dangerous. But if you are dangerous, go punch and kick passersby. Why turn back to hit your own father?"

"Yes, I am wondering the same thing. Even a blind person in the village knows that since Quy's birth, Mr. Quang was the one who took complete care of him; from his education, to his marriage, to building a house, buying clothes and stuff. He not only took care of his son, he also helped all the grandkids, male and female."

"He makes tons of money."

"He has money but is stingy and tight; don't expect him to pull cash out of his pocket."

"He helps others, so why should he ignore his children? But I think that Quy relies on being the oldest when, according to tradition, the oldest has the right to inherit because he has to take care of funerals for the parents. After the parents pass away, he has to worry about marrying off his siblings. 'The brother takes over from the father' . . . this phrase from many generations."

"You take over from the father only after he dies. But Mr. Quang is still very much alive, straight like a post; next to his son he is ten times better-looking . . . talking about replacing the father is premature."

"Yes, that's the main issue!"

Slowly enunciating each word as if he were a village teacher, the henpecked one spoke as if he were reading the conclusion of an essay:

"The son calculates the scenario that the father will die so he has to rely on him, to see who will wear the mourning cloth, who will hold the stick and roll on the streets, who will summon the horns and the drums, who will order food for the soul; then after the funeral comes the forty-ninth day's offering; after the forty-ninth day comes the fifty-third day, to invite the soul to the temple for prayers; then comes the first anniversary, the second one, and the third one; then comes the cleaning of the bones to put them in the terra-cotta urn; after that a permanent grave will have to be built. All the customs for the dead are too complicated. Everybody worries that after death the children will ignore them. Therefore, one has to swallow the bitter pill to please them. Because of that fear of being left to become a hungry ghost, people are willing to salt their faces to ignore the corruption, disgrace, in the family. Relations between parents and children are often a show for the village and neighbors to see. It's rare to see through to the reality; it's rare to see it exposed sincerely. That is why we have this proverb: 'When she was alive, you didn't feed your mother; when dead, you gave an oration to the flies.'

"Nobody knows for how many generations this sad song has been sung. Nor for how many generations parents have had to clench their teeth and endure ungrateful, inhuman treatment hoping for a proper burial. Children, except for filial ones, often abuse this psychology to make demands on and to pressure their parents. Looking at Mr. Quang's family situation, you will see that clearly. But the main problem in this family is that the son was thinking about death a bit too early. Old people when facing death are usually shaken with fear, losing all their confidence as well as their authority over their children. Additionally, Quy holds the position of village chairman. He has clout with the neighbors as well as the rights belonging to a family's oldest son. But Mr. Quang does not yet fit the profile of a village elder, even though he is sixty-one. He is still healthy, with eyes shining like stars and a mind moving faster than electricity. He still makes money. He does not yet think about death. He still likes to live, still thinks about sex with his new wife. That is why the son was not able to intimidate him. Without a qualm he ran Quy's whole flock, wife and kids, out into the street. Thus the son made a misstep in the chess game; a misstep that cannot be salvaged. That's my thinking, am I right or wrong, gentlemen?"

"One hundred percent on the dot."

"Right, I concur. One says that when the toad opens his mouth, it's not just empty chatter, nor just for fun."

"One's life is such. When you look sideways you think it is a joke, but when you look straight it becomes a tragedy."

"That's how we know—to live is tough."

"You turn this way then that way, old age dashes in. Not behind your back but smack in front of you."

All became silent. Suddenly both rooms were dead quiet like an empty temple because this was the first time they had looked straight at what they feared. This fear coexists with them forever and ever, like a shadow, but nobody dares speak its name, nobody dares articulate its meaning. People avoid the topic, they cover it up using every sort of pretext, like family honor, like the sanctity of blood relationships, like parental responsibilities. But in reality, it hides in the darkest corner of one's soul: those irreverent children, those tactless ones who do not hesitate to bring their feelings out into the open, to parade them in broad daylight. Without anyone saying it, people still remember every word, so strident and bitter, from Old Lady Cuu's daughter-in-law:

"You think having an old mother is a light burden, don't you? We enjoy the house and your fields, yes, but you are sick, one has to buy medicine for you. When you die, one has to do a funeral, a banquet now and then, and one has to wash your skeleton to replace a wooden box with a terra-cotta one; all that requires money, don't think that we just clap our hands and it all gets done."

Not every family has a cruel and greedy daughter-in-law as did Mrs. Cuu; but since life is hard, whether you like it or not, one needs to look at realities clearly. But people's hearts usually reject hardship. Besides, the hearts of people need some sweet illusions. Children come from us; they grow thanks to the blood and milk of their parents. Who wants to believe that someday they will hand you a chipped bowl to use for your rice?

After a moment of silence, a man spoke up: "Children are gifts from heaven. Parents give them life but heaven gives them character. Then and now, everyone relies on sons. So within this very hamlet, I can't say more, is there any father whose funeral was more elaborate than Mr. Do Vang's?"

"Miss Vui is a special case; why bring her up?"

"One father and one child, when he died he had nice brocade garments. There are some who have seven children, working hard like buffalo all year round and going bankrupt raising the children to adulthood. Yet when they lie down, they have to listen to them arguing about how much each should contribute to the funeral costs. In this life, we are better or worse, all thanks to our good deeds in past lives. In the morning, nobody can foresee what the night will bring. Nobody can plan the time when we go to the grave. Enough, gentlemen, pour me some wine. In spring swallows fly to and fro. Let's empty our cups to celebrate the New Year. Miss Hostess, please join us."

Miss Vui quietly finished her cup along with the men. Nobody said more. The villagers had come excitedly to her house to gossip about Mr. Quang and his sons, but that story ended up trespassing on the secret, private lives of each of them. And those secrets often told more about the winter of life than its spring. The committee secretary recognized that point. After the round of wine, she requested that the youth group sing to gloss over the gloom. However, the guests left in groups of five or three at a time. She was sure they would continue the discussion in their homes, because underlying the gossip was the fundamental foundation of everyone's life—where happiness and pain intertwine to make a single thread constituting one's destiny. Perhaps what happened between Mr. Quang and his children was an alarm, preparing each family for all the storms waiting for them—a cry from the seabird that warns boats to be careful before an unseen iceberg or surprise tempests in the dark ocean ahead.

The group of young people then left as well. Miss Vui sat in front of the altar and looked at Mr. Do's photograph and whispered:

"Father, you were wise in life and divine in death, please come back and show me the way."

Mr. Do looked out straight at the face of his daughter with a most stern expression that she had never seen before.

"We made the wrong move, totally wrong. Now we have to find a way to undo it."

She pondered and considered what she had done. She had gone all the way to Khoai Hamlet to investigate Miss Ngan's family and the love affair of the mismatched couple. She was the only person who knew the beginning and the end of such things and thus was the one to report back to Quy and the villagers. People would eventually ask: Whatever prompted her to be so enthusiastic? Not because she was submissive to the chairman's request, because she is never submissive to anyone. She had done everything according to her own thinking. Therefore the argument "the secretary was following the chairman's order" would not persuade many people. It would be as if a worker were digging a deep well in the dirt to find the water main below; the villagers would dig to the end for the reasons that compelled her to spend her time and money to go all the way to Khoai Hamlet. They will find them with little difficulty. And then the arrowhead will point her way:

"From just last night to tonight, the situation has turned upside down. Can anyone predict when a move will be made?"

She let out a sigh. Last night, before New Year's Day, the whole village had listened to her report, happily laughing, lifting up and lowering down their wine cups, and carrying her up to the blue skies because she satisfied their curiosity; they looked at the saga of Mr. Quang's family as a fun comedy for spring festivities. Today, Act Two had been quickly performed, but it was no longer just the personal story of Mr. Quang's family; it suddenly touched upon the affection between fathers and sons—as an emotional rope wrapped around a large tree trunk, very close to the old saying: "Pull the rope and you shake the forest." She instinctively sighed again with the thought that she had been clever but not wise: pulling the rope without thinking of shaking the forest. Now, given what had happened, there was no way to reverse events. After a moment of hesitation, she recalled what her father had taught her:

"Hold out your hands to catch water from heaven; how can you ever catch everything that people say?"

That clever saying brought her some calm. She consoled herself: "To heck with life. Isn't it useless to worry about catching the rain from heaven?"

Thus, again as always, Miss Vui was her father's daughter: Mr. Do Vang, the one with a pragmatic mind. She knew that she could ignore all the village gossip, because in the past such gossip hovered like kitchen smoke over the roofs of those who had clout or who stood out from their neighbors. Something she could not ignore was Mr. Quang himself. For a long time, she had known that he was a popular person, with a good heart and generous to his neighbors; but, too, he did not shy from pulling out a sword to confront those with wicked hearts. Even though she had let her imagination fly around the man with a thick beard, she could not have foreseen that he would calmly speak loudly for his children and the neighbors on all four sides to hear the truth: "Before I married your mother, for a whole year I took her to Truc Vang mountain." If he dared speak so boldly, what would keep him from insulting her to her face in a rude and cruel manner when he learned that she had gone all the way to Khoai Hamlet? Just thinking about this made her whole body hot and her face feel as if burned. With sweat breaking out on her head and on both temples, she looked back at Mr. Do and spouted out these words:

"Dear father, divine and wise father, please show me the way."

Mr. Do did not say a word, but stared at her sternly. She suddenly remembered a comment from someone in the crowd: "The father is so good-looking; why is the son so homely?"

She had never fully thought about that point. It was clear that when Quy stood next to Mr. Quang it was like trees of two different types growing next to each other. The father openly resembled a gentleman; the son totally the opposite—not only so skinny but with a face dark like the inside of a closed jar, and a stare distant and dangerous. Miss Vui had never seen Quy look anyone straight in the eye. His eyes, sunken in their sockets, under a constant cloudy shadow, would dart, if not to one side, then often down, as if he were searching for something underground.

"Like that, but still Quy has been village chairman for several terms. And at every election the Party secretary from the district personally came to work with the village committee for that result."

A thought suddenly crossed her mind and she cried out: "Oh my god! And nobody knows!"

The morning of the second day of the New Year, Miss Vui rode her bicycle down to the district town. There, it took her a long time to find someone selling tea and sweets. Business was bad; sellers put up stalls on the side-walks hoping for customers spending their spare change on the New Year. Normally a cup of tea cost 50 cents, but that day, the stall keeper charged five times more, 250 cents, when no privilege was given to buyers to bar-gain, because it was still the New Year holiday. The street was deserted, only a few kids out playing with firecrackers on both sidewalks. To please the seller, Miss Vui drank three cups and ate three overripe bananas, left over from the previous week. Then she gave the owner 3,000 cents and said:

"These are both to pay you and to wish you a prosperous New Year."

"Thank you."

The seller smiled broadly out to the ears in front of a rural customer who was ten times more generous than one from the town:

"You are so generous, heaven will bestow on you goodwill to enjoy and keep."

"Thank you, ma'am," she replied amicably, and asked her the way to the chairman's and secretary's homes.

"Our village is very far, many urgent issues had not been solved in the year. Therefore, I have to come to the district on the first day of spring to resolve them."

"No matter how urgent they are, you should wait until the sixth day, miss. I've done business here for more than ten years. Customers like you come mostly from faraway areas like yours to take care of problems, public and private. Nobody dares to walk into the chairman's residence before the sixth day."

"I don't intend to bother the leaders at their office, but my village has some farm products I want to give to the district cadres to show our grati-tude for the concern shown by the Party and the government."

"Ah, I understand."

The stall owner laughed more loudly, then with her eyes looked over her customer with her bicycle up against the sidewalk. Miss Vui quickly added:

"My task is only to find the right location. Tomorrow or the next day, our village chairman will personally bring the gifts up."

"Of course."

Not waiting for the owner to ask more, she pulled out a 5,000-dong bill and put it on the cigarette plate.

"Here's for you, to make up for the time you gave me."

"Thank you, miss. I will take you right away," the owner answered and without hesitation turned to the alley and shouted,: "Hue, where are you? Come and watch the stand for your mother. Quick!"

Hearing no reply, she shouted again: "Hue! Come watch the stand, Hue!" She called out relentlessly, knowing that selling tea all day would never bring as much money as accommodating Miss Vui. A young girl about seven or eight finally popped out from the alley, her feet trudging in an old pair of sandals.

"I am here, Mother. Where are you going?"

"I have an errand; you don't have to ask!"

The child sat on a chair behind the stand, curiously looking at the big female customer, as imposing as a temple guardian statue, setting her bicycle down on the street as her mother climbed on behind, holding tightly on to Miss Vui's back, like a tiny frog hanging on to a watermelon.

Thus, Miss Vui came directly to the residences of the Party secretary and the district chairman. After her ride, sweat trickled down her spine. Now, all the ten things she had suspected were true. Quy owed his position as village chairman to the directing hands of his father and not to some good fortune; nor especially to his own prowess. Miss Vui stared at the houses of the two district leaders: each had two stories, with four rooms on the lower level and three on the upper one; each with an open yard about thirty square meters surrounded by a wrought iron fence, so that each owner could sit and drink tea while looking at the moon for some night inspiration. Each house had stairs inside and outside leading all the way up to the top floor. Each had a large patio down below with a walkway filled with white gravel. Each house had a pair of concrete and steel phoenixes on the roof—all upper-class decor and architecture. The very same style as graced the new home of the teacher in Khoai Hamlet.

It was dusk when she returned to the village. The sounds of a drum arose from the empty lot. Afraid that villagers would involve her in an entanglement, she went around on the other side of the bamboo ridge. The detour was long because there were more than ten separate ridges on which grew all kinds of bamboo, forming necklacelike strands of pearls. The beaten path was uneven, so her bicycle bounced up and down like a wild horse. But her heart jumped more wildly than her iron horse when she pedaled past the foot of the Golden Bamboo Ridge, the highest ridge, which was thick with golden bamboo. That golden color was the same as wedding threads on the bushes of mums in the country gardens. That golden color spilled in the afternoon sun like thousands of gold threads or a piece of superior silk. That golden color shimmered as in a king's palace or in mandarin robes. Miss Vui looked into the golden bamboo forest on a spring day and thought of a woman who had been there hundreds of times with her lover, but was now lying in peace in a tomb. Will she return on another old spring day or not? Then she thought of herself: Why had nobody ever taken her into that grove? Her secret dream dissipated into smoke, and she wondered if, from then until she lay in her grave, some man would ever extend his hand to her and say:

"I love you . . ." or: "Dear Vui, from now on we will live together!"

She arrived at the alley at dark. For sure, no one saw her rush the bicycle to the middle of the patio. She tied the gate tightly. Then she opened her door and dashed into the house. She did not bother to change her dusty clothes, and, throwing herself on a pile of quilts, she began to sob. She sobbed in rhythms, at times in a crescendo like an injured boar. She cried to the full, overflowing, without restraint. She cried madly. She cried more sadly than on the day Mr. Do had died. She cried with all the passionate hurt she didn't know she had, like a hungry child that gobbles up the bread given him. It may be that with all those falling tears, her soul became lighter.

The next morning, on the third day of the New Year, Miss Vui, dressed formally and most properly, carried a large branch of cherry blossoms to Mr. Quang's house.

"This man does not lack anything but white cherry blossoms."

All night she had debated the idea back and forth. As soon as morning came, she took a saw out to her garden and cut a large branch that had both blossoms and buds to take as an offering.

She had guessed correctly in her choice, because there were only peach blossoms in Mr. Quang's garden and not the blush and white cherry variety. White ones are hard to propagate and need special care and Mr. Quang, away the year round, was unable to grow them. In the village, scores of people grew cherry blossom trees but most cultivated the yellow variety, with skinny branches and small flowers. Only her garden had white cherry blossoms, a large kind with branches full of flowers that spread out evenly. They were the imperial type of cherry blossom for which Mr. Do had gone all the way to a village growing Japanese trees to get proper seeds. When he was alive, he had guarded the tree like he would gold. After he died, Miss Vui continued to care for it as he had, even though she was not as passionate about it as he had been or enjoyed the pleasure it could provide as he had. But Mr. Do had been her sole idol: whatever her father wanted or did, she wanted or did, no matter the cost. She had no expectation that, just then, the white cherry blossoms would be her savior.

When she approached Mr. Quang's house, no other callers had yet arrived. Miss Ngan and Mrs. Tu were sitting in the middle of the kitchen, plucking chickens. Seeing her, they both stood up to greet her. Miss Ngan smiled.

"Good morning, sister, I present to you my New Year's wishes."

Mrs. Tu was bubblier:

"On New Year, a dragon comes to the shrimp's house; we will certainly have luck this year."

Miss Vui tried to look at the black jade eyes of her eighteen-year-old hostess. Smiling when she presented her New Year's wishes to them, her heart was beating hard in her chest. Then Mrs. Tu called out:

"Big Uncle, a guest has arrived!"

To Miss Vui, Mrs. Tu urged, "Please go to the front room, we are finishing up our task."

"With your permission," she replied and walked up the three steps. Standing in the door, Mr. Quang waited for her, wearing an old-fashioned silk suit.

"The old man plays tough; his style is so different," she thought to herself as she bowed her head, greeting her host as the cadres in town would do, while silently evaluating the way a hero like him dressed. She had expected that with a young wife, he would wear a white or egg-colored shirt, at least a "blouson," with a pair of straight-leg pants, according to contemporary urban styles. But, Mr. Quang had adorned himself with a local silk suit like the elders, worn quite loose. Additionally, he did not have his hair cut short, but left it shoulder length, tied up with a rubber band as did carefree travelers in the old days. His beard was jet black and circled his jaw, bushy like grass and curly like those of Westerners. Strangely, in that old-fashioned outfit, all his chest and shoulder muscles stood out handsomely. In this outfit, he was extremely handsome, the incarnation of a great warrior, which would be hard to find not only in Woodcutters' Hamlet but anywhere in the district.

She instinctively bent forward and stepped back, because Mr. Quang's breath bathed her face like the hot wind of a muggy summer, a summer full of storms and lightning.

"Greetings, miss, early in the year."

"On New Year's, I wish you all things well," she replied while leaning the large branch of cherry blossoms against the sideboard next to the altar.

Mr. Quang looked at her. "Please sit down. We have tea perfumed with jasmine or with white mums. We also have tea from Snow Mountain and red cherry blossom tea, too. Which would you prefer?"

"As they are all your own teas, they must all be good. Please choose whichever one you like," she replied, finding her voice trembling. Not yet knowing why, she felt a lump rising in her throat with a strange feeling impossible to control, like a wild stream running through the fields of her soul, a vast and deserted field, actually. Frightened, she thought: "This is goofy; why am I suddenly feeling this way?"

Forcefully, she tried to restrain herself but to no avail. Miss Vui hurriedly bent down to fix the back strap of her sandal, her eyes intentionally staring at her toes, scrubbed clean, above a green floor:

"Look at this! Look at this! I do not have dark feet like the women and girls in Woodcutters' Hamlet."

She repeated it several times to herself and her pride enabled her to regain her calm. No woman or girl—in Woodcutters' Hamlet or in the entire district—had feet as fair as hers. Even though she worked hard, Miss Vui protected her skin and her feet as others would care for their eyes. Whether rain or shine, in summer or in winter, she always wore thick socks and canvas shoes with rubber soles, just like Westerners. One time, a delegation of Russian professionals visited the village; Miss Vui thought their complexions as fair and fine as rice paper. She thought they preserved such complexions by wearing socks and shoes all year round. Then Vui was only thirteen but a precocious awareness of beauty had already obsessed her. From that day on, she demanded that Mr. Do always buy shoes and socks for her; since then her wearing shoes and socks had become routine, just like eating and drinking. When all the working villagers went barefoot or wore skimpy sandals, people found it weird that a young girl would adopt the foreign custom of wearing shoes and socks all year. Because tropical summers are long, to wear shoes and socks is torture. Sweat quickly wets the socks and makes them smelly. Moreover, wearing shoes and socks was a public challenge to common custom that others dared not make. But Miss Vui could not have cared less. For her, all gossip, all harsh criticism from villagers, was just like a hatching of cicadas that live for only a summer. Come fall, whether they want to or not, they all have to crawl back into the ground.

When she looked at her feet, which were white like peeled boiled eggs, she knew they were her way out—a lifebuoy thrown right when she was about to drown. After locking the aluminum clasp in a meticulous manner, she looked one more time at her fine skin, fairer than that of city girls, to find a point of emotional support as a fighter finds an auspicious position in the ring. Looking up, Miss Vui was now able to speak in a formal manner, as she did when having to open meetings of village committees.

"At the New Year, here is a branch of white cherry blossoms as a gift from a poor family; please do not think unkindly of it."

"You are poor?" Mr. Quang said, laughing out loud and asking further: "Do you think that because I make my living elsewhere, I know nothing of what is happening here?"

"No, of course not," she replied, bashfully looking down because her host's teeth were white like pearls, and even. They shone like white lightning when he laughed. She asked herself: "Does he smoke a pipe or cigarettes? What man can keep from smoking? How does he keep his teeth as nice as the teeth of those who are only eighteen or twenty?"

Mr. Quang continued: "The villagers told me that you acquired a generator of the best quality, and have the most up-to-date storm lamp, better than my own lamp. Pretty soon, you will be the wealthiest one in the hamlet."

"I don't dare."

"But you have the heart to give me the cherry blossoms. I accept. For me it is indeed the most perfect gift for spring. We have a vase with brass handles, later I will put it in."

He poured tea. She looked at the rising vapor, dreamily asking herself why she couldn't be the one to arrange the cherry blossoms in that vase. Why not? Perhaps because a long time ago heaven or some spirit had forgotten some duty that should have been done?

Daydreams flit away very quickly. Miss Vui resumed the imperative mission she had come to accomplish: removing herself as a target for the man now sitting in front of her.

"On the coming of spring, I come to present my wishes, to congratulate the new arrival and to bless the new happiness. But I also have something to tell you. I'm not sure whether you will welcome this."

"Oh, I am not a district or provincial Party secretary, so you don't have to beat around the bush. We are neighbors, in a village, in the countryside; we can talk about anything."

"Then I wish to set a time to meet after the five days of the Tet holidays. When you have time, please stop by my house for a visit."

"That's fine; I also must go and present my New Year wishes. What goes around, comes around."

Miss Vui had not finished her tea before guests began noisily pouring onto the patio. She stood up to leave, but, before she left, she stopped by the kitchen to politely say good-bye to Miss Ngan and Mrs. Tu, where those two had retreated into their kingdom. In the kitchen, pots and pans were scattered all about. The aroma of coconut sticky rice mingled with that of honey-glazed fried chicken, making an overwhelmingly sweet fragrance.

That noon Miss Ngan said to her husband, "Hey, you handsome old stud, that big gal who came early this morning has a crush on you. Do you know it or just pretend not to?"

"How could I know it?"

"Right, why should you know everything? West, east, north, south—all four quarters and eight directions—there are plenty of people under heaven," Mrs. Tu interjected, clearly proud.

Mr. Quang looked at his wife, curious: "Why do you think that she has a crush on me?"

"Oh my god, really?"

She pouted. "The way she looks—as if she is high on the pipe. If it is not from a nightmare, then it comes from having a crush on a guy."

"Truly? Like what?" Mr. Quang asked again, and then laughed loudly. "Hey, little one, if I hadn't been destined to meet you, then there would be plenty like you wanting to enter my doors. I do not have to carry a gal as big as a temple guardian back home so that day and night I would have to work out to win a family competition."

"Exactly," said Mrs. Tu, quickly slipping in her opinion.

"For a year now, there have been so many who sent me betel nuts, bean cakes, and even Hai Duong black cakes. Thanks to your charm, I have had no time for a matchmaker because I was full of sticky rice and sweet soups."

Miss Ngan looked at her husband then at Mrs. Tu, shaking her jade earrings and giving a broad, satisfied smile: "OK, I give in to the two of you, uncle and niece! It's so clear that you are one pillar, one post."

Miss Vui walked home troubled, wondering if Mr. Quang was aware she had gone to Khoai Hamlet. Because his laugh had been both open-minded and playful, she could not divine the answer. The same with his look—it showed cheerfulness and forgiveness when he beamed; when it turned darker, reflecting a vague bitterness, she could not detect the cause. Besides, she knew that after the first day of New Year, people had flocked to Mr. Quang's house, the ideal location to enjoy traditional hospitality. His generosity as well as his classy style were beyond all competition. She visualized the huge patio, the spacious rooms furnished with first-class wooden furniture that he had bought from those brought low by the land-reform campaign; the tea sets displayed on the sideboard; the antique celadon plates and the vases with brass rims that no other village family could afford. She also brought to mind the muscular yet slim body in the silk outfit, the bright smile like pearls in a basket. She suddenly felt like a papier-mâché puppet that had collapsed, ripped apart by that man's sharp insightfulness.

"Maybe the old man knows everything. Not just maybe, but for sure he knows everything. From yesterday to today, he has had one guest after another. For sure someone has retold everything that happened under my roof."

She recalled the deep wrinkle on one side of his mouth when he had laughed and asked flippantly, "Am I a district or a provincial Party secretary?"

This last detail convinced her that Mr. Quang knew everything. Now she could only hope to benefit from his generosity.

Arriving home, Miss Vui was very tired; a degree of weariness she had never experienced as an adult. Letting herself down onto a chair, she reflectively looked at her feet, the fair pair of feet in the blue rubber. She wore shoes and socks all year round to preserve her white skin. But today, when it was cold, everyone could see that she was showing off by wearing rubber sandals. Someone as sophisticated as Mr. Quang would not say anything, but would know it full well. Oh, those white feet of hers. They took so much work to maintain but did nothing to change her physique.

"I am still a woman who wears shoe size forty-three. All my life these feet have found leftover shoes. These feet are permanently sentenced to project masculinity. These feet cannot be cut down or repaired. Nothing can hide them."

Tears welled up in her lashes, and for the first time in her life, she turned toward Mr. Do's image with resentment, saying, "Father, why did you make me? Giving me a life so that I have to endure so much pain and hardship."

Tears clouded her eyes, such that she could not see clearly the image of her father. Then, on the altar, Mr. Do also cried.

From about the tenth to the end of the first month, rain fell nonstop. People looked up to the sky and complained:

"How strange, it's only the first month and we already have this kind of rain."

"This temple-cleaning rain comes early, it means we won't even have rice porridge."

"Pray to heaven; don't let the people suffer anymore. We just had an epidemic of grasshoppers, then one of worms."

"You can't rely on what people can do for themselves but only pray to heaven."

"People's capacity has limits; heaven's rule is limitless. Our ancestors prayed to heaven for thousands of years, so today I, too, pray to heaven."

"OK, after you're done praying to heaven, we have to find a way to plant some potatoes. If we lose the rice harvest by bad luck, at least we will have something to feed our stomachs."

People collared each other to plant off-season potatoes. Afterward, they went together to harvest mushrooms. During this season, mushrooms grow like figs; with luck you could fill a sack with fourteen pounds or more. Fresh mushrooms stir-fried with pork fat alone is quite tasty. Wealthier families would add a few grams of beef marinated in garlic and thorny basil and stir-fry it with vermicelli for a divine dish. For families with small children, the women could chop fresh mushrooms and add pork and scallions to make meatballs to add to rice or wild cress soups. In addition, village families could dry mushrooms and sell them to urban restaurants, from the capital to towns in the lowlands as well as the highlands. That year's mushroom season marked the first time Miss Ngan went up into the woods with a team of women from Woodcutters' Hamlet. It was also the first opportunity for this nonlocal bride to participate in a community undertaking. First she went with Mrs. Tu because Mrs. Tu was her guardian angel and the person closest to her after her husband. And when her relationships with neighbors grew warm enough, or appeared to be warm enough, she went with the ladies and girls living next to her house. Each group included from

five to ten pickers. They brought along food and antidotes for poisonous
snakebites. Each year there was only one official season for harvesting
mushrooms, so every girl and woman in Woodcutters' Hamlet would go
into the woods.

Quy's wife and children also went but with another group, and both parties found ways to avoid each other. Inevitably, though, there were times
when the two groups would touch noses, and clashes between the adversar-
ies were unavoidable. Each time, people would recount the details openly
all over the village, as if they were reporting on national or international
soccer matches.

According to the general assessment of villagers, Quy's family held two
positions: first, they were local people and the saying "the old bullying the
new" reflected a custom that had been practiced for thousands of years. Second, they were more numerous, being three, while the opponent was by
herself. But even so, those advantages could not touch even a hair of the leg
of Mr. Quang's green-shirted gal. Villagers related in a very detailed manner how on the first encounter, Quy's wife cast a look filled with taunting
and disdain at Miss Ngan. Right away Miss Ngan turned her head and stared
squarely at her adversary, not backing off even an inch, completely over-
whelming her husband's daughter-in-law, who was bone-skinny, weighing
less than ninety pounds, and all wrinkled like an old shrew. When Quy's
two daughters spat at her once, immediately Miss Ngan spat back twice.
Those encounters were usually silently witnessed by other villagers; everyone looking the other way and feigning ignorance; nobody daring to ask for
a halt or to offer mediation. Once, though, Quy's youngest daughter stridently offered a challenge:

"Are you good enough to dare?"

Miss Ngan smiled drily and tilted her head:

"Don't you bank on that adage, 'two against one'; if you don't lose an eye,
you will be crippled. Me here, I'll go three against one. Are you up for it?"

That time, Quy's three family members swallowed their rage and kept
quiet, given the fact that this former painter could strike them left and right
with her husband's rod and smash them hard. And for sure, none of the
neighbors would side with them to strike back at the "green-shirted whore."
The patio of the "green-shirted whore" had become a club for the villagers,
and it was now many times more merry than when Mrs. Quang had been
alive. People ate and drank, talked merrily about this and that under the
roof of the house; now even if they had wanted to, they could not turn on,
and hit, one who had received them with such hospitality.

During that time, the village chairman was not to be seen. All administrative paperwork for the villagers was done by the assistant chairman. It was said that there was a twelve-day training class for the village chairman up in the district and following that, a ten-day training session for village Party secretaries. Quy was both village chairman and an assistant Party secretary. After his training with the government, he would stay on to attend the Party training course in place of the village Party secretary, who was at home with his wife and their new baby. Before he left, he had called on Miss Vui.

"Does my father know about your visit to Khoai Hamlet?"

"You think we can hide it from him?"

"Did he ask about anything?"

"You don't understand your father. He does not even care to touch that subject. Not even a word."

"My father is no dummy."

"You don't have to tell me."

"So, what did you two talk about?"

"How to raise cherry blossoms, pink and red ones. How to raise bees, change species, use pollen, or improve the hive. There is no end to his interests."

"Let me ask you this: Do you think the two of them were able to register at Khoai Hamlet? Because the teacher there is nephew to the village chairman."

"People guess they did; no one is sure. On one hand, the village chairman cannot tell on his nephew. Because if he openly registered Miss Ngan's marriage, it would be a slap in the face of his nephew. On the other hand . . ."

"What other hand?"

"I don't know."

The secretary dropped her sentence halfway. In her mind appeared all the houses that Mr. Quang had handily built. The Khoai Hamlet chairman could never otherwise get an opportunity like that; at the very least he got a new tile roof and bumpy and crooked walls were replaced with smooth brick, plastered with cement from top to bottom and painted a bright yellow. Additionally, borders filled with white gravel like in public office buildings ran along the foot of the walls; for people in Khoai Hamlet, this was very classy living. Thus, even though his house had only one story, it looked attractive, majestic like a peacock among a flock of thin-feathered and

scrawny ducks and chickens. Quy was impatient with Miss Vui's nonchalance. He gruntingly hardened his voice:

"What do you say? Why are you half closed, half open like that?"

"I don't know."

"If you don't know, who does? You are the only one from Woodcutters'
Hamlet to go all the way to Khoai Hamlet."

"That is why I am going to endure your father's blow. And you cannot
even cover me with your back," said Miss Vui, now mad and screaming
back, staring at Quy; after a heinous look passed between them, the two
allies quickly became enemies. After a second of stillness, the spinster suddenly stood up, shoved her chair, and moved her arms as if to chase chickens:

"I said I don't know. That means I don't know. If you want to know the
whole thing, go investigate in Khoai Hamlet."

Quy did not say another word; his face darkened like clouds before a
storm. He walked to the door while Miss Vui turned to go into the inner
room. Neither said good-bye.

Down in the district, Quy's stomach churned upside down as if he had
eaten raw opium. It was like a piece of cloth caught in a wheel, rage making
him dizzy and relentless. He could not see anything but "the green-shirted
whore." The green-shirted whore—someone who suddenly had fallen from
the sky or blown in from a strange land in a whirlwind.

"That green-shirted whore! My mortal enemy. That green-shirted
whore!"

Where had such animosity come from? Quy was unable to fathom his
own rage because he lacked both intelligence and courage; he did not understand why he was so furious over a woman from another area. It seems
that animosity is like a kind of alley cat or lost dog that suddenly runs
straight into the yard to howl bitterly and bark madly. Or a kind of bitter
seed that a wandering wind brings over and plants in people's hearts, where
it sprouts and grows leaves and clumps of roots faster than weeds do;
spreading, crawling deeply into each cell until the person is nothing more
than a corpse operated by animosity's pulsating wires. The usual words appear in his mind, the usual voice rings in Quy's ears:

"The green-shirted whore, the one who takes away the house that I have
the right to inherit; the one who shatters my family; who separates father
and children and who makes my mother bitter in heaven."

Thus Quy never dared admit to himself that this "green-shirted whore"
made him completely lose his balance each time they met, that even the first

time, his whole body felt paralyzed, like a crab within the grasp of a toad, its eight claws shriveled up waiting for death, or like a kind of mouse that is totally stiff from the hypnotizing eyes of a snake and losing all ability to defend itself. During that moment, his whole body went rigid like a dead one, then afterward burned as if on fire. Those conflicting and extreme feelings played out back and forth inside him. He felt that his destiny was now in the hands of another person, and the body wherein he resided was nothing more than the shell of a boat with its wheel and sails directed by the hands of an invisible and powerful wicked spirit. From that day on, every time he saw those shiny black eyes of hers, the blood in Quy's veins quickly came to a boil. The boiling blood flowed up to his face like a fire, making his skin burn and his head turn, and everything suddenly became vague and unclear as if seen through the smoke of rice hay burning in a dry paddy. He did not even catch that when he saw her, his throat suddenly choked, like someone eating yams and swallowing the wrong mealy type without a drink of water; and his breath suddenly became short as in one who climbs a high mountain but lacks endurance. On the first day of the New Year, to keep his calm when dealing with his father, Quy had to pinch his palm until it bruised with black blood. And when his father had chased him out along with his family, he still felt the half of his face that looked toward the kitchen frozen by the expectation of seeing the "green-shirted whore" once more. A hidden expectation, invisible and uncontrollable, made him walk like a soulless one imitating a zombie's stride. The familiar patio of his parents' house suddenly turned into an unstable desert. And the door frame of the kitchen turned into the opening of a mysterious cave holding the potential danger that a transcendental animal would appear with the ability to take one simultaneously to hell and to paradise. He had crossed that patio with a hurricane blowing in his soul. But Miss Ngan had stayed inside. His attack had completely failed, leaving no hope of consolation or salvation.

Now each day the antagonistic encounters between the "beautiful whore" and his wife and children grew more and more tense while his own rage escalated.

"That Vui has betrayed me; she does not want to help us anymore. That female elephant without a mate has fallen for my father. That old man eats up all the good fortune out there."

Painfully, Quy realized that he could never measure up to his father. And this feeling was eating away at him day and night. After one of these sessions of torturing himself over his shortcomings and shame, sometimes he would sit up and calculate the ages of his father and himself. This was the only way

Quy could find some consolation. Without question, he was still young, and youth is the strength of champions. Heaven had given him time and heaven gave him opportunity. There was an undeniable difference, a deep pit that could never be filled, between an old man of sixty-one and a man of forty.

"I cannot accept being pushed out to live empty-handed. The fight cannot end that simply. I still have ways to act. I don't need that big broad, I can still do things by myself."

This last thought preoccupied Quy during the entire three weeks of orientation from district and provincial cadres. When the sessions ended he skipped the celebration and headed straight to the city to the district construction complex. Villagers had told him that Mr. Quang was still in Woodcutters' Hamlet, helping his young wife to dry mushrooms. It was a lucky break, actually. At the complex, Quy avoided the area for contract workers because most of them had been recruited by Mr. Quang from the district. He lingered along the rows of food stands outside for a long while, to spot the house where the workers from Ha Tay—the gang of "Coolie Girls"—resided. Finding the cave of the "green-shirted whore," Quy went on sitting at a food stall until dark, then ambled over to the construction complex after buying two packs of cigarettes to give to the night watchman.

"I have a brother who works in Mr. Quang's masonry group. He wants to find out about a girl painter from Ha Tay. My uncle and aunt asked me to check her out to see if she behaves properly before deciding to go on with the marriage. For such an upright purpose, I hope, Comrade, you can help me."

"Comrade, do you have papers?"

"Right here."

Quy handed over the cover letter that came with the instructions to attend the district and provincial orientation sessions. The entrance guard bent over to read. Then he looked up at Quy and with a flattering manner said:

"Please do enter, Comrade. Be careful, part of the road is still slippery because by this time we have turned half the lights off and many parts of the public area are still muddy. May you find success."

"Thank you," Chairman Quy replied with satisfaction. The reserve of the entrance guard made him more confident and excited.

It took over half an hour to walk from the entrance to the complex where the workers lived. On his way over, Quy contemplated how he could chat up the painters, whom, by a bit of bad luck, he didn't know. Once

again, the imposing shadow of his father came down and completely enveloped him. Quy knew he had no skill in persuasion and lacked interpersonal
charm. Things that Mr. Quang could have said easily in minutes were difficult for him to think about, much less find words for. As the father enjoyed
all the gifts of destiny, the children had to endure bad luck.

"Heaven gives to one what it takes from the pocket of another!" Quy
thought to himself, certain of this truth.

The rooming house reserved for female workers was noisiest after dinner
when the women gathered around for games or chitchat. There was a nice
smell of roasted corn; those of middle age ate popcorn and candy while playing cards. The youngest ones put their faces close to a mirror to better trim
their eyebrows, the cheapest way to maintain their beauty. Quy had to stop
at the door because of the sharp sounds of cards turning, the loud laughter,
and the high-pitched and rather unpleasant voices, a new experience for him.
Women in Woodcutters' Hamlet never laughed loudly like that; they didn't
even scream and shout like men caught up in card games. As a matter of fact,
the women of Woodcutters' Hamlet were not even allowed to play cards.
They had too much to do around their houses and in their kitchens.

"No doubt, these are the whores in the construction trade; people are
not off the mark calling them just that. They are like female horses running
wild outside the paddock," Quy thought to himself, elated that the "green-
shirted whore" had come from this environment, from among these women
with no virtue. His father had no reason to be so proud of a young wife like
that. While Quy was lost in his thoughts, a young woman who had just finished trimming her brows stepped outside. Seeing the shadow of a man in
the dark, she hollered:

"Oh, oh! Who is it?"

"It's me . . . me . . ." Quy awkwardly replied: "I am a relative of Miss
Ngan . . . of Ha Tay . . . I am looking for her."

The young woman's shout drew all the others to the door. They surrounded Quy, some still chewing on popcorn, others still holding cards in
their hands, the whole group staring at him, making his legs turn weak as if
they wanted to run away from his body.

"Which Ngan? The one with stinky ears or Ngan Quang?"

"Ngan . . . of Ha Tay . . . of Khoai Hamlet. . ."

"Ah, that's Ngan Quang. She is married; you are a relative and you don't
know?"

"I was away in Ninh Binh for a few years . . ." Quy answered.

The women looked at him curiously from head to toe then one suspiciously inquired: "How are you and she related?"

"She and I . . . we are cousins."

"Cousins or siblings? Just tell us the truth and we will tell you how to find her."

Quy was quiet. His face was suddenly hot and the veins in both his temples pulsed. He did not know how to handle these bossy women, who started laughing, turning left and right as if they were watching a funny comedy. Their mischievous stares at his face were like needles pricking his numb skin. After a moment, he cleared his throat and made an effort to speak slowly and calmly:

"You girls tease too much; really, I only come to inquire."

The older woman with the mostly manly laugh, after wiping her tears with her sleeves and bunching her cards together, said to Quy, "OK, if you are sincere, we will tell you the truth. We're just having some fun. Whether you are cousins or lovers, it is none of our business. If you are sure it's Miss Ngan of Khoai Hamlet you are asking about, she has left the complex and gone with her husband to work on a farm. Her husband is Mr. Quang, the managing boss of city workers, not like us, hired hands from elsewhere. If you want more information, go to the A7 or A8 housing units. The workers there are all selected by Mr. Quang. They know more than we do."

"Thank you, ladies. So when did Ngan get married?"

"Sorry, nobody knows."

"I thought when workers get married, the site organization is supposed to assist them."

"There are workers and then there are workers. We are only dirty-feet country people hired temporarily and not government civil servants. We have no right to make demands. Besides, Ngan's family situation was rather complicated. They cannot be married normally like others."

A young woman next to her added, "I heard she was properly married."

Another interrupted immediately, "Properly married my foot!" And she turned to the other impatiently: "If she were married, why was she so hushed-up about it?"

"She did not invite us to have noodles with roasted pork and sweets on the day she departed."

"Leaving is one thing, proper marriage is another. You're so big yet so dumb!"

The older woman with the manly laugh scolded the girl. Then she bent over to look at the deck of cards in her hand. Quy knew it was time for him to leave. He nodded to bid farewell to all:

"I thank you, ladies."

"At your service . . ."

As soon as he turned his back the peals of laughter rose anew. In the bright door frame, girls passed back and forth, some in white shirts, some in purple, and some in pink.

"Some horsey whores out of the paddock," Quy almost blurted out loud, but was able to control himself.

His eyes stayed glued on the bright rectangular opening; something there pulled him like magnets pull iron. He did not understand. Standing awhile in the darkness, clandestinely looking at those girls, he suddenly felt as if he had just lost something, but could not find words to describe it. He tried to figure out what was going on in his heart but could not, asking himself, "What is this? What did I lose? What do I want?"

There was no answer.

Then all of a sudden a bitter anger could be felt in his throat and he said out loud:

"Just a gang of man-hungry whores; any guy who takes one will fall apart sooner or later. Definitely 'Coolie Girls.' A few months ago that other whore was parading just like this."

In the night, his voice resonated loudly, bouncing back from the rough and empty buildings. He panicked, fearing the people inside could hear him. He turned and ran. The path in the complex snaked around piles of sand and gravel, scattered heaps of bricks, piles of wooden timbers, of half-wet cement mixture covered with many layers of wet jute bags. In the dark with his soul in flight, Quy stepped on a stone and fell forward into cement that was still soft. The wet mixture covered his face, one shoulder, and an arm. After he was able to stand up, Quy started to realize his situation:

"How can I show my face in the streets like this? But before I get to the streets I have to pass the guard at the gate."

He put down his leather attaché case and looked inside to find some newspaper with which to wipe his smeared face. At that moment, the lye water entered one eye and irritated it. The stinging multiplied, a terrifying development. That physical pain crawled up to the top of his head and mixed with another pain, more devastating—a realization of his inability and humiliation. His tears flowed, mixing with the lye to make the whole area around his eyes and cheekbones burn as if they were cut. The pain caused him to sob and he found that he could not stop his crying. In front of

Quy's eyes there was only a vast space where black water would not stop falling. It seemed as if all the blood in his veins now became black, totally black, inky black. The dark blood spread all over his body. His whole body shook in an insane desire to cut someone's throat, to crack someone's skull, to stomp someone under his feet, to relieve the pain he was enduring. While wiping his slush-smeared face, Quy closed his eyes tightly to let tears wash out the lye that clung to his lashes. Then, in his mind, he carried out many scenarios for revenge: he would burn down the majestic house of the provincial Party secretary; he pointed a gun at a gathering crowd like a child who smashes an anthill; he sat on the head of the provincial Party secretary, the guy with a big belly who once scolded him as if he were a three-year-old child during a provincial conference of cadres; he pointed his penis and squirted urine on the guy's slippery and fat face; he spat on his beautiful gray hair always straight-parted; he climbed in the Volga car, took the driver's seat, and made the old man run behind the car to eat dust.

The final image seen by Quy's burning eyes was one of himself riding on the white chest of a naked woman. He kneads her breasts, pinches them, bites them. Her small nipples are almost severed, they are dangling and attached to the breasts only by tiny pieces of skin, looking like two lotus seeds. He bends over and pulls them off with his blackened fingers, with the delight of a child who has just pulled the legs off a grasshopper. Then he rapes her, rapes her with all the passion and hatred piled up over so many lives; he rapes as if it were the only way to exist on this earth. He rapes her insistently from moonrise until noon of the next day. He rapes her until her skin, fresh like congealed fat, fresh pink like eggshell, becomes floppy, discolored, and pale, and at the end transparent, like frog eggs. Beautiful like a rose, she is raped until she becomes weak, exhausted; until she barely breathes. When he stands up to button his trousers, she turns totally into mush. What is left on the ground is a pile of some shapeless and torn rags.

A pile of green rags.

The season for mushroom gathering passed as if it were a festival. People say that January is the month to have fun, but for Woodcutters' Hamlet, January is the month of hard work. On the seventh, eighth, fourteenth, and fifteenth, villagers go to the temple and don't think about money or food. Otherwise, every day is translated into money:

"Today, how much did you get?"

"Five point seven kilos."

"Only so-so."

"How so-so? It's less than Minh's family down in the lower section. They are also only one mother and one child like me and on average she gets seven point five kilos."

"Can't compare with them. Both mother and child are strong like bears. They climb mountains like the San Diu, San Chi people."

"You are doing pretty well, too, each day almost ten kilos."

"All three of us work without stopping for breath, with sweat running down our backs. At night the thighs are painful. But, thank goodness, it's worth it. This year's mushroom harvest is three times better than the cassava one."

"You are right, growing cassava brings nothing."

Miss Ngan was a newcomer, but she kept up with them all; even though she foraged by herself, every day she collected more or less four kilos of mushrooms. Mrs. Tu boasted to everyone:

"Auntie Ngan came to live in Woodcutters' Hamlet, yet without even warming her seat, she already works better than thousands of others."

"Thousands of others" here included the three members of Quy's family and the gaggle of know-nothing women whose tongues itched with envy: "With that little red-and-green blouse, how can she climb the mountain? No doubt, though, that she can climb on top of her husband's belly!"

Only Mr. Quang could confirm the point about "climbing on top of her husband's belly"; but climbing the mountain to pick mushrooms was common knowledge. Every day, the whole village weighed and counted. Each family had a notebook for record keeping; it was a competitive practice among families as well as a way to indirectly encourage effort; but oftentimes it only created jealousy. Thus, at the end of the mushroom season, those who pouted their lips and despised the girl "in the red-and-green shirt looking like a grasshopper" were all embarrassed and hung their heads in silence. The painter from the city had done better than all the local women. Many a time, children playing on village paths sang:

"Red blouse, green blouse.
It's a grasshopper.
From where, from where,
Did you fly here?"

Mr. Quang understood how those old lines were picked to point to someone. His wife never wore a red shirt—the only color she liked being green—but the phrase "red blouse, green blouse" was used by villagers to expose women who paid extreme attention to their looks. By her own labor, his wife had the right to refute any defamer. As Mrs. Tu said: "From now on, to anyone with a loud mouth saying bad things, Auntie Ngan only has to take a stick and throttle their throat . . ."

Of course, Mrs. Tu did not say this only once, but over and over, again and again, wherever hearing it would have the most effect. Such tough words were taken as a most official and most acceptable form of warning, the kind that women in Woodcutters' Village traditionally used to defend their honor.

By the end of the mushroom season, only a few families—those without any or with lots of children—continued to glean in the far corners of the woods; most villagers were now staying home to undertake the final, laborious task of drying and bagging the mushrooms. All over the village the fragrance of mushrooms made the air sweetly intoxicating. Smoke from the drying ovens rose, delicate and light, spreading up like an unraveling bundle of floating white threads, surrounded by mountain clouds striped white, and the large, infinite white steam rising from rocky cracks—all forming an exquisite painting, where the white colors mixed against the blue background of the expansive, enveloping air. The mushroom season gave safekeeping to many happy memories of working together as well as to hearts warmly indebted to heaven for its gifts.

In Mr. Quang's house, after the last bag of mushrooms had been filled and closed, the time came to prepare for celebrating the first anniversary of his wife's death. Two days before, cousins had erected tents to cover the patio and set up tables and chairs. Probably there would be more than one hundred trays, because guests would eat from noon to evening on three occasions, each time consuming thirty-five trays.

Always the first anniversary of a death is the most important one for those alive as well as for the deceased. For the deceased, it is the moment for the soul to rest eternally in peace, not wanting to return and disturb loved ones after having received in full measure incense and flowers as well as repayment of past love expended. For the living, it is the moment to display responsibility along with appreciation and love for the departed. It is the opportunity to openly show your attitude toward others and also to prove how strong your moral character is. Given the unusual circumstances in Mr. Quang's family, these expectations were bound to be examined very carefully from every point of view. The host was clearly aware of this challenge, so preparations were executed to perfection. The responsible party of course was Mr. Quang himself, but it was Mrs. Tu who actually took charge. Miss Ngan did no more than assist her, doing only what was assigned to her like anyone else among those neighbors who came to help. While she had always worn green blouses, from the lighter green of rice plants and banana shoots to the darker green of coconut palm leaves or moss, she wore black on the day of Mrs. Quang's death anniversary—a clear statement of mourning for the deceased. Next, her voice and speech became demure and light, no longer spontaneous and youthful as was her natural habit, nor as strident as when she had to counter her opponents. Therefore, the most censorious of villagers would have no pretext to open their mouths in criticism.

As for the physical preparations, Mr. Quang paid very close attention, for there is a saying: "Even in living spiritually, one must eat first."

Those who have life are not allowed to forget this basic principle. The banquet for Mrs. Quang on the first anniversary of her death had to be far more sumptuous than any previous wedding celebrations. Though there were plenty of neighbors ready at hand to help him, Mr. Quang still hired three chefs from the city, who brought along a van full of spices and ingredients as well as all sorts of cooking gadgets and supplies that one could not find in the countryside. The banquet thus became as elaborate as a fair or an exposition. Was it to be a five-course or a seven-course banquet? Because the host prepared the banquet according to urban preferences, with big bowls and large plates placed on tables, not on trays, it could not be measured by accustomed criteria. All bystanders agreed that no family had ever presented a banquet this classy and tasty, since the founding of the village. The banquet would consume one day; two days were required for preparation and one day afterward to clean up and distribute gifts and food to all the helpers, both relatives and neighbors.

In all, Mrs. Tu counted about 180 large service trays with each one holding enough food for six people. She said, "Even with this we won't have enough. To provide for all, we would need easily two hundred such trays."

"To provide for all" in her statement pointed to the absence of Quy's family and his connections. He performed his own anniversary celebration of the death, of course, because his father had disowned him. From the power point of view, he clearly lost out to his father. In his relations with relatives and neighbors and in the way he connected with others, he was far inferior. The only power he held came from the official stamp in his possession, an advantage that people knew was neither a potato nor a piece of dry clay used for forgeries. That was why anyone who might come to the village seeking an official seal for some document was forced to come to Quy's house to attend the "first anniversary" of Mrs. Quang's death there. They would have a gift in one hand and a carefully prepared envelope in the other. Besides those who needed a favor, Mr. Quang's in-laws on his son's side—the parents, uncles, and aunts of Quy's wife and her siblings—dared not set foot in Mr. Quang's house. The core group of village cadres, those who daily sat at the same table with the chairman, including the party secretary, the police chief, the women committee's head, the heads of the village clinic and stores, also had to come to the son's house. Miss Vui sought the upper hand—attending neither. The majority of the villagers attended both celebrations because they thought it their business to ignore the divisions and to be anywhere that the spirit of the dead was present. They were at the father's banquet at midday; in the afternoon either returning to their homes to rest or gathering somewhere to chitchat; and then at the son's celebration in the evening. "Since I was born I have never gone to an anniversary of the dead twice like this."

"Me neither."

"Has any family fallen into this kind of mess before?"

"How could they?"

"A long time ago, during my great-grandparents' era, there were two brothers who didn't get along and they would not see each other. On the father's and mother's death anniversaries, the older brother did his separately and the younger one his. Relatives and others had to attend both."

"That's the right way to go; whatever the conflict, they are still family. As for outsiders like us, our duty is to 'value harmony' above all."

The "scary" thing that made the people of Woodcutters' Hamlet suspicious and frightened, something they could not explain, would soon expose itself. Twelve days after the first anniversary of Mrs. Quang's death it rained hard. People could not go up to the woods or to the fields. Everyone sat at home to pan-fry green rice, cook sweet soups, or play cards. In the wee hours after the third day of rain Mr. Quang's horse could be heard neighing loudly for joy. Mr. Quang's kitchen was lit up by a fire: Miss Ngan was cooking plain white rice, then steamed sweet rice for Mr. Quang to take on the road. They ate together in the kitchen. Afterward, the green-bloused woman wrapped her arm around her husband's back and walked with him to the hedge where the carriage was waiting. The sight of the two with their arms around each other was an unfamiliar one in Woodcutters' Hamlet and it quite upset the neighbors. Miss Ngan did not know, but Mr. Quang surely realized that hidden behind doors, at the corners of walls, in bushes, many pairs of eyes discreetly watched them. Even though he knew how people thought, he still acted according to what the elders had taught:

At fifty, you know what Heaven plans for your destiny;
At sixty, act as you wish.

Stopping at the gate, he bent over to kiss Miss Ngan before he climbed into the carriage and whipped his horse into a trot. The sounds of the horse's hooves, fast and hard, broke the calm rural air. In the pace of a horse that had been kept enclosed because of the rain, one sensed an uncontrollable force mixed with the unsettling danger of a freedom that had endured repression. Miss Ngan stood there to look at the carriage until it disappeared in the row of trees.

Most of the people in Woodcutters' Hamlet stayed at home that morning. Many called out to one another to go up to work on the cassava fields, but in the end they dallied around home to launder piles of clothes, to rake up scattered hay, to clean and straighten up their rooms. Many things had mildewed after all the rain.

Close to noon, as the women were getting ready to cook lunch, loud footsteps were suddenly heard on the paths. First came small children; then curious teenagers; finally, villagers, men as well as women: all had dropped whatever they were doing to go gawk at "Miss Ngan being arrested." They were neither hesitant nor shy about loudly calling out to neighbors, from the patio of one house to another, from this hedge to that one:

"Hey, do you know yet? Mr. Quang's young wife has been arrested by the police. Let's go see what is going on."

"Hey, stop what you're doing. Did you hear the news? Mr. Quang's green-bloused girl has been grabbed by the neck!"

"What did she do to deserve this?"

"There was a warrant from the province saying she laundered money and specialized in scamming wealthy families."

"Scamming Mr. Quang? That's really insane. He doesn't cheat, so how could there be such a silly thing?"

"Everybody knows he's clever, is street smart, and has eaten with the best and worst. The important point is that he's frustrated. His wife was sick for almost a year and then she died almost a year ago; when has he touched anyone?"

"Don't believe that. He traveled widely and often; there was no lack of women."

"You think it's easy? Why don't you try it?"

"Why do I have to try? With my wife at home, anytime is a good time; I just lie down. I only worry that my strength isn't enough for the game."

"That is why you can easily exaggerate. Say your wife dies, I dare you to touch the clam of your neighbor. They would slash your throat with a knife."

"There is no lack of singles and widows."

"Single like Vui? I invite you to try! Widows like Huong with the chicken pox face and Lan with infected eyes down in the lower section? If you will play there, I will treat you to three feasts with wine and steamed rooster in rice. Well, will you do it?"

"Nah, not those women. I pass."

"That's life: either too high or too low. The ones you like: off limits. With a bed or a mat all ready, one cannot even stick it up. Therefore, frustration. Frustrated like that, when a girl as beautiful as a fairy appears and prepares a pipe, even the most saintly ones would succumb, no less Mr. Quang."

"I don't see a con artist behind her face."

"How can one know the inside of the dragonflies' tangled nest? Those women who turned regimes upside down or destroyed families were and are always beautiful. Average women like your wife or plain ones like mine never get to eat more than rice husks; even if they wanted to cheat, it wouldn't work."

"All you do is think of sullied things."

"I eat rice with salt and touch my knees, I tell the truth. I don't talk flowery or curvy."

"But I can't believe Mr. Quang was scammed. It's like the story of a rooster with four spurs or a horse with four manes."

"Mr. Quang is really smart, but if you look at his background he is only a muddy-footed country person like us. Being good at networking and having all his life made his living elsewhere makes him sharp, but no matter how sharp you are, there comes a time when you must bow your head to that thing hanging in the crotch of your pants. Do you know the line used to humble intellectuals?"

"What do you mean by 'intellectual'?"

"Those wearing long robes, with white feet and hands, the opposite of those like us who work with the hoe or cut wood, sporting short shirts and black feet. The saying goes: 'First come the intellectuals, and second the farmers.' Intellectuals are the literary ones, the gentlemen, all the high and low mandarins, and all those who administer the capital and the villages. Another saying: 'Even when filled with literature and learning, if you're obsessed with a cunt, you will still fall into big muddles.' "

"Really! I wouldn't know."

"If you don't, then you must listen before you talk. What makes you think and insist that Mr. Quang cannot be fooled? Life is not as simple as you think."

"Yeah, possibly."

The villagers poured out into the streets to look at the young wife of Mr. Quang: she was cuffed at the elbow and led by some twelve men of the village militia, with rifles on their shoulders and faces as stiff as stone, with the police chief at their head. This display of force was not impressive, because their enemy was only one young woman, with no weapon in her hands, and tears of fear pouring down a pale but still so beautiful face. Walking behind were more than thirty curious youngsters, a volunteer audience and very attentive. Once in a while, a soldier wanting to show off the power of the government would turn around and shout aimlessly:

"Disperse, you hooligans; disperse!"

"Go home and study; this is none of your business."

"Go, I tell you; go home!"

But all their threatening was like water off a duck's back. The group of curious children ran alongside the police all the way to the village office, making a parade without drum and horn. At the office, they ran this way and that when they got shooed away, but when the militia guards were inattentive, they again impudently sneaked back to watch "Miss Ngan of Mr. Quang" being tied up, a scene that had not taken place in Woodcutters' Hamlet since the land-reform years. They followed when she was led off to the cell in the village storehouse, a five-minute walk away. It was a small house, all closed up like a box with only one heavy wooden door locked by a huge key, with four walls of double brick and no opening or window for ventilation. Long ago that house had held tea for the governing mandarin. In the time of the land reform, the revolutionary government had used it to sequester powerful landowners. Once, more than ten people were detained in that closed space, eighteen square meters. One corner had ashes for a toilet. In the opposite corner was a broken vat holding drinking water for the prisoners. After the land-reform rectification campaign, there had been an order from the district to demolish the building, but the village chairman had second thoughts because it was still of some use. He had people come in to clean it up and paint it white to erase all the bitter memories and neutralize all the remaining stench. Since then the building had been used as a storehouse for the village, to keep tables, chairs, pots and pans, trays and basins, plates and bowls and teacups—all the objects needed for celebrations and receptions for official guests. The village literary group, operating only seasonally, also stored banners and signs there. In another corner, all mixed up, were drums without rim or with holes, two rusted horns, a guitar, two stringless mandolins, and a bunch of moth-eaten flags.

When the police chief turned the lock, a whole bunch of rats jumped out, crawling between his legs, rushing to get outside, and disappearing into the hedge on the side of the road. The air from this holding cell escaped like a breath smelling of rat urine and wetness and blew right in people's faces.

"You, sister, go in."

A militiaman led Miss Ngan up to the door and began to untie her. At that moment, everyone saw that her blouse had been torn at the armpit. When she had been arrested, she had resisted and a struggle had broken out between her and those who were trying to do their duty. She had cried quite a bit and looked exhausted and absentminded to the point where she could not even move her arm. The soldier who escorted her had to untie the rope until the very last knot:

"You, sister; go in there! Are you deaf just standing there?"

Miss Ngan still stood silent, as if she did not hear the order of her jailer; her eyes, filled with tears, were blurred with fear and fatigue.

"You heard the arrest warrant, why don't you comply?" the police chief shouted. After that, seeing that the suspect did not acknowledge his words, he raised his arms and pushed Miss Ngan's back: "Go inside!"

Pointing at the room scattered with stuff, cheap and moldy, he sharpened his voice: "Go in. Now your home is in there."

Miss Ngan was pushed in like she was a sack of rice husks The police chief pulled the door, locked it, and said to the air, "Sometime between now and night someone will bring you food."

After that he turned to his aides and gave an order: "Find someone to bring her a meal. Tomorrow, the government will decide."

Then, he took a few steps toward the curious children and other onlookers, casting a stern look at each one. They were as silent as a pile of unhusked rice, staring back at the human face of power. A fear long buried suddenly popped into life, turning them confused and reticent. Waiting for the silence to pass, the police chief cleared his voice like an actor preparing to step out on the stage. "Folks: please listen carefully. The duty of each citizen is to work; because work is glorious. Therefore I ask you all to resume your tasks. We should not let productivity go to waste. As for social evils, we, representatives of the government, have the duty to rectify them. First, I, individually and as village police chief, promise in front of you all that these matters will be diligently pursued. We will destroy to their roots all harmful dangers and so defend the life of our community as well as the happiness under each roof. OK; anything to say?"

The man stopped and looked at each one.

"Hurrah!" someone yelled, certainly one who needed to curry favor with the village authorities. But the rest of the crowd remained silent, perhaps because the just delivered official discourse had not yet worked its way through their brains. or because the sight of a woman tied at her elbows reminded them of what had happened to many during the great proletarian land-reform campaign. Past fears returned. The one who had shouted "Hurrah!" seeing no one else echoing his sentiment, quietly slunk to the back. The police chief saw that his heartfelt lecture had fallen flat. Embarrassed, he changed his tone and shouted:

"If no one has anything to add, then disperse!"

With that, he ran off immediately. His subordinates followed. The curious onlookers stood where they were, gazing in silence and apprehension at the huge lock. Some inquisitive children ran over and stared through the crack of the door, hoping to see the prisoner, but the heavy wooden doors were so tightly fitted that there was no opening even for a pin or a toothpick to squeeze through, so they grew disappointed and left.

As the sun reached its zenith for the day, even the most curious had to depart—they were hungry. They hurriedly cooked their meal, hurriedly called for their children, and hurriedly ate so that they could go to Mr. Quang's house and see what was happening. There the gates were open wide, but no one could go inside, because Mrs. Tu was sitting squarely on the steps to the central room. From there she could see each person as they crossed through the gate. She spoke up cheerfully as if nothing at all was going on in the world:

"Please do enter and enjoy some water, ladies and gentlemen. Today take the opportunity to rest in the shade. This sun fries the cassava fields like coal feeding a furnace. About an hour or so ago, I was weeding cassava and my nephew told me. The two of us ran back like mad to arrive just as Miss Ngan was being taken away. Quy's wife and kids were standing on the patio. They had been summoned to watch the house. I chased the bunch of them away."

"How could you dare do that?"

"Why couldn't I? Quy may be village chairman, but in the family, he must still look up to me. His mother gave him birth sick with seizures and all by myself I took care of him. When he was seven, he had a skin infection for an entire spring. I had to bend over to clean his scabs until my back hurt and my eyes got blurry. It was me again who boiled water with herbs to bathe him and rubbed on ointment to cure him. His mother was useless; she didn't know what to do. From the very day he got the chairman's position until now, he's been snotty and conceited. The public security militia and the village police chief would not dare take a step like this without an order from him. A son who ignores the face of his own father to this extent is not human."

"I heard it might be an order coming from the provincial authorities."

"If the province had ordered it, then the provincial police should have taken care of it, not those coolie faces from this village. Of those twelve militiamen who came to this house and tied up Auntie Ngan, six slipped out of their mother's pelvis to me, who cut their umbilical cords and washed them up. I will go to each of their houses, flap my skirt in their faces, and wait to see what they will dare do to me."

"They're just low-level flunkies. Big shots give the orders, they just bow and jump to it."

"During the land reform there was no lack of big shots who denounced their fathers, their mothers, spitting on their parents and calling them oppositionists and traitors. And what did they ever achieve?"

"True enough, they are not human; but when they are put to orders, how can they dare resist?"

"Gold is tested by fire. The good separate from the bad during hard times. When it's easy, everyone smiles; when times are happy, who doesn't clap their hands?"

Abruptly, Mrs. Tu ended the discussion and, in a flash, changed the subject:

"In this house we have very superior raw sugar. Anyone who wants chrysanthemum tea with very superior raw sugar, please ask."

"Marigolds, yes?"

"Sisters, you know nothing! You can't use marigolds for tea. If you do use them, you have to throw it out, it's too harsh. One uses only white mums or the tiny yellow ones, the kind that is small like a shirt button."

"Who can brew tea as well as you to know this!"

"In hot weather drinking chrysanthemum tea is refreshing. Well, please do have some."

The way Mrs. Tu had ended her disquisition and changed the subject was more clever than what a professional stage director would have done. The villagers wanted more details but dared not ask any further. The wall clock in Mr. Quang's house lazily struck three. The visitors bade their hostess farewell and left. No one had any desire to go up or down to their fields. They all went home, freshened up, turned blankets and mats to dry, trimmed branches in garden nooks, weeded—tedious tasks undertaken to run out the afternoon, as they waited for a chance to gather after dinner.

As the sun finally began to set the evening meals were set out. The villagers ate hastily, eager to get back outside. Without any plan or forewarning, everyone from all sections of the village began to gather in front of Secretary Vui's house—an entire crowd, some carrying flashlights, others storm lanterns, others oil torches that burned effusively. But the front gate of Miss Vui's house was locked and both the yard and the house were pitch dark.

"How strange! Where can she be?"

"Some saw her this morning in the store buying materials."

"Maybe she's at that joker Quy's house! When Miss Ngan was grabbed, there were only the police chief and the militiamen. We didn't see Quy at all."

"That Quy signed the order for the police chief to execute. He's hiding his face now; of course that's so. How can a firstborn son bring police to collar a stepmother like that? Only a gangster!"

"So why is Miss Vui hiding her face?"

"You forget that she took Quy's order to go to Khoai Hamlet to investigate Miss Ngan's background and there learned the story of Mr. Quang building a house for his wife's father? In this whole village she is the only one who went all the way into the dragonfly nest."

"Under the circumstances, if she's not the chairman's right hand, then she's his left hand."

"No wonder: I saw them gossip with each other. It looked really cozy."

"Oh well! Climb a ladder and ask heaven. People blow hot and cold. These two don't look each other in the face anymore."

"How do you know that?"

"The day I pulled some sacks of charcoal past Miss Vui's house, I saw Quy coming out, his face dark like a water buffalo's vagina. I ran across Miss Vui a couple of days later and when I pretended to inquire about Quy, her face ballooned like a cracked vat. She said, 'I don't know and I have nothing to do with Quy!' "

"Oh-oh! Are you in trouble now! How dare you compare the chairman's face with a water buffalo's vagina? If I squawk, you're finished."

"I dare you to tell. 'Dark like a water buffalo's . . .' is merely an old saying. I just use it as it is."

"I am just joshing you a little bit. I didn't expect them to split so fast."

"What do you expect? People hook up with people like a latch knot: you undo it, then tie it; tied, you undo it again—like a game. There is nothing permanent in life."

"But Quy is the chairman. How dare the committee secretary undercut her boss?"

"That, only heaven knows. OK, time to sleep. Tomorrow morning I have to weed cassava. If we don't do it tomorrow, in a few days the tubers will wither and there will be no crop. All the work of planting and tending will go to waste."

"Absolutely correct! True that cassava doesn't bring us money, but it does let us feed pigs and gives us flour for rainy days. We should not let the crop go to waste. Time to go."

Thus the villagers encouraged one another into leaving; they had wasted the whole day following this dramatic play. Whatever would happen tomorrow, would certainly happen in any event. For the villagers, the rows of cassava were waiting.

The flickering lights moved along the winding paths, past the gardens and the lines of hills. The chatting melted away into the spacious envelope of the mysterious night sky.

At the top of Lan Vu mountain, there was a sudden slash of fire that resembled a shooting star. Someone said, "Oh! A shooting star. Why is there a shooting star in the spring?"

"It's not a shooting star; it's a falling star. When a star falls, someone has just died."

"When an owl or hog bird cries, a person has gone on. But a falling star tells us that a saint's exile on earth has expired and he is returning to paradise."

"Is that true? Heaven and earth are hard to explain."

The next day, rain cascaded again. So plans to work up in the cassava fields were canceled. People sighed, because the more the rain fell, the thicker the grass grew, its roots plunging into the ground as fast as a wind blowing, in no time flat growing right through the cassava tubers. Cassava that has been invaded by grass either rots or has no taste, or tastes faintly bitter, useful only for feeding pigs, not people. They had to put on raincoats to go weed the fields; if they didn't do that, they would have to do some other chore. Not here the smooth white shirts of those who have the leisure to just enjoy their time on earth.

Past noon, the rain completely stopped just as lunch was finished. Sitting around to drink water and pick their teeth, the villagers heard the blowing of a car horn on the rural road. It was a rare noise that was heard only several times a year. At New Year, it had to be the sound of the drama troupe's vehicle. Once in a blue moon, it might be the sound of a medical team coming to inspect for serious diseases such as malaria, hepatitis, or diphtheria, or to check the gynecological health of women and young girls. For inhabitants of Woodcutters' Hamlet, the noise of a car was thus synonymous with a happy event. With it came the presence of a fairy with lipstick and blush, with brilliant skirt and shirt under the lights, or doctors in white lab coats. On that afternoon, when the horn was heard, everybody was puzzled and asked one another:

"How strange, what team is this?"

"Why didn't we get any word? Not from the chairman or the vice-chairman, or the women's secretary or the youth secretary."

"It can't be a birth-control campaign."

"That birth-eradication program has been stopped temporarily. I heard the central government is reevaluating it."

Villagers came out to see who it might be, just like those gawking city people who usually form a crowd to watch a demented and naked patient escaped from the hospital, showing her breasts and butt on the streets. On the sandy road running through the three sections of the hamlet, a jeep painted the color of harvest gold was inching along slowly like a beetle. The road was narrow and bumpy. The jeep went straight to the upper section, followed by twenty kids, all loudly screaming while running behind it. In the middle of the upper section, the driver stuck his head out and asked those standing along the side of the road, "Will you please tell me where is Chairman Quy's house?"

So it was discovered that it was a police vehicle, full of policemen. A quick bolt spread fast among the crowd along the road:

"The police are coming to Chairman Quy's house!"

This is the first time they had seen a police car since the land reform.

"For sure the car comes to take Miss Ngan to the provincial capital."

"Correct! Only the province has the authority to sit in judgment. It's not land-reform time, when villages could set up courts. Whoever said yesterday that village officials could investigate her is wrong."

"The village police chief—who else?"

"If he said that, then it was a lie. If villages could investigate and sentence, then heads would roll and blood would flow; later on, rectification of errors over and over again."

"Why didn't you speak up yesterday? I saw you in front of the storehouse where they shut in Miss Ngan."

"I eat when invited; I speak when asked. Obviously, to speak to the air under heaven is for the demented."

"OK, be quiet and watch! They have arrived."

The villagers crowded the way to Quy's house. About twenty minutes later, the team of provincial police returned with Chairman Quy. But the chairman had not one bit of the bearing of someone who holds power. Those standing farther away saw him walk with his head bowed, his face emptied of blood. At the door of the jeep, he climbed up and slid inside, sitting all the way in the corner so that he did not have to see anyone and no one could see or bother him. Those standing close by could see clearly the sweat dripping from his forehead and temples down his long and pointy face all the way to his chin. They also could see clearly his hands shaking madly and his lips quivering white. These strange sights made the crowd hold their breath; their instinct told them that something important was about to happen. When the jeep turned around to approach the storehouse, villagers stepped back to both sides of the road, no one saying a word. When the car then moved forward, they silently followed it, walking as if in a funeral procession rather than as a gaggle of onlookers looking to satisfy their unhealthy curiosity.

The jeep stopped in front of the storehouse and the team of provincial police jumped down first; then it was Quy's turn. He stepped up to open the lock, but he struggled and could not. One of the provincial policemen snatched the key and opened it himself. Two others entered the temporary prison and a minute later emerged with Miss Ngan, her face full of red pimples from mosquito bites. The last officer, probably the leader of the team, turned to ask Quy:

"Have anything else to say?"

There was no reply.

The policeman who had opened the storehouse door now pulled

handcuffs out of his pocket, opened them, and handed them over to Quy, saying not a word more. Quy, silent like a corpse, put both hands in the cuffs before the shocked bewilderment of all the witnesses, including Miss Ngan.

The policeman looked at the victim who had just been released:

"Do you need us to take you home?"

"What?" Miss Ngan replied mechanically, as if she had not understood what had been said.

The policeman repeated in a softer tone: "Can you go back to your family on your own, or do you want us to take you there?"

"Ah, no . . . I can . . . Thank you all."

"Then, good-bye to you and we wish you a speedy return to your normal life."

He spoke in a calm manner but could not hide the natural attraction that any man would feel when standing before a beautiful woman.

"OK, I bid you all farewell and thank you all again," Miss Ngan replied. Her liveliness began to return.

The police team put Quy in the jeep and took off. The people of Wood-cutters' Hamlet stood dumbfounded, staring at the vehicle as it left their village. They just stood like that until the dust totally settled and the noise of the motor could no longer be heard. Then some woman suddenly said:

"The poor young miss, her face is covered by mosquito bites just like dry oatmeal covers the bottom of a bowl. From only one night. During the land reform, my sister was imprisoned for several months."

"Talk about the land reform: then people turned into monsters and monsters took on human shapes."

That very night Mr. Quang returned.

His closest neighbors heard the young bride screaming like a kid being whipped when she opened the gate: "Holy God! Where did you go to let your son torment me like this? What did I do wrong to endure this, humiliated like a whore? Only because of my love for you, for being your wife, did I have to go through this."

No one heard Mr. Quang's voice, even those with keen hearing. The neighbors listened and waited but there was nothing, so they reluctantly went to bed, their hearts unsettled with anxiety after two turmoil-filled days.

After midnight, the air was cold and full of fog. From the top of Lan Vu mountain, the dew spread down to the lower peaks and from there down the slopes to the hills and the gardens; taking a leisurely stroll over tea stands, cassava fields, and, last, the rice fields. In the white net of thick dew sleep intensified. The crow of a rooster also sounded reluctant, as if it, too, were sleepy. And night shadows in the heart of the woods often set off strange dreams. Around three in the morning, a lad named Hoa in the middle section threw off his blanket and ran all over his house, shrieking like a slaughtered pig. His parents had to hold down his arms and legs and pour warm ginger water on him to wake him out of his dream. After opening his eyes, Hoa cried and asked that lights be lit from the house to the garden, then he slept sitting in a chair. Each time the lights went off, he opened his eyes wide and screamed. The family had to leave the lights on all night long.

The young boy slept until noon. When the sun was shining brightly at high noon, he then told of his terrifying dream. In his dream, he saw a gigantic boa that had scales like a fish, claws like a dragon, a slit tail like a centipede, a long tongue like a watchdog, and a crest like a parakeet. The huge thing rose up from a deep hole and sprawled along the crest of Truc Mountain. When it opened its mouth, a male water buffalo could fall inside. The mouth was bright red like blood, while the whole body was black with horizontal cobalt and yellow stripes. Its scales were hard as if made of coal, and shaped like a gecko's. The giant creature rolled from the crest of Truc to those of the green and yellow Cuom mountains. When it crawled, its tail swished from side to side and flattened forest trees as if they had been blown over by a storm. Across the mountain ranges, the creature dashed to the top of Lan Vu's peak. Halfway, it suddenly stopped and roared with agony. Its huge belly undulated like waves on the ocean; one could see clearly the thrusts of a small animal kicking and struggling inside. Agonized, the mother creature was writhing on the ground, her eyes bulging as if they would pop out of their sockets, her nostrils blowing out hot breath, her mouth spitting out bursts of loud roaring like that of thunder. After some time, her belly slowly cracked open; from the crack appeared a head identical to that of the mother—same shape, same color—as well as with the fierce look of the bulging eyes and the bright red and huge crest like that of the parakeet. This second head grew fast, similar to a rubber ball being inflated. In an instant it had grown as big as the mother's head. After growing to a length equal to that of its mother, the head of the second monster let loose a terrifying roar, then struck the head of the mother a determined blow that injured her. From that wound, blood squirted up—like tree sap but purple like plum juice. The mother monster stretched her neck to roar, and the battle began. Young Hoa stood at the foot of Lan Vu Mountain, right where he usually played badminton with his friends. The two monsters tore each other apart at the heads; he was terrified that their huge claws would destroy the mountainside on which he was no bigger than a fox. He wanted to run but couldn't. Around the mountains suddenly appeared walls woven from sharp thorns and vines. First the bushes were knee high. But in an instant, these thorny plants grew in a rush, close to the height of an adult, branches intertwining, weaving one into another. At the same moment, vines from the corners of the dirt suddenly sprouted into thousands and thousands of hairy tubes, gripping tightly to the thorny walls, making this rampart thick and dense, so that even a cat couldn't crawl through. Young Hoa looked carefully and he suddenly realized that on all four sides there were plenty of poisonous thorns and leaves; the kind of thorns whose prick will turn skin to pus, the kind of leaves that will make you will break out in hives like smallpox if you touch it. Desperate, he called out for his father and mother. No one heard his cries for help. A more terrifying thing was that his belly had started to undulate, too. He looked down, horrified to see that it was moving up and down, like curling waves, totally like the belly of the monster. He visualized his belly splitting in two and, from there, a head that looked just like his appearing, with the same split chin, same slanted eyes and turned-up nose, and also with the name Hoa. And the second Hoa would turn around and bite his neck just like the monster on the mountain and a battle would eventually commence. He was scared out of his wits, running around frantically, trying to escape. Thus, in that fit of terror, he became a sleepwalker.

From that night, young Hoa dared not sleep with his siblings, even though he was the oldest at eleven years of age. His parents were compelled to let him sleep with them, in the middle. Moreover, all night, they had to leave a lamp on in the corner of the room. The neighbors were curious about the conjugal arrangement and the two of them acknowledged that on nights when they felt passionate, they would wait for Hoa to fall sound asleep, turn up the light to make the room real bright, then quietly take their blanket to another room to carry out the insurrection.

Rural people still looked upon dreams as omens from heaven and earth, or as threats from evil spirits. Some dreams foretell good happenings, others bad ones. Often, after bad dreams, heavenly disasters or earthly tragedies do occur. And so those on earth must endure sufferings for long stretches. Whether it was only a coincidence or a divine intervention to teach humans, the dream where parent and child did battle occurred right after Mr. Quang's family drama. Thus all over the three sections, inhabitants of Woodcutters' Hamlet were perplexed day and night. Perhaps only just before sleep could one lie down quietly with hands on forehead to ponder life; and from sunrise until dark, villagers discussed and passionately argued over this episode. In the evenings, they would gather by threes and fives, but not on the patio of Mr. Quang's house, nor now at Miss Vui's—those considered the main characters in the "current drama."

Two days later, the village Party committee met under the leadership of the hamlet secretary. Chairman Quy was sitting in the provincial jail charged with abuse of power and imprisonment of an innocent person.

It was 100 percent certain that Quy would lose all Party and government positions, and be expelled. Thus the Party section for Woodcutters' Hamlet had to meet to quickly elect a new chairman and assistant secretary, decisions that would be ratified by the villagers without dissent. In that meeting, the hamlet secretary declared clearly that the committee secretary, Nguyen Thi Vui, had played an outstanding role in preserving the Party's moral prestige. Thanks to the firm spirit of Comrade Vui, who had acted quickly when village authorities had abused their powers and intimidated an innocent citizen, the district commissar had been able to thwart what might have been a very regrettable incident. For that, the district commissar highly respected the spirit of responsibility and the management skills of Committee Secretary Vui, a most outstanding Party member.

With so many words of praise from the most powerful person in the entire district, naturally Miss Vui instantly became village chairman and assistant Party secretary, to the enthusiastic clapping and heartfelt approval of Party members and assembled voters. After her induction into office, there was a fabulous celebration. Hundreds of banquet trays were scattered around the meetinghouse as well as on the patio; the aroma of wine mingled with that of roasted pig and beef, making the atmosphere happy and intoxicating and letting people forget the reason for their celebration. They didn't even notice the absence of Mr. Quang, Miss Ngan, and Mrs. Tu during the two entire days of meeting and eating. While everybody was enjoying clinking cups with peers, friends, and elders, nobody was foolish enough to broach sensitive subjects that could easily hurt people's feelings and give them headaches. But no matter how enjoyable, every party must come to an end.

The people of Woodcutters' Hamlet had ample reasons to turn their heads and look at Village Chairman Miss Vui with critical eyes after she had received the transfer of power and sat with ease on the chair where Quy had sat before. By that time, those dishes of roast pig, grilled beef in lemon grass and lard, had had time to turn into shit. Therefore, within only some five to seven days, all over the cassava beds, on the tea slopes, people brought up the story of the "Old Maid Dragon" for critical commentary.

According to the accepted account, Quy had stolen from the home of a cousin on his mother's side an arrest warrant for a prostitute. This cousin was an assistant investigator with the provincial police. It was an old order left in a stack of documents waiting to be filed away. Such saved materials, if not used in appeals or in subsequent investigations, are to be destroyed after twenty-five years. Not at all suspecting his cousin the village chairman, the assistant investigator let Quy sit in his office while he went out to buy beer and snacks to share with his guest. After stealing the order, Quy used a solvent to erase the name of the old defendant and the old date, and replaced them with Miss Ngan's name and an appropriate new date. Thus, when he read the order sealed by the provincial police and signed by a cadre in the office of investigation, the head of the village police suspected nothing. Besides, because they were colleagues who had worked with each other for many years, he was ready with enthusiasm to do whatever Quy asked. That is also why an entire squad of militiamen poured into Mr. Quang's house to "apprehend one who deceives men and undermines wholesome customs, Ngan by name." On the very afternoon of the arrest, Miss Vui had ridden her bike immediately to go tell Mr. Quang. What followed then fell out openly before everyone's eyes, leaving no need for background explanations.

Rural folk really despise those who undertake clever and dangerous maneuvers, even though they themselves always use little tricks here and there to advance their interests. To them, those who plot cleverly always constitute a dark force that can destroy not only an individual but even an entire family; sometime a hamlet, a village. Those with such dangerous abilities bring to mind old-time sorcerers, who once used magic charms to pull people into blind passions of love, hate, revenge, and stupid acts that drain away one's humanity. If such a sorcerer was female, then fear and hatred increased geometrically because women were created each with two breasts and two buttocks: the breasts to feed children; the buttocks to make husbands happy. A woman should never act contrary to the nature heaven has bestowed upon her. A woman who in the past presumed to sit on the chair of a village or hamlet chairman was an unpleasant sight to see. But when such authority was seized through a betrayal, such transfer of power would meet with the utmost contempt, according to the old rule: "An honor that thousands see fit to spit on."

Thus if Miss Vui were smart enough, she would have guessed exactly how people would criticize her behind her back. But with fortune in charge, all intelligence has limits, and so Mr. Do's daughter became completely intoxicated with the happiness belonging to someone in power, someone who was all caught up in building a nest, rallying allies, and building up defenses around the chair that comes with being chairman. Those tasks diverted her time and attention away from understanding the level of criticism about her among the villagers, those who would dig up every mystery in her heart like the investigator who exhumes the corpse in some unexplained death. The investigation had the feel of "people's justice," as all the relevant facts had the character of belonging to the "masses" rather than to some single storyteller. Young and old, big and small, boys and girls, all took part, even though the ones who could officially jump into the discussion were those with formal positions:

"Do you all agree that we are old and stupid? The whole flock, everyone from the upper section down to the lower one, gathers around to listen to the story of Mr. and Mrs. Quang, like a bunch of kids who gather to watch shadow boxing without any idea of why they love it so enthusiastically."

"Who knows? I thought because of recent wealth, Chairman Vui likes to put on airs, act like patronizing everyone, thus competing with Mr. Quang."

"Sure, sure . . . That one cannot be generous or open-minded. The other day my grandchild had the fever with caked tongue. Out of honey, we went to ask her for some. She gave only two spoonfuls."

"You lie. . . . Who would dare put out a hand to a neighbor with only two spoonfuls of honey?"

"The little cup where I keep the honey is still in our cupboard; come over later and look for yourself."

"That's the truth. She suddenly became so generous only because she wanted to be on warm terms with her neighbors, but she also wanted to use gossip to destroy her opponent. It is not that she sacrificed her time and money for nothing, renting a car and going all the way to Khoai Hamlet to investigate the happenings of another woman. A stable person would be crazy to do that."

"At that time I simply thought she had followed Quy's orders."

"An order from the chairman is only that effective if your heart gives it a push."

"How true. Now I remember; I may have had eyes but I was blind. I am the very one that stood close to her during Mrs. Quang's funeral. I saw her lighting incense three times and doing all three bows."

"To bow low three times so that the poor dead soul would agree to her stepping into the conjugal bed with the widowed husband."

"Neighbors and relatives should bow only once; that's proper etiquette."

"It was so obvious but nobody noticed; her tactics were most discreet."

"Not so discreet really; we were blinded by a ghost so we saw nothing. I guess that Mr. Do is at work helping his beloved daughter find a husband to give him some grandchildren perhaps. She's over thirty; there's no time to wait."

"No ghost closed our eyes. We're just oblivious. This spinster girl has a strategy. After thinking about it, I realized that it is right on the button that she chose Mr. Quang as her target. In this village, he has wealth and guts, has lived the most, been out in the world for how many years now? Who here beside him would dare to touch her?"

"That's exactly it! But being clever can't overthrow heaven's plans. Without heaven's OK, a hundred thousand strategies will all come to naught. Because of this they say: 'Luck is better than brains.'"

"The delicious reward fell from her mouth, so, in revenge, she followed Quy. She thought she would surely find a place on Mrs. Quang's classy bed. There was the chance to form a large estate; he is half a pound, she is eight ounces—no big difference between them. She didn't expect some faraway woman to fly in like a swallow to land right on the branch of her dream lover. That destroyed everything."

"This time she miscalculated. A cultured gentleman pays no attention to his wife's possessions. Only gold diggers think of the purse. 'He is the captain, she is the ship.' A real gentleman chooses beauty and virtue."

"Exactly. Mr. Quang has too much money to look for a woman with means. He carries one as beautiful as a fairy, young and fresh, with fragrant skin. To be sixty and have it like that, to die there are no regrets."

"To sum up, the spinster is not that clever."

"Don't rush to judgment. Miscalculating, but still supple with maneuvers. Her head holds more strategies than do all of our empty heads put together. I challenge you all to shift position as she did. She was on Quy's side but with a quick leap she becomes Mr. Quang's ally. People say 'troubled waters protect the heron.' So it is."

"We must admit this woman is a terror. Mr. Quang is as secretive as a sphinx but she discovered that his influence with the district, the province, was as strong as split bamboo. She must have an ear on the inside: a relative sitting with those in authority. Never underestimate a woman who can run from here to there, who can leave the east for the west, as fast as a flip of the hand."

"Unable to hold Mr. Quang's tuber, she got her hands on the seal of the village committee instead. Now she is in the first ranks of those in power, the boss of over two thousand people in Woodcutters' Hamlet. So, didn't she win big?"

"A huge victory for sure; nobody denies that. But I ask you all: Her head is full of strategies but does she have any gravel inside her turtle?"

"Yes; yes, she has. Pay attention and listen when she walks by: a row of gravel on each hip rattles away."

"You're dead now! Tonight I will tell your wife that you always tilt your head to listen to Vui's bell ringing. She will pull your ears for sure."

"Oh well! Telling my wife would be useless. She knows that on seeing that old maid my pair would wilt and the hour hand would right away swing to the number six."

"Poor baby, with great power and high position, with a large house and patio, yet her turtle is all moldy. Perhaps if we hit it now, it would sound like a temple's wooden gong."

"Insolent! How dare you compare one with the other? It's out of order; the elders will slap you and give you a swollen mouth."

"Sorry, I beg you all to forgive, I am silly and my tongue slips."

"Be quiet! I have a challenge for you men, also for the ladies if you wish to participate. I ask you: From now on, what trees will Chairman Vui plant?"

"Why do you ask such a crazy question? Who sits in her brain to know?"

"But I know; what will you give me for telling you?"

"Agreed: drinks with fried catfish."

"That's too puny, I won't do it."

"A second round of drinks, this time with a young chicken steamed with salt and lime leaves."

"Still not enough."

"Add a third round with entrails over thin rice noodles, seasoned with shrimp paste and basil."

"I accept! Now, open your ears and listen. From now on, our village chairwoman will pull up all the trees in her yard and replace them with only banana trees. A kind of banana tree propagated in Hung Yen, also called the 'propagating' banana, or the 'show off' banana with each fruit weighing a pound or more, bigger than the pestle housewives use to pound up crabs."

The women immediately screamed as if they had been bitten by a centipede or doused with boiling water:

"You scoundrel!"

"You dirty old man!"

"You devil; heaven will hit you hard!"

Then they laughed furiously, madly, with shrieking noises like those of the insane; laughing so hard they started to choke and cough. Thus, these kinds of discussions always climax with such a strange and obscene metaphor, where the imagination of rural folk is used to the maximum to gather up all the burdens hidden in their souls and then shoot a machine-gun belt of bullets at someone being pilloried before an ancient and permanent court of justice.

Such half-serious, half-joking stories about the powerful woman were in fact a way to obtain revenge; an unconscious way, but one as old as the earth. When emotions bring turmoil to a community, people must find a way to restore balance, to reinforce faith in themselves, and, in the end, to prepare themselves for the future. The most convenient course is to find an object to offer to a formless deity, a divine and most powerful one with enough magic power to melt away all ills. In the past, people took the most beautiful girls in a region and threw them into the deep sea to satisfy the king of the sea dragons, who would have a name like Royal Green Dragon, White Dragon, or Black Dragon, depending on which part of the sea received the offering. Nowadays, however, people living in Woodcutters' Hamlet could not throw their own daughters into deep ravines as offerings to formless gods. So they sacrificed at the burning stake of public opinion the one who had the most vulnerable reputation. In this situation, no one was more deserving than the newly appointed village chair, Nguyen Thi Vui. The nightmare of a child in the middle section had spawned a storm all over the region, but mostly over the people of this one village—a gigantic monster fighting with its own child, which had just come out of its womb. Wasn't that an image of what is most terrifying and feared in life: no good fortune, no virtue, and no moral conscience?

Every family—classy or humble, rich or poor—counts on the relationships between generations as the most reliable protection for their lineage. Maternal love, like paternal concern, has always been regarded as humanity's most sacred emotion. Right after birth, a child hears this lullaby:

A father's work is like the Taishan mountain;
A mother's devotion is like water from a spring.

This cradle song will be repeated over and over throughout childhood. And when the child becomes a young man or woman, on their wedding day—the most auspicious day of their life—he or she must kneel before the altar to the ancestors and honor those who gave it life and nurture. This ritual demonstrates appropriate respect and gratitude; this ritual gives a warrant to filial piety.

Circumstances change. Weddings under the revolutionary authority have no betel nuts, firecrackers, or silk scarves. Enamored, boys and girls just glance at each other the night before; the next morning they make an announcement to the whole community, to the Party, to various groups, or to the women's committee of the village. Parents now have no opportunity to say anything, the children having already received an official seal on their marriage license. As soon as the ink dries, all the groups stand up to make announcements and speeches, advising the newlyweds to be unified, to be conscientious in their work, to execute all the duties to the nation and the family. After that, it's peanut brittle candy with green tea in lieu of large or small wedding banquets; hand clapping replaces red firecrackers and silk scarves. People must bend their heads before power and its new protocols. But revenge hides in the silent shadows. And when the time comes, scores are settled.

Thus, the nightmare of the young child in the middle section poured a tempest of fear and anger into the villagers' souls. Except for the demented, no one would want a child to turn around and put a knife in their parents' back. Those who are parents usually sacrifice without reservation so that their children can benefit from food and education, and can become "somebody" better than themselves. We have been taught for many generations that only a mother pig would roll over on her piglets; only a bitch would fight over her chow with her puppies; and that humans cannot behave in such ways. It is parental sacrifices like that that entitle them to demand filial piety from their children. This self-evident logic, shaped by natural laws, always succumbs to a destructive reality. The dream of moral reciprocity is indeed large like the sea, but the reality of human love, of selflessness, is like a meandering river flowing between low and narrow dikes. For years, life proceeds as the water flows between the two banks of hope and deception, of trust and mistrust, of love and resentment. Similar to the earth turning around the sun: an endless motion, a nonstop rotation until the day when the cosmos becomes some insane spirit's pile of ashes in its last turn. Trapped by the law of this tireless rotation, we must salvage our self-confidence in the moments of greatest danger. Without faith—even insane faith—how can there be life? Rural people need to protect their homes; they need to trust that their children will become aware of their sacrifices, that they will become filial ones meriting all the hardship, the weariness, and the devoted sacrifices of so many years. Parents need a warranty that, one day, when they lie in the coffin, the children who follow behind the hearse will shed tears of genuine love and not cry just because they have to perform for the sake of the neighbors or just because they want to pay back the expenses of the household and the patio and the money left for them. Parents need to be compensated with fairness, just as love should be compensated by love.

At its start, the drama of Mr. Quang's family was only an entertaining opera, but slowly it evolved into a clandestine tragedy, more exciting by the minute, resonating with the perpetual worries simmering behind the doors of so many households. When the "mother fighting child" nightmare of young Hoa in the middle section happened, the gnawing and hidden anxieties in people's souls suddenly burst over the community like a storm, and people changed the name of the "mother fighting child" nightmare into that of "father-son blood fight" to better reflect reality.

The "father-son blood fight" had mysterious elements that could not be explained. The village police chief himself, after being questioned for "acting in a sloppy, mechanical manner, not clear minded and after careful investigation," recounted that when he came to Mr. Quang's house to read the order and ask that Miss Ngan demonstrate the legality of her relationship with Mr. Quang, the young wife had spoken loudly:

"We are legally married. I will show you the marriage license."

Her voice had been decisive. Then she had hurriedly gone into an inner room and unlocked the imposing, three-compartment cabinet made from heavy wood to look for the paper. Her confidence had disturbed the police chief, because if her marriage was indeed legitimate then the order to arrest Miss Ngan as a prostitute would be false. In such a situation, he would be charged with the crime of being accessory to a fraud and harassment of a citizen. His heart had started to pound. But the more Miss Ngan searched, the more desperate she became. In the end the frightened woman cried out:

"Who has stolen my marriage license? I swear with you all that we had registered properly in Khoai Hamlet; my own uncle, the village chairman, did the paperwork." But then all her screaming and crying were useless because the police chief and his militiamen posse believed that their order to act was indeed legitimate, and, if it was a legitimate order, they had to punish an "immoral woman who undermined society's wholesome moral values."

The strange thing was that once the district reported to the provincial police, the latter had immediately dispatched agents to release Miss Ngan from detention. At that same moment Mr. Quang had brought their marriage license back to his young wife. It was he himself who had taken it and not some unknown burglar. No one dared ask about these unusual developments but it was the subject of universal gossip. Some advised that Mr. Quang had guessed events beforehand and lured his son into a trap. Others believed that Mr. Quang had taken the marriage license from fear that his son would steal it and destroy it. The imposing cabinet was an heirloom from prior generations, and as the firstborn son Quy had the right to keep a key. The father's carefulness had unintentionally coincided with the bitter son's effort to humiliate his stepmother, who was the same age as his own daughter. Some people thought that what had happened had been crafted by some devil or divine spirit, as no right-minded child would have behaved as Quy had. Furthermore, because no ordinary father would have harmed his own son. That this had occurred is what people in the past would have called a "witches' brew" and this family must have had connections with the world of spirits, for that was how such unusual things happened. The mother had been captured by a hungry ghost; now the son had been blinded by a devil. All acted insanely as if they were manipulated by a wicked witch, or an invisible demon. They were moving corpses, or wooden puppets under strings manipulated by a world of ghosts.

There was no lack of theories or shortage of analysis. The war of chattering mouths dragged on for days, for months. But everyone shared one sentiment: fear of a devastating reality, a reality that shook the hearts of all parents. They tried to find the truth.

One day, Mr. Quang's younger brother mustered enough courage to ask him:

"How long will Quy be incarcerated after the judgment?"

"Four years and six months."

"So now Vui sits firmly in his chair."

"That is up to the authorities, not us."

"But he is your son and my nephew."

"Everybody knows that."

"Why don't you find a way to reduce his sentence?"

"What do you mean?"

"What I want to say is that, with arms as long as yours, you can keep him in the seat of village chairman."

"You regret the loss? I am his natural father and look how he harassed me; how would he treat those outside the family?"

The brother dared say no more.

A few days later, he came to Quy's house and scolded his niece-in-law:

"Your husband is more stupid than a dog. He doesn't even know when he is lucky. Since you two married, the big house, all of it, was yours thanks to his father. You two had children but all their food and their clothes and shoes came from their grandfather. Even the village chairmanship: How could your husband have got that without him? With him, not only your whole brood but all our relatives benefited from the shadow of a tall tree. Your mother-in-law passed away; whomever he then married was his own business. How was it your business to stir things up? You're a pig-headed bunch. Now your husband is in prison; you, the wife, are at home. Worrying over two meals a day will use up all your spirit and stretch your neck out like that of a goose. Do you think this is happiness?"

This awakened thoughtfulness as well as a moral conscience. Was it not a lesson reasoned from old teachings? In studying for entrance exams, moral conscience is the slow learner. Always, virtue finishes last.

Chairman Quy was sentenced to four years and six months in prison.

Everyone knew that fact. But in a year he returned for all to see. Those who were not in the fields or who were working at home that morning heard the clanging of horseshoes on the country road by Mr. Quang's house. It was the clacketing tempo of a purebred with a smooth, velvety, reddish brown coat, with a long mane like one of those horses in an antique Chinese painting. The clanging of his hooves in time with the bells tinkling on his neck brought a familiar music to the residents of Woodcutters' Hamlet, reminding them of the busy life in a city. Hearing those sounds, they would always peek through the gate or the fence to admire the horse and greet the owner. That early morning they saw Mr. Quang sitting in front, his face sad and his hands absentmindedly holding the whip. Behind were Quy and his wife, sitting like two rag bags, silent like mounds of dirt facing each other. That strange silence prompted people not to offer normal greetings. They pretended not to see anyone or to hear anything. But on the evening of that day, they whispered with one another, passing on the news from hamlet to hamlet. "The father stretched his arms to take his son out of prison. Well, good luck indeed."

"This development will surely make the son open his eyes wide on the outside to better understand life and on the inside to better understand himself. From now on maybe he will find the road to redemption."

"I heard he had to bow down before Mr. Quang right at the prison gate, just as the police read out the order to release him before the end of his term."

One talks, the other remains silent, or looks up at the sky, or over toward the hedges, the tree line, with eyes half attentive, half absentminded. After a silence deepened with concern, people sighed with relief as if a heavy burden had been lifted.

"Life does not change over thousands of years: blood flows and the heart softens. Even a tiger would not eat its cub."

Perhaps it really was a solace, a kind of spiritual and protective wall, a defense against all the storminess that might come from a distant and foreign ocean to pulverize their soft hearts.

Quy's return passed in silence. For one week he stayed at home, not even taking a step beyond the gate. One morning the following week he and his two daughters carried baskets to the cassava field. From being the most powerful person in the village he became an ordinary citizen. This alone was an extraordinary personal challenge, yet he was also a convict rescued by his father's personal intervention. The neighbors had predicted just as much. Given this, in a kind of virtue that has been handed down for thousands of years in the community, the people of Woodcutters' Hamlet pretended that nothing had happened, as if Quy had only returned from a trip and no more. All conversations proceeded calmly just as vegetation grows:

"Hello! Today you and the girls also pick cassava."

"Yes."

"Cassava here is twice as good as the ones by my home."

"No; only so-so; thank heaven anyway."

"Miss Dao and Miss Man work hard in weeding cassava. Next year will see good starch. At New Year we can make plenty of sweets."

"Yes, my kids love sweets. Their mother is unskilled in many things but she knows a few tricks in that regard."

"Do you plan on reviving the bee harvest?"

"No plans yet. Just waiting to see."

"So are we. Last year we had a bad season for pollen, the bees were re- duced by half."

"Farming is gambling. We have to accept setbacks."

"There's this saying: 'A harvest is lost, that must be due to some natural calamity; a bumper crop, now that must be thanks to the Party's ability.'"

"If you were still chairman, I would not say it even if my teeth were pried open. But now that you are a regular citizen like us, we do not have to be so restrained."

"Really?"

"Now, everybody is bold-mouthed and speaks frankly to you about life."

"Really?"

"Yes!"

"Only now do I know. That quip is really good. Whoever thought of it is a genius."

"Kid: Are you serious or joking?"

"Why are you asking?"

"Well, all these years sitting in the chairman's seat, you only heard or- ders from the Party and the government. Those silly songs never reach the ears of those who hold the scales and ink."

"That's true. But time in prison opened my eyes to the truth of life. In there are so many who are so much more intelligent and bright than those district cadres sitting above me."

"Is that so?"

"Why shouldn't it be so?"

"I'm just chatting."

From that day on Quy's "prison story" suddenly became double-edged. No one felt embarrassment, no one was shy, in touching someone's pain. With bravado Quy spoke freely about his "cell mates," taking pride as if meeting them had been a boon and as if they had been the first ever to teach him life's magnificent lessons. Villagers found Quy to have turned into a totally different person. He didn't hide it. Not once but many times Quy would loudly say for people to hear:

"Before I thought the graveside statue was large, but now I find the rock by the pond bridge where we clean our feet is a thousand times larger."

"You speak in riddles, kid; only those with a belly full of words could understand you. Those like us who plow have dull wits."

"Let me explain. Before, the whole village, the whole hamlet, competed and fought. Adults competed in work, in increasing productivity, in sur-passing the goal; children competed in collecting manure, in picking up leftover rice; in school they competed in learning, to be on the honors list, to receive awards—to get a red cloth flower for their chest was the ultimate happiness. So many years living like that—now I realize that was all frivo-lous. Actually, our lives center around three holes: a mouth high up and two others in the crotch of our pants. If we fill up those three holes, it makes for a full life in this world."

"But there is . . ."

"There is nothing more. If there were, we would only be dupes. There are a lot of delusions. Let me explain to you all: we're all impotent. Men have had their tubes tied or use condoms to avoid pregnancy. Women have IUDs inserted—from the one like a worm to the round one like a top. Their complexion goes green like a frog's behind, their faces get so pale it's as if they had caught a toxic breeze, but they still wear the coil to carry out the family planning policy and get recognition badges from the district and province. Meanwhile, do those who order us to become impotent practice what they preach? In prison I learned the truth. In prison, too, I learned that while most people eat only cassava and sweet potatoes, others have a monthly meat ration from seven to sixteen ounces. The mighty official who has a Ton Dan ration book can stuff whatever he likes into his mouth. Sat-urday, Sunday, the masses labor for the socialist regime while wives and children of the cadres dance or beckon for male prostitutes to come to their rooms and serve them. Every New Year, the government asks the people to be frugal while its officials have plenty of expensive herbs and cinnamon and their kitchens are full of the most rare and delicious dishes. If this is not being swindled, then what is?"

"Well . . . for sure, we do not know."

"That is why I understand that that gang standing on our heads and step-ping on our necks only cares about filling their three holes. Why don't we get smart and flush our own holes?"

The neighbors all fell dead silent at this, partly because of embarrass-ment, partly because what Quy had just said was so new to them they had no idea how to react. Some said he was irreverent to draw attention to his "lessons from prison" while forgetting all the low things he had done. Some thought that Quy intentionally exaggerated the truth to show that he no longer cared about living, that he had not an inch of conscience, that his time in jail had been only a lark and a frolic.

It turned out that the neighbors were wrong. Several weeks later, crying, Quy's wife ran to the village committee to ask that Miss Vui sign an order to remove her IUD, for the reason that the husband wanted lots of kids, because, after a thousand years, people still thought that a family with many children has "lots of good fortune." She said that if she resisted his wish, Quy could chase her out the door immediately and bring home a city girl, young and pretty—a thousand times better than "that whore Ngan." The new chairwoman understood that she was dealing with a real jerk, that "even a king gives way to the insane," so she took up her pen and signed off on the order as requested. The next week, Quy's wife went to the hamlet clinic to have her IUD removed. That same afternoon, Quy sat drinking in the middle of his patio, wobbling like an old man of seventy. Halfway through the carafe, he raised his voice to curse:

"The old maid knows her fate, bows her head to sign the order. If not, I would show her the martial arts of a 'hero from the jail.'"

Then Quy ordered his wife to bring him more alcohol. Half drunk and half sober, he told his two daughters and son, "Now, me—I have no Party membership nor committee responsibilities; nothing ties me down. I and your mother have the freedom to make babies, until we no longer have eggs. Now it is your turn, too; paternal and maternal grandchildren, they are all gifts. From antiquity, the elders have taught us: "to have bodies is to have wealth." If our family is large, we can fart all together and blow their house down."

"Their" here referred to Mr. Quang, his wife, and their recently born son—Que. While Quy was in prison, Miss Ngan became pregnant. Most pregnant mothers are sick for several months, but she threw up not even once, even though she ate such unsettling things as green guava, fresh limes and chili peppers, and bitter eggplant. Mr. Quang's wife grew even more beautiful during this time; like spring flowers her complexion and skin were smooth and her cheeks pinkish red. When her tummy grew to the size of a drum she still ran around briskly, still went out to the burrows and fields, laughing merrily like popping New Year firecrackers and with not a hint of weariness. Mrs. Tu took her down to the district to give birth, and boasted that the baby boy was born with rings of flowers around his neck. As soon as the rings were removed, he started crying so loudly as to be heard throughout several rooms. Even though he was a first child, he weighed nine pounds and was over twenty-three inches long; with those numbers, he was indeed the largest newborn in the region, not only in Woodcutters' Hamlet but in the whole district.

Mr. Quang waited for his wife in the halls of the clinic. When all was done, he stepped in and placed around her neck a necklace with a stone carving of the Guan Yin Boddhisattva. All women giving birth in that region would envy such a gift. When the child reached one month, Mrs. Tu prepared a thirty-tray banquet and invited relatives from near and far. The father instead of the mother held the child when greeting arriving relatives, something he had never done with the children by his first wife.

The relatives from both sides—paternal and maternal, close and distant—almost had to admit that they had never seen a child as beautiful as Que; that he deserved the pride felt by the entire family; and that, if, in this life, an old and lonely father like Mr. Quang could have such a child, then millions of people could dream about such happiness for themselves.

All that happened under his father's roof reached Quy's ears, giving pain to his vengeful heart. His words—half sober, half inebriated—could not hide his toxic bitterness. People understood that imprisonment had not brought an awakening to the son, but, on the contrary, had exacerbated bitterness toward the father.

The nightmare of the "father-son war" lingered; it haunted the people continually. In the dark night, the residents of Woodcutters' Hamlet would look up to the dark cloud-covered skies, and worriedly sigh.

That next New Year, Quy gave away in marriage both his daughters at one time. The wedding ceremony took place just when Quy's wife was packing her clothes to go to the district to have a baby. Her small belly was in the eighth month. And their fourth child came just as the "presentation" ceremony of the daughters ended. It was a boy and they named him Chien, or "Fighter"—a word that embodied the father's wish as well as his determination. Chien was just nine months when Quy's wife again became pregnant. The following year she gave birth to another son, named Thang, or "Victorious," also a name full of implication. That same year, the two daughters gave life to two little girls, the older sister one month, the younger sister the next. The two granddaughters were just weaned and barely a year old when the girls again became pregnant, their faces as green as leaves. The babies drank bad milk, constantly coming down with diarrhea. So this family became a reproductive assembly line, ignoring all neighbors' opinions. With two weak-willed sons-in-law, even though the father had lost his position, he was still intimidating, so Quy's dream that "our family is big, we can fart all together and collapse the roof of their house" became a reality.

Nevertheless—because reality always kicks in with the word "nevertheless"—nevertheless, while working to put his crazy dream into action, Quy did not plan the logistics necessary for such a large army. The sons-in-laws' families were poor, classified among those that regularly received assistance from the village. Very poor, yet they had the carefree habits of those who might live or who might not, as the elders said in the old days: "If my meat is raw, I'll eat it raw; if it's well cooked, I'll eat it, too."

The new in-laws had not even a penny to their name. From the betrothal to the "new age banquet," there were only cookies, candies, and tea, and still they had to borrow from neighbors, and after the day of "presentation," Quy's wife had to slip envelopes to her daughters so that they could cover the debts. After each "presentation" ceremony, the young couples returned to stay with the in-laws because they could not afford their own private room. On the wedding night, the parents-in-law had to relinquish their only bed to the newlyweds, taking a bamboo settee out to the veranda to sleep. Thus Miss Mo's and Miss Man's families shared the five-room house of their parents. Each family had two rooms, while the fifth was for storage of all their farm products as well as farming equipment. With such an outstanding record of procreation, Quy's family suddenly fell straight down, from the kind that lives on wealth to the kind that struggles to move forward while mired in the mud of poverty. The money saved vanished like dry leaves blown away in a winter's tornado. Quy's stamina was not that robust; nor was his business acumen. For the previous three years Quy tried only to stabilize his family's economic situation. Under his dominion, the two sons-in-law were docile; they listened to him. But the head of this family had no experience in production and the sons-in-law, born and raised in indigent families, were hopeless. Many people lived in the "big" house. One would think that the circumstance could have brought warmth, vitality, ample rice paddies, and much cash flowing in as well. But fate did not smile on Quy; the genie of good fortune was grinding its teeth and throwing cold water in his face.

For several years in a row, even though the cassava was planted separately for family appropriation and the earned labor points were sufficient, whatever might have brought Quy some cash totally failed. During the mushroom season, only the three men went up into the woods to scavenge, as the women in the family were either expecting or had just had a baby. With one child on the hip and another on the back, caring for the children exhausted them. That no women were available to dry and bag the mushrooms left Quy and his two sons-in-law in charge, and a significant part of the harvest was ruined. The endeavor that should have brought in the most money—beekeeping—was also a disaster. First, Quy's bees had diarrhea. Then they had green fungi growing on their backs, and in only one day the infection had spread all the way to the base of the wings, causing them to fall off. The hive died out.

Many people whispered behind his back about his family's mysterious misfortune; others were too afraid to talk about it. If you passed by Quy's gate, you would see the three families sitting on a mat—no table—having dinner on the patio, entirely like a very poor rural family in days far past, looking puzzled, with a powerless gaze, without even the capacity to feel ashamed. During that time, Quy's family became the very first family in Woodcutters' Hamlet to eat rice mixed with cassava. Meanwhile the storm lamp still shone brightly over part of Mr. Quang's large patio, a setting where neighbors were generously treated to chicken and rice as well as many other goodies. Nobody dared raise a concern. Their anxiety looking at such contrast twisted their hearts into knots so words froze at the tips of their tongues. Quy's plan of "many children making grandchildren; plenty of good fortune" hit the wall of dire poverty.

Dire poverty is a bad-tempered acquaintance, an opponent well deserving caution, giving its victims blows that can never be healed. Forever in the past, one relied on the reassurance that "paternal concern will prevail." So it was expected that, sooner or later, Mr. Quang would reconcile with Quy so that there would be someone to hold the bamboo cane and wear the gauze mourning headband and mourning coat when he came to lie down for the last time. Quy never imagined that someday the man he called "Father" would look at him as no more than a passerby crossing the street.

One morning, Quy and his two sons-in-law went up to the forest to cut firewood. In the early new dew, the air of the mountains was still rising thru the cracks, giving everyone goose bumps. The three men shivered in clothes that gave no warmth; they kept stepping on one another's feet as they rushed forward. It was a steep climb and there were many large stones made slick by the dew that caused the path to be very treacherous, especially for those wearing rubber sandals. It was bad luck that Quy had left his old canvas shoes at home that day to wear light, six-strap rubber sandals. He slipped and began to roll down the ravine; midway down the stony slope, an old thornbush full of dry branches stopped his fall, saving him from death, but he broke four ribs. While he was held by the thornbush, waiting for his sons-in-law to rescue him, he suddenly looked up at the top of the slope. Mr. Quang was standing there, looking down into the ravine. For an instant, their eyes met. For the first time, the son understood that all was over—forever. He caught in the eyes of his father a terrifying coldness— the type of frigid cold brought by the north wind in December. He shivered and quickly closed his eyes.

Quy was hospitalized for more than two months. During that time, he learned pointedly what it is to be dirt poor: how humiliating it is when you don't have enough money for hospital expenses; how excruciating it is to have just a bowl of rice with plain watercress soup while others enjoy soup bowls full of chicken meat and drink milk; how injurious it is to one's pride when you cannot afford a pack of cigarettes to tip the orderlies, or candies to give to the three-year-old son of the nurse who gives you injections or changes your dressings. His four ribs healed slowly due to his poor nutrition. When his wife and the family walked into the hospital room, he had the opportunity to look at them objectively—his own blood and flesh, the large army for which he had such vivid hopes. The army named Chien and Thang was not even a gang: they were disheveled, skinny, with privation showing on their faces. When they came and went among the bamboo hedges of Woodcutters' Hamlet, their poverty was not that obvious. But it was a different matter at the clinic.

When he got back from the hospital, Quy assembled his family and ordered a cease-fire:

"Now it is more difficult to feed people than before; you should stop temporarily. When our family regains its prosperity, we can have babies again."

"Whatever you teach, Father, we will put into action," the two sons-in-law responded obediently.

The order from the head of the family came a bit late. Quy and his wife already had three sons: Phu, Chien, and Thang. Because of the saying "three sons, no wealth; four daughters, no poverty," they therefore sought a fourth child. This time it was indeed a girl, but she died twenty days after birth from untreatable pneumonia. The daughters Mo and Man each had little ones on their backs and four-month-old babies in their wombs. They gave birth to these babies almost at the same time, but neither child ate adequately. Both mothers and babies were pale like green leaves. Quy's wife was only seventy pounds, with skin folds on her neck. The two daughters were not much older than twenty but their cheeks were full of lines that looked like cat's whiskers. For this large army, worrying about food was gut-wrenching. There was neither time nor money left to worry about pants, shirts, and blouses. Therefore, villagers chatted with disdain every time they saw the family:

"Look there, the girls Mo and Man are now older than Miss Ngan by ten years."

"Exactly. Thus the grandniece-in-law is older than the step-mother-in-law. How extraordinary. The stepmother-in-law is prettier and younger each day. In the old days our elders compared an exquisite beauty to a fairy descending to our realm. A descending fairy is as good as it can get."

"They are so wealthy, why don't they have more babies?"

"I heard the wife wants to but he doesn't. He said, 'One little Que is worth ten other children. One can be precious; not many.'"

"Yeah, you have a point. One piece of gold in the hands is worth more than ten pieces of lead in the pocket."

"That family is really happy: a beautiful wife, a handsome son, the husband maybe old but still good-looking. As the saying goes, 'One eats white rice with a bird's egg omelet.'"

"The husband is handsome, the wife beautiful; they just need to look at each other and they are full."

No one could ever deny that Mr. Quang's young wife was a living embodiment of this saying: "Mother of one; one for the eye." Many villagers felt she had kept her childhood looks. After giving birth, Miss Ngan's lips seemed redder and fuller than before, like a fruit full of juice, promising the taste of orange in her kisses. Her breasts were more ample, too, like two grapefruits hiding under a thin blouse. And her thighs, like the rest of her body, evoked an overflowing feeling of blooming flowers, full of love's fragrance.

On days when they went up to the woods to cut firewood or down to the fields to farm—tasks for men only—residents of Woodcutters' Hamlet gossiped quietly with one another:

"In our lives, only Mr. Quang is really happy. At best, a king could only wish for his wife to be that beautiful."

"Yeah . . . in Russian movies, many of the stars are her inferior. Mr. Quang was right to spend his money and wealth on a house for his parents-in-law. How many can produce such beauty in a child?"

"I heard she is being selected for the national artistic troupes."

"What a pity. If she is in the national troupe so many will be washing their eyes."

"Stupid . . . to go national, then she will never want to set foot in this very remote place."

252 Duong Thu Huong

"Oh yeah . . . I forgot."

"Now, I want to ask you one thing: Suppose you could sleep with a beauty like her just once and the next morning go to the guillotine, would you do it or not?"

"Of course I would do it. How long is one's life?"

"Oh, no, I am not that naive. Beautiful she is indeed. Before such a beautiful woman any man would drool, but there is too much else to take care of in life."

"Like what?"

"Family, clan, grandkids' futures, graves of the parents. It's stupid to obey the tuber's priorities."

Such conversations blew like gusts from this mountain to that, from one valley to another. And life in Woodcutters' Hamlet continued on in the calm rhythm of farming communities. Villagers continued to see Mr. Quang's horse cart coming and going to the fast tempo of jingling bells. Each time he returned, the light in his patio shone brightly and there was cheerful chattering blended with voices from the Suong Mao radio, sometimes the news, sometimes the high-pitched singing of performers such as Thuong Huyen:

*"Quietly listen by the side of the stream, a birds flits from here to there . . .
Quietly listen to my heart, it sings my love for you."*

Dying away, winters called out to spring. Summers were barely over when shivering dew arrived to announce long and stormy autumns. Time went by and little Que turned five, the age when children in Woodcutters' Hamlet must begin their formal schooling. The village had but one elementary school. But the upper, middle, and lower sections each had their own separate kindergartens, each with two divisions: a lower one reserved for kids three and four; an upper one for kids four and five. The five- and six-year-olds were put together in a starter class that taught writing and simple math, preparing them for the first year of elementary school. There, the children also learned how to dance, to sing, to draw in the sand and on the chalkboard. They learned the first lesson in relationships. For these good reasons, every village parent understood that kindergarten was in reality the most important class of all. In truth, little Que should have started school long before, but being an only and a precious child, both his mother and Mrs. Tu spoiled him, so he skipped the lower division of kindergarten.

At home, the two women taught him words, how to count, and to add and subtract simple numbers. When he turned five, they had no reason to sequester him any longer in their loving arms.

"This year, little Que has to go to class like all the kids in the village," Mr. Quang ordered.

"Yes, I thought about it," Mrs. Tu said.

Miss Ngan was silent, but she opened the cupboard and handed Mr. Quang a brand-new bag full of books, notebooks, pens, and chalk . . . all the necessities for Que's first day in class.

Year had followed on year—life had flowed on like a large river ever shoving forward its sediments, trash, and foam. It seemed as if Miss Ngan had almost forgotten the terrifying, brutal events that had occurred after she had first set foot in Woodcutters' Hamlet, forgotten those people who had stood in the dark shadow of her husband's past. And them? For sure, they remembered her, because those who stand in dark shadows usually see very clearly those who stand in the bright light.

When the day came for the beginning of kindergarten for children in the upper section, each mother had to bring her child to school. Not only the children, but also the mothers were nervous. That day, with excited hearts, mothers held their kids' hands to take them out of family territory and entrust their care to people under another roof, turning them over to strangers, like a mother bird pushing her babies out of the nest in order to teach them forcefully how to fly—with hearts a bit torn, a bit worried, a bit hesitant, but, in the end, full of hope.

As there was only one building in the entire section for the initial learning and starter classes, an encounter between the two hostile families was unavoidable. The school sat on top of a hill, under the cool shadow of an old, spreading elm, with its leaves green and birds singing cheerfully. In front, there was a large yard with a fairly smooth gravel surface, in the middle of which was a tiny flower garden surrounded by grasses. At recess, the children were free to play and roll. The side of the hill slanted down to a row of eucalyptus. That row of trees ran along the country road, where mothers would arrive from two directions, corresponding to the two resident quarters of the upper section—one to the north and one to the south.

That morning, Miss Ngan fed her boy earlier than usual, and gathered with the mothers of children from the north quarter. More than ten mothers and almost twenty little students formed a happy group. As soon as they passed the row of trees and saw the top of the hill, the children all ran up. Those from the south quarter had arrived first. The air filled with smiling chatter; mixed with the singing of birds, the happy sounds deepened the hue of the blue autumn sky.

As with the other mothers, the excitement of that first day of school made Miss Ngan happy. Like them, she also talked and laughed excitedly and ran after her boy. The kids were always faster than the mothers when they wanted to escape encircling arms. Miss Ngan finally got hold of young Que when everyone was in the school yard. Before them the teacher, Ton, stood properly with glasses on the bridge of his nose, a shirt with buttoned collar, the opened registration book ready in his hand. On each side were two young lady teachers, each one proudly wearing a fine, flowered blouse with a ribbon in her hair. The three of them stood according to their class: Ton taught the initial-learning class in the middle room; on the left was the lower kindergarten class and on the right the higher class. The three class- rooms were separated by brick walls whitewashed and adorned with red cloth flowers. On the main wall hung a poster of honor with large letters that read: "Smart students, well-behaved children."

Every mother's eyes focused on the pair of spectacles sitting on the bridge of Ton's nose; he was the most important person: the one who would lead their children in their first, tentative steps toward adulthood. Ton had taught the initial-learning class since he was a young man. War, revolution, resistance war, land reform, then rectification of errors in land reform, di- vision of rice fields, then reassembly of plots, division of rice fields, then reallocation back to one party, confiscation from one party to divide some land into "100 percent family ownership" because of the threat of hunger— all those changes had not touched one hair on the legs of Teacher Ton, which was very strange. Some said he had led a moral life and therefore was pro- tected by a good spirit, but others said that in every generation people want their children to become good and so must respect those who teach the young. So even the stupid, wicked, or the most cunning when they rose high enough during the period of enforced land reform to become this lord or that lady dared not humiliate or maltreat someone like Ton, who was looked upon as the embodiment of the spirit of responsibility and love of youngsters. As school started that day, all glued their eyes on the pair of glasses sitting on the bridge of that nose, with respect and utmost attention. The slender and stern old man waited for everyone to gather; he looked at the four sides to survey for the last time whether anyone was not ready to pay attention. Then he lifted the registration book to his eye level. The calling-out of names began, alphabetically by first name. Given the place of the letter "Q," Miss Ngan knew her son would be among the last called. But she paid attention to the names of other children because they would be her son's classmates.

She was startled suddenly when the teacher called the name: "Lai van Chien."

The frail voice of a woman replied, "Please, my son is here."

The teacher continued to read: "Lai van Thang."

Having read this name, the teacher looked up at everyone and explained:

"Student Thang's name starts with the letter T, but his family requests that he be assigned to the same row of chairs as his full brother, Lai Van Chien. That is a legitimate reason, which is why I skipped the proper order to please the family. Is student Thang here?"

"Yes, he is here," the woman with the frail voice replied, but no one saw where she was.

Someone spoke out: "Bring him to the front row. Why be so awkward?"

The mother remained silent. Then Miss Ngan realized that the woman with the frail voice was Quy's wife and the two kids whose names had been called were her sons. A whole set of people emerged from the foggy past. The darkness she thought she had left behind, then returned. Lai Van Chien, Lai Van Thang—branches connected to the root: Lai Van Quang. Those branches were pulling at her beautiful son: Lai Van Que. And later for sure, these little men carrying the family name Lai would run and jump together, tumble down the side of the hill full of grass or frolic in the shadow of the elm tree. That thought was both obvious and strange, making her puzzled for an instant. Then she saw Ton adjust the glasses on his nose, his eyes looking around:

"Will the two brothers Chien and Thang step up to the front row so the teachers can see you clearly? The two of you will sit in the same higher class of kindergarten, right?"

"Please, teacher, let them be in the lower class. The older brother is only one and a half years older. I kept him at home to play with his younger brother so that they could go to school with each other."

"That is all right, it's convenient. Now, bring them up here," the old teacher answered, smiling. Those standing in the front silently stepped back to permit the mother to come forward holding her sons' hands. Then, Miss Ngan recognized Quy's wife and immediately a shivering overwhelmed her like an electric shock. Before her was an emaciated woman looking like a bag of rags, with a face shrunken like that of a bird with a pointy beak.

Dark rings under her eyes gave them the appearance of a pair of faded brass death coins. Her eyes resembled those of one inflicted with the white blood disease when the last breath is inhaled. Her complexion was almost that of a cadaver, with wrinkles along each temple in long lines like the folds of a fan. There were dark spots from her forehead to the base of her ears. No one could believe that she was a woman of just over forty. She seemed even older than a woman in her sixties, because over that devastated face was a flock of dry hair with patches of gray.

Miss Ngan must have voiced some startled cry or made some gesture, because everyone turned to look at her. Then they remembered that Miss Ngan had not been witness to the agonizing decline of Quy's family. The others had seen the decay growing day by day, week by week, month by month. They had seen Quy's wife and daughters void their strength with childbirth and hunger; had seen their children grow swollen bellies from lack of nutrition. For the villagers, those images were so familiar they had been stamped solid; only Miss Ngan had stood outside this reality.

As she noticed that everyone had turned around to look at Miss Ngan, Quy's wife was forced to lift up her head and glance at her nemesis. One look met another. Miss Ngan uttered a sound that seemed equally one of shock, fright, or pity. Then tears flowed over her lashes. The young woman bit her lips, trying to control the shock to her emotions, but finally burst out with a rush of crying. At the other end of the yard, Quy's wife was also shaking like a heron in a storm; she also cried loudly, bending her head down, doubled over in pain and humiliation. All looked squarely at the two of them. The women's eyes were red. Some girls sniffled and wiped their noses. Ton stopped calling out names. The young children went silent. In that space, suddenly, was only the sound of wind accentuated with the melody of unconcerned birds singing.

Some moments passed in perplexity. Then Ton spoke:

"Now, student Chien, student Thang, come here."

When the two boys reluctantly come before him, the old teacher took them and walked toward Miss Ngan and her son.

"This is the student Lai Van Que. You all share the same descent. From today on, you will study under the same roof and play in the same grassy yard. Please greet one another."

The three boys understood what was being asked of them. Confused, the brothers and Que looked at one another. One was tall, with fair complexion, clean, and smelling good from head to toe. The other two were skinny, faces messy and poor. Then Quy's wife stepped forward and pushed her sons forward:

"Say hello to your uncle. Say, 'We salute you, Uncle Que.'"

After the first day of school, the residents of Woodcutters' Hamlet were excited. The tears from the two formerly hostile women had stirred up a healthy breeze. Aren't tears the streams that cleanse animosity, like clear fresh water where people can dive in to erase black spots in the mind? Rural people do not like such cute suppositions; they pay more attention to all that happens before their eyes. Realities perceived by the senses are most important. The first reality they saw was that Miss Ngan had paid all the school expenses for Quy's two sons. Later that day when school was over and Mr. Quang had returned home from work and was at home to welcome neighbors, Chien and Thang were told by their mother, "Go in and greet the young mother. Then if she gives you anything, bring it here."

The two kids went to Mr. Quang's kitchen while Quy's wife stood next to a nearby hedge. Later, the kids returned with curry rice and chicken. The three went home, like a squad of soldiers returning to their barracks with trophies. That first time, they were clumsy and shy; from then on, things proceeded more openly and naturally. Meeting up with villagers and neighbors, Quy's wife always initiated the conversation: "There's a banquet up at the kids' grandfather's; grandma wants us to have a part."

The villagers were happy for them, but couldn't help being curious. They wanted to know Quy's reaction.

Once, on an occasion when everyone was in the forest cutting firewood, one daring mouth asked Miss Mo: "Well, the rice and the chicken and goodies from the grandfather, does Quy eat them?"

"No. Not only will he not eat, but the first time he saw my mother bring that food home, he smashed a teapot."

"Why so?"

"Because my father is angry. He cursed us: 'You humiliate me. My wife and children are all miserable, good-for-nothings.'"

"Does he still feel that way now?"

"No. After the second time, he didn't curse anymore. He lay down in his room. My mother told everybody that we cannot eat in the yard but in the kitchen."

"Why so?"

"So as not to irritate him."

"Standing on ceremony!"

"Who can know what is going on inside someone?" Miss Mo concluded, mysteriously. People did not ask any more.

At the end of that winter, Quy got a cold and was temporarily admitted to the district hospital. The two sons-in-law had to carry him there.

Certainly his illness was the consequence of so many years of setting his mind on revenge; failure and bitterness had depleted his spiritual and physical strength. Flu is a condition that everyone encounters, except those with steel feet and brass skins; ordinarily, when you have a cold, the cure is to extract the toxic forces through vomiting or a bowel movement or by having your back scraped using ointment or steam, to be followed by watery, hot rice soup and bed rest. A flu that requires hospitalization happens only with people who are exhausted, whose bodies have no ability to fight off the invading infection. Serious cases can cause death; the less-serious ones still require good medicine and nutrition over many days. The afternoon Quy fell ill, he had just come back from working in the fields. He went to the well and poured water on himself but collapsed immediately, his whole body stiff like a stone, his complexion dark purple. As he passed them by on the way to the hospital, villagers lifted the covering blanket and looked, shaking their heads. Quy's wife ran behind, numb, her mouth crooked, tears falling down her cheeks.

Quy was lucky enough to have an outstanding doctor and he was saved. Unconscious for three days, he opened his eyes on the fourth day and slurped down almost a full bowl of rice soup broth. Quy's wife returned to the village, having hundreds of things to do while her husband convalesced. That afternoon Mrs. Tu had already taken young Que to their gate and said:

"This is brother Quy's house. He is the father of Chien and Thang. You just go straight into the house and greet their mother."

Que crossed the yard to the house, just as Mrs. Tu had told him. There he gave a thick envelope to the mother of his nephews.

"My mother said to give this to you."

Villagers standing by outside anxiously listened in. At the end, everyone sighed with relief:

"Life has been always this way: blood flows and the heart softens."

And people look up to the summit of Lan Vu Mountain, as if quietly praying to divine beings to diminish humanity's conflicts, to resolve the "father-son war," and to bless their lives with faith and dreams of peaceful goodness as had been vouchsafed since days of old.

ACCUMULATED REGRETS AND NOW AFFECTION FOR HIM

1

The president opens his eyes. It is three in the afternoon.

He has never had an afternoon nap so long and so heavy. The short, frightening dream had merged with images and thoughts that had remained after his learning about the deceased woodcutter, pushing him down an abyss. He feels as if he has just participated in a parachute operation where he was a frightened soldier pushed into the night through the plane door to let his body drop into a black hole full of danger.

It was really horrible.

He steps out onto the veranda. Sunshine covers more than half the patio; a clear kind of light yellow sunshine without a hint of warmth. The cherry tree branches shake in the wind. He looks at them absentmindedly. From the temple on the other side of the patio, sounds of the wooden gong mix with chanting. One could discern the voice of the abbess from the higher pitches of the nuns. He listens to the chanting for a long time to make sure that the dreams are completely gone and that he now lives in the present. The young and chubby soldier sleeps soundly on a hammock hung at the veranda in front of the temple, his face pinkish red. For one so young, his snoring is quite loud. That snoring sound pulls him into reality, out of those dreams that had sunk his soul like a boat stripped of its sails, capsizing, and sinking into a muddy bottom.

"Oh no! I am done . . ."

The young soldier suddenly stands up and lets out loudly: "I am sorry, I overslept . . ."

"Don't worry. I myself also overslept. It's very cool today."

"Thank you, Mr. President. Please give me a few minutes. I will make some tea right away."

The soldier hurriedly folds his hammock and starts boiling water. The administrative office had provided an electric kettle so that now he does not have to boil water over in the temple's small kitchen. The president looks at him quietly. Daily tasks come and go without variation. Suddenly, he recalls his youth and cannot help reflecting to himself:

"How can he stand to do this boring work all his life? Work that is not remotely appropriate for a lad only twenty. Is it perhaps out of respect that people sacrifice their other passions? Or that they don't have any passion more inspiring than being in the army for a vocation, drawing a paycheck to carry out boring jobs?"

He swiftly gets rid of this train of thought; he has suddenly and somewhat surprisingly become fond of this young soldier. It is a genuine affection. He does not want to hold any thought that might not be worthy of the lad.

"Mr. President, please come in and have some tea."

"Thank you. What kind of tea did you make?"

"Jasmine; just like the other day."

"Good, I will come in."

He turns to the room; the air is filled with jasmine fragrance. Steam comes out of the pot of newly brewed tea. From the full cup, he slowly takes small sips. During the time when he was still in the Viet Bac maquis, he had a jasmine bush planted right by his house. That bush grew faster than weeds, in only one year it spread itself out to the size of a sleeping mat. During both the muggy summer afternoons and nights of trickling rain, the intoxicating jasmine fragrance enveloped the house. How can such tiny flowers exude such a strong scent? Many a night, he had stood by the window, looking out to the pitch-dark forests, filling his lungs with forest smells mixed with jasmine scent. Then when he had her around, he saw jasmine flowers more often because she liked to tuck jasmine flowers and magnolia blossoms in her hair.

"I had her in my arms in 1953. She was over twenty. The afternoon I met her sharing figs with her friend in the tree, I had to wait two more years; two years of longing, excruciating longing. I did not love a minor. By law, I committed no crime. That old woodcutter guy married a girl younger than she, only eighteen."

The cup of tea is empty, only a dry jasmine petal is left at the bottom. He stares at the dry petal and suddenly feels jealous for the time past. Jealousy, how very strange, a weakness that is hard to acknowledge.

He re-created in his mind the incongruous setting of that night: the smell of Craven A cigarettes mixed with that of the Gauloises he lit continuously, one after another in a desultory fashion, smoking like a machine, without any appreciation of taste. He remembered the ashtray filled with butts and the stack of files that he had turned page after page without being able to absorb one single line. The first night they made love. The first night her smooth white body appeared before his eyes, uncovered by any bra or blouse, just pure flesh, the pure beauty created by nature. Old folks say: "Clear like jade, white like ivory." He had heard that saying before but not until that night had he thoroughly understood each word, each phrase. Her beauty was indeed as of a precious jewel. He recalled her laugh, in the soft light of the lamp in the corner of the room, her teeth shining like jade. That was an instant that both the past and the present could sustain, when space became dreamlike and the barriers between two living beings just collapsed. She was inside him, melted into his own flesh, kneaded into his soul. Forever, forever . . .

But this is quite strange: Why is he so jealous? In the many meanderings of his life's journey, he had not lacked encounters; he had not gone without the warmth of women. As a philanderer, he is certainly someone who has lived. Thus he cannot escape this ordinary, low-down feeling. After making love, he had told her that he urgently needed to read a stack of documents and he had left the room. But, sitting by the light, he had turned each page while trying to imagine who those others were who "had been" with her. Who had been the first one to have possession of her gorgeous and enticing body? He knew she was a girl from the highlands where life flows free like streams and forest clouds. Boys and girls there make love freely at puberty. For Easterners, people in the mountains are by that very token very much "Westernized." A healthy and pretty girl like her, there had to have been dozens of guys who had taken a good look, especially those fellows growing up in the same region, by the same streams and woods.

"I cannot escape these so ordinary feelings," he thought to himself. "It's hard to understand: after all, I am a guy who spent twenty years in the West—and the first woman in my life was a blond with white skin."

Instinctively he lets out a sigh:

"The first time I had sex, now that's over half a century. To be more accurate, about sixty-five years ago. Nobody can really measure time, because it expands and contracts with one's memories."

Pouring himself a second cup of tea, he sees that first woman in the steam rising from the cup's rim: "A widow. A woman in an alley. A seamstress, big and grotesque—my first sex teacher . . ."

Her face now appears opaque like smoke, but he can never forget her panting and interrupted screams during the lovemaking. They were both renters in a house in the short alley off Rue St-Jean, next to a waterless fountain that stood there rusty amid a flock of old pigeons. She was much older than he; her husband had worked for the post office and had died a few years earlier. Three kids of uncertain paternity were kept locked inside the house. Back then, he was just twenty, at an age when youth exudes seductiveness like a muskrat leaves a scent to attract a mate. One afternoon, the widowed woman had passed him in the alley; she lived in the room built for the housemaid, facing an old garage. She was a seamstress in a small shop that made sleeping caps. Most likely a family business; she had worked there since she was thirteen. They silently walked side by side for a stretch; then all of a sudden the widow smiled and asked him:

"Well, is everything all right?"

"Thank you, I hope so," he replied, but inside he was quite depressed, because his legs were tired from searching for a job and there was not a hint of hope.

"Good," the woman said, then she lowered her voice: "Tonight, at one a.m., my door is open. Will you come?"

He was shocked, not knowing what to say. The woman held his elbow, squeezing it hard while repeating: "Don't forget! One a.m. tonight!"

Then she turned to her apartment. He continued down the next stretch to the last house in the short alley, then climbed to the seventh floor. There he drank water and ate a piece of dry and hard bread from the day before. Cold water and plain bread, with no butter or milk or meat and fish, but his blood managed to stir. The hardest organ in his body could not wait until one a.m.; it had stood up like a mast. He had to walk back and forth in his room; he could not do anything else. His heart beat fast from anticipation but his intellect forced him to smile with bitterness. He had dreamed so often of the first time he would make love but had never imagined it would arrive in such crude circumstances. There was to be no princess of his dreams, no prince of her heart; just a widow needing to fill an empty space in her bed. In those days, even though young, he was already quietly bitter about his fate. It has never occurred to him that the first one who would possess his young body would be a widow twice his age and with blond hair and white skin but no beauty. Nevertheless, he waited with excitement like someone who had never tasted life but was ready to eat his first feast. Then it was time. He silently walked to the already opened door. The woman, too, said nothing; she pulled him to the private room, which was in the old garage, walls hung with loud, flowery wallpaper; it had an antique bed, a quite large one filling the whole room. This confirmed that the postman must have been larger than average.

"Strange! Fate takes care of everything; any path will bring you to where you are supposed to be."

Also strange is that while he had almost forgotten the widow's face, he recalled the tiny room very well, especially the old bed with iron posts holding globes on their tops. One could feel that this solid black bed was like the gravel-making machine that had survived since antiquity and would continue to exist for many centuries. He remembers vividly the brown sheet with large stripes, the bed cover colored café au lait. He remembers the ways she taught him how to love. The arms of that seamstress were hot but her muscles were flabby and her hands large, full of calluses that hurt him when her caresses became wild. He remembers the gestures, determined and at times rough, when she took her nightgown off over her head to throw it on the floor. He remembers the glass of hot milk she offered him, the sounds of the spoon clacking in the late night; he was scared because the kids were sleeping on the other side of the wall. All the details of practice preliminary to lovemaking. His twentieth year was thus marked.

"A bigger worry than the jealousy she stirred up in the neighborhood has been the jealousy of other women that I am still ashamed of."

That little quarter of Paris was full of women without men in their lives: wives of soldiers unable to be with their husbands; widows from the ongoing colonial wars from Africa to America; Italian women who had escaped their own country. There were too many reasons those beds were cold. The postman's widow hung tight to her twenty-year-old lover as a drowning person would hold on to a float. At first she was somewhat shy; later she became to him like a prisoner's warden. And the other women, younger and prettier and no less daring, started throwing swords at the one who had gotten there before them. They stirred up jealous passes around the young and fresh Asian fellow who was crunchy like an apple. He was ashamed. He could not accept the way they used him as bait. He quietly looked for another place in another quarter. And one night he took his bag and left.

"Mr. President, are you done with your tea so that I can clear it?"

"Thanks, I am done."

The soldier carries the tea tray outside, and he, by habit, pulls over the stack of materials in front of him and turns the pages, while musing to himself:

"I turn these pages not unlike that time long ago. People sometimes can be so mechanical; their automated gestures take up most of their time. Really, living life is only the tip of the iceberg—always the small part."

Another thought rushes in quickly, like the crest of a wave thrown back on the rocks: "Those little parts are actually life. If they melt away, then our living can have no meaning at all, can only be a copy of a picture in which what we see is no more than an approximation of what is real."

That comparison suddenly reminds him of the darkroom where he once made a living by printing photographs, a boring and ungrateful occupation where one was imprisoned all day in darkness with the smell of silver salts. In the afternoons when you stepped out of that little prison, your eyes blurred and your back hurt.

"Actually, no, that old darkroom was a place I chose so that I might buy lousy bread to get through the days. Now, here is my real prison with a whole army of guards. Why? Why did I let them push me into such deprivation?"

In the end, he is incapable of forgetting; nor can he escape. He is trapped to return again and again to the frightening dream he had just experienced during his nap. He cannot avoid her. She stands somewhere, right behind his back. She casts a huge shadow over him, looking lovely and lonely. He feels she has just emerged from somewhere frigid, from a spacious, snow-white space where rivers freeze into clear crystal, where woods of dry trees and grass leave imprints in the wild space of dark branches crooked like snakes, where flocks of blackbirds fly while uttering imploring cries like peeling bells to summon the ghostly spirits. How strange! She never set foot across the border; she is locked in the sleeves of his shirt; she offers a life of fleeting happiness later to be thrown straight down into hell. Then in his dream she becomes an eternal companion. Wherever he lives, her shadow is there. He sees her on the boat across the sea; he sees her in the alley in Paris; he sees her wandering on the street of a quay:

"My beloved! When are we going to see each other again?"

That lyric rises up in the empty air and hits his heart. More and more he feels that his soul is akin to a mountainside confronting an ocean on a stormy day, where the thoughts advance nonstop like the ocean waves crashing against the cracked rocks, in an eternal struggle without a victor.

"I could have had happiness with her. I should not have backed off before them. Those who had warmly called me 'Venerable,' 'Eldest One,' and those who I had considered my soul mates, close brothers who shared with me their handful of rice, real 'pals' as they used to call themselves. Turns out all those 'should bes' and 'can bes' were misunderstandings. In a special instant, all values turned upside down just as if we had believed films about life and then life itself appeared."

On that day when he had requested the Politburo to make public his relationship with his young wife, all the smiling faces of his "buddies" suddenly became dour:

"Mr. President, you should never bring this subject up. It is 'taboo,' to put it exactly and accurately."

This from Thuan, who was pretty fluent in French. Only half those present understood the term he has used—"taboo." Those who hadn't understood that word expressed themselves brutally and without mincing their words.

Sau followed Thuan. He stared at the president as if he were surprised. Theatrically, he suddenly pursed his lips and firmly asserted, "Women. I think, Mr. President, you bring up this subject to please Miss Xuan, and that is your only purpose. I am sure this request starts with Miss Xuan; or from the coaxing of her family. And our president is far too smart to recognize that this is something that is unacceptable."

"Naturally it is impossible. *C'est sur,*" stressed Thuan, using French as was his habit.

Waiting for the uncomfortable feeling to pass among those not familiar with "the language of the enemy," another leading comrade, named Danh, said, "Even if it is Miss Xuan, we cannot be lenient. Women only think of the roofs over their heads, their own self-interest, but the president must respect the interest of the nation and the people over all other considerations. Our revolution is successful because all the people together trust your leadership. Your image brings strength to the nation. We cannot let that image be defamed."

Comrade To raised his voice to object: "How 'defamed'? We should not use such loaded or extreme words."

Immediately Sau turned around and retorted strongly, "We need not be shy; we don't need to weigh our words. We face the life or death of the revolution. The needs of the revolution are at stake; we must protect those interests at all costs. Thus, now is not the time to play with words or choose one over another."

"Comrades, don't be so harsh. In the end, all questions are to be resolved in a calm manner by consensus," Thuan intervened, lifting his arm and continuing in a firm manner as if to have the last word. "I believe that all of us are of one mind: the matter of recognizing Miss Xuan cannot be done. We cannot even think about it. I hope that, in a spirit of high responsibility before the whole nation, Mr. President must accept this decision. We have no alternative."

"Mr. President is the elderly father of the nation."

Sau followed with his lips still pushed out in a subtle smile: "The elderly father of the nation is the roof that shelters the people. For years now, the people have known this metaphor. Mr. President needs to remind Miss Xuan about this point, if she continues to demand that she be officially recognized."

At that moment, he felt his tongue stick in his throat. Sweat ran down his spine and his feet were cold as if they were soaking in ice water. Those well-known faces had suddenly become plastic masks all puffed up, twisted, and bumpy. How could he find understanding and trust among those deformed people? All that he had firmly believed in had been a complete misunderstanding. A high wall just collapsed inside his heart. His soul emptied; his brain became paralyzed. He suddenly became mute. He could not move his lips. After a moment, his powers returned. A fleeting warning came on, making him quiver. He had to calm himself first before he was able to speak:

"If the Politburo has decided, obviously I have to accept. But, dear comrades, do not forget that Miss Xuan is my close associate, together we have two children, and these children are my own blood and flesh."

"Be assured, Mr. President: all your loved ones will be treated properly. Just as long as they willingly live out of sight, behind the revolution," said Thuan, who reputedly was the most mature and courteous member of the Politburo. He also was reputedly a man of moral character, which meant that, unlike his other comrades, he was monogamous. Thuan had only one wife. With that woman he had five children.

The president no longer remembers the end of that meeting, what happened after he had received what felt like a sentence of death. He had felt as if his heart were led up to the platform where the blade of the executioner's sword came down. The last impression in his soul was a realization of his powerlessness. For the first time, he saw himself as just a colossal wooden statue hollowed out by termites. All those buddy-buddy comrades standing in his shadow just to seek some power. In reality, they were his bosses, such brutal and immoral cronies. The whole gang lived only for what could happen below their belly buttons. More than half of them had two wives and a gaggle of mistresses. The one who appeared to empathize most with him had been Do, for he understood the life of one who has been castrated. Do's wife had been inflicted with a delusional condition since youth. After childbirth she became a schizo. She was treated in the hospital and at institutions reserved for families of Politburo dignitaries. Do had to endure a period of no sex for a while, before taking up a clandestine relationship with a singer in a theater troupe from Zone Five, with whom he had a son. But Do was always in the minority; besides, his temperament was weak and submissive. All his life he was only an actor. For a long time, he had volunteered to be a marionette.

The one with the most respectable reputation, who spoke in a high moral tone and who took a firm attitude during that meeting, was Thuan. He had once and for a long time been his most effective right-hand man.

"But he was never deprived of sex," the president thinks to himself. "He had only one wife, and with her he has five children, and both during war and in peace, the sex life of this man has run without lapse."

The president remembers a celebration in the Viet Bac zone. That day the cooks had been authorized to kill a cow. Local villagers provided plenty of rice whiskey. After eating, all were tipsy and happy. Suddenly, a woman's screams were heard coming from the family quarters, a male voice mixed with the woman's curses and cries. Horrified, the chief office administrator ran over to inquire. He returned a bit later and reported that the wife of the warehouse warden was in difficult child labor. The more pain this coarse woman felt, the more she cursed her husband. Those around her offered encouragement. When her pain subsided temporarily, the women's association took her to the clinic.

This incident triggered an explosion of crisp laughter mingled with jokes, both new and old, among the revelers.

Some guy asked, "Any of you ladies here ever curse your husband when you were in labor?"

"None of us!" the wives replied in unison.

A more daring wife said, "Even if we wanted to curse, we'd grind our teeth and do it quietly to let off some anger."

"Maybe you're the most honest one here!"

The president smiled in praise then continued to tease them: "But why get mad at the one who shares your bed and pillow?"

"Because . . . because . . ."

The woman hesitated, part of her wanting to respond, another part still unsure. Then he heard Thuan laughing; it was he who responded on behalf of the woman:

"Because when you are happy there are two of you; but when you suffer, you bear it all alone. That's what you feel facing the injustice of heaven and earth. That's what anger demands from the Creator."

"You have a wonderful talent for getting it right," the president said, his voice raised in praise, and then he turned to Thuan's wife:

"Knowing how to speak like that, he must also know how to be an ideal husband. Am I right?"

"Ah . . ."

Thuan's wife also hesitated like the other women. She glanced at her husband and again he laughed out loud, this time without concealing his pleasure:

"Mr. President, on this topic you are pretty naive. Theory and practice are always like two parallel lines that never meet. My wife was just nagging me all night because I broke a rule."

"Broke a rule? What rule?"

He had asked the question out of genuine curiosity because he was not clear what kinds of rules there were between the couple. For his whole life, women had passed him by like rain or clouds, temporary like an inn, dreamy like a fictional beauty. Family life for him was an unexplored continent. While looking toward Thuan, the wife's face became red like a ripe fruit, while Thuan smiled the largest smile he could manage. Then he slowly explained:

"There are lots of rules, but no rule can withstand youth and all the rushes of one's nature. For instance, our elders taught us that after a wife gives birth, we have to restrain ourselves for one hundred days, that was the official position. But I don't believe any husband can fast past twenty-one days. Behind our wives' backs, quietly I asked ten husbands: all ten admitted they broke that rule. Then the doctor has his rule: when a wife is nine months pregnant, it is absolutely forbidden to come near her bed. Me, I practice *'jusqu'au bout'* (until the end). The day she went into labor, the night before I was knocking away."

"Will you stop now, you devil," Thuan's wife screamed, almost crying of embarrassment.

The whole group burst into laughter, with an obvious air of complicity. He hurriedly intervened:

"OK, OK . . . when the lady speaks, it's an order. I recommend that we turn to another subject."

A time to remember; a time to love; a time to take revenge.

An old verse suddenly returns. He suddenly sees the logic of the ordinary. It's correct that there was a time. A time to remember.

A time that has passed—a time of all those who had lived in the jungle, who had together sung the same military songs, who had marched in the same formation, who had shared bowls of rice, and who had had the same hopes. A time of suffering and dreaming, when each could share with the others all things in an easy manner. A time when people thought that love and friendship were the strong ropes that bound them tightly, despite all barriers, despite all changes.

"Why does this revenge arise? From hidden envy or from power crucified?"

Those two alternatives put him at a fork in the road where either way had snakes and centipedes underfoot. So many years had passed, but still he did not fully understand the reason for this communal betrayal. Could it have been that her beauty brought jealousy to the heart of his comrades? Or had his love for her undermined the power of the organization?

Before he had met Xuan, the resistance movement had decided to find him a woman who would be the future "Mother of the Nation." His rejection of that proposal, followed by a torrid affair with a girl from the mountains, was the hammer that had decidedly smashed the sculpted image that his comrades had readily erected for him.

"Who appointed them matchmakers? Everything that has happened feels like a stupid game as well as a plan of some ghost taking me to the grave."

He cannot remember for sure when, but about the winter of 1947 or the spring of 1948, the office had come to report:

"The Politburo has met without you and decided that a female comrade from the women's association will be assigned to service you."

"Why wasn't I informed of the purpose of that meeting?"

"Because, Mr. President, your responsibility is to be the highest leader of the resistance; thousands of matters await you. Thus, you do not have time to worry about your personal affairs. The Politburo had to step up and make the arrangement."

"But feelings between two individuals cannot be addressed in such a simple and mechanical manner. You all set the tasks, but the woman does not have any passion, so then the arrangement is a punishment for her."

"Don't you worry, Mr. President! To serve you is an honor."

"But me, I'm human, too; I have to feel genuine emotion for the whole thing to work out well."

"Yes, all the officials of the Politburo say that to carry out this decision is to safeguard your health, Mr. President. According to Hai Thuong Lan

Ong's *Encyclopedia of Medicine*, if your yin and yang are not balanced, then all kinds of ailments will come. Your health secures the destiny of the people and the future of the nation. The whole administrative office has the obligation to take care of your health."

"I understand. But you cannot use that reason to solve everything so pragmatically."

"Mr. President, the women's association has briefed Comrade Thu. She has agreed that serving you means to serve the revolution."

"What?"

"Mr. President, the administrative office informs you that it will commence this Saturday."

"You don't have to rush things like that. I have lived a few years without a partner and nothing happened," he replied, an annoyance invading his heart. But the chief of the administrative office hurriedly went out. His quick footsteps could be heard at the top of the stairs. Then an aide stepped in and asked him to go to General Long's bunker for a meeting. This meeting had been scheduled two weeks ago so he went right away, but his annoyance remained, similar to that feeling from the past when the widow in the short alley off Rue St-Jean had pursued him and stalked him in a blunt manner in front of all the neighbors.

As soon as he had stepped into General Long's bunker, right away he asked about this decision. But this fellow pretended not to hear anything; he kept busy pouring tea. Then he said slowly: "It's only temporary."

He understood that they had found for him only a temporary remedy, but it was still a forced arrangement. He felt his freedom being violated.

At the end of that week, on Saturday, he saw the shadow of a woman appear. Routinely each Saturday everyone went to the family compound except the bodyguards. Their shelter was only a few yards from his house; one could hear noises from either side of the walls. He seemed to have forgotten about "the female comrade serving the resistance." He seemed quite surprised to see a woman approaching his quarters as the evening meal had just ended; in the sky only a bright yellow cloud remained that shed colorless rays on the deep black trees of the forest. In that light and in the desolate space, the image of the woman was most frail and lonely.

He wondered, "Who can it be? Who is coming here at this time?"

In principle, the guards were not allowed to receive family members in the off-limits area. If a family came up to visit, guards could take a break and meet their loved ones in an area called "Reunions" or, more romantically, the "House of Happiness." That house was about a stream and two hills away. Curious, he continued to peek through the window, following the one who walked with her head down. It seemed as if she were carrying some objects that made her gait both hurried and quite unbalanced: an uneasy and painful gait. The image did not stir any feeling of admiration, only pity. Pity for a man is bad, but twice as bad if it is felt for a woman.

"What a stupid business," he said to himself in an unpleasant manner, as if against himself. Then he looked down at the pile of documents. But an intuitive feeling told him that the woman with the unsteady walk was of concern to him and not to the guards. He then recalled the "temporary solution" that General Long had talked about and immediately a cry pierced his heart:

"Hell! This is the woman they have chosen for me."

Putting the materials down, he sat absentminded.

There were no good-looking single women left in the women's association. All had been taken. Top among the fair ones were Van, Vu's wife; Sau's second wife; and Miss Tuong Vi, who came from the central performance troupe. These latter two were nicknamed the Two Ladies." Then followed the "Three Dainty Ones," Lan, Hue, and Nhi; three women well known in the resistance zone because of their graceful looks and domestic skills. They were tasked to assist all the international welcoming ceremonies and important celebrations, making flower displays, cakes, and all the popular dishes, as well as teaching the other women how to apply makeup. Even though they lived in the woods, these women were all pretty stylish, and spoiled with shipments of luxuries, silk, cosmetics, and French cigarettes.

On this subject, he had declared, "It is a habit. At my age, habit is stronger than one thinks."

The women relied on that to make their demands: "It might be the jungle, but we're still women."

It was he who had supported them. A handful of annoyed ones commented behind his back:

"He lived with Westerners for twenty years. He likes to drink French wine and is gallant like the French."

During celebrations, he saw that the women discreetly sprayed perfume on the collars of their dresses or on the satin ribbons in their hair. The nice smell and their smiles made the forests less somber.

Now he thought that of all the women he had seen, not one of them had this twisted walk, and nobody had the name Thu. It was clear that all the beautiful women already belonged to somebody. Left was this "comrade who serves the resistance," who must be the ugliest one left in the women's association, from whom even men who were deprived would turn away their face. That fact was undeniable.

"However, she will still come."

He sighed and stood up, rearranging his clothes. At that moment, the guard entered and said, "Mr. President, the female comrade from the women's association is here."

"Thank you. You may retire."

The guard walked out in a flash. Detached, the president looked after the young lad then wondered, "What am I going to tell her and still be polite? Because I didn't choose this woman. If it is a meeting forced by destiny then it is worse than what happened with that Paris seamstress, because it is tied to prior events. That would make him and her most uneasy: a lovemaking without love; not even mutual agreement to release a body's pent-up physical needs, but simply an act to support the resistance. This is both hypocritical and senseless."

The thought depressed him. But he still remembered that he was expected to be the host when a guest was coming. He stood up and walked out under the sloping roof to greet her. The woman, as he guessed, had just put her feet on the first step of the stairs. From on high, he saw the top of her head first: a small head with thin hair parted on both sides, and tied in the back with a shiny aluminum three-prong clip.

"Her hair is as thin as that of an eighty-year-old lady," he thought to himself. "How painful. I have never seen such thin hair, to a point where I can see clearly her scalp. And it is not white but brownish."

That thought floated on by. He remembered, while in Paris, he had often met old women who had lost almost all their hair, exposing pink scalps. Those women had passed beyond the age of emotion and desire, and had lost all ability to do anything useful; they walked slowly on the sidewalks all day long, or in the parks alone, or around the water fountains to look at the trees or to feed the birds. They always wore cloth or wool hats; only on extremely hot days would they unwrap their protective covers and reveal for all to see their pitiable bare heads: the mark of old age, the undisputable verdict of time!

"This woman is still young, why did she lose her hair so quickly? Because of the mountain climate, the stream water, or the hard life? But these bad conditions are shared by all. Why do the other women still have the right to 'display the shiny flock of hair,' to speak like a third-class poet?

By this time, the guest had taken the last step; she looked up. Their eyes met; her whole body suddenly shriveled up, from narrow shoulders to peanut-size knees; it all gathered in out of embarrassment. He did not know why but he, too, was embarrassed to witness the unconcealed fear of the woman, and he felt that this encounter was brutality.

"Mr. President . . ."

Her lips quivered for a while before she could utter those words.

He quickly replied, "Miss, please do come in."

"Yes . . ." the woman answered, breathing heavily. As soon as she was inside the house, she took her bag from her shoulder and hung it on the back of the chair, and then she laid the mat and the blanket she had carried under one arm down on the floor. He glanced at her and right away saw a white pillow within the quilted blanket, both wrapped neatly in the individual mat with several rounds of parachute strings.

"Those strings will be used to hang the mosquito net after the duty is completed," he thought quietly to himself. The organization must have briefed her carefully that she must hang this net in the front room of the house, where it would be concealed by the large bamboo curtains hanging from ceiling to floor. There, there is no other pillow, no other blanket, no room for a second person. Thus she has to bring all these things with her. The careful and neat preparation is like a small unit of sappers preparing to attack a large fort. How pitiful!"

Visualizing the woman crossing the stream and traversing two hills with the mat and blanket, he says to her, "You've been walking; please sit down and rest."

He went to prepare a new pot of tea. The water had boiled at three in the afternoon and had not retained enough heat to keep the tea leaves settled, so they were floating on top. He had to shake it awhile for the water to turn a light yellow color:

"Please have some tea. I just received a gift of some cane sugar."

He took the jar of Quang Ngai cane sugar and put it on the table:

"Miss, please . . ."

"Mr. President, my name is Thu, Minh Thu. The association has another Thu, Bich Thu."

"Yes? So there is another one, named Bich Thu?" he repeated mechanically. He racked his brain trying to remember if he had ever met a female comrade named Thu but came up empty.

Meanwhile, the woman drank some tea. She seemed to be truly thirsty after walking to his residence, even though it really wasn't that far. Her wrists were small and skinny like those of a child; her neck displayed long, twisted veins that could not be shielded under her light blue shirt. Sitting in front of him, he could see clearly her thin hair sticking to her scalp, exposing brown spots. Her skin was brown but not the honey-cake color that people thought so highly of.

He dared not look at her long, knowing she was fluttering like a snipe. His heart was filled with boredom mixed with pity. Pity for whom? Perhaps for both of them—the poor woman and the president. Life is a cruel drama, truly; full of scenes that are impossible to anticipate. Or is it no more than a traffic accident?

Turning his head toward the window, he looked at the afternoon light, which had taken a slightly purple tint, then said aimlessly, "Does the women's association grow lots of vegetables?"

"To report to Mr. President, our garden has all kinds: green cabbage, chrysanthemum leaves, cabbage, and kohlrabi. Eggplants and tomatoes are very good this year."

The poor woman had seized the silly question as her way out, replying enthusiastically with a flourish.

"Really? You gals are pretty good."

"Yes. The leading ones are very enterprising. We had to send people down all the way to the border to buy the seeds."

"Have you ever been near the border?"

"Mr. President . . ."

She looked up toward him with a terrifying air, and immediately he recognized he had made an unforgivable mistake. Those assigned near the border, or down in the cease-fire area, were those full of energy; besides having strength, they needed to be quick on their feet, intelligent, with attractive physiques. The woman who sat curled up in a chair before him met none of these criteria.

"Oh, I just asked that. You can go only when the office assigns you."

"Yes."

"All of us have to do what the revolution orders; the duties of the organization."

"Indeed, yes."

"Miss Thu . . ." He almost asked a stupid question: "Miss Thu, how old are you?" Such questions were permanent fixtures in his head to use with the youth groups: "Little Hong, how old are you? Come get the candies and give some to your friends"; or, "Little Thanh, how old are you? Now you get the gifts. Will you save some for your parents?"

Those questions were still fresh in his brain because just the previous Sunday he had distributed candies to some children. The president cleared his throat as if a cough had stopped his question:

"Miss Thu . . . Miss Thu, do you hear from your family regularly?"

"Well, I have nobody besides an older sister. But she followed her husband to Thailand for business when my parents died. I could not keep in touch with her. For me, family is the revolution."

"Good. The revolution is the extended family; it is the communal roof over all of us," he replied, suddenly realizing that he had turned bland. He no longer used the sharpest words, even in his meetings with the motivation cadres. His words were like wilted vegetables, warmed-up soybean husks, foods reserved for cows or pigs. But the woman seemed satisfied. She looked at him, blinking her eyes, and it was not clear if she was flirting or just showing her happiness.

"Not only is she homely but she looks really dumb. For sure, there is not a thought in her head, except for whatever was stuffed in by others," he silently observed

Suddenly his limbs felt tired:

"I will have to hold this woman, will I not? In a few minutes I will have to do to her all that sex requires. This is not avoidable. I will have to release my body from all the pressure. I will need to keep my wits sharp because the resistance will go on for a long time. Because of this, nothing will be better than to annihilate all the hopes that any normal man might have; to bury the world of feelings. I represent responsibility. What I do is carry the nation's weighty load. If in the old days there was someone who, in the name of duty, had to marry Chung Vo Diem, now I have to copy that old hero and perform."

Even after all that reasoning was concluded, his spirit was not at all convinced. The will just disappeared.

"How strange! All of a sudden I have no sexual desire. Totally empty; totally unfeeling."

He knows that the man in his body is extremely robust and that his sexual needs exceed normal limits. Many times he had told his buddies, "I am only an old man from my head to my belly button. Below it, I am still young."

That statement had spread like a fairy tale.

And yet . . . and yet . . .

Standing before this woman, the part below his belly button turned into that of an old man, too.

He panicked: "How pitiful! The hand of the clock points at the number six. It is something nobody predicts. When I lived alone, it was wild like a fighting horse, now it gathers all four legs to surrender. Demonic! Can it be that this woman can destroy the sexuality of anyone who stands before her?" he wonders.

And the answer comes right away:

"There is no doubt. If not, she would have married. At the front, there are ten times more men than women. Women choose their lovers; men have no right to pick a wife. It's clear that this woman's ability to destroy the urge for love is great. Is that why they chose her for me?"

All of a sudden, he was angry. Scattered thoughts pounded in his head: "Those people are really bad! What allows them to treat me like this? What power prompted them to arrange this for me?"

Blood rushed to his face; he felt hot. He quickly poured a cup of tea and took little sips to control his anger, a longtime habit of his. Meanwhile, Miss Minh Thu had drunk many cups. She sat there waiting with an air of acceptance like a dog in his master's yard. His anger made him forget the presence of the tiny woman, shriveled in her blue blouse. The anger made him walk with long strides around the room, a cup of tea in his hand, his eyes looking straight into enemy space. Then he suddenly realized his rudeness. He quickly returned.

"Will you forgive me, Miss Thu? I have too many things to think about."

"Yes . . . Mr. President," she replied sheepishly, her head bowed.

He put the teacup on the table and pulled a chair close to the woman.

"I am sorry . . . Thu, OK?"

He purposely became intimate. At the same instant, his heart was boiling because of a sudden rage:

"Why am I acting out this miserable play? Why don't I tell her directly that my sexual machinery is now incapacitated because it was violated? That it is her who destroys all the desire in the man. That any man would become impotent or incompetent if he had to go to bed with her."

While his brain was churning with those insulting thoughts, his face was as calm as that of someone meditating. He lowered his voice and said, "I sincerely apologize to you, Minh Thu. I do not feel well today. Perhaps I have had a fever since yesterday afternoon and have not had time to take medication."

"Yes . . . well," the woman confusedly answered, her head bowed lower. Suddenly, tears dropped slowly along the bridge of her nose. Miss Thu wiped them with the sleeves of her shirt. He quickly stood up with the intent to find her a clean cloth. Unfortunately, he was using the only dry one. The others were soaking in a basin of soapy water. He just stood there silently, looking at the pitiful woman who sobbed in humiliation. Because she hadn't brought a handkerchief, she bent down and took an undershirt, probably meant for sleeping, out of her bag to wipe her nose.

"I have never met a woman with so little charm," he thought to himself while looking at the tears rolling along the sides of Miss Thu's nose, a small nose, turned up and crooked at the tip. A predestined imperfection. According to Asian physiognomy, the shape of one's nose reveals both one's career and the character of one's mate in marriage. A man with a crooked nose will most unavoidably marry an unintelligent, ugly woman; but if she were to be attractive, then she would be a chanteuse, actress, or whore. A woman with a crooked nose will not find a husband; but if she should marry, it would not be to a gentleman.

"Definitely I cannot be Miss Minh Thu's gentleman. No nice gentleman could look at his wife as if he were looking at a head of cabbage displayed in a produce bin, as I am doing now. Still life paintings would move me many times more."

In the past, whenever he had stepped into the Louvre, he had felt an extraordinary stirring before a painting, even though he was no artist.

"But this woman . . . bad fortune indeed—both for her and for anyone who beds her. Others can be vulgar or rough; antagonistic and stubborn; submissive or gentle. But they all exude the scent of a woman who can arouse a man's enthusiasm. Maybe not burning feelings but at least some warmth of feeling. That hat seamstress, though not refined, still possessed traits that made her a full woman."

He reflected.

The sleeping-cap seamstress had hair thick as a horse's mane, the golden color of hay. When she let her hair down, her back was showered with a golden waterfall. He had often caressed that hair, curiously examining each curly strand, thinner than worm silk. One time, after lovemaking, he had gone back to his room and inadvertently found a few strands of her hair; curious, her took one and tied it to his watch. He shook it back and forth like a yoyo, totally amazed that the thin hair could hold an object a thousand times heavier.

Then he saw another face; this one proud with eyebrows slanted at the sides. His heart blurted out a silent greeting: "Hello, dear; an old friend . . ."

"Oh, it is her, the soul mate."

The woman looked at him full of threat, then suddenly burst into laughter. He smiled, too, because this gesture, if truly hers, was from the one who had made his heart crazy, even though that madness had been just a fleeting fever.

"Hello, my dearest; my dearest comrade!"

Because she was a comrade, according to the real meaning of the word, referring to those who share the same steps on a road, pursue the same goal. The look on her square face was both determined and daring, her words were incendiary, her resolution close to that of a dictator—all those striking traits of her personality made her the model representative of the revolution. The revolution roared on this planet because of people like her, beings with both brilliance and blindness, as all their enthusiasms and their passions were led by the prospect of victory, a crucial motivation of ancient warriors when they engaged in battle. This passion for victory was a ghostly force guiding them along the whole journey forward, carrying them to all corners of the struggle. Believing that their action was for the common good, in reality they were just looking for a way to subdue the hot, untempered blood of youth, to satisfy their thirst for power, though they nevertheless borrowed the cause of all to justify their actions.

"Enough: no more discussion. I think it's time for a decision."

"Enough: no more extended excuses. The revolution is waiting for us. Now we have to go!"

He recalled her choppy speech, often having the last words at the end of a meeting because the men did not want to antagonize her when her cheeks were very red and her eyes shone with anger.

In their short affair, she had often interrupted him when she was annoyed, in that same bossy manner. He remembered the way she threw her arms up to show her superior authority; the way she had leaped up to kiss him instead of using words of apology when she had realized that she had been wrong. And the way she had enjoyed sex. She always went first; she often cheerfully rode him like a professional comfortable atop a devoted horse.

"Yes, even with that one, I find traits that are worth liking. When she was angry and pouted, her dimples deepened and turned her strong words childish and you could not disagree. After voicing those extreme words or presenting those extreme programs, she knew how to withdraw awkward ideas by bursting into laughter. That genuine laugh both made fun of herself and was an apology offered to others, which swept away all difficulties."

While he was drowning in memories, Miss Minh Thu had suppressed her sobs. She straightened herself up, lips tightening. Her face, no longer startled or afraid, showed stubbornness. Her hands still gripped her under-shirt, which had been crumpled into a ball and perhaps soaked with tears. She looked, not at him but straight at the opposite wooden wall.

Then darkness overtook the day. The president suddenly recovered himself to say, "Are you calm now, Miss Minh Thu?"

"Mr. President, I am."

"Very good. Let me turn on the light. That will make us more at ease."

"Yes."

He was a little surprised, as her tone seemed to have changed. It seemed strong, distinct, as if she were careless. He lit up two lamps at once and put them on the table:

"Miss Minh Thu, do you want to go to bed?"

"Mr. President, my bedtime is eight thirty."

"Very good. I might find something to serve my guest. At least tonight is Saturday evening."

He looked for something to serve his guest, but in his cupboard were only some cigarettes and a can of Bird brand milk.

While he opened the can, Miss Minh Thu went to the veranda to fetch some kindling for the stove. Seeing the woman return clutching a bunch of branches, a slight feeling of compassion engaged him. A feeling complex and vague took over his soul. It might have been pity, nostalgia for all the seeds of happiness that had no sooner sprouted than they had quickly died during an uncertain life, full of changes and hardships. Perhaps it was a deep understanding of humanity, empathy for another wandering being, one like himself also indicted for life, though for different reasons.

Or, because the evening dew was starting to spread in the evening cool, perhaps feeling the fogginess of the earth had awakened all that was foggy in his soul.

He no longer knew, but when the woman bent her back to put the wood in the stove and stretched her skinny neck to blow on the fire and sparks from the wood flew everywhere, he suddenly felt sorry for her as one would for any life spent in misery. He gave the glass of milk to Miss Thu, saying:

"Please drink the milk, then I will hold the light to hook up the mosquito net. Hopefully next time, my fever will be gone and the situation will be better."

Next time was the following Saturday. He had returned after a long trip to inspect a war zone. His clothes were stained from dust on the roads. Sweat had dried on his skin, causing it to itch. This time he again forgot that it was a Saturday. Then, when he had set his foot on the stairs and saw light flickering from a fire, he raised his voice and asked:

"Who is up there? . . . Why light the fire so early?"

No answer. The bodyguard whispered in his ear, "Perhaps the woman from the women's association."

"Yeah . . ." He suddenly remembered.

The bodyguard asked, "Do I need to stay to prepare water for your bath?"

"Of course."

For a long time now that guard had always prepared hot water for him to bathe. The pot was fairly big, made of heavy copper, and the wooden container to hold the water was also very large. Only the strong arms of young men could roll it around. After two days on the road, having a bath, cleaning up, and changing into new clothes were happiness for him; a small happiness but happiness nonetheless.

When they entered the house, Miss Minh Thu was already there by the stove, knitting away: the traditional epitome of a wife waiting for her husband. He felt trapped and uneasy; nevertheless he had to smile in greeting the woman. The guard went directly to the bathroom then turned around:

"Mr. President, there is hot water in there. Now I only need to get your clothes ready, then I am done."

"Thank you."

He turned to the woman and asked, "That tub is pretty high, how did you manage it?"

"Yes, I could do it."

"Thank you . . . Next time let the guard do it. He is at the young age when he can break buffalo horns."

"Yes."

He walked into the bathroom, stripped off his sweaty and dusty clothes, but suddenly sighed. Outside, the young guard had withdrawn, his footsteps heard on the stairs. When he withdrew farther, the only remaining sounds were of the fire—the bubbling of the wood sap and the crackling of the charcoal. In this familiar space of his where he had been the only resident, now there was that strange woman sitting there. From her awkward movements it was clear that she had never handled knitting needles before and that she had been put up to learn this craft by her comrade sisters in the association.

They cast, choreographed, and directed actors, especially among the poor. He felt sorry for them both: for Miss Minh Thu and for himself.

"C'est la vie; toujours la même comédie!"

The first bucketful of water he poured carelessly over his head and his eyes smarted. He quickly wiped his eyes with a dry towel, cursing his own inattention. Waiting for the burning to subside, he continued to bathe, while remembering the promise he had made to the woman. The situation did not look any brighter, especially after a long and weary journey.

"It's terrible. The fates don't smile on her. In which hour was she born to be so unfortunate?" he thought to himself. And a real fear took hold of him.

"But I cannot twice push her into humiliation. She is a human being nonetheless, a woman. Humiliation can drive a person to seek death . . ."

When young, he had read quite a few tales of palace life. He remembered deaths by the poison-filled golden cup, by slashed throats, or by a piece of white silk hung over stair rails. From queens to concubines, from ladies-in-waiting to maids . . . how many women had sought death to end humiliation arising from unrequited love? But the majority had been real beauties. Miss Minh Thu was not a beauty, of course, but had accepted the mission of "serving the revolution." Her reaction thus would be increased manyfold. No need for a rich imagination to know that after the previous Saturday she would have confessed to her superiors: "To report, I did not accomplish the mission assigned to me." The older sisters had met, and all week had looked for ways to help her. Luckily for them, he had had to go to prepare for a forthcoming military campaign, giving them time to work on a plan: "The lady will prepare scented water for him to bathe and sit by the fire knitting."

Pity the fate of humanity!

But even if he complained on his or her behalf, he could not forget that in a little while he would have to "enter the room," according to the old saying. But what was under his belly button still refused to play its part. This worry over failure mixed with fear of all the consequent humiliation that could set in made him lose his bearings. But at that moment the work of toweling dry brought to him an old but always effective solution. He caressed himself. He brought vividly to mind a memory of the most sensual woman he had ever met in his life, the one with the slanted eyes. He visualized the sight of her straddled on his stomach, her flesh, her breathing, her charcoal black hair spread on her forehead shining under the light.

And his youth returned.

The loud ringing of the telephone startles him and wakes him from his revery. He is about to get up but the guard runs straight into the room and picks up the phone.

"Mr. President, Vice Minister Vu."

"Thank you, leave it there for me."

He holds the phone to his ears, hearing the panting breathing on the other side of the receiver.

"What happened to you? Do you have bronchitis?"

"No, I just have a cold from yesterday afternoon."

"Be careful. You may be much younger than I, but you're no longer so strong and youthful. Don't tease the Big Boss."

"I know. Are you well, Eldest Brother?"

"I am OK. After you left I had someone bring me more money to offer to the woodcutter's family. They had prepared the envelope too skimpily."

He hears Vu's laugh on the other end of the line, then continues:

"We always forget the details. We are always indifferent to the concrete facts."

"But those very details and all such ordinary calculations are life."

"Agreed. These days you have the inclination to become a philosopher of dialectical materialism. Do you plan a transfer to the training department?"

"What?"

He hears Vu burst into laughter in his familiar playful manner.

"What? Will you spare me!"

He also laughs and quickly changes the subject:

"What is going on in Hanoi?"

"Tomorrow there will be a wind from the northeast. Don't forget that it will be cold for a long while."

"I do not forget: in January it's a drawn-out cold, in February it's a fortunate cold, and in March it's Lady Ban's cold."

"Yes. That's why I'm calling you. With the north wind, it will be cold up there first. Don't take a walk in the woods; a sudden rain will bring the flu."

"I will remember."

"I have to go now. They just informed me of a sudden meeting at central administration, followed by dinner . . . after dinner, for sure we will continue the meeting . . . Eldest Brother, take care."

"You, too," says the president. "Give my best to Sister Van. You are lucky to have her. She is beautiful both in person and in character."

"Yes, thank you," Vu replies in a joking manner that the president has not heard before, and repeats on the other end of the line: "Eldest Brother sent me congratulations on the beautiful woman with attractive character."

Then, right away, the younger brother turns back to the phone to say, "I am going now."

The president hears a strange noise when Vu hangs up the phone. A suspicion flashes by. But he is unable to guess what.

2

Hanoi becomes cold. The north winter wind returns.

The rows of trees turn deeper green in the freezing cold and the surface of Ho Tay Lake ripples with millions of wavelets. The rows of jacaranda along the lake's edge are purple, a solitary kind of purple. Pedestrians pick up their pace along the Co Ngu road to shield themselves from the strong, wild wind blowing above the water. Right at that moment, too, a pair of lovers sits at the edge of the lake holding each other, their faces toward the wind.

Vu casts his eyes in their direction and thinks to himself: "How long will those two be able to live out their dream of love? Who knows in what year, in what month, on what day they will have to cry in regret because of their passionate embrace today?"

Pairs of curled-up men and women hold on to each other under their transparent rain gear, shields too delicate to ward off the cold February wind. Leaving the Co Ngu road, Vu finds a tea stall, a folksy hangout, a tiny and deplorable "private enterprise" that has permission to operate in the exclusively government-run economy. The stall is sheltered by deteriorating old panels with used newspapers glued to them. The pot of green tea sits warmly inside a large cozy lined with hay. The cups are chipped, stained with tea residue; they are placed disorderly on a large tray that is no less dirty. But this scene of utmost poverty and frugality befits the society in which he lives. Because it does not invite jealousy. Because it can evoke only pity or disgust. Things considered diseased or cursed in a prosperous society are right for this society. For a long while, these suspicions have been gnawing at him.

"Lean the bicycle on a lamppost and lock it. Caution is the mother of success," says an obnoxious and disdainful voice. The tea seller had seen the strange guest and raised his voice to guide him:

"Don't you see that lamppost over there? Put your bike there so I can watch it."

Vu looks up and around for a while and sees a lamppost on the other side of the street somewhat hidden from sight by a cart drawn by a cow and filled with watercress in long bundles. He walks his bike to the other side of the street and leans it close against the cart and carefully locks it.

The tea stall owner watches his every movement carefully with an inhibited curiosity. Then he waits until Vu walks into the stall and sits on the long bench with his back against the panel holding out the wind then asks, "What do you want to drink? Green tea or black tea? Or if you want to enjoy a glass of rice wine, I have that, too."

Vu is surprised: "A tea stall also selling wine?"

"Why not?" the old man asks back with an air of daring mixed with playfulness: "You think that people need only tea and not wine? You think that if the government forbids selling something people must go along?"

"I do not think it is that simple. But . . ."

The old man laughs hoarsely: "But I find you a good person, that's why I said that. If it were someone else, I would bend my tongue in another direction."

Vu also laughs along: "Thank you. You find me a good person, really? What does it mean, 'a good person'?"

"A good person is one who is not sneaky; who is unable to be a lowlife or be disloyal. Not like those who come here begging me, asking me, to sell them wine to drink. After they are done drinking, even before they take time to pee, they go and report to the police."

"And then?"

"And then?" the old man repeats with a faint smile full of spite. "The police are what they are. Many know how to drink wine. In cold weather like this, a sip of wine is warmer than a swallow of rice gruel, thin like snail water. Therefore, even if they pretend to confiscate my bottle of wine, three days later they have to return it anyway. The only thing is, when they return it, there is only the empty bottle. I continue to call the people in the countryside to bring up more wine and everything is normal again."

By then, the old man has bent down and pulled out from under the settee a basket covered with a jute bag. Turning over the jute bag, he shows Vu the wine jug in a jade color with a large, open spout.

"Do you see it now? Top-rated sweet rice with yellow blossoms is of superior grade."

"Such a beautiful jar!" says Vu. "The wine must be good. Please give me a cup to warm up."

"Ah ha . . ." The old man starts laughing loudly, making his beard shake hard. "The nice vessel does not guarantee good wine; like good paint does not warranty good wood. But my wine is guaranteed to be good."

That said, he bends down and opens a wooden box with two brass handles; he takes out a shiny clean porcelain cup, then pours one full cup and gives it to Vu.

"Taste it and you will know what wine is!"

Vu holds the cup, bemused. The porcelain cup is blue with a painting of a phoenix. Its rim is encircled with brass. It is the kind his father had used to drink wine. In the afternoon, after his gardening chores, his father used to put a small brass tray on the sitting platform. On the tray, there would be a drinking set that held one cup, one tiny wine jar, and a small plate of appetizers. He would sit there contemplating the scenery, sipping his wine while waiting for the evening meal with his family.

"Well, take a sip to see if I tell you the truth or only joke!" the old stall owner urges. Vu lifts the cup to his lips; the fragrance of the fermented rice touches his senses before his tongue touches the liquid of the Luu Linh wine. That fragrance invokes the harvest, the warm countryside of the fields of his youth, where golden waves of harvestable rice overflowed and covered the surface of the earth, where one was surrounded by outlines of villages with rows of dark green bamboo, and where the shining and silvery streams by the paddy fields were bathed in the whispering songs of the wind. The wind during the harvest gave off a special scent. He takes a sip and voices his praise:

"Splendid! I never had wine this good."

The old man is elated. "I knew right away. Nobody has complained about this wine. The people in my own village brew it. But in the whole village only Mr. Khai's family reaches this superior grade."

"Really good."

"So many times production was stopped, swept away. From the guerrillas to the police: they sneak up to confiscate the equipment and throw it in the river. Half of the village loses their work. But the remainder carries on; they live here, they live there, but they still live. As long as there are people who want to drink wine, those who can brew it still exist."

"Aren't you afraid, saying that?"

"Like I told you: I find you a good person, therefore I tell the truth. With others I change my tune. Like this kind of wine."

At this moment, the old man pulls out another basket to show Vu: inside is a vat made of plastic, washed clean and full of wine.

"My gosh, why are you storing the wine in this plastic vat, isn't it toxic?"

"To each its own device. With you I offer my superior wine served in the blue phoenix cup. With others I sell this kind of wine from the chipped cup. Our elders say: 'Of people, there are three grades; of things, three kinds.'"

"But . . ."

"It was different in the old days. Nowadays it's different, too. Don't you see that the situation has turned upside down? I display the good vessel and the pretty cup to let the rotten ones report that I am suspect, one who opposes the revolution."

"Yes, now I understand . . ." Vu slowly replies, and a pain penetrates his soul as the wine stirs his nerves: if drinking from the blue phoenix cup makes you a suspect, then his father was among those in opposition who were subject to suspicion. It was fortunate that his father had died before he could have been tripped up by the revolution, which his own beloved son supported.

Vu takes the last sip of wine then hands the cup to the old man, who immediately puts it back in the wooden box, because, just then, a new customer had walked in.

"It's cold, old man . . . give me some wine."

The customer rubs his hands while talking. He stands instead of sitting down. A wide-brimmed hat still on his head, he looks like someone who recruits workers for construction jobs or factories. He not only rubs his hands together wildly but his legs shake uncontrollably. His body rocks back and forth in an odd manner.

Without looking up, the stall owner says, "Yes, really cold," as if he is repeating the chorus of a song. Then he pulls out the plastic box and pours wine into an old cup taken from among the chipped and stained ones.

The customer takes one gulp, then hands the cup back: "One is not enough, pour me another one."

"Yeah, the February cold is very, very cold," the old man replies, pouring a second cup.

Quietly Vu looks at them and pursues his own thoughts:

"We had the revolution to liberate the people, but, at the end, what we have is only a miserable drama in which decent and honest people can find no place to stand. Those who can make it are forced to be dishonest and disloyal. Or at best, little people like this old man must look upon life as having two sides—like some kind of reversible armor. When I was still young, people were not that bad. It's the new society that pushes them down the slope."

"Well, good-bye, oldster. I'll stop by and pay you tomorrow," the customer says loudly, then lays the empty cup on the settee and walks out.

Vu waits until he is far away then asks, "Do all your clients drink on credit like that?"

"It's not on credit, it's theft. They say that but they never pay a cent."

"Why is that?"

"Oh, clearly you are someone who doesn't hang around stalls. When I first saw you I knew that already. A guy like that was called an 'informer' when the French were here. If I do not give him free wine, he will find stories to tell the police and spoil my business."

"I see . . ."

The old man continues: "You guess correctly. I do not have a lot of time to play around. Today I have a bad headache so I am looking for some diversion."

"That's it. That's life. Everyone has issues that cause headaches and heartaches."

The old man lowers his voice in a consoling manner, and, a few seconds later—as if he wants to express his sympathy in a more effective way—he asks: "Do you wish to have another cup of wine? This time it's on me."

"Thank you, sir. I am not a heavy drinker, even with your wonderful wine here," Vu replies.

At that moment, he sees his wife with a bicycle on the sidewalk. Even from a distance, he can see she is looking pale. Because of the cold weather, she is draped with a large blue woolen scarf, making her face sadder. Vu stands up.

"It's so cold, what are you doing outside?"

She looks up quietly with a reproachful air. Guessing their situation, the proprietor quickly says, "Why don't you give your bike to your husband to put across the street? I guarantee no one will steal it."

"Thank you, sir," Van replies and gives the bike to Vu. Then she sits down in the stall, shivering from the cold.

"Please warm up with some ginger bud tea," the proprietor cheerfully offers.

"Thank you, sir. Here you also have ginger bud tea?"

"I have everything. For I have lots of regular customers. Those ladies prefer only ginger bud tea."

Again he bends down under the settee, pulls out another box containing

many dark brown lacquer cups decorated with golden flowers. At that moment, Vu returns. He is surprised to see this owner like a magician with all
sorts of boxes underneath the bamboo settee. He says, smiling:

"How many other boxes do you use to store your various cups?"

"I already told you. Special guests deserve precious objects. To such a
beautiful person, I dare not sell tea in a ceramic cup."

"My goodness: such gentility!"

"Not really. I am just clay feet that happened to be born on the Yen Phu
dike," he remarks, his voice as if in song, his face full of pride. "My parents
were not wealthy, but they had enough to get me educated through high
school. Thus people say: 'Not gentlefolk, but at least comfortable.'"

"You must have been very talented when you were young," says Van.

"Oh, please don't. It's too much. But, in reality, during my youth I was
not bad . . . *Pas mal.*"

The old man's French surprises both Vu and Van. Vu smiles.

"You still remember French? That's very strange; people in your generation have given all their learning back to their teachers."

"I am half a century old; my brain is slow and my tongue stiff. But there
are some words scattered in my head. It's like sprouts of watercress in the
early January fields. They still threaten that French is the enemy's language,
so I challenge them by once in a while using a few words to see what they
will do to me."

"Aren't you afraid some will snitch on you?"

"I worry more if they will snitch about my wine. But snitching about
some broken pieces of French does not concern me. I do not fear reprisals
as would a government official. I am a black ass who sells drinks by the sidewalk, the lowest-down-in-the-abyss kind of person. Is there any lower place
that you can fall to?"

Silent, each follows his or her own thoughts. Then a very young but already heavyset woman with reddish complexion steps in. She cheerfully
greets everyone, then turns around to ask the owner:

"Old man, sir, you open your stall so regularly. It is cold, why don't you
wrap yourself in a blanket and sleep?"

"If I could sleep like you all, I would be a young man, not an old one."

"You may be an old man but there are plenty of interested ladies. In Yen
Phu village alone, there are seven at least."

"Wash your mouth out; you talk nonsense."

"You wash my mouth! Who is going to cheer you up? Who else brings you rice cakes and pressed sticky rice every day from those interested ladies?"

The woman giggles with devilish delight, and the stall owner, Vu, and his wife laugh along. Piles of flesh shake on her ample body, her face bright red with simple happiness; she makes the little stall warmer. When she is done laughing, she takes out a cloth to wipe the sweat on her forehead, then says, "I am leaving. In the afternoon when the little boy comes over, please feed him."

"Don't worry, you don't have to remind me," the old man says, scolding her.

The young woman cracks a broad smile: "These days this old man is quite arrogant. With only two weeks without inquiry from 'the ladies,' he turns sour."

She doesn't wait for the old man's reaction, turns around, and bids farewell:

"You two, please stay and enjoy. I am going."

Then again not waiting for their reply, she briskly crosses over to the other side of the street, takes the handles of the watercress cart, and pushes it down the street. After turning the cart toward Quang Ba, she firmly moves it along.

Vu looks in her direction and says, "That woman is really strong and is definitely a good person."

"Her look tells her character," the old man observes. She may be cheerful, but she was widowed when she turned twenty. She raised three kids by herself. She does not refuse any work. She works like a buffalo from early morning until dark. Thus she never opens her mouth to complain."

"Why did her husband die so young?"

"They are both people from my village. They were friends from the time they wore open-crotch pants, and they married just when they turned eighteen. When the wife carried their third child, the husband was drafted. He never even set foot on the battlefield, but just as he crossed the border with Laos, he was blown up by a bomb."

He stops talking and pours himself a cup of perfumed tea and drinks it straight down as if to swallow something. Vu thinks silently as he remembers the banners hung at the intersection of Quang Ba road:

"Eldest Brother is right to say that this war shall become the greatest regret in history; that this defeat—the most bitter in his life—could not have been prevented. For him, this war is actually a national decapitation under the pretense of having the people drawn and quartered. It is the four wheels of destiny's cart and our people are the ones who will be pulled and severed to death."

All of a sudden a car's repeated honking bursts out loudly. Vu steps out of the stall and looks. A convoy of military trucks has been blocked by a train of carts carrying quicklime left standing in the center of the road. The haulers had stopped at some tea stalls to warm themselves. Hearing the honking, they now all hurriedly step out to push the carts up onto the sidewalks. Instants later, the liberated trucks, covered with camouflage tarps, zip noisily by.

The stall owner, looking at the dust flying on the street, tells Vu and his wife, "Sir and madame, the two of you should not stay here longer; the place is going to be very noisy and dusty. In a little bit, a flock of construction workers, carpenters, will stop by. It's better if I move the hot teapot and the stove to the back room. I don't have a lot of money but my property is fairly large."

"You are most sensitive and considerate. We do not know how to express our thanks."

"Please don't stand on such ceremony! I don't have much opportunity to meet people I can talk to openly from my heart."

The old man stands up briskly and with an agility belying his age. After the tray of tea is prepared, he takes his dear guests to the rear, explaining, "My parents left me a garden over a thousand square meters, thinking I would have lots of children and grandchildren and so later I could build more houses. They did not expect my fate was to be single; it is already tiresome to look after some of the houses they left behind."

He leads them across a patio made of leaf-pattern tiles with three houses on the shore of Ho Tay Lake. This house is only for drinking tea or contemplating the view. The middle house has a pond with goldfish; the inner one a rock garden with bonsai landscapes.

"Oh my; the patio is so large, why don't you put the fish pond outside?" Vu says.

The old man replies, "I know that putting the pond outside would give it the right look, but the neighbors have a ghost cat. Anyone with a pond outside would find the goldfish all eaten up."

Vu has never heard of cats eating pond fish before, but he dares not ask more. The stall owner puts the tray on the low table, between two armchairs.

"Why don't you two sit here, you can drink tea and chat. Here it is shielded from the wind, but I will bring out a little stove because it is cold. At the stall I have a bigger one to heat water for tea."

The old man turns around and leaves; he later returns with a little stove with red hot coals that he lays in front of them.

"In two hours, there will be a street vendor with sweet rice cakes and pressed sticky rice. Do you want to call her in here?"

"Yes, thank you, sir. This is more than enough. Later if we are hungry we will call for more," Vu replies.

The old man smiles with satisfaction while with his hand he scratches his beard, grown long down to his chest.

After he leaves, Vu tells his wife: "Now is a time for us. In such an idyllic spot it would be regrettable to speak of what is sad."

Van is silent; she is giddy in the oversized armchair. Finally, she finds a blanket that she rolls up and puts against the back of the chair, and then she leans on it. Vu glances at the dark circles under his wife's eyes.

"What is so urgent that you had to look for me in this cold weather?"

"I am your wife, isn't that enough?" she retorts in a taunting manner.

He does not answer but looks out to the lake. Since their discussion near the cornfield along the Red River, they no longer shared a bed. He had moved down to the first floor; he now worked in the living room and slept in the children's room, for they no longer lived at home. But one time, seeing him asleep in Trung's bed and not in their son's, she had screamed:

"I know why you sleep in that bed. What can you say about a father who does not choose the warmth of his own son?"

He had coldly replied, "Because there is no warmth but only a bad smell!"

It was true—Vinh has bromidrosis, a genetic condition passed from Mrs. Tuyet Bong and Master Tung down to their son. Not just in his armpits but all over; if he goes even one day without a bath, all the creases of his shirt smell rancid and grow black with stains. Thus, to avoid further issue with her sickening jealousy, Vu had brought into the house a low, foldable bed, which he slept in at night in a corner of the living room, with an old green curtain surrounding it. His sleeping area was simple, like the overnight accommodation given a guest from the countryside or a soldier on emergency leave.

Left to herself, Van had hung a beautiful Ukrainian lace curtain in place of the blue one. She replaced the old lights with a most sumptuous chandelier from Moscow. She acquired a living room set just like the one in the living room of the Russian Embassy. She had obtained a Rigonda phonograph, with all the records that the sophisticated have. Then she acquired a new glass cupboard to display all her Bohemian crystal glasses and cups and all her Chinese tea sets of paper-thin porcelain. Opposite that cupboard was placed an impressive buffet, in which were stored all kinds of cookies and candies along with many foreign wines brought by hand from Moscow, Prague, and Budapest, the places most favored by officials of the Ministry of Foreign Affairs. These were—undeniably—objects of the utmost luxury for the tens of millions of little people who daily lined up to get their rations of mildewed rice. Her bedroom could not store everything, so she took over his old office for that purpose; her bedroom was no longer a place for sleeping but an extravagant living room, full of light and very inviting. Nightly she turns on the three-tier chandelier, the lamp of the wealthy, to admire her looks as they are reflected in the glass windows. Or she turns up the volume of the record player to lie in bed and cover her ears so that her eardrums will not burst. But when she sees the neighbors poking their heads out their windows and looking toward her house with inhibited contempt, she hurriedly turns it off out of fear. All these things she does to taunt him are ineffective. Maybe the love he had for her has died. It drowned in the Red River. Now it is only a ghostly corpse, decaying at the bottom of the abyss. On the other hand, she is not able to love him, or more accurately, she cannot stop loving him despite the mismatch and differences between them. Maybe because of those contradictions she loves him more, which makes her miss him more. Such a tormented marriage is a misfortune, because at the dawn of old age, everyone should live with a spouse in harmonious affection, tightly spun out of all the preceding years and months.

Many a time, she had told herself, "I have everything. Only one thing I have not dared. Maybe I should and see what happens."

Just the thought made her face burn hot from shame. What she had wanted to try is exactly what she had often spoken of with contempt.

Thus, she did not expect that he who had stood indifferent to all the tricks she had deployed would be the first one to bring the subject up. At lunch one day, as they sat silently eating, each looking in different directions as they had done at all meals since they had slept separately, he suddenly told her: "You have done everything. What about the last one, why don't you do it to make the circle whole?"

"What do you mean by that?"

"I am not a nosy one, but, because I left a book in a drawer near the bed I was forced to go up to get it. I see that you have a living room that is identical to that of Fishmonger Tu. As to the last trick, why don't you do it?"

"Are you trying to humiliate me?" she screamed.

Calmly he replied, "In this life, no one can humiliate another. One can only humiliate himself or herself."

"Each of us has only one life," she responded with an enraged heart. "Why not enjoy it? Only those who are stupid or blind or missing something in their character would not find out how to live for themselves."

Then she told herself, "I will do it. I will do it! But then, don't you complain!"

She imagined her gorgeous living room full of young men, with loud music and red wine and champagne pouring out in streams. Scenes of pleasures would happen not only in movies but under the light of her own chandelier.

That imaginary episode of revenge lasted only a few seconds until she saw herself as that ugly and decadent woman Mrs. Tu, which made her want to puke. She returned to her private hell of unrequited love, a hell that cannot be driven from her mind.

"Why don't you drink some tea, dear?"

Seeing his wife quiet, Vu pours tea and gives it to Van. Not refusing but not saying "thank you" either, she takes the cup from his hand, puts it to her mouth, and swallows several big gulps. He pours himself a cup, and then also drinks it quietly. Before them, the big lake shines silvery gray. Not a pleasure boat in sight; only fishing boats that bobble on the water in unrelenting competition to make a living. The wind is strong. As soon as a net is thrown it is blown back against the side of the boat, making the boat shake with its nose diving forward as if it were being pushed down to sink. The fisherman drives his boat in circles to dismantle the net and to avoid the wind. Thus, life continues. Vu contemplates that little drama and wonders, "If I lived as that fisherman, would I be happy, or at least would life be less troubled?"

Such questions have no answers, so he continues drinking his tea. He realizes Van is looking at him.

"Tea is spilled down the sleeve of your shirt. This material cannot be cleaned. Cleaning will tear it."

"Sorry, I didn't pay attention . . ." he says, adding, "You are indeed perfect . . . on the material side."

"On the spiritual one, I am a zero, a despicable one. Is that what you want to say?" Van responds, rolling her eyes like one ready to dive into a fight. At the same moment, her face becomes pale and her heart begins to beat nonstop. He looks at her with a hint of surprise and hesitation, and an un-avoidable feeling of pity.

"Do you need to be reminded of the talk we had yesterday afternoon? You were also there when I was speaking in the living room. Eldest Brother congratulated me for having a wife like you, beautiful both in person and in personality. I know for a fact that, since the resistance war until now, he has sincerely admired you."

She blushes but does not reply.

He insists: "Or do you think the Old Man was being diplomatic?" Van is silent. He continues: "You do not want to answer because you know that what the Old Man said is totally genuine. Your nicknames of 'Miss Battle-field' and 'Miss City Beauty . . . it was the Old Man who named you so; no one else. Isn't that true?"

Still no reply from her.

He smiles. "Yesterday, I reminded you of his compliment because he re-quested it. He sent his regards to you."

"But you reminded me in a mocking manner! You know that," she said, exploding.

"I already said no one can humiliate you but you. The same with mock-ing; only if your true self does not mock."

Her face is white pale. After some inner debate, she bows her head and says intelligibly, "I kind of know that. That is why I came up here to look for you."

"Ah, that's why . . ." He lets out a cry, an unconcerned, almost insignifi-cant one. In the meantime, his eyes never stop following the fishermen's boats, which increasingly fade away on the silvery waves of the lake.

"He does not care about me. He does not love me any longer, not even a little bit," she thinks to herself, and in her despair, she suddenly screams:

"You are a miserable husband. Why don't you turn around and look at me? At least I am still in front of you, talking to you. Not even a hint of courtesy left."

"Oh, is that so?" Surprised, he turns around and looks at her. "All right: now I turn and look at you, I will try to be courteous to please you and try to be like a gentleman . . . Is that all right?"

She does not answer and he continues: "I'm listening to you now. Will you go on?"

"You can't drop that style of speaking, can you?"

"I myself do not understand when I start talking like that. Maybe it be-comes a habit that is hard to break."

"Vu, dear, we've had some very happy times together. Do you miss those days at all?"

"I miss them terribly, if you want to know the truth. I miss them and I am very unhappy, many times more than you can imagine. But I am not one of those who pretend to forget, who pretend to be blind or deaf. This is the crux of all the misfortune under our roof."

"I still love you. Or else things would be different."

"I know. Thank you." He laughs reflexively. "But now you can do anything; including taking up Fishmonger Tu's lifestyle. I will not intervene. You have the freedom to act to your satisfaction."

"You do not want to understand the truth. You didn't change, even after half a century."

"What truth?"

"The truth that you always look at life your own way, just your own. But life follows its own course, not yours; and that is why, always, you stick your nose out to get it hit; always, you stand against rivers and in front of storms."

"I am sorry. I'm forged and nurtured by my parents. When I met you, I was middle-aged. I cannot change to satisfy your wishes."

"This government has only a few hundred with your rank. No one has to bear all the hardships and shortcomings that you do."

"You can free yourself from your ties to me. You have the full capacity to start a new life."

"But I love you," she shouts, tears streaming down. "Why? Why can't you understand that simple fact?"

Vu is silent. A question sneaks inside his head: "When a woman loves, she believes she can do everything, even the craziest, the most illogical of things. All in the name of love. Is that really love? Or is it a way to accommodate some spiritual demand? Or a means designed to satiate corporal desires? 'Love'—maybe the most un-thought-through term in the human vocabulary, the one that is the most abused and carries the most hidden meanings."

Van cries. She pulls out a handkerchief to wipe her nose while he turns the empty cup in his palm. The wind off the lake howls and reddens the coals in the stove, making them pop. Warmth spreads and envelops them. Vu looks at the stove, waiting. But his wife cries for a long while, so he pours himself another cup of tea.

"Have you calmed down?"

". . ."

"We are getting old. No need to shout like that. I do not want the stall owner thinking that we're not stable mentally."

"I only want one thing. That we love each other as in the past."

"I also want that. But time does not turn back. Time has its own law, like you just said. Life goes by only on the path it draws for itself."

"I will do anything you wish, as long as you love me like before."

"Thank you. . . . But I firmly believe that you can only do everything according to your wish, and because you——"

"You refer to the living room upstairs? I can ask the workers to carry all that stuff to the dump tomorrow."

"That only creates gossip. You are aware how people look at that kind of woman."

"So what do you want me to do?"

"I cannot 'want'; what I 'want' for you is impossible."

"Impossible because you always look at things in a wrong way vis-à-vis others. It was like that in the war zone. Things that people find obvious, you fiercely oppose. Things that people think are impossible, you find ways to get done."

"What you are trying to say? Really, we seem not to have a common language anymore. Strange. Will you please explain?"

"Don't pretend!" she says, her voice rising again.

He turns to look back as a signal that the stall owner can clearly hear their argument.

She stops and finishes the cold cup of tea to regain her calm. Then she continues: "At the front line, everybody agreed with the choice of Miss Minh Thu for the president. You were the only one who vehemently objected all the way to the end. You alone cast a vote for Miss Thanh Tu. Do you recall the journey to recruit soldiers in the cities in the lower plains? It was Sau who gave that order so that everything could go smoothly."

"I remember. I understood that, back then, that people purposely pushed me away so they could do as they wished."

"But that was the responsibility of the organization, for the Old Man. How was it your personal responsibility?"

He looks at his wife, as if he were looking at some strange woman from another land, from the Sahara Desert or from the Antilles Islands. And she turns red at his glance. She repeats, with less confidence:

"That was the organization's task. How can it be wrong for me to say that?"

He slowly asks, "Van: If I were one-eyed, buck-toothed, and only three feet tall like a circus midget, would you nevertheless have loved me and married me?"

She remains quiet.

He looks at her attentively and continues: "Or if I were an albino, or had rickets or six fingers and toes, would you have married me?"

She does not answer and turns away to look at the west lake.

He continues his line of argument: "I remember the first time I met you, the hamlet high school girl, leaning her back against the door, with dreamy eyes, holding in her hands *The Hunchback of Notre Dame*. Perhaps I fell in love with you out of that vision. Now I ask you: If I were Quasimodo, the hunchback, would the beauty To Van agree to take me as her husband, or would she not?"

She continues to look at the lake and not answer.

Then he keeps on, asking, "Those things you don't want, why do you force them on others? Why did you impose your cruel wish on someone as decent to you as the Old Man was? Was it you who gave the idea to the association chairwoman to send Miss Minh Thu with her sleeping gear to the big house?"

Van turns around, looks at her husband, and says, with a natural manner mixed with some surprise, "Because Brother Sau asked for my opinion; because everyone agreed with my idea; because the Old Man was not normal. Why can't you see that?"

"The Old Man was the nation's president. He was the soul of the revolution. Anything else?"

"The Old Man is the Father of the Nation . . . you forgot that title."

"So?"

"Your question is silly. As the Father of the Nation, the Old Man cannot live like ordinary people. If you are full of rice, you have to stop eating meat. You are a learned and intelligent man, how can you not understand this small fact? Brother Sau and many others asked me that."

"Ah, ah, ah . . ."

Thunder rings in his head, not once but many times. The string of thunderclaps mimics the peals and clangs of fate that will explode on Doomsday. Vu feels that thousands of strings of mines have been placed in his brain, and now the first one has exploded, triggering a second one and making for a chain reaction.

In a storm, lightning always flashes before the thunder. That sequence happens to him in reverse. The thunder explodes first before bundles of bright lights arrive. All things appear so clear down to the very smallest details, as mountains appear in the horizon of a clear autumn, as gardens appear when fog evaporates away under the brilliant sun of June.

"I begin to understand people's logic; when you are full of rice, then you must give up meat. When you are made a saint, or the Father of the Nation, you are not entitled to ordinary happiness. That is why they forced upon him an old woman, one that had many times been offered in marriage from one unit to another, like a charitable donation, and no one wanted to take her. An old maid, of eighty-four pounds and thirty-four years.

"Why didn't they think of the Old Man as a king? A king in the old days had the right to fulfill all his sexual desires, no matter how brutal or immoral. If the Old Man had a young wife, that would have been only a very humble consideration.

"Why didn't they think that if the Old Man enjoyed a little happiness, he would have been more whole both physically and mentally, and thus could have done more for the nation?

"How could they have given themselves the right to unanimously torture the one that they hid behind to seek popular support as well as power?

"When you are full of rice, you have to forgo meat . . .

"It is with such logic that the cruelty of humanity manifests itself. A pleasure that hides discrimination and envy."

A concern suddenly rises. He turns to look into her eyes.

"Now I understand everything. In those days I truly believed that you would also go out to the mountains to do assigned tasks while I was away at the front. Now I know you didn't go anywhere. You stayed to assume the role of an assistant, to push at all costs for Miss Minh Thu to go over to the Old Man's big house. If you had not taken the opportunity to get everyone in that position, they would probably have assigned Miss Thanh Tu."

She does not answer, but her look reveals that this was true.

He asks again, "When did you learn how not to tell the truth?"

She turns her head away.

He continues: "In summary, how many times have you lied in your life? How many times since you grew up? How many times since we became husband and wife?"

" . . ."

"Now I understand that I am stupid. But that's not all. Besides me there is another one as stupid; so stupid as to trust and admire someone as mean as you. Tonight I will call the Old Man and tell him this: 'Dear Eldest

Brother: don't think you are ever so clever and proper. You don't know how stupid you are, and in a big way.' "

Van bows her head, her cheeks pale. Then tears start rolling down her once beautiful but now wilted face. Wrinkles have appeared around her eyes. Her lips, once vibrant red, now are pale even under her dark plum lipstick.

As for Vu, he buttons tight the two panels of his vest; clearly a mental shock is accompanied by a physical one. Suddenly waves of pain course through his chest and all the upper part of his body. Clutching his stomach, he recalls the look on his mother's face when he first fell in love with Van. His father had seemed calmer, while his mother appeared really upset. He had caught them whispering to each other. Those exchanges stopped when he appeared. Then, a few months later, his mother had confided to him with carefully chosen words:

"Dear son, it is taught, 'When you take a wife look at her family environment; when you take a husband consider his genes.' Miss To Van is indeed pretty, she looks like Teacher Luong but we do not know her character. The raising of the children in a family is mainly by the mother. The father's role is like a big pole to hold the roof up firmly. A woman like Mrs. Tuyet Bong is not likely to produce a nice girl. I am not the only one to notice that To Van does not socialize with other pretty girls. Anytime her cousin Hien Trang, who is both pretty and gifted, gets near her, she becomes uneasy and moves on. Miss Hien Trang tells people that To Van said that she only likes to be with people who are uglier and more stupid than she is. It is as if she is looking for a setting in which to stand out. If, at her young age, she is that self-conscious, she is cruel."

At that time he had found many reasons to win over his parents. Then he was in love, passionately. Blind are all who love too passionately. Now he understands that his mother had been completely correct; that his wife had purposely encouraged everyone to choose Miss Minh Thu and she had found many ways to push Miss Thanh Tu away. She had acted based on her selfish instincts: she had wanted to accentuate her own attractiveness by taking advantage of the homely women around her. What was worse was that other people also had taken pleasure in this cruelty.

" 'When you are full of rice, you should give up meat.' This woman has just opened my eyes. After thirty years of marriage, now I see clearly the personality of the one I called 'wife' . . ."

His heart roils in fiery waves. He feels his head and his whole body torn in two; both bobbling like two boats tossing on top of ocean waves. In this turmoil, he can't understand why the president's smile comes back to him. It is an image from the celebration of the border campaign when the Old Man lifted his wine cup to congratulate everyone and to pronounce these concluding words:

"Best wishes to the entire organization, especially to those men with beautiful wives. Given that criterion, Brother Vu has to drain three cups of wine!"

"How bitter," he thought to himself. "It was the Old Man who was first to honor her beauty. He had no inkling that such a generous compliment would come to cause him harm. They made him miserable quietly and with complete premeditation . . ."

Restraining the effects of his pain, he looks over at her and smiles. "How strange fate is. Why didn't you marry Sau? You were most compatible of all with him. How ironic. Why did you choose me?"

"Because I love you. Because I love only you. If not, all things would be . . ."

"If not, a bed was always ready, and making love would still have been so relaxing, whether in peace or war. Right?"

" . . ."

"But the irony of fate is that, most often, those with cruel intentions are not likely to become a couple because they want to safeguard their singularity and their own destiny. Between such accomplices, there can only be a temporary union; for their security they plan behind the scenes to choose those who are nice and stupid, because life is long and full of changes. That's the main reason you chose me to love. Just like Sau: he did not choose you but another woman."

Van remains silent as Vu slowly goes on, dropping each word as if he wants to hear the echo of his own voice.

"It takes thirty years to understand a person. What a nasty game the Creator plays. Compared with history, thirty years is like the blink of an eye. But with people, it's a lifetime."

She looks into his eyes and sees the deep despair. The eyes of her man— the one she can't stop loving and longing for, or stop wanting to possess with absolute ownership and sovereignty. The years have not changed the delicate traits of his face. Vicissitudes have not beaten him down but have enhanced his beauty. It's possible he does not even notice his beauty. But for her, she can see it clearly through her own nonstop longing and through the looks of other women.

"Don't you still love me?" she asks, even though she knows the question is out of tune. The fear of an open breakup makes her lose her better mind:

"You no longer love me?" she repeats one more time in a higher pitch, with a maddening anticipation.

It seems he does not hear her question; he is somewhere else. After a while, he turns and looks at her in a dreamy way, as if examining an old picture or a moldy, long forgotten knickknack:

"Hey, Van, do you ever probe your conscience?"

"What do you mean?"

"I would like to know if you ever question whether what you did was right or wrong? Do you ever feel your conscience not at peace? Or do you even understand the thing called 'conscience'?"

"I don't know. I live like all the others. How other women act, so do I."

"Liar. Other women are not able to sit in Sau's office for hours, talking and plotting. Other women do not know how to influence the chair of the women's association with a bunch of little tricks. Other women are not titled by the Old Man 'Miss Beauty of the Front' or 'Beauty of the City.'"

"I will not answer you any longer. You have no right to question me. This is not the Hoa Lo prison."

She grimaces, but her nostrils are red and she is about to sob. She knows she has lost the contest. The man standing before her is no longer inside the chalk circle that destiny drew for her at her wedding. He has crossed over permanently, without a hint of regret. Her pursuit has been in vain. But her passion thus increases manyfold; like the fox chasing its prey, she will not abandon the hunt. She coughs, covering her mouth with a cloth. She needs to find another way, one more effective. Over on the lake, the boats still sail by. The waves are whispering, as is the wind. Here, the wind cannot enter because walls face north. The charcoal stove is bright red in front of them. But she still coughs. The intentional coughing does not catch his eyes. Nor does it move him, at least at this moment.

Not bothering to look at her, he says, "Now I understand why—all these years—we had a hard time conceiving children. Women like you cannot become mothers. Because, if you were to have a daughter, when she became a woman, you would be jealous. Like the stepmother queen in the fairy tale who was jealous and chased Snow White. There have been your kind of women for thousands of years."

"You need not talk anymore. That's enough," she retorts.

But he does not stop. She no longer has power over him. Her famous charm of love has lost all effectiveness. Bewildered, she looks down at her dainty fingers, which are full of rings. The fingers are still delicate but their skin has become wrinkled with tortoise patches. Meanwhile, he continues to pour out his rage:

"One thing: women like you lack practical brains. No beauty can survive over time. What lasts the longest and is best in a person is love and moral integrity."

"Moral integrity?" She starts a taunting laugh. Her face suddenly burns like fire: "The most moral person in this world is your mother. Why don't you sleep with her?"

"Oh . . . oh . . . oh . . ."

He opens his mouth wide, an unconscious gesture. He cannot control himself. Is he trying to scream or say something? But a black and dark wave, high like a wall, suddenly stands in front of him like the waves of Quang Ninh Sea in the old days when there was a big typhoon coming ashore. The angry wave falls on his head and pushes him into an abyss of rocks.

3

When Vu wakes, he is lying in the Viet-Russian hospital.

It is lunchtime, patients are sitting up in their beds waiting for their families to bring their food rations. His cupboard is full of all kinds of fruit and cakes, all starting to wilt because nobody has touched them. Vu feels his head heavy as if a stone is pressing on it. He tries to turn it to both sides to stretch his neck muscles. These movements give him a sharp pain.

"I am old . . . This painful episode just whips me down," he thinks to himself but patiently continues the exercise.

The patient opposite him looks on and inquires, "Are you all awake now? Congratulations."

"Thank you . . . I have been unconscious for how many days?"

"Three and a half. Ah, yes . . . altogether four days. You were brought to the room noon last Saturday. Today is Wednesday, eleven thirty Wednesday."

"Here you count each hour?"

"A hospital is similar to a prison; a day is longer than a century. You have not had a long stay, therefore you don't know."

"True. Visiting people, I have. But myself, it is the first time."

"I heard that." He starts laughing: "Just stay here a few weeks and you will see clearly. Before you heard people threaten: 'Staying in here a few days is longer than a century, don't believe it.' Once in here the truth becomes evident."

"Is that so?"

He also laughs. Even the laugh makes his face painful and stiff. However, he is awake. His body cannot be destroyed so quickly. This is a reward from a life of healthy living, with moderation, and with so many *chi gong* classes. He rubs his cold stiff hands together, waiting for them to warm up, then he uses them to rub his neck.

"I will not submit to failure before I fight back. Old age: I accept thee but in the spirit of competition. I won't be your servant."

The doctor in charge steps into the room. A man in his forties, calm and weary. He approaches the bed and smiles: "Greetings."

"Greetings to you, too," Vu cheerfully replies. "I live thanks to you, therefore I welcome you. That's more accurate."

"Not quite. You have a strong constitution, which is why you recuperated so quickly. If it had been another, it . . ."

"Another person would have died?"

"I didn't mean that. But if it had been another, it could have had long-lasting consequences."

"Because the side effects of a brain aneurism can be total body or organ paralysis or at least a twisted neck, crooked mouth, and so on . . . Is that right?"

"You know the prognosis like a professional."

"I read medical books. Not much but enough to have simple knowledge. When I opened my eyes I know that I was lucky. As our elders said: 'Meet the right doctor and you get the right medication.' If I say more, people will say I am pompous, but, whatever, I still have to say thank you. Thank you very much."

"Don't mention it. It is our duty."

The doctor seems embarrassed. He quickly says good-bye then leaves the room. Later, a nurse comes in.

"Today you drink milk. Tomorrow, too. From Friday on your diet will change given your health situation. The doctor said you might want to eat rice porridge today but that would not be helpful."

"Thank you. I will follow the order. No need for you all to be concerned."

"Should I mix you some milk now?"

"No need. I am not hungry yet. Later, I will help myself."

The nurse walks away. He continues to rub and shake his neck. He figures that during his days lying unconscious, people had continuously fed him with IV fluids, sugar and minerals, which explains why he does not feel depleted. There is only a feeling of stiffness all over his body. Twenty minutes later, he sinks into sleep. He sleeps straight until nine o'clock before waking up, feeling hungry. He scratches his stomach. He sits up. There is a moment of unsteadiness but later all his movements become accurate and sure. He stands up, mixes some milk, and drinks it. While drinking, he listens to his body slowly coming alive, the warmth spreading from his chest out to his limbs, feeling his blood moving in the veins—all in all a brand-new feeling he has never had before: revival!

"I am your neighbor. Do you remember me?"

He hears someone talking at his ear. He turns over to see a meticulously dressed man leaning against the wall, looking at him with a pair of warm eyes, smiling.

"Maybe . . ." he replies with embarrassment, trying to recall this stylish look, the fashion of the 1940s, the hair wavy and a light-colored shirt collar turned out to cover the dark jacket:

"The truth? I kind of remember . . . It is old age . . ." he replies, one more time trying to conjure the identity of this hefty man with hair à la Yves Montand, the eyes in parallel, the nose bridge regular and the mouth bright pink, lips turned up, definitely the kind of man who is talkative and . . .

"I am Tran Phu, not the Tran Phu who was general secretary of the Party during the First Uprising, but the one who was a classmate in 1947, during training at Nam Mai Hamlet. Do you remember now?"

"Ah, ah . . . now I remember," Vu answers. "Because you said you were a neighbor, I kept searching among my acquaintances in the old hamlet, my birthplace."

"Lying next to each other for two months, hammock to hammock, foot touching foot. We were more than neighbors. It's lucky that we were of different dispositions, or else things might have happened."

"True," Vu confirms and bursts into laughter.

Tran Phu asks, "Are you still tired?"

"It's better."

"Sit up to straighten out your back then try to get off the bed and take a few steps. After the first few steps, you will want to go down the hall and back at a speed just enough to carry you forward. That's the best way to get your blood flowing. You will recuperate very quickly; I believe that."

"Thank you. I also hope so."

Casting his eyes in curiosity to watch the other, Vu says, "And you, what is your secret that time seems not to have touched you at all? It has been more than twenty years. After the first few minutes of surprise, I find you keep most of your old demeanor."

"I have changed quite a bit. Twenty years is not a moment. You do not see my tummy?"

At that moment Tran Phu pulls the lapels of his blouson to let Vu look. Vu finds his stomach to be quite ordinary. Very normal even for a man of forty.

Vu says, "I see nothing. At the most the waist is eighty centimeters. Compared with others, that is an ideal number."

"Oh, no . . . I cannot accept it. Do you remember in the old days I was famous in the front as 'Tran Phu with the frog's waist'? My waist was sixty, not a millimeter more. My stomach was smaller and firmer than those of the ladies."

"Are you crazy? That was more than twenty years ago."

"The fact is that it is a weakness to let ourselves atrophy over time. I know an old man who is over eighty and his skin has no wrinkles, his waist is still sixty-eight, not more nor less."

"Eighty and skin without wrinkles? You are joking. Sorry, but I can't believe it."

"You must believe. Then, you'll come to believe. I will explain to you right now: beautiful women keep their beauty by rubbing their face. Massaging is a traditional method to keep beauty as well as health. In Persia people sell hundreds of different perfumes for bathhouses to serve customers; of course those customers are only royalty, aristocrats, or wealthy businesspeople. But even massage cannot prevent skin from wrinkling, as the masseuse has to pull the skin across the horizontal, forcing it to expand. When it expands, it changes form. Thus, massaging makes the blood flow and the skin pink, fresh, and healthy, but still the skin continues to wrinkle. To correct this shortcoming, people have to adopt a new method."

"Your theory sounds very appealing. Now I am growing very curious," Vu replies with a smile that is both open and full of awakened alertness.

Tran Phu also smiles. "You don't believe it yet. Whether you believe or not, it is all the same to me. I am not that Son Dong character who sells medicine in the middle of the market just to pull some coins out of your pocket. I act only according to the motto 'If you see something nice but don't tell anyone, you are too greedy; and if you see a hole in the middle of the road but don't yell out a warning, you are too nasty.'"

"Oh . . . don't swing a big hammer like that . . . Well, tell me about the special techniques of that eighty-year-old man with the smooth skin."

"That old man is a master of the Nhat Nam teachings. He lives next to the Dong Da dike. If you wish, I will take you there for a visit, and at the same time you can watch his disciples practice. I believe you will fall completely in love with this martial art. And the technique to keep skin from wrinkling is very simple: slap yourself!"

"Slap?" He almost can't believe his ears. "What did you say? Slap?"

"Slap!"

"Slap? I don't understand."

"Slap, but it is not slapping your enemy, nor slapping until you see fireflies in the eyes, nor slapping to make the nose and mouth bleed, nor slapping to dislocate the jaw and break the front teeth. It is not slapping the other to inflict injury or death. It is still slapping, but just enough to make the blood flow, to ward off the process of aging while preserving the original resilience of the skin. Here, I will show you how it's done."

Tran Phu then lifts both hands up at the same time to slap his face, first both sides of his jaw, then slowly up each cheek to his temples until his hands meet on his forehead: smack, smack, smack, smack . . .

Vu can't stop him, being both surprised and confused before that exciting demonstration. A moment later he lowers his voice and whispers, "Stop, stop! I understand now. We should not disturb the people around here."

Tran Phu immediately lowers his voice, too: "Why even pay attention to those walking corpses? To live cheerfully, just pretend they don't exist for us to see."

Vu is frightened by the arrogance of Tran Phu's manner, so he hurriedly stands up, even though it makes him a little dizzy.

"Let's go out to the hall. I will try to see."

"Good, let me escort you," Tran Phu replies, then wraps his arm around Vu's back. His hands are warm and firm, the sign of a steady body. Vu feels comfortable walking beside this man, a reassurance of security and warmth. They walk along the hall. With each step, Vu's memory slowly fills with flashbacks of those nights in the woods more than twenty years ago. Back then, the officer named Tran Phu was already very well known as a commander full of potential; all day long he would boast to the enlisted men about his 'frog's waist.' Everywhere he went, soldiers would flock around, mouths open, to listen to his stories. Nobody knew for sure what kind of stories, but they certainly were frivolous, because after a silence the whole group would burst out laughing. They laughed crawling around; they laughed as if they had communal epilepsy; they laughed like the demented. Even though they trusted him due to his battlefield experience, his superiors remained suspicious about the odd persona of this lad from Hanoi.

At that time, they had to attend training sessions during the day. At night, even once he was up in his hammock, Tran Phu still would not want to sleep; he would poke his foot over to Vu, forcing Vu to crawl outside his net and listen as Phu whispered all kinds of comical stories. The two of them had to cover their mouths to laugh quietly. In those days they were young men. Now, that springtime of their lives is just a memory. Tran Phu, too, might also be thinking about something, because his constantly moving mouth is silent. In quiet they walk many rounds up and down the hall then sit down on a bench.

"Are you tired yet?"

"At the beginning, a little fuzzy. Then after completing the first round it felt normal."

"That's good. Your body will heal satisfactorily."

"Who tells you that?"

"The doctor."

"The head of the ward? The one I met this morning?"

"Exactly. You are lucky. He's the one with the best credentials in this hospital. He decided to extend your coma to let your body heal more quickly. I monitored your breathing as we were walking, and I recognize that this fellow is experienced."

"I find you no less experienced. . . . Did you study medicine?"

"No, but I read. I direct a publishing house for culture and information. Thus, I am forced to read. Also, when we reach old age, sooner or later, whether you want to or not, diseases will come. The best course is to understand them first before those uninvited guests invade your home."

"When did you switch your profession?"

"Right after the liberation of the capital."

"But . . ."

He is about to ask something then suddenly stops. During their friendship, Tran Phu was commander of Battalion 507, assigned to the capital district. He was valued as a most outstanding officer, thanks to his knowledge, his initiative, and an unusual power of intuition. This lad from Hanoi with mincing gait and bright red lips, both talkative and sensual, had, of course, made many ladies fall madly in love with him. He was also the kind whom superiors trusted, being able to ask soldiers to jump fearlessly into the fire. Why had he wastefully left the army when his career had been so promising? Vu asks himself. But then, he knows that there are truths that lie outside ordinary logic. And the ordinary logic of the majority contains nonsense when we look at things from another angle.

Perhaps Vu has had to pay a high price to attain this insight.

As if Vu had guessed his secret thoughts, Tran Phu opens wide his mouth and laughs: "You regret my military career, right? Because many soldiers under my authority are now wearing big medals, while I am only a mere cultural assistant, not even a commissar, not even climbing up to get the title of office director. But this was out of my own free will; my own choice. When the nation was in danger, as a citizen's duty, I had to hold a sword. But the battles are over; I hand it to others to keep. An officer's career is not what I am fond of. Between hats and uniforms and a life disengaged, I chose the latter."

"Before now I might have been puzzled, but now I know you had a reason."

"Thank you. My motives might be unreasonable to someone else. That is why my words might offend others; those in your office, for example. But life is not long enough to please everyone. We have to do what we desire as long as it is not immoral or inhumane. Now I will accompany you to your room. Take another glass of milk before going to sleep. I guarantee that tomorrow you can eat rice porridge with meat."

They return to Vu's room. Obediently he drinks a glass of warm milk before going to sleep. And indeed, his sleep turns out satisfactory. The next morning, he wakes up and sees Tran Phu already chatting with the head doctor. Both seem excited.

Seeing Vu awake, they turn around and say, "We wish you a good morning."

Tran Phu says it first. The doctor follows, smiling.

"Today you will eat rice porridge with meat. Congratulations as you transition to another phase of your recovery much faster than ordinary people."

Vu smiles and replies, "It must be my kind friend who proposes to the doctor that I am making progress?"

"No. No one has the right to propose. Professional decisions are always one-sided. Professional advice is always arbitrary. It follows professional principles only," the doctor answers while raising his arm to bid farewell, as others are calling noisily for him at the end of the hall. Tran Phu enters the room under the cold looks and harsh stares of people hanging around. But he appears oblivious to all of them. At the head of Vu's bed, he goes through the pile of oranges, bananas, and all kinds of cakes and candies in the little cupboard.

"You should not eat these. Let me give them to the other rooms. Even though this is called the Viet-Russian hospital, reserved for high-ranking cadres, many people do not have enough money to buy fruit. These packages of cakes we can give to charity. At your age you should not eat these 'state-enterprise' candies and cookies. I will share mine with you."

Without waiting for Vu's answer, Tran Phu leaves the room and returns a little later with an aluminum basket in which he puts all the fruit and candies, taking it away without saying a word. Vu says nothing. He silently mixes his milk, quietly embarrassed because of the attentive looks from bystanders. But the hunger that has returned with racehorse speed reassures him. While drinking his milk, he looks at the trees swaying outside, feeling as if he were in a strange land, a place where he had never before set foot and thus distinct from the world where he had lived. It is a permanent disruption from all the days that are now behind him; a new continent that has opened up upon his return from death.

After the meal, Tran Phu returns with a basket full of fresh fruit. He arranges them nicely on the cupboard at the head of the bed, saying, "You have started to eat savory porridge. That means you can eat all of these fruits. No more restrictions. Here are flan and the madeleine made by my sister. You can have them when you drink your milk or hot tea."

"Thank you. I feel bad that you have spent so much time on me."

"Not as much as you thought. All is prepared by my younger sister. I have been spoiled since I was young, even though there were many mouths in the family. Go take a nap; we will see each other again tomorrow."

"Let me see you out, so I can exercise a bit."

"Agreed."

When they reach the stairs, Vu whispers in Tran Phu's ear, "Why do the people around my bed look at you with strange eyes. Why is that?"

"Why?" Tran Phu asks with surprise. "You do not know the simple explanation?"

"I admit, I don't know. I cannot pretend that I do as my heart is full of quandaries. Please forgive me."

Tran Phu turns to look at him attentively, perhaps puzzled, perhaps moved. Then he lowers his voice: "If someone else were to ask this question I would think he is acting up like 'the lost old deer.' But with you, I believe your question is genuine. Perhaps this naïveté governs your persona, and perhaps that is why we love you, you who are the last hero of the epoch."

"No."

Now it's Vu's turn to be puzzled. He is not used to hearing people voice their feelings so directly.

Tran Phu continues to look at him intensely as if gazing at a painting in a gallery, then says, "You don't know that our society is intensely and savagely divided into classes, even though it is regularly advertised as being egalitarian, free, and democratic? Even here, people still distinguish class from class, and watch one another from the standpoint of rank. Those in your room are all professional experts in grades eight and nine, which are at the bottom of the hierarchy for professionals and experts. Meanwhile, I am only an assistant grade six, just high enough to gain admission for treatment here. That is why they despise me. While they flaunt their rank, from the human point of view, they are only zombies. Have you noticed the way they stir their bowls of porridge with a spoon or pick up each grain of rice and put it in their mouth?"

"Not yet. I haven't dared look at them or chat with them much at all."

"Because of my presence. And because they look with unfriendly eyes. Thus you learned that they cannot empathize with you."

Vu smiles instead of agreeing.

Immediately Tran Phu laughs loudly: "I am right! You are kind of accommodating. Your personality is more educated and polite than mine—even though I am from Hanoi and you are from Bac Giang. But inside me there is always someone carefree, provocative. I look at nutty people like them as puppets made of paper. I crush their conceit, making them die choking in the mud of jealousy. Look here . . ."

Tran Vu rolls up the sleeves of his shirt to show his arms still full of muscle.

"No matter how many grades higher than me, their legs are not much bigger than my arms. We might have been born in the same year, but their teeth are now all fake while I have only lost tooth number eight. In the morning, I quickly finish a bowl of pho with two drumsticks while they stir a bowl of thin porridge with their spoons. At lunch I eat two bowls full of rice with homemade braised fish while they chew nonstop on the hospital's stir-fry of tough beef. There: those are the reasons they look at me with those jealous eyes, if you don't want to say it straight—those enraged eyes. People have been like that for generations, even as they stand on the edge of their graves. Don't worry yourself about it. Now: go to your room to rest. I'll come tomorrow."

Tran Phu raises his hand in farewell then goes down the stairs. Vu hears Phu's footsteps treading lightly on the stairs, and with those steps, hears him softly singing:

> *"Then the waves will erase all on the sand beach—*
> *The footsteps of couples and lovers . . ."*

A song from the 1940s: dreamy students and slender girls in flowing white *ao dai* dresses. Ah, his youth. Phantoms from that era return with the old song. But he drives them out because a fear suffocates his feelings.

"No! No! No . . ."

He hurries to his room, gets into bed, hoping to find some sleep, but sleep does not come. Finally he tosses off the blanket and sits up.

The patient across from him opens his eyes: "You give up, Uncle? Can't sleep?"

"Yes."

"Me too. No one wins over old age."

"Yes."

"That handsome friend of yours, is he coming to visit you tonight?"

"No. He said tomorrow."

"He does not remember me, but I know him well."

"Is that true?"

"Before, I had the same rank when he was in command of 507."

"Then how long after that did you change your branch?"

"I didn't. I am still in the military."

"Oh, really?"

"You want to ask, Uncle, why I am lost in here and am not being treated in the 108 hospital, right? I am here like a horse lost in a goat pen."

He closes his eyes. His dry and dark lips expand and contract in a grinning and bitter smile.

"Because the director of that hospital is my mortal enemy. I will not take my body there so they can slaughter me as they would a chicken."

Vu keeps quiet, not knowing what else to say.

The grin stays on the other patient's lips, making his face look like a wax mask. His breathing is fast and comes with strong husky noises, which at times sound like a ghostly hissing wind.

"Everything leads to some end. Each turn of the road will lead to that last destination. But in the journey toward death, people still live with all their grudges, all their entanglements which they cannot undo." So Vu thinks to himself while looking at the pitiful person in the bed next to his. Then he gently gets up to go out. At that moment, the patient speaks even though his eyes are shut tight.

"Uncle, will you tell Tran Phu that he is a smart and lucky guy? He knows how to live life his own way."

"Yes, I will tell him."

"Don't tell anything about me . . . Just say an officer of his rank said so."

"Yes."

"That I wish him the older he gets, the more cheerful he will be."

"Yes."

"I . . . also wish you, Uncle, the same . . ."

"Thank you. I am not lucky to have such an uneventful life as my friend."

"I know. I know, Uncle . . . who you are," he says before stopping to catch his breath.

Later he adds: "Nonetheless . . . I still wish you, Uncle . . . happiness."

A grinning and bitter smile appears again on his dark purple lips. It worries Vu. He asks: "Uncle, do you want me to call the duty doctor?"

"Thank you. I know my illness. Go out, Uncle, take a stroll and relax. Go, go!"

Not knowing what to do, Vu steps out into the hall in a hurry and makes his way downstairs to the hospital yard, where he stands like a statue, his eyes glued to the shadow of the trees, looking for a shelter for his trembling state of mind. Fear is after him.

"Well, a few days earlier, was I that deplorable? Did I have a face that was gray like dirty beeswax? Was my mouth wide open like the mouth of the dead fish in a market basket? Was I drooling like those lying in the same room? Oh, heaven: how horrible is one's incarnation in this life!"

The thought starts him shivering like when you catch a cold or listen to ghost stories.

"I need a healthy and useful life. And later, when heaven is not hospitable, I will seek death in a calm manner. That will be the ideal liberation."

In front of him, the big trees, all in a row, sway under the sun: the old sapindus trees, the mother-of-pearl trees, and the jacaranda trees garlanded in purple blossoms. They have grown close to one another, not in any particular order but forming an island in the huge yard. This luscious flora has calmed many patients in their mental agonies, as it does for him at this moment.

Vu sits down in a chair and closes his eyes to listen to the brushing of the leaves and the sounds of the birds fighting. Suddenly, something wet falls on his nose. He opens his eyes wide and realizes that some irreverent bird has pooped on his face. He looks inside his pocket for a cloth to clean himself. While he is busy looking, a hand spreads in front of him and gives him a handkerchief:

"You are lucky. When a bird poops on your head or neck you get a reward. If the reward is not big like a gold bar, a small reward can be a cake or some sticky rice."

Not looking up, Vu hastily grabs the cloth and wipes his face.

"Where do you come up with such a theory?"

"That is an old theory, my great friend."

A very strange voice makes Vu look up: Tran Phu is not alone; he is with another man. It is this guest who has challenged him.

"My great friend, don't you know that in the old days, people believed that dreaming of feces brought good luck?"

"I heard it a couple of times but never paid attention," Vu replies.

The other man widens his mouth in a smile. His mouth is huge, pulled all the way up to the ears to boast a set of teeth yellowed from cigarettes, eyes blinking behind thick glasses. His face is very dark, with not one attractive feature, yet it projects an attractive aura that is hard to explain. He continues to expound on his theory:

"Because we live where we grow rice in water, we are forced to learn the meaning of dreams about feces." He smiles.

At that moment Tran Phu introduces them to each other: "This is Tran Vu, the contemporary hero. This is my friend, the writer Le Phuong. We both left home to join the revolution in 1945, when we were just twenty."

They shake hands. Then Tran Phu proposes going to the hospital cafeteria for refreshments. It is a large room with a few dozen rows of tables and chairs. They pick what seems to be the least dusty table, near the merchandise case and close to the window.

As the counter is abandoned, Tran Phu calls out: "Hey! Little ones in there . . ."

Hearing no response, he raises his voice and shouts: "Hey, ladies of the cafeteria!"

No response again.

Then a customer who is eating sesame balls suggests, "You have to go to the middle of the yard to call. Those girls are fooling around where the guards are quartered."

"Thank you," Phu replies, and then walks briskly to the yard, where, standing right in front of the door of the guardroom, he asks, "Who is selling in the cafeteria today? We have waited a half hour already."

"Here! We are here . . ."

Two or three girls answer then the whole group runs back to the cafeteria, giggling as they run.

Tran Phu turns around, his tone no longer playful but annoyed and threatening: "Hurry up! Two filtered coffees and a number one teapot. For your sakes I will overlook this negligence."

"Thank you, Chief . . . We apologize, please . . ." a few girls answer, no longer smiling but starting to feel frightened. One girl hastily takes out a cloth to wipe their table. A second girl makes tea; a third puts ground coffee in the filter.

"Older Brother Vu, did you see that?" asks Tran Phu.

"Yes, I did."

"I wonder what that famous and dour Tran Phu, the secretary general of the Party, would say if he were alive?"

"Enough. Let's change the subject."

Le Phuong then speaks up: "Going into this kind of conversation is like crawling on the horns of the buffalo. A tunnel without light. Who would have thought what face would mark the society that Tran Phu and his comrades were creating? A revolution is like a pregnancy, and the baby who comes into the world—even if not a monster—will be totally different from the dream or imagination of those who created it. We return to our little lives. Today is a happy day, because Brother Vu is the person I have secretly wished to meet for a long while."

"No, I am humbled."

"A long time ago I read Lermontov's *A Hero of Our Time*, knowing full well that it was an autobiographical novel about a very handsome character. Now that I meet you, I find you just as handsome."

"No, you are too generous. I am no screen actor," Vu replies, feeling his ears grow warm with embarrassment.

Tran Phu and Le Phuong look at him attentively like furniture merchants admiring a sideboard carved with dragon, unicorn, turtle, and phoenix, then Phu says laughingly:

"We are happy on behalf of whomever became your wife. Such a handsome man who blushes with shyness in his fifties."

"Well . . ."

Vu does not know what to say. These two guys are strangers from a strange land. Their words, their expressions, and their thoughts—all are completely foreign to his world, the world of those who run the machine of political authority. He decides to lead the conversation in another direction:

"Last night I kept thinking, Hanoi is so small, yet how is it that we have never run into one another before today?"

"Because we turned at different intersections, and those turns led us farther and farther apart as time went by. Then we meet again here because this is where life meets death. Those who set foot here are those who, since long ago, have been chosen by the lord of death. They all try to put off that last and eternal surrender for as long as they can," says Tran Phu.

"I find you more like a businessman ready to marry a concubine than one prepared to go to the cemetery."

"You are half correct," replies Tran Phu. "I am here because of my prostate cancer. The doctor wants to operate but I refuse. I combine the medications with taking foods that have good pharmaceutical properties, like raw carrots, fungus, raw tomatoes. Especially no meat: neither pork nor beef. Once in a while, chicken and duck are allowed, on condition that the skin and fat are removed. My main foods are freshwater fish and shrimp. Of course, these things are provided by the family. After four months I had an examination, and the abcess in my testicles had shrunk by two hundred grams. Now I am looking for a young nymph who can make me an active 'revolutionary' to an extraordinary degree. If it can be done, then all swelling will disappear."

"I think you said that to be lighthearted," Vu replies, and then Le Phuong butts in:

"You have your reasons and Phu has his. Because our views about life differ and our experiences of life also differ, our faiths are not the same. But if you do not remember our sayings and proverbs, I will offer this: 'Empty bladder, good food.'"

"I had heard that but totally forgot. You two are really masters. How can all those ancient sayings still be stored in your brains?"

"Because we live according to the truth of the downtrodden," says Le Phuong. "That truth is a commodity put in storage but which never mildews. Whenever necessary, it can be taken out and used right away. No need to cook or add onion and garlic. According to that learning, if a man resurrects his sexual life, his weak organs will be renewed."

"Wow, your wisdom is quite dangerous. It will prompt men to leave their families to look for adventure and erection."

"Exactly. Not only men but women, too, because the two halves—yin and yang—are always equal before the devil in their ability to sin. The problems to resolve are concrete cases and persons. There is no common denominator for all humanity in its pursuit of happiness. There is no limit to the number of adventures. The main thing is . . ."

Le Phuong stops talking. He pulls from one shirt pocket a large pipe and from the other a packet of dark loose tobacco. He slowly packs the tobacco into the bowl of the pipe. Vu finds this writer's style of conversation akin to that of a Chinese novel: he makes you wait for the clincher. Ugly as he is, he nonetheless must have seduced quite a few women with his innate charm.

"You trigger my curiosity," Vu says, smiling.

"I'll go on," Le Phuong replies, but he takes his time lighting the pipe, inhaling the smoke, then leisurely exhaling. Vu can clearly hear the bees flying in the garden outside, buzzing over the green tamarind trees.

"Not only for men but women, too, because the two halves—yin and yang—are always equal before the devil in their ability to sin. Why am I aware of this at my age? Everything comes too late."

That thought brings Vu back to the image of his woman: to Van! For the first time since he opened his eyes from the coma, that name returns.

"No . . . No . . . No . . ."

He reacts strongly because he feels that the storm is about to break over him, leaving him in danger of being thrown into that strong wind.

Turning his head around, Vu forces himself to concentrate on the dialogue with the writer:

"Then what happens? I am waiting to hear more."

Smiling, Le Phuong says, "Why would a respectable person like you, Older Brother, ever listen to the silly theories of your younger friends, us studs who love to play around with life?"

"Why do you make that distinction?"

"Because you, Older Brother, you belong to those who work on great national tasks. Us, we like to live only as we want to live. We fear our careless words won't be accepted by our big brothers."

"Oh, I have heard all the comical stories that Phu told in the jungle years before. No reason to hold back."

"Yes. But more than twenty years have passed and time does make a difference."

"So true."

Instinctively, Vu lets out a sigh and slowly continues: "Time sorts out people, not just individuals but all of humanity. However, we still have valuable things in common; for example, goodness, or friendship, or family bonds. Those feelings cannot disappear in the comings and goings of time and space."

"Yes."

"During the hardest times of my life, I always asked for help from Eldest Brother. He could understand me when I was silent. He was ready to shoulder the family, to let me roam freely."

"Yes."

Vu stops because he realizes that he is opening up his heart before these two men; one forgotten for more than twenty years and the other known for just half an hour. He has never done this before. He takes several small sips of tea to conceal his confusion. And then he asks of Le Phuong:

"And you, you are here to treat what illness?"

"Me?" the writer replies. "I have no illness whatsoever. If I had, I don't meet the conditions to be admitted here."

"What do you say? You were in the revolution since '45, the same year as Tran Phu."

"Yes, but I don't meet the criteria for joining the Party. If you are not a Party member then, for sure, for the rest of your life, you will never get a decent position. Not only that, I am guilty of always loving young and pretty ladies. For me, the Party is noble in theory, while young and pretty ladies are perfection in the practical side of life. I do not like 'setting bait only to catch a shadow.' I chose what has value in life, and Party greatness I leave for others to enjoy."

At this point, the two pals laugh loudly. Vu is forced to laugh along, suspicious, not knowing if these two playful guys are telling the truth or joking. As if they understand his concern, Tran Phu chimes in with his friend:

"Le Phuong is right. He doesn't meet the criteria of being at least Assistant Grade Five to get treatment in this hospital. But he comes every day to visit me. His highest duty to fulfill is to 'raise a comrade's morale.' Each of your Party cells has three members. Ours has only two, established in 1945 and until now unusually strong—no dagger in anyone's back yet."

"That's exactly right . . ." Le Phuong confirms. "Our comradeship does not rely on the grand theory of a 'united world proletariat.' Our cell relies on a foundation of ordinary and small-scale relationships, of pusillanimous concerns, in fact. For example, when I was in the jungle in the north, whenever the family sent provisions, whether a lot or a little, from money to clothing to medicine, it was always divided in two. When we were sick, one carried the other on his back. When at peace, we relied on one another to 'attack.'"

"Attack?"

Seeing Vu's puzzled look, the two men crack smiles at each other. Then, Le Phuong turns and tells Tran Phu, "Older Brother has no concept about the language used by those who 'play around in midlife.' Enough; thus it is an opportunity for us to entertain the older person at the time when he is in need of rest. I will unravel all the small secrets of our insignificant lives. Is that OK with you?"

"OK. The cell adopts the motion," Tran Phu replies with his everlasting happy face, which has turned red out of excitement.

Le Phuong pulls his pipe from his mouth, and carefully resting it on a lacquer ashtray, says, "We were not as lucky as you, or all the men like you, who have a beautiful fairy for a wife and who are satisfied till the last moment of their lives. Our wives—or to be more accurate, 'those deserving old ladies who bore our children'—always have a firm conviction that we are their prisoners for life, for life under their management, just like the heavy settee or the heirloom cupboard that sits for years in our house. Because they take us for granted, whenever it suits them they can display us from one day to the next as if we were their property, with the calmness of a judge before the conviction."

"You have to say it clearly. Brother Vu does not understand what you mean by that word 'property,'" interjects Tran Phu.

The writer nods, winking. "Property means accessories that are now old and torn. I am sure Older Brother has seen houses with peeling walls and leaky roofs, sinking or broken columns. Try to visualize people as if they were a house being hit by bombs, or storms, or by destructive time. Please, Older Brother, disregard the vulgar comparison. But it is hard to find more exact words to describe the thing. But the 'property' of these ladies is sagging breasts, soft, fleshy, and saggy thighs that spill over into the crotch of their pants, and pairs of eyes that no longer exhibit any brightness but only crust and pus. Not to mention ladies who sport outrageous or dirty clothes."

Le Phuong then clears his throat like a singer about to go onstage and empties his coffee cup. Vu cracks a smile, knowing that Le Phuong is now ready for the main story, a chapter pretentiously titled "Little Secrets of

Little Lives." But the writer puts his dragon-decorated cup on the table, turns to his friend, and says, "Tell them to brew new filtered coffee. This coffee is worse than sock laundry water. Our traditional foods have been destroyed by all these state enterprise products."

"You're right. It is disgusting," Tran Phu replies, then turns to tell the girl attendant: "Brew me a double-filtered coffee and charge me double. Just like yesterday morning."

"Right away, Chief."

Le Phuong turns back around to Vu with a twinkle in his eyes: "Definitely the things I am about to say are forbidden in your circle, Older Brother, and definitely after these confessions, we will seem to you to be immoral as compared with people of rectitude."

"Oh, don't beat around the bush. Each of us lives as we see fit. Don't compare one to another."

"Most inconveniently for all of us, each person is indeed different, in different life situations, but within one common sense of what is valuable. And this value system is set in place by law and power, which forces everyone to conform. Thus, it is like setting out one standard bed and asking everyone to do whatever they can to fit on it. Perhaps you do not recall, in the old days, they used a steel bed to torture and ill-treat prisoners. Those who were longer than the bed had their feet chopped off, and those who were too short had their arms and legs stretched. Enough said. We are, nonetheless, sitting in this room, enjoying this ease—an occasion that has been long awaited. Whether we go up or down in your estimation is of no importance to me."

After these words, Le Phuong grins and waves his hand at the cafeteria employees, who hastily bring out the coffee. This time, the steam holds some fragrance. The two golden friends gleefully drink the hot coffee while Vu sips his tea. He does not know why he feels so lighthearted while sitting with these two talkative men; it has been a long time since he had felt this way. It made him think of the idle talks of his youth: a bit vulgar, a bit light-headed, and a bit playful; but not a hint of plotting or behind-the-back meanness.

"Now, this is almost coffee. But compared with coffee from Hanoi this deserves to be called dishwater."

"If we keep talking about the old days, we could spend all day complaining: What happened to the green rice cakes, the candied lotus seeds, the jasmine tea of the old days? But enough: don't say any more, as it saddens Brother Vu. He is one of the most enthusiastic authors of our new society."

"Correct, I am most heartbroken," Vu affirms. "But I am waiting to hear more about how you 'attack.'"

"Well, we are just ordinary people who love to live ordinary lives. Therefore we always follow the call of what you called the new sources of inspiration. Our soul is divided in half: one is for duty and the other for oneself. We have to make sure our conscience stays intact but we cannot let our souls molder and wither. That is why our lives are a series of plots mediating between the two itineraries of our way forward. Monthly salaries, social benefits, we turn over to our wives on schedule, because they care for the kids and manage the home. Whatever else comes in we call the 'black budget' and is set aside for fun. To prepare escapades of fun, we must get to know the whole network of accommodations for relaxation. To be more accurate, we must look for all the ways in which to get close to the group of cadres who run those rest houses. This task we call 'assuring the safety factor,' a necessary but not sufficient condition. To reach sufficiency, we need to hold in our hands a stack of blank travel permits. When we start out, we only have to fill in a day, month, and add a scrawling dragon signature and it is done. Lucky for us we have stupid wives. They read well but can't tell if the signature or the work order is genuine. Those two priority requirements are Tran Phu's responsibility because he is a Party cadre and thus has more power than I."

"In this sense, the Party is useful," Tran Phu adds joyfully. "Every time he accepts an assignment, I force Le Phuong to sing this song: 'Forever Be Grateful to the Party!'"

"Exactly," says Le Phuong. "When you eat fruit, thank the grower. I have sung this song for more than twenty years, and hope to continue singing it. Now I will let you hear about all the fun that those who look at life as a game of enjoyment can have. Outside our duties to our wives and children and to our work, a new wind blows in every once in a while, a rose suddenly loses its way and enters our lives—some fresh and pretty girl who is lonely or sobbing because of a lost love, or who is horny and wants to escape from the steel cage of the family, or is tired of a weak husband, or is unable to endure the attacks from a witch mother-in-law. In short, gentlemen that we are, we are willing to help out in all such circumstances. If the pretty swallow flies to land on Tran Phu's shoulder, I am the one who will write and sign the order: 'Immediately investigate the N, A, Z case.' Or: 'Make a detailed report on national festivals, in cooperation with the Ethnographic Institute.'

"Or vice versa. In all the investigations there must be two people. I carry a bag to Tran Phu's house to let his wife and kids see clearly that two patriarchs are on the road to carry out their duty. We eat a last meal before departure with the solemnity of the Japanese warrior who drinks the 'Determined to Die' wine cup before getting into his plane and diving into the American warship."

At this moment, Tran Phu suddenly bursts into loud laughter. "Do you remember the time we went to Tam Dao?"

"I do, as if it were yesterday," Le Phuong replies and turns to Vu to explain:

"This is a recollection that belongs to the category of 'never to be forgotten.' That time, there was an apprentice actress who had been fired from her troupe because she was pregnant out of wedlock. I do not know the reason or who told her to come to my house crying. I was scared because it was after ten in the morning, just an hour before my wife and my two kids would return for lunch. If they saw her crying on my shoulder, I am sure the tray of food would have gone flying out to the patio followed by other noisy chaos. But I could not rudely force a pretty girl like that to leave the house. For the longest time, I could not find a solution and the hands of the clock zipped around the dial. In the end, too terrified, I took her to the flower garden, bought ice cream for her, and went to Tran Phu's house. Down at his gate, I called up to the second floor:

"'Phu: get dressed right away. Doan is dead!'

"Tran Phu's wife stuck her head out:

"'How can he die so quickly? Last night he was here drinking until dark before he left.'

"'I don't know, I just heard the news that he is dead, therefore I quickly ran here.'

"After I said that, my tongue froze. I had no idea why I had made up such a crazy story. But then I heard Phu's wife rush her husband to get dressed, followed by the noise of his steps on the stairs. We looked at each other then burst into laughter, not suspecting that Phu's wife was also running downstairs. I just had time to say:

"'There's your wife!' Then I bent my back, bowed my head down to my stomach, and began to cough loudly. One series of coughs led to another. I couldn't stop it. Tears rolled down, and when I stood up straight, I definitely had the face of someone who has the croup. I took out a cloth and wiped my tears. Before me, Phu's wife also sniffled:

"'Tell me when the funeral is. He was strong like an elephant and died so quickly. Nobody ever knows the plans of heaven!'

"'That's all right. Go back up. When the agency decides on the funeral

I will go with you,' I said and then told Phu to get in the car to go to the flower garden. On the way, Phu cursed:

"'You crazy bastard! Why make up such an outrageous lie?'

"Then I felt remorse because Doan had been Phu's loyal friend since childhood, but facing a very stressful situation I could not find a more appropriate tale to tell. Because I had to get him out of the house immediately, only an accident or the death of a close one could ensure complete success. Taking my friend to the flower garden, I introduced him to the beauty as the gentleman who could protect her. Then I left the two of them together to reach a mutual understanding. I rushed home just in time for lunch, the old woman who had given birth to my kids annoyingly looking at the hands of the clock. If I had come twenty minutes later, the bean and fish sauces would have been spilled on the tray followed by a never-ending presentation of recriminations."

Vu bursts out laughing. Surprisingly, he is drawn to the story, and, perhaps because of his honest disposition, he worries for the two old playboys:

"So how did you explain the pretended death?"

"Oh, every tall mountain has a trail to the top. After eating, I waited for my wife to go back to work and for the children to return to school. I then sat at the table to write Phu's wife a short letter saying that there had been a misunderstanding. My cousin in the countryside named Toan had just died but, when I received the telegram, in shock I had read it wrong as 'Doan.' In short, everything was fine, except that I had to go to the village for the funeral. After the letter was written, I asked a colleague to take it immediately to Phu's house."

"I doff my hat to you guys!"

"I already told you, people with hats and formal gowns like you take care of the big things. We only play little tricks to enjoy some fun and we harm no one."

"So how did you help that unfortunate actress?"

"She hooked up with Phu, becoming his mistress until love's debt matured. Her coming to me was a mistake, like sheep ending up in a duck pen, because she only ever fell for guys who are good-looking cads like Don Juan. People are stuck with their looks. Once you pick a standard for what is beautiful, it will stick with you forever as the epitome of giving and receiving love. Given this understanding, she would pick Phu because he is much more handsome than I. As for me, I am both small and ugly but good at talking, so those who liked to hear sweet words would lean on my shoulders. That was the allocation according to the law of 'natural selection.'

Nine years of protracted resistance taught us the spirit of supporting the attack and the ability to take care of each other. Between us the tradition of jealousy and animosity that is notorious among Vietnamese has had no effect. That national character doesn't enter into our friendship. That is why, after twenty years, this cell is absolutely rock solid. That solid frame of our friendship rests on the rule of complementarity and mutual support. Phu is handsome; I am dark and ugly. He is generous because he is a dandy from Hanoi; I am tight—'Eating small shrimp and shitting out hair; exchanging nine pennies for a dime'—because my parents died early and I've had to take care of myself since I was ten. He is more fastidious than those well-groomed women, like a duck taking a bath every day whether winter or summer. Before he goes anywhere, he grooms in front of a mirror. He puts his nose on the collar and to the armpits and sniffs to see if it smells good, because, if by any chance a woman were to lean her head on the shoulder of a hero, then they would not faint because of a bad smell. Me, on the contrary: I don't like to bathe. In winter, I do not go into the bathroom for one or two months, but my conscience is fine and my soul shows no pain. Sometimes my wife could not stand it; she would pour crab or meat soup on me to force me to take a bath."

Vu cannot help but laugh again and asks, "If the ladies poured broth from steamed watercress soup over you, you would not go bathe?"

"No! Vegetable-flavored water is like plain water. I would just change my shirt. The leaders often boast that in the imperialist prison, they defiantly made public the revolutionary organization. I think when ten of them talk, not one is to be believed. But me, I am much more convincing. If you are not really dirty and there is no urgent need to take a bath, then I wouldn't bathe. Now, to satisfy your curiosity—you, a person who has no inkling at all about the ordinary and irrelevant lives of playboys—I will tell the ending. We took the pretty and pregnant actress to the rest house in Tam Dao. There she played the role of Phu's wife. Me, I took the rest-house manager to hunt quail in the neighboring forests. After three weeks, the manager was dead tired after all kinds of comical episodes. Every evening he stuck to me like paint. After dinner, we'd go through two teapots while chatting. In the fourth week, almost at the end of the assignment, I asked his help in taking the pretty lady to a clinic for an abortion. He enthusiastically agreed. The next morning, a car from the rest house came to take Tran Phu and his 'wife' to the hamlet clinic to end the sad situation, which had occurred due to 'bad planning.' In summary, everything was arranged to perfection. When we returned to Hanoi, the pretty young lady was already laughing happily, no sign of despair or fear on her face as on the day she had climbed the stairs of my house. Then, three years later . . ."

"You are wrong, more than four years. To be accurate, it was four years and two months."

"Well, I forget. It's been too long to remember exactly. Four years later, we helped her get selected to join the troop of the General Political Department. In her new environment, she found her true love—an average actor but an ideal husband. The day before her wedding, we organized a farewell dinner. It was as elaborate a meal as it could have been, given the living conditions in those days. The farewell meal was intended to recall all our memories together. A few sad tears were shed and a few heartfelt thank-yous said. After that, the road took many turns. She left—forever a pink shadow. And us, we returned to our respected ladies that had birthed our children."

The writer stops talking, lifting his hand to adjust his glasses on his nose, then asks Vu, "Well, have you ever heard such silly stories before?"

"No, for sure not," Vu replies, somewhat embarrassed. "In my department, such goings-on must be brought before the cell for grading and the cadres must undergo discipline."

Both Le Phuong and Tran Phu burst into peals of laughter. Then Le Phuong wipes his tears and asks Vu: "Then, do those who must impose the discipline dare open their mouths to propose that the cell grade the behavior of higher-ranking leaders? Because everybody knows that more than half the Politburo members have two wives. And General Secretary Ba Danh not only has two wives but, in addition, a harem of women pretending to be nurses."

"Of course I have thought about it. But I am a lone rider and of no effect," Vu replies, sighing helplessly.

Le Phuong continues: "This gigantic machine of dominance just keeps turning; just keeps chewing up so many people with its stinking pretense of morality and its injustice."

Not knowing what to say in reply, Vu remains silent. His soul is overwhelmed. What this dark and ugly guy has just said is not news to him. Vu has thought about it, but only clandestinely, and has never dared, or wanted, to believe that it was the truth.

How could it be that the idealism of his youth and the idealism of so many others who had sacrificed for the revolution had come to this miserable end? How could it be that the blood of so many people had been spilled, so much gold and wealth contributed by so many generous people spent, to produce a filthy and inhuman government like this? That filth and inhumanity were well known to him, but still he wants to believe that only a few in the machine of dominance are contaminated. Such power struggles are the curse of humanity; they strip away all good attributes and leave only corrupting greed, conniving plotting, and perpetration of cruelty. However, he does not want to admit that the entire society, in which he had placed so much hope, is immoral and sneaky. Nevertheless, it had been a gamble for which he and so many others of the same generation had pawned their whole lives. It was a joint undertaking, a communal pregnancy. What mother would acknowledge that she has given birth to a monster?

In hearing these stories, this troubling doubt from the mouths of total strangers, Vu understands that what he has suspected with fear during many sleepless nights is seen by the public as a visible and present truth. But he, like someone confined in a quarantined palace, can see only rebels as the walls collapse and fire breaks out on all four sides.

Bending his head to look thoughtlessly at his fingers, Vu sees that his nails are long and untrimmed; he clicks one with another.

Le Phuong looks at the gesture, smiles, and continues: "Now you understand why we choose to be playboys, satisfied with a small life and its tiny pleasures. It is also the way that the old folks called 'to live while hiding.' Because right after the liberation of the capital, we knew that the 'Great Task' had been wrongly done; that the love boat had foundered; and that dreams had been illusions. The day we started on the road of resistance, all had the same dream. A revolution for a backward society or a people in slavery is to be a great cleansing—like a storm that sweeps away all the garbage and brings after it a new life of fortitude. For that reason, people accept death on its behalf. To be precise: people will die for their mountains and rivers because of a brighter future. All real revolutions always liberate productive forces and expand the space of freedom. But this revolution, aside from what it did to emancipate the people, neither brought freedom nor expanded productive capacity; on the contrary, it totally destroyed all the valuable culture that had made our nation, while also destroying its productive capacity. The land reform was actually a systematic and organized slaughter of all talented and effective people in the rural areas. Thus, from the social point of view, this revolution accomplished only a disgusting dredging up of layers of mud from the bottom of the pond to pollute its surface. With that mud came the dead bodies of frogs and toads along with junk and weeds."

He stops talking. Vu feels as if he has been slapped by someone; a strong blow. But the fellow had not taken aim at him personally. He had only announced a truth. A truth that is the price to be paid for putting one's neck in a noose when young; a price paid by so many other young men who had died without justice following a hallucination. When the writer spoke about this, his eyes were so sad; the pronounced wrinkles on his face deepen when he does not smile. Are his lighthearted and silly stories really a way to disguise a huge disappointment? A disappointment for an entire people!

All three of them fall silent. The other customers had left long before; there are now only three waitresses, busy plucking their eyebrows.

Tran Phu comments: "Those three girls must have just come from the countryside. If we stay here longer, they will take off their shirts to pluck the hair under their arms."

"Yes, don't rule out that possibility. Because they have no need to pretty up or play coy for three old men."

"Have we really turned into some torn rags?"

"Not quite, if we look at it more objectively. The merchandise can still be used if it meets up with ladies in their thirties and forties. But these ones are very young and fresh, about sixteen or seventeen at the most—the age of our own children and grandchildren."

"Oh, old age! Old age sneaking up behind our backs. Hey, Brother Vu, what is your take on old age?"

"I embrace it and live with it peacefully, to the extent I can."

"That's a smartly masterful reaction," Tran Phu says, then he stands up. "Well, it's almost time for supper, the patient must now return to his room. Le Phuong, will you accompany Vu back to the treatment ward? I will settle the bill and catch up with you."

As Vu and the writer step out to the yard, they hear Tran Phu loudly call out to the girls: "Hey, if you want to groom yourselves, you should find an appropriate place. This is not the place to display womanly utensils."

Hearing no one reply, Tran Phu suspects the girls are afraid to answer. A little later he catches up to the other two. They leisurely return to the building reserved for high-ranking cadres then part ways at the foot of the stairs.

"We wish you, Great Brother, a speedy recovery. Today, meeting a hero, I am completely satisfied," says the writer to Vu.

When Vu gets to his room, he sees a group of nurses surrounding the doctor, a mature woman in her fifties. They had carried in an artificial breathing machine for the patient in the bed opposite his. His face is all pale; his eyes are shut tight; his lips are compressed, leaving only a dark line. Vu steps in just as the nurse puts the oxygen mask on the patient. He quietly walks behind them to his bed.

4

It rains again, the shy rain of spring.

The drops fall singly, dropping lightly on the ground without bravado. Then it stops. The wind from the Eastern Sea rolls in and chases the wandering clouds across the deserted sky. Clouds the color of eggplant, reminding him of the garden in his birthplace, a home village that seems so faint and distant that no more than some delicate and mysterious memories remain. The purple reminds him also of the fields in Provence where people grow the fragrant herb called lavender to make perfumes and soaps. The first time he had ever stood before such a vast and purple field, his soul had frozen still before the beauty of the foreign land. And he had then cried silently in his heart:

"Oh, when will our local fields and the vast and sunburned hills of central Vietnam be covered by such an exquisite blanket? Oh, when will the peasant farmers of my country walk in their fields with the tranquil faces of those in this country? Oh, when will the kids who watch cattle in our country be dressed properly like those kids here who leisurely walk their cattle in the shadow of poplars lining the roads? When and when?"

For many months and years, his heart raged over these questions. For many months and years, he was obsessed by a parallel image—a comparison that was painful and that could not be forgotten: the leather shoes and warm socks of French farmers seen next to feet that were cracked, with muddy black nails, with toes that were crooked because for a thousand years they had had to take hold in the muddy fields. That pair of images had followed him like a shadow, appearing to him during noontime dreams or when he was tossing and turning in the middle of the night; when he was sitting in jail as well as when perched honorably on a dais. His suffering people. The hard fate reserved for them by the Creator. So many tears he had shed over that bitter destiny. Everything he had tried to do had been in the brave hope of changing their condition.

"I love my people so much. Why don't they love me? Why can't they give me just a tiny bit of happiness, the same as in other, ordinary lives?"

"Oh, the people: it's an abstract concept, a formless crowd, a cacophony of the sea breathing, the pounding knocks of the waves of time. Those who have prevented you from living as a true human should are your very close comrades, but most of all it was my own fault because I took up the role of a saint."

"But my nation is small and weak. To have stimulated their trust and courage, could I have acted differently?"

"You chose the easier path, one most appropriate for your people's intellectual capacity. That is why you have had to pay a price. The game of playing the saint is not a new one in human history. What altar has not been decorated with fake flowers, even though, in the past, it was made from silver or brass or, today, of pliable plastic and synthetic diamonds? Every game has its price. In this life, nothing is given free."

The one in dialogue with him has the last word, with a teasing smile on his lips. Then he disappears with the wind; a warm and wet wind that leaves him cold, making him shiver. He casts his eyes as if he could follow the unfortunate fellow, as if he had come from the left side of the temple, crossing the yard and the cherry blossom garden. Then he had disappeared in the same direction. That fellow looked exactly like him, but with a complexion greenish like a banana leaf and a look full of contempt.

"Mr. President, please come in, you are cold."

The chubby guard is already behind his back; the sudden voice quite startles him.

"All right, I will come in," he replies with a little anger that he does not want to show. Whether he likes it or not, he is under surveillance from all sides. Not a minute of freedom. His life belongs to the people. His health belongs to the people; his time belongs to the people. Is there nothing left for him? The game is really wicked!

Dong, dong, dong . . . The temple bells suddenly ring repeatedly, briskly, one after another. *Dong, dong, dong* . . .

He turns around and asks the guard, "Why is the temple bell pealing like that?"

"I forgot to tell you that the abbess herself is presiding over the cleansing ceremony for Mr. Quang. The temple bells will ring and there will be more chanting than usual. Please be sympathetic, Mr. President."

"Here we are staying on temple land. They may do what they please."

"Yes, but nonetheless . . ."

"What kind of ceremony? I did not hear clearly."

"The cleansing away of bad fate and the dust of life for the deceased. . . . The woodcutter from the hamlet has been dead for forty-nine days now."

"Already forty-nine days? So fast."

"Yes. Yesterday the hamlet chief came all the way up to ask that Brother Le permit Mr. Quang's family to come up here for the ceremony. When they come up, the company will increase security."

"Here, really it is their business. Increase security for what? To make sure that I don't fall down before the woodcutter's widow? Otherwise, why would the country people want to harm a president?"

That hidden thought runs through his mind, like a joke and a question.

"Please have some tea while it's hot."

"Thank you."

"Will you place the rocking chair near the door for me . . . There, I can read the paper with the natural light."

While drinking his tea the president thinks that in a little while he will see clearly the woodcutter's whole family, first the oldest son. This story has become an ongoing obsession since he first learned of it. An uncontrollable curiosity gives him this need to look at the personalities revolving directly in the tale of this mismatched couple. "So, you thirst to see the faces of these people as a mirror reflecting back your own life. A perfect reflection but from an opposing vantage point. For the woodcutter was no saint. He lived out only an ordinary destiny. He conquered all the misfortunes that he had a chance to encounter, while you were vanquished under the awning of power and glory. A silent, wretched, defeat."

"Mr. President, is it OK like this?"

"Back up a little bit. Better if they don't see my face. That would be distracting to both sides."

"Yes."

"Is that Le's voice?"

"Mr. President, precisely. Brother Le brings reinforcements. The woodcutter's family will arrive after these soldiers."

"Tell Le that I am reading documents. Have him put the men outside; no need to come in to greet me."

"Yes."

The chubby guard glances at the chair to see whether it is properly placed then goes out to greet the augmented force. Carrying the stack of documents to the rocking chair, the president takes the best position from which to observe the mourners who will pass before him as they proceed to the principal hall of the temple.

The air fills with the smell of incense. The sound of a wooden gong rises loudly after the bells stop ringing. He hears soldiers' footsteps. They line up in a row right in front of the hall. All are solemn like wooden statues, facing the far side, their backs turned toward his room, where the door is half closed, half open to hide the person sitting inside. Perhaps Le has guessed his wish, because he stands in some out-of-the-way corner. His absence makes it more comfortable for the president.

The sound of bells arises again to announce that the mourners are approaching the temple. The abbess steps out onto the patio, her two hands in lotus position to greet the guests. The first person he sees is not a member of the family but a monk definitely older than fifty. Behind him are two more monks, then comes Mr. Quang's oldest son, Quy. The president recognizes him at first glance and is somewhat disappointed. His appearance creates no impression. A small man with uneven shoulders, his face is pointed. It exhibits no feature of the father nor the slightest evidence of masculine charm. He wears an old winter uniform, which is usual for village cadres. He does not have a beard, nor a sharply defined jaw. Even his gait is strange, exactly like that of women who must accept the fate of singers or actors; it is both twisted like a slithery snake and on tiptoe like a sparrow. Even though he displays such a sad and weak physique, the oldest son emanates a dangerous power that is hard to describe or explain. "Here is a model of the pseudo warrior," the president thinks. "His movements look like dancing steps but they are aimed at where his opponent is most vulnerable. When making his move, he can finish an opponent most unexpectedly. In other words, this kind of warrior never enters the ring; this kind of swordsman does not appear by day but, in the dark, puts his enemy down with a stab from behind. This type of person will never retreat from any obstacle blocking his ambition, giving no heed to conscience or the contempt of others. But Quy's guardian angel lacks the clout to help him succeed, so the struggle of one without a father only spawns malnourished and neglected offspring."

So he quietly thinks as he watches the family come forward, all dressed in white mourning clothes and lined up according to lineage rank. Behind the family comes a group of old men and women. They must be close relatives of the deceased. At the end is the young wife and her child with a good-looking young man that he guesses to be the student Quynh. This group leaves no special impression.

The president instinctively closes his eyes. A fixation returns him to the image of the oldest son, who is already inside the temple.

"Such a pitiful and weak son adamantly opposing his father; using his position to turn him into a slave? How absurd is life? Someone living under the protection of the family head but who wants to apply his own power over him: Is this a unique madness or a common denominator of all species? Do all children have to kill their fathers and do all grown animals have to eliminate the old ones in search of food? Are humans and wild animals not so far apart?"

Beyond the patio, the bells slowly ring. One set stops as another continues; the vibrations overflow the mountain ridges and penetrate the empty spaces around Lan Vu Temple with waves of magical enchantment. The temple patio is deserted as everybody is inside. Left are scattered yellow leaves in piles. The president looks at the blue sky to find an answer, but none is available. Because he has no direct evidence, because he loved his own father, and because he has no need to fight for power with, or to destroy, the one who gave him life, he does not believe that all of humanity has such a need.

"Perhaps because I left the family too early, and I always missed my father, therefore in my heart there is only longing and sadness. Millions of others live tranquilly with their parents. A drama as in the woodcutter's family is the first such that I have heard or seen. There are children who are filial and others who rebel and are ungrateful. But if ambition turns you into a warring and blood enemy of your parent, you would be abnormal. If deep father-son affection still exists, then those who so love ignore those who are of different blood and cold hearts."

At the end he finds that he has returned to his familiar purgatory, to the tribunal where he is both judge and defendant.

From the temple, the noise of the group chanting rises. The wooden gong sounds in regular measure to mark the song of the bells, mixing with the chanting. Those in the temple are living as they wish and in their faith. They believe firmly that heaven and the divine saints understand their pure-hearted wishes; that they are freeing the deceased from all wrongs and all the shortfalls he had endured in silence, erasing his mistakes, and restoring the honor that had been stained. And last, to open the path that leads to Nirvana, which will receive the one that has left the earth. As for him, what faith does he live with now?

A pain runs down his back, turning his thighs freezing cold. The president shuts tight the doors, turns to his room. He lies down. He never lies down at this time of day except when he is ill. Today he is not ill but he wants to lie down. He feels weary—a weariness both physical and mental.

He cannot sustain, and does not want to, the bearing and activities of a warrior king. Nor does he even want to be a leader with endless strength, to work like a machine that will never rust.

"All my life I have had to maneuver, to strive to work like a hard steel machine. But a man is not a machine. A man will rust out with time," he thinks quietly, but before he lies down he glances at the clock on the wall and hesitates a moment because the clock only shows 9:30 in the morning.

"At this moment, what's the use of exemplary spirit in an old king who is confined? Enough. Accept the reality that my life has limits and my strength is not a stream that will flow forever. I am more than seventy. At this age I should not stick with any illusion. All my life I sacrificed for big dreams, the kind people often call ideals, or lofty goals. All my life I kept myself facing the altar at which people unselfishly offer up their youth as well as their fate. But in the end, I finally find that the ideal is also illusion. It's like a mysterious castle standing in the fog on the other side of the river, enticing those on this side. People get out of their boats to swim over. But when they reach the far shore, the boats have split into broken timbers and there is no sight of the castle and its treasure. There is merely a deserted beach by the river's edge; besides the crumbled mounds are a thousand pieces of broken glass that reflect rainbow-colored lights."

That thought weakens his legs and arms and unmoors his soul like a corpse bobbing in the waves. Immediately, an anger explodes. He raises his voice to blame himself:

"Well, don't be shaken by such pessimistic thoughts. Don't walk in the footsteps of those who have no principles. Do you want to follow their example or not? Or rather follow the cult of nudists and live a life with vegetation and animals? Over all this time, the revolution has made a long journey. Accepted or rejected, the truth will appear in front of your eyes like the five fingers of the hand spread before you. To state the facts: we have a free country, we have our own national flag, we have a government, armed forces—the realities of a long-held dream nurtured on the front lines."

The man with the face green as pale banana leaves turns around, stands leaning against the wall, curls his lips, and says, smiling: "But what's the government for, the national flag for, when the people live more miserably than before? What good is the state machine if it's used only to benefit a small number of people who oppress the majority and push them into mass murders, the biggest of which is this very war? Your own comrades dream of a large arch of triumph to glorify themselves. They dream of a war ever more great and glorious. 'Greatness and glory' are always whoring, eternally out to trick us all. Even for you—you have been mesmerized by them. Wishing to be the guiding light for the people, to be great, to become a great chief of state, you volunteered to play a saint. In the process you harmed her, a simple-minded woman, who wholeheartedly trusted you. Is all this true or false?"

He dares not answer. He has no courage to answer. His provocateur no longer smiles but contemptuously shrugs his shoulders. After throwing him a condescending look the specter steps over the president's head to leave through the window.

The president feels his nostrils burn.

"Oh my god, why am I shedding tears so easily? Old age, infirmity, or for other reasons? A man should not cry so easily like this. I have changed. When did I go bad?"

He curses himself fiercely, but tears keep falling, slowly rolling down his temples then soaking his hair. And in his ears, the doctor's familiar singing is heard:

"My beloved one . . ."

"Ha, ha, ha . . ."

"Ha, ha, ha, ha, ha, ha, ha . . ."

Fits of irreverent laughter break out and immediately he sees the large round face, the drooping cheeks and chin of Chairman Man. He appears in the ashen purple light; his complexion the striped green of a gecko. With a solicitous, cheerful manner, he examines the president as a child might examine a cricket.

The president raises his voice angrily: "Why are you here, Mr. Chairman?"

"You imply that I am an uninvited guest?"

The president is quiet.

Chairman Man smiles: "Why don't you answer directly? This is no longer a game of eventualities, or playing around with diplomacy. You and I are yin to the other's yang, but whether we like it or not, neither of us now has any influence on the politics of the two neighbors. Nevertheless, you are now like Napoleon on St. Helena; you have no reason to be circumspect."

"Mr. Chairman, I don't know how."

"Well, you're very polite, with the politeness of whites. But you and I both come from simple rural people. I am from Hunan and you from Nghe An, the dirt-poor city where the farmers chew on sweet potatoes instead of rice, more miserable than the Hmong hill tribes who make corn cakes and corn soup. Being a rural person, just act according to your roots. Why show off the kind of politeness you learned elsewhere?"

"Would you please consider changing the subject, Mr. Chairman?"

"What will you do if I do not change the subject?"

"Dear sir, don't forget you are a guest."

"Oh, I have long forgotten the difference between host and guest, even though I still play at diplomacy. For me, all those in front of me are but game in a struggle with the Lord of the Jungle."

"I know you see yourself as the true Lord of the Jungle, and the Americans and the Westerners are only a bunch of paper tigers. If you so believe in your own strength, why don't you take direct responsibility for this war?"

"You are wrong. If indeed the Americans and white-skinned Western devils are just paper tigers, then why did we let our vassals in the south start the game? I am not yet able to swallow the white men because, to my mind, they are too big a bait for my throat. Did you ever read the story of the boa swallowing wood?"

"My country is small, my people are poor. I have no intention of becoming a boa, therefore, I don't concern myself about swallowing others."

"That is your first stupidity. If you are a king and just tie your thoughts up in a dream, then you don't deserve to sit on the throne. The king must dream differently from ordinary folk. One who rules is not on a parallel path with those who are ruled. Because of such demeanor, you lost the struggle. Also because of such behavior, you are ruled by your own subordinates. It is the old saying: 'Many tigers defeat a ferocious one.'"

"The 'many tigers' act under your direction. Thirst for glory clouds their conscience and blinds their eyes. Because of dark amnesia, they are flattered by those shining words from the big brothers, therefore they are determined to throw themselves into this war at all costs. They trust your encouragement: 'Hit the Americans, they are only paper tigers' . . ."

"Ha, ha, ha, ha . . . You're not bad! All along I thought of you as the best little soldier and the most feared from the south. My estimate is not wrong. Intuition never misleads. On the contrary, it is to me the most thoroughly reliable of all our mental faculties. You are pretty good! I confirm that you are worthy of being a gentleman. The only regret is that you lacked 'opportunity.' Then and now, when we discuss heroes, we tend to emphasize military experience. I am more practical. I believe in heavenly destiny. Heaven did not support you. Or, to be more accurate, your destiny is softer than mine, therefore, you cannot win this round. Such as this the old ones left to fate. Heaven decides. That is why you have eyes but are blind, a chicken becoming a crow; you put power into the hands of betrayers. Because heaven dictates is why your subordinates trust the words I say as if they believed in the gods. Even if we painted the rocks white, they would not turn into cotton balls. A square cardboard box will not change into a brick. I, forever, am King of the Northern Palace, and your world is forever just a gate for the little people in southern China to use when they need to borrow some pepper. The little piece of land you claim to be your fatherland of mountains and rivers is only an isolated district that we, sooner or later, will seize. Now you understand that this war is one of the best games I have ever played; a little game that costs nothing. In this game, I don't really need any plan or schemes, but only need reuse one of the ancient thirty-six strategies."

"Yes, all that I have known from the start," the president responds. "You did not come up with the strategy of 'Tigers Fighting in the Mountain' but copied it from ancient commanders who had used it many times. During the Sino-Japanese War you rang bells and blew whistles and said, 'Resist Japan; save the nation,' but your army hid along the border roads to safeguard your forces, leaving the Nationalist Army to fence with the fascists alone. In reality, you used the Japanese to destroy your political opponents. Waiting for the big war to end, you kept your army secure gathering strength to destroy the Nationalists. Now, not only the Chinese people but more than half of the world besides thinks that destroying the fascists was your work. But history is not written only once as letters are engraved on tombstones. All deceitful schemes sooner or later will be exposed. Future generations have the right to rewrite all the histories, and their power lies beyond your reach."

"Future generations? I have yet to see the faces of future generations. At least as of now. My shadow will be over China for a very long time."

"Do you need glory like one who gets to be remembered in a shrine? You can create glory with fraud?"

"Only idiots don't cheat in the game of political chance. You seem to know everything, so why can't you imitate me?"

"Because I am me and you are you, Mr. Chairman. No one can change their place; also, no one can teach how to be smart, because humans vary one from another. However, I know that this war is destiny's cruelest playground, and, if our punishment is to be drawn into pieces by four chariots, then the most brutal charioteer has been directed by your own hands."

"You know, I acknowledge what you say. But you only know it after your hands and feet are all tied up. You know it only when you have become a living ghost. Someone who is king but no longer has soldiers is only a dressed-up puppet."

"My life of struggle did not teach me with sufficient experience to predict and resolve all contingencies."

"I feel you have had sufficient experience. Your weakest link is your conflicted stance between East and West. That unresolved orientation has planted a seed of destruction inside you. First is your understanding of democracy, a kind of bread baked by the white devils. Here is the root cause of your failure. You were an obedient student of the West, while your closest subordinates were indigenous only. Therefore they simultaneously suspected that you had affection for the French and took advantage of the Western principle that the majority rules to bind you like a butcher ties a pig before bleeding it to death. The blood that flows in you is Eastern and calls you back to the old temples, wherein for thousands of years Confucian literati lit incense and bowed up and down praying before the teachings that the virtuous should rule. You forget that no one ever saw the faces of the mythical Sage Kings, Yao and Shun, in this life. Those two puppets really were created by the government to educate a bunch of underlings and to tame the masses. You allowed yourself to embrace the passion of sacrificing for a cause, of sacrificing for the common good; therefore you had to follow your subordinates like an idiot. You forgot that those in the East eat with chopsticks and distinguish kings from subjects very distinctly. Between a king and his subjects there is no equality, nor any trust. There is only use or rejection. The word 'comrade' I borrowed from the West to direct the mandarins and the little people exactly as a magician directs his army with charms and spells. It was like a lemon rind, a ghost's shadow, and yet you believed it to be the meat of the fruit and a real personage. Death comes to you because of this misperception. Oh, 'comrade'! A fancy word created by a few guys with beards. Do you see how I treat those I call 'comrades'? I suck the blood from their veins as a farmer releases water from a field. I take their blood to clean the steps that lead to the throne, because the color red is the color of power and glory. Nothing can represent the color red better than human blood. Those who stand to the left or the right of the king are always the warriors of his bedchamber. You have to know how to kill them right away before they take time to think about hiding knives in their shirtsleeves. That is the art of governing. It has been well tested for thousands of years. As a king in the East you didn't even know that law. You wanted to build your nation according to Western standards, so you let someone else manage recruitment and placement of personnel. It was like giving a sword to a cabal of enemies. In the game of power we cannot even trust blood relatives, so how can we trust strangers?"

"On this point you might be right . . ."

"Not 'might'; I *am* right. Right meaning 'uncontestable.' Don't hesitate at the frivolity of words. People pay dear prices for misunderstanding them. But I, how am I to explain your misunderstanding?"

"Perhaps due to my lack of experience or my lack of intelligence. Perhaps in the special situation of our country it was hard to find a better solution."

"You're pretty smart when considering the big picture. But you're stupid once you mix up what is true with what is not, it's just playacting without having to live that role for real. Being king is the greatest role on life's stage. But one has to realize that it is an act. And that insight must be preserved, nurtured regularly just as people must regularly maintain both their souls and their bodies. Your misery is that you have an actor's blood and sometimes you cry, you smile, for real; you put your true self into the character. Therefore, you cannot keep up the role of a ruler all the way to the end. Now I will tell you the difference between a king and a little thespian. A king acts but always knows he is in a role. Anytime he takes off the mask and throws it in the cupboard, he can do anything he wishes even if totally contrary to his role, but he forces the courtiers and the people to accept it as natural. Emperor Ch'ien Lung of China was the most appropriate example of this. He was extremely smart, very literate, and accomplished in martial arts. His calligraphy was beautiful and fairylike; his poetry glossy like green jade. He fully taught his officials and the people the Four Books and the Five Classics and other moral principles. That was when he assumed the role of ruler. In other moments, he could take off the face of kingship and throw it somewhere in a corner, and live true to his own self. Do you remember the tale of his kicking his queen until her fetus died?"

"I remember."

"Do you remember his love affair with Ho Ch'in?"

"Of course I do."

"Very good, thus do you remember that Ho Ch'in had plotted to kill the crown prince, Fu Ching, how many times?"

"Twice, if I am not mistaken."

"Right, twice. And if Minister Liu had not insisted, the crown prince would have become dust. And still Ho Ch'in was favored. His personal wealth was more than the state treasury. This demonstrates that Ch'ien Lung's adoration of Ho Ch'in had more to it than the life of the crown prince and the national interest. And definitely Ch'ien Lung was not a weakling or a frivolous dreamer. What, then, prompted him to behave like that, if not satisfaction of his sexual appetite? If not to caress until satiety a body that contained the soul of ruler? As a bisexual, Ch'ien Lung was passionate for both man and woman but I believe that in reality his homosexual proclivity was stronger and the more dominant. Because in those days, homosexuals were despised and teased, that is why he built a series of pavilions for them in the inner part of the palace to hide them from the people. If the court had released his harem to the countryside, for sure two-thirds of them would still have been virgins. There: open your eyes to see the game as played by real rulers. Not just Ch'ien Lung; rulers of every dynasty were the same."

"I know. And you are sure that successors should follow this tradition?"

"You rank me too low; to be accurate, you look at me with irreverent eyes. That same irreverence of the ancient clans of the hundred Viet peoples in southern China. You need to understand that I am not a successor but a founder. I laugh at how the old kings and lords used women at such cost but with such little effect. I don't need to build red chambers and towers. I don't need to check expenses for red bodices and trousers. If you drive them into a corner, the female cats will scratch each other and disturb my sound sleep. My home is mobile. A modest vessel on dry land is a thousand times more convenient that an extravagant oceangoing sailboat even though it can visit the six continents. The land is vast; the mountains and rivers grand; I select women from wherever I happen to be. Not twenty-year-old mountain girls as you did, but all youngsters ages twelve to sixteen. The younger they are, the fresher their life-giving sap. I regain my youth and nourish my libido thanks to those growing girls."

"Of course," the president says, smiling and puckering his lips, "I know your famous saying: 'I wash my sex organs inside them.'"

"What are sex organs? Indeed, you really are one who takes your words from those with big noses and blue eyes. I am only a person from Hunan. I like to speak like local farmers: 'I wash my cock in the alleyways of young girls so they can stimulate my energy.' There, do you hear it clearly?"

He starts to laugh after these words, in a playful and provocative manner, his tiny blinking eyes shooting out devilish sparks. The president sees clearly his two rows of very even and yellow teeth. He remains silent, not answering. A moment passes. Then Chairman Man clears his throat and says:

"After I pop their cherries, I return these 'female comrades' back to the local cadres to manage. They must give them a raise, enroll them in units or the Party; if unemployed, find them manufacturing jobs. If they want to go to school, then institutions will open their doors. If some are weak and die, it is but the falling of a peach or two from the peach trees of Yunnan. A lucky one gets my love and is honored with carrying my seed. She will be well cared for and her child will be raised in secret and sent to the child-care center of the Party's central leadership. Don't you see my capacity for initiative? Don't you see that I am better than Ch'ien Lung in enjoying games?"

He again laughs robustly.

The president quietly looks at the apparition opposite him. The folds of flesh overflowing the high collar of his cadre-style shirt are also lined like lizard skin, reminding one of a pile of soggy and mildewed dough. His full chest stretches his shirt. But from his stomach area down only a blanket of fog appears. When the president was young, he had heard people say that ghosts never have legs. They glide over the grass and can be seen only from the knees up. Now he knows it is true. The strange thing though is that this king of the north is still alive, arranging the executions of his subordinates; so why does he appear to the president as a ghost in his dreams, whether at three in the morning or in the afternoon? His laughter creates sounds that are both sharp and flat. If one could put a color to the sound it would be black steel mixed with brass rust. It's not obvious why Chairman Man's laughter makes him sad while his arrogance no longer makes him angry. At first, he feels an unrelated sadness, an odd melancholy as when you read a romantic story. Chairman Man seems surprised to see him quiet. He lowers his voice:

"Why? Are you nostalgic for the past or do you regret things you ought to have done?"

"No. Regrets are useless."

"So what are you thinking?"

"I think yin and yang are unbound. You—a nemesis—bother to come visit as an honored guest. But all the advice given out in life is worthless because individuals are different."

"Right. Sheep graze grass and vultures devour corpses. But anyone governing a large kingdom with prowess or just caring for a small island must study the art of governing. Even Africans know how to retain sovereign power. You are a thousand times more intelligent than they: why you let subordinates push you to this extremity is something I would like to know."

"You have nothing else to do down in this sad and gloomy country? Have all the relatives of those you harmed up on Chinese soil really lost their smarts or come down with dementia? You think they will always remain silent in the presence of millions of innocent corpses?"

"Believe it or not. Is it so important? The game is over. The chess pieces are back in their coffins. Now I am looking for new lands. You are an object that excites me. All excitement is linked to curiosity. But for thousands of years China and Vietnam have been enemy siblings. You and I, too."

"I find you pretty honest."

"Yin and yang take different paths; the game of being diplomatic—no longer useful."

"If you already confirm our kinship of brotherly enemies, why do you come?"

"You ask a stupid question. I come because of that kinship."

"To give your power an official stamp; to prove that as head of state you are outstanding; to say that during all your life you were full and satisfied in every way and your personhood was always on a pedestal looking down on the interests of your country. That is why you never hold your hands back from any kind of destruction. That is also why you became the 'Great Helmsman.' Because your people are so used to worshipping great ones who stand on arches of triumph built from human bones. Given that you want to stand on a high pedestal, the higher the pile of human bones, the more beautiful the result. And, finally: Is this the best way to educate those who want to be kings?"

"In reality, it is. Now, you are extremely intelligent. I came here to advise you or to humiliate you—however you want to see it! Because always, words just whore; a gentleman from the southern capital or from the northern one just jumps into bed. I am here to teach you that acting the role of a king is day and night different from the skills displayed by any old actor. You should study acting or else retire to the calm life of ordinary people 'under a thatch roof; two shining hearts.' To be king, such work demands different behavior. Rulers can never forget two basic rules. The first thing is to be able to release your semen perfectly. This is hygienic for the body and must be done to keep the brain clear and the blood flowing. The second thing is to know how to use the blood of others in cleaning the steps to the throne. Because blood is the only liquid that can water the garden where the fruit of power and glory grows. Do you see any tree that is not watered producing leaves and fruit? These are the two golden rules by which to nourish the mind and body and to preserve the throne. Kings and mandarins in years past all knew how to apply these two principles. And you can't. Worse: you went against them. This was the biggest mistake in your life. This fault not only destroyed your life's work but also pushed you into a life of imprisonment. Imprisonment on two fronts: your body suffering from clotted blood and your mind in agony because you are in the state of being used. Your subordinates used the Kwangchou rest house as a place to tie down your legs. If I am not mistaken, you were settled in there about six, seven months, started to get used to the terrain, to like the food there, to love looking at pretty local girls. So why did they send you here?"

The president is silent. A misty white shroud from the ghost shadow flows toward him. His face goes frigid, especially his cheekbones.

Realizing that there will be no reply, Chairman Man smiles and continues: "Oh, I am just joking when I ask. How would you know? The bowl holds the fish; the cage the bird."

Then, shaking his head as if in pity, he waves his hand and disappears.

Loud knocks on the door startle him. The hands of the clock are lined up on the number twelve.

"It's lunchtime already."

"I have a headache," the president says. "Just leave the food on the table and return to your company."

"Yes."

The president continues to lie down but he is nervous. Ten minutes later, he stands up, washes his face, and steps beyond the bedroom. Some cozies cover the bowl of rice and several stir-fry dishes set for him on the table, but the nutritionists and the doctor still stand out in the hall. They have not dared return down the mountain but have gathered behind the guard booth, contemplating the temple scenery. On the other side of the patio, the din of the wooden gong and the little bells intermingled with chanting continues. The president steps outside to inquire:

"Why haven't you returned down the mountain? It's OK; later the guards can prepare my meal."

"Mr. President, we must do our duty."

"All right. If so, come in and prepare the meal for me then clear it away when convenient. Really, today, I don't feel hungry."

"Dear sir, today the cook has made the eggplant-and-tofu dish and the stir-fried pumpkin blossoms that you like. Please, Mr. President, try to finish it."

"Fine . . . I will try," he says. Sitting down before the tray of food, he suddenly remembers the words of Chairman Man:

"You forget that those in the East hold chopsticks and distinguish ranks very clearly."

Holding up the black wooden chopsticks, he gazes at them as if seeing them for the first time.

"Why make such a big point of it—the differences among those who hold chopsticks, or forks, or eat with their fingers? What is the meaning of any difference in habits?"

That thought floats past him, passive without feeling, like a face strange and cold. He starts to pick up the purple basil scattered on top of the plate of eggplant and tofu. He has always enjoyed this dish. When he used to teach in Phan Thiet, his neighbor married a woman from the north; she had introduced him to eggplant with tofu. She had been a homemaker worthy of the name; she lived with the single aspiration of caring for her family and keeping their home tidy. Her husband, a savvy businessman on the north-south railroad, who, all year round, enjoyed banquet food and restaurants with his business buddies as well as those who owned government franchises, nonetheless admired his wife's culinary skills. It was she who had exposed the bitter truth to him:

"If you want to talk about dragons and phoenixes, be my guest; but if you are dirt poor, how can you ever have good food?" Then she raised her voice: "But even if wealthy, you may not know how to eat well. With your coffers full of cash, sometimes you still eat from containers and drink from vats; or waste your money bringing junk home."

Inadvertently, her frank words shamed him when he thought of the pride that people in his native region took over their shiny eggplants: it was nothing but a mask of confidence used to cover up their poverty. That merchant's wife had also opened his eyes to see that people's tastes differ according to customs and culture. She taught him how to appreciate good food. Eggplant cooked with tofu is one of the everlasting memories from his youth, connected to Phan Thiet villages with their hills full of lush vegetation and lonely Cham monuments on sun-bathed red sandy hillocks.

One afternoon after he was done teaching, he was returning home at the same time as the respectable merchant. Before they had reached their common destination, rain started pouring. Both of them had to duck under the eaves of a prayer shrine. They may have been neighbors but they had never sat together or chatted with each other. Their relationship was based mostly on greetings politely exchanged by the fence. The rain provided an opportunity for them to talk. The merchant seemed open and friendly. When the rain had stopped and it was almost dark, he said:

"It may be too forward of me, but may I invite you over for dinner? . . . You are single; it might be inconvenient cooking for yourself."

"Thank you. I am used to living alone."

"I was single like you before I married. But we are neighbors; you have a career, I have mine. There is no relationship. You don't compete with me nor I with you. It would be very good if we became close."

He had been amused because he had never met a merchant who spoke so "straight as a stick." It put him in sympathy with the neighbor and he had accepted the invitation. After changing clothes, he went to the merchant's house. The latter had stood at the gate to wait; a maid was feeding the youngest child in the compound's yard. They sat at the table right away.

"This is an ordinary meal. Because we trust that you are easygoing, therefore we presumed to invite you over. Please forgive us should there be any shortcoming."

The neighbor had then said, calling out to his wife: "Mother, you do not have to worry too much. Today it's just a simple meal to open a relationship. Having a party for our guest in a few days would still not be too late."

He had been quiet, thinking to himself: "A simple meal like this is better than a New Year's banquet in my home village."

The merchant's dining table with its marble top was very large, but places had been set for only three. On the empty chair the host had put a vase full of large mums. This gigantic vase was more than a meter high and it presented itself more seriously than would another guest. It added elegance to the room and put everyone in a comfortable state of mind. On the table was a porcelain tureen of rice covered with a basket opposite a pitcher of wine brewed with many medicinal herbs. Seeing the dishes in the middle of the table, his mouth watered intensely. He swallowed quietly, but was unable to suppress this traitorous reflex. The wetness could not stop, because the flavors and the colors could not but excite. First was a spring hen braised in a clear broth of sunflowers, a bantam chicken with paper-thin skin, yellow with fat, coming with the nice fragrance of fresh shiitake mushrooms, which were left whole and surrounded the chicken like the petals of a chrysanthemum, one on top of another. There was a fresh whole fish with oranges swimming in the middle of a clear broth holding specks of chili flakes and minced coriander leaves. He had never seen fish with oranges so prepared; each flavor of spice was pronounced but all blended splendidly. On that night, as he recalls, he had eaten the oranges and fish as if he had been drinking soup. He had felt a bit ashamed but at the end he told himself, "A woman eats like a cat; a man like a tiger. I am full of youth."

He ate the next dish—braised garlic eggplant—in the same quick manner. In his village, people were used to eating eggplant slightly pickled or deeply immersed in salt —a hand-me-down recipe for all poor farmers, not only in central Vietnam but also in the north. There is a saying that makes fun of stingy, wealthy men harshly using their prospective sons-in-law:

In five years of servitude to my future father-in-law
Your mother has used up three vats of pickled eggplants.
Please get me to the well quick, for I am dying soon
Of thirst from eating her pickled eggplants.

That meal had taught him that people could make something of this vegetable totally different from what he had known at home. The braised eggplant dish that evening had included crisp, deep-fried soft tofu, slightly burned cubed pork cutlets, and a bright red tomato sauce. In addition, there had been plenty of garlic, both fried and fresh.

As he later walked along his paths of destiny, he had eaten dishes from East and West, but nothing ever compared with the flavor of the braised eggplant by the woman in Phan Thiet.

"Mr. President, please start your meal before it gets cold."

The group of soldiers who have done the cooking are still outside the window, still looking at him.

"I will eat now," he replies, then mechanically picks up some braised eggplant. He smells the garlic, the grape and perilla leaves, the fried tofu, the grilled pork, the eggplant fried in lard. But these smells do not come close to the ones he knew before. They are only a faint reminder. His mouth does not water and the food tastes bland. His youth, too, is gone; gone, too, is a far horizon enticing him forward; gone, too, is his faith. And likewise the braised eggplant dish is no more. What is left before him, in an expensive gold-rimmed dish, is its ghost. A ghostly shadow of that evening meal a long time ago in Phan Thiet.

"Mr. President, is the eggplant dish I cooked OK or is it undersalted?"

"Good, very good. And the frying in lard was perfect, not too much, not too little," he answers quickly, intentionally picking up some raw garlic and herbs to please the cook. The food sticks in his throat. He has to take some soup to wash it down. The cook still observes him attentively and respectfully. He tries to finish the bowl of rice, sticks his chopsticks into the second dish, and nibbles on the red fried pumpkin blossoms before placing his chopsticks down.

"Please clear all this. The food is very good today but I am not feeling well. Maybe a headache. Your duty is successfully completed; I did my part poorly. Old age is something we cannot avoid."

"Mr. President, you did not finish one third of your food."

"When you reach my age, you will understand," he says, making a gesture to pacify the group and to close the conversation. The on-duty doctor steps in to prepare his medications.

On the other side of the temple, the sounds of nonstop chanting can still be heard. There was no stopping for lunch. "How can they endure all their lives such a strict regimen and still stay healthy?" the president thought to himself. "If I am not mistaken the founder of this religion lived until his eighties. What strength nourishes them besides their faith?"

The sounds of the bells synchronizing with the chanting return him to reality. The congregation is praying for the soul of a father who had been assaulted by his own child. Is it performed genuinely with full regret by the guilty child or is it just for show? Further, if this father had not died abruptly by accident, and if he were alive with all the operative strengths of body and a clear mind, would the child still display heartfelt repentance?

"Alas, the answer already comes to mind given the arrangement of the ceremony."

Suddenly, a curiosity arises in his mind: "When I die, will the cadres who betrayed me cry?"

He imagines those people in a group standing on the platform in Ba Dinh Square, with of course everything being as it must. Above their heads would be the flag at half-mast, his portrait surrounded by a black border, and so many heartfelt and powerful slogans, such as:

"From Generation to Generation We Mourn Our President, the Great Father of Our Mountains and Rivers," "The President Will Forever Live in Our Hearts," or, "The Country Survives; the People Survive. The Thoughts of Our President Are the Compass Showing Us All the Way."

Perhaps all those beautiful words will be used to praise his public achievements. Beautiful words cost least of all; they call for lots of saliva but very little morality and intelligence. Besides words, there will be music, because, always, music has been an effective charm and hypnotic. Will they not look for both old and new songs to make the national funeral more heart-wrenching? More tragic? Will they play the Sa Lech Chenh tune? Or the Nam Binh or Nam Ai song? The Ly Chieu Chieu or the Nghe Tinh marching style? Oh, what a country brimming with sad tunes to see people off to heaven. Suddenly he sees clearly before him events at their comedic best and so he imagines the delegation standing on the platform for his funeral, all using handkerchiefs to wipe away tears, real or fake.

"They will be forced to pretend that they are crying but in their hearts will rise the loud noise of teeth grinding: 'Why did you wait so long to die, you hunchbacked old man? We wasted so much building the public edifice to speed your passing over to the other side but your stubborn will to live hung on until this minute. Too much to endure . . .'"

But they could also be crying real tears.

"Tears mixed with salt really will roll down from their eyes, because they will cry first of all over their fate. Because they know for sure that someday they, too, will go down to the grave, the last place for every human life. A place for gathering in—common to all—that none of us can miss. There, they will have to face me!"

That thought makes him shake his head, depressed. He quickly drinks a sip of tea because he fears the soldiers will notice his mood. They would think that he has lost his self-confidence, has become an old, enfeebled patient. Many times in the past he had passed on the streets of Paris old people who walked while talking or laughing to themselves. He thought: "Pity to watch the old ones."

Now could such pity be directed his way? A muffled laugh rises in his thoughts: "If only I could laugh to myself and talk to myself as they did! . . . But—the worst thing is that I don't even have that much freedom. Even worse, my memory is not fatigued from traveling over the years. It refuses to sink into the fog. It does not want to fade with age. The biggest punishment for a person is to have their old body house a sharp memory. Memory forces me to live in hell day after day. Memory is the one who builds you a permanent court of justice. Memory is the one at your side from whom you cannot run nor can you dare repudiate. Without our memories, would not life be lighter?"

He bends his head to continue drinking tea, looking at the yellow liquid that resembles the color of the curry he had eaten before he had left Guangzhou in China. The rest house at Guangzhou—a vacation that had been exactingly prepared like a contemporary over-the-top Broadway play. The whole time he had been there, the cook had made only Vietnamese and Chinese dishes. For his last meal, the Chinese cook had gotten the idea of cooking Indian food for a treat, knowing that he was soon to leave. The meal had been good. Before getting on the helicopter he could still taste the flavor of curry mixed with oil in the rice. It made the color of the dish quite attractive: a smooth and shiny yellow, a color depicting warmth or happiness.

A military helicopter had taken him that night back to Hanoi. They had told him they had to use a helicopter to fly real low and so avoid the antiaircraft defenses. War often turns misjudgment into farce. To ensure his safety, they had been forced to use a ragged, obsolete piece of machinery.

The pilot had seemed nervous, even agitated. He wanted to say something but stopped. The president had looked at the soldier and immediately felt confident.

"I have ridden in carts drawn by buffalo. Riding in your plane is a luxury. Don't worry."

"Yes, sir," the pilot had replied, then sat down at the controls. The president's four bodyguards had sat at each of the four corners as specified. The flight began. When the helicopter had risen up the necessary height over Guangzhou, it had shaken and bumped around like a buffalo cart rolling over crumbling mountain roads. The moving air around them was like many waves continuously dropping down, mixing in with the clouds. The night was ink black. He could see only a vast black space, with no moon or stars. And so they had flown in silence to the next zone. But once the helicopter had crossed the border, tracer antiaircraft rounds shot up, plowing narrow lines of red fire. Each time, those lines of fire had come closer. He knew that they had entered the no-fly zone defended by the antiaircraft units in the northeast area, from Lao Cai to Quang Ninh. The pilot brought the helicopter down under the red streaks made by the tracer bullets. His stress had caused his eyes to bulge out from his face and sweat to roll profusely down his nape, soaking the collar of his uniform. Sweat had also run down to his hands. The president still remembers the image of those hands, thick and firm, with hair on top and on the last knuckles of the fingers. He recalls fixating on those hands, as did his bodyguards. They had been unable to do anything but breathe anxiously and glue their eyes on the hands of the pilot. That had been the longest plane ride in his life. Each minute going by had been an anxious one—listening to the puffing sound of the old engine, waiting to see what would happen. The pilot and the four very young guards dared not say anything: he knew fear had turned them so stonily silent.

Finally, the pilot breathed a sigh of relief and showed him the Long Bien bridge. He tilted his head to look through the glass to see the familiar bridge in the faded light of a city during wartime. Without turning his head backward, he said, "Inform the president: we will land in a few minutes."

Hesitating a little, he had continued: "If nothing special happens."

The president had replied, "If something special happens or not, one person is in charge. On this plane you are the pilot, not me."

"Yes, sir," the pilot answered, eyes looking straight ahead. At that moment, the helicopter started to circle. The soldiers, who had just begun to relax, now again were afraid, and their worry contaminated the small cabin.

The plane circled a second time, then a third.

Silence weighed heavy in the air. Strangely, however, at that moment a calm suddenly came over him followed by a playful smile.

"Certainly, every game has to end. At least, the people will see the last scene of this play. Won't that have some benefit?"

The pilot suddenly turned around and spoke: "Mr. President, the landing lights are placed in the wrong position."

"Are you sure about that?"

"Yes, Mr. President, one hundred percent."

"What does that mean?"

"It means that if we land based on the landing lights as positioned, the plane will fall right in the middle of Dinh Cong Lake."

He was quiet; he could almost hear the wild beating in the chests of the four guards. After a few minutes, he asked, "Have you been flying for a while now?"

"Mr. President, not quite as long as some others but I know all the airports of the country like the palm of my hand," he replied with the determined manner of one who is cautious and has a sense of responsibility.

The president was satisfied, because from the start he had trusted this person, a soldier among thousands whom he had met only for the first time. He smiled and said, "In the old days, great weavers wove in the dark. They only needed to hear the sound of the shuttle and the tempo of the thread bobbins to know what was going to happen. The palace selected outstanding weavers for the court using this criterion. We call such proficiency a test that challenges the skills of expertise. I find you are a good pilot. Therefore, just use your expertise."

"Yes, sir," the pilot replied. He finished flying his fourth circumnavigation then began to set the helicopter down in the middle of a pitch-dark area. Suddenly, the guard on the president's left grabbed his arm and squeezed, half in seeking comfort and half in wanting to protect him from danger. The grabbing fingers—hard as nails—hurt him, but quietly he bore the pain. Then they heard the wheels touch ground.

The pilot had turned around to ask, "Mr. President, should we keep the lights on or turn them off?"

"Keep them on to give us light," he had replied.

Right then, like magic from a devil or a saint, an entire building materialized before their eyes: the central building of the military airport. All the glass windows were brightly lit but no one could be seen. By instinct, he turned toward the line of landing lights, and caught the gaze of the pilot at the same time. This row of lights was placed along the lake. Black-painted steel posts kept them off the surface of the water. The instant when they clearly could see the scene was when all the lights were turned off like the torches of flying ghosts. At the same time, the large doors of the central building of the military airport had opened wide. Out from the hangar had stepped a group of people, eight in all: Ba Danh, Sau, four bodyguards, and two others, for sure high-ranking cadres at the airport.

"They will die tomorrow, those with unlucky fates. The four bodyguards will be destroyed instantly," the president thought to himself. "But the two airfield officers? Will their lives go on for one or two more days, or the whole week?"

The lights on the grass had started to come on. The pilot asked, "Mr. President, can I turn off the engine?"

"OK, it's time to do that."

A stepladder had been brought over by the airfield officers. The president stepped down, and warmly shook the hands of his two subordinates.

"So glad you are back, Eldest Brother. Welcome."

"Greetings to you, Mr. President. Were you pleased with the scenery and the friendly people of Guangzhou?"

He had smiled. "Yes, I am very pleased, extremely pleased. Thank you, younger uncles."

And his life then had returned to its normal routine.

For many days afterward, his mind had been preoccupied by the image of the helicopter pilot. For sure, he had lost his life along with the four young soldiers. He had never seen them again. His regular guards were rotated periodically, faster than the wind changes the season. What about the gifted pilot?

In his eyes, that pilot had saved his life. His was one of the faces that obsessed him almost all the time. That face was a mirror reflecting back such a bitter truth: he was powerless vis-à-vis those to whom he was indebted.

"I am the most powerless among the powerless. I am so grateful but am the most faithless one among all those who don't repay their gratitude. It is a truth that no one can believe. It is also a humiliation that I cannot share with anyone."

5

Vu puts on his coat and walks into the hallway.

He sits on a wooden bench and listens indifferently to the noises coming his way. Earlier that morning at about five a.m, the patient opposite him had breathed his last. The doctor on duty summoned the morgue attendant and the personnel management cadre to come and complete the procedure to transfer the corpse to the morgue. The other patients wiggled their necks somewhat like worms to observe everything with unfocused, dispirited eyes. Terror has turned their already pallid faces into completely colorless ones. The atmosphere got so stifling that Vu put on his coat and silently left the room.

The hallway is deserted, with only dim lights along the wall shining on the green benches. The quiet temporarily alleviates his mood. With his back against the bench, Vu looks at the opposite wall and sits thus for a long while, without thinking of anything in particular. A moment later he can hear birds chirping; dawn was breaking.

"What charm makes me pay attention to these birds singing in the early morning?" Vu asks himself, for during the years he had spent in the Viet Bac woods he never paid much attention to them. Not finding the answer, Vu closes his eyes and continues to listen to the chirping. For some reason, all these bird songs bring him an extraordinary joy in living which nothing else at the moment can.

Just at that moment, the rolling gurney approaches carrying the dead man, who is covered in white. The person pushing it is the morgue attendant, a big man with a swollen face and expressionless eyes. His facial complexion has the yellow tone of a corpse. Following him are a few administrative personnel and nurses. The doctor on duty stands by herself at the end of the hallway, leaning out the window to look at the trees in the garden. Perhaps like him, she is listening to the birdsong. Now Vu understands why he is paying so much attention to the birds singing at dawn; it was like that on the morning he first heard of Xuan's murder. He recalled how he had suddenly stood like a statue to listen to the birdsong even though the driver had started the engine in the driveway. It had been a mere instant but a fateful one. The little birds did not know that they brought him strength; they were actually the buoy that saved him at the very moment he was about to sink.

And this is the second time.

This time, however, it is the death of an unknown person but it comes just when he feels threatened. For he is in shock both bodily and spiritually. His situation makes him feel like a sinking boat being battered by the waves and nearly capsizing. It is a call to find a purpose for his life.

"I am seeking this song like a drowning person grabbing at a raft that a savior has just flung down. The song of birds, the immortal beauty of nature. Are you, then, our companions, companions who never betray us, the very support of mankind, a support that never collapses?"

The doctor steps toward him. A night of hard work has left wrinkles on her forehead. For the first time he takes note of her: an average face revealing deeply engraved traits from the countryside. When she comes face-to-face with him, she stops and says with a smile:

"Good morning, did our work keep you from sleeping?"

"I have plenty of time to make it up. Don't worry."

"Will you have visitors today from your office or your family?"

"Oh yes, like usual. Thank you, Doctor."

Having just been transferred from a military hospital, she hasn't had enough time to learn that, when he had been hospitalized, the doctor in chief there had requested that Van not be permitted to visit him. For it was precisely arguing with her that had caused his spiritual shock, which had led to his sudden arterial tension and his passing out. They were forced to conclude that she was the pathological agent; therefore, contact between the two of them has to wait for the doctor's recommendation. Vu feels quite at ease. He's free. Initially he wasn't the least bit interested in his family, and had forgotten her name; her image was gone for good.

But today, as the gurney takes the dead man away, he is suddenly assaulted by a concern: "If I go unexpectedly, what will happen to Van and the boy?"

As soon as the question occurs to him, he smiles to himself.

"I am still reminded of her. Is it out of love or just from my sense of responsibility? Or perhaps I miss her as a slave misses his master, as a masochist misses his sadistic torturer, as one condemned to death thinks about his executioner. A pathological memory. This proves that, at heart, any person is just an animal enslaved to habit."

Vu jumps up and walks along the hallway, afraid that if he keeps on sitting there his own contempt for himself will crush him. As he walks, he still looks down at the hospital courtyard. The gurney carrying the dead man is crossing the main courtyard heading toward the morgue, a tall white concrete building lying behind the funeral parlor. On the stone benches laid out around the flower urns, people are already sitting here and there. They may be recuperating patients out to enjoy the fresh air and get away from the stuffiness of the hospital rooms. They could also be families of patients. He has been in the hospital for two weeks now, and is used to the rhythm of his new life. After coming out of his induced coma, he recovered very fast, but at the same time, he could hardly stand a patient's life. The various smells of injections and medications, of diseased and debilitated bodies, of disinfected bathrooms and toilets; the faces of patients, which for the most part remind him of wax masks or starched shrouds. Eyes half dead as if they have lost their life shine, at times abject and pleading and at times showing curiosity or despair, lust or envy . . . In brief, a psychological world so terrible as to make him shrink in horror. But gradually, because he had no choice, he has found loopholes through which he can breathe, can help himself to brush off all sad thoughts. He ironically compares himself with those living underground or in tunnels, gluing their noses to ventilation hoses to get some oxygen and smell the sky. His biggest life jacket is the central garden in the hospital. He is in the habit of loitering in it whenever he has free time. Even when it drizzles, he still walks slowly around the flower beds, looking up at the vaultlike bowers of the trees to spot birds and listen to their querulous songs. In his pocket he always has ready a couple of napkins, for he is often the victim of the birds, believing in the peasants' credo "seeing shit means that wealth is coming your way." He only wants to be close to an animated, inspirational world such as that of the birds. The songs of these little ones are angelic, a gift from his guardian god, a raft mysteriously thrown down by the creator in an invisible great flood.

His wanderings have brought him in contact with a number of patients who more or less share his mood. They, too, cling to the garden as if holding on to a remaining corner of paradise. They run into one another, bow slightly in a friendly and silent manner, then go on their way. When tired, Vu will go to the canteen and sit at a corner table near the window overlooking the back garden of the hospital. There, for a couple of hours, he will sample the contents of a teapot with a madeleine, listening to the humming bees behind him, to the salesgirls chatting away or the hospital guards.

This is the quietest moment, allowing him to talk to himself about life, ideals, his job, his family, the roads that he has traveled and those that remain ahead.

"Has the Great Task turned rotten?"

That question turns around and around in his brain like the dharma wheel. That soft, almost teasing question from the guy with thick lenses—the thickness of a bowl's foot—works like a death sentence: Has the love boat smashed its hull and his dream gone up in smoke? Has the revolution to which the entire people committed themselves ended up as no more than the stirring of thick mud at the bottom of a well so as to expose the dead carcasses of marine animals or ill-smelling seaweeds and mosses? How can he swallow such bitterness? How many people have fallen? How many young men's lives have been cut down like spring grass mown by the scythe of Death? Oh, how many, how many?

With time, what had started as a suspicion is in danger of becoming a certitude.

"It's not that I am swayed by what those two talkative guys said. The reality has been sinking in for a long time now but no one is courageous enough to face it. Those standing outside the power structure surely must have a more objective view of things. It's possibly because of their station, or more precisely because they have chosen to roam freely that they look at events in a more detached way. For it's impossible to deny that the majority of those around me are no more than toads and tree frogs living in the mud."

Together with this bitter thought, he reviews the long line of faces that crowd around him on the reviewing stand. These drivers of government include scoundrels and cheats, robbers and thieves, and low-class prostitutes . . . all of whom can be summarized in a word: trash. Wealthless and without principles, they move according to a violent passion, a passion that allows them to accept all sorts of cruelties, all measures of inhumanity. Their underlying strength is the thirst for power. Their licentious and limitless greed grows out of their original misery—an unsatisfied need for unconscionable revenge owed to sufferings, losses, hatred and vicious enmity accumulated over many months and years!

Memories of the Ninth Central Committee Plenum have not yet faded. It marked a fateful turn in the nation's life and had brought the fall from grace of the one who had worn the most beautiful armor.

It had been a muggy morning, as muggy as the atmosphere suffocating the entire gathering. Though all the ceiling fans were turning at their highest speed and the standing electric fans were sweeping and blowing, everyone was stifling in the heat. Now was a most crucial moment, for they were casting their votes for the nation's political future. Of the more than three hundred and fifty representatives, the faction for war had a crushing majority whereas the peace party numbered fewer than the fingers on both hands. But courageously they held out to the last, out of a sense of responsibility for the fate of the nation. The first to stand up was Le Liem, vice minister of culture. Because Vu was in the row right behind him, he could clearly see the sweat soaking through the back of Le Liem's shirt. Nonetheless, he went on speaking, not sparing one word or omitting one idea:

"I think we represent an independent nation," said the vice minister. "We have the right to choose for ourselves the optimum policy in line with our national interests. The resistance war against the French was concluded only yesterday; there remain tons of problems that need attention. We are not sure that the minefields in Muong Cum and Him Lam have been thoroughly cleared. Rice has yet to cover all the old battlefields. The wounded in many camps must still be nursed and helped. And the people still lack many essentials such as food, clothing, medicines. And we have not yet touched upon the books and notebooks and school supplies for our young ones. In such circumstances we have no reason to commit ourselves to a new war just to prove the superiority of socialism. Two opposing camps can coexist on one planet, for our earth is large enough to sustain different countries and different political systems. We can triumph over the Americans without having to go to war. We can triumph over them through scientific competition, industrialization, and economic prowess."

While Vu does not remember exactly what Le Liem said thereafter, he is able to recall in detail how those surrounding him cast hostile eyes at the vice minister. Those sitting in the front rows turned themselves fully around to stare with bloodshot eyes at the man holding the floor, frankly promising that he would be stoned or have a knife stuck through his neck. Those sitting in the back rows showed their anger and protestations toward "this revisionist" by comments and loud cries . . . After a moment, a delegate jumped up, got out of his seat, went over in front of Le Liem, pointed his finger at Liem's face, and shouted:

"If you don't shut up now, if you go on spitting out this revisionist line, I will hang you, you hear!"

Liem stopped on the spot as if someone had hit him in the back of his neck. He looked intensely at the guy who just tried to shame him, Vice Minister of the Interior Le Chi Than, a crony of Quoc Tuy. Taking off his glasses, Liem blinked, somewhat embarrassed. He was at a loss as to what to tell his antagonist even though he was known for having cutting rhetorical skills. The entire plenum also went quiet. This was the first time that they had witnessed a situation where "comrades" were treating one another like the scum of the earth. More than three hundred people had to look down in shame.

On the dais Ba Danh and Sau were speechless as well.

After a moment, the president of the plenum stood up, turned to Le Chi Than, and in a natural voice said, "If you want to hang Le Liem, then you have to hang me first."

Le Chi Than shut tight his lips, looked down, and regained his seat. The assembly was quiet for a short moment.

Sau then rang a small bell.

"Refreshment time. Please take a break."

After the plenum, Le Liem wrote the Politburo a letter requesting that the Party's top leaders correct this excess, for he did not believe that the Party could tolerate hoodlum language and behavior among members of the Central Committee, who represented the people.

The vice minister of culture was much too naive. He was an aesthete. But aesthetics had no place in this country. The Politburo, which he expected to arbitrate between him and the one who had humiliated him, was cut from the same cloth as the latter. To create a monumental Arch of Triumph, the Party necessarily needed people with monumental capabilities to destroy and to exterminate. War needs criminals—professional and amateur murderers—among which those who excel are precisely the hired guns and executioners, soon to be recognized as the flowers among the grass. Their achievements had been recorded in lists and put into charts. But come to think of it, the majority of those in power also came from crooks and thieves, the very replicas of those unprincipled proletarians! . . . Wolf howls normally make every other species shudder but are reassuring if you happen to be of the same breed. It's people like Le Liem who were the odd ones out. While waiting for a response from the "comrade leaders" he was at once expelled from the Party, relieved of his post, and put under house arrest. A few days later, General Dang Kim Giang, director of the Hoang Minh Chinh Institute of Philosophy, the literary author Nguyen Kien Giang, and nearly one hundred other personalities—those identified as having been poisoned by the thought of the archrevisionist

Khrushchev—were arrested. During the same week, more than twenty generals were thrown into jail because they had undergone long training at the Kutuzov military academy or were close to General Long. The following week, more than five hundred officers from the rank of colonel down, officers who had collaborated with or who had held posts under the direct command of General Long, were also arrested, one after another. They were picked up in trucks belonging to the Second General Directorate of Internal Security, then incarcerated at the Thanh Liet prison on the outskirts of Hanoi, and, additionally, in two other centrally run prisons in Ha Tinh and Thai Nguyen provinces.

The war was only just starting.

The people's itinerary changed destination.

Together with it came tragedy to all those who had been close to Vu.

6

Fresh from sleep, the president notices that plum flowers have blossomed white outside his window. Is this spring's last showing of blossoms? He stands up and gazes at the flower-covered branches, which look like the snowy cotton hanging on a Christmas tree, like crystal petals carved from white dew. The white plum garden makes him think back to the Parisian sky on snowy days.

Paris, a far horizon that he misses all the time.

Paris, city of passionate love and bitterness.

How many winters did he spend in that city? Oh, how many times had he stood there to watch snow fall on the uneven roofs, filled with complicated feelings of alienation mixed with intimacy, of sadness with delight? Being short of money, he always had to rent attic rooms, the kind let out to poor students or workers from the provinces, or miserable exiles. In those attics he had to endure bone-chilling cold, but in compensation he felt himself that much closer to the sky; the flying snowflakes whirled and whirled in spectacular fashion before they fell to the earth. At such times, when the city was deserted, Paris became incredibly forlorn, so forlorn as to no longer look like Paris but only a snowbound plain. During chilly sunsets, the snowflakes flying obliquely in the air blurred the weak light of the streetlamps, making the cloudy sky appear mysterious, as if it were a witch-drawn painting. On other occasions, he walked on the snow-packed sidewalks, watching indifferently as the white carpet was sullied by the black boots of pedestrians. During those Paris winters, the rich aroma from the bakeries was the warmest, sweet-smelling thing that he, a man from Asia, had ever encountered. Very often he found himself walking back and forth, dozens of times, in front of a shutterless window that opened right onto the curb, with black vertical bars looking somewhat like the windows of a prison. From these totally unappealing windows came the intoxicating smells of newly baked breads.

Paris!

Oh, why this sudden gnawing memory?

These white plum branches floating in the white mist of the Lan Vu peak brought back memories of a world both far and near. A glorious stage of his life. His youthful days. For far too long he hasn't revisited that city. Has it changed a lot or is it still the same, he wonders. The old cafés no doubt must have changed their furniture and decor; the houses must have changed owners, the old-fashioned streetlamps must have been replaced by more modern ones. But in the end, how could the Seine change its course? And the trees bordering Ile Saint-Louis still must shed their leaves in great numbers during winter. He misses Paris as if missing an unfulfilled and unforgettable love.

Suddenly, a wind arises and stirs the plum blossom branches. Masses of petals are scattered at each gust, making them look exactly like the snowflakes of yesteryear. The first time he had seen those snowflakes the size of popcorn he found himself exclaiming, "Oh, how pretty they are, these tiny flakes!" Many years later, he still laughs at himself over such naïveté. In his case, these memories of snow have become an eternal sorrow, a sorrow associated with lost youth. After he had become a sophisticated person, on days when snow had fallen, his mind was still entranced by that old song "Snow Falls!" Could it be that the white of the falling snow has become part of his life, an integral part? Could it be that those old lyrics, once they became part of his inner being, have turned into an undying refrain that survives all the ups and downs of fate, the collapsing journey of time?

". . . *Snow falls*
You are not coming this evening
Snow is falling
My heart is dressed in black . . ."

All his life he has been missing love. All his life this song has echoed in him as an endless refrain. Sadly, he could not fill this gaping hole. He feels pity for all those who, even when white-haired, still remember this song, "Snow Falls," and whose hearts still twinge with unrequited love.

"Mr. President, please have some hot congee."

"Oh, have they served it?"

"Yes, sir. The doctor asks that you take this at breakfast so that, if you prefer, lunch can be reduced by half. That would do your health good."

"I have heard him explain it to me. But I have long been used to two meals a day."

"Yes, sir . . . The doctor, though . . ."

"OK, I'm coming."

He steps into the outer room. An unusual aroma coming from the patio makes him stop. It reminds him of the Paris bakeries.

Somewhat doubtful, he takes in a deep breath. Seeing him doing so, the guard says right away:

"Mr. President, what you smell is the mung bean paste coming from the temple. This morning, the abbess wants to show that she can make good fried mung bean paste."

"Is that so? It's so different."

"What is it different from, Mr. President?"

"Oh, I mean that it is unlike the aroma of other dishes."

"The smell of vegetarian food is definitely different from that of ordinary food."

"Of course, otherwise how would people call it vegetarian?" the president said, laughing.

The guard looks at him inquisitively and asks, "Mr. President, would you want to try the temple food?"

He shakes his head: "Don't bother them like that. That we live here is already intrusion enough into the territory and freedom of the nuns."

"Not really, sir. The abbess brought us a big plate. The fried paste is still piping hot. May I bring up some so you can have a taste?"

Before he can reply, the guard runs out like an arrow and disappears in the huge white cloud floating over the patio. A minute later, he comes back with the dish of fried mung bean paste wrapped in a thick cotton cloth.

"Please, sir. Have some while it's still hot."

"Thank you."

He picks up a piece of the fried paste and tastes it in front of the anxious eyes of the young guard.

"It's truly very delicious. This is the first time I have had this."

The guard is beaming: "Fried mung bean paste is one of the most delicious vegetarian dishes. But they prepare it only on special occasions, for it's rather time-consuming."

"How do they do it?"

"First of all, they have to steam the mung beans as they would any steamed rice dish. After that, they have to pound it in a mortar to make it into a thick paste. You mix this paste with some starch so as to make it somewhat gluey. Then you add a pinch of salt and spices. You then mold it into patties and have them deep fried. Today, the abbess used peanut oil to fry them. But they would taste better if they were deep fried in sesame or sunflower oil."

"How clever you are. You can become a chef anytime."

"This morning I helped the abbess with pounding the mung beans, and I was able to hear her explain all sorts of vegetarian dishes."

"It seems that life in a temple can be quite a rich experience, doesn't it?"

"Yes, Mr. President."

"I ask only as a joke. Life for a monastic person is truly very simple. The difficulty lies in keeping and adhering to that simplicity."

"Yes, sir."

Knowing that the young man might not fathom what he had just said, the president pats him on the shoulder.

"Stop. You don't have to stretch your mind fighting with these intellectual debates. Just trust that their lives are entirely different from ours."

"Yes, sir," the guard answers happily, as if he has just been able to rid himself of a big burden. He then takes away the food with an elated mien as if he were a general just coming home with a whole convoy of war booty. The president has finished the deep-fried mung bean paste, but did not touch the cook's bowl of pork congee.

Only a few seconds later, the guard can be heard loudly laughing on the other side of the patio. He cannot see him because of the unceasing movement of the white clouds floating across it, which are like a band of God's oxen being herded over a fairy meadow. Those white oxen keep walking past his eyes. Suddenly, his solitary situation meshes with those white clouds to send a chill through his heart. The president is taken aback; never has he felt such terrible solitude as he does today. A strange loneliness to the point of crunching chill, of limb paralysis. Lonely as if there were an invisible net dropping on him, tying him up in its cruel mesh. He becomes short of breath. He feels that he cannot endure even one more minute of this crushing loneliness even though all his life he has had solitude as his constant companion. He suddenly shudders with fear.

"How can I be so weak? Is it because of old age that I have become a stranger to myself, a miserable person even in my own eyes?"

So he berates himself. While sipping his tea, he looks into the bottom of the cup, trying his best to find in the gently rocking yellowish water an association, a memory about streams, a thought of long ago about tea parties, thin wisps of steam that wave over still hot dishes. Anything that would make him forget his solitude. But that is impossible. For his solitude is the twin of his forgetting. The more you forget and run away, the more solitude comes back to haunt you: two garrotes tightening around his neck.

He stands up; if he were to stay seated he would suffocate. Throwing his long coat on his shoulders, he walks out. As soon as he opens the door, the white clouds rush to his face, wetting it. The large tiles under his feet slush with water as if rain had just fallen.

From the other side of the temple, the guard yells: "Please go in, Mr. President. It's very cold."

The guard flies across the patio and takes hold of his waist as he is about to descend the stairs.

"Mr. President, please go back inside."

"Oh no. I get a headache sitting inside the whole time. Besides, I have to go and say thanks to the abbess for her deep-fried patty."

"Mr. President, it's already a great honor that your chopsticks touched our vegetarian food. You don't really need to come over."

It is a nun speaking, her loud voice reverberating from the other side of the cloud. She is only a couple of dozen steps away but he can't see her through the white fog. It is truly a setting from the extremities of a mountain. Only when he puts his feet on the threshold of the middle temple building can he see that the nun is sitting and pounding betel leaves for the abbess. Before he can say anything, the abbess walks out and says, "Please, Mr. President, please go right in because it is very cold. Should you by mishap catch a cold, we would not know what to do to redeem ourselves in the eyes of the people."

"Please, you are even older than I," the president replies, walking inside.

The nun abandons the mortar and steps in right after him, closing the door. The screeching sounds of the closing door startle him. Then he realizes how familiar this screeching sound was to him in his youth. The old wooden houses were all built on the same model, and the sound of the doors screeching on their wooden posts makes him sad, thinking of days long gone.

The abbess asks him to sit down facing her, on an antiquated ironwood chair, which despite its age is still very strong with a patina that reflects like a mirror. The guard sits behind him, on a stool of woven rattan that the nun brings over to him. In the middle of the room, a brazier is crackling as it burns. From time to time, the nun takes a stick and pokes around so as to make the coal burn red. The whole room gives an air of simple warmth and antiquity. The nun pours tea water into a set of rare Bat Trang cups to honor the guest. The nuns drink *nu voi* (lid eugenia) boiled with ginger.

The smell of the tea water brings back memories of his mother: "Venerable one, *voi* with ginger is very flavorful. Do you use this refreshment also during the summer?"

"Mr. President, in summer we consume fresh tea leaves or dried mum petals."

She turns to the nun: "You have mung bean pudding for dessert. Why don't you offer some to the president?"

"I am sorry, venerable teacher. I am so forgetful."

The nun goes to the next room, where the soft pudding is being kept for guests. He quietly looks after the woman in a long saffron dress, then vaguely thinks: "Why doesn't she seek a family like so many other women? Is this place really a prayer hall or is it only a temporary shelter for her, somewhere to hide and forget a past of suffering, filled with unhappiness? A kind of surrender to Fate, just like me, an old king stuck in a hole on top of Lan Vu Mountain."

The nun comes out with a dish of mung bean pudding topped with white cornstarch.

"Mr. President, would you taste this pudding, us poor nuns' fare?"

"Thank you very much. I just had a taste of your deep-fried bean patty, it was excellent. I am sure your pudding must taste just as good."

So saying, he takes up a piece of the pudding and bites into it. He then washes it down with a sip of the *voi* tea prepared with ginger. It was simply wonderful. He realizes this tea ceremony is helping to alleviate his depression. He looks up at the ancient wooden structure, wondering why it has taken him so long to visit this place. The tiled patio is like a wall separating the secular world from that of the monastery, and crossing it seems like crossing a frontier between two kingdoms that are, if not hostile, at least incompatible. Why should it be so?

"It's truly delicious. This goes marvelously with *voi* tea." He then laughs and adds: "I have been here more than a year, yet only today do I dare come into the temple. I didn't realize what I was missing. Had I taken the liberty of troubling you sooner I would have had a taste of this pudding long ago."

"Mr. President, the living quarters of a monastery are certainly not elegant enough for us to dare invite you," the abbess answers, smiling. Her two rows of teeth are still intact, solid and brightly black.

Smiling in turn, the president replies, "We are neighbors, we should have gotten acquainted a long time ago. It's my mistake for being so busy."

As he finished the cup he continues: "Venerable Abbess, the other day, apparently, you had a requiem for the newly deceased woodcutter?"

"Yes, sir. You have such a busy schedule and yet you still have time to be concerned with the fate of a common person. This shows that your compassion is very vast. I learned from my nuns that you went all the way down to the village to attend his funeral."

"Oh, I only dropped by to pay him a visit."

"But that, sir, is already a great honor for the dead man's family."

"By the way, Venerable Abbess, would you be kind enough to explain to me what a requiem achieves in Buddhist terms? Do all deceased persons need a requiem or only those who have had an unusual, particularly painful, fate?"

"Mr. President, the Buddhist faith is not strictly tied to any rite. There is no regulation as to who needs or who doesn't need such a service. Everything depends on the compassion of the living. Only compassion can open our minds, enlighten us to what is needed; and only when enlightened can one have what is needed to see through one's karma. We in the temple only do what is requested by the living survivors. It is said, 'When your heart is moved, the spirits will know.' We monastic people know that when your Buddhahood is illuminated like a lamp, it shines not only on the spirit but also on the earthly body of the people. It shines across the seven skies to open up the lotus blossom of your plenitude."

"Venerable, we are outside of your faith. No matter how we try we cannot readily understand the scriptures of your religion. However, from a secular standpoint, we are very much concerned with the story of the father woodcutter and his son. I wonder how you can explain that conflict."

"Mr. President, the Supreme One taught us that in everyone's life, greed is the one predominant drive. It is greed that blurs our conscience just as a black cloud covers the sun or the moon. Feelings between father and son, teacher and student, brother and brother can all be maligned and destroyed by greed. In one of the many lives of the Buddha, even the Supreme One was also murdered by his close cousin, the monk Devadatta. In dynastic histories, from time immemorial, there are many cases where a crown prince would kill his own father, the king. I am sure that you must have read a lot more than me, a poor nun."

So saying, the abbess again smiles benevolently. And again he notices the two rows of black and shining teeth.

"Clearly she is an old Vietnamese lady, with black teeth and a satin skirt. Seventy years ago, she must have been a bright and lively village girl, full of spirit. But she refused to accept a normal life with its normal pleasures in the village; instead she has spent time learning scriptures in order to become a disciple of the Buddha."

So he thought to himself as he replied sympathetically, "Venerable, your explanation is just superb. Clearly you have spent lots of time on the scriptures."

"I dare not accept your praise, Mr. President. Anyone who has 'begged' at a temple door, or who has read carefully the words of the Supreme One, can explain this a lot better than I, your humble servant."

And without waiting for him to respond, she turns toward the back room and asks: "Don't you see, my child, that the pudding dish is near empty? Our temple may not be rich but it never lacks hospitality."

"I am sorry. I was so caught up listening to you."

He smiles at seeing the venerable abbess still so sharp. Her way of avoiding topics that she does not wish to discuss shows that her reactions are still very quick. He finishes the last piece of pudding in the fashion of neighbors well acquainted for more than half a century, saying, "The pudding was simply delicious. Venerable, let me thank you as well as the nun here for your wonderful hospitality. With your permission, I would like to come back sometime and bother you."

"Mr. President, that you set foot in our place is a big honor for us humble folks."

He stands up, as does the abbess, who brings her hands together in a lotus gesture.

When he gets back to his room, the clock shows nine twenty-five. That means that the conversation in the temple lasted an hour and a half. In that time, the aroma of *voi* tea boiled with ginger and the beautiful smile of the abbess, with her two rows of shining black teeth, had saved him from the chasm of despair. Now he is alone with himself once again. He sits down on a chair and resumes being afraid of the time stretching before him. His solitude returns. Where can he run to and hide? Should he go into the woods? That's not possible. Should he go down the mountain? There's no reason. Besides, he will not turn himself into a mental case in front of those charged with guarding him inside this beautiful prison. His self-respect does not allow him to act irresponsibly. Looking up at the bookshelves, he notices dozens of volumes that he has left partially read, books marked with bamboo wafers. Pulling out three of them, he begins to turn one, page by page. The lines of type go past him like so many soulless dots, with no meaning whatsoever. Sighing, he folds the book closed, putting the bamboo wafer right where it was. On the temple patio, the enormous white clouds still keep going by one after another. And the plum branches filled with white flowers still slightly sway outside the window, making his heart ravenlike, gnawed by memories of white snow.

"I cannot go on enduring these pangs of conscience. This is worse than death."

He stands up and picks up his cotton-padded coat, intending to walk out again. But the wet and cold coat forces him to realize that he cannot go any-where at the moment. He has no choice but to sit down again amid his four jail-like walls, face-to-face with his own tribunal, which is himself.

Rehanging his coat on the hook, he lowers himself down on the chair. Watching the white clouds roll through the patio like so many pieces of cot-ton, he remembers the abbess's words.

"Even the Supreme One was once murdered by a follower, one who had put on his monk's robe, one who had become a priest—even such a one was motivated by greed. How can one then blame a common person? Let's not hold a grudge toward those turncoat comrades. The one to blame first of all should be myself. Yes, me. Either because I am a coward or a dummy, or both."

This time, he no longer feels like defending his record. Is the attorney in him dead? That thought indifferently goes through his head as he thought-fully watches a tattered cloud dragging itself across the patio. The form of this cloud suddenly makes him self-conscious:

"The roads of life being twisting and turning, how can one know which path to take? For our people I went to Paris yet destiny took me to chilly Moscow, fate chased me back toward Eastern shores. My whole life, I have been formed and pushed by chance. Is a man's life a sequence of 'drifting duckweed and floating clouds'?"

"The France of Diderot and Voltaire opened its doors and invited me in. But another France, that of top-hatted bureaucrats attired in shiny, gold-buttoned uniforms, slammed its door in my face, just like a butler slams the door to beggars. The enslaved people of small and weak countries are chased away from all the roads leading to happiness, and the only cobble-stoned slope that welcomes us is the very one leading directly to hell. By the time I realized this, it was already too late."

And that hell has unmistakably arrived, no doubt this is true. But who can be courageous enough or contrite enough to dare open their eyes and look into it? He remembers the shock when, for the first time, he saw people queuing for their turn to buy food. His car had black windows and no one realized that he was inside. The car sped by but there had been enough time for him to see the common people. And that image of misery hit him like a hammer. That year, his heart was still humming joyfully the melody of "Forward to the Capital." Two years had not been enough time to blur the glorious colors of victory or to cool the ardor in his veins. Busy with work, he did not have time for going incognito among the people. Whatever little time he had, he had spent it with her, but their rendezvouses were always after midnight, when all the activities of the common people were over. On that morning he had had an appointment with a foreign history professor. Because the subject of the meeting had to do with the national museum, he had suggested that they meet there. He had then asked his driver to choose a new route so that he could see something of the people's lives. Since leaving the maquis, that was the very first time he had had an opportunity to observe the people's activities. What he saw was not as pretty or as reassuring as he had expected. The masses appeared before his eyes—in person but fighting and in wild confusion—as if they were a herd of sheep contesting their way back to their pen. The faces that caught his eyes were thin, hunger-ravaged ones; faces dark and resigned, marked by patience and shame; faces in terror as they were repressed by fear, waiting, suffering, and hatred. Faces of people who were at the edge of going into institutions for the mentally infirm.

Repressing a sense of shock, he had tried to ask the driver naturally, "Does your family have to wait in line like that to buy rice?"

"Mr. President, we're lucky to belong to the priority list. The government has rice and food items brought to our very office."

"Who is in this privileged position?"

"All of us, Mr. President, who directly belong to the Administrative Office of the Central Management Committee of the Party. Besides those are the special offices belonging to exceptional ministries like the Ministry of Interior and the Ministry of Defense . . . and, above all, the Ministry of Trade and Food because that is precisely their preserve. Personnel belonging to those ministries are considered like the children of kings and lords in the old days."

"And what makes one a child of kings and lords?"

"That expression, Mr. President, implies that they are entitled to the highest level of privileges. They have the same rice ration book as the rest of us but it's for fragrant rice coming from the most recent crop; the common people, however, are reduced to eating moldy rice because the government sells them only rice that has been kept in storage bins for five or six crops. Likewise with pork: they take for themselves the best cuts, leaving the belly cuts, the lard, and the head of the pig to sell to the people. If you don't belong to the privileged group, you have to put up with lots of shameful belittlement before you can get a piece of real meat—just as if you were someone condemned to quarry stone. My eldest brother works at the National Library; he is a leading cadre and therefore is entitled to buy five hundred grams of meat per month. Once a month, his wife has to get up at three in the morning to go get in line at the Hom market. Every time, though, she ends up with pieces of pig's head or pork belly because those in the government store smuggle the good pieces to their own folk and to those government offices that have something to trade: for instance, stores selling rice or fabric, sugar and milk, or some other necessities. It's only once they have satisfied these privileged exchanges that they look after the people."

"How come the leading cadres of the government are not aware of this?"

The driver was at a loss as to what to say. He briefly eyed the president, both to guess what he meant and to check for some ulterior motive. Then the president realized that he had uttered an extremely stupid question.

"Maybe they know it but they haven't had time to report it upstairs."

He had answered his own question. And the driver was quick to respond.

"Yes, Mr. President, it must be so."

That night, he sat watching the moon. His quandary made it impossible for him to sleep. It was a crescent moon, looking as deceptive as a rice stalk's leaf, and reflecting no light. He looked at the moon and thought of the inevitable decline of everything.

"Life is an insistent, endless turning; a mulberry field can transform itself into a seashore, while people come from nothingness to return to nothingness. Why, then, am I so depressed? Is it because that dying moon is somehow secretly linked to the country's destiny? And is it an omen for the collapse—sooner or later—of the regime, a finality that must come to pass?"

That thought felt like a sharp sword that an executioner had placed against his neck. Suddenly he felt a terrible chill run down his spine. In front of him once again there appeared a mass of thirsty and hungry people crowding in a shameful mass in front of a counter distributing rice. He saw arms raised, clawing and pushing at one another; eyes showing only the whites and necks stretched out toward the barred window with all the crazy focus of wild animals lunging after their prey in their gnawing hunger. God, these are his own compatriots, citizens in the society that he gave birth to; people for whom he had nurtured the dream of liberation. Was this an illusion or a reality? Could it be that all his efforts had been mistaken or that what he had dreamed of was only the reflection of a palace upon the waters of a phantom river? He asked but dared not answer. A terror enveloped his mind. The faces that he had seen that morning were like a herd of ill-treated animals tortured by lack of food, no more than beasts in a stall waiting for the hour when they could put their heads in the manger. For if people could still feel outrage, they must no doubt nurture hatred, waiting for the opportune moment to cut the heads off those who guarded the prison, those who kept them in this beastly life.

Alas, could it be that the regime that he had done his best to build was, in the end, no more than an immense sheep pen? Or was it, more correctly, a gigantic prison, one that kept people down at the lowest level of their material needs? A place over which the most extreme mass self-shaming ruled; a school for cows that they might lower themselves before clumps of grass; or worse, a school for training robbers and thieves, for educating disturbed or schizophrenic people? For no other conclusion was possible. And if there was no other explanation, the present society must then constitute an unimaginable regression, even when compared with the misery of years ago.

Oh, dear gods, how many people have sacrificed themselves, how much wealth has been expended and destroyed, how many ups and downs have his people endured, only to end up with this barbaric life? If that were the case, then this revolution was the most dicey of all life's possible undertakings. And if that were the case, then his life must be accounted a tragic failure without equal.

Now in the Lan Vu temple, he feels goose bumps all over. Chills running down his spine are such that he cannot help but cry out loud, which brings the guards on duty and the doctor rushing in. He has to come up with an imagined physical pain so as to deceive them.

370 Duong Thu Huong

At the Politburo meeting that had followed his first glimpse of the people's misery, he had asked that the economic policy be reversed so as to find a way to save the situation. He stressed the meaning of the word "happiness." Liberation is meaningless if it does not make people happier. All revolutions are crazy and cruel games should they fail to bring freedom and a worthy life. It is the same with independence. Independence is valueless if the people of an independent country do not find themselves able to stand on their own two feet as far as the most essential necessities are concerned.

No one had contradicted him.

But no one had listened to him either, even though all thirteen of them (including himself) sat around a huge table. He understood this as he had looked at their inattentive eyes, at their fingers as they indefatigably flicked the ashes from them. Yesterday, they had still been comrades fighting for an ideal. Now they were sitting there thinking of other schemes. The war of yesterday was over. Today was when the generals divided up the war booty in the palace. Yesterday in the woods they had all received the usual portions of rice and water from the springs, there being nothing to envy or to scheme for. Today, things were different. The social rank of each one sitting there needed to be accompanied by thousands of measurable and immeasurable rights. They were no longer concerned with the things that concerned him, because personal interests are always closest to us and seduce us the most effectively. The things that bothered him that day, to them had become tasteless or even incomprehensible. A whole machine was now serving their own persons or their families irrespective of time or limitations. They lived absolutely in accordance with the golden principle of communism. And that golden principle was meant for only one group of people and excluded the rest of the nation, a nation of sheep and cows that were jostling with one another, waiting to be let out onto the grass.

He had repeated what he had to say twice, three times. No one had objected. No one had responded either. No one had felt the need to dispute his ideas. Then came a break for refreshments, after which another topic had come up, which had more real, more concrete urgency, than the shame and suffering of the people. For other people's suffering is always immaterial and difficult to internalize, and the suffering of the people is even fuzzier and harder to feel. For the people are very abstract, formless, having no feet with which to run, no wings with which to fly, not even beaks with which to sing. Independence was then no longer the great aspiration of a slavish and suffering nation, it had become a concrete war booty, somewhat like a boar that has been brought down by the lance of a hunter. With such meat, there is only enough for those who know how to handle spears and halberds; as for the masses who stand apart, they are merely bystanders or gossips. When necessary, he had realized, people can easily become deaf and dumb. Likewise, they can easily become heartless. Yes, those who crowded around him, who had divided up the meat of the freshly killed boar . . . they had become estranged from him. And he had become difficult for them to understand. The continent had ruptured; he stood on one side and they on the other. That had been the first time he had understood the breakup of relationships among those who had once called one another "Comrade" or even "Brother," associations that had been woven over decades or even longer. The cutting asunder could happen in a moment once the sword of power had been brought down. Before that blade, all past associations, simply, would be fragile spiderwebs.

"I should have understood this since then. I should have changed my game after that day. But I was not fast enough, so now I am washed away in floodwaters.

"Oh, they are much too many while I am one, by myself. It's terrible to think that I consented to go along with them, believing that compromise would save the great work. I thought that, if I sacrificed for them, then—out of respect for what was greatly righteous—they would forget their personal ambitions. That was my stupidity. The chess game moved toward mate. They took advantage of that compromise to push me into the back rooms.

"But where does it lie, the root of my failure? Was it my stupidity or was it only fate's twisted road? I journeyed in the same ship with them but when we reached the other side of the ocean, how could it be that only I was left behind on a forsaken island? Could it be that I am fated to be a lone wolf that can't survive long in any gathering?"

Was it fate or wasn't it?

These questions go around and around unceasingly in his head. His old, tired heart palpitates.

The clouds still roll unceasingly on top of Lan Vu Mountain. The snowy season of Paris and reflections of a youth long past also float by. His brain is racked by suspicions. Then his melancholy heart suddenly turns back to a Western city, a place known forever as one for love and short-lived love affairs. Only his soul remains behind like an orphan left on a deserted beach after the noisy days of a summer with lots of visitors. Paris! Strange that after leaving it, he had looked back as if it were no more than an inn; yet now that city appears in his heart as a port of last resort, very much inviting to a traveler. He misses an absent child because, after he left the apartment in the alley right next to Rue St-Jean, a baby girl had seen the day. A baby girl with a name extremely popular in France—Louise. He did not suspect that the nights spent with the seamstress had left a forbidden fruit. It was dumb negligence on his part. It was not until seven years later, on a chance encounter with the mother, that he had learned of this. He realized that it was simply the unexpected result of bodily urges. Nonetheless, the child still carries his blood, his very own blood. He had always meant to go back to the old alley and find the seamstress and Louise, but he did not have enough money in his pocket to buy her a proper gift. Then the tornado of revolution carried him away. In the end, he never bought for his daughter a single skirt or a pair of shoes. He has yet to hold her in his arms and look into her eyes.

"By now, she must have become a grown woman, for sure. She must be married with children. Does she ever, I wonder, search for the image of her absent father? Does she ever entertain, I wonder, the idea of going to Vietnam, a faraway tropical land, to watch an alien people who somehow are still related to her by blood? Or has she simply forgotten all about me even before getting to know me, deliberately so?"

This last thought makes him feel numb. He touches the teapot; he wants to take a sip but the tea is already cold. His face is reflected clearly in the mirrorlike surface of the table. He leans down to take a look at his silhouette. In silence. And a whisper is heard in his mind:

"This man is the worst possible father on earth. One of these days, you will have to come face-to-face with loved ones in the supreme court of your heart. The Autumn Revolution of 1945 will eventually be lost in the on-flowing river of history, just like any other revolution. Like the earthquakes, the tsunamis, the volcanic eruptions. Time will efface all traces. In time, all the crowns on earth will be shredded. All illusions of glory will be shattered. But the supreme court of the heart will always be there on the grounds of a secular world and that court will also be there on the other side of the river of illusions, where the souls of the dead are crowded together on boats made from ashes and dust, with empty eye sockets and three pennies placed on their silent tongues."

An invisible net closes on the president, nearly asphyxiating him.

His head feels ice cold but his entrails are burning. He thinks this must be his own private suffering, only his. For he is a materialist, he does not believe in telepathy. From the beginning, he only knew the visible world, only considered real things that impacted the six senses, like most people.

Yet the president's suffering is precisely the result of sympathy with other people's sufferings. For on this earth there is another person in exile. An anonymous person. A person whose name he no longer remembers; whose face he does not know. A shadow of nothingness. Yet that shadow is still and always a living being in the flesh. That other being never stops thinking of him. That unfortunate person is linked to him because of an unusual destiny, a constant suffering, and a tragic chase. But the irony of fate makes it so that all the things happening to that other person must remain in the dark, beyond his understanding and imagination.

THE UNKNOWN
BROTHER-IN-LAW

1

According to an announcement from division staff, the entertainment that evening would not start until 7:00 p.m. But dinner had been moved up from 4:00 to 3:30. After eating, the soldiers gather in large numbers in front of the stage, noisily chatting, with all the excitement of men who haven't seen women in a long time. Some greedy fellows still have in hand a big chunk of burned rice, which they crunch while expectantly looking up at the curtains as if they would like to find behind those garish veils their "dream princesses." Actually, those princesses are still having dreams in the trenches of the command post, partly because of fatigue after the long trip, partly because they all have a pale complexion and white lips due to malaria and thus they have no interest in showing themselves to people without makeup. They all sleep rolled up with one another like silkworms hanging on a board, trying to catch a few more hours before they have to appear on-stage. The division command promises to wake them up at 5:30. But well before five, the soldiers outside are already yelling:

"Fairy ladies, why are you sleeping so much? You haven't been to see us for several years, how can you have the heart to go on sleeping?"

"Little ones, wake up. We have been waiting and waiting for this day."

"Where are you, princesses? Let us have a glimpse of your beauty."

All these calls and shouts, the teasing and joking, get so loud that the women cannot go on sleeping, so they get up. Every one of them keeps yawning so hugely that their jaws nearly go out of joint. The assistant to the division commander clears his throat several times before putting his head inside the trench:

"Please be understanding, the soldiers haven't seen even the shadow of a woman in a long while now. More than three years have gone by without a troupe coming here."

The deputy head of the troupe responds, "It's the same wherever we go, you don't have to worry. The battlefronts are too far apart and there are not enough troupes to entertain them."

"Thank you, the division is lucky to have you. Now the cooks are bringing you dinner so that you can have something before you put on your makeup."

"Where is the troupe leader?"

"She has eaten with the commanding officers out there. So have the male actors."

The deputy head of the troupe turns back and yells, "You see? We were privileged to go on sleeping. Everyone else has eaten and is setting up the stage. Anyone who wants to yawn, go ahead and yawn, then we will get ready for dinner."

The actresses do not have time to respond, for the cooks are already coming in with their clanging pots and pans. They feel lucky, as if they have found some gold, for they are privileged to see the girls first, when the latter have not yet even put on their cosmetics. Needless to say, they feel at home, for if they were strangers to one another they would have to be entertained in the sitting room; only close friends or relatives could have the right to go into the kitchen:

"Today we specially prepared banana flower salad mixed with chicken and we made mung bean pudding to give you a treat. We hope you enjoy it."

"Thank you, friends. With this pudding we will be so much more graceful in our dancing."

The girls gather to have dinner while the three cooks sit around. Finally, the assistant looks at his watch then asks:

"It's five twenty already. How long do you need to do makeup and change into your costumes?"

"Twenty-five minutes, not more."

"Bravo, I will let the guys know."

He leaves. In a blink one can hear loud clapping of hands and shouts coming from the soldiers.

The deputy troupe leader smiles. "They are fine, the guys in this division."

Another girl rejoins, "They are all northerners."

"Right."

A second girl joins in: "They have been waiting for us partly because they want to see a fine performance but also because they wish to see people coming from their native provinces. I heard that the last troupe to visit them a few years back was a folksong group from Interzone Five."

"Where's Interzone Five?"

"What an ignorant girl! You have been serving in the army for the last five or six years and yet you can't even tell the differences between the military zones."

"Whoever asks doesn't know. We just go where we're told. Everywhere we go, all we see are springs and woods . . . Woods and springs, then springs and woods. After a Van Kieu village, we would go to a lowland Lao village, then to an upland one. Everywhere we go all we do is follow the walking stick of the guide between two locations."

"Same here, I have no idea what an interzone is. Everywhere we go, all we do is to look at the backside of whoever is in front."

"You'd be lucky to be able to see the behind of the guy in front. Do you remember the time we went up Monkey Piss Mountain? The slopes were like cliffs, the sole of the guy in front touched the head of the person who followed. No chance then to watch the guy's behind or ass."

"Yah, that was terrible, that time. Clouds wrapped all around us, and we had to climb as if we were blind. It was good karma inherited from our ancestors that kept us all from falling down into an abyss."

The girls have yet to finish changing when the assistant to the division commander can be heard clearing his voice outside. The deputy troupe leader announces: "Exactly another seven minutes." Then she turns to her companions: "Come on, gals, quicker. The guys out there are causing a riot. This division must have been stuck in this deep jungle for much too long. These soldiers are not as patient as the last ones we entertained."

"I guess. Last time, they did not yell in confusion like today."

"Well, as I have said, they have been imprisoned here too long."

"But here is where?"

"Who knows? I heard from the commander that we are in Laos. And far into the Laos jungle at that."

"Is that so? It's all mountains and forests everywhere you look. If one gets lost here, one's bones will have a new home. There is no finding a way back."

"That's for sure. But we each have our fate when it comes to dying or living, so why worry? Only when all the soldiers die will we run into a sad fate. We performers are the spice of their lives, true gold in war. No one will let us get lost."

After making up and changing into stage dresses, the girls file out of the trenches. The soldiers crowding on the two sides of the tunnel's leading to the performing stage clap their hands and shout vociferously:

"Hey, pretty fairies, why don't you say something so we can hear your northern accent?"

The deputy troupe leader smiles right and left and asks, "What can we say?"

That is enough for the soldiers to begin talking all at once:

"Say anything . . . Or you can even give a shout."

"Darling, we are from Hai Hung. All you have to do is to call out 'Oh, Hai Hung!' That would be enough to soothe us."

"What do you mean, calling out just Hai Hung? How about Hanoi, Ha Tay, Ha Bac, Vinh Phu: our home provinces? Are these provinces just for dogs? How selfish!!"

"And how about Hai Phong? If you forget the city of the red flame tree, American bombs will get you all."

"Stop complaining! Ladies, you can just cuss them all and their fathers, too."

Then arms stretch out to touch the girls' shoulders and dresses, or caress their hair. As they walk, a crowd of soldiers follows in their wake. From a distance, the division command staff smile and watch the procession with undisguised envy. However, in their position as leaders, they have to restrain themselves, whether they like it or not. In traditional fashion, the girls split into groups of two or three to chat with the soldiers before going onstage to perform. But this time that way of engaging will not do, because the division has just been reinforced, so there are too many of them. More than a thousand soldiers jam the place, in serried ranks. The deputy troupe leader orders:

"With so many of you we cannot possibly entertain you all. I suggest the girls split into teams by province, to sing and entertain you outside of the main program. The musicians also should split likewise."

With that, the leaders of provincial groups call out in confusion:

"Hai Hung, where are you? Follow me to the left of the stage, right next to the speaker here."

"Hanoi, where are you? Those from the capital, go to the back of the performance stage. Be orderly, will you."

"How about Ha Tay, land of silk? Let's gather next to the Hanoi bunch, on the right side of the stage."

The soldiers assemble according to their province of origin, shouting to one another, even louder than a market fair breaking up at the end of day. The deputy troupe leader is seen gesticulating to the musicians, apparently negotiating in view of some tense assignments. Thereafter, some can be seen taking their organs, others their guitars or mandolins, others yet their flutes and bamboo flutes, and going to different groups. This brings a strange sense of animation to the whole forest clearing, which normally would hear only the wind rustling the leaves, or rain pattering on the fronds, soldiers talking or arguing among themselves, or bombs exploding.

Company Commander An stands there, absentmindedly looking at the joyous crowd. Suddenly someone taps his shoulder:

"You couldn't find your Lang Son group?"

His battalion commander is right behind him, smiling behind a pair of thick glasses.

"I report to you, Commander. I am the only one here."

"Aren't there a couple of ethnic Tay in Battalion 2?"

"Sir, they are Tay from Cao Bang, on the border with China. I have never set foot in their territory and they have never been to Lang Son, to visit Dong Mo, my native place."

"Is that so? So you are all Tay, yet you live in different territories and your customs also differ. Me, I am an ethnic Vietnamese and I can't tell who is Tay from Lang Son and who is Tay from Can Bang. They all look alike."

"I report to you, sir, we are not all that different. But since the troupe told us to gather by province, there's no reason for us to form a Tay group from two different battalions."

"That's the right principle. We cannot tolerate differentiation by ethnic group within our nation, among people who all carry the same Vietnamese nationality."

"Yes, I understand."

Nha, the battalion commander, pulls out some cigarettes and offers An one. On the stage, the assistant to the division commander looks around, with a loudspeaker in one hand and a notebook in the other. At a favorable moment, just as the songs stop temporarily, he yells into the loudspeaker:

"Hi, hi . . . Attention, please. The performance program is being delayed by one hour and a half, so the curtains will not go up until eight thirty. This is because there suddenly is a new development: we have to wait for Battalion 209, which is a reinforcement from the north. They are right now encamped on the other side of Panda Mountain. They do not belong to our division, but are an independent combat unit. However, because we are on the same battlefield we have the duty to wait for them so they, too, can enjoy tonight's performance. In the meantime, the troupe will continue performing among the provincial groups already gathered, supplemented by local talent from our units."

At that the soldiers all jump up, their yells ringing through the forest:

"Hurrah, hurrah . . ."

"Headquarters can go on delaying the performances, even until midnight. In fact, the later, the better."

"This will be the most marvelous night in the last three years. Those who have a favorite song can start practicing it. For we have musical accompaniment and our local talent will have a chance to show off."

Nha, the battalion commander, asks An, "Do you know how to sing?"

"I am afraid I am totally ignorant on that score."

"Likewise here. We can then take advantage and have some rest before the curtains go up. We still have two and a half hours to go."

Just at that moment, the division commander walks toward them, and warns loudly: "Looks like you two are thinking of slipping out of here. How can you leave a good party and waste it?"

"I report to you, sir, I don't know how to sing. Besides, I am nearly fifty and my vertebral column is not standing up well."

"Am I any younger than you?" retorts the division commander.

Indeed, he is older than Nha by a few years, but being a fisherman originally, he still shows an abundance of energy. And despite all the ravage of the war and years, he still has rippling muscles. His shoulders are broad and even and, because he is not very tall, his build is almost square. Whenever he walks by the side of the battalion commander, he is often compared by the literate soldiers with Sancho Panza walking with Don Quixote, his superior. Instead of being upset, he would return the compliment:

"They say, first comes the look, second the air, third the voice, fourth the appearance. You outshine me on the last item but I am better than you on the third one. That's why I am a division commander while you only command a battalion."

It's true that when it comes to voice, no one can best him. And not just in the division. In the whole front, where four divisions are in place, no one can mistake his voice. If he were a tenor, his voice could break many layers of glass. His voice is stentorian, the kind of voice that has been trained through many generations of yelling over the waves. You have only to listen to him speak to know right away that he is the kind "who can stand firm and even melt stone." That is why the battalion commander replies without hesitation:

"Oh, you are old but you belong to the type that is both old and tough. You are not an empty crab shell like me."

The division commander has to give up: "I raise my arms and surrender."

The battalion commander continues to tease him: "You being tough, you should stay and compete in singing with the young ones. Please pardon such brittle-boned and flabby guys like the two of us."

So saying, Nha drags An away. But whereas Nha goes back to the underground compound to grab some more sleep, An quietly goes to the stream for a bath. This immense stream is even better-looking than the one in his home village. They call it a stream but it is no less broad and long than a true river and it flows into the largest river in the region. The stream water is crystal-clear and it does not display any moss or bronze color as in the case of more poisonous mountain runs. The rocks on its bank are clean and shining, well fitted for one to lie on or for drying one's clothes on sunny afternoons when the sun beats down on them. The banks of the stream are gently sloped and filled with white shining pebbles. If one hikes up less than one hundred meters one runs into Elephant Thundering Falls, which, with its ten-meter drop, makes the stream below churn like boiling water. Oftentimes playful soldiers break off dry branches and throw them in the cascade. The branches are immediately carried away, turning in the process into arrows sharp enough to pierce anyone trying to wade across. Each time he comes here, An's reminiscences arise inside him. He shakes off his clothes and begins to wade into the stream. But when he is about up to his knees in the bubble-filled water he suddenly feels a chill. He returns to the bank and puts on his clothes. Is there a ghost who happens to be around and forces him out of the water? Or is it a premonition of things to come? He doesn't know. No one can understand everything we do during all our time on earth. But this time, he feels absolutely confident that an invisible power has pushed him to action.

"Is that you, darling, truly you? Or is it the Little One? There is no mistaking that one of the two girls has stretched out her arm to impede my going forward." So he softly wondered.

But there is only the wind in the leaves, and the singing carried from the other side of the tree line. The eerie music seems to blow a vague chilly breath onto his back.

An folds his arms above his knees and listens to the waterfall rumbling upstream. As usual, that fall recalls the sound of another fall, a smaller, gentler one of no more than three meters that did not threaten anyone, nor was it an omen predicting injury or death. That fall was called Nightingale, for nightingales nested in the forest on its two sides, and their songs made an interminable music that resonated in the quiet environment of those faraway woods. From Nightingale Falls, one crosses a forest clearing and a valley and then reaches Ban Xiu, An's native village. The place where he left his heart while his two feet have taken him ever farther, and it is impossible to know when he will return.

"But who would I see if I did return, if ever that day should come?" he thinks to himself. "The two persons closest to me are already under the black earth. My uncle and aunt are, by now, likely to have passed away, and my little cousin Mai must have gotten married and moved away. There remains only an old one but soon he will have to follow the tracks of the ancestors."

When An left his village, his father-in-law had been sixty-nine. Twelve years have now gone by. Even if he were still alive, it is doubtful that he could take a bundle of firewood from under the house on stilts up to its kitchen.

"I wonder who will still be there once he is gone?"

Oftentimes that is what he keeps repeating to himself. But a birthplace remains one's birthplace, a never-ending echo that follows us throughout life. We think that we have forgotten it but suddenly it comes back to haunt us unexpectedly. A tree branch breaking off in front of one, a pebble falling near the bank of a spring, the song of nightingales in a cliff . . . they are all insignificant pretexts summoning the echo back and causing one's heart to be in pain. On occasion when he woke in a dark underground tunnel, An would imagine sun-bathed mountain flanks, where the indigo silhouette of his loved one would appear. Sometimes she would be by herself, at others she would be accompanied by her sister, who was nine years her junior. Though they were sisters they almost looked like mother and child, for she had had to raise her sister from birth. When the young sister had been born was also the day their mother left this world. As for the two sisters, because one was born in the winter, she was named Dong (Winter), and because the other was born in the spring she was named Xuan (Spring). In An's mind they always manifested themselves in the bright yellow sunlight bathing the mountainside, always walking toward him in the magnificent beauty that they had inherited from their mother. An could see their shiny black eyelids closing as they laughed, and the crystal-pure bright sun reflecting from their doe eyes. He could see their vermilion lips—the color of wild banana flowers. And the silver bracelets that rang against one another on their milk-white wrists. In the little village called Xiu (Tiny), heaven had blessed these two girls with extraordinary beauty, so that they had to pay for it with equally extraordinary misfortunes—on a scale to match their beauty.

"What did they ever do wrong?"

"They never harmed even a small bird, let alone another human being!"

"Why was it, heaven, that they had to meet with such calamity?"

His soul does not stop yelling out these questions. An does not believe in heaven, but he invokes it as a habit, just as anyone would when in trouble;

clearly, though, he has fixed in his mind the faces of flesh-and-blood murderers.

"Maybe they are too powerful while I am all by myself. In other words, I will have to stomach this offense and hold it until the grave. If so, I shall pursue this injustice into the next life. And if one life is not enough I shall ask heaven for another incarnation. I will go to the very end of hell to find those who killed her and her little sister."

Beyond the trees, one can hear the hubbub of a combat unit arriving. As the forest opening is narrow and the newly arriving troops are rushing pell-mell to get in, the noise they make echoes from all directions, reverberating from the mountainsides and woods. Realizing that Battalion 209 has arrived from Panda Mountain and that it's time for the evening's performance to begin, An gets up and returns to the stage area. Sunlight has long since disappeared and the grass public area is now flickering with lamps like some kind of enchanted land, as large headlights illuminate the whole stage. The new arrivals assemble in the assigned corner, each drenched in perspiration but happy like a kid receiving candy. The performers have gathered behind the sides of the stage. The soldiers have split from their provincial groups and rejoined their units. Whistles and catcalls come from everywhere.

Nha, the battalion commander, apparently restored after his nap, is now back in charge of his troops. An gazes at the whole spectacle somewhat puzzled, for he is still haunted by his memories of loss. He somehow feels left out of the party. Leaning on the base of a tree, he looks toward the stage as the soldiers from Battalion 209 keep surging forward from behind him to occupy the patch of ground reserved for them.

"Chi Van Thanh! Chi Van Thanh!"

A sudden call explodes right beside him, making An jump up. He unconsciously turns back. When he realizes that it was a mistake to do so, a guy has already come close, face-to-face with him:

"Brother Chi Van Thanh."

"! . . ."

"Thanh, don't you recognize me?"

A smiling face in the dark. An leans back against the tree, his whole body shaking like he is being electrocuted: "Comrade, you must be making a mistake. I am Hoang An."

"Brother Chi Van Thanh, I am Ma Ly. Don't you remember me?"

"But I am Hoang An."

"Oh . . ."

The new arrival turns the flashlight toward himself so as to throw light on his face, which is drenched in sweat and sort of plump, like those of some women. The eyebrows are short and slanted and the eye slits really deep as they twist into a smile. The man has a short nose with open nostrils, and two rows of small teeth. An shudders, for there is no denying it. This man is indeed a former companion-in-arms—Ma Ly, of Meo origin, deputy squad leader in a company that An used to command. It was An who had suggested that he be promoted to that post. An takes Ma Ly's arm and squeezes it, pulling him near.

"My name has been changed to Hoang An. I forbid you to use my old name. Understand?"

The other guy nods his head repeatedly in agreement.

An then says, "Go on watching the show. We will talk later on."

Ma Ly agrees. "Don't forget, will you? It's quite a while since we have seen each other."

An nods and says, "How long are you going to be here?"

"Only God knows," Ma Ly replies. "Our battalion commander says we will have to be stationed here for quite a while to practice and wait for the order to integrate into an understrength division on the western front. It might be a few months."

"In that case we still have time to run into each other. We often go that way."

"Good. We must see each other. I'm going now."

Ma Ly runs after his comrades. In a minute, everything becomes an indistinct crowd mingled with the trees in the woods, an undifferentiated black block. An suddenly remembers something. He springs up and runs after Ma Ly.

"Ma Ly, Ma Ly! Wait for me, Ma Ly!"

He brushes aside soldiers from Battalion 209 as he runs after his old comrade-in-arms.

"Ma Ly!"

"Here I am."

An looks in the direction where the voice is coming from, and notices someone standing beside Ma Ly, so he hides himself behind a tree, waiting. In the dark he hears Ma Ly say:

"We are old comrades-in-arms . . . You go ahead, I will look for you later. We will assemble with our units after the performance."

"Agreed."

"Let me borrow your flashlight; mine is about to go out."

"Be careful using it. We still have a long way to go."

"OK."

The other guy disappears in a flash. An stays in the dark for a couple of seconds before he walks out and faces Ma Ly.

"Let's see the show together. I have many questions for you."

"Agreed."

They both join Battalion 209 to get closer to the stage, for, as guests, the 209 guys have been given half of the left side facing the stage, making the other soldiers green with envy. An and Ma Ly sit down together.

An looks at his watch then says, "I can only watch until nine fifteen. After that I have to stand guard."

"You have to do it yourself?"

"My company is in charge. As its commander I do not have the right to sit here and watch while the younger soldiers have to leave and go on patrol."

"You're always the model soldier. I haven't forgotten that. Ever since . . . we have known each other."

"It's not just me. In every division the cadres must act that way."

After a moment of silence, Ma Ly asks, "Is this a dangerous place? I have heard that this is our rear area, like the 'safe zones' before."

An laughs. "True, we are far from the battlefield. But there is no lack of enemy recon probes. That's why we had to wait three years before we could have tonight's entertainment. The soldiers, though, still have to go on patrol."

"The enemy dares to venture even this far?"

"Are you joking? This is not like the Ha Tay boot camp twelve years ago. We are at war now. Do you think they are all just flabby pots of flesh or only wooden puppets?"

Ma Ly is quiet for a moment then asks: "You have given that many years and have only made it to company commander?"

"Do you forget that I was pursued so that I had to change my name? How about you?"

"I, too, am a company commander. I am told by higher-ups that should things develop well, next quarter I may be upgraded. A Meo who is especially loyal to the revolution and really courageous in battle."

"Congratulations . . ."

"Oh-oh, the girls are coming out . . ." Ma Ly says, pointing to the stage.

They watch as the red curtains rise and a girl walks to the mike to give a very graceful bow as the master of ceremonies. She is dressed in a green four-piece tunic with one shoulder piece in red and another in purple over a chicken-fat-colored pair of pants, and the soldiers began to clap as if they have lost their regular minds. Then the music arises in all its splendor and excitement. The whole division has been waiting for this moment of happiness! But An no longer hears anything, no longer sees anything except the sweat-drenched face of his old comrade-in-arms. Ma Ly is giving all his attention to the MC.

"How will he behave?" An wonders to himself. "Perhaps he will stay mum because he is a friend, because I was the first one to help him understand the most elementary things about people living downstream. I also recommended him for a rise in rank, then helped him with some money so he could go home and take care of his father's funeral. Or will he accuse me so as to show loyalty to his superiors and get a very special promotion? How can one predict all the tricky ways people behave?"

Twelve years have gone by but this fellow seems hardly changed. Still it is impossible to read those small and deep-set eyes. Hoang An quietly watches Ma Ly. The Meo must be in agony because he is in heat, yearning for a woman. His eyes are wet with longing. His breath is heavy and he constantly licks his lips. Randy people, whether men or women, can never resist this gesture. An recalls the time in the old unit when Ma Ly had been desperate, looking for a woman. And even though he was a full-blooded Meo, freshly come to the lowlands, he had been clever enough to find a half-nutty gal in the village who could take care of his pressing need. Now he is open-mouthed, looking at the fairies all dressed so gorgeously on the stage, dancing the Lamp Dance.

"How do you like it? Is it better or not as good as the Conical Hat Dance of the Thai people?" An asks.

"Better, much better," Ma Ly answers without taking his eyes off the stage.

"Do you like the *khen* dance of the Meo people?"

"No," Ma Ly responds emphatically, which surprises An. The Meo explains: "The Meo people don't have a very sophisticated dance. The best dancers are the people in the central highlands, whether they are Rhade, Bahnar, or any other group."

With that, he suddenly exclaims: "Oops, it's over."

Smacking his lips and shaking his head in regret, Hoang An laughs. "I didn't know that you were so in love with these performances."

"Are you thinking to denigrate us by suggesting that we Meo do not know how to appreciate art and literature?"

"No, I didn't mean that. This kind of appreciation is a personal matter, it doesn't have anything to do with an ethnic group. In my village we are all Tay but some of us love the flute so much that we can stay up the whole night playing it, while others know only how to drink wine until they collapse into slumber."

"I am passionate about these things," Ma Ly responds, then after a minute of hesitation, adds, "But I only care for dances with the women. I don't like to watch men dance and sing."

As he says that, the curtain again rises. An keeps quiet, as he does not want to disturb this Meo. It looks as if his entire mind is turning around and around under the stage lights. And that is how things go until 9:15. An raises his wrist to note the time, then says:

"Time to change the guard. I'm going."

"Yes. We'll see each other."

"Agreed. After the performance, please try to wait for me."

"Rest assured. I'll wait for you."

Hoang An retires toward the back. After gaining some distance from the crowd, he goes deeper into the forest and finds a good observation spot where he can entirely wrap himself in the darkness. Before him is a black immensity; where Ma Ly once had been is lost to him entirely. Ma Ly is of small stature like the majority of Meo men, normally about the height of their wives' shoulders. It is said that when a Meo couple embrace, they look just like a big frog hanging on to a cucumber. The curtains keep rising and falling as one performance follows another. The watch shows twenty to ten. An feels his breathing starting to come more easily.

"Maybe he is not wicked enough to report me. Maybe he hasn't forgotten the good memories of the past."

But just as a sense of optimism returns, he notices the small silhouette of a man standing up and distancing himself from the crowded spectators in the dark. The silhouette finds its way between the ranks of soldiers and continues walking toward the stage where the division command officers are sitting in the front rows next to the commanding officers of Battalion 209.

"So, what I suspected is now inevitable," An thinks as he watches the man. He feels a little bitter, a little sad, but at the same time his heart resumes its normal beat. The doubt he felt and the thin expectation he had are now burned to ashes. A mood of frozen chilliness invades his soul, and his brain is now vacant and transparent.

"That's something that had to happen. Now is no time for hesitation;

only action counts. I didn't want this to happen but it did. So: I must be ready for any eventuality."

He puts out his hand and touches the submachine gun by his side, the way a farmer touches the back of a buffalo before stepping down behind the plow or a rider smoothes out the mane of a horse before getting it to gallop. This had been a habit of his ever since the age of thirteen, when he followed an uncle out to the woods in search of game. When An's fingers touched the cold iron of the gun, a strong wave of emotion spread throughout his body, reaching all the way up to his brain and bringing along a sense of power, faith, and iron will all at the same time. The chill of the weapon passed a torch through him. Touching it was like the people of old touching the tablet to make an oath, it made him feel quite at ease. To An, the weapon was like a faithful warhorse or hunting dog. It was no longer an inanimate object but had become part of his own body and will.

In the dark, a twisted smile crosses An's face.

"I don't want this! I absolutely do not relish this hunt. But now that I am hunted, I must become the hunter."

He watches Ma Ly sit down with the commanding officers. No doubt he is reporting briefly on the situation and suggesting that the division chief watch An because of "a military secret of national import." So An guesses silently. As it turns out, a moment later, Ma Ly stands up together with the division commander, and both of them begin to move along the front edge of the stage to go toward the back.

An cannot figure out where they are heading. If they are going toward the back of the stage, then it will become extremely inconvenient for him because the engineering team running the generator will be right there. But this presupposition is probably incorrect because it would be too hard to reveal a big secret given the noise of the generator and the curious stares of the electricians. Will they go into the deep woods surrounding the clearing? But should they do so they might run into the patrolling soldiers. On the other hand, with the division commander having a very loud voice, perhaps he will take the Meo to the stream, where his voice will be carried away by the noisy falls and thus not heard by anyone. Fortunately, that will be the most favorable spot for handling the situation because on the other side of the stream is what is called a "death zone," a cliff wall that goes straight up, and on that huge wall not a single bush can push its way out into the air. That is why not only men, but even antelopes, dare not climb it. It was not the northern soldiers but actually the military recon troops of the South Vietnamese that gave the region the name Death Mountain.

An follows the two men—now his prey—hiding behind trees as he goes along. As he thought, the division commander is taking the Meo to the bank of the stream. Since it is quite a distance, the music fades to be replaced by the increasingly loud rumbling of the waterfall. Like a leopard An follows them. He does not realize that the wind has changed direction, turning the leaves backward, making the forest move so that the steps of the prey as well as those of the hunter become lost in the overall symphony of the leaves. After about ten minutes, they arrive at the bathing spot, almost exactly where An had been sitting earlier in the afternoon. An idea flashes by, like a lightning shaft through the air:

"Could it be that a few hours earlier, I hesitated to bathe in this stream because I would have to take care of them in this very spot?"

He does not have time to think much more, because the conversation has begun, with every word quite audible:

"Dear commander, we Meo are absolutely loyal to the revolution, that is why I think I am duty-bound to report this to you. An extremely important affair."

So Ma Ly begins in a trembling voice. Maybe he is not quite himself. Maybe he hesitates between his own fear and the fear of his conscience, "the conscience of someone loyal to the party and government" . . . Or perhaps he is in a quandary, caught between his fear of An, one who has already escaped from an entire army, someone to be feared, and his own thirst for power. Or maybe he instinctively feels the danger to him lurking in this game. An cannot figure out the reason but there is no mistaking Ma Ly's trembling voice and his shortness of breath.

An curses him with deep contempt. "Son of a bitch . . . You shake as you fuck . . ."

At this point, the division commander's voice can be heard firmly saying, "All of us are duty-bound to be loyal to the revolution. It's good that you spell out your thoughts clearly like that. I am ready to hear you out."

"Commander . . ."

Ma Ly begins again, his voice no longer so shaky: "Commander, isn't that true that in the division there is a company commander named Hoang An, a Tay from Cao Bang who is fighting directly under your command?"

"Correct! Company Commander Hoang An is a bold, clever, and promising leader. It can be said that he is the right-hand man of Battalion Commander Dinh Quang Nha . . . But his native village is in Dong Mo, Lang Son, not in Cao Bang. I know by heart the bio of Commander An, the way I know the CVs of all the battalion commanders in my division."

"I report to you, Commander, that Hoang An's native village is actually Xiu in That Khe district, Cao Bang province. He used to be the third company leader of Company 1, Battalion 109, a unit with special assignments stationed in Ha Dong in 1957. At that time I was deputy squad leader in his company. His real name is Chi Van Thanh. He was recruited as a Party member after he joined the army, in September 1951, three years before the liberation of the capital."

"What did you say? He has been a Party member before?"

An notes how the division commander's voice has grown louder as he posed those questions. When he had joined the division under the name of Hoang An, he had used the papers of a dead comrade who was not a Party member. And he had been newly recruited into the Party exactly two years ago. It was the division commander himself who had ordered that he be recruited into the Party on the spot after a series of combat successes achieved by An's unit. An now hears Ma Ly laugh ironically; after a moment of silence, Ma Ly goes on:

"When I joined the army, Chi Van Thanh had already been a Party member for six years. He was recruited right in the Viet Bac resistance zone."

"OK, then. Go ahead and tell me more. I am listening."

"Chi Van Thanh motivated me to join the Party and proposed that I become deputy squad leader."

"Then?"

"Then, one day he simply disappeared, saying he had a chance to visit Hanoi. The command did not know the reason for his departure and ordered that he be found, but without result. After about a week, the command staff sent someone down to officially report that Chi Van Thanh was a spy planted by the puppet army in our ranks so as to sabotage us from within. Because his identity was about to be revealed, they had reported, he had fled together with another spy in the guards. Both of them are Tay from Cao Bang and natives of That Khe district. Border defense soldiers went in pursuit, even crossing the Viet-Lao border, but all they could find was two tiger-eaten corpses and two abandoned rifles."

"If he has been determined to have been eaten by a tiger, then how can he come back and live under another name? Especially when two rifles have been abandoned. Do you think, Comrade, that an escapee can throw away his rifle and survive in the woods with only his bare hands when in front of him are both wild animals and the enemy?"

An gets the feeling that his division commander does not believe what the Meo is telling him and that he is trying his best to lead him toward another explanation.

In hesitation, Ma Ly mumbles for a while but then speaks in a most decisive way: "I know. What you said makes sense. But I cannot be mistaken, since Chi Van Thanh also recognized me. He even told me not to call him by his old name, that he had been pursued and that he had changed his name and family name."

Suddenly, whistlings and passionate shouts echo all over the woods:

"Bravo, bravo . . ."

"Encore; one more dance . . ."

"Once more! Hurray . . . Once more, please!"

"Once more! Please do it again."

An is sure that the Cham Rong dance must have just been performed, the dance of spring, the dance of love, of festivals and of aspirations. He imagines the crowd's excited faces under the headlights. At the same time, an idea comes into his mind:

"Dear commander, you and I have no enmity or hatred, we don't have any unhappy memories of each other. You have been like a generous brother to me but right now I have no choice. Please pardon me."

An points his gun at Ma Ly's back, aiming at a span and a half below his left shoulder, and pulls the trigger. An explosion. Surely the Meo's heart must be a mess. Moving his gun half a millimeter to the left, he shoots two bullets into the other, much larger, man. The whole thing happens in a blink. Both bodies fall forward almost at the same time, in the same direction.

An lowers the gun and puts it down at the foot of a familiar tree, where he used to sit by himself in the afternoon. The reflection of the fireflies in the water on the other side of the stream and the uncertain light of the phosphorescent balls under the tree bushes are all he needs to find everything. After hiding the gun, An walks toward the two corpses, which are piled one on top of the other. Both corpses are warm. First he carefully takes the pants of each man so that the blood from their chests does not smear their pants. The he picks up their weapons and flashlights, their cigarette packs and lighters, the nail cutters in their shirt pockets, notebooks and pens, and stacks everything on the grass. Then he takes off their shoes and socks. Figuring that all has been taken care of, he carries the Meo upstream to Roaring Elephant Falls.

Stopping to breathe a bit, he then throws Ma Ly's body down the falls. He hears the corpse drop into the water and watches as the black body is carried violently downstream. Coming back, An tries to pick up the division commander. He is very heavy. Finally he gets the sturdy body over his shoulder and walks step by slow step to the falls, where he puts the corpse down on the bank. He then pulls from his pants pocket a parachute string and ties one of his legs to a nearby tree. Gathering all his strength, he picks up the corpse and throws it down the cascade. The momentum from his throw makes him fall after it, but the string stops him. An then jumps up and unties the string, then goes back downstream, where he immerses himself in the icy water to get the blood out of his clothes. He then picks up the flashlight and submachine gun, intending to go back to the underground chamber. But as he looks up, suddenly he hears running feet and glimpses a dark silhouette disappearing among the black trees. Though he does not get a clear look, it is for sure a living creature, not some ghost.

"Was someone watching me?" he thinks to himself, immediately going in pursuit of the dark shape.

Whatever made the noise might as well have been a fox or some other animal. It disappeared in a flash, leaving no trace, as if it had blended in the woods. Nonetheless, An tries to follow, pursuing it all the way to the edge of the forest, where finally he stops. Though the prey he was after might be human or a ghost, or even a fox, he lets it escape. To follow any farther would put him in danger of getting caught with the trappings of a murderer, wet from head to toe.

"Well, I will take care of you later," he resolves, and proceeds back to the underground chamber. Luckily for him, the quarters are totally deserted. Hanging his wet clothes on the drying rack, An stands there a moment looking at the fire in the brazier lit to dry clothes in the damp underground chamber, feeling at once sad and indifferent. He feels like sleeping. But, that being impossible, he puts on fresh clothes and goes back to the clearing, joins his unit, and quietly hides himself behind his troops as the performance continues.

After about ten minutes, he puts a hand on the shoulder of the fellow in front of him:

"Having a good time?"

Taken aback, the fellow turns around and looks at him.

"Where did you go, Chief, to be here only now?"

"Commander Nha told me to go with him and take a nap in the underground chamber. I overslept."

"You missed half of the evening already, you know."

"So be it . . . But at least I had a good rest. Besides, being ten years older than you, I no longer yearn as much as you do for the pretty girls. Isn't that right?"

The soldier laughs heartily. "To that question I have no answer."

"Go ahead, enjoy the show, lest you lose out on the fun," An replies, putting a sudden end to the conversation. He then uses his right hand to squeeze a vital spot on his left shoulder. Only now does he feel his whole body aching after the strenuous and tense episode he has just passed through. His eyelids start to weigh heavily like lead and it begins to seem as if they will no longer obey the will of their owner.

"I can't sleep now," An thinks to himself. "I have no right to do so. Having just declared to everybody that I got a good nap with the battalion commander, I cannot have a reason for napping some more."

But, starting to yawn, he pulls out his pack of cigarettes and lights one of them. As soon as the smoke spreads, five or six heads turn around, greedily looking to share in a smoke. Arms spread toward him:

"Me first, Commander. I had my hand up first."

"Liar, I was the one to raise my hand first. Sitting where you are in front, how could you smell the smoke before anyone else?"

"I am third. Please do not forget me."

"How about me? Is not an old soldier entitled to a smoke?"

"I thought you all were fixated on the show," An replies. "That's why I dared open my pack of cigarettes . . . You all certainly have keen noses."

The cigarette then passes from hand to hand through the ranks with its butt burning bright then dimming then burning again. In the end it disappears even as more hands are raised in expectation. An looks up to the stage but in his ear he can still hear the thud and the gurgling sound of the water when the body of the division commander was thrown in.

"He certainly was a strong man. He must have been an authoritarian father to his children and an exhausting husband in bed. People from maritime provinces consume lots of fish, so they are born potent, needing no bear or tiger paste. His heart was really pumping blood. It spurted out like water from a sprinkler."

So thinking, An instinctively put his hand on his neck to ascertain whether he was entirely free of the commander's blood. On the way toward the waterfall, blood from the commander's corpse kept flowing out, gooey and warm, soaking the base of his neck and then flowing past his chest, his navel, all the way down to his pubic hair, making him feel extremely uncomfortable. It had then split into two streams flowing down the interior of his thighs, feeling a bit sticky like a sauce coming from a stew pot. It made a very strong impression—an unforgettable one. The blood felt like a kind of thick tree sap but it was warm and gave a slightly fishy smell. All of a sudden, An feels his limbs go weak. A hatred rises up and becomes a whisper in his heart:

"Why couldn't you just shut up, you damn Meo? I didn't do you any personal harm. Besides, you have no idea why I had to flee my home province. How can you understand the pain of someone forced to leave his homeland? What dark wind blew in your direction so that you dumbly listened to others? What wicked black veil covered your eyes so that you looked on me blinded by such a poisonous thought?"

Onstage, they are performing a short piece of *cheo* theater from the traditional ethnic Vietnamese playlist. The piece is called *Xuy Van Gia Dai* (Xuy Van Feigning Madness). An cannot recall any of the details of the story, only that it is about a woman betrayed in love who has gone mad. The actress onstage wears a bright red skirt the color of kapok flowers with a white magnolia flower in her hair. Her confused movements and her beautiful, thoroughly sober look don't seem to go together at all. Her singing is mournful, imbued with authentic melancholy, but at the same time quite alluring. To An, it isn't the singing of a madwoman, but rather that of a female bird calling for her male companion.

"Male and female birds call to each other in the spring, coo throughout the summer, make love throughout the fall, and take turns brooding their eggs over the winter. Those are the happy birds. Only we suffer. Now we can never call to each other or carry out a courtship with our words and songs. We can no longer make love and never will we have children to cuddle and nurture like little birds that are taken care of by their parents."

As these thoughts slowly pass through his mind, they cut like a knife heated hot in a furnace and now applied to his skin and flesh. He can almost feel his skin and flesh sizzling under that horrible knife. He misses her, the pretty wife he had. His first love but also his last. The one and only woman in his life. Fused with his flesh for sixteen full years, she will live forever in his soul.

"Dong, where are you now? My lover, please ride the wind and the trees, please borrow the voice of birds and beasts to give me an answer. Where are you? And where is your little sister?"

Dong and An had become lovers at the age of fifteen. But they had known each other since they could barely walk. They had been the closest neighbors, their houses separated only by a mountain slope. Both their mothers had become pregnant in the same year, and had given birth to each of them in the same moon, her at the beginning and him at the end. The following month, the two families agreed to take the full-moon day to celebrate the first full month of both children. The mountain village people had gone to her home to kill a cow and celebrate at noon, and in the evening they had come to his family's house to roast a pig, boil chickens, and have a feast. The festivities went on until very late and everyone stayed the night, not returning to their homes until the next day.

The immense flank of the mountain had been their playground during childhood. It was where she would follow him into the bushes to find ripe fruit, catch May bugs and ladybugs, or dig up cricket holes. When they were five, he had taken her on their first adventure, leaving the familiar hill to go look for the springs that brought water to the village, then up the mountain to where one could hear the sporadic songs of the nightingales. In the winter of that year, a pharyngeal epidemic had spread throughout the district. Xiu Village was lost in an isolated, faraway valley yet it, too, could not avoid the common plague. Since then An had been an orphan. His father had died one day, and the next, his mother also passed away from an epidemic that killed mostly young ones. His parents were its only adult victims. What had been odd was that he was living in the same home yet he stayed in splendid health. His parents and the young dead had to be collected, put on the same pyre, and buried together in a corner of the valley so as to prevent the epidemic from spreading.

The saying used to go, "With father gone, there's still the uncle / With mother dead, the aunt will still give suck." That was all one needed in a traditional Nong clan. After the funeral, An's uncle and aunt sold their house to a neighbor and moved into his parents' house on stilts so that they could take care of their nephew. At the time they had been a young couple. Not until four years later, when he turned nine years old, did they have an only child, a girl called Nang My. There had been nothing to set off one child from the other and they loved each other as if they had come from the same parents. Nang My had been born the same year as Dong's younger sister, called intimately "Little One," and thus, in their case also, those two girls— niece and aunt—had become fast friends from the time they were toddlers. At the age of seventeen, his uncle and aunt had married him to Dong. After the wedding, seeing that her father was by himself, they had been allowed to go and live in the house on stilts on the other side of the mountain. It had been a marriage made in heaven, as it was like a series of honeymoons. Or better yet, one unending honeymoon. Two weeks after the wedding, he had gone down to That Khe district town to continue his studies. Once a month, the lovers had been allowed to be together. At that time, the district school did not have enough students, so the program dragged along. For that reason, it took him more than ten years to complete his secondary schooling. At the graduation ceremony that year, he, Nong Van Thanh, was the only Tay to graduate—the pride of Xiu Village, who had achieved a dream shared by all prominent Tay families.

Growing up under the protection of his aunt and uncle, An could do no more than submissively comply with the orders of his uncle, who one day said to him: "You have become quite a grown-up man but you are still in your youth. I have hesitated for several years, but now you must go and join the resistance. We are a small village with not many households but we cannot afford to become the laughingstock of the larger villages."

"I understand, Uncle."

"Your aunt will take care of your clothes and medicine and some cash. Is there anything else you need?"

"I just need a few days to go and say good-bye to my friends in the village and to go down to the district to take leave of my teachers."

"OK. We have five days before you need to go to camp."

After a moment of hesitation, An had added: "I haven't done anything to help you, Uncle. Ever since my childhood, I have done nothing but take your money and rice to go and study. Now that I am on my way, I leave back here my family burden."

His uncle smiled. "We raised you so that you could become a useful person. That was my wish. Now that you are enlisting it's because I realize you cannot avoid your duty toward the country. As you are going to be on your way, be at ease. At home we will take care of Nang Dong, your wife. Besides, Mr. Cao, your father-in-law, and I are friends . . ."

An had not dared say anything further. What more could he say to a person who was both his uncle and father? Besides, he was very much in the prime of his youth and had wished to be on his way into the world. New horizons had beckoned him. Echoes of war from far away had called to his soul; many of his classmates had already enlisted. Even Nang Xuan, "Little One," had left the village at the age of thirteen to join other young cadets in the maquis. And pretty soon, his own sister would possibly be sent to the Soviet Union or China in accordance with the mobilization and training plans of the revolutionary movement. In such case, how could he stay put? The quiet valley, which was his birthplace, was bordered on all sides by the forests. He knew every path going through those gentle woods. In the familiar surrounding hills, he was fully cognizant of all the falls that trickled onto the rocks and cliffs. Nightingale Falls in particular had been singing its eternal song from the time he had been a baby till he knew how to make love. The footprints of buffalo on the muddy paths leading to the village on a rainy day—the jingling bells under their necks resonating in the deserted sunsets—was all too familiar to him, familiar to the point of his not noticing them. He realized that he must leave this valley to learn a little more of the outside world. He must go out even though he very much loved Dong.

"Once you go, how long before you will be back?" she had asked.

"I am going to war. Once the war is over I will be back."

"I'll miss you," she had said, starting to cry.

"I will miss you, too. But to do my duty to our rivers and mountains I must go. If you love me, then wait for me. For surely I will be back," he had replied. The same answer that soldiers for thousands of generations had given to their young wives before leaving their villages. Such consoling words are always meant for those leaving as much as for those who stay. She had let her face fall on his shoulder and her tears had soaked the indigo shirt he was wearing. Her tears had been warm and very wet. Warm and wet the same as . . .

The recollection stands An's hair on end. He at once closes his eyes. A chilly wind is blowing from the direction of the stage onto his face. Just at that moment, the singing of the madwoman in the red skirt fills the empty space.

In silence An tells himself: "Life is full of deceit. Like the wild rooster eating in the company of peacocks. Your innocent tears rendered my shoulder warm one night long ago. Tonight, however, my shoulder has been warmed with human blood. The blood of a traitor mingled with that of another innocent person. The same way, I guess, as the wild rooster ate together with the peacocks. That is, however, fate's way. I had no way to avoid my fate. I will have to continue on that road so as to find where you are living now. You and our Little Sis."

"Hurrah!"

"Bravo, bravo . . ."

Everyone is standing up around him. An quickly follows suit. The performances are over. All the performers and the musicians rush to the stage to take a bow and take leave of the soldiers. The commanding officers go up onstage to present flower bouquets. The accordions play at full volume in front of the sound system so that both the performers and the audience can sing the finale before parting. Those onstage wave their bouquets, the soldiers below clapping hands in time with the drums.

The clapping of hands resonates over the mountain and into the forests. Then, after a few minutes of boisterous noise, the deputy division commander walks up to the mike to thank the performing troupe. At the same time he wishes the units present a fine training season. An noticed how he looked right and left for something before he stepped up onstage. For the person who should be saying tonight's closing words is the division commander. But he has mysteriously disappeared.

Then the units of Battalion 209 start to check their ranks before retiring. The soldiers of the division disperse in every direction to their encampments. An sees Nha, the battalion commander, looking for him. An raises his hand and waves.

"Commander, our company is over here."

He then gives an order to the platoon leaders: "You comrades can go back to your barracks. There is nothing left to do here by the stage. Tomorrow, I am sure the division leaders will let you sleep in a little in compensation. That's my guess."

"It makes sense to let us oversleep a bit, sir. It's already two thirty-five."

The Battalion 209 units begin to leave one after the other. Drumrolls of thunder arise over the forest.

"Quick, you bum! How can you be so awkward?"

"How can I speed up? The path is so narrow!"

"Then move aside and let me go forward."

"What are you quarreling for? Whether you get ahead or fall back, you gain just a few yards. There's no escaping the rain. If you know what to do, you'd better take out your plastic poncho."

"Let's pray that it doesn't rain right away. Heaven: please let us get back to our barracks before it starts raining. Then you can pour down all you want."

"Maybe we will escape in time. 'If thunder peals in the east, one should watch out while running.' But tonight the thunder rolls in the west."

"What a dumb ass. 'Thunder in the west means rain pouring and winds gusting.' The rain might come late but it will be much worse, ten thousand times worse."

"We'll see."

The night wind howls above the gigantic trees. Branches crack as if they are breaking off right over one's head. An waits for all the soldiers to go by before he leisurely walks toward Battalion Commander Nha. The latter stands in a circle with the deputy division commander and the officers of various battalions. When An arrives, the circle opens up as a way of welcoming him. An understands that the information they seek is known to him alone.

"Sir, did you, Comrade Battalion Commander, call me?" An asks, stopping in front of Battalion Commander Nha.

"Come here, come here!"

Nha then speaks in a worried tone: "It's not just to meet me but the whole leadership here. We are all concerned because it's not at all clear where our division commander has gone. About midway through the evening, he went out with a cadre from a company in the guest battalion. And they have yet to return. Battalion 209 reports that before he came into the clearing this Meo company commander met with you. Then both you and the Meo fellow went to sit with Battalion 209."

"That is correct, Battalion Commander. I sat with him until past nine. Suddenly I had a stomach cramp and had to go back to quarters to get my medicine. When I returned I joined my company because I was afraid that my soldiers would get concerned not knowing where I was."

"You were a former comrade-in-arms with this Meo?"

"Yes, I was in the same company with Ma Ly when we were in the Viet Bac. But at the time he was only a runner outside the unit, since he was not old enough. After the liberation of the capital, some recruiters came and got soldiers to cross into Laos for special missions. A number of us volunteered and I was one of them. Thus, in fifteen years we haven't seen each other."

"When you were still buddies in the Viet Bac, did you know anything about his particulars?"

"I don't know much because of our different ages. He was more buddy-buddy with a couple of San Diu and San Chi guys from Lang Giang and Ha Bac than with me. But from time to time, a number of us belonging to six different ethnic groups also pooled resources to have a party. On those occasions, Ma Ly would brag that the blood flowing in him was not pure Meo, instead it was a kind of mixed blood. His maternal grandmother was an ethnic Vietnamese seller of dry fish. During the war she had been robbed of everything so she had to stay up in the mountains and ended up marrying his grandfather, a famous opium dealer in the region. When we met earlier, he said he would look up a cousin he knows to be in our division."

"Could it have been our division commander?"

No one had an answer. An then asked them, "Did you say that our division commander went out with Ma Ly?"

"Right, after the sixth number with the *cheo* buffoon," replied the deputy division commander.

"I wasn't back then," An says.

The officers all open their eyes wide looking at one another, each one searching the faces of the others, looking as if they were kindergarten children considering an arithmetic problem on a blackboard. An waits for a few minutes then turns to Battalion Commander Nha.

"I think they may have gone to the other side of Panda Mountain before the evening was over. Should it turn out to be true that our division commander is related to Ma Ly, then Ly will have to call him Uncle on the maternal side. In the case of ethnic Vietnamese, the paternal side is considered more related but in the case of the Meo, the maternal side is the more important. After so many years of separation, they must have a lot to say to each other."

"Maybe . . ." Nha answers.

One peal of thunder follows another in the west. A few lightning flashes cut the coal-black night sky. The deputy division commander looks all around and says:

"At any rate, we have to wait until morning before we can know what happened. It's really strange. For if it were so important, he should have warned me, at least."

He takes a watch from his shirt pocket then continues: "It's three a.m. already. Let's go back underground. Tomorrow morning, at nine thirty, let's get together. The soldiers can go on sleeping."

Turning toward An, he says: "Thanks, Comrade. Sleep well."

The group splits up, going in different directions as they return to their quarters. Battalion Commander Nha goes with An in one direction. On the ink-black path, Nha suddenly lets out a long sigh:

"Don't know why I suddenly feel extremely dreary tonight. It spoils the whole party."

"It's true," An agrees.

Another peal of thunder suddenly explodes. A chilly wind blowing vigorously through the clearing makes their faces feel frozen.

"Let's run. The wind has changed," says Nha.

"Yes."

Both start running fast. Their flashlights throw erratic beams into the night darkness. Ten minutes and they are already in the underground quarters. Just at that moment the night bursts with more lightning and the wind begins to gust as a heavy rain whips down in lashes. The trees twist back and forth in all directions. An and Nha stop at the entrance to the underground bunker. For just a second, they look at the sky.

"Wow. It's just as they say, 'thunder in the west means rain pouring and winds gusting.'" Nha remarks with assurance.

"Yes," An replies, nodding.

"Now we can sleep in all tranquility," says Nha. "At least for one night—tonight."

"Yes," An rejoins, "it's war. Each day we get to live is a good day."

Then both of them go below.

Once in his mosquito net, An listens to the pouring rain, which makes a sound like a waterfall cascading. He tells himself:

"Tomorrow, there won't be any trace left on the bank of the stream. A hundred microscopes will not discover the murderer's fingerprints. Oh, Division Commander: don't hold a grudge against me—I am to be pitied. You had power in this infernal apparatus, so the higher you rose, the greater the danger to you. The more glory you have, the more shame you must endure. This has been the story forever. Please rest well in the Nine Springs together with my loved ones down there . . ."

He sighs deeply, then immediately falls into a deep sleep.

2

His sleep that night brings neither nightmares nor beautiful dreams; not a trace of the past, nor a premonition of the future.

His sleep is black like a winter night, thick from December fog, and ponderous like a cart carrying thick logs. It is like a skiff floating on an immense body of water that is neither river nor lake, neither pond nor troubled sea. An oversleeps the next morning, until ten. The leaders meet, and Nha has to send someone to wake him up, as he is late for the meeting. An jumps up and goes off to meet the other officers.

In the underground command chamber, everyone has assembled, with some standing and others sitting, gathered into small groups. Seeing An finally arrive, Nha goes out and welcomes him:

"Did you oversleep? I had breakfast and started out right away, I did not go back to the bunker. I had thought that you would remember and get up in time."

"Chief, you know me, I love oversleeping. When I woke up it was still the dark of night, so I lay myself down to sleep some more. It's always dangerous to go back to sleep. How's things? Do you have news of our division commander yet?"

"No, we haven't found anything . . . but . . ."

"But what?"

"The soldiers have found their pants, together with their weapons and other belongings on the bank of the spring. Division is of two minds right now: either to report it upstairs and wait for the verdict or to find the real reason to explain this. The deputy commander and all of us are hoping that you will have a suggestion. You are the only one to have known the Meo platoon leader, the supposed agent."

"I thank you for your trust. But my knowledge here is very limited. Ma Ly is a Meo. He lives in an earth home and grows poppies—their main occupation. I am a Tay tribesman. We Tay live in houses on stilts, breed cattle and chickens and pigs, grow dry field rice, and eat long rice as well as sticky rice. Our environments and our customs differ. Besides, we haven't seen each other in fifteen years."

"At any rate, both of you were comrades-in-arms. Besides, both of you are mountain people."

An laughs out loud. "Now, every one of us here is a mountain person, for we are living in the Vietnamese Cordillera. If you lump all mountain people together, it means you have no idea about who we are really."

"Sincerely speaking . . ."

Nha seems embarrassed, trying to formulate a plan of action. He takes off his glasses to clean them, a regular habit of his when in a situation like this. Just at that moment the deputy division commander notices An and quickly steps toward him, along with the leading cadres of the various battalions. After the greetings, everyone has gathered around An in expectation. But An turns to Nha and says:

"First, I would like to know what they have found on the bank of the spring. For I don't believe that Ma Ly would invite our division commander to take a bath, especially when it's pitch dark and the water has gone chilly. In all frankness, the Meo don't like to bathe. They are in the habit of 'fire bathing,' especially those who have acquired the long habit of opium smoking. Do you know, at one time opium was considered like white rice in the Meo kingdom?"

"In truth, that's the first time I've heard this. My native village is on the bank of the Red River. Ever since I joined the army, my contacts have been with ethnic Vietnamese. You are the first tribesman that I have known."

"Meo territory is right in the middle of the Golden Triangle, where they grow poppies and produce opium for half of Asia. The Meo king, Hoang Su Phi, used to lead a very efficient army charged with protecting the opium caravans crossing the border. They are capable of fighting any national army or forest bandits. The Meo people therefore had to grow poppies for him in exchange for rice, salt, dried fish, and oil. After many generations of such culture, they have grown addicted to opium the way we are used to white rice. I am not too sure why but opium addicts have a great fear of water. Very rarely do they bathe themselves in a spring or boil water to take a bath inside their houses. Instead they take off their clothes and sit next to a fire so that they sweat all over, thus opening all the pores of their skin. Then they use their fingers to roll the dirt into tiny balls, which they throw away."

"God, is that true?" a battalion commander bursts out in surprise.

An turns toward him: "Do you, Comrade, think that I am just fabricating that? Or that I am prejudiced and trying to slander the Meo?"

"That was simply an expression of surprise," the deputy division commander interjects. "Don't misunderstand. Even me, I have never known that."

An realizes that talking about Meo bathing habits has made them all very curious, but that they dare not ask for more. One only has to see them exchanging looks to know.

Nha tells the deputy division commander, "Comrade An wants to go see the crime scene because he does not believe that the two of them wanted to go take a bath. I hope that the soldiers have kept every trace intact."

"You can be at ease. I have ordered that the place be kept exactly as it was. You can take Comrade An there to have a look."

"We will be right back after the inspection," Nha replies. Then he walks out of the underground command chamber.

An follows him, with his salt-and-pepper hair covering his faded shirt collar. He's only fifty but looks more seasoned than the division commander. In this war it's clear that the people from coastal provinces and from the mountains endure much better than those from the Red River delta. Flowers that can blossom on the banks of the Red, or Luoc, River fade very fast under the mountain sun.

It is 10:20 a.m. but the soldiers are already gathered in groups of five or three all over the encampment. Actually, they could have overslept or stayed indoors and played cards, but the gossip has gone from ear to ear, and by the time Nha and An arrive at the stream bank, soldiers from the division are already there in great numbers. A parachute string has been strung from three large trees, forming a protective boundary around the crime scene. The squad normally guarding command headquarters is keeping the curious outside the string.

An takes a look at the bank. Traces of last night's flooding rain can still be seen on the sand beach and on the pebbles. The belongings that the night before had been neatly piled up are now scattered everywhere. The two pairs of pants had drifted down the stream for a couple of meters before getting caught in the root of a tree. One flashlight is now planted in the sand while the other has been carried down the water some thirty meters until stuck in a stack of dry, fallen branches. As for little things like the toothpick tube, the cigarette packs, the lighters, and the nail trimmer. . . they have disappeared without a trace. Only the two pistols are still there, at the original spot, together with one shoe. They are covered, however, with sand and mud. Truly, the rain last night was a masterwork, a high-class act of sorcery that turned everything into something else.

"Comrade, look," says An. "Look at the mud stuck to the shoe . . ."

"It really was something, that rain last night," Nha says, nodding, and then he goes on: "During the rainy season last year, this very stream even washed down a couple of deer. The guys in Division 89, who were stationed downstream, saw them still struggling in the water. They took out their guns and shot them, then threw out some cords to drag them in to eat. But in pulling in the deer, one of them fell down and he himself was washed downstream with the flood without being able to even cry out."

"I wonder why I don't remember that incident?"

"How could you? The story was circulated only among the leading comrades in the division. For who would admit to such a truth?"

Nha smacks his lips and lowers his voice to the point of a whisper: "So sad! A human life for a piece of venison."

Looking at the stream, An tells himself, "Last night if I had not tied one of my legs to a tree, I would have ended up like that guy with the deer."

In turning back, An sees the soldiers with all eyes on him and Nha—spectators in a mystery without plot or even a stage set. The protagonist is not present. Only a few pieces of clothing and some personal effects lying here and there. But the play is arousing so much curiosity because it dramatizes both a physical and a nonphysical death. Even if it is not yet an absolute death, it nonetheless has severely damaged the reputation of the leadership. Less than three months earlier two soldiers had been sentenced by a military tribunal to death by firing squad for having raped a Van Kieu woman who was burning coal in the forest. News of the execution had been disseminated to all four divisions operating in the region as a severe warning. Yet now the commander of the most famous division in the whole battle zone, the one with the most unit commendations, has disappeared in the night with some Meo, the only trace of them being two pairs of pants snagged on the side of a stream. Clearly it does not require much intelligence to imagine what is going on in the minds of the soldiers crowding around.

"Can we return to the command post now?" asks Nha.

"Yes . . . We have observed enough," An responds, and the two of them go back. "I am sure they went out looking for a deserted spot so that they could make up chicken-style," a soldier suggests. "They picked the right moment, too. With the soldiers wrapped up in watching the girls in the show, they went out there to take care of their choked-up balls."

"What do you mean, chicken-style?" asks another soldier.

"Damn you, don't play the innocent. If you don't know, then who else would?"

"You want to pick a lump of charcoal and put it in the hands of another?"

"Fire and charcoal. Who the hell told me the other day about the Lao being expert at ass-fucking?"

"You mean chicken-style and ass-fucking are the same? Oh, then I know now . . ."

"Hell with you, joker!"

"If I am not the joker, how can you have such a hearty laugh?"

An observes Nha walking really fast with his head down, as if trying to flee from the rowdy comments of the soldiers. He must feel awful, thinks An. Normally he is a well-spoken man, if somewhat simplistic, but all offenses against the more spiritual side of life always take him off guard and affect him more than others.

An catches up with him and says, "No one is born to be a soldier. War is something imposed on us. You shouldn't give those comments too much thought."

"I am someone not given to quarreling. But in this case you can't just stop wondering. How do you explain this affair?"

"I, too, am at a loss."

"How are we going to explain it to our colleagues?"

"If we don't understand it ourselves, then it's better not to give any explanation."

"But you can't do that. Whether we want to or not, there is no way for us to escape giving some explanation in front of everyone. In the army, each death must be explained clearly, for it also concerns the family of the deceased. Either it's the shameful death of a traitor, or it's a sacrifice out of one's duty to the people, in which case the family is entitled to some compensation."

"Yes," An responds as he bitterly thinks to himself: "But life is not all that simple. There are lots of deaths lying outside the boundaries that you are drawing. There are unjust deaths, stifled and quiet deaths, unintended and unconscionable deaths, deaths that steal upon you like poisonous snakes, these poisonous snakes of Fate that no one can prevent or fight off."

Soon they are back at the command bunker, where everyone has been silently sipping tea or smoking water pipes while waiting for them. An knows that they are all waiting for an explanation. There has to be an explanation. Concluding that it is best if he speak first without waiting for entreaties, he announces:

"I report to you, Deputy Division Commander and leading cadres . . . Battalion Commander Nha and I have carefully observed what remains on the bank of the stream. I feel certain that our division commander and Ma Ly could not possibly have gone out together for a bath because although he was in good health, our commander was already over fifty. At that time of day, the water is freezing. Second, I am sure Ma Ly would not dare go into the water. The whole time I lived with him in the Viet Bac, I witnessed him taking a bath only twice, and on both occasions it was during the middle of a hot summer when he was enticed to do so by his San Diu, San Chi, friends. Normally, Ma Ly would never volunteer to sink his body into the water. Even when he had to, he would quickly dry himself so he could put his clothes on right away. We used to call the Meo 'water-shy cats.' Thus there is no possible reason for both of them to suddenly and crazily step into the water for a bath in the middle of the night. As for other explanations, I do not have enough time nor experience to guess . . ."

After he finishes, he sits down by Nha. The others are shell-shocked. Someone coughs dryly. Then the deputy division commander, with all seriousness, states:

"Comrades, I am forced to ask that all of you give your opinions so that we can come to a final decision. We have responsibility for solving this situation, as it relates to the honor of each one sitting here. We have to confront the anxieties of more than one thousand of our soldiers here as well; after that I am sure public opinion will spread to other friendly divisions. Furthermore, we cannot just report the situation upstairs and wait for the higher echelons to come and open an investigation, then write up a file to submit to the military tribunal as usual. That is out of the question. It would take half a month, minimum, for the paperwork to move up and down. Besides, it will only take a heavy rain tonight for everything to be washed away if we do not gather whatever is left on the bank of the stream. These mementoes need to be kept for the families of the missing men. I use the word 'missing' here because we are still uncertain as to the fate of our division chief and the Meo fellow. We hope, of course, that they are somehow still alive in some way that we don't yet know."

One officer says, "I believe we should rule out that they are missing, for it would not be very persuasive. Can you imagine two naked persons alive without a piece of clothing on? Who could have forced them to do something like that?"

Another reminds him: "A year or so ago, did not enemy rangers catch a whole bunch of our troops bathing naked in a spring? If I am not mistaken, they were from Division 887."

"Oh yes, I had forgotten all about that incident."

"You certainly have a short memory. It happened just last summer and you had already forgotten?"

The first officer replies, "I am forty-nine already. 'Can't be too smart when young, or keep it all together when too old.'"

Another comments to the group: "I say this—and I hope you don't think I am superstitious. I don't believe that our commander is alive. At six o'clock this morning when I woke up, I heard lots of vultures croaking on the mountain. Ever since Thang's troops stepped on mines, did you ever hear the vultures in such a ruckus?"

"Right," says another. "I also heard them, and the sound gave me goose bumps. At that time, it was barely light, and yet the vultures were out in great numbers. This must mean that they have found their food. Their cries come from the direction of Beak Mountain. That's where the stream runs into the Nam Khuot River."

The deputy division commander turns to his staff aide: "Comrade, tell us how much time it would take from here to there."

"Around twenty minutes by helicopter," the aide replies. "But a walk through the woods would take at least five days minimum. From where we are stationed to the Nam Khuot River there are no blazed trails through the woods, nor is there a road going through our encampment. Following the stream is also out of the question since the part of it right below us, less than two hundred meters down the mountain, becomes a rocky cliff that is exactly like Death Mountain on the other side. There is only one way, and that is by following the trail used by the Van Kieu people. And that trail would take no less than five full days,. The vulture cries that you heard could not possibly have come from the Nam Khuot River. It's three kilometers away, and no bird cries can be heard from such a distance. I suspect, however, that these vultures once they find a carcass may have a way of telling one another, of communicating by crying that way. It may be a way to call the others to come."

"I think so, too. Our military staff assistant's analysis is entirely reasonable," agrees the commander of Battalion 2. He then turns to the deputy division commander and asks: "Do you think we can find a helicopter?"

The deputy shakes his head. "Our battle zone has never been granted such a favor. Even in the Peacock Hill battle, when our wounded were in the hundreds and lying all over, we could not get a helicopter, so how could we in this case?"

"Does the general staff think we are rear-echelon soldiers?" retorts the commander of Battalion 2.

"Not quite rear-echelon, still deep inside Laos. But the Lao front is understood to be less dangerous than other fronts in the south where the Americans are. Did you forget what Senior General Dong said the other day?" the deputy commander replied.

After a long moment of silence, Nha suddenly says, "Should we send someone down toward Nam Khuot River to find out? At any rate, we must do our very best. That way, we won't have regrets later on."

"Are you dreaming?" The deputy division commander gives Nha an unhappy look.

Nha is still uncertain how to respond when the commander of Battalion 2 turns around, taps on his shoulder, and says:

"Man, where is your head? Is it up there in heaven or down in the sea? All it takes is from now until this evening. There won't be a piece of skin left. Did you not see what happened when Thang's soldiers ran into the minefield? Eighteen guys altogether and yet it took the vultures only two days to clean them out."

An watches Nha shudder. Nha then tries his best to regain his composure by putting his hands into his pockets and hanging his head. Normally the staff meeting is limited to battalion commanders, but because this is serious business, the deputy division commander has decided to open it up down to the level of company commanders. For the first time An has had a chance to observe his immediate superior at work. Clearly, Nha is somewhat less sharp than the commanders of the other two battalions. Yet, his men's prowess in battle has always been exceptional. Maybe it is a case of heaven favoring the simple ones. In fact, Nha looks more like a student than an army officer.

After a moment of silence, the deputy division commander declares: "I suggest that you all take turns to speak up. This is totally unexpected. I have spent several decades in the army, yet I don't have enough experience to solve this. That's why I have decided to get a collective opinion, and we will take collective responsibility for it."

More silence.

Everyone looks at everyone else, as if calling for assistance or looking for sympathy. For everyone realizes that they are at a dead end. The deputy division commander takes out his tobacco pouch and begins to roll a cigarette. Other hands spread toward him. The tobacco pouch is passed around, each man taking a pinch and tearing off a piece of rolling paper. When the pouch comes back to its owner, there is left only one last pinch, enough for a second cigarette. Having finished the first one, the deputy division commander rolls another, then puts the pouch in his pants pocket.

The men smoke silently. After a while, the commander of Battalion 3, who had been mum from the beginning of the meeting, suddenly raises his hand:

"I have an idea."

"Ah, the toad finally opens his mouth," An thinks to himself.

"We're listening," the deputy division commander says.

"I think . . ." the Battalion 3 commander says, but then stops to take a sip of tea. Although anxious, everyone has to be patient, since he is known to be very deliberate and very sparing in his choice of words. He takes his time to drink his tea down. Then, he leisurely clears his voice before he goes on:

"I believe we have forgotten an important link in the chain. The Meo guy asked our division commander to go with him. Among us, Comrade Hoang An is the only one to have known him, but that was some fifteen years ago. During the following fifteen years, no one apparently can describe what he had done or was like. The information we get from Battalion 209 is minimal. Even that battalion itself was formed from two battalions under strength after severe losses in battle, and from a number of new recruits. This Meo company leader himself is part of the reinforcements from the north. Now, I assume . . ."

At that point, he slightly closes his eyes, as if watching the imagined scenes in his mind. The whole group holds its breath in expectation. An wonders what is flashing behind those half-closed eyes. Then the battalion commander suddenly opens wide his eyes and peers at the deputy division commander.

"I am assuming that the company leader has struck a deal with the Meo king, Hoang Su Phi, a redoubtable enemy of the revolutionary forces before the liberation of the capital. I take it that he has a kinship relation with Hoang Su Phi or owes the latter a debt of gratitude. In which case he must entertain a very profound, deep-rooted enmity toward the revolution. It's obvious, then, that he would take advantage of his kinship on the maternal side to take revenge. Comrades, you must not forget that we have had severe losses in the fight with the Meo king on the plateau of Dong Van at the northern border. Comrade Hoang An also knows that the Meo king's troops are very experienced. Being natural mountaineers, they climb the rocky mountains or trees with ease, whereas our soldiers coming from the lowlands are not used to the cold up here and are unable to master this rough terrain. The Meo are fed well and learn to shoot at the age of ten. They are renowned to be sharpshooters who can hit their targets every time. Hoang Su Phi, being very rich, was able to equip his troops with more modern weapons than our troops could afford at the time. With all these advantages and superiority, they controlled all the one-way access roads, and from up in the mountains they could shoot down at our troops. We have thus lost I don't know how many comrades that way. The victory on the Dong Van front had to be purchased at a very high price. I am recalling all this so that you can grasp the background behind this affair. Now, let us assume that this company leader Ma Ly is a descendant of Hoang Su Phi who has changed his name and surname to be able to infiltrate our ranks. Meeting with our division commander is the best opportunity for him to exact his revenge. He was thus able to eliminate a high-ranking officer of our army; he could smear his reputation as well. We have lived with him many years. No one could believe that he would be doing something indecent, especially in a difficult and strange situation like that. I believe that the Meo fellow referred to relations dear to the family of our division commander, then shot him surreptitiously. After that, he pulled off our commander's pants and his own so as to leave the impression that they were having crazy sex. My hunch is that our commander is dead but that the other one is still alive and has gone into the woods. The whole thing must have been prepared carefully before he went into action. You should not forget that we, being ethnic lowlanders, are not familiar with the woods and the night, which to us are a strange and fearful world. But with the Meo, they go into the forest as fish go back to the river."

Everyone gasps in agreement.

"Of course!"

"It's so simple yet no one had it figured out."

"We all are in debt to you, Comrade. As they say without exaggeration, 'When the frog opens its mouth, it's well worth a listen.'"

All of a sudden everyone is talkative; now everyone can breathe. Every face is now at ease. In the end, they have found a way out. The opinion of the Battalion 3 commander is a light at the end of the tunnel. Not a single person contests his idea. The deputy division commander reaches across the table, taps his shoulder, and says:

"Marvelous!"

An looks around and secretly tells himself: "You Meo son of a bitch! In the end, you are the one marked as having changed names—not me. Now the sentence has been pronounced: you are the murderer. And so we end with the truth—that was the way it was."

As an irony of fate, in his ear he can hear the lyrics of "The Wild Rooster":

Wild Rooster,
Why are you eating in the company of peacocks?
Why are you deceitful, O Wild Rooster?

Right after the meeting, An returns to the underground bunker, slings himself down on the bed, and goes to sleep. Even at lunchtime he does not wake up. The deputy company commander comes and pulls him up.

"Are you sick? To the point of skipping your meals?"

"No, I am not, but I am extremely sleepy. It looks as if I'm going to catch malaria again."

"Get up and have lunch. The kitchen says you have skipped breakfast this morning."

"My tongue tastes bitter."

"I have with me here some malaria prevention medicine for you. But you cannot take it unless you have a full belly."

"Well then, I'll try. Getting sick at this point will inconvenience everybody. Let's go. Have you eaten?"

"I waited for you. Today the cooks found some wild vegetables. And there is some broth to go with them."

"Are the guys in our company done eating?" An asks, then buttons up his shirt and walks out of the bunker.

His deputy follows him and answers lackadaisically: "After the meal the guys went back to their quarters to play cards or catch some sleep. They don't have anything else to watch. Out at the stream, the on-duty guards have collected the material evidence and taken it to division headquarters."

"Is that so . . ."

An bursts out laughing at the way his deputy has replied. He then asks another question: "Has the leadership given an explanation as to what happened?"

"Not enough time for them to come up with one. But the guys overheard things and already have a good idea. The information went from the division headquarters down to the battalions, then it went from the battalions down to the companies—just like an arrow."

"That's because we're here in the forest. . . . What is there to divert them?"

"Yes, they had to wait a couple of years before they could have a night of entertainment. Who would have thought that with it would come a murder?"

"Do you believe in fate?"

"I believe a hundred percent. They dare not say it but everyone believes it to be so. In the battlefield who can say he will sidestep the bullets? It's the bullet that chooses its victim. If it were not for fate, how could it be that a bullet would hit this one and not another in that same place at the same moment?"

"Fate is something that exists and that doesn't. For if people truly had a choice, they would never willingly take themselves to the battlefields to face arrows and bullets."

"Ah, this question, if one were to trust the fortune-tellers, relates to the destiny of a nation, a common fate that belongs to a collective. The destiny of a nation turns on whoever leads it, not on ordinary soldiers or common people like us. In the old days, it depended on the king or emperor. Today, it turns on the president."

"If you are right, then our president must have a truly rotten horoscope to have led our people into living deep in the jungles and forests like we do now."

"Oh, I don't mean that. Please, Comrade, don't put things in my mouth," the deputy company commander mumbles, his face turning pallid.

An reassures him: "Don't be afraid. I am the one who said that, not you. Neither am I intelligent enough to raise such issues. I heard it from a

Vietnamese astrologer who has lived many, many years in Laos. I have merely repeated what he told me."

"Yes," the deputy replies and then, lowering his voice: "Do you know, I have heard one person say exactly the same thing. But he was not an astrologer, he was a historian."

"Yes, a historian also must have a brain full of pebbles like an astrologer. We are approaching the dining hall, though. Let's keep this between you and me."

"Yes," his deputy answers, almost in a whisper.

After they are through, the clock shows 1:30 p.m. Only two of them remain in the five huge wood-built dining halls. Outside, the sun is shining full blast everywhere. A gentle breeze runs across the range of trees, which are heavy with scintillating leaves on which dew still hangs in the thick leaf funnels. On the edge of the forest, wildflowers are in gorgeous bloom. The deputy company commander looks at the petals, which are like butterflies displaying their vying colors, vermillion and purple, then sighs:

"How I miss my home! These flowers make me remember the mustard fields along the river. In the spring the mustard flowers bloom yellow, attracting butterflies in the thousands. When young I used to run after my mother to go out and pull up those mustard plants. Then, when we were of marriageable age, we went out to various festivals in the first month, and we could find these yellow mustard flowers all along the foot of the dike."

"Right, I remember a folk song of the ethnic Vietnamese:

'The first month is for having fun all month,
The second is devoted to gambling and the third to drinking.' "

"Yes, that's a folk song from way back. When I was home we would try to get people to work starting with the fifth day of the first lunar month. But even as they worked in the fields, they would find ways to hold spring festivals, for that was the custom."

"It's the same way with us in the mountains. We prepare various kinds of cakes, make crispy honeyed rice balls, then play cards all of the first month. Even when we don't have festivals, there is not much to do since it drizzles all day long. At that time of year, the rice is maturing while the weeding is done in the dry cassava fields."

"Up there do the festivals last as long as they do in the lowlands?"

"Not as long but enough for people to have fun all around. After the

Spring Music Festival is over, we call on one another to go see the Ball Throwing Festival of the Thai, then the Khen Playing Festival of the Meo. Only the strongly built young men in the village, equipped with good steeds, dare go far. As for the women, all year 'round they stay in the village."

The two fall silent for a long while. Then the deputy asks, "When will the war be over?"

"When?" An echoes.

No one has an answer to that difficult question. A moment of silence follows. All of a sudden, the deputy company commander asks:

"Do you remember Tiny-Eyes Toan?"

"Of course. He's the buffoon in Company One. Wonder whether his bones have disintegrated by now? It's been over two and a half years. And there the soil is humid all year 'round with dew settling, intermittent mountain rain, and moss-covered ground all the way from the foot of the cliff down to the gulley below. In that kind of soil no bones can remain intact."

An does not hear his deputy reply. Turning, he sees the man bite on his lower lip, his face smeared with plentiful tears. His shoulders quiver in waves as if he has malaria. An looks around but luckily there is no one to see them at that moment. After clearing the tables, the kitchen staff had gone back to their chamber to nap. The only souls stirring are probably just the chirping birds in the nearby forest. Raising his hand to console his companion by rubbing his back, An says:

"It's very good that you can cry like that. Go ahead and get some relief."

A second voice is heard in his own soul at the same time: "You are lucky to be able to cry with me. As for me, I can only cry by myself. And I will have to do so till the end of my days . . ."

The two of them sit there until the deputy gets hold of his emotions. On the other side of the grass clearing one can see vague images of naked soldiers. Surprised, An asks:

"What are they doing over there?"

The deputy blows his nose and answers, "They are scooping the gulley water to bathe."

"Why don't they go over to the stream? It's very easy to catch a cold bathing with gulley water. By now the springwater has had time to warm up a bit."

"Have you forgotten that our division commander has just drowned? This morning they all rushed out to watch right and left."

"The water flows unceasingly, washing everything downstream. Besides, the stream flows through so many areas, how can one count all those who have drowned from its source down to its lower reaches?"

"That's true . . . But our commander died right here, at this stream, so the guys are very afraid. Maybe, being a mountain person, you do not know the fears of us ethnic Vietnamese. . . . We people from the Red River delta or in other river valleys are all obsessed by the unceasing and wicked pursuit by water ghosts. According to our legends, water ghosts are the innocent souls of those who have drowned. For when they are forced by others to drown in the rivers, they have a chance to escape from hell, and can reincarnate into another life on earth."

"Is that so," An answers. And a second voice arises in him: "If that were the case, then the first one to have been forced to drown would have been me. For it's not just one water ghost but two who would look for a common enemy to take in exchange for their lives. But for a long time now I have no longer known fear. Fear has long since abandoned me, both in my soul and in my brain."

An stands up and says, "I feel so much like taking a bath. Would you want to go to the stream with me?"

The deputy looks at him, flabbergasted. "Me? . . . I had a bath yesterday afternoon."

An laughs and tells him, "There's no fear. I just need you to sit on the bank and watch me take a bath. If we cannot get rid of this superstition, how can we solve regular problems in the lives of our soldiers? Should more than a thousand guys have to fight for a few drops from this tiny gulley—not much more than a cow's piss—they will surely come to blows. While this stream, nay this river, is left untouched. I just don't believe in water ghosts."

"Yes."

"Follow me."

"Yes."

The deputy answers An mechanically, then he also follows him mechanically. The two of them go to the bank of the mountain stream. Several groups of soldiers who have been in the forest follow them out of curiosity.

Arriving at the stream, An loudly asks: "Who would like to come down here and have a swim competition with water ghosts?"

"Sir, we are not all that courageous."

"Wait and see."

So saying, An takes off his clothes and steps into the stream. He goes all the way out to the middle and plunges down and resurfaces several times just like a professional athlete. So doing, he turns his eyes toward the white foaming Thundering Elephant Falls.

"No one is suffering more than I right now. No despair is deeper and heavier than the one right now in my heart. Thus, no force can stop me before I take this revenge."

The soldiers on the bank clap their hands. Seeing An smile, they clap even louder because they think he is laughing with them. But in actuality, he is laughing at the bitter fate that has befallen him.

3

In the fall of the year Quy Ty (1953) An had been stationed in Tuyen Quang. When a relative in the people's labor force who carried provisions saw him, she eagerly told him:

"Little One has been presented to the president king, do you know that? The revolutionary organization had found an ethnic Vietnamese for him but he prefers our Little One, so by now your sister-in-law has become the queen, do you know that? Her name has now been changed to Chi Thi Xuan. The twelve families in Xiu Village changed their family name to Chi after they learned the news."

At the time An had been in the army for two years. For two full years he had not had one single piece of news from home. This run-in with his relative made him happy for months. His joy was like a slow-burning coal, which kept the fire going without getting extinguished.

On that very day, An went to his battalion commander and said, "Report to the leader: from this moment on I am no longer Nong Van Thanh but Chi Van Thanh."

"Why?" asked the surprised battalion commander.

"Because my uncle who is the chairman of the village committee has so decided. My village contains only twelve households, so whatever he decides, the people in the village just do as told. A relative whom I've just met told me so."

"Is your relative among those serving in the people's labor force being bivouacked right in front of our camp?"

"Yes. That's precisely true."

"Nonetheless, there must be a reason to change one's name or family name. For who would suddenly decide on something like that, out of no-where?"

"I report to you, sir, there surely must have been a reason. But that rea-son is known only to my uncle and the old learned scholars in our village. We, as the younger ones, are not entitled to ask," An smilingly responded.

So seeing, the battalion commander also laughed along and said, "That's OK. We'll respect the decision of the local leaders."

So saying, he quickly gave an order to his assistant. The latter took out the unit registry, rubbed out the word "Nong," and replaced it with "Chi." That was it. In the maquis everyone was a volunteer joining the army to fight; nobody needed any advantage or privilege, and thus one's wishes could be easily addressed. Additionally, he was from an ethnic minority and the minority peoples were the firm foundation of the August Revolution and of the protracted resistance. Every leading cadre knew this principle: "In all situations, minority cadres and fighters are entitled to privileged treatment."

"Our Little One has now become queen!"

An's joy at that fact had stayed with him throughout the remaining days of the resistance, together with his new name, Chi Van Thanh. It seems that the new name brought An much good luck even though no one in the bat-talion, from the officers down to the soldiers, quite knew the secret source of this good fortune. An was promoted beyond normal expectations be-cause of his fighting valor. The luckiest stroke, however, was that, having gone through many battles, he was still whole, not even grazed by a bullet or anything else. He did not have a chance to meet with Little One although he knew that she had left Xiu Village to go and live in the government's headquarters in the Viet Bac maquis. His pride in her lightened his soul. As far as he was concerned, she was like a little sister or even a daughter to him. He wasn't quite sure. The ties that bound him to her were nothing like the normal ties between a brother-in-law and his wife's sister.

Nang Dong being his companion since infancy, when Little One was born it had been he along with Nang Dong who had taken care of her. Her father, Mr. Cao, who was multitalented and also lived a multifaceted life, had left the village and gone into the wide world until the age of forty-two, when he came back and married a beautiful girl twenty-three years his ju-nior. When she died giving birth to Xuan, he was already over fifty. At that age no man could be expected to carry around a baby or feed it with bottle and milk. In his huge house the sawmill occupied the main room, the altar to his wife the outer room. As for the inner room, which was used as a kitchen, he had divided it with wooden partitions into three smaller ones. This is where the two children, then aged nine, had taken care of the half-orphaned sister, still red in a cradle. For two full years An had lived in one of the three small rooms, the middle one being used for holding the baby's cradle, and the last room reserved for Nang Dong. Mr. Cao slept right in the kitchen so as to keep the fire going. In front of the baby's room a dish holding a candle burned all night. When the baby woke up it was either Nang Dong or he who would rise to change her diaper or feed her. In rare instances when they had trouble waking up, Mr. Cao would ring a bronze bell to shake them out of sleep. The sound of the bell ringing in the deep night left a memory that would never leave him; it was like some sort of rudimentary but lively music that joyously sounded in his childhood days. He also recalled with fondness the deep ceramic dish that held beeswax with a wick made up of rough cloth the size of a chopstick. The flickering light would project their silhouettes on the walls.

He could still remember as if it were yesterday how to slow-cook a congee made of half sweet rice and half mung bean; how to sift rice gruel so as to have rice milk to keep in a thermos; how to milk a female buffalo, wait for the milk to curdle, and then keep it in such a way as not to produce whey. In Xiu Village, there were no cows, as people had raised only buffalo. The babies were fed only buffalo milk. An could also remember the wooden basin in which Little One used to be bathed, with him on one side and Nang Dong on the other, both dipping their hands in the water and rubbing the dirt off Little One. That was real life, yet it felt like a game. For they themselves, An and Nang Dong, were still in their early teens. That "game" linked the three of them in a strange love. That was why, even though he had been married to Nang Dong for ten years by the time he went into the army at the age of twenty-seven, no one had questioned why they did not have any children. Also, at the time, the fact that a couple was slow in having children was not something as serious as would be the case today. Nonetheless, it was still considered an irregularity. Little One lived wedged in between the two of them, surrounded by a very colorful love. All three had felt satisfied with what they had, so neither Nang Dong nor he had sought out a doctor to treat her infertility, as advised by their neighbors.

The resistance war ended suddenly one year after An changed his name. He did not have an opportunity to return to Xiu Village, because his wife found him on exactly the day the various columns were getting ready to liberate the capital. Nang Dong clung to him, laughing and crying all at the same time. Tomorrow, she would be living with Little One in the city of Hanoi. How about him? Fate had once more smiled on him, for his unit was stationed in Ha Dong, a mere ten kilometers away from Hanoi, not more than one hour by bicycle. In their case, it seemed as if the doors of Paradise had opened for them.

However, from the very first day he had come to visit them, An was not pleased. Walking along the long and dark corridor, he had wondered why they could put Little One in such an ordinary apartment, even though it had three high-ceilinged and roomy chambers, along with a separate kitchen and closets. Even so, it was simply the upper floor of a common person's house, the home of any well-off urban resident. His Little One was now the queen. Could it be possible that a queen would be put in an ordinary basket, to live among the common people? Could it have been because they were Tay tribespeople? Could it be that a Tay queen was not entitled to the same privileges as one who was pure Vietnamese?

Though torn by these thoughts, An had not given them any voice. For both women were at the zenith of joy. The war was over, now they could be certain that they would live. After so many years of separation, now was the time of reunion. No one could ask for more than that. Now all three of them could sit around the same tray table of food. And if it was not quite like being in the old huge house on stilts, surrounded on all sides by deep forest, it was still the comfortable upper floor of a small house, the dwelling of city people.

After dinner, An had asked Little One, "Is the president happy that you live here?"

"Oh yes. He says that we have to live simply. Like the common people."

"It means, then, that you are happy, right?"

"Yes . . . I am happy. I love him."

"Does he love you?"

"Of course," Little One had replied, raising her voice. "He's very much in love with me . . ." Her cheeks had suddenly reddened. "He's a very good husband."

That night, while cradling Nang Dong, An asked, "Let me know, is our Little One truly happy?"

"Yes, she is. You don't have to worry. She is very, very happy. Though he is old, the president is still potent in bed."

"How do you know?"

"Being from the mountain, we are not shy about these things. I have directly asked Little One about it. She says that in having sex with the president she is happier than with her first lover."

"Is that so? In that case I can feel at ease."

He was at ease for about two years. At times though, he became unhappy when he rode his bicycle around the quarters reserved for the generals and the main architects of the regime and observed how their ethnic Vietnamese wives lived in separate villas, surrounded by trees and gardens, with guards standing in front and Volga cars to run their errands.

Then when the president's first child, a daughter, was born, joy made him forget both his unhappiness and his jealousy. Each Sunday, An would ride into the city feeling like a child going to a festival or an adolescent guy going to meet his love. Now he could be a father and Nang Dong a real mother. They no longer had to slow-cook mung bean congee and milk female buffalo. Life in the metropolis may have been confined somewhat but things were much more convenient, and both of them found themselves as excited as a forest going into spring whenever the baby laughed. All that time, the baby's real mother could afford to sleep her fill or watch them take care of her bastard child with eyes full of satisfaction.

An never met the president in that house because he could stay only until 6:30 p.m. on Sunday. After dinner, he had to ride his bike back to Ha Dong before the night bugle sounded at 9:30. He knew that the office of the president usually had Little One summoned to go to the palace to be with him, but on occasion when he could arrange it, the president would go to visit his wife and daughter around midnight—it was the president himself who had given the daughter her name. An ancient name, ethically meaningful: Nghia ("Duty").

When first told of this, An was somewhat frustrated: "There're lots of fine names, why give her, my niece, such a straitjacketed name? In my company there are at least three guys with that name: Tran Trung Nghia, Dao Duy Nghia, and Ngo Thanh Nghia . . ."

"Oh, don't be angry." Little One smiled. "She's the president's daughter."

His wife, Nang Dong, also joined in: "She's right. Being the father, he has the right to name her."

An didn't answer.

But starting the following week, he started calling the baby by the name that he had come up with for her: "She's born in the year of the goat, so I'll call her Mui. In this way she will be easy to take care of. Come, Mui, come here to your uncle."

"Ba . . . ba . . ."

The baby could emit these sounds by the time she was nine months old. Her tongue was found to be pointed. No other baby could speak as early as she did. Her lips were the red color of a lobster while her smile was an exact copy of her father's.

The following year when Mui was one full year old, An bought a rattan chair and attached to it a bicycle frame. Putting the baby in it, he carried her around to all the surrounding streets. On many occasions, uncle and baby went back and forth in front of the president's palace. The baby would babble away while he peered at the palace as if he were looking at a mysterious castle or a ghostly fortress. To the man who lived there, the man An had never met or exchanged a word with, he would whisper: "Mr. President, do you see your daughter sitting on this simple bicycle of mine? You may be the most powerful figure in this land, but you are only a brother-in-law to me. For I am married to the older sister while you are the husband of the younger one, so if we were at a wine party now you would have to pour wine for me to drink. That's how it is with the customary law of the Tay."

Years of plenitude and seasons of abundance usually come unexpectedly. Who could have predicted that, when Mui was eleven months old, Little One would become pregnant for the second time? She had suddenly become sleepy all the time, drifting off even during meals. And little Mui, still nursing, had come down with diarrhea. No one was quite sure what was happening when an old lady neighbor said:

"This means that the mother is pregnant with child, so her milk is now contaminated . . . If a baby drinks contaminated milk, then nothing can stop the diarrhea. How come no one knows this?"

"Oh, truly, no one knows this," Nang Dong had replied.

It was clear that little Mui had to be weaned right away. Fortunately, being a very good baby, she cried for only two nights then turned to taking powdered milk, sucking loudly on the bottle. It was also the case that she had been sleeping with Nang Dong, to the point where she was much more used to the smell of her aunt than to that of her own mother. It was said that the firstborn in any family tends to be somewhat slow, not very smart. But Baby Mui was extraordinarily smart. On Saturdays, as soon as the sun started to set, she would go out to the balcony to wait for her uncle Thanh.

The flow of people rolling through the street did not confuse her. Sometimes she waved her hand as soon as she saw him stop for a red light at the intersection. The black Vinh Cuu bicycle without mudguards was well known to her, as it promised many a fun ride. As An pulled the bicycle up on the curb, he would look up to the balcony and could see her right away with her ingratiating smile, her face radiant and her black eyes shining. On occasion An almost felt like he were still living in Xiu Village. For, in those faraway years, in the evenings when he and Nang Dong would come home carrying firewood, Little One would be waiting for them at the corner of the house on stilts with the same quiet and radiant smile now displayed by little Mui.

Their gentle, sweet life continued until the day Little One gave birth to her second child, in the year of the monkey, Binh Than (1956). One Saturday afternoon, when he was just about to step into the house, Nang Dong rushed out, took hold of his neck, and, with a face showing both pride and mystery, solemnly and mysteriously whispered: "A boy. Three point six kilograms. Fifty-eight centimeters long."

"Oh, that's wonderful, we have now both sweet and long-grain rice," he answered.

Nang Dong was taken aback for a second then looked at him and said, "It's funny what you say."

"How? Did I say anything wrong or mistaken, making you laugh?"

"No, it's neither wrong nor mistaken." She smilingly looked at him: "It's not just a question of sweet rice and long grain. Do you forget how extremely important a boy is to a father?"

"Of course, I understand the importance of a boy to continue the line. From now on I will let you take care of the new baby, the VIP, and I will take care of little Mui, since she is the less important one."

"Are you going to the hospital to visit Little One?"

"No, tomorrow I will go to the market, prepare dinner, and take Mui to the zoo so she can watch the tigers and the bears. Going to the hospital will be your responsibility."

An did not understand why he reacted so. He can still remember the wild-eyed look of his wife at his answer. That look followed him as he went inside. It obsessed him like a problem without a solution. It was not until very much later that he realized it was instinct that had told him to behave as he did. That he already had the premonition that black and sinister shadows of vulture wings were spreading above their heads at the moment Nang Dong told him the news, news that should have brought extreme joy to anyone. The next day, he took Mui to the zoo on his bicycle. On the way back, she insisted on stopping in front of the president's palace so she could watch the guards. But they had not been there for more than a few minutes before the guards approached and asked for their papers. An showed his military ID.

The guard examined the paper carefully, then said, "This is a protected zone. You should take her to another place."

"I didn't want to bother you. It's only that she wants to see."

At that moment, little Mui spoke up: "I see soldiers."

Probably because of the innocent babbling of the child, the soldier felt softhearted so he went away. Nonetheless, An's heart clouded up. He looked at the house behind the pruned trees.

"What happiness is it when the father lives in a castle while his daughter sits outside looking in? What use is this twisted love affair? Had Little One failed to catch the eyes of the old king, she would have found a husband more fitting for her circumstances. In the countryside there is no lack of happy marriages. Our house on stilts was three times as large as these cramped homes in the city. Particularly the house of the father-in-law: a whole sawmill could fit in just one of its big rooms. We had land, buffalo by the herd, and pigs galore. The hundreds of hens we had laid so many eggs that we couldn't eat them all. We had woods and streams, wild and domesticated bees, and animals to hunt. Sure, life is more convenient and civilized here but land is at a premium and people's generosity is a luxury. Did we make a mistake by leaving the mountains to come here?"

He had not finished thinking along those lines when another soldier from the guard post approached. He looked to be the officer in charge of the guards. He said in a dry, unmistakable voice, "This is a zone that requires strict security. I suggest that you take the child elsewhere."

Not bothering to answer him, An turned to Mui and said, "We can't stay here, baby. Uncle will take you to Ngoc Ha market and I'll buy you a ball. Do you hear?"

Then he climbed on the bike and pedaled away. He could not help but feel angry:

"Hey, man, you who are the father of this little girl here," he whispered to the brother-in-law he had never met. "Could you ever have imagined this situation? A child stands in front of her biological father's house yet is not allowed to enter; nay, not even to look at it. A child who is chased away from the entrance to her father's house. Does a crazy situation like this, I wonder, make you feel bad, my president? Now your daughter is too small to understand it. But later, when she grows up, will she consider you to be a decent father or will she think that you have been an insensitive, heartless person willing to throw away the very blood of your offspring? Can it be that your splendid, magnificent palace does not have a room to accommodate your wife and children? Or is there a secret, a black reason, why you accept our Little One living with the common people? Could it be because she comes from the mountains that she is forced to undergo the persecution of your court? The very court that periodically comes out with orders that ethnic minorities are to be privileged!"

The suspicions and anger that had been buried in his soul all these years suddenly surfaced. So did curses; they sprouted and multiplied in his brain like a forest of bamboo shoots emerging in the spring. Without noticing, he ended up biking around and returning to Hoang Dieu Street, so he could further mark in his mind the appearance of these magnificent palatial residences now occupied by the pillars of the new imperial order. Afterward, he continued riding through Phan Dinh Phung Street so as to take another look at other residential palaces, palaces the occupants of which he had learned by heart, so that hatred and grudges kept on boiling in the quiet lake of his soul.

"These are palaces reserved for tiny-eyed and black-lipped society ladies and not for our Little One, even though she is a thousand times more beautiful."

As he processed these thoughts he noticed a minister's wife ride by in a Volga, her neck shortened by the layers of fat that rose all the way to her chin, and her eyes tiny slits the thinness of a thread watching the streets in full haughtiness. That afternoon the weather was gorgeous but An could not escape being drowned in dark thoughts. Was he pitying Mui? Or Little One? Or could it be that he felt his impotence before fate? It was not until that evening when his wife came back from the hospital with the happy face of a child who had just gotten a gift that he could temporarily put aside his bitter observations.

Nang Dong told him, "In three days we will bring Little One home. I won't have to take the meals in to her."

"Is she in good health?"

"Our Little One?" His wife laughed. "She is fine and happy. But I can see that you are biased toward women. You don't ask about the newborn."

He burst out laughing. "It's because the whole society is already biased toward the males, that's why I do the reverse. Don't you like it?"

"Yes, I do," she responded at once. An knew that Nang Dong was extremely happy to be by his side. He was a liberal type who did not care for richness or wealth. Neither did he care too much about descendants. The years of study at the district school had given him an outlook entirely different from other men his age. This came somewhat like a gift from the creator. On many occasions his wife had asserted, "Oh, how lucky that we live on two sides of the same hill!"

And he would rejoin: "Lucky that I had a neighboring girl already waiting for me when I was born."

Nang Dong gave a twist to his answer: "You mean because I am older than you, by fifteen days?"

"You could have been older than I by fifteen years, you would still be my wife. That was what destiny had in mind."

"Gosh! . . ." his wife burst out. "You must be the most clever liar on earth."

Their conversations always ended in laughter. An had yet to see another couple as close as they were. When they were young, he did not in the least doubt his happiness. But after Little One gave birth to the boy, a cloudy premonition lodged permanently in his mind, even when he was at his happiest. He would remember the quotations he had learned from the history professor, the one teacher to whom he owed most while studying in That Khe district.

"Beautiful women are like flowers; they blossom early and die in the evening, because blue heaven has bestowed upon them a gorgeous beauty that causes many people to covet and envy them."

The beauty of Nang Dong and her sister had only grown more and more pronounced, to the point of surprising him. Time, it seems, had no effect on them; on the contrary, the months and years seemed to have matured their beauty, making them more attractive, more mysterious. On numerous occasions An had witnessed passersby stop, struck dumb by the sisters' beauty; they looked at them as if they were seeing river or mountain goddesses. In Hanoi, one could "light torches to illuminate the forest" and never find that kind of beauty—enough to make fish stop swimming and birds fall to earth.

An felt like he had been in love with Nang Dong since the day he was born. It was only much later that he realized his wife surely must have provoked desires on the part of men who came across her. In that way, he came to understand why the old king could fall head over heels in love with Little One. It's impossible for any man not to be moved by the sharp-swordlike beauty of such women, who, besides, have simple and holy souls that promise years of family happiness. Although Nang Dong was totally un-aware of all these things, An realized that he was in possession of a mag-nificent fortress. To protect that fortress, one needed both intelligence and courage. The pride inside him was always accompanied by vigilance. In the case of Little One, did the old king think like he did, he wondered. Or could it be that, given the fact that he was the king, instead of treasuring the rare love of a soul like hers, he would give himself the luxury of considering her beauty to be no more than an exotic dish?

These dark thoughts he dared not express to anyone. An did not want to burden the minds of the two sisters, whom he loved more than he loved himself. He became a silent witness to all their happy and joyful and hopeful conversations.

"Will you go to the Presidential Palace tomorrow?"

"Yes. A driver will come for me at nine."

"Have you thought really hard about what you will need to tell him?"

"There is not much to prepare. I will tell him only one simple sentence: since we have now both a boy and a girl, we need to legitimize our relation-ship before the law."

"That will do. Tomorrow will be a busy day. I will prepare dinner earlier than usual, and you should remember to breast-feed the boy at eight."

The following day was a Sunday. An took little Mui out in the morning, telling the two women that he would be home late. At lunch, he took his niece to a pho restaurant, then to the circus for the three o'clock matinee. After the circus, they went home. Little Mui went straight to sleep while he quickly gobbled down some food so he could get back to his barracks. He did not ask at all about how Little One's meeting with the father of her chil-dren had gone. An still remembers the questioning look of his wife as she was ironing her sister's dresses. As for Little One, she was so busy feeding the boy that she did not have time to worry about the unusual silence of her brother-in-law. Or it may have been that she was so filled with happiness and projections of the future that she was not paying much attention to what was going on around her.

An blamed himself for having been so strangely indifferent; an inde-scribable sadness was tearing him apart. So one day passed after another. Whether he was in training or out on exercises with the soldiers, An felt like he was living in a dream, as if his feet were not on the ground but walk-ing in the clouds. He could not understand why. Sometimes his memories took him back to Xiu Village, with reflections on happy days. At other times memory took him back to That Khe town, to the school where he had stood way above the other students. Or he would picture the tea-fragrant house of his history professor, whose wife was a jasmine tea merchant. He had sometimes come by to help the family fold tea bags while listening to the professor tell all sorts of stories, both apocryphal ones and official ones from Chinese history or from Vietnam's own dynasties, tales from the *San Guo Ji* (Romance of the Three Kingdoms) or *Dong Zhou Lie Guo* (The Vassal Countries of Eastern Zhou), which the professor knew by heart. At other times he felt his heart oppressed with a vague concern that was surrounding him like a gigantic spiderweb.

One Saturday evening, after military exercises, An grabbed a bicycle. After going only a few hundred meters, the front inner tube exploded. He found a repairman, who explained, "Sorry, Comrade. There is no way to fix it. You need a new one."

"Please try real hard. We don't live in a time when I can be given a new inner tube."

"I already looked carefully. I promise you: if I can't fix it, no one can. That's guaranteed."

There was no option but to take the bike back to camp and borrow one that usually carried food. Because the food bike had priority, its inner tubes were always new. The food team lent him the bike on the condition that it be returned the next day at noon so that they could have enough time to get to the afternoon market. After arguing awhile, An was able to extend the time to 3:30. That would give him enough time to take Mui to see the music and dances of the town's youth group. Content with his victory, An hurriedly pedaled to Hanoi. By the time he arrived, the streetlights were already on. Mui was not standing on the balcony waiting for him as usual; he was definitely late, he thought to himself as he walked the bike through the long hall under dim lights. In the yard, he saw little Mui playing with two other kids, the grandchildren of an old lady in the neighborhood. Seeing him, the little girl rushed out to kiss his cheeks.

An wanted to take the girl to the house, but the old neighbor said, "Just leave her here to play . . . her mother told me so . . ."

This seemed odd, but An didn't feel comfortable asking anything further of the old lady. He went upstairs, where the two women were waiting for him by a tray table with food. Seeing their faces, he understood half of the truth, but he said, laughing, "You must be about to faint from hunger, right? Sorry I'm late. Let me wash my face and then we can eat. I had to borrow the bike from the food team; mine has a burst inner tube."

"The army doesn't even have enough inner tubes to use?" his wife asked.

"Inner tubes are rationed for all government-issue bikes. And the priorities do not extend to shirts, underwear, rice, and food. What do you have to feed me today?" An said, changing the subject.

Dong replied, "Today I made banana shoots with steamed pork and Vietnamese shrimp paste."

"Next meal, I suggest you cook traditional sour beef soup."

"People say that the sour beef soup of Lang Son is better than ours in That Khe, because they add spices to the broth—grilled onion and ginger, cinnamon, star anise, and other things—as secret ingredients. If you want, when I am free I will go to Mam Street to try it out. After eating it a few times I will figure out the recipe."

"Yes, why don't you try that? Lang Son sour soup has been famous for a long time."

Thanks to this dialogue, they were able to forget temporarily all the troubles and finish their meal. But when tea was served, he could not pretend to be cheerful. The gigantic spiderweb encircling them was pulling tight its choking threads. He was the male, the eldest of the family; he must be the first one to speak the truth:

"Now, let's deal with our issue. I am waiting to hear."

Little One was still silent but his wife said, "On Sunday, the issue was presented to the president; he agreed but had to wait for the consensus of the Politburo. On Monday the subject was brought up because that was the day of a regularly scheduled meeting. But the president's idea was not accepted. Not one supporting vote."

"For what reason?"

"Because they do not want the president to have his own family. They want the president to be only the elderly father of all the people. Thus . . . thus, that was the resolution of the Politburo."

"They forced the president to accept their decision? Or did the president want to follow them?"

Dong remained quiet. Neither his wife nor Little One could reply. But An wanted to get to the core of the issue. He asked Little One:

"You saw the Old Man what day after that meeting?"

"Friday. Around eleven a.m., the president sent a car to pick me up."

"How did he explain it?"

"The president said that, by Party principle, the minority has to surrender to the majority."

"Did he say anything else?"

"He said that he knows I have suffered lots of disappointments . . . that we have to be patient and live in the shadows for a while to wait for an opportune moment to persuade the Politburo members."

"When he said that, how did his face look?"

"I don't remember, because I was bent over, wiping my tears."

"Was he smiling or crying?"

"The president was also crying. He held me and said, 'They really lack compassion, they have no empathy for us.'"

"'Us' here is who?"

Little One looked at him as if she did not understand what he was trying to say.

An answered himself: "'Us' here means he, you, and the two kids. To speak naturally: four individuals in one family. If it were a normal family, then it would be a complete family.

In the same instant, another bitter question arose in his mind: "Unfortunately there is another and different 'us.' That 'us' is a small group that includes me, my wife, and you—three related people who cannot be separated; a relationship that is living and intimate. This relationship stands outside the president's awareness as well as his concern. But ironically, what happens to him will strike our heads like the sword of destiny. It will not bring on glory or wealth but, for sure, nothing but painful loss. Intuition never lies to us."

He looked at Little One's sad eyes and his heart hurt. What would he do now? What could he do to salvage the situation, to protect his loved ones from the wicked wind? He: the only man in this tiny family. Why did destiny push them to this point? An felt suffocated. He stood up to open the windows facing the yard. He turned around and said:

"Dear one: now we must be calm to think. I do not clearly understand the Politburo's intentions. In the past vigilance was needed when a king became too enamored of a queen. Especially when the king was old and the wife was young and beautiful. The worry of our national leaders is based on the corrupting experiences of history: Duong Minh Hoang was passionate about Duong Qui Phi; Tru Vuong was enamored with Dat Ki. In our history, General Trinh Sam was passionate with Dang Thi Hue. But all these cases are totally different from our situation. All these beauties of Chinese kings lived in luxury with silks and precious jewelry. Each step Duong qui Phi took was on a water lily made of gold. Dat Ki's castle was decorated with silk and brocade and each of her meals was worth several taels of gold and her coach was carved from jade and made with gold from its cushions to its roof. Then, court mistress Dang Thi Hue of our country, relying on Lord Trinh Sam's love for her, freely abused gold and silver, brought many relatives to the court, and covered for her brutal brother Dang Mau Lan. Wherever he went, Mau Lan robbed people of their wealth. Whomever he met, women or young girls, if they pleased his eyes, he would order his soldiers to set up curtains in the middle of the marketplace so he could rape them over and over. Whoever dared resist, he would kill them right then. His brutality and troublemaking angered both the people and the court officials. Many complaints submitted to the king requesting punishment for Mau Lan were all ordered by his relative in the palace, Mau Phi, to be torn up or burned. In the end, an officer stabbed him to death then voluntarily turned himself in to Trinh Sam. In contrast to those three cases, we have no connection to luxury or brutality. We live here like below-average people. I am the only male in this family, and I have never robbed or raped anyone. Your children were born in the most plebeian of clinics, with no medical staff from the president's office. Little Mui and her sibling have grown up just like any other kid in a low-level cadre's family. We have never had any benefit or advantage; we have never touched any property or power of the state. How can they treat us like this?"

Nobody could answer him. Both women cried gently, their heads lowered. An understood that no one could answer him other than heaven itself, but only if heaven would be moved by compassion for their situation. But he had never encountered such a heavenly being. The various spirits and the souls of all the ancestors that they worship were often mere smoke that floated over the altars on New Year. Now he did not know where to find the mind of heaven.

"Do you dare ask the Old Man directly about what I have said?" An asked, his voice rising, and Little One cried louder, her sobbings more pronounced. His wife looked at him, begging. Anger continued to overflow in him as a pot of rice soup comes to a boil on a simmering fire.

"Little One, you must ask him for clarity, for your life, and the life of your children."

"I did ask, but the president said he must live as an example. And that, if I love him, I have to accept that. And when the two children grow up, the situation will change."

"When the kids grow up? Heavens, he is now over sixty! Will we have to wait for him to get to be eighty in order to live in an official manner with the people? How sad for our Little One! How bitter for the children of an old king! Our nephews—kids who, whether they like it or not, are related by a blood tie . . ."

Then another question rushed to him that he could not suppress: "Dear one: Do you truly love him?"

Little One looked at him, perplexed: "What are you asking?"

"I want to ask if you truly love him or do you love him just because he is the country's president?"

"I love the president . . . I love . . ." she replied, then burst into stronger sobbing.

Dong looked at him, angry: "What's the matter with you? Did a horsefly bite you?"

"No," An replied awkwardly. He realized that his anger had pushed him too far. Perhaps he had wished for his sister-in law to have a different destiny. The strings of a tragic destiny had tied her up with an old king—an old king she happened to love. Love is so tauntingly unsettled! Not because he was someone with high position but foremost because he was a good husband, even though only a husband on occasion.

"Is this old man a good talker, a great flirt with women?" he wondered to himself, but immediately he intuited that this old king was not a good talker in that way but was able to move Little One's heart with soft and passionate words that younger men couldn't summon forth; that he could make her love him by tender and sweet gestures that locals were incapable of performing—all the foreign manners that he had acquired from the West. Such strength was not that of a hunter who raises his rifle to aim at his prey, because it was not intended to harm the prey but only sought to conquer its heart. Such strength was shapeless but he sensed it forcefully as if it were a fire burning. Such strength he had held in his hands as well. He thought back to warm nights in Xiu Village, when he would return from the town of That Khe. In the spacious house with dancing light full of neighbors, his uncle would have prepared a large container of wine. The deep wooden tray would be full of savory appetizers along with cakes and fruit. His aunt would have roasted a basketful of sunflower seeds before preparing tea to serve the guests. The neighbors, old and young, would sit around the room. Standing in the center, the student would recount all the stoic, pastoral, and magic stories of the lowlands as well as ones from other mountain regions—the complete warehouse of knowledge that his teacher in the district school had handed down to him. His uncle, sitting next to him, would give him a look both loving and proud, bending his head to conceal his pride from the guests.

His uncle was renowned for his salve made of tiger, bear, and deer horn gelatin. Knowledgeable and wealthy people everywhere would come for gobs of the thick, pasty ointment produced in his house. The very money the uncle had made from selling those jellied ointments had been used to pay for seven years of An's education. But when hearing An praise the sound of a Truong Luong flute or comment on the death of Quan Van Truong or describe the Bach Dang battle with a shout of "Sat That," the uncle would feel the admiration of those who are illiterate before one who is fluent in reading and writing. And that admiration walked very close to the edge of fear or passion. The conquering power gained by becoming cultured had been the most important conditioning agent during An's youth, even though he had been only a secondary student. An understood that all he knew was only one small grain of sand compared with the president, who had traveled to the four corners of the world for twenty years, who spoke both Chinese and Western languages. His stored intelligence was thousands of times larger than his own, and thus, that Little One loved him was not a strange thing.

"Yes, you are a thousand times capable and powerful. But nonetheless, you came into this family's home after me. Before the ancestral altar of the two women, I have the right to light incense. Now, under these circumstances, my wife and I are those who will care for your offspring. In the end, you will be indebted to us, dear old king."

That evening passed ponderously. Later in bed, Dong held him tight. They made love in a quiet way, like their first time by the stream of Son Ca Falls, at the age of fifteen with all the welling up of a wild and boiling zeal. He slept till nearly noon the next day. When he woke, his wife had gone to market and Little One had taken the two kids down to the yard to play with the old lady neighbor. An opened the window wide to look at the three of them playing under the old tree. His eyes were glued to that scene but his mind was all foggy, and totally empty; not one thought appeared distinctly. Not one feeling could he put into words. An felt that he had become a wooden statue that could walk around and talk, but was devoid of feelings. He remained in that unreal state for a long while until his wife returned. Dong put the food basket on the floor and looked attentively at her husband. Then, as if feeling his strange mental state, she took him into the bedroom, where she held his head gently, pressing it against her bosom. Her familiar warm flesh and the tender softness of his love made him slowly rise from the cold water of his emotional numbness. He burst into tears. He cried loudly like a woman; painfully, like one who is hungry and cold; he cried like a child lost in a train station.

4

The following Saturday, An would have no time to cry.

As he pedaled his bike up to the house, three soldiers dressed in civilian clothes, including Nong Tai, the only Tay tribesman in the security guards, looked at him with dark eyes like those of the monster bats that live in deep caves. It was as if their gaze contained a frightening but silent scream, a suppressed fear. An nodded his head in greeting, then walked to the corridor. Those dark looks from the security guards followed him, withering his spine like a kind of hot, molten lead. But his heart did not pound hastily as before. A week had been enough for him to have thought about and planned for all contingencies that could happen to his family. The treasury of history stored in his memory helped him prepare to act. Stepping inside the house, An closed the doors behind him tightly and was surprised to find the two women holding each other and crying. It was all they could do. Their cries were ones of fear and rage. It was no longer sadness over their destiny but the reproachful lament of those who had been stampeded, raped, who live in fear before a death that slowly approaches like a hearse that will someday haul them away. An stepped forward, not waiting for the women to speak. He saw right away the swollen, purple, beaten face of Little One. He sat down, holding her arms and pulling up her shirt to see the scratches, bruises, and scars left by the ropes.

"Who tortured you?"

"Quoc Tuy!"

"The minister of the interior? The one who ambushed you when you were at the northern front?"

Little One nodded.

An turned to his wife and asked, "Where were you then?"

"I was in the yard with the children and the old neighbor. As I stepped inside the house, he chased me back into the yard. I could not resist because he pulled out his gun and threatened to shoot out my brains if I screamed."

"Even if you screamed, it would only be heard by the old lady and the three guards. It is not without reason that they arranged for all of you to be in this house. That miserable bastard came here what day?"

"He came every day from Monday until today. Each time at about three in the afternoon. Each time he ordered the soldiers out to the streets to stop anyone who might enter the corridor. Each time they beat and tied up our sister." Then his wife screamed: "It is so humiliating, Husband."

Holding the smooth arms of Little One, he asked, "What did he say to you, that dog from the highlands?"

"He said he had had eyes for me since the resistance, when he met me crossing the stream; that if I were smart, I would have agreed to be his wife since that day; that he had sworn that, sooner or later, he would have me."

"Then what?"

"I told him I am the wife of the president; that we have a son and daughter, that he cannot rape me. He showed his teeth, laughing that the old man of mine was far away; that he wouldn't hear my screams. Here he is the king, he said; he can have whomever he wants. If he wants to kill someone, the person will be killed. Now he wanted me to lie under his belly. Because that was the Politburo's order. The Politburo had decided that I will be his wife. 'Think about it,' he said, 'I am much younger than that old man of yours. If his stick is made of wood, mine is made of steel. If he takes you to the third heaven, I will take you to the ninth one. If he gives you two kids, I will give you twelve, one after the other. Be smart, shut your mouth, and spread your legs.'"

At each part of her recounting, her tears flowed.

An felt red-hot steel pellets rolling around in his heart. An episode from history returned, resonating in his ears: "The government was cowardly, therefore Dang Phi slept with the Ngu military lord, leaning on this officer to protect her troubled and promiscuous son, Dang Mau Lan."

He thought: "My sister-in-law did not decide to sleep with a Ngu military general, but she is raped, humiliated, and tortured. Then this old king is ten times more cowardly than were the Trinh Lords of years past. The peril cannot be overcome. If I don't run fast and fly far, my whole family will be turned into headless ghosts, wandering forever in darkness. My sister-in-law's painful injustice will be permanently consigned to silence and then forgotten. Each woman's life will be abandoned like a corpse bobbing on waves. My sister-in-law did not sin. From childhood to adulthood, she never said one word that hurt anyone. Her soul is childlike and pure. Her goodness measures three times more full than that of all the people who surround her. I have to survive to clear her of dishonor. I have to live to be witness to this horrible, brutal act."

The teacher in That Khe district had taught him that the profession of writing history is the profession of heroes, daring to exchange their own lives for truth. Because all kings fear truth, they want historians to bend their pens to write as commanded. So many heads of historians have fallen under the swords of imperial executioners, but history is continuously written with their dry, blackened blood.

"Thus I must become a historian. Not one who writes about the nation's history, but one who will record the lives of my loved ones."

He held both women tight, looking at them for the last time so as to permanently register the images in his heart as well as his mind. Then he asked his wife, "How many rings do you have left?"

"Altogether five."

"Keep the smallest one I made for you when we married. Give me the rest. As for cash, maybe we do not have much, but give me some to spend along the roads."

"No, we have quite a bit of cash stored since last year. Let me give all to you."

"How much?"

"About fifty thousand."

"I only need half of it. Keep the other half for food."

His wife went into the bedroom. He looked at her svelte back and thought: "You will not have the chance to go to the market, or cook Lang Son sour soup, my beloved wife. Our life together has been cut short like a stalk of rice at the harvest. Oh heaven, the day Little One was presented to the king was the very day disaster came to roost in our family. And changing our surname from Nong to Chi was about as stupid as you can get."

Dong returned with a stack of paper bills in one hand. In the other she held a small case the size of a chicken's gizzard. Putting the pile of money on the table, she opened the case and pulled out a string of rings, of the large size without stones or carvings, the kind long-distance merchants carry as cash.

"You must put the gold in your underwear. I sewed a pocket inside the waistband."

"I understand."

"Put the bills into many different pockets in your clothes. If you lose some from one, you will still have more in the others."

"I understand."

"And you must take along the vial of ointment for colds and the medication for stomachaches. There is also a flashlight, a lighter, a knife for the woods, and snakebite antidote. Is it complete?"

"All are in the duffel bag."

"Let me see your duffel bag."

"Nothing is missing," An answered while thinking to himself, "The one most important thing missing is you, and our Little One; because I cannot take you along on this journey of misery. But we will see each other in the other world, another land, the meeting place of all living things. We will meet again. But all my beloved ones, before we meet again, I must do this to make things right."

For the last time, he bent down to embrace the two women with a hard squeeze, to smell the intimate scent of their shiny and straight hair, rubbing his face against their smooth faces. Then he stood up.

"Don't go to the door. Don't follow me. Kiss the kids for me."

"You . . . !" Both cried out.

He lowered his voice: "Don't cry. Look as if nothing has happened. We have no other way."

He went down the stairs, not turning back even once.

In the hallway, An called Nong Tai over and said, "Do you have money in your pocket? Can you lend me ten thousand? I planned to buy some stuff and ask someone to bring it back home, but I did not take enough money."

Nong Tai looked at him. "When will you pay me back?"

"Next week. Oh, I forgot . . . Payday is in two weeks, at which time I will repay you right away, not a day later."

"In my pocket I have only enough to buy a couple of sesame balls. I left my money in the barracks."

"It is almost time for changing the guard. Will you see if the comrades will let you leave one hour early?"

"OK, let me ask."

The corridor was long enough that their conversation would not have been heard by the two other guards. He knew that the ruse would succeed because usually highland people do not know how to lie. Three minutes later Nong Tai returned.

"Let's go; the two comrades agreed I can leave early. We will go to where I left my bike so we can cycle back to the camp."

"Agreed."

They left together. When Nong Tai had his bike, the two quietly rode through three streets; they were convinced that nobody had followed them.

"Let's stop at the sidewalk," An said.

Nong Tai understood him immediately and got down from his bike. The two went up on the sidewalk and stood under the shade of a tree.

An asked, "Do the other two guys know that sooner or later they will die?"

"Nobody says anything but all three of us quietly understand it will be so. We have the afternoon shift. The thing always happens in the afternoon, therefore only the three of us witness it. The other group has the shift from midnight until noon the next day; they know nothing."

"So why didn't you three plan an escape?"

"Where to escape now? Every morning they call roll before going to exercise; in the afternoon they do it before bedtime. However, if they want to escape they will not talk to me because I am a Tay. And I, I cannot plan with them at all. Because they are Vietnamese. Minister Quoc Tuy is Vietnamese like them and Miss Xuan is a Tay like me."

"Do you think they suspect that I have asked you to escape?"

"No."

"Why?"

"Because they think we are people of the mountains: trustworthy and stupid; that we would not dare to do so."

"Good. Because we are stupid, we will escape death. And they are from the lowlands and smart; therefore, they hold in their hands certain death. Now there is not much time. We have to get to the train station; hopefully we will not miss the train, thanks to the public security pass that you have."

"But . . . what about my clothes and money in the barracks?"

"Are you crazy? It's better to live naked than die draped in a military uniform in a coffin. Let's go."

They biked straight to the Hang Co station. There, the two bought tickets for Vinh to the south. As An predicted, Nong Tai's public security pass helped. It gave them priority to buy tickets under the justification of being sent on "special duty." As soon as they boarded the train, its engine whistled and it pulled out of the station. An put down his duffel behind his back then sat down, his eyes gazing out the window.

"Farewell to you, city of my enemies; a city I had dreamed of for so many months when I was still at the northern front; a city I thought was a paradise but which has now turned into a hell. This is the very place that will be the dark tomb in which my loved ones will be buried forever. Farewell, you gigantic and atrocious monster."

So he thought as he set eyes on Hanoi for the last time.

"Brother Thanh," said Nong Tai, "Brother Thanh, I am thinking . . ."

"About what?"

"Why are we going south? By advancing deeply into the flat plains of the central provinces, we will be like foxes caught in the open fields, like fish thrown up on the hills. Why don't we turn back to That Khe? There we know all the main roads and shortcuts. We know the streams and forests. Anywhere we hide, we can dig up roots or trap animals to keep ourselves alive."

"Stupid: That Khe is the first place they will look. We cannot hide forever in the woods. Moreover, even if we escape the encircling net and cross over the border, we will fall into the hands of Chinese soldiers. They will immediately turn us back over to the Vietnamese government."

"But in the central provinces, a strange place?"

"Only in a strange place can we hope to escape. It is much shorter from Vinh to the border with Laos than from our homes to the northern border with China."

"How do you know that?"

"I must know to save myself. I must learn all the necessary details before I start the journey."

"But on the other side of the border is the land of the Lao. Do you know them or not?"

"The Lao and the Chinese are like the deer and the tiger. We cannot compare one with the other."

Their whispers were buried in the loud grinding of the steel wheels on the rails. Then An said, "Go to sleep."

"I am not sleepy yet. And it's hard to sleep with an empty stomach."

"Right. Nobody can sleep when they're hungry. Go to the cafeteria to buy some bread. After we eat, we will drink lots of water. It's easier to sleep with a full stomach. We must sleep to have strength for tomorrow."

Nong Tai got up and went to the cafeteria at the end of the train to buy two big loaves of bread sprinkled with salt and pepper and two containers of water. The two ate quietly then fell asleep sitting up. The train shook their heads as if they were bouncing rubber balls. They slept very soundly until the loudspeakers announced:

"The train is arriving at Vinh. Please check your luggage."

An opened his eyes wide. The train moved forward then stopped completely, and they got off, passing along the station platform in a fog. It was only four a.m. Horse carriages were lined up in a row outside the station. Their drivers sat around drinking tea or wine in the row of stalls along the street. To get government transportation you had to line up for at least ten hours until you could purchase a ticket.

An took Nong Tai for a stroll then focused on a driver with a daredevil air and a handlebar mustache.

"Hello to you. We have a special assignment up on the border. Do you think you can help the two of us?"

"Who are you?"

"We are public security and a military officer. Here is an identification certificate for the two of us."

"Public security and a military officer enjoy priority for government transportation. Every three days there is a car going to the border crossing. You comrades rent a room and inform the local police to make arrangements. There will be a departure the day after tomorrow in the morning."

"Our assignment is an emergency. We cannot wait."

"But you comrades cannot hire our horse carriages. Going up the mountain road is very expensive. Here, we usually take passengers going only to towns around Vinh."

"We can pay no matter how expensive. The agency will reimburse us."

The horse carriage driver looked at them with suspicion: "A carriage usually takes eight passengers."

An interrupted him: "We will buy eight tickets plus the cost of luggage for eight. We hope you accept."

"OK . . . let me see."

"And we will pay additionally for the feeding of the horses on bad roads. If you need to change the horses along the road, we are ready to cover that, too. As long as we can make good time to complete our assignment."

"OK!"

The driver stood up with an unexpected swiftness. He pulled out some change to pay the woman for his tea then took the two men to his horse carriage.

An gave him two-thirds of the fare, adding, "The balance I will pay when we see the border post appearing before our eyes."

"Comrade, you are a very generous person. Therefore heaven has led you to meet up with me. To say it straight, my horse is number one among all the horses that run in this town," he explained with great pride. "No horse would dare go against mine up the road to the border, because I am the only one who feeds his horses corn mixed with honey. The others feed their horses only hay all year 'round."

After carefully putting the money in his shirt pocket, the driver climbed onto his seat and turned the carriage completely around to go west.

As he listened to the galloping of the horseshoes on the road, An stuck his neck out to look around.

"Vinh is not much larger than the town of That Khe. But the style of the houses here is a bit different. Why are we seeing all these red-painted barrels like that one?"

"You comrades are here for the first time, right?" asked the driver.

"Yes. Exactly correct," An said.

The driver pointed his whip to the rows of rolling mountains at the horizon ahead and said, "The Lao wind blows from the west. It is so fierce that wherever it blows, everything dries and easily burns up. The government distributes those red-painted barrels for families to store water. Lazy ones who let the barrels get low will be reported and will be warned or disciplined."

"The city fire department is paid with government salaries to do this work. Why force all the people?"

"The fire department here is three times larger than in other cities. But even if there were twenty times more firemen, they could not put out the fires brought by the Lao wind. The Lao wind is also called a fire wind; it starts the fires, no need for people's negligence in addition."

"Really! That is scary," An replied, thinking to himself: "Lao wind! How dangerous; and we are going toward that cavernous oven. No disasters are more dangerous than those created by people. There is nothing in nature more cruel than people going after one another."

Then he turned to tell Nong Tai, "Did you hear what the driver said? From today on we are going to operate in this hot Lao wind. Now we sleep to get some strength."

"The road shakes us like dice, how can we sleep?"

"Then just close your eyes."

The driver turned and added: "It's true; any minute you close your eyes is good for that minute. In a little while, when the sun rises, your eyes will be blinded as if needles were piercing them. Visitors from the north all complain about the hot sun of Nghe An."

"The birthplace of the president with the surname Chi!"

"That's totally correct," said the carriage driver, who then started singing: " 'A poor land gives birth to heroes . . .' "

"You sing really well," An praised him, with this thought in his mind: "Yes, indeed he is a hero. But he is also the greatest coward on this earth, a husband who cannot protect a wife; a father unable to protect his children."

Outside the city, houses became sparse. Looking back, Vinh was now only an undifferentiated mass under a couple of tall chimneys spewing dirty black smoke.

An asked the driver, "Can we get to the border before nighttime?"

"It depends: on the running legs of the horses; on whether it shines or rains. This time of year the weather is unpredictable; it may be sunny with bright blue skies, then suddenly, thundering, stormy rain comes. The meteorologists never predict accurately storms in the central region. But if we are lucky and the horses do not act up along the way, we will be at the border post when the sun is still high at one pole over the top of the mountains."

"About four p.m. then; is that what you want to say?"

"I do not look at time much. This profession binds us to the road day and night. But I remember when the carriage has reached there, the sun is higher than the mountain on the west by about one pole."

"The sooner the better. After the border, we still have to walk a long way."

An looked at the rows of dry hills ahead, which they must cross before reaching the border: they were empty and spacious; one could cast one's eyes all the way to the foot of the sky. Not a wood, not a mountain, but never-ending naked hills with low-growing thorny plants no taller than an arm is long and other kinds of ferns. If you were being chased here, your death was guaranteed.

An wondered if the That Khe border office had received an order to look for them yet. He can easily imagine what is going on back in Hanoi. First his own division, then that of Nong Tai, would report the disappearance of two from the "minorities." According to regulations, it would then take twenty-four hours for a search order to be issued, but, in this case, Minister Quoc Tuy would probably make a move sooner. On all the boats going up to Lang Son and Lao Cai, soldiers would be put on the lookout to catch the two "defectors." They would probably charge them with some crime to justify the order to "hunt down the criminals." If not a crime of robbing and killing, then it would be spying for foreigners. And that one would be the most convenient crime with which to arouse the hatred and spite of the people:

"They have become dangerous spies plotting to overthrow the government and taking money from foreigners. There is no other explanation."

An recalled all the times he had stood under the flag to swear loyally to fight for the nation, to destroy every enemy who threatened the socialist principle of the people. Now he has become that very enemy—he and Nong Tai sitting there, looking at the scenery. Life is a terrible fraud indeed that so many million people had become a powerless mass—each and every one of them hooked by the nose like a herd of buffalo.

An's thoughts continue:

"And the two women, what will they do to them?

"They will do nothing because they are prisoners in that upper room, and they have no way to fight back. But the two guards will be called in and advised to keep quiet.

"Would those two pitiful ones have guts enough to escape?

"No! Even if they have the guts, they will have no chance to do so. After Nong Tai's escape, they will constantly live under the surveillance of guards. They will swallow bitterness and pretend to be mute and deaf, to be just walking corpses, or else wooden figures standing in long halls without sunlight.

"The sex-addict minister will not soon change the guards. Perhaps in a week, or two, or three? It will depend on his sexual appetite. After he has satiated his bestial desire, the two women and the guards will all perish together. As he himself had done, those two soldiers most definitely had also raised their hands thousands of times under the flag, swearing to destroy the enemies of the people and protect the nation!"

"Why are you laughing? What are you laughing about?" Nong Tai suddenly asked.

An quickly replied: "I remembered a funny story."

"Then tell me, I am bored."

"I cannot. It's very gross."

Nong Tai was silent and annoyed.

An caught on that he had a tendency to force laughter when pain gnawed at his heart. This strange habit—just formed—had become a skill as if it had been part of him forever.

"The man from Xiu Village is completely dead, I don't see him anymore," he thought, and a few moments later a pitiful question arose:

"And the two children? What will these dogs do to them?"

He visualized little Mui's black eyes; her sweet breath when she whispered in his ears; the gentle swish of her hair brushing his cheeks; the warm and sweet feeling each time the little girl put her tiny hands in his large ones—the hands of a hunter. At the thought, An felt a sharp knife scraping his heart as blood dripped from the wound.

"No! I must not think of these things anymore. Just believe that behind me is a silent and dark grave. There is nobody left. No Xiu Village; not even my uncle and aunt or my parents-in-law. All are removed from this earth. I will be the last one. The last one must live to report on these Vietnamese executioners. I must do that at all cost . . ."

Suddenly An felt weary. He told Nong Tai, "Let's lie down. My back really hurts. The bench is long enough for four people, therefore we can stretch our legs comfortably. Don't forget that past the border post there will be no horse or buffalo cart, but only a pair of feet. The road is long and steep, it will not be easy."

"Just rest, Comrades. I will let you know when we arrive," said the driver.

"I will pay you the balance when we see the border outpost," An reiterated. "If the horses are well and we are earlier than usual, I will pay you extra to buy corn and honey to feed them."

"That will do," the cart owner cheerfully answered. He then started singing an old-style song that An had never heard. His voice was warm and resonated loudly in the deserted hills. He must have been a singer during his youth, just like the artists who had played the flute all night in Xiu Village. He lay down on the bench, listening attentively to the song. The local verses mixed in a coarse manner with poems and proverbs, rather ordinary:

Dear lady from the other side of the river,
You in the bright shirt, wrapped in a pink scarf,
Are you married or waiting for someone to come and ask?
If you are married but your husband is away, come here to me.
Here it is deserted and quiet, nobody will see.
Don't be shy; life is short; no more than a hand's span.
Pretty one, trundle on over here.
The panels of your dress fly up; exciting my burning heart,
As if I walk on fire, sit on charcoal . . .

The horses' footsteps on the road created a sad melody that blended with the driver's lament. Slowly, sleep came and pulled An into pitch dark waves.

5

"Wake up! There's the border defense fort," the cart owner shouted, waking them.

"Hell, it's too bright!" Nong Tai cried out, removing the hat covering his face. An immediately closed his eyes because the bright light was like a thousand pins poking them, immediately causing them to water.

After keeping his eyes shut for a while, An covered his face with the hat to get used to the intense light. Then he opened them. The cart owner said:

"I warned you already. People from the north who come here all complain about the sunlight in Nghe An. Nonetheless, you are lucky because today the Lao wind is not blowing."

"If it does blow, then what happens?"

"Comrades, you are about to go over there. No need for curiosity, you will soon know."

"Where's the border fort?"

"See it yet? The highest red dot; that's where the defenders put their flag. Before it was the French flag. After the revolution it's a red one with a yellow star."

An counted out some money and gave it to the cart owner. "Please take this. There is extra to buy honey and grain for the horses."

The owner put the money in his pocket then bent over to pull out of the cart packages wrapped in dry banana leaves.

"Comrades, you are too generous. I, too, must know my duty. They say that giving and receiving makes everybody happy. Here are two kilos of very good cane sugar. Comrades, in the jungle you can suck the cane to quench your thirst. If you are lucky enough to make it over the pass at the border outpost, then you can give half to the soldiers. Up there they are bored, so every time strangers pass, for fun they find many reasons to make them sit around and wait."

"Isn't there a rule?"

"There is no rule, but there they are bored. Very seldom does a horse cart go up here; mostly military vehicles. Civilian cars don't come here. If you were locked up in that post all year, you would do just the same."

The cane sugar smelled wonderful. An said, "We need give them only half. We need to go while there is still light."

"If you had no cane sugar, you two would probably end up sleeping there overnight; not until morning would you be allowed to go on into Laos. Most of the detachment is from the north. They tend to fuss over all kinds of anecdotes about their native region."

An was quiet. But Nong Tai looked out for a moment, then turned around to tell him in a terrified way, "Brother Thanh, they stand in line to meet us at the top of the hill!"

He looked up and saw the red flag clearly. Indeed, the soldiers were standing in line to block the road as if an ambush was being set. Instinctively he touched the gun on his hip. So, at the same time, did Nong Tai. The two looked at each other.

An lowered his voice and asked the cart owner, "Why do they stand in line like that?"

"Out of boredom," he replied tersely, without stopping his whipping of the horses. "Anyone in their shoes would do the same. They come to see the horse cart. Later they will look at you two comrades. Then they will gossip. We only hope that they will quickly let you go on."

"Ah, like that huh?" An said, already thinking of what to do next to get through this stretch quickly and safely.

"Lucky that we're crude," An went on. "We don't much know how to chat with citified soldiers."

Thinking a bit, he then said, "You are a good-hearted person. Can you stay for a while and chat with them so that they will let us leave quickly? The jungle road at night is not easy going but spending the night will make us breach our duty. We can give you more money."

"You don't have to buy me with money," the cart owner replied briskly. "I take only my fair share as well as that of the horses. If I'm too greedy, heaven will hit me with one calamity after another. But I promise to help you, Comrades. I will sit and chat with them for half an hour. The sun will still be on the mountaintop for about one and a half rods."

About ten minutes later, they reached the top of the hill. The soldiers immediately surrounded the horse cart, their faces excited as if they had received a gift.

"Hello, Comrades!" said the cart owner in a loud voice.

"Hello, Uncle. It has been a while since a horse cart has climbed up here," one of the lonely soldiers replied.

"Yes; a horse coming up here just once takes a month to recuperate. I only use the whip on special occasions. Today, I carry two military comrades for a special mission."

"Whatever the mission, there must first be a stop here for a good chat."

An and Nong Tai jumped down, pulling out their orders for presentation. One of the soldiers seized both passes and put them in his pocket, not even caring to glance at them. Then another, wearing the insignia of a captain, said, "Please, Comrades, do come into the fort."

The soldiers entered first, An and Nong Tai following.

As if he could see the worry on their faces, the cart owner said, "You just go in, rest, and have some tea. I will feed the horses and join you soon. Remember the two packages of cane sugar."

"I have them here," An said.

The defensive fort was built above a ravine, three buildings placed in a U shape in the style of Vietnamese living in the plains, with a stone patio in the middle. A small cement blockhouse sat next to the main building, definitely built under French rule. Next to it stood a wooden watchtower. Behind the building on the left, about fifty meters down the hillside, was a horse pen with about ten horses grazing grass; they were the main means of transport for the soldiers assigned to the fort.

"Tomorrow, these horses will undoubtedly chase us as we try to get away," An reckoned. "In the worst case, we will have to send at least half a dozen of them to hell before we die."

They entered the main building, which was quite spacious, with a large Ping-Pong–like table in the middle covered with scattered teapots, newspapers, a radio, cigarette packs, knives, flashlights . . . Glued up on the walls were photos cut from picture magazines of beautiful girls from performing troupes. The senior captain, obviously in command of the fort, threw out an order:

"Someone go boil water for a new pot of tea."

A voice from the courtyard immediately said, "I am reporting that we have the fire going."

"We will die stuck here with them. I must find a way to escape . . ." An thought, but he said, "Reporting to you, Comrades . . ."

"That's fine. You can report after we have a drink. We are all soldiers. You are infantry; I am with the border defense guard. We get up like anyone else when we hear the horn in the morning. We don't often meet each other. There's no rush—even if you were to leave now, you wouldn't have enough time. It may be sunny right now but darkness comes on very quickly. This place has lots of light during the day but at night the mountain fog comes thick like cotton."

An began to get nervous. This "lovelorn" soldier clearly presented a danger. Luckily, just at that moment, the cart owner returned. He walked slowly into the building while singing a song about flirty girls:

"Maybe you're married but your husband is away, come here by me,
It's isolated and lonely here, but no one can see. . . ."

The senior captain turned to the cart owner with a big smile: "Why do you, old man, ask someone's wife to come over and not fear doing wrong?"

"I am not asking anyone over. That's a song of the old guys in the old days."

"The old guys in the old days were quite disgraceful!"

"Those guys also had tongues to twist and two eyes to ogle girls just like we do now. But even if we wanted to criticize or straighten them out, they are sleeping soundly now under three meters of dirt. Nobody can take them by the nape anymore to ask them questions." Saying so, he looked toward An, as if to tell him to calm down.

Seeing that, An said, "Uncle, have the horses finished eating yet?"

"How could they be finished? They take their time. And you, Comrades, have you presented your papers yet?"

"I presented both our passes but the captain's subordinate put them in his shirt pocket."

"Hey, a lady in a red shirt; hey, one with a pink cloth tiara . . ."

The driver continued to sing another verse, then turned to the senior captain: "These two comrades have to carry out their orders immediately; they can't wait for a military bus. That is why the Thanh Vinh police recommended me. Not to make any money did I come up here with my horses. These two don't have time to drink tea with us. But they have very good cane sugar. They gave me some pieces to suck in the cart. It tasted good, like flower pollen."

Turning to An, he asked, "Comrade, will you offer some to these guys in the post? We will sit and drink tea to soothe our throats."

An put the package of cane sugar on the table, then said, "Here. A gift for you, Comrades."

He smiled and looked at the captain. "I am a first lieutenant, lower than you by one rank. It would be fun to chat if we had time. But unfortunately we must take care of urgent responsibilities."

"Really?"

The captain stuck his head past the door frame and asked the group of soldiers gathered outside on the patio, "Who of you kept the military orders of these two comrades?"

"Me."

"Have you checked them?"

"Yes. They are First Lieutenant Chi Van Thanh and People's Police Master Sergeant Nong Tai. Both of them belong to the Tay ethnic minority."

"Give them back. Bad luck that they are on an urgent mission."

The soldier returned the passes.

The captain said, "Well, we will see you when you return. My cousin married a Tay girl. She is cute, really cute. Her skin is fair like cotton, more beautiful than that of the wives of the Russian and Czech advisers. Next life, if I am lucky, I would like to be a Tay son-in-law. OK?"

"Thank you."

An and Nong Tai said good-bye to the soldiers then turned back to the road. The singing of the cart owner followed them:

"The panels of your dress fly up; exciting my burning heart,
As if I walk on fire, sit on charcoal . . ."

An said, "If we get out of here, we have to thank the cart owner a thousand times."

The two looked toward Laos, bowed their heads, and walked away with a running gait.

They walked like that for one full hour, sweat running abundantly down their faces and wetting their backs. The sun was now hanging lightly like a bright globe to the west just above the mountain in front of them. The sunlight threw a wide blanket but the air had cooled. Slowing down their pace a bit, An felt the cold on his shoulders. Behind them, rows of hills ran to the horizon. Before them, only a patch of road before they reached the forest. Its dark border appeared along the full stretch of the valley.

Nong Tai cried out: "Here's the forest. We made it alive."

"Divine beings: please protect us. But we must go faster. Behind is empty space with an empty road. But if the horses of the outpost chase us, there is not much chance of escape."

The two continued to head toward the forest, running fast. They looked at the sun as if it were some clock timing a race of life or death. Feeling tired, An slowed his pace, but Nong Tai said, "We can't slow down now. The forest here is open, horses can run freely. We have to get to the heart of the forest where the path is large enough only for feet to hope to be out of danger."

After speaking, he moved to walk ahead of An and set the pace, as if to encourage his companion. Walking in the shadow of trees, they grew less anxious. The two passed through a part of the wood that sloped downhill. Ten minutes beyond that, they arrived at a flatter part of the forest where it was full of vines. The path was now wide enough for only one person.

As he wiped the sweat off his face, Nong Tai said, "Not quite the heart of the forest, but horses will have a hard time because the vines here make a trap."

"Yep, really lucky for us," An replied as he glanced at the vines dangling overhead, the protruding arms of the trees looking like those of an octopus.

Along the path a thick waterfall of small and large vines hung down, some long, some short, but each like a noose that would snare any horse entering the forest. It would be more difficult for a herd of horses. At the very least, someone would have to open the path with a machete, cutting down the vines in order for the horses to make any headway.

Nong Tai turned to tell An, "The jungle where we live does not have these vines."

"Yes, but we have bigger trees."

"The vines here have interesting colors. Look, the ones on our left are orange. And the one around the trunk of that tree is of an eggplant purple color."

"Yes, different soil, different jungle, so the trees are different, too . . ." An replied as he continued to look up at the vines dangling among the scattered rays of light coming from the setting sun. Nong Tai did not say more, but walked quietly along. Suddenly, An heard a sound—*thump*—a low but heavy sound, followed by a terribly bad smell. That nasty smell brought back memories from past nights in the jungle around Xiu Village. Tiger!

Leaping forward three steps, An grabbed the trunk of the nearest big tree and climbed up with all the strength he had left in him. Scrambling up to a big branch near the top, he sat with his legs wrapped tightly around the branch, his arms around the trunk of the tree. Only then did he dare look down: the tiger, which had pinned Nong Tai under its forelegs, lifted its neck and looked up at him. Their eyes met. He felt cold sweat on his back. The eyes of this king of the forest widened, sending rays the color of hardened steel mixed with yellow straight into An's eyes.

He thought, "That tiger knows there is a second prey. It will continue to watch until I fall down. Now I must be very calm to escape this danger."

An tied his body to the tree with three loops of parachute cord, which he had in one of his pockets. He placed the revolver behind his back for easy access. Then he looked down to contest the animal in a hypnotic stare. Poor Nong Tai: he must have died from the fierce animal's initial attack without being able to utter a cry. The tiger was clearly one that was used to eating people, one that had realized humans were top-quality prey. Meeting such a tiger automatically opens the door to hell.

The tiger looked to be about six feet long in An's estimation. It couldn't have been too old, as its fur was still yellow and its black stripes were precisely edged. An couldn't stop looking at the animal, perhaps out of fear, or perhaps only out of curiosity. From the age of thirteen he had followed his uncle and the other hunters of Xiu Village into the forest. His uncle had killed many bears, horses, wild boars, buck deer, and more than a dozen tigers. An himself had never been so close to a tiger, nor able to observe how it eats its prey. Never.

The tiger put a foot on Nong Tai's head and flipped it back and forth in the manner of a child playing with a ball. Then, suddenly, it opened its mouth wide and snapped once at the victim's neck. An heard the sound of bones being crushed. The tiger took a second bite, severing Nong Tai's head from his body, and pushed it away with its foot as one would flick away a little marble. An watched the bright red head of his companion roll several times before landing in a nearby bush. He couldn't breathe; terror paralyzed his limbs. At the same time, a warm stream of water from somewhere ran down his rigid body. An realized that, without knowing it, he had wet his pants. The urine ran along his thighs and continued down to his feet.

Down below, the tiger was tearing up Nong Tai's clothes and beginning its feast. An couldn't look.

"Oh, Nong Tai: we ran away from one death but another was waiting here. Just when you thought you had walked through the door of life, it turned into a door of death. Please forgive me because I did not have enough strength to protect you. Please forgive me because I did not do my duty as your guide. I should have gone first, not you. But your fate or just bad luck has taken you to death. From now on, your death will burden my shoulders as well as your loved ones."

It had been a short friendship, one that had lasted no longer than two days and one night. Still, it had been a real friendship because it had led them to cross the porous boundary separating the fields of life from the shores of death; such a bond will last forever.

Through the forest's leaves, the sun's rays were no longer yellow, but the lighter color of a ripe lime. Night would come in no time. He had to escape this forest before then. An began to rub his hands vigorously to make the blood flow. When he put them to his cheeks, he felt them as warm as usual. Then he pulled the revolver from behind his back and cocked it. The target was close at hand but difficult to pinpoint because the tiger was busy eating, so its neck and head moved around constantly. Only its back and hips pointed toward An, but those were not the parts where a bullet could put the animal in mortal danger.

Suddenly an idea flashed in his mind: "Why do I have to kill it? If the border defense guards find the tiger's carcass, they will chase me all the way to Laos. The best thing is to let the animal escape, and to pretend that I, myself, have also been chewed up by the tiger's jaws. That would be the most certain escape under the circumstances."

An aimed at the hip closest to the gun barrel and squeezed. With a terrifying roar, the animal turned in his direction. Its eyes shone straight at his with rays of mad anger. It let go of its prey, turned around, and jumped up. As An had calculated, the animal couldn't reach where he sat. Not able to grab its prey and wounded, the tiger walked unsteadily around the tree for a few steps, then backed up, roared a second time, then jumped again. The gun in An's hand fell to the ground, bounced, and fired another bullet. The animal turned sharply, and leaped toward its small, strangely shaped enemy, biting with all its strength and flowing fury. Then it roared weakly from the pain of biting on the steel. Looking up at the tiny prey in the tree with a surprised gaze, it darted into the bush and disappeared. Waiting for a long while to make sure that the tiger did not return, An untied the parachute cord and climbed down. Something was sticking to his butt. Then he realized that he not only had wet his pants but had pooped in them, too.

"Yes, people say that you shit from fear, and that's true all right."

An took off his shirt and tore it into many pieces to dab the smeared blood under Nong Tai's head, then he placed the head in a thick and thorny bush so that no hunting dog, wild fox, or boar could go in after it. Then he threw his blood-soaked, tattered shirt over Nong Tai's headless body and threw his gun close to that of his companion. Looking at this terrifying sight one last time, he turned around and ran straight ahead, toward the sound of a running stream. Kneeling down by it, he wanted to clean up but a strong urge to vomit overcame him, and a green liquid residue mixed with yellow came up, followed by black bile as from a fish. It felt like his gut had been cut with an invisible knife; pain curved his body as if it were a shrimp cooking in boiling water. He put his face on the grass, then lay down on his side. At that moment, a stream of feces came out unexpectedly. He had no control at all over his body. He waited for the terrifying illness to pass. When there was nothing left in his bowels, he began to shake from cold.

Reaching to open his pack, he pulled out a blanket that Nang Dong had meticulously sewn stitch by stitch for him from a parachute taken as a trophy during the battle for Dien Bien. He covered himself with it. Closing his eyes, he took long breaths and waited for his body to warm up.

"I must escape. I must live at all costs," he told himself. That resolve kept repeating without pause, like a breeze blowing gusts into a charcoal stove. Repeating this mantra over and over, his frigid body finally began to warm up; after almost twenty minutes, he could feel his heartbeat return to normal. Pulling the blanket aside, he sat up and went to the stream to clean up. He washed his soiled clothes and wrapped them in a raincoat, which he tucked carefully back inside the duffel bag. Then, after crossing over to the other side of the stream in his clean clothes, he resumed running. It was getting late; in another ten minutes he had to take out his flashlight. From then on, his life had only the forest trees for protection. He had to be frugal with each flash of light. He also had to be frugal with each piece of dry cake still left until he could find shelter. Dizziness forced him to stop. Reaching inside his pack, he pulled out a piece of cane sugar and put it in his mouth. The sweetness penetrated his tongue and made him less shaky on his feet. Later the sugar melted down and even revived his empty and damaged stomach, and he was able to move with more confidence. He continued along the dark path, but an hour later, he suddenly heard the rushing galloping of horses mixed with screams. "Why do the galloping horses sound so close? Have I ended up getting lost or turned around? Is this worn path taking me back to where Nong Tai was eaten by the tiger?"

He turned off the flashlight and crawled into a thick bush, knowing that when one is not sure of an escape route, it is best to sit tight in the dark. It was less dangerous than making squishing noises and revealing his location with the flashlight. Indeed, the sounds were getting closer and the wind brought the cursing of the soldiers to his ears:

"Slow down! Your mare bumped into my horse."

"I can't help it—it's so dark."

"We have to wait for them to cross the road before we can move forward. Don't push your horse."

"I did not. It just jumped on its own."

A voice intervened, surely from the fort's captain: "Enough, you guys. Don't fight with each other. When we return, there will be a pot of chicken soup to fill us up."

The soldiers kept quiet.

The captain again said, "Let's speed up a little. Don't forget that these hill people know the forest ways a thousand times better than us. They are born with the forest trees."

"Reporting, Captain: we are really trying but there are too many vines. This stretch of road is a bitch."

"Because it's a bitch, we need your professional skill with a knife. Try hard. I think we are almost there. No matter what they do, they cannot be faster than the horses."

The sounds of their movements mixing with the hissing of the horses became even clearer. Soldiers in the front slashed at the vines, preparing a way for the horses to advance. Since the sun had set they had been under orders to chase down An and Nong Tai, but their horses had been blocked from entering the forest. If the worn trail had not been covered tightly by the hanging green vines, the soldiers would have already caught him when he was lying under the blanket next to the stream, in the most compromising situation imaginable.

"Now I have regained my composure, and if we do clash I can still take out some guys before I die."

That thought was a consolation to An. An insect bit his neck; the pain was so excruciating he almost cried out. Reaching back with his hand, he seized a toxic ant the size of a black bean. He squeezed it to death but the ant still managed to bite the tip of his forefinger, which started to burn from the acid pain. At the same moment, a scream was heard:

"Tiger! Tiger!"

A hail of bullets erupted right after the terrifying scream.

An smiled to himself: "Those are too many rounds to deal with the king of the jungle."

After the firing ended, An clearly heard the captain's voice:

"Do you see it?"

"No. Reporting, Captain: right by the horse's foot I saw a bunch of bones from a torso with the flesh all eaten."

"Where?"

Then he heard the outpost commander shout: "Dismount. Bring the electric lantern over here."

There were footsteps running; talking to horses; the slapping of riding crops on backs; then silence. Perhaps the soldiers were tiptoeing around Nong Tai's headless body and bones. Then the captain spoke in a tremulous voice:

"Two guns? This tiger finished both of them?"

"Yes. It must be a big one."

"I never heard of a tiger eating two people at the same time."

"Reporting, Captain: tigers do not kill two people at one time because when a tiger catches one victim, the other one has time to run or shoot. But it can carry a cow on its back and still run swiftly. This time, perhaps the two highlanders met their last call; perhaps they sat and rested; perhaps they walked close together. They may be woodsmen but they underestimated these forests."

"We cannot locate the heads."

"Tigers never eat the head; only foxes and wild boars. Foxes do not eat at one place; they normally fight each other and take their prey far away. I believe foxes have dragged one body and both heads. It must have been one big pack of foxes."

"That's right. Only foxes and wild boars could clean it up this fast. I believe the round of bullets we shot chased them away. Looking at the pile of ribs, we know they were really famished."

Another moment of silence passed, then a soldier said, "Captain, let's return. Here the blood stinks."

"Pick up the two guns," the captain ordered. "Our mission has been accomplished without wasting one drop of our blood. Those who betrayed the nation and are foreign spies have been punished by wild animals instead of a people's court."

An heard repeated coughing from a soldier; it must have been the unlucky one who had to pick up the two guns smeared with dried blood. After that: the sound of horses being mounted, the whipping of crops, whispering, and, at last, galloping horses. Then the sounds grew fainter and fainter.

Waiting for the noise of the running horses to completely subside, An came out of the bushes, knelt down, and reflected:

"Oh you, King of the Jungle—you saved my life!"

From that year on he lived in an isolated hamlet of the Van tribe, so remote that not even Lao would set foot there. Two years passed in the belief that he would never see his country again. His country was no longer Vietnam, because that name only evoked rage in him. On the back side of propaganda pamphlets that he would pick up in a tiny market in a Lao village, he wrote out with a bit of pencil the sordid story of his family. In the third year, he began to understand that he must return to the hostile territory that was once his homeland, to Hanoi, a city hell he thought he would never see again. In the middle of these mountains, among a people who spoke another language and lived a different culture, he could write thousands of pages that no one would ever care to read, and thus his escape would become pointless. He had prolonged his life to vent his rage, but, in the end, this longer life had sunk him in useless darkness.

He realized that he had left so that, someday, he could return. He must now return to that very place where cruelty had spilled forth; where the souls of his loved ones were waiting for him. Back then, just to stay alive, he had left any way he could. Now, similarly, to get revenge, he must return in any way he could. Return, return, return!

So decided, it still took five more years before he could find a way. It happened when scores of the first North Vietnamese soldiers began to pass through the Truong Son Mountains in preparation for the fierce war to liberate Saigon and, after that, to expand Vietnam's border all the way to Siem Reap in Cambodia. It was the year of the cat, the springtime of that year. The previous fall, enemy planes had started hunting down frontline soldiers in the forests of the Truong Son Mountains. Bombs started falling in areas marked on maps as unknown or as having North Vietnamese soldiers working away, hidden under camouflage. Because America was a great munitions warehouse, the Saigon army could drop bombs generously, like the Bac Lieu gentlemen throwing money into gambling under the ancien regime. Thanks to that development, he encountered a group of soldiers killed by bombs and thus rejoined the North Vietnamese army with a stolen military identity card: First Lieutenant Hoang An of the infantry, ethnic Tay, from the city of Dong Mo in Lang Son.

He was placed in a new unit made up entirely of survivors from battalions, companies, and platoons that had taken so many casualties that they had been stricken from the order of battle. Hiding under the name of someone already dead, he understood that his life now had only one purpose. That day, he swore before heaven:

"Nong Van Thanh has died for eternity.

"So has Chi Van Thanh.

"Only one name, Hoang An, is left on this earth."

FINAL SUPPLICATIONS

1

Clunk, clunk, clunk, clunk . . .

Clunk, clunk, clunk, clunk, clunk . . .

The steel panel hanging from the tree oscillates wildly. A large, awkward, and mean-looking fellow, most likely recently selected from the rock pile or the sawmill, swings a huge hammer against the panel to announce breakfast. This rudimentary instrument appears to be effective, as its long-lasting sound resonates all over the hospital compound, almost as loud as a fire truck's claxon.

When the sound stops, the cart comes from the end of the hall bringing that morning's food to the patients. From the rooms, people who care for the patients start bringing containers or bowls and plates out to receive breakfast portions for their loved ones. Vu observes them quietly: a society withering away; a battlefield for life and death; a place where fear and pain and hope converge; where time effaces and smudges; where life for the living is but repetitious habit.

"This kind of life is not just the nameless people in row upon row of suffocating houses. Even the extremely intelligent, or at least those who could be a model for clear thinking, integrity, and self-respect, have many times accepted this life of routine, no different than unsophisticated country women who elbow their way to the food carts.

"Thus, they don't have to keep their eyes glued on the ladle that stirs the pot of meat porridge, or to count the rice rolls that the attendant doles out to see if there is a full set of eight pieces and not seven only. Thus, they are not unhappy for not having a winter blanket or some money to give to their sons on the day they enlist. But, to be exactly truthful, they live only through movements already determined by machines or, more accurately, as puppets moving to a script written for them."

The morning when he had received word that Miss Xuan had been killed, Vu had met with those he considered "role models of conscience." As it was before office hours, it was to their private homes that he had rushed. First, he met with Prime Minister Do. He did not have to wait even one minute because the prime minister was already up, dressed, and sitting in his office. In front of him was a cup of coffee and his copy of the old fifteenth-century court history of Vietnam—a book that was on the table every time he paid the prime minister a visit. That perennial book was open and the host was reading it attentively, his face bent close to the page. When Vu entered, the prime minister hurriedly got up, not to shake his hand but to shut the doors. When he turned around, his face was covered with tears:

"Brother . . ." Vu said; the prime minister quickly waved his hand to signal silence. Then he closed his eyes and from them streams of tears rolled down without stopping. Losing control himself, Vu also wept. The prime minister was leaning against the door; Vu stood in the middle of the room. The two men faced each other without a word and wept together as other men would drink tea or sip wine. They wept clandestinely, suppressing any louder sobbing for fear that the guards in the hall outside would hear. They wept, controlled and in silence. Then Vu understood what pain and humiliation were. Those overflowing tears were in regret both for the life of a beautiful and unfortunate woman, and to release the turmoil in their hearts. A powerless man is ten times worse than a weak woman. They had been born to be men, beings meant to embody strength and power. A man who cannot act knows only how to drown bitterness and rage with tears, no differently than a child of five. Realizing this fact first, Vu looked up and wiped his face. The prime minister continued to weep, his long and thin fingers covering his square face. Vu focused on those fingers because people usually called them "spear" fingers. They shook from the root to the tip, similar to wild grass shaking in a strong wind:

"Was it because of his scholarly disposition that he was squeezed and turned into a kind of brainy doll encapsulated within this power machine?"

Vu kept thinking about this possibility while waiting for the prime minister to regain control of his emotions. Do had been crying for a long time, even before Vu had stepped into the room. The history book was open to collect the stream of falling tears. Two pages were swollen in spots.

"He weeps not only for Miss Xuan. He weeps for himself, too. That's for sure!"

Vu walked over, putting his hand on the prime minister's shoulders as if to say good-bye.

"We won't find any help coming from the brainy doll, not a drop besides his flowing tears. The magnificent building before us is just a little row house bereft of all hopes. But we cannot give up. Where there is water, you scoop."

On reaching the street he told the driver, "Let's go to the house of Comrade Deputy General Secretary. As of now he is not yet in his office."

"Yes. Offices will open in ninety minutes."

The driver turned back to Hoang Dieu Street, famous because it held the former residences of the palace majordomos. Two rows of trees stood firm like marble in the cold dew. Vu told the driver to stop and let him out so that he might find a stall to get breakfast. Then he leisurely walked to Deputy General Secretary Thuan's house. This house had been the substantial villa of a French official, but the Party's Central Committee had renovated it to provide better security. They had replaced fences with masonry walls, adding a second gate and a watchtower, so that people looking in had the impression of a seminary or ammunition warehouse. Vu stopped before a huge barrier gate, painted in stripes of white and red like a gate at the train station. A large lock, bigger than a hand, dangled at the main entrance. It was not yet time to open the main gate, but the guard had seen him. Hurriedly he had come over and opened the secondary gate for Vu to enter. Then the guard climbed back up the watchtower to observe him. Vu felt that gaze sticking to his back. Instinct told him that from now on, everywhere he went, he would be watched closely by naked eyes as well as through officially issued binoculars.

"I did not expect things to get to this point. But if you want to play, you accept the rules. Let's see what they can do to me."

Though his disposition was rather sweet, Vu could get stubborn when challenged. He walked straight to the villa.

Then the owner called to him from the garden on the left: "I am here, Vu, my friend."

"Good."

"I am over here. Don't you see rows of yellow roses full of blooms? Come here. These flowers last for only a couple of weeks, and this kind of rose is especially rare and hard to grow."

Thuan had been standing in the garden, wearing blue pajamas with white stripes. Indeed, the garden of yellow roses was in full bloom. The petals were soft like thick velvet. Their color was between the color of ripe lemon rind and the yellow of an egg: a soft and dreamy yellow; a gentle fleeting color like a suspicion, as if it could fly and rest on the wing of a dragonfly or a butterfly, as if it could vaporize like fog.

Under normal circumstances the small vista would have been worth admiring. But at this time, beauty just inflamed him.

"Your garden is really beautiful. Your roses are exquisite," Vu said as he approached his host. "I have never seen roses this fresh and beautiful. Paradise cannot exceed their perfection. In this life how many are able to enjoy such things?"

Thuan remained silent before this question, which contained no hint of reproach. Putting out his hand to shake, he walked toward Vu, then whispered: "I stand here to wait for you. You don't have to fight with me. We can go to the end of the garden to talk safely."

They walked beside each other between the rows of roses toward the end of the garden, where irises circled a plot of needle grass that ran along the foot of a wall. The two stood in the middle of the tender green grass.

Looking around, Thuan acknowledged, "Here the reeds cannot grow." Then he turned to Vu and asked, "Who gave you the news this morning?"

"A disguised voice, as if the nose was covered or was stuffy from a cold. And you?"

"Also the same voice informing me, not quite at five thirty a.m."

"With me, also about that time."

"Who do you think informed us, with such an intentionally distorted voice?"

"Why are you asking me? You belong to the Politburo—assistant general secretary of the Party. To refer to old times, you are one of the four pillars holding up the dynasty. Me? I'm just a marginal guy, so many ranks below you. Properly speaking, I am the one who has the right to ask you."

Thuan quietly sighed, looking down at the grass near his feet as if the answer could be found among the tiny shoots. Pausing, he then slowly explained: "I know I am at fault, because, in a Politburo meeting on the issue, I promised to guarantee the safety of Miss Xuan and her two kids. I did not expect things to happen like this."

"You didn't expect? Perhaps you did expect but washed your hands and let others act."

Thuan looked up at him. "I am well bred and well educated, Vu, my friend. Therefore, I ask you not to suspect me of doing anything so grotesque. If not for my sake, then at least with a forgiving heart in respect for the departed spirits of my parents. They were good people. I do not lie, above all with someone like you."

His voice was shaking and his thick nostrils started to redden. Vu knew that he was being truthful, and that eased a bit the rage burning in his heart.

"My mistake was the very fact that I did not learn what to expect," Thuan continued. "I didn't expect all the dark turnings of human hearts. I was thinking as if I were still living at the front: when all in the Politburo were of one mind, then everything would proceed exactly so; no need to be concerned. This event takes me aback. The game has changed; the times are different but my simple thinking is stuck in the past. Now, it has happened. What to do?"

"It has happened and now you just whine about what to do? That is really the simpleminded talking!" Vu interrupted. "Thuan, just once, try to put yourself in the place of others. At this moment, you are standing here and talking to me. Later, you will walk fewer than a hundred steps and you will be in a majestic house; in there, your wife, your kids and grandkids—the whole crowded flock. In that company, nobody must endure isolated loneliness, and none of your little ones will have to worry about being orphaned or exiled; exiled in their own country."

To escape his inquisitive and angry look, Thuan looked over at the lichee bush in the corner of the garden next to the main gate. Then, lowering his voice, he said, "I know I have failed the Old Man."

"What do you think about that person? Now, how will the Old Man live knowing that those who claim to be his comrades have killed his loved one? Do all of you—twelve people with the most power in this country—think that the Old Man is not a person but only a rock? Because you were the first—and you were the one who spoke up strongly—to oppose the recommendation to normalize the relationship between Older Brother and Miss Xuan. Because your words were decisive, having power to obtain consensus from the others. I carefully asked Do about that meeting."

"I know that you are extremely angry, not only with me but with all those who opposed that relationship. Really, we acted in the interest of the country, and also because of the Old Man's prestigious stature."

"I think all the time about the notion that you usually call the 'charisma' of leading cadres, that those who lead the way for the people must be role models or idols. I find that an odd and imposed concept. Life is filled with old men who are madly in love with younger women. Not only royals but little people, too. If I am not mistaken, your paternal grandfather had a twenty-year-old concubine when he was seventy-two. Is that true or not?"

"It is true, even though my grandfather was only the chief of a small district. I still remember the sight of my grandfather taking a nap, his head on the lap of the beautiful twenty-year-old as she gently fanned him. I also remember my grandmother eating her meals with those two people in the main house, and our family taking ours separately in the side residence. I also remember the concubine could sing the '*Kieu*' poem very well, and when my grandfather was inspired he usually asked her to sing to entertain guests. All that is very true, Vu, my friend. But when it comes to Elder Brother, such cannot be accepted, because he does not live for himself alone. He is the compass, the torch to light the way, for all the people."

"And because of that shining torch, the Old Man must be castrated like the eunuchs were in the old days, or forced to live in hiding like a smuggler? All of you invented this role for him; starting with Miss Minh Thu carrying her sleeping things to the house at the resistance zone. If the Party were to ask you to marry Miss Minh Thu instead of the woman you are bedding now, how would you take it?"

Thuan was silent. He cast his eyes down and continued to look intensely at the grass under his feet.

"I do not fully understand the terms 'comrade' or 'brother-in-arms' that you speak as if singing with the tip of your tongue. Really, I don't understand," Vu continued. "For all time, people have bonded together through understanding. Little people with little voices still know the saying 'Everyone has bones and skin; cut anyone, blood flows.' Any Buddhist most likely understands the famous teaching of Gautama: 'All blood is red; all tears are salty' . . . Catholic teaching also says, 'Treat others as you want to be treated.' Whether the religion is Eastern or Western, this is what is taught about good behavior."

"Dear Vu, but there is only one thing . . ." Thuan replied.

"What?"

"That the Old Man agreed to pay the price. He himself had no objection."

"Given the procedure on decision-making, by himself the Old Man could not carry the day against twelve. To be more precise, only Do wanted to support him. But in the end he was pressured by the majority, therefore he changed his mind to follow you all. Thus, for good reason, the Old Man was an absolute minority. The Old Man relied on your understanding, you who had been both his comrade and his younger brother. From the beginning of the revolution until now, everything was done based on feelings of brotherhood. But the Old Man did not realize that things had changed; that the convivial past had died. And its dying really began right after the army left the mountains and jungles to control the cities. From that point on, all brotherly comrades became no more than merchant partners with their goods on a ship in the ocean; to protect their interest in the cargo, they would throw anyone overboard just to lighten the load. Then, as you looked on, the Old Man was no longer a beloved older brother but simply an animal to be sacrificed up to the god of the revolution. Above all, this revolution brought profit to all of you worthy beneficiaries. Am I right or wrong?"

Thuan did not answer; he stood like a statue, his eyes glued on his slippers, the kind made from perforated leather with open heels for use inside the house. Vu looked down on those fancy shoes; without knowing why, the sight of them intensified the fire in his heart.

"You are more lettered than the other eleven Politburo worthies. You are fluent in both Chinese and French; by heart you know the old and new annals. You knew damn well that when the Old Man married Miss Xuan, one man married one woman who married one husband; it was not some polygamous arrangement like that of our famous mandarin under the Nguyen dynasty, Nguyen Cong Tru and his third wife. Tell me clearly: Why was it OK for Nguyen Cong Tru but not for the Old Man? Did you ever think of that before?"

"To tell you the truth, I never thought about it this way."

"Well, to tell the truth, what were you thinking of? What was in the brainy skulls of those who considered themselves the Old Man's trusted younger colleagues?"

Thuan did not answer.

Inside himself, Vu felt a falling wall of flames pushing him down, almost turning him into ashes along with all those who were related to him.

"I have to get away from here," he thought to himself. "I have to go right away. I cannot stand this guy in the striped pajamas and open-heeled shoes. This man who nonchalantly smells his fragrant roses in the garden."

Trying hard to suppress his rage, he said, "I must go; there are the Old Man's two children. I want to warn you up front: if you do not immediately stop them, these hoodlums will carry on and those two kids will perish. Then you yourself will not survive if you still have a conscience, or whatever's left of one."

"Hey, Vu," Thuan said, still looking down, staring at the grass as if seeking moral support or consolation from the green stalks, "I know you are very angry with me. It's lucky you haven't reached the point of rage or revenge. Because everybody knows that, emotionally, you are closest to the Old Man; that in the resistance zones it was you who went to the city to meet Miss Thanh Tu; that it was also you who intervened to stop Miss Minh Thu from bringing her sleeping gear up to his house; that it was you who took Miss Xuan over there, too; that you were the one person Miss Xuan trusted and relied upon to organize her entire life; that you were the only one with whom the Old Man could talk about everything without reservation or formality. We have not forgotten all those meetings. We only needed to hear the two of you laughing to know how deep the affection was. Then, we were all very grateful to heaven for providing the Old Man with such a sympathetic and companionable younger colleague. Because all of us were busy with family, only you could volunteer your time to be with him. We also know that it was because of that closeness that you were shortchanged, as the Old Man held himself back, never proposing any favor or any special promotion. As for you, you also held back because of that relationship, so you silently accepted the downside. For that sacrifice, whether or not we wanted to, we had to respect you. For me, I ask for your understanding, if that is possible. Really, I didn't expect things to turn out so terribly. Really, I wish the Old Man had kept his private life in the dark, to thoroughly validate the image of a father of his people, a patriarch filled with feelings and convictions for the extended family of the nation. I believed that our arrangement made good sense. It was I who suggested that Miss Xuan agree to live in a little second-floor flat in the old quarter just like any other citizen. Because I believed that providing such an uncomplicated example would bring the Old Man more prestige in all our eyes."

"So: it was you! It was you who made that decision?" Vu said with surprise, continuing: "I argued so many times with the Party's Central Administrative Office. Perhaps because of that they kept silent before all my screaming. Now I know that you were the culprit and that they were the ones who had to throw out the garbage."

He stopped a few moments to process his many memories, then asked, "But, if you were using simplicity to create prestige, why didn't you personally practice it first? Why didn't you ask for a simple thatched-roof house with climbing vines on the fence out in the suburbs, rather than live in this overly imposing house?"

"You forget that I must administer the work of a nation."

"So the Old Man is just a puppet for you guys?"

"The Old Man is higher than us by a head. He is the top leader of the people."

"Because the Old Man is the top leader of the people, therefore the woman who sleeps in the same bed had to live in an ordinary flat in a narrow alley. And the woman who sleeps with you lives in this spacious, majestic villa. Because the Old Man is the top leader, the very soul of the Fatherland, his young wife had to be killed by you all, killed as if she were a rabbit, while the women who sleep with you all—I want to emphasize here that this includes my own wife—can ride in Volgas to go shopping, to buy clothes, candies and cakes, and cosmetics, at the international stores. By what moral principle do you guys authorize yourselves to do such things?"

Thuan did not answer; he squished some invisible thing on the grass; he did not look up. A lonesome and cold spring breeze was blowing. After a while Thuan cleared his throat.

"I apologize. I am disappointed that our talk has hit a dead end."

"We hit the dead end because you all refuse to assume responsibility. You are all just like kids who throw rocks at a bird's nest: when a stone hits someone, cutting his head, and he falls down and bleeds, they all run away. Is that comparison accurate or not?"

"I have never had a concrete answer from Brother Sau. When I called this morning, he was not home. The secretary on call said that he was running in the sports center. I think her death is an act of overreaching excess by the minister of the interior. It's possible that Sau only gave some general instruction. Quoc Tuy acted according to his own hoodlum instincts. They assigned him; I had warned Sau about this minister's criminal past, but Sau ignored it, saying that we should trust the innovative and constructive abilities of revolutionary cadres."

"What that means is that this is beyond the scope of your duties. Or more accurately, you have no responsibility whatsoever."

"I am very sorry that things turned out this badly. I will try my best. Nevertheless, you should try very hard to understand our situation."

Then Thuan waved his hand to show the rows of iris with curly petals bordering the lawn like lace around a woman's shirt. "You should look over there."

Vu bent down but he did not see anything besides the purple petals; they were shiny, full of water, and cared for regularly. The garden was really beautiful. But that exquisite beauty angered him all the more.

"I don't see anything at all besides the beauty of this garden. But that beauty is now like thorns that prick my eyes."

Thuan's face was somewhat puzzled and sad. He pulled on Vu's sleeve and showed him a large spiderweb between two iris stalks. On it was a fly, caught but struggling.

"Do you see that fly in the spiderweb there? Doesn't it bring some analogy to your mind? Prime Minister Do as well as I can easily meet the same fate as this miserable insect. Previously I had never thought of this. It is the death of Miss Xuan that has opened my eyes. Things have changed. The game has taken a new turn. Just look around us: sentries, bodyguards, the cook, the gardener, the driver, as well as the house servants and the garbage collector for this area, all belong to them. In just a few years everything has changed. Two years ago, we shared a meal of red rice with salted fish in the mountains; all were of one heart and one mind. Now, with a house and a large garden, nothing is as it was."

Instinctively, Vu shivered. He suddenly visualized the cowardly pettiness of people, including those with power and position—the most enlightened minds of the nation, pillars of the state. Looking straight into the deputy secretary's face, he smiled and said, "The most important and most decisive thing is this change: when we were up in the mountains, we all were committed to the big cause, ready to accept any sacrifice, even death. Now, because of large houses, servants, and sentries all around the yard, no one retains a warrior's honor. Wealth and glory have turned people into docile horses and sheep."

The secretary's face reddened; his fleshy nostrils quivered. He turned away to avoid Vu's look.

Vu continued: "Whatever happens, we have to protect the Old Man's two children. And for you, your conscience will tell you how to act."

Then he turned his back and walked away.

"Good-bye, Brother."

"Let me walk you out," Thuan said, and the two strolled away from the rows of roses to the gate. While walking, the deputy secretary said the final words: "I will bring the subject to the Politburo. I will intervene with all my ability. I will beg the Old Man's pardon and hope he will forgive me."

"It's up to you," Vu replied coolly, extending his hand to shake with the same coldness. Then he walked toward the main gate because now the barrier had been raised and the two heavy steel doors were open wide. The shiny Volga approached from the garage, stopping in the parking lot. Fifteen minutes were left before offices would open. He saw Thuan hurriedly go up three steps and into the house. There was enough time for him to change his clothes.

2

"Uncle: your ration of morning porridge. Go to your room and eat it while it is still hot."

With a broad smile the nurse gives Vu his breakfast. Vu looks in the enamel bowl: meat porridge cooked in a huge pot then scooped out into large aluminum saucepans to be divided among the one thousand people in the hospital. A quiver shakes all of Vu's body. Suddenly he is afraid of this communal dish. Perhaps some heavy memories check his appetite; perhaps the death of his roommate makes the porridge stale in his mind.

Vu looks around at the few female relatives who are there taking care of the patients in his room. Among them, he notices a bony woman, quite tall. He had seen her before, carrying her husband to the bathroom as if he were a three-year-old. The story was that this husband had left her in their village for fifteen years while he had lived clandestinely with a female cadre at the front. And, after the liberation of the capital, he had then bedded a city widow. Now, close to earth and far from heaven, he could rely on no one, so he'd had his children summon the "skirted woman with the blackened teeth" to care for him. This country woman doesn't like the hospital's food. Now she is in line, holding out an aluminum plate, waiting to receive her husband's portion of rolled rice-flour pancakes.

Vu immediately presents his bowl of porridge: "Hello, Sister, I don't feel like eating today. Can you help me out?"

"Yes, that is so nice of you, thank you, Uncle," she replies cheerfully. "I'm waiting for the pancakes and will take them to our room."

Vu then walks toward the end of the hall. He thinks of strolling around the garden a couple of times; when tired he will go to the cafeteria to drink coffee and eat sesame balls. At least they are not as awful as the thin meat porridge. Vu purposefully goes down the stairs. He does not notice a man running after him.

"Brother Vu . . . Brother Vu . . . Brother Vu . . . Wait for me . . ."

The guest calls three, four times.

Vu turns around. "Brother Bac!"

The older brother wears a palm-leaf hat, his clothes the brown outfit of a real farmer, his hands full of small and large bags.

"Forgive me, I was busy walking . . ."

The two men stop in the middle of the stairs and look at each other. The older brother says, "Nobody told me until yesterday, when Thao's daughter stopped by the house."

"That's true," Vu replies. "Van couldn't tell you because she caused the physical and mental breakdown that led me here . . . And the organization, I asked that they not tell you, to spare you worry."

"You're mistaken! You and I—we come from the same stock, why hide it?"

"Because you already have too much to worry about," Vu replies.

"What is all that you have brought?"

"Oranges and bananas from our garden, and honey from our own hives . . . Only some ocean shrimp did I buy to grill them myself."

"You still treat me like a little child."

"Well, child or grown man, you are still my kid brother."

The two look at each other. Two men with salt-and-pepper hair, the younger one with more salt than pepper, the older one with more pepper than salt. There is a moment of emotional silence before the older brother awkwardly smiles and says, "How awful. You worry too much, therefore your hair is much whiter than mine. A farmer's fate has its hardships but also its blessings. Each day we eat simple meals; when the sun rises, we start singing; not a worry."

"You: not a worry?"

"Now, let me put these bags away and we—two brothers—will go down to the cafeteria for some refreshments. In the hospital, it doesn't smell nice. Just stay here and wait for me."

Vu takes the bags back to his room, and after arranging them neatly in a small cabinet, returns to the stairs and the two brothers head to the cafeteria. There they sit in silence with a teapot. Both think about the last time they had seen each other. Then, almost simultaneously, they blurt out:

"It has been two and a half years."

"Two years, seven and a half months," Bac says, correcting Vu.

Both remain silent as if waiting for the other to speak first. After a long while, Vu cries out, "I really miss Mother, dear Brother Bac."

"Me too." After a pause he adds: "So strange: as we grow older we are like kids. We miss Mother like when we were six."

"This morning when the hospital served meat porridge, I remembered the fish porridge Mother cooked in the old days. Just thinking of it made me salivate."

"Yes, Mother's cooking was famous throughout the whole region. Thus, anyone who had a big banquet would call on her. Do you remember once when she cooked catfish porridge for everyone in the family?"

"Yes, I can still smell the nice aroma of fresh chopped ginger, dill and green onions, crushed pepper and fresh hot chilies in fish sauce. I still remember the large ceramic barrel under the eaves where she put the catfish to use up slowly. The fish jumped friskily all night."

Vu stops, as if he would cry if he continued. The two brothers often goofed off around that great pot of fish. One time, playing war with other kids in the hamlet, he had taken the role of the mighty hero Dinh Bo Linh.

Wanting to impress the neighboring kids, he had demanded that his mom cook porridge as a treat. Of course she refused, because no one would ever spoil a child by doing such a crazy thing. The next day, waiting for his mother to go to the market, Vu had emptied a whole bag of powdered chili into the container of fish and had killed them all. After this wicked act, he had sneaked over to his grandmother's. Back home, his mother had taken control of the situation. She was forced to turn her anger into something useful, so she had cooked close to twenty fish to make a huge pot of porridge to treat the little army of the hamlet's Dinh Bo Linh. More than forty little guests were invited to enjoy the fish soup and many sweet desserts. His older brother, on behalf of "Warrior Vu," had stood up to announce the reason why "Warrior Vu offers his army a victory celebration." When the party was over and the kids with their full and happy tummies had left, Bac was punished. He had to lie facedown on the mat in the middle of the room, to receive on his buttocks twenty strikes from a bamboo stick for the crime of abetting the killings. Meanwhile Vu, unabashed, enjoyed safety in his grandmother's protective arms, even though he had missed a meal of tasty fish soup. In exchange he had good beef soup and other goodies. Four days later his mother had come and called out from the street:

"Vu, I forgive you. No more running away; come home."

This memory fills his heart with nostalgia. He thinks to himself, "He always took punishment for me. He always had to extend his arms to help carry heavy burdens. Not only during childhood, but until now, too . . ."

Instinctively he looks down at his brother's hand on the table: the hand of a real farmer with coarse fingers, all brown from sunburn, nails dark from tree sap. By contrast, his fingers are fair, like those of women during childbirth. It has been twelve years since Bac left his family in the city, turning the management of his carpentry store over to his son-in-law, in order to live in the countryside with the pretense of caring for an unmarried, childless aunt on his mother's side, but in reality to raise Nghia, the daughter of Miss Xuan. The day Miss Xuan died, Vu had sent word for him to come, because he could not find anyone else to assume this responsibility. It was already too much for his wife to take in Miss Xuan's son. Moreover, everyone knew that Van disliked those of her own sex. She could be friendly for a while with a few women who were clueless or ignorant, taking advantage of them or turning them into her pawns, but in her heart she wanted no friendship with any female whatsoever. She could befriend only men. She had real feelings only for those of the opposite sex. She loved him, and, besides him, she wanted a regular contingent of men around her from different walks of life; this flock of men, old and young, all circled around the city beauty like little satellites orbiting a sun, ready to serve her as needed. They admired her beauty, concealing their lust in their afternoon or midnight dreams. Thus, Miss Beauty To Van—without having a throne—had always enjoyed the pride of being a queen. Though without an official title, there had been no absence of a bright halo highlighting her name. And so heaven could not endow her with enough kindness to care for an orphaned girl. There was nothing else to do but to turn to his own family. He had asked the driver to deliver a letter of one sentence: "Dear brother, I need to see you right away, the sooner the better."

The car had left early, returning to Hanoi at dark with his older brother. At night, after dinner, they had gone to the garden to smoke. Bac had asked: "Will they let the child live peacefully in the countryside? Don't forget that the farther you are from the capital, the darker it is. It's easier for hoodlums to strike."

Vu had replied, "I think farther is safer for the child. She's a female, not someone who will extend the patrilineage, therefore she won't be on their radar. Farther away, they pay less attention. Less attention—less viciousness."

Then the older brother had agreed: "If so, all right. If you gather enough clothing for the girl, I will take her immediately tonight."

"You don't need to go immediately tonight. The driver needs sleep. But tomorrow morning, I will ask the driver to take you and the little girl very early. However . . ."

Then it was Vu who was hesitant.

He was bothered by imposing on his brother to leave his family and his work to move to the countryside, to a life without prominence, without all the regular means of living comfortably. From supervising a large carpentry business in three hamlets, he would be forced to harvest, to garden, to pull a rickety cart to sell jackfruit, guava, pineapple, pomelo, and lichees. No longer enjoying the position of boss with staff to make your meals and get you drinks, he would have to live in a house with three large rooms in the dim light of oil lamps; he would have to cook his own meals in a kitchen filled with smoke from husks and straw. He would endure the absence of his wife and kids and his trade, because he was a craftsman with golden hands: everything he made was considered across the region as a piece of art. His mother-of-pearl-inlaid furniture was not for use but was regarded as heirlooms for children and grandchildren. Every family tried to buy some work of his—a sideboard, a buffet, or a sofa with kneeling feet—so that they could proudly boast to their neighbors, "They are Mr. Bac's!"

Thinking of all this, Vu had become embarrassed: "However, I think . . . really, I have done you wrong."

Bac had shaken his head. "Don't be concerned. I have known my fate for a while. When you were at the northern front, Mother was sick for six long months. Before dying, she reminded me, 'Your brother at old age will encounter much hardship. Don't leave him alone. Others may say: "Each brother has his own fate," but in our family we must follow this: "Brothers are like arms and legs." ' "

Then, he had put out his cigarette and gone to bed. The next day he had taken the child to the car when the dew was still wet.

Twelve years had passed; Bac had become a real farmer, just as Vu had predicted, even though he did not harvest. His monthly rice ration from the city came from his wife, who bought it and took it to him; this had given her opportunities to visit him. In the countryside, he had taken care of the gardens; he had raised poultry and had twelve beehives. All day, from morning to night, he had had no lack of things to do. Thus, he had raised Nghia since she was two; she had become a young woman who knew how to care for a house, how to help the father push a cart to sell fruit or animals on market days. The neighbors called them the "carpenter father and daughter," because Bac had brought some of his tools, and, when he was free of chores, he would engage his hands in carving. The aunt had died seven years earlier at eighty-two, but Bac had remained in the countryside with the young child.

After some silence, Vu asks, "How is she doing?"

"She is healthy and a good girl. She is sweeter as she grows up. I fear she is too sweet and shy."

"Like mother, like daughter. Her mother was as sweet."

"The thing is: this year she reaches puberty."

"My gosh! How could I have forgotten that?" Vu cries out. "Oh my heaven, time flies like an arrow."

"Yes, you and I, we have aged quite a bit."

"Twelve years, you had to be separated from your wife and the kids to carry my burden."

"Don't say that. Your responsibility is also my responsibility. I don't mind it. Now, there is something bothering me: the little girl has grown. If we let her continue to live in the village, she will become a real peasant. In no time she will fall for some village guy and then will turn into a farmer. Thus, we will shortchange the young girl's potential. Even though she lives under our protective arms, she really is a princess."

"Yes, you are right," Vu says. "This is totally my fault. I am so preoccupied and did not think sooner about this."

Vu then grabs his brother's hand. "Look here, Brother, your hands are rough and dark, mine are white. Thus you carry all the heavy burden in the family on my behalf."

"You are joking; everybody who works in an office has a white face and hands."

"I cannot use my mouth to thank you because words are ordinary and bland. But, according to the old ways, I must kneel down and bow to you."

"Now, Brother Vu . . ." he says, shaking his head. "Don't say that. Don't ever say that. You and I are from the same womb. A burden on your shoulders is a burden on mine."

Tears well up in his eyes and also begin to roll down Vu's cheeks. Vu turns toward the yard at the back of the hospital to avoid curious eyes. Bac also looks down, and drinks cup after cup of tea.

After a long while, the older brother looks up. "The business between you and Miss Van: in what way has it been solved?"

"I have not gone through the process of separation but will move into the office complex. When little Trung has summer vacation I will take him there. The other day when the secretary came to visit me, he requested that I prepare all the formalities so that, when I leave the hospital, I can go straight to the new place. Van will stay in the villa with Vinh, and, certainly, her brother will crawl in there."

"It's hard to resolve amicably. I think she will not agree to it."

"As of now, I cannot find a better solution."

"In this situation, it is hard for you to take in Nghia. Let me take her to the city with the family. Whatever happens, a girl from the city is always less deprived than a peasant from a farm."

"I am indebted to you, but I will manage to find help somewhere. In truth, the little girl is really at a disadvantage."

Bac gets up. "I have to return before I miss the afternoon ferry. I am not comfortable leaving the girl alone overnight. Perhaps I will have to make arrangements to sell the house and garden or hire someone to look after it when I take her to the city, the sooner the better."

Hesitating a moment, he sighs and adds: "Do you know that plenty of guys stalk the paths day and night? She is not yet fourteen and she is quite attractive. That is why I dare not leave her by herself."

He rubs his brother's back. "Take care of your health. I feel all your ribs here."

Putting his hat on, he leaves.

Vu sits down and looks at Bac disappearing into the bustling crowd of people entering and leaving the hospital. He does not like emotional good-byes in front of a crowd, which is why he does not walk his brother out. In his family, often an opposite scene was played: on his visits to Bac in the town, when it came time to leave, the two brothers dragged things out for a good hour, unable to separate. Bac always found excuses to accompany Vu to the car, then would take him around, stopping here for a while to drink tea, there to watch a fish pond or a rock garden. Then, at the end, Bac would suddenly cry out:

"Oh, my goodness! I forgot to give you a pack of tea. The lotus-smoked tea from Mrs. Lieu of Cham Lien village. During the lotus season, flowers from all the large ponds are brought to her to sell. Her toasting hand has no equal. Hanoi people always come down to buy." Or:

"Oh, my goodness! I have packed some fish in a bag of water and have forgotten it in the kitchen. Wait for me. These fish are superior river fish. Bother yourself a little to take them back and put them in a great big ceramic pot. Ask Miss Van to make porridge or put them in wine and ginger to eat." Or:

"Oh, my goodness! The ocean shrimp I carefully grilled—I forgot them in the chest. Wait, I will get them. Take them back to Hanoi to enjoy with beer."

Each time, he found many different kinds of such "forgetting," which enabled their partings to be drawn out for a little more time. On the contrary, when Bac visited Hanoi and it came time for him to leave, he would quickly run alone to the car while the younger brother looked quietly on. Their personalities were different; so were their behaviors.

"He is a worthy man: a brother replacing a father!" Vu thinks to himself a little later. Then, "He replaces the father but has no brotherly authority!"

It is indeed true. Vu was responsible for all important decisions in the family, but his brother carried out the most arduous duties. When they were little, their mother often told their father, "Our family's two sons seem under a love charm for each other. But the little one has a big head and always bosses the older one."

Vu smiles as he drinks his tea. As Tran Phu and Le Phuong cross the yard arm in arm, an idea suddenly pops into his head: "These two fellows! It could be these two fellows. Why not? For sure, I can rely on one of them. My intuition tells me that."

Putting his cup of tea down, Vu runs to the door and calls out to Tran Phu. Both men turn around immediately.

"Hello, great man . . ."

"Does the great man have an appointment with someone or does he just want to hide from people?" Le Phuong asks with a smile.

"Hide from people? What do you mean by that?" Vu replies.

"To avoid those comrades of yours in the ward. Regular encounters with those comrades does not make you comfortable either physically or emotionally, right?"

"Well, that's true enough," Vu admits. Then he turns to tell Tran Phu, "Do you remember the patient adjacent to my bed? The officer that knew you when you headed up Battalion 507?"

Tran Phu looks at him, puzzled. "I have not found my bearings to recall that time so very far in the past."

"Well, he's a military officer but dares not go to Hospital 108 to be treated, so he sneaks in here. He sends regards and says that you know how to correctly choose one's way in life."

"Ah, now I remember. The guy with purple lips like Lang Son plums, right?"

"Exactly . . . He died this morning."

"Really?" Tran Phu blurts out, neither surprised nor sad. Then he turns to tell Le Phuong, "That lieutenant had a stormy life and, of course, plenty of a loner's regrets. I will tell you more when I am free. A novel could tell it all."

To Vu, he says, "After he died, the hospital staff took him to the morgue, and no close relative came; is it true?"

"How did you know?"

"Because I'm kind of nosy; I want to know what happens to all in our generation. So I opened an investigation immediately."

"He died about three or four o'clock this morning. Since he was admitted to the hospital, no one set foot here. The sideboard at his bed never had any oranges or foods brought by others. The doctor said he had been here almost three months."

"That is the extent of a life. But enough, let's change the subject, we need not bother ourselves with such a person on a beautiful morning like today."

"You are right," Vu says. "Because I personally am having a headache and want your help."

Both burst out laughing; people around them become curious and glance over. "A big shot like him speaking humbly before two carefree playboys. Honorable One, are you joking or are you serious?" Le Phuong asks.

"Never in my life have I joked with anyone," Vu replies, and his serious tone shuts the two men up.

"You two know that I agreed to raise two children of a . . . big brother . . ."

"Yes, we heard."

"The son lives with our family. But the girl had to go to the countryside to live with my older brother, in an isolated village all the way up in mountainous Thai Nguyen. Now she is thirteen, I want to take her back to Hanoi but don't know whom to entrust her to."

"Is she indeed the firstborn daughter of . . . the most elder uncle?" Le Phuong asks, taking a few minutes to find the right word for the mysterious father, while preventing the ears around from guessing to whom he was referring. "This is the very fruit from the last blossom in the life of a great man!"

"Exactly so," Vu says. "The two kids are only twenty months apart."

"The girl has lived in the countryside since she was young?"

"Yes, since she was two, to be accurate. Now she is almost fourteen. If she is not brought back soon to Hanoi, she will surely become a peasant and so she will live out her whole life as a gardener or a laborer."

"I understand," says Tran Phu, nodding. "A woman's life is quite short; especially those from the countryside."

"I know that this is an extremely difficult situation," Vu goes on. "I am reluctant to ask even those I have been close to for many years for assistance in the matter. But now my intuition tells me to ask the two of you for help."

Smiling broadly, Tran Phu says, "The sixth sense always provides the wisest compass. You are right to ask us. Because we sit with our butts on the grass. Only those who have dirt on their butts would dare to get involved in such a thing."

Vu is puzzled. What does Tran Phu mean by "dirt on their butts"?

Seeing this, Tran Phu explains: "There are two kinds of people with muddy butts. One kind are farmers or dirt-poor people. They would have a hard time helping you even if they wanted to, because they lack ability—

intellectual as well as financial. The other kind are those who voluntarily live outside the circumference of power. They choose to live like that because they are able to see the failings of those who govern. Moreover, they equip themselves only with minimal financial support—enough to sustain their survival with a little extra to cover others when needed. Thus, they are relatively free."

"Yes, now I understand. However . . ."

"However, you are still hesitant because doing this would really be a crime for those who are still living in your world. We understand that very clearly. When living in the world of power, the hierarchy of position rules over everything. The more power you have, the more you want, and the more you belong to it. But we—we are like those who stand at the sides of the machine. Even though my friend is the director of a publishing company, his position is like a piece of stale bread compared with the other cushy jobs. A stale piece of bread with no butter or jam spread upon it; one munches on it only when one is very, very hungry. Nobody wants to live on it forever. Especially when age starts to slide toward the end and we need to protect our upper and lower teeth."

Stopping, Le Phuong turns to ask his friend, "Am I right or not, Mr. Director?"

"Correct one hundred percent!"

Both burst into deep laughter that leads to coughing.

"They seem oddly very happy," Vu thinks to himself. "I wonder, are they serious or are they joking?" He asks after taking some sips of beer, "Will you be able to endure threats or interference from this machine or not?"

"I may joke and laugh but my mind has covered all the implications of what you are suggesting," Tran Phu replies. "I know that you worry a lot. In addition, all your life you have used the correct terminology, the serious language of politicians and administrators. It is understandable that you are a bit apprehensive when dealing with a couple of unsettled guys like us. Therefore, I will explain everything carefully to put you at ease."

For the first time since they had met, Vu sees that Tran Phu is serious. "I have a sister who has married a medical doctor—she brings the food here for me," Tran Phu begins, going on: "The couple is childless. For a long time they have wanted to adopt. Everyone, especially me, has discouraged them. Adopting a child is a dangerous venture, because most kids given away or sold have an abnormal history, or are full of elements not beneficial to their psychological and physical development. However, we know also that taking care of an abandoned child brings auspicious fortune. If this is possible with ordinary adoptees, why not more so with the kin of a distinguished person? Don't worry. I have not asked my sister but I am sure there will not be any problem. We shall announce that we have found a girl for her to adopt; and it is you who has brought her to us, right here, in this hospital. Whatever the truth, I will say it as it is, in the context of having known you since the northern front. Our knowledge has limits, not an inch more. A girl of thirteen with no prior convictions; never cheated or killed anyone. If concerns are sought, it is hard to find any basis."

"Thank you," Vu replies, both anxious and moved. However, he still doesn't completely trust what Tran Phu is saying. It is too good to be true . . .

"Let's pretend," he says, "that . . . that the entire truth could be openly told . . ."

"It cannot . . . And if someone dares say anything, I will declare him a traitor, who accuses and defames the highest leader," Tran Phu firmly replies. "For years, the Party and the government have always used propaganda to teach the people that our leader is the Father of the People, the one who always fought for independence and the nation's future, and therefore who has no personal happiness. I will accurately quote one hundred percent of all the teachings of the Party's Central Indoctrination Office. I will repeat exactly all the things they have asked me to memorize all these years. I will throw in their face exactly what they have vomited out systematically."

"Splendid!" says Le Phuong. "There is no better way than to pick up a stone lying in front of the house of Mr. Tu to throw at the guava trees of Mr. Tu; it's like taking the cane from the canton chief to hit the head of the canton chief . . . This type of counterattack, of turning the tables on the big shots, has been used for thousands of years. Now they explain it in a more modern way: the action of a boomerang."

Vu remains worried. After a few moments, he says, "I don't know, perhaps this is too much trouble for the two of you; I'm still a little uncomfortable with the plan. If you agree, I could certainly ask my secretary to bring money and food, monthly, as a contribution to the family."

"We don't have need of your food ration," Tran Phu replies. "In reality, these ration cards don't provide enough to feed a cat." Lowering his voice, he goes on: "We are not as well off as the people were in old Hanoi, but now we know how to tighten our belts. We cannot trust any directions given to us by those who once sat on sidewalks pouring cash out of cans to count what the passersby had contributed and then, the next day, thanks to the generosity of the revolution, sit in the finance minister's chair. No, we are not that stupid. Our money cannot be deposited in government banks, nor can it be declared to these officials who once were beggars. We have to find ways to transform it . . . as if we might bury it at the foot of an orange tree. It is that simple. Now, are you comfortable or not?"

"Yes," Vu replies, though his face is hot as if someone had just slapped it. This is the first time he has heard such words. Unfortunately, they are true.

At that moment, a loud clang sounds in the yard. Looking out, they can see a large, perplexed fellow forcefully hitting the steel sheet. The three stand up.

"It's lunchtime," Vu says. "Good-bye to the two of you. I have to go back to my room. Thank you for all you have said."

"Oh, Older Brother, don't stand on ceremony," Tran Phu replies. "Everything is within reach. Now I have to see a friend off to the city center. Have a good lunch. Please make preparations for the young girl. Whatever can be done, we will do it; it doesn't have to be perfect. What's left, my sister will take care of. Next week we can pick her up."

The two men walk arm in arm to the doors of the hospital. Vu returns to the patient section, his step light and bouncy as if walking on clouds, murmuring to himself, "Too good to be true."

At the top of the stairs, the duty nurse comes up to him, smiling happily. "Please come and eat your lunch while it's hot. I put it on top of the cabinet."

"Thank you very much. I will be there soon."

She quickly walks away but, suddenly remembering something, hurriedly turns back to say, "You got some mail. I put it in the drawer so that no one else could try to open it."

"Well, thank you. You may be young but you are very careful."

"You are kind. I have never been called 'careful.' At home my mother called me 'the crow with its insides out.' But in the village, my mail was often opened, therefore . . ."

"I appreciate it," says Vu warmly. He hurries to his room, curious as to who might have sent him a letter. "Could it be Sau?" he thinks to himself. "Sau's letters come in the form of some scrawled lines on a page torn from a notebook and never put in an envelope, so whoever delivers the letter can read it freely. Most often these notes are sent when he needs to have an urgent meeting. He knows I am in the hospital and can't go out for meetings, so it can't be him. Then who? Could it be Van? Perhaps she desires that we make one final attempt at reconciliation?" Vu goes to his room and pulls the envelope out of the drawer. Tearing it open, he sees that the letter is written on the kind of ruled paper that students use.

"A letter from the young boy. Thus, he knows how to write. The first letter in his life."

He holds the letter, thinking back in time to when the boy had started to walk and begun to talk and to feed himself. All this seems like yesterday, but now here he is composing letters like an adult.

My dear father:

I am sending you this letter, knowing that you are in the hospital and there is no way to leave this place to come visit you. From the school to the hamlet is more than forty kilometers but there is no bus, only a horse cart. Father, please forgive me that I am not able to comfort you while you are sick. I can only pray to heaven for your speedy recovery and return to your regular activities. Here, we study well. Once in a while Vinh stays home because he has a tummyache, but I take notes for him. Last week, Mother Van came and visited us. She was very strange. I do not know what happened in Hanoi, but Mother Van stared at me and suddenly said: "Because of you our family is destroyed."

Dear Father, it is very painful to think that I am the cause of this. I only need to know that I am your own son, which is in itself happiness. I do not want to make Mother Van suffer or to deprive Brother Vinh of his share. Maybe you could let me go down to the country to live with the older uncle. After the summer, I can transfer there, it would be no problem. As long as the family is harmonious, Mother Van and Brother Vinh are satisfied. I believe that Sister Nghia will be very happy and older uncle there will not be so lonely. Thus it would be less of a burden to you and everybody would be happy.

I also want to inform you that Mother Van came with a tall man with sunglasses. I never saw him before at the house and his behavior was very odd. While Mother Van spent time with Brother Vinh, he pulled my ear and said, "I want to know if your ear is soft or hard," then he lifted me up. It hurt really bad: I had tears in my eyes. I almost screamed but I ground my teeth in fear of Mother scolding me. This man made me very scared. I don't know why he was so cruel to me. Dear Father, please let me go to the countryside and every now and then you can come and visit both of us. Thus, everything will be more peaceful.

I am always trying to study so as not to worry you. I wish you a speedy recovery so that we can see you very soon.

Your son kisses you: Tran Trung

As Vu finishes the letter, dizziness comes over him and he has to lean against the wall. "Oh, my dear son. It is so sad," he thinks. "A boy who is filial but who cannot be a son. A child born full of compassion who must live in a world of heartless and inhuman people. . . . Oh, it's so sad for me, too—with the title of father but unable to protect the child who lives within my arms. . . . And I myself never had the chance to have such a good child as this. . . . My love with the beautiful woman only created something immoral, incompetent, and full of flaws. My miserable patrimony got lost in a dark body and in a darker soul. This truly is a complete failure. . . .

"Why does she behave so cruelly? . . . A woman that I held over thirty years. . . . It is so strange that it is only now that I come to really know the person with whom I shared a bed with for so long. . . . Life is like an endless performance; not until the curtain falls do we know what is black and what is white. . . . Oh, it's no coincidence that for thousands of years people read and reread the Lieu Trai story, because there has been no shortage of those who lived in passionate love until they awoke one day to find out that for so many years they had taken pleasure with a skeleton. . . . My wife! When did she become an enemy? That guy with sunglasses is none other than Sau's henchman! They play the game of ill treating the boy; it is a sign that they are mobilizing me for some demand on the real father. The survival of this person becomes the stick that directs others. . . . This blow is nothing new, but the surprising thing is that she accepts the agreement. Is it she who leads the enemy on? Why is it she?"

Black waves suddenly appear before his eyes, rising up and then crashing down, leaving him with the impression that his whole body is breaking into foam. The moaning of the receding tide is terrifying and mysterious; it feels as if it is no longer the noise of the moving sea but the roaring of gigantic beasts from the Jurassic period. All of a sudden, the edge of the low tide disappears and in its place is a horde of dragons running wildly over a vast field of vegetation. Chasing after them are giant tongues of flowing fire, climbing one on top of the other. Wherever the wind blows, the vegetation turns into a roaring fire pit. The firestorms encircle, entrap, and consume the animals. He feels that fire burning him and making his own eyes shoot out sparks of fire.

"Why am I turning into a Jurassic beast? Is this real or a dream, very strange . . ."

He hears clearly the fire being fanned by the wind blowing around him. Then the fire slaps his face, making him want to scream: "Water . . . Give me water . . . Call the fire truck . . ."

But he is unable to open his mouth. He falls down at the giant feet of one of the dragons and sees before him what will become a pile of crumbling bones once the fire is finished with it.

Then he hears vaguely, calling from somewhere: "Doctor . . . Call the doctor . . ."

"Where are the emergency aides? Bring the oxygen here."

A dreamy thought comes to his mind: "Well, they are bringing the oxygen for the officer with the wheezing breath, with lips dark like the Lang Son plums. Strange, though: this guy is dead but still he needs lots of oxygen from the hospital?"

Suddenly he hears a fish twisting in his ears. It makes the same sound as the fish jumping in the container where his mother had kept them. The fish had noisily fought all night. Above that container was the tile roof. And above the roof was the sky, a high, open space filled with sunlight, a light blue . . .

3

Military Field Hospital 306 sits at the jungle's edge, not too far from a stream, in a fine setting for a multispecialty facility. The buildings are clustered together up high under the shade of bushy trees that are so dense, even during bright summer days sunlight cannot break through. In that permanent shadow, clusters of wild orchids and crow's-nest plants dangle. Behind the hospital is a large stone cave into which as many as thirty seriously injured soldiers can quickly be moved when bombs fall. The kitchen, the communal dining room, and a storeroom are shoved into an area close to the cave's mouth.

It is the spring of 1969 and the hospital is full of injured soldiers. The number of those waiting for surgery is three times more than normal, forcing the doctors and staff to work around the clock. The screaming and moaning, along with the angry fighting of the crowd of injured soldiers, has turned the hospital into chaos.

Among the injured soldiers appears an alluring prince, a delectable prey for the twelve girls who work at the hospital and stand shakily on the divide between their last moment of youth and the time of loss. It is Lieutenant Hoang An. Hoang An is considered a manly ideal not only for his looks but also because of his unusual courage. He did not utter a sound during an entire surgery performed without anesthetic. A piece of shrapnel had cut

Hoang An's left arm; on arriving at the hospital, the wound—tourniqueted too long on the road—had become infected, and they had to remove the arm from the shoulder down to save him. Oddly, Hoang An healed very quickly, almost magically. The injured soldiers around him, even though some were half his age, looked at him with admiration and envy. Even before new skin had grown to cover his stump, he was strolling all over the area, setting up traps to catch porcupine and fox for the kitchen to prepare for meals. After he had fully recovered, he volunteered to help the girls carry stream water up to the camp; With only one arm, this lieutenant could carry more than many men with two arms. He had the legs of a hunter and he climbed the slopes like a gazelle. The girls of the hospital looked at him with adoring eyes. But Hoang An shared his goodness with everyone, thus there was no fighting among the girls waiting for life's chances. So when he was completely rehabilitated, the head of the hospital kept him there instead of transferring him to another post. Eventually, Hoang An became a member of the hospital staff without specific duties. He seemed extremely pleased with his new role. Nobody said anything, but people understood that soon he would be sent to the rear because he could no longer fight. Until then, it was best to dedicate himself to helping others.

One frigid morning, with fog covering the mountains, the loud horn of a vehicle is heard. From the truck comes a shout: "Medical supplies from the regional command have arrived . . ."

Everyone in the hospital rushes out, surprised.

"The telegram said two more days before the ambulance would arrive . . ."

"Who knows? Perhaps there was no bombing so the road was open . . ."

The staff, including Hoang An, go down to pick up the medicines and medical equipment. It is indeed true that the American bombers have taken the weekend off, which has left the road safe to travel. Everybody is happy because, besides medicines, there are also food and loose-leaf tobacco. When all the packages have been unloaded and lined up neatly along the sides of the road, the driver starts the engine and immediately takes off for headquarters. As the truck rolls a few meters, he suddenly cries out, "I forgot!"

Bending down under the seat, he takes out a tattered and dirty backpack.

"Does this hospital have anyone by the name of Hoang An?"

"That is I."

"Headquarters sent along this backpack, which belonged to a martyr. Was he truly a relative of yours or not?"

"If not my relative, then why would they send it to me?" Hoang An replies, with doubt in his mind. He wonders whose pack it could be—perhaps that damned Meo tribesman Ma Ly.

The soldier looks at Hoang An and explains: "Not that I am nosy, but the address is very vague. Moreover, in this military region there are six named Hoang An. The administrative office was skeptical of sending it to you because your birthplace is Lang Son but this martyr was a Tay from Thai Nguyen."

"Ah," An says, smiling. It is beginning to make sense to him now.

The driver turns over the backpack and squeezes his hand. "I wish you good health."

"Thank you. I also wish you safe travels."

Hoang An looks down on the dirty, smelly backpack; it is like a beggar's bag. He guesses it had been thrown in a stone cave for a while, at least a year or two. That would explain the moldy, dried bloodstains and the many holes made by roaches eating the canvas. Attached to the pack is a faded piece of white paper on which someone had written not too long ago.

Remnant belonging of Lt Hoang Huy Tu, Battalion 115, Zone 18, Company 3, Platoon 1; martyred at the battle of Thuan Hoa. Suggest forwarding this to Captain Hoang An, of the First Battalion; Battalion Commander Dinh Quang Nha

An is lost in his thoughts for a moment. The name Hoang Huy Tu evokes a time of warmth and happiness. He had been the husband of An's sister My. Tu's family had lived close to the town of Lao Cai. His father had been a famous welder. Hoang An has fond memories of his sister's wedding; it was the first and only time he had set foot in Lao Cai.

After everyone returns to the hospital and the medicines and food have been stored away, An takes Tu's backpack and walks toward the stream, where he can be alone. He carefully opens the pack, which contains a fall-winter outfit, a dry tube of toothpaste, a brush with worn-out bristles, a small horn comb, and an envelope sealed by layers of plastic. A smell of mildew is mixed with that of the damp cloth.

"This is all that is left of a handsome and healthy man. All that is left from a husband and a father. The possessions of Lieutenant Hoang Huy Tu. Precious items that someday I will turn over to My and her children."

He sits there for a while before the insignificant items. Then he opens Tu's letter. It is written on the ruled paper of kindergarteners.

Dear Brother,

Since the day I saw My off to go to Lao Cai, so much time has passed and so many things have happened. Even though we have had no opportunity to meet since then, I have never forgotten you because My always reminds me of you. We have two children, both boys. My family moved to Thai Nguyen after you enlisted, because there my father found a connection to do big business and the welding shop had potential to grow. My father is also old and the production for which we are responsible required hiring almost ten workers. I have nothing to complain about, except among the three brothers, two must take the road. With no clear news about the youngest brother, tomorrow I have to fight in Thanh Hoa. Soldiers sent there have little hope of return. It is said that the earth is hard and narrow, therefore corpses are not buried singly but mostly piled up by five or seven. This afternoon, the whole company is writing letters to their families. I am writing to you. Everybody thinks quietly that it is the last letter they will ever write as a soldier.

Dear Brother, there is something you have surely guessed about but didn't know for certain. Miss Xuan and Miss Dong were both killed in the year of the rooster (1957), their skulls smashed with a wooden mallet. The body of Miss Xuan was thrown on the side of a road outside Hanoi, making it appear that a car had hit her, pretending it was a traffic accident; and Miss Dong was thrown under the bridge across Khe Lan, on the road to That Khe. I only learned about this three years after the fact through an acquaintance. My parents-in-law and Mr. Cao were all killed in the winter of the year of the dog (1958), a year after the deaths of the two women. When I returned to Xiu Village, three weeks after that disastrous night, only ashes remained of the two houses. The hamlet people said that one night they had suddenly heard a helicopter landing by Son Ca Falls. Because it was so cold and dark, nobody went outside to look. About half an hour later, the two houses went up in flames. When neighbors arrived, they smelled gasoline and the fire was high like a dragon lick, so they could do nothing. Looking through the flames, they could not see one person. They stood there like statues, watching each beam fall. The fire burned until the next day. Later the charred body of Mr. Cao was found among the ashes. My parents-in-law were missing, invisible. The district proclaimed that a company of American lackeys from South Vietnam had flown up to start the fire and bring havoc to our people. But I know that the killers were the same ones who killed Miss Dong and Miss Xuan. Our Tay logic tells me that.

Dear Brother, early tomorrow morning we have to leave. Surely there will be no return. Please live to revenge this by any means. Please protect My and our children. If you do, even in the grave, I will owe you a debt forever.

Your younger brother, Hoang Huy Tu

The signature is firm, not a bit shaky; the writing of a welder who had used a hammer since youth. Hoang An puts the letter down. An emotion shakes his body. Then thoughts run through him one after the other like rats.

"They murdered the women with a wooden mallet because that was the most frugal and simple way to kill. They stabbed Mr. Cao, letting people think that his death was due to some score being settled among playboys because Mr. Cao had left the hamlet to run around for twenty years. They kidnapped my uncle and aunt in an airplane and killed them, then threw their bodies in the woods of another town, making it appear as if bandits had murdered them, because my uncle was then village chief, the lowest position in the power machine. All my loved ones destroyed as chess pawns. I have no one left in this world . . . no one."

The flames in his head burn like the fire of the two houses. The rats inside his head do not stop running back and forth, jumping around. The thick smoke rises right to the top of his skull and a sharp pain erupts in his stomach, overflows his throat, and pushes into his lungs with a burning hot steam, as if his chest is now a pressure cooker ready to explode. Suddenly, he lets out a terrifying scream, one that makes him dizzy; it sounds like the roaring of an odd monster who has borrowed a human throat.

Everybody comes out to look. They have never heard such a horrifying scream; it sounded like wild waves twirling with a terrifying force. People are so scared that they stop breathing. Such a scream could only have come from a river demon, a mountain devil, or a demented, wicked giant who was extremely agitated.

But there is nothing to see other than Lieutenant Hoang An sitting by himself at the side of the stream. As he hears the footsteps of the approaching group, Hoang An turns around, his face pale but smiling broadly.

"This is my brother's backpack; he died in the Thuan Hoa battle. I could not bury him nor can I cry for him. I screamed from rage. I hate America's lackeys."

"Comrade An . . ." The head of the hospital gently puts his hand on his shoulder. "Please go back to the hospital to rest. It is war. We are all here because of this war. All of us hate America's lackeys . . ."

4

The president awakes at midnight from very heavy dreams, his heart apprehensive and tense. From the two guards outside comes the sound of the slapping of cards. It's 1:25 a.m. He pulls the blanket to his chin and absent-mindedly listens to their whispering:

"Eight."

"Ten."

"Queen of Spades."

"King of Spades."

"King of Hearts . . . you're about to die, kid."

"Dying, no shit. The red king is hot. I'll wait to see what you drop."

"Kid, it's the end of your life. . . . Ace of Spades. Where is the joker? Play it. If not, just surrender . . ."

"OK, I accept defeat this time. If I'd had the joker I would give you a sticky face. Now it is eighty-three. You still owe me five rounds. It'll be hard to undo tonight, mister."

"They are really happy, these lads who play at cards," the president thinks to himself. "In victory, they eat a couple of sesame or peanut candies. In defeat, the opponent will paint their face with ashes. Their game hurts no one; no blood is shed, no heads roll, no one harbors hatred."

A face appears in the president's imagination—the face of the wood-cutter's son. He sighs.

"My own son: if the traitors leave you alone and don't kill you, for sure you will live as just an ordinary person. You will mix with those at the bottom of society. Someday you will play cards for sesame candies and get a mustache like those guards. Who knows, maybe you will be satisfied with such anonymity. Perhaps games that pay off in candy might bring you real happiness."

To chase away these obsessions, he reaches out to turn on the light at the head of the bed to read but suddenly remembers that doing so would interrupt the game of the young men, who would then fret over why he wasn't sleeping. He lies back down, pulls the blanket to his chin, and stares at the dark ceiling. At the base of one wall, there is a tiny night-light the size of a firefly. In his childhood, he and his friends had caught fireflies and put them in eggshells; at night, the eggshells would light up. That summer of fireflies had been the most magical summer of his life.

"Nowadays, I wonder, does the boy make firefly lights?" the president asks his imagination. "He now lives in the countryside with his classmates and around them are gardens, grass, and a village cemetery full of vegetation like when I was still in Nghe An."

But his son will never know where that ancestral hometown was, and nowadays no child would play with fireflies. The nation is at war; instead of the twinkling lights of stars, bullets blaze the night sky red, making a light that spreads terror and death.

"War, war, war . . . A history thick with one war after another, thus leaders become obsessed with victory, seeking one more with this war. A war without end—both in mobilized efforts as well as in all the blood and bones. What a stupid war. A war carried out as the punishment of a people, a colossal meat grinder for a bloodbath of brothers, a thousand times more terrifying than the ancient two-hundred-year conflict between the Trinh and Nguyen clans!

"What can I do now that the game is lost? When I must become a hand-carved wooden puppet for these murderers? All my traitorous brothers: Why did they purposely turn their backs on conscience—because competition for power gives more pleasure than does ensuring the happy fate of a people? Oh, ambition and glory . . . the kind of people with whom I can't eat, can't sleep, can't be close—but they have frightening power to destroy, not just individuals or factions, but an entire race.

"But for what reason do I still passionately care for and still suffer for this nation? The nation that needs my life as if it needs an animal to sacrifice to its gods. The nation that smiles aimlessly but with satisfaction; that cheers for me as it would a great king; that admires me as officers admire a fabulous marshal who has never lost a battle, and does not understand at all the nagging suffering of my heart, and does not have enough goodness to bestow upon me even a tiny bit of happiness? For what reason do I tear myself apart for this selfish and uncaring nation, though mine it is?

"Damn: always the masses are no more than a gust of wind, a wave, a tornado, a hurricane, a fire. The mass is nameless, senseless, and takes no responsibility for what it does. So I have no grounds to complain. Whether wanted or not, this people remains my people.

"It is the meaning of my life. My heart's most painful suffering is because of it: a people doomed.

"Because we are born in this land, a muddy, unhappy acre of dirt. Because the thin, resonating cord of the nation's soul vibrates in mine as a thousand years of humiliation penetrate all my cells—from my skin, my blood, and my bones to the way I want to live. This is where I am permanently condemned to suffer. From here I must repay the mountains and rivers, which have lasted a thousand generations!"

Therefore all paths lead him back to the hell that is himself. There is no escape . . .

The president moans but immediately stifles it for fear that the two guards will hear. His heart begins to thump; he can feel each laborious contraction.

"Would that instead of having a human heart, a person could use a pump for the blood, a tool to maintain circulation but cause no pain. What if I had such a different heart, and a totally different mind: Would I live in tranquility?

"Why do I bring on myself such endless turmoil and nagging regrets?

"Why can't I just put it out of my mind? Does not the dredging up of memories just bring me before the most supreme court to hear its verdict?" Hearing a soft laugh by his ears, he opens his eyes. The man with the banana-colored skin is again standing with his back against the wall, looking dapper in a suit of his favorite ivory color. He still remembers his excitement the first time he had had enough money to have a suit like that made for him in Paris. His first stylishly impressive suit, and now this guy is wearing one, too; turning the collar of the shirt as he had and tying in the same old-fashioned way as he had the same tie of navy blue with white polka dots. But this is not a young man, rather someone in his fifties, appearing as a carbon copy of what he would have looked like at that age. Once again, he recognizes his double, the man he could have become.

Leaning against the wall, slow and mannered, hands in the trouser pockets, eyes looking straight at him attentively, the double says, "Aren't you crying?"

"Excuse me?" replies the president. "I don't like your question."

"If you feel like it, just cry a bit to lighten your soul. I am rather tolerant of weak people."

"I am not as weak as you think."

"We'll see."

"That comment is meant for someone young. I am more than seventy. What you say has no meaning for one like me."

"Even if you return to your ancestors tomorrow, that comment is still germane today."

The president remains silent because the guy is right. But he cannot acknowledge his failure; it's best to keep quiet. He looks up at the dark ceiling.

The guy smiles and continues: "At your age you are still trying to answer existential questions. That is to be commended."

"People can be tormented by such questions until they go to their graves," says the president. "That's why searching for answers is so natural."

"There are thousands of questions to which humanity never finds the answer, because the heart of life is a guessing game and a challenge. This determines where humans are in the natural order and their relationships both with other groups of people and with other individuals, one on one. Look to your past: you will see many empty spaces, weaknesses, splinterings, and defeats. These things happen when people lose the ability to control what drives life itself."

"I will offer some evidence for your deduction."

"Don't try. Just turn your head and look at things more objectively. The evidence lies all spread out over the road behind you."

"I always try to analyze things objectively. That is the most important demand to be made of those in power."

"That most important criterion usually is what is lacking among those who make decisions. The collapse of regimes, the disappearance of dynasties, all occur because of the lack of objectivity. I have come back to show you the greatest shortcomings of your soul. Thus, I can help you attain liberation. I will pull you out of this hell."

The president is quiet; it is true that he was genuinely waiting for help from this other man, and that fact is humiliating. Finally, he musters the courage to ask, "Yes, I am waiting to hear what you have to say."

His double smiles with the debauched seductiveness of an Yves Montand. Looking deep into the president's eyes, he says, "I will start with that neverending torment of yours: the death of a beloved woman. When Miss Xuan was murdered, what did you do?"

The president is quiet because he does not know quite how to answer. That day, he had phoned General Long, but when the general came, they had only discussed international relations. He had waited for General Long to raise the killing of Xuan, but though their meeting had lasted for longer than four hours, he did not bring that subject up. And he himself had not dared to open his mouth. He had understood that, at the time, only General Long held enough power to put a stop to Quoc Tuy's intolerable abuses. All the generals and the Defense Ministry were at his beck and call. But like the others in the Politburo, General Long, too, had wanted the president to be just an old father of the people, with no hint of a personal life becoming public. This acting as a living saint fostered indifference throughout the entire machine of power, since no one ever declines a tasty morsel that comes with having power and prestige.

"You did nothing and your mouth was closed like a clam, right?" says his double, knowing full well that the president lacks the courage to answer.

"To tell the truth, you were expecting General Long, your closest ally, to act. And you, you didn't raise your voice, because in your mind, you were afraid that history would condemn you: your emotional weaknesses had brought havoc upon the nation. Everybody had realized that the only way out of it then was to have the military seize Quoc Tuy, while simultaneously stripping Sau—your foremost betrayer—of power. But if that had happened, there would have been blood. And you feared for your name not being recorded in the nation's history books as an immortal hero of the people. After all, it was you who had authored this romantic mantra:

Unite! Unite! Great Unity.
Succeed! Succeed! Great Success.

"Your idea was beautiful and indeed effective. But only for a certain time; only for one set of circumstances; a virtuous ideal only for those living deep in the mountains and jungles with babbling streams and chattering monkeys. You did not understand that such a mantra was no more than a slogan for guerrilla warfare. Once the power machine was institutionalized, your lofty idea became only a pretty bird that was not allowed to sing or fly because it had been stuffed and mounted. Your mantra was fit only for the vehicle of resistance and could not apply to the workings of a dictatorial party in power. You were too enamored of your pretty words and your ideas and you did not understand that language—like all things in this world—has not only life, but death, too. Power is power and can't get along with beauty or morality. The strike on your young wife was indeed a dagger aimed at you, a very serious challenge to consider. Because you tied your hands then, later on, your opponents stomped all over you."

"But I couldn't possibly have asked General Long to strike. That would have led to the shedding of too much blood. The country had just gone through nine years of war; the people had not yet enjoyed any peace and happiness."

"Well: so you wanted to avoid bloodshed. It is still flowing. On this planet has there ever been a cease-fire? The current war is the most atrocious in our people's history; a war that makes the demons cry from sadness, because the dead will be more than all those sacrificed in the struggles against the northern invaders from the Mongols and the Ming dynasty to the end of World War Two. Am I not correct?"

"You know I did everything to prevent it. But . . ."

"But—you fell off your horse in the middle of the front line. Let's consider this scenario: after your young wife was murdered, you had organized a counterattack but instead of putting your opposing subordinates in a make-believe prison, you had imprisoned them in a real one. Who knows but that you could have avoided this catastrophic war and preserved so much blood of a good people?"

The president sighs quietly, while the man shrugs him off and continues:

"Never mind; let's not consider 'ifs.' That word is candy for three-year-olds. Let's return to your family drama. And this time I am not using 'what if' but confirming that General Long kept silent then because he wanted to take advantage of the game in which you played the role of a living saint. By keeping under the shadow of the saint, how many got their allotment of pressed sweet sticky rice? And the one who got the most was he himself. Your name was connected to his in the Dien Bien Phu battle. Thus, this general also wished to confine you forever in a temple. Well, playing a saint is the nastiest game of all: a one-way street that can go up but provides no way back down. One who assumes sainthood is a cadaver standing on his own pedestal; dead in the cold and stormy wind; encased in absolute and permanent loneliness; lifeless forever in the form of a statue, not able to be buried like others. It is a very fatiguing death; a death that does not allow for lying down, which is a tiredness that extends over many generations. A fantastic punishment of the creator. Am I not right?"

He starts laughing, mockingly. The president's face is hot but his whole body turns to ice.

"You were completely paralyzed, because you had no clear idea how to direct an action at that time. You wished to fight back against your enemies but dared not mobilize your close friends. You had forgotten the decisive principle of self-protection leaders had used for a thousand years:

Those who touch my left and right cut my feet and hands;
Those who touch my blood kin reach to the pupils of my eyes.

"You should have pointed out the danger to General Long and his faction—that, if he were silent before Sau's abuse of power, then, after this exploratory blow, he would be the first big tree that would have to be cut down next; that someone who steals an egg today will steal a rabbit tomorrow, and a cow the day after that; that power walks only down its own path and never looks back to reflect or to regret. If you had been wise enough to realize all this, I am sure all your followers would have immediately lent you their hands, without any hesitation or uncertainty. At all times, people act swiftly when they feel their fate being threatened. Selfishness is an old instinct and humanity's strongest motivation. But instead of acting with all

the force of reason, you were silent, waiting for some repressed understanding from your followers. That silence did not necessarily mean that
you were entirely stupid, but that you were caught between clarity and ob-
scurity. That blurred state of mind paralyzed you. There were two ways of
looking at it: on the one hand, you were embarrassed and so you did not
protect your beloved, because she was too young and too beautiful, a delectable taste in an old king's mouth; and that was why, even when your heart
was churning with love, you were shy and dared not openly defend that
love. In this instance you were infected with unfortunate emotions. If not
this, then there is only one other explanation: you were ecstatic playing the
inspiring role of a living saint, that game satisfying your pride, therefore you
had to give up a normal man's enjoyments; you had to sacrifice her, the
woman you loved most. In this instance, you were . . ."

The man goes on, but by now the president's ears are ringing and all he can
sense is the sound of rain falling somewhere, noisily, on a corrugated roof,
perhaps the roof of the port prison. Fits of angry rain. Above the roof is the
sky; sometimes light blue, other times dark with storm, then thick with
smoke and fog. Heaven: only those imprisoned can understand completely
changes in the sky's appearance. So many days, he had looked at the skies
over the port to remember those of his hometown. Then suddenly she appears on the corrugated roof, looking at him with a young and innocent
smile; exactly like the nineteen-year-old girl she had once been, sitting on
a branch eating fruit, in the woods of the north, two rows of teeth white
and shiny like pearls and lips stained with the juice.

He calls out to her but his mouth is glued shut by some kind of sticky sap,
and his tongue can't move.

"Is it possible that I have died and they sealed my mouth with this sap?"
he thinks, but then he hears the sound of cards being turned outside his
room. When he opens his eyes, he sees clearly the blue night-light.

"No, I am here . . . I am on top of Lan Vu. Opposite this building is the
temple complex, where the Abbess with shiny black teeth lives with her
disciples. Clearly I just went to visit there and they treated me to ginger tea
and rice porridge, the kind that is soft like ripe bananas."

He composes himself, and looks around the room one more time. The
elegant guy in the ivory suit has disappeared. Where he had leaned his back
against the wall is now the black-and-white photo that he likes a lot: cherry
blossoms. That picture had been a gift from her when they had their daughter. There is not a day when he does not look at it. It is all that is left of her;

all that remains of her in this vast and isolating world. Cherry blossoms. Messengers of spring. Cherry blossoms. An undying reminder of a love short lived. . . .

He tastes a saltiness. Are they his tears or lost seawater returning?

"Oh! . . . my youth . . . the old song . . ."

He begins to remember that song, then another one returns, churning within him down to painful longing:

Even though separated, my heart does not stop remembering . . .

The singing resonates inside him, digging down into his every cell; it makes his body and soul dissipate like grains of sand. He feels the waves whip him as his flesh and bones are ground down and mixed with the troubled air of the storm. He knows he is no longer himself, because he sees himself bobbing on the tips of the waves; a cluster of sea foam longingly clinging to the moving seaweed of hatred and desperation.

There is a loud knocking on the door, which then opens. The electric light outside is bright. He hears the doctor's voice:

"Mr. President, please allow me to see you. The guard heard you, so he called me over. Please stay in bed."

He is silent. The doctor listens to his lungs and heart. He shivers when the stethoscope touches his skin. But the doctor's fingers are very soft and warm. The touch of this man provokes secret thoughts:

"Warmth is the best substance for life. Warmth both shapes and sets borders to the fire of passion. My life's most passionate desire was to ignite the flame of revolution. But that revolution did not bring happiness to people. A smaller fire of passion burned in my heart for her. In the end she was destroyed by the fire of that hell. Oh, how sad to see a useless waste of human striving. My life erupted like a savage fire, a misplaced fire, an insane use of energy. I am inferior to any normal person, like this doctor, for example. He can use his energy to warm up patients, to warm a woman's body or to sing love songs."

"Mr. President, you seem to be fine but full of troubled thoughts, therefore your sleep is not calm. Will you agree to take some sedatives?"

"Oh no. Losing sleep is part of old age. And talking in your sleep is for the young. However, in old age, people tend to dream, a symptom of dementia's onset. Tell the truth: Do you find me starting to be confused?"

He laughs, and so does the doctor: "Well, that is funny."

The president continues, "I hope I don't become confused before I get into the coffin. But now, go back to your room and resume your sleep. Don't worry too much about me. I no longer have the right to eat fully or to sleep soundly."

"You will be tired with little sleep."

"Tomorrow morning I'll make it up. Tell them not to wake me for breakfast."

"Yes, sir."

"Don't worry; go back to sleep. And you, you have the right to sleep late tomorrow because you had to get up in the middle of the night. What time is it now?"

"Three twenty a.m."

"Very good. There is plenty of time for more sleep."

"Good night, then!"

The doctor closes the door. He hears him telling the two soldiers to move the table and chairs to the other side of the main temple so that their voices will not be heard so clearly. He suddenly remembers his surprise at hearing the doctor sing; his voice was sweet and the words pierced his heart with brutal strokes:

My Beloved, when will we see each other?

He realizes he has returned to the monument, where her face is opposite his and between them is a crystal net woven from a thousand teardrops. He calls her but she does not reply. Why did she remain silent for so long? Why didn't she complain or curse him, even once? That way, his heart would be lighter. Her silence is like an oil vat that, in hell, feeds the flames forever burning his soul.

"Her silence sentences me to life. Before her pure soul, her naive trust and her true and passionate love, I am a criminal for a thousand generations."

But not him alone. Those who killed her will also have to pay the price. Only a year after she died, Ba Danh and Sau had a special prison built on the island of Tuan Chau with the intention of keeping General Long there forever. But after some discussion, they feared international protests, so they forced him to go work at the planned parenthood office, with the responsibility of putting IUDs in women. Was not all this dirty comical game the Creator's revenge? Because her heart had been so pure, because her beauty was God's gift, her goodness was recognized by both saints and devils. Therefore, those who looked the other way when she died now endure misfortune, mishap, and humiliation. When for any reason whatsoever, cruelty takes a step through the temple door, it will continue straight on into the hall and no sword or dagger will stop it.

In the morning, Vu telephones and says just one sentence: "Elder Brother: the great task has turned rotten."

Shocked, he wants to ask more, but on the other end Vu has already put the phone down. Le had told him that Vu had entered the hospital three weeks earlier, having fainted unexpectedly, but he had received no further medical report about his friend's condition. Thanks to the phone call this morning, he understands why Vu's health had taken such a turn for the worse. And he knows that the doctors could do nothing to cure him. That's how life goes.

"Heaven, the great task has turned rotten!"

The last shroud of hope has fallen away and the truth is exposed. The exquisitely beautiful fairy of the imagination is nothing more than a disgusting fox in real life. After hearing Vu's thick and hoarse voice, he understands that this is the end.

"I have no further reason to sustain this corrupt and brutal regime, a regime that I created but which has betrayed me after it betrayed the people. I cannot continue to coexist with it. It's become a monster that came to term inside the country's well-meaning heart, but, right after its birth, bit the neck and sucked the blood of the mother who had carried it and painfully given birth to it. My heaven, how horrific that bloody and painful birth. Horrific to my people and horrific especially to me."

The darkness before him suddenly turns into pitch-black ink, the Chinese kind that calligraphers use to write on red paper. His mind brightens with an old image, how each spring Confucian scholars would sit grinding the ink they would then use to write poems about their dreams and hopes for the future. Those sacred characters materializing on bright red paper while outside the rain would be falling gently on the garden of cherry blossoms, and farther away white herons would be gliding over the bright green fields. How beautiful were these odes from the spring; the Chinese characters undulating like curving dragons, like curling clouds; the black, so very black; the red, so bright red. Life is always the intertwining of extremes, it seems. Why not then employ the dynamic of this competition? The thought comes abruptly, surprising him:

"Why can't I use my death like the old scholars used the black ink to glorify the vibrant red, to symbolize a glorious future for the people? Why didn't I think of this stratagem before? It is perfect for my next move on the chess board of circumstance. This is the most effective way to choke the monsters to death, to compensate the people for my mistakes. It is also the quickest way for me to find my love."

Immediately, his heart seems lighter, like that of someone who for a long time has felt his way through the darkness to finally discover the light.

"How splendid! This death will bring both escape and rescue. Why do I think of it just now? Well, my useless brain, you are really to be blamed . . ."

He pushes the blanket aside and sits right up. For a long while he has known his horoscope as well as the palm of his hand; he knows that the day to return to dust is the Mui day of the Hoi month in the Tan Hoi year (1969). He turns on the light and removes from the cupboard his old torn horoscope, the one that he's had for more than sixty years. Opening the chart, he reflects on the unfavorable alignment of the stars on that day when Death will come to shear off his life with a sickle. There is nothing out of place; his memory is totally accurate.

"Well, why live another two years in this imprisoned and absolutely hopeless life? Why go on playing the role of a wooden puppet inciting innocent children to join a miserable and stupid war, only to be sentenced later by history as an old king who was a coward and had no conscience? Departing in such a way will offer the best chance to be redeemed; it will give me calm when facing the soul's highest court of judgment."

He folds the chart, puts it back in the cupboard, and then goes to the desk, looking in the drawer for the last testament he had partially drafted the year before. He will finish it tonight because he has decided to die on the coming September 2. According to the old customs, anyone who dies on the anniversary of the founding of a dynasty, religion, or sect of martial artists demonstrates a fated rendezvous with death that cannot be denied by its followers.

The next morning, the chubby soldier comes to begin the new shift at 7:30 as usual.

The president says, "Let's go up the mountain and then have tea when we return."

"But . . . Mr. President . . ."

"I want to climb the mountain to stretch my legs. I am not hungry yet."

"Mr. President, I have to get the doctor's approval . . . I dare not . . ."

"Don't worry. I take full responsibility. The doctor is still sleeping."

Then, without waiting for a reply, he steps forward. All the chubby soldier can do is quickly follow him and take his arm.

"Mr. Chairman, let me lead you. At this hour the road is very slippery and dangerous."

"No." He turns around and says, smiling, "The old man in Woodcutter's Hamlet fell on a dry day, with the sun just past noon, right? Then, there was not a drop of dew on the grass."

"Yes, that is correct, but . . ."

"Don't be so cautious. Just walk behind me. The mountain road is so narrow, if we cling to each other it will be more difficult."

The soldier is obliged to follow him. The president takes off so quickly that all the soldier can do is hold the hem of his shirt. The farther he walks, the deeper he begins to pant because of his heavy body and the brisk pace. The flaps of the president's quilted coat slap hard on his legs and the tail of his striped scarf flies behind him like a kite being blown by the wind. He walks straight to the top of Lan Vu, to the highest point, where he has never before set foot. There, he stands on a big rock and looks out. Floating clouds glide around the top of the mountain, then swim down to the lower peaks. Farther beyond are hills and fields stretching out to the horizon.

Well! His mountains and rivers . . . there is only one reality: it is his land; it is tied to him, and he to it, forever. Everything he had had, everything he had lost, all that he had ever done, and all that remains as a debt . . . all this had started from, and would end because of, this land. A suffering homeland, a people enslaved. A history without the sound of flutes—only the rattles of daggers and swords.

"Well! This is my last battle. And this is my last prayer for my people!"

He tells the chubby soldier, "I want to stand here a little while. I have never before set foot on the top of this sacred mountain. And that is sad."

"Yes. We, too, have never climbed up here either. I heard that kings in the past came up here every three years to pray and make offerings."

"Who told you that?"

"People in Woodcutters' Hamlet."

"That's true. The top of Lan Vu is a place where the cosmic energies of rivers and mountains unite. The ancients openly recorded this fact in the histories. Trouble yourself a bit to read them and learn."

"Yes."

"Go down there and wait for me where the pine trees grow in the crack between those two rocks. I will call you when it is time to return."

"But, Mr. President . . ."

"Go down there and wait for me. No need to worry."

His voice is firm and somewhat cold, and the chubby soldier has no choice but to go where he had been directed.

Left alone, the president turns his back to the Eastern Sea and faces west. Standing as still as a statue for a few moments, he then closes his eyes, opening his entire mind to hear the voice of his heart loudly, to let the most secret sounds of his chest spread wide and resonate up to all the deities:

"Hail to all the sacred saints of the nation; to all the great spirits of brave heroes and kings who have explored and protected these mountains and rivers. Though your bodies may have decayed, if your spirits still walk abroad and permanently watch over the nation, please come here to assist me.

"Hail to the Buddha: I have not followed your way but I am lucky to know your devoted disciples here and I understand your strong influence over humanity. If your spirit always watches over the western skies, please add your strength to that of my country's deities to help me achieve my last wish:

"I, who gave birth to Communist Vietnam in the fall of the year At Dau, 1945, on the second of September in the Christian calendar, request to leave this earth on that day of that month this year, the autumn of Ky Dau. My passing will announce the end of a cruel and traitorous regime and provide its death certificate.

"My death will be my last gift to my people.

"My death will be the last victory, to compensate for all the failures and mistakes I made during my whole life.

"My death will be my most sincere apology before the highest judiciary of all existence as well as of conscience itself.

"Thus, I passionately beg all of you: help me attain my wish!"

Ah . . . ah . . . ah . . .

Ah . . . ah . . . ah . . .

Ah . . . ah . . . ah . . . ah . . .

He hears thousands of dreamy sounds, like a choir from the Eastern Sea that resonates, overflows, and rolls with the waves. Then it sounds like the whispered chattering of thousands of years being restored. He sees shadows of people clear like water in crevices, delicate like foam on the waves, dressed in old-fashioned clothes, from the Ly to the Tran dynasties, from the founder of the Truc Lam Buddhist meditation sect to General Dinh Bo Linh to General Quang Trung; also there is the Le king along with his general Tran Nguyen Han; General Nguyen Xao in the shape of a ghost without a hand; and Nguyen Trai as a headless ghostly shadow. It is a gathering of those who loved Vietnam the most; among them so many had been friends but then became enemies as time passed.

Behind this group of people, at the bright yellow horizon to the west, there is a tall person with a calm face and a perpetual relaxed smile. He knows it is the reverend Buddha.

Thus his prayer has been witnessed.

He stands there for a long time, feeling a happiness he has never experienced; one that is totally different from that obtained by a victory or cigar smoke; a happiness beyond words.

"Mr. President, please . . ."

He opens his eyes and sees that the chubby soldier has returned to his side.

"Sir, I saw you standing still like a statue. Then your face suddenly got red as if you were drunk. I have no idea why."

"There is nothing to worry about. People's faces get red either from shame or happiness, right? So what do you think I am: ashamed or happy?"

"Sir, I am afraid . . ."

"Don't worry. My heart is beating normally. Well, we will go down now."

Then he slides off the rock and returns to the beaten path that leads to the Lan Vu temple. The soldier runs wildly behind, holding on to the back of his quilted coat.

The soldier says, "Mr. President, now I cannot hear you. One is more likely to fall when going down than when climbing up."

"Yeah . . ." He smiles, letting the soldier hold on to his coat in the way children hold each other's shirts in the game of dragon tug-of-war.

"I have to brew some tea," the soldier says. "After your tea, you have to do your exercises before breakfast."

"No. From now on I will not exercise."

Surprised by this response, the soldier is quiet for a little while. Then, not able to restrain his curiosity, he clears his throat and asks, "But . . . you always tell us that exercise is discipline."

"That is the strictest discipline to be observed to maintain physical health. However, each circumstance requires an appropriate exercise. From now on I will practice the most appropriate one for leaving swiftly in the fall. If I know how to nourish my body like a mechanic maintains an engine, I will be able to shut my living machine as the temple's caretaker snuffs out the candle at sunrise."

The path curves around a deep crevasse; the dripping of water blends with the singing of birds. Sunrise in the mountains is always mysterious and pure. Everything is laced with white clouds and drowned in birdsong. The president walks briskly like a young lad and feels as if he is seeing all of this for the first time. Suddenly, as the path opens out of the woods, the Lan Vu temple appears like a painting.

"Wow, that's fast!"

"Yes, sir . . . going down the mountain is always ten times faster."

As they cross the gate to enter the temple patio a large field of white hits his eyes, blinding him. The president realizes it is the cherry blossom garden reflecting the sunrise.

"Well, cherry flowers blossom all over the patio," he cries out. "When we left I didn't see them."

"Sir, when we left there was still some lingering fog. You also were in a hurry and didn't pay attention. This is the second time they have blossomed. After this, there will only be some late-blooming branches. The abbess told me that."

"Is that so?" He stops and touches some clusters of flowers. The cold, wet, soft petals are caressing and comforting on his skin. The light from the east reflects off the diamondlike dewdrops on the tips of the leaves. He shuts his eyes to enjoy the gentleness of the petals and listens to the whispering of the early wind. When he opens his eyes, her face has risen on the other side of the garden, opposite him. She is fresh in a dark blue tunic; her gaze is soft and clear, her face pleasing and bright. He knows that it is her: her today, her liberated from hatred and humiliation, her at the age of twenty, with an undying love, waiting for him on the other side of U Tich River, waiting . . .

He speaks: "Now, I tell you, Love, a gentle and lovely woman, a passionate wife and so naive, my own little bird. Dear lady, I am preparing to leave to meet you."

THE BRIGHT LIGHT

The president died exactly on National Day, September 2, the year of the rooster, 1969. His traitorous followers knew that this coincidence carried a curse and would lead to a punishing blow to their position from destiny. Therefore they tricked everybody by reporting that he died on September 3.

From the moment he shut his eyes, it rained for an entire week, a pouring rain as if from a waterfall; white water swept the earth and sky. The Red River billowed with water; there had never been so much water in an autumn. Usually at that time the riverbed would withdraw and the lakes become so still and clear that one could see the weeds at the bottom. But that September, the Red River was foamy red, noisy and wicked as if it were the stormy season. All over Hanoi, the water had no chance to run off. It flooded the sidewalks, overflowed the thresholds of houses, circled around in the intersections. All over the country, people clustered around the foot of lampposts, listening to the speakers describing the funeral. They cried as if a communal assassination had taken place in their nation.

The funeral was held at Ba Dinh Square under a downpour. Soldiers stood in line, in their soaking wet uniforms. People spilled out from the square into the side streets, wearing black pants and brown shirts with mourning ribbons covered in plastic. The official pillars of the state stood on the dais with guards holding umbrellas to protect their heads. The speeches were emotional like the emotions in life. Words of gold and jade were poured out to applaud the accomplishments of the great leader of the nation, the father who had given birth to the revolution, the one who had led countless followers, who had trained a successor generation to carry on with loyalty and dedication!

During the funeral, who knew where the trembling soul of the president stood? If it was smart, it should be under the shade of the trees by the gate to the Ministry of Defense, even though it would have to bear the cold water like a whipping. Wherever it was, surely it could observe in its entirety all the acts of the play. The people wept; of course the little people, but even those who had plotted him harm cried loudly as if their own father had died. They cried miserably with overflowing tears, with their throats obstructed by pain, their noses running. Their speeches were punctuated with noisy nose-blowing, and this unattractive sound was amplified when broadcast over the public airwaves.

The president's prediction proved correct: they cried for real.

But his explanation proved wrong: they did not cry from a realization that, someday, they would have to face him before the tribunal of all existence; they did not cry from shame or embarrassment over an encounter that would occur on the far side of the U Tich River. Oh no, for none of these romantic reasons.

They cried because they could no longer harm him, because they could no longer search for him and wish for his death, because such is the game of power. The ultimate reason that they cried: they understood truly who they were. To understand oneself is the most difficult learning one can obtain in life. One can discover this self-awareness only in special circumstances and by rubbing elbows with others, because the features of a person can be recognized only in the mirror of others. His death provided that very opportunity. For many years, they had held the country's power, having at hand an entire hierarchy of lackeys from high ranks to low, from pillars of the dynasty to the guards in all the camps or those who gave out merits and demerits in the countryside. His traitorous subordinates had believed in the efficacy of their structure, that they were the reigning king on the throne and he was the abdicated monarch living in the back palace who had to do whatever they asked of him; that they were the genuine heroes and he only a gilded plaque where heroes who have decomposed into the mud were listed; and that the arch of triumph they were building would stand on this land forever and that his accomplishment was only a prelude like the vestibule one must cross before entering the main hall. At the funeral all those dreams turned to smoke. They understood that his power could only generate resentment on their part but could never be appropriated.

His power had been a compass created by the hand of a saint or a devil; the evocative impact of a saint in the imagination of many; the unusually innovative ability of an unusually seductive charm. A champion's strength in belief, in emotion, in hallucination—all mixed, intertwined, and set over time and forever lodged in the soul. Full of magic containing simultaneously every contradiction—the culmination and the sediment of a great game.

Thus, at destiny's call, they understood that they were nothing before this old man—even though they had invested so much effort to promote themselves as "stars brighter than a thousand candles" that appear in the skies over the nation.

Like a storm or a flood or a fire, this communal emotion spread during the funeral. They understood that he still lived even thought his heart beat no more; that they had to continue to use his shadow to cover their heads; that their arch of triumph would never be erected if they could not rely on the name of their Elder Brother. Because, in the end, even if they suffered from wounded pride, from their hatred of their own inability, or from the unfairness of the Creator, they were only foxes jumping around looking for food under the tiger's tail. They needed him, even after he had eluded them with his death.

The old tiger was dead. But his continued presence was an essential requisite to ensure their power as well as their glory in the eyes of their subordinates, so at all costs they must have a corpse filled with straw. That is why, almost immediately, the Ba Dinh tomb for him went into construction.

Thus, they continued to betray him, because the president had officially written in his last testament that, upon his death, his body must be cremated, its ashes spread evenly over the rivers, and afterward his name should be carved on a small rock on the modest hill in Vinh Phu province. But betrayal, just like wickedness, never stops once it starts.

However, since the second day of September, the year of the rooster, 1969, a sword has hung dangling in the Hanoi sky; a huge and visible sword. One can clearly see it on fall days when the skies are a cloudless, crystal blue after a stormy rain. That sword blade aims straight at the flagpole in Hanoi, waiting for destiny to fall at any time and cut down the red flag with the yellow star, to end the fraudulent and brutal regime, to destroy those monsters who sucked blood from the necks of the very people who had nurtured them.

In this way, the president's wish had a witness. The divine and immortal souls of all the brave heroes and the great kings who had built and preserved the nation presided over the seven levels of cloud covering every region of the land, mountains and forests, rivers and ponds; as well as the divine Buddha traveling in the western sky, understanding and approving this passionate wish.

What is left is only anxious waiting for the final moment—when the Vietnamese will know the full truth and understand his last wish.

Paris, January 2, 2007